'Robert Kn Miller
New

'The adventure is nonstop, the characters powerfully endearing, and the world-building meticulous'

Paul Di Filippo

'A massively entertaining roller coaster ride that culminates with a final epic confrontation ... Fantasy at its best and the reason I read and greatly enjoy it'

Fantasy Book Critic

'A very rewarding and enjoyable tale, well told'

Bookgeeks

Also by Robert V.S. Redick from Gollancz:

The Red Wolf Conspiracy
The Rats and the Ruling Sea

ROBERT V. S. REDICK

The RIVER of SHADOWS

Copyright © Robert V. S. Redick 2011

First published in Great Britain in 2011 by
Gollancz
An imprint of the Orion Publishing Group
Orion House, 5 Upper St Martin's Lane,
London WC2H 9EA
An Hachette UK Company

This edition published in Great Britain in 2012 by Gollancz

1 3 5 7 9 10 8 6 4 2

A CIP catalogue record for this book is available
from the British Library

ISBN 978 0 575 08185 7

Typeset by Input Data Services Ltd, Bridgwater, Somerset

Printed and bound by CPI Group (UK) Ltd, Croydon, CR0 4YY

www.redwolfconspiracy.com

www.orionbooks.co.uk

Para Morgan y sus padres, con amor y avena

What can you do against the lunatic who is more intelligent than yourself, who gives your arguments a fair hearing and then simply persists in his lunacy?

Orwell

The disease has sharpened my senses — not destroyed — not dulled them.

Poe

I

Lost Souls

It might have been a palace window in Etherhorde: round, red-tinted, firelit from within, but it was a living eye set in a wall of sapphire lunging east through a cobalt sea. Beneath the eye, shattered scales, and a wound that gaped long and raw as the opened belly of a bull. Lower still a mouth like a sea-cave, and from it a hot, salt, rancid wind that took the little skiff in a foul embrace.

No one moved. The beast had come upon them so quickly that they'd not yet even turned the skiff about. The quartermaster tried to squeeze out a command, but no sound came. On the second try he managed a whisper: 'Lie down. Lie down!'

The others obeyed him, curling down against the deck, and the quartermaster, dropping the helm, did the same. The skiff had been tacking neatly across the inlet, but as the monster closed it began to buck and heave like a wild stallion, and they clung to the thwarts and cleats and oarlocks for dear life. The creature had a serpent's body but its head was leonine, maned in shell-encrusted hair, the strands thick as old halyards and shedding tons of seawater as it rose.

Thasha Isiq lifted her eyes. It was close enough to touch with a boathook; she could have leaped from the skiff right into that blue-green mane. She felt someone tugging her arm; she heard the quartermaster, whose name was Fiffengurt, begging her not to stare. But she could not look away. The eye blinked, huge and terrible and desperate and sad. She saw chipped fangs and a black torrent of tongue. She saw an iron collar buried in the mane, and a bit like a rusted tree-trunk cutting into the flesh at the back of the mouth. She saw the chain fused to the bit whipping up out of the foam. All this in a split second: just before the chain struck the hull and jerked the boat half-out of the waves and snapped her head sharply back.

When the red flash of pain subsided Thasha raised her head again. The waves were smaller, but the boat had sprung a bubbling leak. Frightened curses, desperate looks. Pazel Pathkendle, Thasha's closest friend in the world, was pointing at a spot some twenty yards off the stern. A huge loop of the serpent was rising there, turning like a section of a gigantic waterwheel, each blue-green scale as large as a soldier's breastplate. Further east another loop broke the surface; and beyond it that terrible head rose again, and the wound flexed and twisted like a second mouth. The beast was heading for the cape across the inlet, with its fishing village and a cluster of rocky islets a few miles offshore. Behind the largest of these the *Chathrand* stood at anchor, waiting for their return. Thasha could just hear the lookouts starting to howl.

'Ent no blary end to that thing!' said one of the Turachs, his eyes on the oozing body of the serpent.

'Quiet, marine,' whispered his commander.

'It is dropping lower,' said the swordsman, Hercól Stanapeth.

So it was: lower, and lower still, until they could no longer see the horizon beneath the loop of flesh. The farther coil was lowering too, and the creature's head was gone from sight. Then Fiffengurt hissed through his teeth. The water around the skiff had begun to boil.

They were in the centre of a vast school of sharks, trailing the monster like a ribbon of mercury, packed so tight that they jostled one another, flicking spray into the boat. The sharks were slender, man-sized, their dead eyes round as coins. Thasha could feel the thump of each snout against the hull.

Their numbers seemed as endless as the monster's length. But eventually the school was past, and at almost the same time the arch of flesh sank out of sight. Nothing remained of the serpent but a trail of foam.

Fiffengurt and the soldiers made the sign of the Tree. Mr Bolutu, the older dlömu, began a prayer of thanks to Lord Rin. But Pazel rose carefully to his feet. Thasha watched as he shielded his eyes, studying the creature's wake.

So little to him, she thought suddenly. A boy barely seventeen, the age she'd be in six weeks, dark like any tarboy, and a bit darker yet by blood. Thin arms, fierce eyes. Did he care about her any more? Did she care about him? Did it mean something, that notion, I care, I love, after yesterday? He might well have despaired. He might hate her casually, as part of hating everything: the new world and the old, the *Chathrand* and the place she'd anchored, the frightened villagers, the savage Gods.

When the prayer ended, Sergeant Haddismal, a hugely muscled Turach with skin like boot leather, twisted around to glare at Mr Fiffengurt.

'Couldn't believe these eyes,' he said, pointing, as though they might have been confused with some other pair. 'You dropped the tiller, man! What kind of mucking pilot are you?'

'The kind that brought us safe out of the Nelluroq,' said Hercól.

'Didn't ask you, Stanapeth, did I?' snapped the Turach. 'But what I will ask, once more, is what in the Nine putrid Pits we're doing out here? What did you lot find yesterday that's got you too scared to let the men set foot on land? It has to be something worse than a few more of these fish-eyed abominids.'

The pair of dlömu just looked at him, silver eyes shining against the black, black skin. Their indifference to his abuse only fuelled Haddismal's rage. He shouted at Pazel to sit down, and at Mr Fiffengurt to bail, although the quartermaster was doing so already. Looking again at Hercól, the sergeant gestured at the mighty ship that was their destination.

'Just tell me the Gods-damned truth. Eight hundred men goin' mad with thirst, and you come back from the village with two little *parlour-casks* of fresh water, and say that's it, lads, make do till further notice. What do we get by way of explanation? Nothing. Soon my men are on riot duty, though they're so dry themselves they'd lick sweat off a pig. What can I tell 'em? Nothing. And then, just to prove that you're mad as moon dogs, you announce that we're going to take a jaunt over to the *empty* side of the inlet, so that you can run about in the dunes. What d'ye find there? *Nothing.*'

'We'll be back on the *Chathrand* by sunset,' said Thasha.

'Sooner,' said Fiffengurt, 'if we get back to rowing, that is.'

Haddismal scowled over his shoulder at the western shore, already a mile behind them. 'Pointless,' he said. 'Why, it's just a spit of sand! Any fool can see— Eh, *Muketch*! Sit your arse down!'

But Pazel, as if he had forgotten the hated nickname, remained standing in the bows. He was looking at the waves around the skiff, and Thasha noticed that they were ragged and oddly churned.

'Sergeant Haddismal?' said Pazel.

'Sit down! What is it?' barked the Turach.

'Take off your armour.'

The soldier's mouth fell open. He raised a hand broad as a shovel to strike the youth. But the hand stopped in mid-air, and his lip curled as if with an unwelcome thought. He glanced at the other soldier, who was already unbuckling his hauberk, and it occurred to Thasha that the previous Turach commander had died in the very act of beating Pazel about the head, and then the boat shot skywards like a rock from a sling, and split across the keel, and Thasha was flying, spinning, shards of hull and mast about her as the tail of the diving serpent snapped like a whip and was gone.

She caught a glimpse of Pazel, arms crossed to protect his face, crashing back into the sea as through a sheet of glass; then Thasha herself struck, head first. She barely slowed: the monster's descent had created a suction that dragged her down, and the cold and terror of sudden darkness nearly made her gasp. But she did not gasp: Thasha was an admiral's daughter, a *thojmêlê* fighter, a survivor of the Nelluroq crossing. She held her breath and tore at her boots.

They were large and came off easily. The woollen coat took

longer to escape; by the time she succeeded the water was black and leaden. Somehow she had the clarity of mind to swim sidelong to the downward current. Eight, ten, a dozen aching strokes. Then the current slackened and she aimed for what was left of the sunlight.

Dark flames, overhead. The sharks were returning. She pushed through them, heedless; all she wanted was air. When at last she broke the surface the dorsal fins were flowing by her like small grey sails.

Her lungs made an ugly croak. There was barely room to tread water among the sharks. She waited for the first bite, cold and angry. But the sharks were dispersing, their collective mind on the serpent and the greater pickings it provided, and not one of them harmed her. On the crest of a wave she saw Pazel, naked to the chest, and Mr Fiffengurt clinging to a broken plank. She heard Hercól shout for Haddismal but saw neither man.

Her head slipped under again. Her remaining clothes were going to kill her. She clawed at the knot that secured her sailor's breeches, but only managed to tighten it hopelessly. Giving up, she shed her blouse, then tugged off the breeches with brute force. Rising again, she found the shore at a glance and knew she would not drown.

There was Ibjen, supporting the younger Turach, who was limp. Thasha kicked towards them, doubting that the boy could swim a mile through swells and breakers with a dying marine. But before she had taken three strokes the other dlömic man, Bolutu, surfaced on the other side of the Turach and caught his arm. Together they bore the soldier away.

Thasha's own battle to reach the land was much harder than she expected. She grew light-headed, and her limbs began to seize with cold. The back-swell fought her, urging her away from the beach like an overbearing host. Blackness, death, come and see, come and see.

When at last her foot grazed the bottom she thought suddenly of her father, signing his letters with the word *Unvanquished*, and dragged herself up from the waves with a growl.

The sand was warm. A mallet smashed at her eardrums with each beat of her heart. She raised her eyes: there were large black animals, walrus-like, lurching fearfully into the waves a hundred yards from where she stood. She fell down and rose unsteadily and fell again. Then she remained on hands and knees and watched a trickle of blood run down her bare arm. A cut on her shoulder, nothing dangerous really. Unless you were swimming, tiring, needed all your strength.

Footsteps, staggering nearer. Someone dropped to his knees beside her and made a choking sound. Pazel. He put his hands on her back and shoulder, inspecting.

'You hurt?' she said.

More choking. Then: 'No ... only the Turach ... he'll live.'

She turned her head. Pazel was naked and shivering and bleeding from the scalp. His whole body caked with sand. Up the beach she saw the others, crawling or rising shakily to their feet. Her vision blurring, she counted them. A miracle, she thought.

'Find ... some clothes.'

A fit of retching took her, but she smiled through it. The nearest clothes were six miles off on the *Chathrand*. She dropped on her side, facing away from him, then reached for the hand that had not left her shoulder and kissed it, and got a mouthful of sand for her trouble.

'No one died, Thasha.'

'I know.'

Then she rolled over, facing him. *No one died.* She began to laugh, and Pazel caught her eye and did the same, and then with a shared impulse they turned their backs to each other, no longer laughing exactly, in fact what was it, weeping, fits of pain? Whatever they were about they did it quietly, convulsed but voicing nothing, showing nothing, least of all faces that might have acknowledged, inflicted, the truth.

The dlömu, astonishing swimmers both, had not needed to shed their clothes. They brought their shirts to Thasha to cover herself, and with an arm over her breasts she thanked them, then looked at each in turn, and lastly at Pazel, until all three turned away.

Ibjen had struggled not to stare. Even now he made as if to glance back at her over his shoulder, but checked himself. Thasha watched him as she ripped his shirt open at the seams. *Whatever else they are, they're men.*

But then Ibjen had been staring at the humans since their arrival the day before. He still jumped occasionally when one of them spoke. The way humans did, Thasha mused, when faced with a woken animal, a creature who used words when they expected brays or screeches.

For in his lifetime Ibjen had never met a human capable of more than that. They were animals, dumb animals: every last human known to exist in this hemisphere. They had, he admitted when pressed, rather less sense than dogs. Perhaps as much as cows or sheep. Thasha, Pazel and Hercól had met a few of these damaged humans yesterday, naked, drooling, clustered about Ibjen's father, gazing at the newcomers in thoughtless fear. He had tamed them, the old man said. He had given them names.

She tied the torn shirt about her waist and pulled the other, wet and chilly, over her head. The sun was low in the west; in an hour it would be dark, and they would be cold indeed if the wind kept up.

Fifty yards along the beach, stranded by some long-ago storm, lay the bleached trunk of a mighty tree. It was a good five feet thick, and Thasha saw that the men had withdrawn to the far side, peering over it timidly as she approached. On another day she might have laughed. Arquali sailors, for all their crassness and carnal appetite, would rather be hanged than spied naked by a woman.

But as she neared the trunk she realised that something had changed. Ibjen was talking, and he looked like a messenger with so much bad news to impart that he expects to be chased off or stabbed before he finishes. Fiffengurt and the Turachs stood motionless, pale. Hercól had decided to tell them the truth.

7

'You are—' Ibjen stammered, embarrassed. '*They* are dying out in the wild, I understand. Winter kills so many. They get sick, they can't find food, and people – dlömu, I mean – aren't allowed to set up feeding stations like they used to. The war shortages, you see.'

Feeding stations. Human beings who scavenged along the edges of woods, the outskirts of towns. Humans who ran like deer when the dlömu approached, or waited, blinking and terrified, for a handout. Humans without human minds.

'We call them *tol-chenni*. That's a foreign word, I forget what it means—'

'It means "sleepwalkers",' said Pazel.

'In Nemmocian,' added Bolutu. 'How very ... evocative.'

'We're breaking Imperial law by feeding them,' said Ibjen. 'The Grain Edict, dlömic labour for dlömic mouths. Some of the men want to drive the *tol-chenni* off into the woods, but they won't cross my father. Besides, there aren't any laws these days. Not really. Not out here.'

Thasha sat down with her back to the tree. 'Out here' was the Northern Sandwall: a ribbon of dunes stretching east to west, horizon to horizon. On one side, the Nelluroq: the vast, vindictive Ruling Sea. On the other, this Gulf of Masal: warmer, infinitely calmer, and such a brilliant blue that it was like the sea a child paints who has never beheld one. Yesterday, quite literally dying of thirst, they had limped into this Gulf around a sandy knob six miles to the east, a place that Mr Bolutu had recognised with cries of joy as Cape Lasung.

They had reached the very margins of his homeland, he declared: Bali Adro, an empire greater by far than the Empire of Arqual, which was Thasha's own country, and one of the two great powers of the Northern world. Bolutu had lived for twenty years in Arqual. Twenty years magically disguised as a human; twenty years with no hope of returning, until he joined the crew of the *Chathrand*. Still, it was not surprising that he knew Lasung at a glance, for a singular landmark stood upon the cape: Narybir, the Guardian

Tower, a weird, waxlike spire of red stone. The tower graced coins, he said; it appeared in murals and paintings and books of architecture. No citizen of his beloved Empire could fail to recognise Narybir, even if, like Bolutu, he had never come near it.

But once ashore they had found the tower abandoned, its doors barred and padlocked, its great stair plunged beneath a drift of sand. A few minutes later they had met the dlömu villagers: coal-black figures like Mr Bolutu, skin slick as eels, fingers webbed to the first knuckle, hair of a metallic sheen and those hypnotic eyes in which it was difficult to spot the pupil. Ten or twelve families in all: refugees, gaunt and fearful, hiding from the war. By day they scanned the Gulf for danger, tended their meagre gardens, snared birds and rodents in the stunted forest of the Cape. By night they huddled in the old stone houses, plugging holes against the wind.

Sergeant Haddismal was shouting: '—ask us to believe that? I *don't* believe it! And why not? Because it's monstrous and impossible. You're trying to play us for fools.'

'Rubbish, Sergeant!' said Fiffengurt, shouting rapidly and with unnatural excitement. 'There's no bad faith here. A mistake is what it is. Humankind wiped out? It doesn't square. We saw a group of men just yesterday, soon as we landed.'

'But *we* saw them up close,' said Pazel. 'Hercól and Thasha and I, and Bolutu as well. It's true, Mr Fiffengurt. They're ... animals.'

'They are *tol-chenni*,' said Ibjen.

'Come come,' said Fiffengurt. 'Yesterday a whole devilish armada passed by in the Gulf – you can't have forgotten *that*, Mr Hercól.'

'I fear I never shall,' said Hercól.

'Right,' said Haddismal, turning on Ibjen. 'We're done playin' this little game. Or are you going to tell us those ships were crewed by your kind alone – dlömu to the lowliest swab? That there were no humans aboard?'

Ibjen was at a loss. 'In cages, you mean?'

'Gentlemen!' said Fiffengurt. 'This is a mix-up, I tell you. A tiz-woz, a garble-box, you follow, Ibjen my lad? Maybe you don't. Or maybe I'm still not following *you*. Don't take it unkindly, but you're not exactly speaking proper Arquali. Your words start all wrong. *Puh* is *puh* and *buh* is *buh*, and they ain't the same thing—'

'He is not speaking Arquali at all,' said Bolutu. 'I told you yesterday, Fiffengurt: your tongue is an offshoot of our Imperial Common. You Northerners are the children of Bali Adro emigrants, whether you like it or not.'

'Well then!' said the quartermaster, pouncing. 'If humans from your Belly-whatsit Empire crossed the Ruling Sea and founded our own, they couldn't very well have been *animals*, now could they?'

'That was before – many centuries before the change.'

'No, no, *no*!' shouted Fiffengurt. 'Hush, listen! I've sailed more than any of you; I know how strange tribal folk can seem – why, some of them brutes back in the Jitril Isles—'

Thasha sank her hands into her golden hair and pulled, pulled, until she felt the roots close to tearing, until she knew for certain the pain was real. They wouldn't believe even this much. How could they possibly face the rest? How was *she* going to face it?

The first part, what had become of human beings: she might still have been denying that, if she hadn't seen them yesterday, in the little square at the village centre. But oh, how she'd seen them. Slack-jawed, fly-mobbed, stinking. Half the women pregnant. The men with coarse, matted beards. Out they had come at the old dlömu's call, shuffling, whimpering, and then—

Something had happened to Thasha then. Something frightful and very personal, like those nightmares that erupt in silence and last just an instant, waking one with an urge to scream. But Thasha could not for the life of her say what it had been. She had not fainted. Several minutes were simply gone.

When memory returned no one was standing quite where they had been. Hercól was blocking the gate that let onto the square, forbidding entry to the rest of the landing party. Mr Bolutu was staring at his hands. Pazel was beside her, pressing a cup of water to her lips, the first long drink she'd had in a fortnight and the most delicious in her life. Pazel told her she'd suffered an attack. He spoke with tenderness, but his eyes betrayed another feeling: for a moment, before he checked himself, they had blazed with accusation.

She had seen Pazel angry, furious, fighting for his life. But she had never seen him turn anyone that sort of look. What could she possibly have done to deserve it?

A distant boom wrenched her back to the present. The serpent had risen again, this time across the inlet beside one of the rocky isles, and with a thundering roar smashed its jaw against the cliff. An echo of steel on stone rolled across the inlet; from the island birds rose in clouds. Again the monster struck, and again.

It was trying to break free of its bridle, the remains of some entangling war-tack. She winced; even from here she could see the fresh blood, scarlet over turquoise. Great shelvings of stone collapsed into the waves; miles away the *Chathrand* was rocking like a hobby horse. *Pain*, she thought. *Pain and death and madness, and enough fresh water to keep us alive.* That was all they had found so far in this new world, this great South they'd reached after months without landfall, half of it in storm, a passage through lunacy in its own right, a nightmare. Hercól was right: the truth might trigger almost any sort of panic once it reached the ship.

They collected driftwood and desiccated grass. Pazel and Fiffengurt, with much swearing and arguing and rasping of twigs, coaxed the brush into flames just minutes before it grew too dark to see. There was plenty to burn: the weather, as they knew too well, had been mercilessly dry.

Hercól had gone away into the dunes 'to be sure they were quite alone'. Thasha went on collecting firewood until the light failed altogether, now and then glancing across the water at the *Chathrand*. They had waved to the Great Ship from the mouth of the inlet, and received a signal in return: *Are you safe till morning?*

A reasonable if disappointing question. The serpent might be gone (it had slipped the bridle at last, flung it high as the tip of Narybir Tower, and shot away into the Ruling Sea) but what else might be lurking in this alien Gulf? No, there was no justifying a rescue by night. They had answered *Yes* and trudged back resentfully to the beach where they'd swum ashore.

In the darkness a small miracle occurred. The beach was etched with faint, zigzag ribbons of light. Scarlet, emerald, shimmering blue: each line no thicker than a shoelace, and fading even as they stared. Thasha walked down to the water, entranced. It was the surf lines that were glowing. Each charge of foam reached its highest point, and there disgorged a boiling mass of shelled creatures, smaller than termites, which somehow gripped the sand and began to glow. For a few wild seconds they crawled and squirmed. Were they spawning, seeking mates? Thasha found she could not touch them: at the approach of her hand their light vanished without a trace.

It grew cold. The men were still embarrassed, but they could hardly deny Thasha a spot by the fire. They held bunches of dried grass against their loins, grass that crackled and poked them and blew about in the wind, and the more the wind blew the closer to the fire they edged, until Thasha feared that someone would go up in flames. Only the dlömu, dignified by their trousers, sat calmly, warming their webbed hands. Pazel was as foolish as anyone, hiding behind the marines.

Thasha found them ridiculous. Hours ago they'd been told that their race was dead or dying across the entire Southern world. What were they thinking, how could they care? And yet she herself was glad to be covered. They made for something normal, these motions of modesty. Something that had yet to collapse.

Hercól reappeared, startling them, for none had heard his approach. 'I have walked along the north beach,' he said, kneeling, 'and I found the memorial: it was not in the dunes at all, but on a black rock facing the Ruling Sea. That is what we were looking for, Sergeant: a war memorial, one we hoped might tell us something about the catastrophe. Alas, I could not read a word of the inscription.'

'We shouldn't have come!' blurted Ibjen suddenly. 'We told you: even if you could find the memorial, and read it, you'd learn no more from it than you would from us. Is that truly why we crossed the inlet? Is that why we almost died?'

'Yes,' said Hercól.

Overwhelmed, Ibjen turned away and bit his lips.

Haddismal laughed. 'What you means is, "*I* shouldn't have come." What are you doing with us anyway, boy? Your old dad punishing you for something?'

Ibjen looked down at his hands. 'I was told there were great ones among you,' he said, 'trying to do something fine.'

'Fine?'

'Something to redeem the world.'

'Who told you that?' asked Thasha. 'Who could *possibly* have told you that?'

But Ibjen just shook his head. 'We shouldn't be here, Thashiziq. We explained everything back in the village.'

Haddismal's lips curled in a sneer. He said, 'You still don't see it. Ain't there a brain behind those fishy eyes?'

Ibjen looked from face to face. 'I don't understand,' he said.

'We needed some proof of your story,' said Pazel. 'We wanted to know if you were mad.'

The dlömic youth was shocked, then furious. He leaped to his feet and started towards Pazel, hands in fists, only to turn on his heel and stalk away into the darkness. Bolutu went after him, shooting an angry look of his own back over a shoulder.

In a short time both dlömu returned. Ibjen, eyes locked on the fire, apologised to the humans. 'I assumed you were like us,' he murmured. 'That was foolish of me.'

'Like you how?' said Thasha.

'I thought you would know how vicious a thing it is to call a person mad. But Mr Bolutu tells me it is no grave insult in your country.'

'Nor was it here, when I departed,' said Bolutu. 'And I've no doubt it became an insult because of the catastrophe. By all the Gods, a third of the Imperial population was human! No one could have been unmoved. We were one people – dlömu, human, Nemmocian, k'urin, mizrald, selk. There were even marriages, occasionally. My cousin Daranta took a human wife.'

Ibjen gave a twitch of disgust, clearly involuntary. The wounded Turach laughed, and everyone looked at him. He flinched at this concentrated scrutiny, pressed his bunch of grass tighter against his waist. 'My sister married a bloke from Noonfirth,' he said.

Haddismal looked at him with vague distaste. Noonfirthers were jet black. Worse, their kingdom, though small by Arquali standards, was peaceful, fashionable, educated and rich. 'You'll keep that to yourself if you know what's good for you,' he said.

Night brought no rescue, but it brought other visitors. Eyes gleamed from the dune grass. Some low swift creatures loped by in the surf, panting like wolves. And when the wind ebbed they heard a rustling all about them, accompanied by a noise like the breaking of small sticks. The sound was persistent and strangely unsettling, and in time Thasha realised that the creatures, whatever they might be, were moving about them in a closing spiral. At last Pazel tossed a burning branch out of their circle, and a half-dozen crabs the size of sunflowers, with translucent eyestalks and the delicate legs of spiders, recoiled into the night.

'*Irraketch*,' said Bolutu. 'Lucky crabs. Don't hurt them. They can be taught to mimic human speech, like parrots. Some part of them, legs or back or claw, is deadly poison.'

Ibjen professed to know nothing of these creatures. He did not leave the village at night, he said. A bit later, as though reaching some difficult threshold of trust, he stated that he had come to live with his father just the year before. All his life his parents had been estranged, he said, and he had spent most of those years with his mother in the city of Masalym across the Gulf. But the previous winter she had sent him to his father's dying village on the Northern

Sandwall, to hide him from the military press gangs that robbed the mainland of its children.

'Don't tell,' Ibjen pleaded. 'None of the villagers know. They'd set me adrift in the Gulf, or kill me outright. They're afraid to harbour runaways.'

'What's the fighting about?' said Haddismal. 'A threat to Imperial territory, is it?'

Ibjen shook his head. 'The enemy is the realm of Karysk, in the east. Not long ago they were our friends – but we are not supposed to say that. In any case I know nothing of the recent war.'

'Recent,' said Pazel, in a hollow voice.

The Turach commander glanced at Hercól. 'I assume,' he said, indicating Pazel with his chin, 'that you'll be taking our genius here off to read that inscription at sunrise.'

'Perhaps,' said Hercól.

'Perhaps?' cried Haddismal. 'Damn your eyes, ain't that what we came for?'

'*He* won't be able to read it either,' said Ibjen.

''Course he will!' said Haddismal. 'Translating's all our *Muketch* is good for. That runt can speak, read and write every language under Heaven's Tree.'

Hercól said nothing, and Thasha waited, perplexed. The Turach was exaggerating Pazel's Gift: it only let him learn new languages a few times a year, during a few days of magical insight, though he never forgot them afterwards. He had acquired some twenty-five languages during these interludes. But they ended in such violent fits that he'd thrown away his savings from five years as a tarboy (an amount Thasha had seen her cook spend preparing for a dinner party) on a cure that had failed. Still, Haddismal's question was a good one. They'd come here to learn something. Why not show Pazel the memorial?

Haddismal clearly thought his question more than good. 'You answer me, Stanapeth. Don't you dare sit there mute.'

'My silence is not meant to insult you,' said Hercól.

'Your blary existence insults me. You're under sentence of death, you and these two brats and the rest of your gang. A delayed sentence, but not rescinded. It's beyond everything that you're still at liberty, defying the ship's commander.'

'*Who?*' said Pazel.

Thasha could have hugged him. Even Haddismal looked caught between amusement and rage. Nothing was less clear than who was in charge on the *Chathrand*.

The Turach threw up his hands. 'I can't talk to you people. You're all cracked – not you, Mr Ibjen, don't get sore, you're quite sensible for a fish-eyed freak. Keep the fire burning, for Rin's sake. Long live His Supremacy.'

He dropped on his side. The junior Turach echoed his praise of the Emperor, then his example, and in scant minutes both men were breathing deep. The others sat up a long time, listening to the scuttling crabs, the wail of night birds, the surf. Their whispered conversations went nowhere; they were, like Haddismal, too bewildered for words.

Thasha would remember their smiles. Bitter, perhaps even unhinged. But none of them cruel – not even Haddismal, at the last, though she had seen terrible cruelty from the man. *She thought: It's the world that's cruel, not its poor stupid creatures. It's the world that stabs a wall of perfect blue scales until they bleed. The world that makes you monstrous, holds you by the neck, tightens and tightens its jaws till something snaps.*

She looked Pazel over when she was sure his head was turned. He would always be thin, light, something less than a deadly fighter. But he was growing, and he'd embraced the lessons she and Hercól had thrust on him. They were brutal, those lessons: every one involved pain, and Pazel had few natural gifts as a fighter. But he wanted it, now, and that made all the difference. 'One day I'll protect you,' he'd told her, 'instead of being protected.' From the far end of the stateroom Felthrup had called: 'You protect us already with your mind, your scholar's mind! You're a genius, Pazel Pathkendle.' Thasha had stabbed at him with the practice sword, because he'd dropped his guard to answer Felthrup.

16

She could see the scar on his hip even now, above his clutch of weeds.

Skinny boy, genius. Someone she loved. Would it happen to him? In three months, six months, tomorrow? Would she wake up and find an animal looking back at her with those eyes?

Perhaps he hates me. The thought ambushed her again. She knew that no one else suspected, and that Pazel himself would deny it to his last breath. Hadn't they been inseparable for weeks? Hadn't he shivered when she kissed him last?

Yet sometimes people knew more than they knew. Perhaps in his heart Pazel sensed what Thasha was already certain of: that she deserved it. Deserved not just his hatred, but everyone's, deserved to be loathed, tortured, dismembered, dead. *Why?* Thasha could not bring her thoughts to bear on that question: there was a gauze curtain between her and the truth, and though it lurked there like some vulgar actor awaiting his cue, she could not yet tear the curtain down.

But she knew this much: if Pazel didn't hate her yet, she would soon be giving him a reason.

A hand touched Thasha's foot. It was Hercól, his eyes stern but kind. 'Brood no more,' he said, and the command in his voice was made healing by their years of trust. His hand withdrew, and Thasha did her best to obey.

They fed the fire. At length they found a way to sleep that cut no one off entirely from its warmth. Thasha lay down, her head bumping Ibjen's knees, her foot on Hercól's shoulder. If anything was still blessed in this world it was sleep.

Night sounds, emptiness, a world without people. She drank it in for what felt like hours. Her mind was alert, but robbed of will and purpose; her heart drifted in a void. She thought that if the wind rose just a little she would float away, a cinder, and nothing in the universe would change.

And then out of the darkness Mr Fiffengurt said, 'There's more to tell, ain't there?'

Deeper silence, suddenly, as though they were all waiting to breathe. Thasha wondered who would answer first: Hercól, Pazel, she herself? And once they answered, who would be the first to go mad?

But she did not find out, for the silence held. None of them, it seemed, was ready to admit to being awake.

2

Love and Cataclysm

The world is a little house. If you listen, you will hear your country's exiles, grumbling. They have been in the next room all along.

Winter Meditations, Vasparhaven

21 Ilbrin 941

Thasha could not recall those moments in the village, but Pazel could. When the *tol-chenni* stepped into the crumbling square she had turned to him with unfocused eyes, clutched his arm, whispered in terror:

'I didn't mean to. It was never supposed to happen. You believe me, don't you?'

Now, some thirty hours later beside the fire, he looked at her – directly, at last, for no one was awake to catch him at it. Only the fire itself was in the way. On one side he saw the bedraggled mass of her hair, not at all pretty, like something that had slithered out of the Gulf and expired by Hercól's knees. On the other side he could see her legs below the makeshift skirt. Bruised, sleek, powerful. He closed his eyes and it made no difference; if anything he saw them more clearly. *Think*, he told himself. *Face yesterday.* If he didn't the fear would come back in his sleep, pounce on him, tear him apart.

Thasha's grip had been close to excruciating. 'An accident,' she'd said. 'I tried to fix it, Pazel, I tried so hard.'

19

With difficulty he had pried her hands from his shoulders, then held her as she shook, repeating her confession and her plea for belief. 'I'm not the devil,' she'd added helpfully. Pazel was shocked by the coincidence of their thoughts. He had made no guesses, diabolical or otherwise. But he was asking himself just who in Alifros she might be.

He gave her water, the cold, sweet water Ibjen had just pumped from the well. Drink deep, drink slowly, he urged. It was the only way to make her stop talking.

For apart from the horror of the mindless humans, there was suddenly the horror of Thasha's claim that she had made them so. From the other side of the world, apparently. What could one say to that?

He had decided to say nothing at all. Ibjen and his father, Mr Isul, were saying enough. They were as excited as children: the visitors were the first 'woken' humans the old man had seen in fifty years, Ibjen in his lifetime. Still working the pump handle, he cried to Bolutu: 'Did you bring them from Masalym, brother? Is there a cure?'

Bolutu just stared at the *tol-chenni*. His tongue had been mutilated by Arunis the sorcerer, and he had only recently regained its use (dlömu, like newts and starfish, could regenerate lost parts of themselves). Now it was as though the tongue had never grown back.

Hercól recovered first. With an oath he sprinted into the gatehouse at the edge of the square, just in time to keep the rest of the *Chathrand*'s landing party from barrelling through. For the rest of his life, Pazel would remember the man's swiftness, his absolute resolve. Hercól was in mourning: just weeks ago the woman he loved had been murdered before his eyes. He had as much right as anyone to paralysis, to shock. In the gatehouse the Turachs raised their spears; Mr Alyash, a trained assassin, sidled towards him with intent. Hercól did not even draw his sword. They could not enter, he said again. They must go back to the ship.

Thasha's mentor was the deadliest fighting man on the

Chathrand, with the possible exception of *his* old mentor, Sandor Ott. But Alyash had also trained with Ott. And the Turachs were lethal: commandos trained to fight and kill the *sfvantskor* warrior-priests of the enemy, and to guard the Arquali Emperor himself. How could Hercól have known they would not attack? The answer was obvious: he hadn't.

And yet there was no bloodshed. The landing party, cursing, retreated to the shore road outside the wall. As soon as they left the gatehouse Hercól turned and shouted to Pazel in his birth-tongue: 'Keep them all inside! The dlömu and ... those others. Keep them out of sight! And bring fresh water: as much as you three can handle alone. Quickly, lad! Without water no one will go back to that ship!'

Pazel obeyed; at that moment he would have obeyed an order to eat sand or jump into the well, anything to break through the drumbeat inside him. *All of them animals. An epidemic, a plague.* By that point several more dlömu had crept into the square, and Bolutu had recovered enough to beg water for the ship. Good-natured, his fellow dlömu had run for casks, but the vessels they returned with were small indeed: not above thirty gallons apiece. Pazel and Bolutu rolled these out to the waiting men, and at the sight of the tiny barrels even Fiffengurt lost his temper.

'That won't come to half a draught per man! We need ten times that just for starters! And the men are hungry, too. What's Teggatz supposed to cook with, bilge?'

'We will bring more when you return for us,' said Hercól. 'Go now, and ask no further questions. Don't you think I would answer if I could?'

'No,' said Alyash. 'Ott's made you as tight-fisted with secrets as I am.'

'Sandor Ott's first lesson was survival,' said Hercól, 'and survival is all I am thinking of. Go, Alyash! We are plunged in drifts of gunpowder, and you berate me for not striking a match.'

They followed (almost chased) the men back to the pilot boat, and watched them row for the *Chathrand*, where men thronged like beggars to the gunwale. Elkstem had tucked the ship in behind the largest island, out of sight from the Gulf. It was a sensible precaution, for they had not been an hour in the vicinity of Cape Lasung when a trio of unknown ships had passed: slender vessels, running east by south-east with all the canvas they could bear. They were battle-scarred, and too small in any event to threaten the *Chathrand*, but who could say what followed in their wake?

The answer to that question, when it came, had brought with it the second terrible shock of this new world. It had occurred shortly after the stand-off at the gatehouse. Pazel and Thasha were searching the village for Bolutu, who had blundered off into the streets, like a dazed survivor of a massacre. Ibjen's father had said something about food and hobbled away. Pazel and Thasha were sweating: there was no breeze inside the wall. From sandy lanes and unglazed windows, the dlömu peeked out at them in awe. Once a boy of five or six burst laughing from a doorway and collided with Pazel's legs.

He saw the human hands first, then looked up in terror at Pazel's pale, brown-eyed human face, and screamed. 'Don't worry, we're friends,' Pazel ventured. But the boy fled back into the house, wailing, and the word on his lips was, '*Monsters!*'

The village was small, and in short order they reached a second gate, the chains of its rusty portcullis snapped, the gate itself propped open with timbers. Passing beneath it, they found themselves west of the village, on a footpath that led by way of grass-covered dunes into the stunted forest. Near the edge of the trees, his back to a small, wind-tortured oak, sat Bolutu. His face was grim and distracted. They were about to hail him when voices from inside the gate began to shout in alarm:

'Hide! Fires out! Wagons in! An armada comes!'

They ducked back inside the wall. No one gaped at them now. Children were running, weeping; a woman swept two children into her arms and dashed for cover. Dlömic boys were crouching behind the parapet atop the wall, raising their heads just high enough to peer at the Gulf. After a quick scramble, Pazel and Thasha found a staircase and joined them.

It was like a vision of the damned. Four or five hundred ships of unthinkable size and ferocity, rushing east to a blasting of horns and a thundering of drums. Ships that dwarfed their own great *Chathrand*, ships hauled by those horrific serpents, or pulled by kite-like sails that strained before them like tethered birds. Ships crudely built, dubiously repaired: fitted with blackened timbers, clad in scorched armour, heaped with cannon and ballistas and strange, bone-white devices Pazel could not identify. A bright haze surrounded the armada, of a sort that Pazel felt obscurely convinced he had seen before, though he could not say where. The haze was brighter in the spots where the vessels seemed most nearly ruined: so bright in places that he could not stand to look at all. Fire belched from cauldron-like devices on the decks, and swarms of figures tended the fires, goaded by whips and spears.

The villagers were as frightened as the humans: they had seen many terrible things, they whispered, but this armada was on another scale altogether. Some looked at the newcomers with renewed fright, as if the vessels flowing endlessly past the Cape must have something to do with their arrival.

'They're making for Karysk,' said Ibjen, who was among the boys. 'They're going to destroy it, aren't they?'

The boys pointed at Bolutu, shaking their heads in despair. He had not moved from his tree by the dunes, and they had no doubt that the armada's leaders would spot him, and send a force to investigate.

But the horrid fleet showed no interest in the village – which was fortunate, because a slight shoreward turn by any part of it would have revealed the *Chathrand*, still as death behind her island. Hours passed; the line of nightmarish ships stretched on, and so did the silence. It was only towards evening, when a breeze off the Nelluroq began to cool the village, that the last of the vessels swept by, and the drums and horns began to fade.

Thasha and Pazel left the village by the same gate as before. There sat Bolutu, as he had for five hours, digging his black fingers into the sand. When they approached him he did not look up.

His voice, however, was soft and reasonable. 'The pennants are ours,' he said.

'The pennants?' said Thasha. 'On those ships, you mean?'

'The pennants on those ships. The leopard, leaping the red Bali Adro sun. It is the Imperial standard. And the armada came from the west, out of the Bali Adro heartland.'

Pazel felt sickened – and betrayed. 'These are your friends?' he demanded. 'The good wizards who sent you north to fight Arunis, the ones who can see through your eyes? The ones you said would come running to our aid, as soon as we made landfall?'

'Oh, Pazel, of course not,' said Thasha. 'They're impostors, aren't they, Bolutu? Flying Bali Adro colours in order to fool someone?'

Now Bolutu did raise his eyes. 'I do not know who they are – madmen, I would guess. Madmen can fly any flag, usurp any legacy, squat on any throne. But listen to me, both of you: *this is not my world*. This wreckage, these illiterate peasants, this plague on the minds of humans. It is not mine, I tell you.'

'You've been gone twenty years,' said Pazel.

'Two decades could *never* work such a change,' said Bolutu. 'Bali Adro was a just Empire, an enlightened one. The years of famine were behind us. The *maukslar*, the arch-demons, were all dead or defeated; the Circle of the Scorm was broken. Our neighbours posed no threat, and our internal enemies – the Ravens I spoke of – they were imprisoned, or scattered to distant lands. We were safe here, safe and at peace.'

'Sometimes things *do* happen fast,' said Pazel. 'Six years ago Ormael was still a country. Now it's just another territory of Arqual.'

'Pazel,' said Bolutu, 'it is not remotely the same. This world is ancient beyond anything that survives in the North. The Codex of the dlömu, from which our laws derive – it was written before the first tree was felled on your Chereste Peninsula. And though your rulers were unseated and your city torched, your people did not devolve into beasts.'

'Well it's blary plain that *we* will, if we stay around here,' said Pazel. 'It may be too late already. We all drank from that well.'

Bolutu shook his head. 'The disease is not contagious. It was the first question I put to Ibjen's father. There he is now, by the way.'

The old dlömu, Mr Isul, was creeping towards them along the road from the forest, carrying a bundle of sticks and a woollen sack. Age had dulled his silver hair, but not his eyes. They were troubled, however, and not just by the hunt for footing on the rutted track.

'How does he know it's not contagious?' asked Thasha.

Bolutu kept his eyes on the old man. 'There were experiments, he says. When it was clear the plague was out of control. They locked unaffected humans and *tol-chenni* together, forced them to share food, water, latrines. But those humans corralled with the *tol-chenni* degenerated no faster than those who had no contact at all.'

'I thought every human south of the Ruling Sea had caught the disease,' said Thasha.

'They have. But not from one another.'

Pazel was losing patience. 'I don't care if they caught it from earthworms,' he said. 'Something in this land of yours gave it to human beings, and made it spread like wildfire.'

The old man was just reaching them; he nodded cordially, but with obvious unease. He put down his bundle of sticks, but kept the sack in his hands. 'Not like wildfire,' he said. 'More like a snowfall. Everywhere at once, but softly, quietly. We took no notice at first. Who minds a few snowflakes on the wind?' He looked up at them, and his eyes were far away. 'Until they turn into a blizzard, that is.'

'The plague has to do with woken animals,' said Thasha. The others looked at her, amazed. 'Well doesn't it stand to reason?

25

Animals bursting suddenly into human intelligence, humans turning suddenly into beasts?'

The phenomenon of waking animals had been a strange part of life in Alifros for centuries. Strange and exceedingly rare, at least in the North: so rare indeed that most people had never seen such a creature. But in the last several years the number of wakings had exploded.

'Are there woken animals in the South, Mr Isul?' asked Bolutu.

The old man's look of worry intensified. 'Thinkers, you mean? Beasts with reason, and human speech? No, no more. They were wicked creatures, *maukslarets*, little demons.' He looked down, suddenly abashed. 'Or so we were told.'

'What happened to them?' asked Pazel, dreading the answer.

Isul drew a finger across his throat. 'Condemned, all condemned,' he said. 'Back when I was a child. And it's still the law of the land: you're obliged to kill a Thinker on sight, before he works black magic against your family, your neighbours, the Crown. You can get away with harbouring *tol-chenni*, if you're careful – in Masalym there's even a place that *breeds* 'em – but get caught with a thinking mouse or bird under your roof, and it's the axe. They're all dead and gone, is what I reckon. And if there are any left you can be sure they won't let you know they can think. You could be looking right at one, a stray dog, a dune tortoise, and be none the wiser.'

Now it was Thasha's turn to look at Bolutu with rage. 'We should *never* have trusted you,' she said. 'They started killing woken animals when he was a *child*? That was a lot more than twenty years ago! Why didn't you warn us? Do you realise what we might have done?'

Aboard the *Chathrand* was a woken rat, their dear friend Felthrup Stargraven. Despite his suspicion that something terrible awaited them ashore he had wanted to join the landing party – to share in any danger, he'd said. They had almost agreed.

The old man put a hand on the side of his woollen sack, probing something within. He glanced uncertainly at Bolutu. 'Twenty?' he said.

Bolutu rose to his feet and dusted off his trousers. 'Mr Isul,' he said, 'be so good as to tell us the date.'

'You know I can't,' said the other, a bit testily.

'The year will suffice.'

It was then that Pazel noticed the tremor in Bolutu's voice. The old man, however, was put at ease. 'That much I know,' he said. 'We haven't lost our bearings altogether out here. It's the year thirty fifty-seven, His Majesty's ninth on the throne.'

Thasha looked at Bolutu. 'You use a different calendar in the South. You told us that weeks ago.'

Bolutu nodded, his face working strangely. He bent and plucked a stick from the old man's bundle. He squinted at it, picked at the bark.

'Of course, after all those years in Arqual, you'd know *both* calendars,' said Pazel.

Another nod. Bolutu raised the stick and considered it lengthwise, as though studying its straightness. It was not very straight.

'What's wrong with you?' said Thasha sharply. 'What are you trying to tell us?'

'If Mr Isul is correct—'

'You don't believe me, go ahead, ask anyone,' said the old man.

'—we have rather misjudged our time on the Nelluroq. By your calendar, it is Western Solar Year Eleven Forty-Four, and we have been two centuries at sea.'

In the silence that followed Pazel heard the drums of the armada, still echoing faintly from the Gulf. He heard the breakers on the north beach, the wind in the forest, the cry of a hawk as it circled the abandoned tower. Then another sound, a faint flapping, close at hand. Mr Isul lifted his sack and gave the contents a poke.

'Wood hens for dinner,' he said.

Now, lying awake in the darkness by his shipmates, Pazel almost wished the armada had borne down on the village, landed some undreamed-of army, slain them all. *Eleven Forty-Four.* His mind still screamed with laughter at the notion – absurd, preposterous, tell me another – but his heart, his body, his nerves were not so sure.

There was the Red Storm. A band of scarlet light, stretching east to west across the Nelluroq. They had sailed right into it. The light within was liquid, blinding; it had filled their clothes, their lungs, eventually their minds, until they swam in the light like fish in a red aquarium, and then it was gone.

And later, when he and Thasha and the others began to discuss it, hadn't they all asked much the same question? How long was I in there? Why can't I account for the time?

His friends Neeps and Marila thought it had lasted days. But Hercól felt it had blown past them in six or eight hours, and Ensyl, the ixchel woman who had become their friend and ally, spoke of 'that blind red morning'. Pazel himself had not dared to guess, and when he had asked Thasha how long she thought they had spent in the storm, she had looked at him with fear. 'Not so long,' she'd said. But her voice brought him no comfort.

Two hundred years. How could he toy with believing that? If it were true then everyone he'd left behind was dead. No more searching for his mother and sister. No more hope that one day his father, Captain Gregory Pathkendle, would return and beg forgiveness of his abandoned son.

Angry now, Pazel opened his eyes. Rin, how he wished he could talk to Neeps. Pazel felt astonishingly lost without the smaller tarboy, his first friend on the *Chathrand*. Neeps was clever and fiercely protective of his friends, but he was also a hothead with a knack for getting in trouble. Look at him now: trapped with Marila and Captain Rose and a dozen others, held hostage in a cabin filled with a poisoned vapour that would kill them if they stopped breathing it. What would happen to them? Would they ever leave that room alive? Every thought of his friends was black and terrifying, like that plunge into the sea.

He studied Thasha again: smooth apple of a shoulder, yellow

lock of hair across her lips. Day by day the way he looked at her was changing. He wanted to be with her all the time. The fascination shamed him, somehow. Thasha was one of just a handful of women on the *Chathrand*, and if Pazel could not stop himself from thinking of her in this way, could not sleep with those smooth limbs in view, could not banish the thought that when the world was ending they could do as they liked in the final hours – then what about the rest of the men?

But you love her, Pazel. It's different with you.

That wasn't the point. Order on the *Chathrand* was breaking down. Arunis was still aboard her, in deep hiding; they could feel the sorcerer's presence like a whiff of something explosive in the musty air. The hostage stand-off, meanwhile, was in its sixth week, with no end in sight. The captain could hardly lead from inside a cage, yet the sailors trusted no one as much as savage, greedy, unbalanced Nilus Rose. He terrorised them, but he kept them working for their own survival. Now they were fighting among themselves: a thing Rose had brutally suppressed. Could even the Turachs keep the peace? When the ghastly news escaped, would they try? It was awful to reflect that their safety hinged on these men, elite killers all, and part of the same Imperial army that had sacked his city and beaten him into a coma. If they despaired it meant anarchy, a doomsday carnival. And who would protect the women in that case? Who would stop men who wished to die from taking their last, low pleasures with Thasha Isiq?

He heard their muttering, vile and explicit (how often they forgot about his horde of languages). What they needed, how exactly they wanted her to touch them, who they imagined she already was—

'Pathkendle.'

Pazel jumped. It was Hercól who had whispered. The Tholjassan lay with his eyes open, looking at him intently, and Pazel blushed, wondering how much Hercól had guessed of his thoughts.

'I wasn't—'

Hercól put a finger to his lips. Then, after a long, listening moment, he rose to his feet, beckoning Pazel to do the same. Pazel stood, balancing carefully among the sleepers. Hercól moved swiftly down the beach towards the Gulf. Pazel followed reluctantly. Two steps away from the fire and he was cold.

The moon suddenly brightened, and looking back Pazel saw it emerging from behind the twisted snag of Narybir Tower. Hercól walked in the foam, through the rainbow threads of surf. 'Do as I do,' he whispered. 'Stay deep enough to hide your tracks. I don't want them waking and following us.'

He started west, and Pazel splashed along behind. 'You're taking me to read that memorial, aren't you?' he asked.

'No need,' said Hercól. 'I told a lie back there, lad. I could read the inscription well enough. It is in their Imperial Common, and even in written form it resembles Arquali. But the message is somewhat terrible.'

'What does it say?'

Hercól paused in his march. He spoke without looking back at Pazel. '"*Here two hundred traitors were thrown chained into the sea. Here the Chaldryl Resistance met its demise. We are Bali Adro, the Limitless; in time we will conquer the sun.*"'

Pazel felt the words like a blow to the chest. 'Oh Rin,' was all he could say.

'I thought it best to spare the others,' said Hercól. 'They have heard enough bad news tonight. Come on, then, lad.'

With that he stepped out of the surf and began to climb the beach again.

'But where are we going?' asked Pazel, hurrying after him. 'Did you find a village, like the one across the inlet?'

'Nothing of the kind. Ibjen spoke the truth: this place is abandoned.'

'Then what are we doing out here?'

'Spying,' said Hercól. 'Now hold your tongue.'

They crossed the beach and mounted the dunes, which were tall and crowned with brush and cast black shadows. It was perhaps the strangest walk of Pazel's life: naked, freezing, the enormous crabs darting suddenly across their path, lifting armoured claws. Spying on whom? Bolutu had claimed that there were still other peoples, neither dlömic nor human, in his beloved South. Was that what lay ahead?

They threaded a path through the dunes, Hercól now and then bending to pluck some small twig or shell from the ground, which he would examine and then toss aside. In this way they slogged a mile or more. It was hard going, but the exertion lessened the cold.

'Hercól,' Pazel asked, 'what's the matter with Thasha? Do you know?'

Hercól stopped long enough to take a single breath. 'I cannot say,' he answered at last, 'nor have I ever known just what ails her, since the day Empress Maisa sent me to Etherhorde, to keep watch over her family. But I think we must expect her condition to grow worse before it improves. Worse, or at the very least more intense. Ramachni, Oggosk, Arunis himself – every practitioner of magic she has ever encountered – has taken an interest in Thasha, and that cannot be coincidental. And now, when we face a deluge of magic, Thasha herself has begun to change.'

'She's changing, all right. But into what?'

'I will not voice my guesses until I can trust them further,' said Hercól. 'Yet of one thing I am certain: Thasha faces a trial that will demand all her strength. And as her friend, Pazel – her irreplaceable friend – it may demand just as much from you.'

He marched on, and Pazel, brooding grimly on his words, struggled to keep up. At last they came to a point where they could hear the Nelluroq booming distantly on their right. Before them stood the tallest dune they had yet seen, a great hill of sand crowned with sea-oats and brush.

'When we reach the summit you must move only as I do,' said Hercól. 'Flat as snakes we must crawl, and slowly, slowly through the underbrush.'

It was a long, awkward climb. Halfway to the top, Hercól stopped for a moment, and pointed silently to the south. Pazel turned, and felt a thrill of wonder: low on the horizon hung a pale-blue light, smaller than the moon, but larger than any star.

'What is it?' he whispered.

'A legend of the South proved true,' said Hercól. 'The Polar Candle, the Little Moon of Alifros. North of the Ruling Sea it cannot be glimpsed, not ever. Bolutu tells me that many in the South think it has power over their lives and fates. Come, we are almost there.'

At the dune's flat summit, the roots of shrubs and sea-oats bound the sand into a fibrous mat. Hercól wriggled forwards, keeping his head well below the height of the grass. Pazel imitated him, cursing inwardly as burrs and thorns began to pierce his skin. There were crawling, biting insects too, and many small burrows from which came scurrying sounds. He would have been miserable, Pazel thought, even fully clothed.

The dune was wide, but they crossed it at last. And suddenly they were lying, side by side, looking down upon a wide sand basin. It was about the size of the village square across the inlet, and ringed on all sides by dunes, except for a narrow gap on the north side leading down to the sea.

In the centre of the basin a fire was crackling, somewhat larger and brighter than their own. And beside the fire three figures crouched.

'They're human!' Pazel whispered.

'Yes,' said Hercól.

'Not, not the—'

'Not *tol-chenni*, no. Be very still, Pazel, and watch.'

They were roasting a small animal on a spit. They wore tattered clothes – but they *were* clothes, not scraps and rags like the *tol-chenni*. Indeed, the three figures had an encampment of sorts: crates stacked up like building blocks, a makeshift tent of rough fabric, jugs and amphorae squatting in the sand. And the figures were armed: swords, daggers, some kind of club. All three looked strong and capable.

Two were men. The figure on the left, turning the spit, might have been forty: he had a severe face and black hair streaked with grey that fell in curls to his shoulders. Across from him crouched a younger and much larger man, big as any Turach. His eyes were shut and his hands folded before him; he might well have been speaking a prayer. The third figure, whose back was to them, was a young woman.

'Then it's not true,' Pazel hissed. 'The mind-plague, it *hasn't* wiped everyone out! Hercól, maybe it never struck anywhere but in that village. And if they're wrong about the plague, they could be wrong about the two hundred years!'

'Gently, lad,' said Hercól.

But Pazel, clutching suddenly at hope, was not to be calmed. 'Maybe the village was quarantined – way off the mainland, see? – because everyone there went mad together, dlömu and humans alike.'

'Come,' said Hercól. 'The humans become idiots, and the dlömu *at the same time* fall victim to a shared delusion about the cause?'

'Why not? It's more likely than what they claim, isn't it?'

'Watch the girl, Pazel.'

Pazel looked: she was lifting a blackened kettle from the embers. Turning, she filled three cups beside her with steaming drink. Pazel saw her silhouette against the fire, and thought his heart would stop.

'Neda,' he said.

'Ah,' said Hercól.

'*Aya Rin*,' said Pazel. 'Hercól, she looks *exactly* like my sister Neda.'

'Perhaps she is.'

Pazel gazed helplessly at the swordsman. He could not speak for fear. It wasn't the villagers, or Thasha, or half the human race who had gone mad. It was just him, Pazel. Actually mad: he would shut his eyes for a moment, and when he opened them again he'd be in sickbay, feverish, his tenth day without water; or still tied up in that cave on Bramian. That was the only explanation.

'When one of the men turns away,' said Hercól, 'try to catch a glimpse of his neck.'

'You never met my sister. You couldn't know what she looks like. I think I'm crazy, Hercól.'

'Enough of that. I've looked at her portrait a hundred times. It hung for years in Dr Chadfallow's study in Etherhorde, alongside your mother's and your own. It hangs in his cabin now. But that portrait must be ten years old. I could not be sure it was her, until you saw for yourself.'

'But how in the blary howling Pits could she be *here*?'

'Look! There's an answer for you, or the beginning of one.'

The older man was reaching for something on his right. He leaned forwards, and his long hair fell away from his neck. The firelight showed a black tattoo, a pattern of strokes and diamonds.

'Lord Rin above,' said Pazel. 'They're Mzithrinis.'

So they were: three citizens of the Mzithrin Pentarchy, the enemy state, the rival power that had fought the Empire of Arqual to one blood-soaked draw after another, for centuries. Dr Chadfallow had always claimed that he'd placed Neda in the hands of a Mzithrini diplomat, to save her from becoming a slave or concubine of the invading Arqualis. It could have happened, Pazel thought: she might have taken on their customs, their beliefs. In five years she might have become almost anyone.

'What should we do?' he whispered.

'I brought you here that you might help me decide,' said Hercól. 'They are Mzithrini, to be sure. Which means that they, like us, have somehow crossed the Ruling Sea. But they are not common sailors. Those tattoos declare holy orders. They are *sfvantskor*, warrior-priests. And if they choose to attack us, they will win.'

'Neda won't attack me.'

'Pazel, if she has taken the Last Oath and become a true *sfvantskor*, she will do whatever her leader commands. In some parts of the Mzithrin the newly sworn are told to leap one by one into a covered pit. Most find the bottom filled with rose petals, but one lands on razor-sharp stakes. The rest honour his sacrifice with prayers, and taste his blood for discipline.'

'That's horrible!'

'No worse than what a Turach endures. Those three, however, may have a special reason to detest us: the loss of their ship. The men were aboard the *Jistrolloq* when it drew alongside us in Simja. I dare say your sister was as well.'

'She spoke to me,' said Pazel suddenly. 'A *sfvantskor* girl in a mask whispered to me in the shrine – she told me to turn away from evil, as if one *could* – Hercól, how can they be alive? We sank the *Jistrolloq* months ago, in the middle of the Ruling Sea.'

'Months,' said Hercól, 'or two hundred years?'

Pazel froze, then lowered his face, grinding his forehead into the sand.

'If we decide to speak to them,' said Hercól, 'let us take care not to speak of *that*. So far it has been a secret among the two of us, Thasha and Bolutu. Let it remain so, for now.'

'It's not true, anyway,' said Pazel. 'That part *can't* be true.'

'Why not?' said Hercól.

'Because if two hundred years have passed, then the whole conspiracy's failed. And the war must be long over, if it ever came to war.'

'Certainly,' said Hercól.

'And your Empress Maisa is dead, and everyone we cared about, everyone who knew our mucking names.'

'Catastrophes are only unthinkable until they occur. You Ormalis should know that.'

'I'll tell you why, then,' said Pazel. 'Because if it's true then I really will go mad. Barking blary mad.'

Hercól's hand slipped under his jaw. Gently, but with an iron strength, he lifted Pazel's chin. His eyes were sharp and wary in the moonlight.

'Please,' he said, 'don't.'

*

The Mzithrinis could smell the rabbit crackling on the spit. It was all they could do not to pluck the carcass from the fire and devour it, raw though it surely was on the inside. They had come ashore ravenous, and found only crabs. They had lived for four days now on crabs – to be precise, on the legs and eyestalks of crabs: the bodies of the creatures had proven so toxic that their leader, Cayer Vispek, had nearly died, his throat swollen until he battled to breathe. When he recovered he cited the Old Faith proverb about the glutton who choked on the wishbone of a stolen goose, and the younger *sfvantskor* laughed.

They had laughed again when he showed them the rabbit, and asked if they would not rather wait for morning. Then it was Jalantri's turn to quote the scripture, as he scrambled from the tent: *'And should the morning never come, how now, my soul?'*

Their master smiled, but only faintly: one did not make light of the soul. It was man's claim on eternity, his gift from the omnipotence that some called Rin or God or the Gods, but which Mzithrinis would never presume to shackle with a name.

Jalantri had scurried like a boy to build the fire. Neda had skinned and gutted the rabbit, while Cayer Vispek walked out to the beach to touch the Nelluroq, and whisper quietly to the five hundred brethren who had perished there.

By the time he had returned the rabbit was sizzling. Now, sipping their brackish tea, they felt as though the smell was already nourishing them, the appetiser to the feast.

Jalantri saw the intruder first. A youth, standing in the brush on the high eastern dune, looking down with the moonlight behind him. *'Vrutch,'* he swore. 'I thought we'd driven them off.'

Cayer Vispek stopped turning the spit. 'He's the first one to come upon us from the east,' he said. 'How peculiar. The land ends in just a few miles that way. Perhaps he smelled the rabbit.'

Neda glanced up at the boy and shrugged. 'He can't have any of mine,' she said.

Jalantri's big chest rumbled with laughter. But their leader stilled him with a hand. The youth had started towards them, slide-stepping down the dune. They rose, tensing. Not one of the witless humans had ever tried to approach them, even in stealth. This one had to know he was being observed, yet on he came. The shadow of the dune hid his features. But there could be no doubt: he was deliberately approaching. They scanned the basin on every side: no companions. Neda drew her dagger. Jalantri pulled a burning stick from the fire and strode forwards, waving it.

'*Ya! Away!*' he shouted, in a voice for scaring dogs. The youth paused. Then he took a deep breath and continued towards them.

Cayer Vispek bent and picked up a fist-sized stone from the fire ring. 'I am going to kill this one,' he informed them rather sadly. 'If they lose their fear they will give us no peace. Don't help; it will be easier if he doesn't run.'

Neda squinted at the figure, intuition gathering inside her like a storm. Then the Cayer walked past Jalantri and waited, turned slightly away from the youth, the stone loose in his hand. He was a deadly shot. The rabbit might have been no closer when he crushed its skull.

The youth reached the foot of the dune. He stepped from its shadow, and Cayer Vispek whirled and threw the stone with all his might. And Neda screamed.

Sound flies faster than any arm – and Pazel lived because the Cayer's mind was faster yet. He skewed the stone with his fingertips as he released it, and the shot went wide. As the youth flinched and ducked, Neda ran forwards, crying his name.

'Stop!' roared a voice from the dune-top. A second figure, a grown man, was flying down its shadowed face. 'Harm that boy and I swear I'll send you to meet your faceless Gods! Damn you, Pazel, I should never have agreed—'

The youth looked at Neda. He was more ashamed than afraid, standing before her without a stitch of clothing. A different body, but the same fierce, awkward frown. She had seen that look ten years ago, him standing in a tiled basin, and Neda, the older sister, approaching with a sponge.

The hug she gave him was pure instinct, as were the tears she shed in a single, toothy sob. But before he could return the embrace she released him and stepped back, glaring through her tears. A *sfvantskor* could not put her arms around him. A sister could not do otherwise.

3

The Orfuin Club

Who has sown the dark waters in sorghum and rye?
Who has whispered to gravestones and heard their reply?
In the deluge of autumn, who has danced and stayed dry?
Let him gaze on the River, and sigh.

Anonymous Hymn, Vasparhaven

'Arunis, what do you fear?'

The speaker was a short, round-faced, pot-bellied man with thick glasses, dressed in clothes the colour of autumn wheat. In both hands he cradled a large cup of tea, the steam of which billowed white in the chilly breeze on the terrace. On the table before him a red marble paperweight held down one sheet of parchment. At the man's feet squirmed a small creature, something like an armadillo, except that it lacked any obvious head, and instead of limbs, two feathery antennae and countless tentacle-like feet emerged from its shell. The creature was foraging for insects; as it moved in the torchlight it became invisible, transparent and darkly opaque by turns.

'I fear that one of us will expire before the woman arrives,' said a second figure – a tall, gaunt man in a black coat and white scarf, ravenous of mouth and eye, who stood near the doorway letting into the club, orange firelight on his left cheek, cold and darkness on his right. 'Otherwise, nothing at all. I have no time for fear. Besides, there is no safer house than yours, Orfuin. Safety is your gift to all comers.'

The doorway was framed by leafy vines, within which a keen observer might glimpse movement, and now and then a tiny form of man or woman, running along a stem, or peering from a half-hidden window the size of a stamp. From within the club came music – accordion, fiddle, flute – and the drowsy chatter of the patrons. It was always late at the Orfuin Club; by daylight the tavern's many entrances could not be found.

'Safety from the world without,' corrected the pot-bellied man, 'but if you bring your own doom within these walls, you can hardly expect them to protect you. What is that thing in your hand, wizard?'

'A product of a sorcery beyond my knowledge,' said Arunis, displaying the shiny, slightly irregular metal cube. '*Ceallrai*, it is called, or *mintan*, *batori*, *pilé*. The lamp you keep on the table on the third floor draws its fire from some source within the metal. It is a feeble sorcery and does not last. This one is dead; the goat-faced creature who wipes your tables gave it to me.'

'That is why he is always opening the lamp.' The man called Orfuin chuckled. 'It was in his sack of trinkets, when he came to me so long ago, fleeing assassins in his own world. He loves that ugly lamp. Arunis, you resemble a human being; did you begin life as such?'

Arunis scowled, then hurled the metal object into the darkness beyond the terrace. 'What can be keeping her? Does she think I have all night?'

Orfuin took a languorous sip of tea. He moved the paperweight, glanced briefly at the parchment. 'You are not a frequent guest,' he said to Arunis, 'but you are of long standing. And in all the time you have been coming here I have observed no change. You are impatient. Never glad of where you are. Never cognizant that it may be better than where you are going.'

Arunis looked directly at the man for the first time, and there was no love in his glance, only pride and calculation. 'You *will* see a change,' he said.

The little animal scurried under Orfuin's chair. The innkeeper looked down into his tea with an air of disappointment. Then he lowered his hand and scratched the little creature along the edge of its shell.

'I thought all *yddeks* had been exterminated,' said the mage, 'but now I see that you welcome them like pets.'

'They were here before us, in the River of Shadows,' said Orfuin. 'They come and go as they please. But they're rare today, true enough. This one swam out of the River while you were inside. He's quite a bold little fellow.'

'He is a masterpiece of ugliness,' said the sorcerer. Then, with a sharp motion of his head, he added: 'I am leaving; I have urgent work on the *Chathrand*. You will inform the woman that Arunis Wytterscorm cannot be kept waiting, like a schoolboy for his coach.'

Orfuin took another meditative sip of tea, then rose and walked to the edge of the terrace.

There was no rail, and no wood or garden beyond. There was only the sheer stone edge, a few vines curling up from below, and beyond them a roaring darkness, a torrent of rising wind little illuminated by the club's lamplight. Orfuin leaned out expertly, gazing down into the void, and the blasting air held him up. When he pulled himself back from the edge he had not even spilled his tea.

'She is here,' he said.

Even as he spoke three figures shot past the terrace from below. They were spectral, blurred; but when the gale had carried them fifty feet above the terrace they spread their arms and slowed, and descended weightlessly, like beings of cinder. Arunis watched them with an expression of nonchalance, but his body was rigid from head to foot. The three figures alighted without a sound.

They were ghastly to behold. Two bone-white women, one black man. All three were tall – one might even have said stretched – with long, gaunt mouths and cheekbones, staring eyes like dark searchlamps and grasping, spindly hands. They wore finery fit for court, but it was tattered, filthy, with an air of the tomb. The

41

nearest woman trailed yards of faded lace. She pointed a lacquered nail at Arunis and shrieked: 'Where is the Nilstone, traitor?'

'A delight to see you again as well, Macadra,' said Arunis. 'The centuries have left you quite unchanged.' He turned his gaze on the other two: a stocky woman clutching a dagger in each hand, and a black man, coldly observant, fingers resting on the pommel of a sword. 'Your friends are younger, I think? But not too young to have heard of me.'

'Oh, you're not forgotten,' said the black man. The woman with the daggers sneered.

'They must depart at once, of course,' Arunis continued. 'You promised to come alone.'

'Promised!' said the tall Macadra. 'That word should burn your tongue. Ivrea and Stoman are here as witnesses. Though if you forget whom you serve your punishment will be too swift for trial.'

Then Arunis walked forwards, until he stood one pace from the woman. 'I serve no one – or no one you dare to contemplate,' he said. 'You may have gained power over brittle Bali Adro, but your Order has stagnated. I have not. Think of that before you speak of punishments again.'

Macadra's upper lip curled incredulously. Arunis let the silence hold a moment, and then continued in a lighter tone, 'But if you refer to my *cooperation* – well, really, Macadra, how could I have done more? You dispatched me to northern Alifros without gold, or guardians, or allies of any kind. Yes, you helped me escape the old regime. But at such a price! You bade me shatter two human empires, to prepare the world for its grand reunification – under the Ravens, of course.'

'Under Bali Adro,' snapped Macadra. 'The Ravens are merely advisers to His Majesty.'

'And a conductor merely *advises* his orchestra to perform.'

For a moment the woman checked her rage. She looked rather pleased with the analogy.

'You have not yet killed the girl,' she said. 'Are you that afraid of her?'

'Afraid of Thasha Isiq?' said Arunis, and this time he won a smile of amusement from all three of the newcomers. 'No, Macadra, I do not fear her. She will die at the appropriate time, as will all of her circle. But why should I rush to kill my greatest accomplice?'

Macadra laughed aloud. 'You have not changed either, Arunis Wytterscorm. Still working with puppets, are you? Painting in their faces, tying your invisible strings.'

'Shall I tell you something, madam?' said Orfuin suddenly, looking up from his tea. 'Life is finite. That is to say, it ends. Why not spend it pleasantly? There's gingerbread fresh from the oven. Leave off this scheming and be my guests. Hear the music. Warm your feet.'

His gaze was mild and friendly. The newcomers stared at him as if unsure what sort of creature he was. Then Arunis went on, as if the man had never spoken:

'I have been splendid, Macadra – that you cannot deny. I took a harmless madman and built him into the Shaggat Ness, a slaughtering messiah, a knife upon which both Arqual and the Mzithrin are preparing to throw themselves. And I managed to let the Arqualis believe the entire affair was in their interests – indeed, that *they* had devised the plot, alone. What general with legions at his fingertips ever accomplished so much? Either Northern power could mount a fight to try the strength of Bali Adro – together, they might even have bested you. Instead they think only of killing one another, and will soon begin to do so with more determination than you have ever seen.'

'Your Shaggat is dead!' screamed the woman with the daggers. 'A peasant boy turned him into a lump of stone!'

'The Pathkendle boy may have started life as a peasant,' said Arunis, 'but he is now a *Smythídor*, magic-altered, blood and bone. The great Ramachni entrusted him with Master-Words, and one of these he used against the Shaggat. But Ramachni's gamble was a losing one, for in so arming Pathkendle he exhausted himself, and had to abandon his friends. And for what? They wish to kill me; they cannot. They seek a new and safer resting place for the

Nilstone; they will not find one. And the Shaggat – he is *not* dead, merely enchanted. He will breathe again, mark my words.'

'Suppose he does,' said Macadra. 'Suppose you complete this journey, hand him back to his faithful on Gurishal. Suppose we help you to that end.'

Arunis bowed his head, as though to say he would not spurn such aid.

'What will we gain for our efforts? All I see ahead is the self-destruction of the Mzithrin in a civil war. And afterwards, the total victory of the Arqualis. You will leave us with one giant foe in the North, rather than the smaller pair we face today.'

'Not if you do as I suggest,' said Arunis.

Macadra smiled. 'I saw that coming ere our feet touched the ground. Show it to me, wizard. I have waited long enough.'

When Arunis said nothing, Macadra swept towards the doorway of the club, never glancing once at the proprietor. She gazed into the warm firelight. A hush fell over the patrons; the musicians ceased to play.

'Where is it?' she demanded. 'Is someone holding it for you at one of the tables?' She turned him a searching look. 'Is it on your person?'

'My dear lady,' said Arunis, 'we must have words about the Nilstone.'

'Are you saying that you have come here *without* it?'

'How could I do otherwise? You offer me no assurance that you speak for the Ravens. I do not even have proof that yours is the same Order that dispatched me to the North so long ago.'

'But how *dare* you leave it unguarded! What possible excuse—'

She broke off, a new thought writing itself in a frown upon her colourless face. With a sharp sound of rage she drove both hands, nails first, into Arunis' chest. Her fingers sank to the first digits, then she ripped her hands apart. The mage's flesh vanished briefly, obscured by a sudden haze. Arunis stepped back, and the woman's fingers emerged unbloodied.

'I told you!' said the woman with the daggers. 'We make the

dark journey in person; he sends a dream-shell, a mirage! He'll never give up the Nilstone! He means to *use* it, Macadra, to use it against us all!'

'As you have just observed,' said Arunis, 'I could not very well leave the Stone unguarded aboard the *Chathrand*. And why not come in trance to the Orfuin Club, this place where all worlds meet so easily – even the worlds of our dreams?'

'You should have come in the flesh *to hand over the Stone*,' growled the stocky woman, 'as you swore to do two centuries ago.'

The black man looked at Arunis with contempt. 'If you do not track this mage to his ship and kill him, Macadra,' he said, 'you are the greatest fool who ever lived.'

'We would not be talking at all if he had already mastered the Stone,' said Macadra. 'Say it, monster. What is it you want from the Ravens?'

Arunis walked to the table and took the parchment from beneath the paperweight. 'You are quite right,' he said. 'I cannot yet use the Nilstone, any more than you or Ramachni or any other since the time of Erithusmé. But you have misunderstood my purpose. I have never wished to make it mine. No, I seek only to finish what I have begun, what you sent me to accomplish so long ago – the ruin of Arqual and the Mzithrin, so that when Bali Adro's ships next assault the Nelluroq, they will find the whole of the Northern world hobbled and broken, and ready for their conquest. And you Ravens, the true power behind Bali Adro – why, you shall shape this world to your liking. One rule, one law, one Empire spanning both shores of the Ruling Sea, and you at its apex. I am making your dream a reality, Macadra. But to complete it I need the *Chathrand* a while longer – and the Nilstone.'

Macadra smiled, venomously. 'Of course you do.'

Arunis held up the parchment. 'This is no mirage,' he said. 'Take it, read it.'

The black man leaned forwards. 'That's a *Carsa Carsuria*. An Imperial decree.'

'Give me a new crew for the Great Ship,' said Arunis. 'A dlömic crew, with a dlömic captain. The humans nearly destroyed her on the first crossing. They allowed her to be infested with rats and ixchel. They let a lone Mzithrini gunship come close to sinking her. They should never have been trusted with such a vessel. Take this to Bali Adro City. Make your slave-Emperor sign it, and dispatch a crew to Masalym with all possible haste.'

'Don't, Macadra!' hissed the stocky woman. 'He'll just slip away again! Don't let him!'

Arunis closed his eyes a moment. 'Your servants prattle like children. I have no desire to *slip away*. Indeed, I hoped to persuade you to sail with me. You could be of great help with the Red Storm – I know how intensely you have studied it, Macadra – and besides, you could keep your eye on the Stone.'

The black man laughed. 'Sail with him on the *Chathrand*. Just walk aboard that spell-ridden hulk, straight into his lair.'

'With a crew that answers to your Emperor,' said Arunis. 'As for the humans: simply hold them in Masalym until the charm breaks and the Shaggat returns to life. After that they are of no consequence.'

Still Macadra did not reach for the parchment. 'We help you cross the Ruling Sea again,' she said. 'We guide you through the time-trap of the Storm, and let you take your Shaggat to Gurishal. He rallies his worshippers, leads them into a doomed but damaging civil war inside the Mzithrin. And when the Mzithrin stands gasping and wounded over the corpse of the Shaggat's rebellion, their old foe Arqual strikes them from behind, presumably—'

'Unquestionably,' said Arunis. 'Their monarch dreams of it night and day.'

'As well he should!' shouted Macadra. 'That is where your plan collapses. It will take us two decades to build a fleet that could brave the Nelluroq and seize the Northern world. How do you propose to keep the Arqualis from using that time to make a fortress of those lands?'

For a moment Arunis looked at her in silence. Then he took her arm and drew her towards the tavern door, not far from where

46

Orfuin sat glumly, the little animal flickering in and out of sight beside his feet. Looking back to make sure the others had not followed, Arunis murmured into her ear.

'What?' screamed Macadra, breaking violently away. 'Are you joking, mage, or have you taken leave of your senses?'

'Come,' said Arunis. 'Don't pretend it's not the solution you've been hunting for. The South is free of humans already, unless you count the degenerate *tol-chenni*. This will merely finish the job.'

'It would finish far more than humankind,' she said. 'You cannot control such a force!'

'I can,' said Arunis. 'Through the Nilstone, and the puppet we call the Shaggat Ness. Help me, Macadra. I know the Ravens wish it done.'

Macadra stared at the parchment. 'You speak as though we were devils.'

'That is what you are,' said Orfuin.

He rose, startling them all. 'The bar is closed. I will give you two minutes to conclude your business here.'

The four mages gaped at him. 'You can't mean it,' said the black man, smiling uncertainly. 'You're famous for your neutrality, old man.'

'That and my gingerbread,' said Orfuin, 'and precious little else. Goodbye, Arunis. Plot your holocaust elsewhere.'

He clapped his hands sharply. At once several dozen tiny figures, shorter even than ixchel, emerged from the vines with brooms and began sweeping the terrace before the arch. The guests within the tavern slammed down their mugs and rose, shuffling for the exits as though obeying some irresistible command. The little *yddek* scurried across the terrace and flung itself into the night.

'This is unprecedented,' said Arunis, 'and if I may say so, unwise.'

Orfuin shrugged. 'Neutral or not, the club is my own.'

'But we have nowhere else to meet!' said Macadra.

'Then you have nowhere to meet.'

He entered the bar and began snuffing lights. Stoman, face twisting with fury, stamped dead one of the tiny sweepers; the rest fled back into the vines. One by one, like wary dogs, the tables and chairs slid of their own accord through the archway. The wind grew suddenly louder. The four figures stood alone.

'Devils in this life,' said Arunis, looking only at Macadra, 'but in the next something else altogether.'

He held out the parchment. Macadra met his gaze, snarled, and took it from his hand. She placed it inside her dress and raised her arms.

'Do not think us fools, sorcerer. We will send you a crew indeed! And when your work is done the Nilstone will return to the Ravens.'

'When my work is done I shall not need it,' said Arunis.

Somewhere a door slammed shut. Then the archway became a wall, and the vines closed in like scaly curtains, and suddenly there was nothing beneath their feet but the roaring immensity of the darkness, cold and mighty as a vertical river, bearing them away from one another and towards the lee shore of their dreams.

4

Brothers and Blood

~⁊⁊~

22 Ilbrin 941*
221st day from Etherhorde

Introductions were strained. The two younger *sfvantskors* had some Arquali, learned in preparation for Treaty Day; Cayer Vispek spoke barely a word. Pazel, on the other hand, spoke Mzithrini better than his sister. Vispek and Jalantri listened with open suspicion.

'You say you learned such diction, such grace with our tongue . . . from books?' the elder *sfvantskor* demanded.

Pazel glanced uneasily at Neda. 'That's how it started,' he said.

'It's the truth, Cayer,' said Neda. 'Pazel is a natural scholar. He taught himself Arquali by the time he was eight. Other languages, too. But they were mostly just nonsense from his grammar books, until our birth-mother cast the spell.'

'The one that changed him, but not you,' said Jalantri.

Neda shrugged, dropping her eyes. 'It gave me white hair for three months.'

Cayer Vispek shook his head in wonder. 'And made him able to collect languages as easily as a boy puts marbles in a bag.'

'Not that easily,' Pazel objected.

Neda sat between her brother *sfvantskors* and looked at Pazel much as they did, with doubt that was nearly accusation. Of course, Pazel was shocked to learn that she had become a *sfvantskor*. But

---

* It should now be abundantly clear that all such cited dates are open to question. – EDITOR.

how much greater had her shock been! During the invasion of Ormael she had watched Arquali marines beat him senseless, while their fellow soldiers rampaged through the family house, smashing everything they could not eat or slip in their pockets. Five years later, hidden by a mask, she had seen Pazel with Thasha Isiq: daughter of the very admiral who led the invasion.

Every Mzithrini youth learned to hate Arqualis. There were reasons of history, war stories from uncles and teachers, scars on temple walls. But few of Neda's age had as many reasons as she.

Nine of those reasons had crowded into a single hour. Nine reasons who had dragged her screaming into a barn.

Now her brother served those same Arqualis – cared for them, loved them maybe. Neda had known about him since the morning of Treaty Day, more than four months ago. But the thought still made her want to scream.

For she too had spoken but part of the truth. Her mother's spell had done more than change the colour of her hair. It was an augmentation hex; it took an innate gift, whatever one was naturally best at, and strengthened it a thousandfold. At first Neda thought that her mother had nearly killed her only to prove that she was plain and stupid: a girl with no gifts to augment. Only years later, in training to be a *sfvantskor*, had she realised that she did possess one gift: a prodigious memory. And as she aged, and so had more years of life to remember, the spell had come into its own.

Now her memory was vast and merciless. It rarely obeyed her will. She might try for hours to summon a specific fact, and fail. But when she made no effort her memory worked on, like an involuntary organ, pumping, flooding her with knowledge she did not want. As it was doing now. The dust sculpting beams of light through a high window in the barn. The nine voices of those soldiers. The underside of each chin.

Cayer Vispek offered to share the rabbit, but Pazel and the Tholjassan man gently declined; they could see that the others were starved. Neda and her comrades attacked the meal in earnest, and as they chewed the man called Hercól Stanapeth began to speak. His Mzithrini was halting, like something remembered from a distant time, but with Pazel's help he told his tale.

And what a tale it was: the lie of the Great Peace, the treason plotted in Etherhorde, the riches hidden aboard the *Chathrand*, the fact that the Shaggat Ness had never died.

At this last confession Cayer Vispek had set down his plate. In the darkest of voices he asked Pazel to repeat Hercól's words. Then he put out a hand to the two younger *sfvantskors*.

'Your weapons. Quickly.'

Neda and Jalantri were astounded, but they obeyed, unbuckling their knives and swords and placing them in their leader's hands. Vispek closed his eyes for a long moment. When he opened them again they were deadly.

'The Ness,' he said to Hercól. 'You have harboured the Shaggat Ness, the Blasphemer, stained with the blood of half a million of our people. The one who broke the Mzithrin family, and beggared us all.'

'Arqual has done so, yes,' said Hercól.

'And he is aboard your ship even now?'

'He is enchanted,' said Hercól. 'Turned to lifeless stone; but we have reason to fear that the enchantment will be reversed. He is to be returned to his worshippers in Gurishal, to provoke a war inside your country.'

A brief silence, then Jalantri exploded to his feet. 'Give him a weapon, Cayer, and give me mine. The Shaggat! This has all been about the Shaggat! They mean to destroy us, to plant their flag on the ruins of Babqri and Surahk and Srag! Don't you, cannibals? Deny it if you dare!'

'The Father was right,' said Neda, with equal venom. 'He warned us that the *Chathrand* was carrying death in its hold.'

'Death in the guise of peace!' shouted Jalantri. 'Monsters! Cannibals!' He pointed contemptuously at Hercól. 'I need no weapon! Stand and fight me, stooge of Arqual!'

Hercól's eyes flashed at the insult, but he made no move to rise. 'Jalantri Reha,' hissed Cayer Vispek. 'Sit down ere you disgrace us all.'

The young *sfvantskor*'s mouth twisted in fury. He obeyed his master at last, but famished as he was he did not take another bite of his meal.

'We will not harm you,' said Vispek. 'But know this, men of the *Chathrand*: the Shaggat razed twenty townships along the banks of the Nimga, where Jalantri's people lived. Sailors in the delta said the river was like a vein gushing blood into the sea. Jalantri's parents met as refugees in the Babqri slums, orphans in a swarm of orphans, a generation without hope. And the Shaggat ordered many such massacres. You would be wise to tell us the simple truth of this business, and not a word less.'

'The truth is not simple, Cayer,' said Hercól. 'But it is true that Emperor Magad and his servants seek the ruin of the Mzithrin, and the expansion of Arqual across the whole world – the whole Northern world, I mean, which is all they comprehend of Alifros. They are meticulous deceivers. They held the Shaggat for forty years, after all, before springing this trap. But there is a subtler enemy than Arqual, and a greater threat.'

Then Hercól told them of Arunis, the Shaggat's mage, hiding even now somewhere aboard the *Chathrand*; and of a certain object that Arunis wished desperately to control. 'It is there in plain sight in the Shaggat's hand,' he said. 'And Arunis has meant all along for the Shaggat to have it, for by its power the mad king might not just weaken your Empire but conquer it – and Arqual as well. He has turned the conspiracy back upon its authors. But neither Arunis nor the Shaggat has yet mastered this thing, for it is an abomination. Indeed, no more deadly thing exists on either side of the Ruling Sea. It has many names, but the most common is the Nilstone.'

Neda glanced sharply at Cayer Vispek; her master's face was guarded and still. The Nilstone! Their own legends spoke of it: an object like a small glass sphere, made of the compressed ash of all the devils burned in the sacred Black Casket, until the Great Devil in his agonies split the Casket asunder. Neda had never known whether or not the Stone was real; if it was, she had supposed it would lie among the other treasures of Mzithrini antiquity, in the Citadel of Hing, protected by arms and spells.

'You stole it, then?' she demanded.

'No, Neda,' said Cayer Vispek. 'That is one crime for which Arqual bears no guilt. The Shaggat himself took the Nilstone from us, in his last, suicidal raid on Babqri.' Vispek hesitated a moment, then added: 'We rarely speak of that theft. It does no honour to the Pentarchy to have lost the Nilstone, though in fact we wished to be rid of it for centuries. The Father spoke of it to me – just once.'

Neda closed her eyes, feeling a cold stab of loss. *The Father.* He was a great Mzithrini mage-priest, and her rescuer, her patron. He had taken her from the hands of a lecherous diplomat and made her a *sfvantskor*: the only non-Mzithrini ever admitted to the fold.

'What did he say, Master?' asked Jalantri.

'That the Nilstone is more dangerous than all the ships and legions of Arqual put together,' said the older *sfvantskor*. '"We could not use it, Vispek," he told me, "and we dared not cast it away. Nor could any power in Alifros destroy it – one cannot destroy an absence, the idea of zero, the cold of the stellar void. In the end we guarded it merely to keep it from the hands of our enemies. And even in that we failed."'

'Not your people alone,' said Hercól. 'The very world has failed in the matter of the Nilstone. We have never fully grasped its nature. Your legends describe a thing of demonic ash. Others call it the eyeball of a murth-lord, or a tumour cut from the Tree of Heaven, or even a keyhole in an unseen door, leading to a place no mortal thought can penetrate. Our own leader, the mage Ramachni, tells us it is a splinter of rock from the land of the dead – and death is what it brings to any who touch it with fear in their hearts.'

'We've seen that with our own eyes,' added Pazel.

Neda turned him a bitter look. 'You've seen many things,' she said, 'but a few you've chosen to forget.'

Pazel looked at her, startled. 'What are you talking about?'

'So many fine friends you've made,' she said. 'Such worthy pursuits. To return the Shaggat to Gurishal, armed with such a weapon! How could you, Pazel? What have you become?'

Pazel's mouth worked fitfully; he was biting back a retort. But Hercól spoke first. 'Your brother has become what the world so sorely needs – a man without blind loyalties. Those who would restore the Shaggat to power are no comrades of ours. Pazel knew nothing of the conspiracy or the Nilstone when he was brought aboard the *Chathrand*, but he has taken an oath to fight these men, and Arunis as well, until we find a way to place the Stone beyond the reach of them all. That is our charge. None of us knows how it is to be done, but we would have failed already without your brother. Several times already the fight has turned on his courage.'

Pazel flushed, more from Hercól's praise than the *sfvantskors*' dubious looks. 'We have some damned good allies,' he murmured.

'Like Thasha Isiq?' asked Neda with contempt.

'Yes,' said Pazel. 'Haven't you been listening, Neda? Thasha was fooled along with the rest of us.'

'And her father too, no doubt,' said Jalantri. 'Tricked into leading fleets against the Mzithrin, all those years.'

'No,' Pazel admitted reluctantly.

But Hercól said, 'Yes, tricked. Eberzam Isiq loved Arqual and believed everything its Emperor proclaimed. The very Emperor who sent a woman to his bed, to become his consort and confidante, and to slowly poison him through his tea. She would have killed him as soon as Thasha married your prince. When we left Simja, Eberzam remained, determined to expose Arqual's plot to the world.'

'Nonsense!' said Vispek. 'We remained in port for five days after you sailed. I myself was often in the court of King Oshiram. There was no sign of Isiq about the castle, nor any mention of a plot.'

Hercól and Pazel looked at each other in dismay. 'They got him,' said Pazel. 'Oh Pitfire, Hercól. Someone got Isiq after all. What are we going to tell Thasha?'

The *sfvantskors* made sounds of amazement. *Tell her!* thought Neda. *She's alive, then! They lied about her death on top of everything!*

Hercól looked deeply shaken by Vispek's words. He steepled his fingers for a moment, then pressed on: 'Honoured Cayer, you can see that Pazel and I speak in good faith. That we come to you defenceless, when we might simply have waited for rescue from the *Chathrand*, and left you here, marooned as you clearly are. I do not ask for trust—'

'That is well,' said Cayer Vispek.

'—but I pray that you will see one thing for yourselves. The world has changed beneath our feet. And none of us will survive unless we also change. Into what? I cannot imagine. But whatever is to come will try us all, and terribly. We need strength, Cayer – strength of mind and heart and hand. The kind of strength your order teaches.'

Jalantri laughed aloud. 'What would you know of our order, stooge?'

'I know it forbids you to challenge another to a duel,' said Hercól, 'unless your master commands it. To do otherwise—' he closed his eyes, remembering '—is to place pride above holy destiny, and anger over service to the Faith.'

Jalantri stared at him, abashed and furious. Cayer Vispek was surprised as well. 'How is it that you quote so confidently from our scripture?' he demanded.

'Every member of the Secret Fist reads the Book of the Old Faith,' said Hercól. 'My copy remained with me when I forsook Ott's guild of spies. You see, Cayer, I know something of change. So does Neda's brother, incidentally.'

Vispek's eyes moved slowly from Hercól to Pazel and back again. He took a long breath, then pointed at the stack of crates across the basin.

'The one on top is full of clothing,' he said. 'Go and dress. Then I will tell you of a kind of change you know nothing about.'

They had numbered seven once. Seven: the Mzithrin lucky number, the standard complement of *sfvantskors* dispatched as a team to a particular Mzithrin King, or an army brigade, or a warship of the White Fleet. The latter had been Vispek's assignment: he was made votary to an elder aboard the *Jistrolloq*, deadliest ship in the Northern world, as famous for her speed and weaponry as the *Chathrand* was for size and age. Neda and Jalantri and several others came aboard after the murder of their teacher in Simja, and had been assigned to Vispek's care. They were still aspirants, barely out of training; by rights they should have been returned to the Mzithrin to do just that. But their teacher had planned otherwise.

That teacher, the great Babqri Father, had long suspected a trap behind the Arqualis' offer of peace. He had lived through more than a century of war and duplicity, but his knowledge was not merely that of years. He was the keeper of Sathek's Sceptre, an artefact older than the Mzithrin Empire itself, and one the Shaggat had not managed to steal. Crowning this golden rod was a crystal, and in the heart of the crystal lay a shard of the Black Casket, the broken centrepiece of the Old Faith.

Through the power of the sceptre the Father had come to sense the evil approaching in the belly of the *Chathrand*. Weeks before Treaty Day, he had come to Simja with his aspirants, and taken up residence in the Mzithrini shrine outside the city walls. There he had held council with Mzithrini lords, merchants, soothsayers, spies, as they congregated ahead of the wedding meant to seal the Peace. And there, night after night, he put his disciples in a trance and sent them into the sea, and by the power of the sceptre they cast off their human bodies and took the forms of whales.

'Whales?' said Pazel.

'Whales,' said Vispek. 'The better to observe your approach, and your doings aboard the *Chathrand*.'

'Your crew spotted us,' said Jalantri. 'We were a rare sort of whale, blue-black and small.'

'Cazencians,' said Pazel. 'Yes, I saw you – but it was here, on this side of the Ruling Sea. Neda, was that *you*?'

She gave a curt nod. 'We trailed you along the Sandwall.'

'Until attacked by sharks,' said Vispek. 'They were vicious and innumerable; we escaped them only by hurling ourselves upon this shore.'

'And these possessions?'

Vispek gestured with a turn of his head. 'Shipwreck. Three or four miles west, along the inner beach. A grim discovery, that. The bark itself was weird and slender, and partly burned; we thought it a derelict. But inside it was full of murdered creatures, like black men except for their hands, hair and eyes. Their throats were slit, all of them. On the deck where we found the bodies a word was scrawled in blood: PLATAZCRA. Can you tell us the meaning of that word, boy?'

He looked expectantly at Pazel, who nodded reluctantly, knowing his face had given him away. He knitted his eyebrows. 'Something like "victory" – no, "conquest" is closer. "Infinite conquest", that's it.'

They all looked at him, shaken. 'The boat was maimed,' said Cayer Vispek at last, 'but only partly looted. We found fine goods – fabrics, dyes, leather boots of excellent workmanship, even gold coins, scattered underfoot. It was as if the attackers had struck in haste, or fury, intent on nothing but the death of everyone aboard.'

'They took the food, though,' said Jalantri, frowning at the memory.

'Why didn't you return to the sea, once the sharks departed?' asked Pazel.

'We could not,' said Vispek. 'The Father tried to give us the power to change ourselves back and forth at will, but he never succeeded. Once we returned to human form, only the sceptre in a Master's hand could make us again into whales.'

'And the sceptre went down with the *Jistrolloq*?' said Hercól.

'I told you that we came here with nothing,' said Cayer Vispek.

57

'Our elder changed us a final time, even as the sea flooded the decks. That is the only reason we survived.'

Neda glanced sidelong at the Tholjassan warrior. *What a sly one. He knows the Cayer avoided his question.* She busied herself with the gnawing of flesh from a bone, thinking how cautiously their leader was handling this moment, how attentive they would have to be to his signals. *Above all we must say nothing of Malabron.*

Inside her the memory blazed, hideously clear. The collapsing hull, the grotesque speed of the inrushing sea, the old Cayerad bringing the sceptre down against her chest and the instant agony of the transformation, no pain-trance to deaden it. Squeezing from the wreckage, the whirling disorientation before she spotted the glowing sceptre again, in the aperture where the old man was working the change on a last *sfvantskor*: Malabron. She had watched his body swell like a blister. Confused and zealous Malabron; desperate, damned for evermore. He had believed in the utterances of mystics, believed they were nearing a time of cataclysm and the breaking of faiths. And with the enemy victorious and their mission a failure, Malabron the whale had done the unthinkable: bitten off the arm of the old Cayerad, swallowing it and the sceptre whole, and vanishing into the sudden blackness of the sea.

They had never seen him again, and Cayer Vispek had not speculated as to what had driven Malabron to such treason. Jalantri merely cursed his name. Neda, however, recalled his furious, quiet chatter, his ravings. In the last weeks they were almost continuous, in the hours when talking was allowed, and so much of it was outlandish nonsense that the others took no heed. But Neda heard it all, her manic memory sorting the drivel into categories and ranks. And in one category, by no means the largest, were his mutterings about 'the path our fathers missed' and 'those who fear to be purified'.

Neda chewed savagely. *You should have spoken. You could have warned Cayer Vispek before it was too late.* For Malabron's words had carried a sinister echo. They resembled the heresy once preached by the Shaggat Ness.

She cringed, feigning some bone or gristle in her mouth. *I couldn't do it. Not to any of them.* It had taken them five years to trust her, the foreign-born *sfvantskor*, almost a heresy in herself. Five years, and all the wrath and wisdom of the Father, taking her side. How could she have admitted that she did not trust them back – even just one of them? How could she have reported a brother?

'Neda?'

Pazel was staring at her. *Devils, I must take care with him!* For her birth-brother's glance was piercing. Even now he could read her better than Vispek or Jalantri.

She was struggling for calm. With an uncertain movement Pazel reached for her elbow.

'Do not touch her,' said Cayer Vispek.

Pazel jumped and shot him a look. 'I was just—'

'Coddling a *sfvantskor*,' said Jalantri, regarding Pazel with a mixture of amusement and contempt. 'Now I see why the Father did not wish the two of you to meet, sister. He knew no good could come of it.'

'Listen to me,' said Cayer Vispek to Pazel. 'The one before you is no longer an Ormali, no longer Neda Pathkendle. I do not expect this to be easy for you to grasp, but know that every parent, brother or sister of a *sfvantskor* has faced the same kind of loss.'

'The same, is it?' said Pazel, his eyes flashing. 'I haven't blary clapped *eyes* on my family in nearly six years.'

'Neda has left your family,' said Cayer Vispek. 'She has become Neda Ygraël, Neda Phoenix-Flame. And she has been reborn into a life of service to the Grand Family of the Mzithrin, and the *sfvantskor* creed. Only if you remember this can I permit the two of you to speak.'

'*Permit* us?' said Pazel, as though he couldn't believe his ears. 'She's my sister! Neda, is this what you want?'

Neda held herself very still. The eyes of all the men were upon her. With a ritual cadence to her words, she said, 'My past is of no consequence. I am a *sfvantskor*, a keeper of the Old Faith, foe of devils, friend of the Unseen. The life before was a game of make-believe. I can recall the game, but I am grown now and wish to play it no more.'

'So speaks our sister in the fullness of her choice,' said Cayer Vispek. 'You must accept her decision or else insult her gravely. Is that your wish?'

Pazel looked at the older man, and his dark eyes glinted with anger. But he held his tongue.

The Cayer watched him a moment longer, as though noting a source of future danger. Then, turning to Hercól again, he said, 'There is more I would know. What sort of land have we come to, where men are killed under the banner of *infinite conquest*? Who are these black beings with silver eyes? And where are the humans? We have only met with miserable savages, hardly better than beasts.'

When the telling was done Neda felt wounded. As if some crushing harm had struck her body, some venom or germ that stole her strength and clouded her mind. She believed Hercól; his voice was too raw and bleeding to be feigned – and she had seen the men he called *tol-chenni*, and had thought them imbeciles from the start. *But a plague of mindlessness.* She squatted by the fire, clenching her fists. *Protect us in this, our black hour*, she prayed. *Defend us, that we may water Alifros with the blessings of your will.* She addressed the prayer to the Unseen, the Nameless Ones, in the Mountains of Hoéled beyond the world. But did the Nameless Ones care about these strange Southern lands, or was their gaze fixed elsewhere? It was a troubling question, and probably forbidden.

Hercól looked up at the sky. 'Dawn comes,' he said. 'Pazel and I must return to our shipmates. And you three must make your choice, for I expect to see a boat from the *Chathrand* approaching by the time we reach them.'

'Choice?' said Neda, the bitterness rising in her again. 'What choice is that? To return to your ship and be put in irons, or stay here and starve?'

'We'll do neither of those,' said Jalantri, 'will we, Cayer Vispek?'

The older *sfvantskor* pursed his lips, and gave a thoughtful shake of his head. 'Perhaps not,' he said – and flew in a blur at Hercól.

The attack was one of the swiftest Neda had ever seen. Cayer Vispek bore the swordsman backwards off his crate, and by the time the two men struck the sand there was a knife at Hercól's throat. Pazel surged to his feet, but Jalantri was far faster, and deftly kicked the youth's legs out from under him. Pazel fell inches from the fire. The *sfvantskor* came down on him with both knees, caught his arm and twisted it behind his back. Jalantri looked wildly at Neda.

'I have him! Aid the Cayer, sister!'

'The Cayer needs no aid,' said Vispek, still pressing his blade to Hercól's neck.

'That's lucky!' snapped Jalantri. 'Neda, you sat like a stone! What ails you? Were you afraid I might give your birth-brother a scratch?'

Pazel twisted helplessly, grimacing with rage. Neda shuddered. She recalled that look of defiance. He had shown it to Arquali soldiers, once.

'It was not luck,' said Cayer Vispek. 'The Tholjassan chose to yield. *Chose*, I say: you saw my intention, didn't you, swordsman? As plain as though I had drawn it for you in the sand.'

'I guessed,' said Hercól, motionless under the knife.

'You are too humble. I saw your readiness even as I struck. You might even have disarmed me, but you chose not to try. That was an error. You are prisoners now, and it may not go well for you.'

'What will you do now, Cayer?' asked Hercól.

'We will take the rescue boat, by persuasion or force, and seek the mainland.'

'If you take us as hostages on that boat, the *Chathrand* will know it,' said Hercól. 'They can see our encampment plainly through their telescopes.'

'They will not wish to see you harmed,' said Cayer Vispek.

'You don't know Arqualis,' gasped Pazel, turning his head painfully in the sand. 'Prisoners of the Mzithrin are presumed good as dead. They'll engage you whether we're aboard or not. They'll blow you to matchsticks.'

'We can take the boat alone,' said Neda quietly. 'Leave them here, Cayer. The *Chathrand* will send another for them.'

'And for you, an extermination brigade,' said Hercól. 'There are over a hundred Turachs aboard the Great Ship, and longboats that can outrun whatever little vessel they have dispatched to collect us.'

'We should have struck an hour ago,' growled Jalantri under his breath.

'Perhaps,' said Hercól, 'but it is too late now.'

'Not too late for one thing,' said Jalantri.

'Cayer—' Neda began.

'Be silent, girl! Be silent, both of you!'

Their leader's voice was tight with desperation. Neda and Jalantri held still as wolves about to spring. *But spring where, on whom?* The heresy of Neda's thought appalled her.

'I fear Neda is right about the irons,' Hercól continued. 'The crew tolerates our own freedom uneasily, since Rose charged us with mutiny. They will never tolerate yours. Nor can we hide those tattoos on your necks.'

'Those tattoos are *never* hidden,' snapped Cayer Vispek, pressing the knife tighter against the other's flesh. 'We are *sfvantskors*, not skulking thieves.'*

'You may be reduced to worse than thieving,' said Hercól, 'if you go alone into this country.'

Neda felt the readiness of her limbs, the killer's focus trying to silence that other voice, the sister's. *Let me do it, Jalantri. If the Cayer commands us, let me end Pazel's life.*

---

* *Sfvantskors* may never conceal or fully cover these marks, which declare not only their tribe but their first master's name, royal affilliation (*pentarchrin*) and stage of enlightenment. Facing execution, a *sfvantskor* will always ask to be stabbed or drowned rather than beheaded or hanged, so that his neck will remain intact, and his spirit pass with dignity through the regions of death. – EDITOR.

'You grow careless with you words,' said Cayer Vispek. 'If you truly know our ways, you know we cannot despair. For those who take the Last Oath it is a sin.'

'There is a related sin,' said Hercól, 'but graver, in your teachings. Will you name it, or shall I?'

Cayer Vispek was very still. 'Suicide,' he whispered.

When Hercól spoke again he did so courteously, almost with sorrow. 'It is a hard thing, Cayer Vispek, but I must request your surrender.'

It was midmorning before the rescue skiff neared the *Chathrand*. Her crew was waiting in a ragged mob.

Some leaned out to help swing the hoisted boat over the scarlet rail. Most stood and watched. Never in all those months at sea had their spirits sunk so low, nor their eyes flashed so dangerously. The thirst! Not one of the eight hundred sailors had known such torturous want of water. The men's very flesh had tightened on their bones. Their skin had peeled and blistered, and the blisters had shrivelled from within. Their lips were cracked like old parchment.

They had watched in silence as the rescue boat tacked across the inlet, empty now of both serpents and ships. Passing telescopes, they had studied the captives, two men and one young woman ('Look at them arms, will you, she's a bruiser, a wildcat, a hellion, why is every blary girl who comes aboard—'), and Old Gangrüne the purser remarked on the way the strange young woman stared at Lady Thasha: with malice, or something very like.

The men had followed the boat with their eyes as it rounded the jetty, passed the great abandoned tower, and finally drew up to the landing near the village gate. They had watched ten or twelve dlömu step forth timidly, and cheered with faint derision when the creatures rolled out three small water casks and passed them down carefully to the skiff. Another mouthful each, they laughed bitterly, while over the tonnage hatch the sixty-foot yawl dangled in her harness, ready to launch, fourteen casks of five hundred gallons apiece lashed in her hold.

They had watched with impatience as Pathkendle and Lady Thasha spoke with the dlömic boy at the landing. The two youths pointed at the *Chathrand*; the boy shook his head. For several thirsty minutes the sailors watched a debate they could not hear. Then the young dlömu had made a gesture of surrender, and all three had climbed into the skiff, and the little boat had started out to the *Chathrand*.

Now they were hoisting it, dripping, above the rail. Six men caught the davit chains, guided her inboard, lowered her gently onto her skids. Haddismal shouted a quick command; the assembled Turachs surrounded the boat. The three human prisoners studied them keenly.

Fiffengurt beckoned at the water barrels. 'Same ration as yesterday,' he declared, and the sailors groaned and snarled, though it could not be otherwise, and the ration, albeit painfully tiny, had been fair.

Pazel Pathkendle and the Lady Thasha leaped first from the skiff, then aided Fiffengurt, who appeared rather bruised. But when the quartermaster's feet were planted on the deck he straightened his back and swept the topdeck with his obedient eye.

The *sfvantskors'* gaze followed his. The sailors looked where they looked, and then Fiffengurt turned to see where Pathkendle and the Lady Thasha were looking, and it was some seconds longer before they all became aware of this circular game, and stopped seeking what none could find: someone indisputably in command.

Of course, Nilus Rose was still their captain. But Rose and thirteen others were hostages, caught in a trap so devious that the men struggled to believe it was the work of ixchel – crawlies – the eight-inch-tall beings that most humans had learned to fear and kill from their first days at sea. The crawlies had introduced a sleeping drug into the ship's fresh water (hence the shortage) and when all were asleep had used ropes and wheel-blocks to drag their victims to a cabin under the forecastle, which they had filled with a light, sweet-smelling smoke. The latter did no harm until one was deprived of it: then, in a matter of seconds, it killed. The hostages, all addicts now, stayed alive by tending a fire in a tiny smudge-pot, feeding it with dry berries provided several times a day by the ixchel. As long as the berry-fire sputtered on, they lived.

Given his plight, Captain Rose had temporarily entrusted the ship to Mr Fiffengurt. So surely Fiffengurt was in command? But Sergeant Haddismal walked free as well – the crawlies had fed him an antidote that morning, fearing the Turachs might riot without their commander. Perhaps it was time for the military to take charge? But Haddismal was not the highest military officer on the *Chathrand*: that was Sandor Ott, the Imperial spymaster, the architect of their deadly mission. And Ott remained a hostage.

All told, an intolerable situation. Mutiny was the obvious answer – but how, and against whom? Kruno Burnscove or Darius Plapp might have led a few hundred gang members in such a rebellion – but the ixchel, thorough to a fault, had seized these two rival gang leaders as well.

So it was that the roving eyes converged at last on a tiny, copper-skinned figure, balanced on the mainmast rail. He was attended by six shaven-headed spearmen, and he wore a suit of fine black swallow feathers that shimmered when he walked. Those who were close enough saw his haughty chin, the plumb-line posture, the eyes that managed somehow to convey both ferocity and fear. It was galling, but inescapable: the most powerful figure on the *Chathrand* was this young ixchel lord, a crawly they could have batted overboard with one sweep of the hand.

'Well, Quartermaster?' he demanded. 'Hasn't my crew thirsted enough? Will you deliver them from misery, or not?'

His voice came out high and reedy: the effect of bending it into the register of the human ear. It was clear from his expression that he found the effort distasteful.

Fiffengurt scowled and deliberately turned away, busying himself with a davit strap. '*My crew*,' he muttered.

One of the ixchel guards snapped furiously: 'You will answer Lord Taliktrum at once!'

Fiffengurt, Pazel and Thasha exchanged nervous looks. Behind them, Hercól Stanapeth leaped onto the deck and bent to whisper in the quartermaster's ear. Fiffengurt nodded, then turned uneasily to face the crew.

'Now, ah, listen sharp, lads,' he said. 'There's danger ashore. The villagers can't let us back inside their walls—'

Roars, howls: Fiffengurt was announcing a death sentence. The only danger anyone believed in was thirst, and the only fresh water this side of the Gulf was the well in the village square. The men pressed closer, and their shouting increased. Fiffengurt waved desperately for silence.

'—but they've agreed to fill any casks we bring 'em, and to hand 'em off right there at the gatehouse. Mr Fegin, get that yawl in the water! Thirty hands for duty ashore! Who's prepared? Volunteers get their ration first.'

Instantly the roars became cheers, this time in earnest. Countless hands shot skywards. 'Let it be done!' cried Taliktrum from his perch, but no one listened to him now. Already Fegin was ordering men to the capstans, and topmen were loosing cables to allow the big yawl to be hoisted.

Pazel and Thasha grinned at Fiffengurt, who breathed a sigh of relief. Bolutu descended from the skiff, pushing his way through Turach spears. Haddismal directed the prisoners to climb down from the boat. 'On guard, marines, those are blary *sfvantskors*!' he shouted over the mayhem.

Haddismal possessed a voice to cut through storm and battle. Yet somehow one of the newly summoned Turachs did not heed him, and in the space of five seconds, disaster struck. The soldier was stationed behind Neda, who had yet to rise to her feet. Leaning forwards, he prodded her with one hand in the small of the back. Then his eyes found a long rip in Neda's breeches. His hand developed a will of its own, and three fingers groped for an instant over the flesh of her thigh.

Neda simply exploded. With a backwards elbow thrust she broke the man's front teeth, then spun on the bench and delivered a lightning kick to the chest of a second Turach before he could bring his spear to bear. Suddenly everyone was moving. Cayer Vispek's boot deflected another spear, then he leaped into the rigging as the startled Turachs stabbed at his legs. Jalantri whirled towards Neda, but Haddismal clubbed him savagely across the face, and three Turachs fell on the young *sfvantskor* like boulders, grappling, while a fourth kicked at his stomach.

Neda instantly pulled her legs back against her chest, then snapped forwards, rolling over the side of the skiff with a violent lurch. She came out of the roll with a twist of her upper body, and rose facing her would-be attackers. To the crew she seemed to have passed through the Turachs like a shadow – except that two lay senseless on the ground.

The crowd drew back. Neda whirled, as though suddenly aware of the vast, empty deck surrounding her, the futility of flight. And now the Turachs had recovered. They did not have the grace of *sfvantskors*, but they were terrible fighters, and they could spear anything that moved.

Neda almost became the proof of this, for eight of the soldiers had taken aim. But before they could let fly Thasha flung herself between them and their target.

Her friends shouted in horror. But the Turachs froze. Neda seized Thasha brutally from behind, catching the younger woman's throat in the crook of her elbow. Thasha gasped but did not fight back.

Half out of his mind, Pazel rushed at them. 'Neda, don't! Thasha—'

As Neda's grip tightened, Hercól lunged forwards and caught Pazel by the arm. 'Hear me, all of you!' he shouted, raising his black sword high. 'On Heaven's Tree I swear it: the one who harms Thasha Isiq will answer to me!'

'Hold, you dogs!' bellowed Haddismal. 'Damn you, Stanapeth, what do you expect of us? The girl went mad!'

'*I am doing kill!*' shrieked Neda, in rough Arquali.

'Neda,' said Thasha, her voice constricted but wry, 'I just saved your blary skin.'

Then Cayer Vispek spoke from the rigging. 'The Turach groped at her womanhood. Perhaps Arquali women brook such treatment, but ours do not. You gave your word she would suffer no man's abuse – and yet it begins before she sets foot on the deck.'

'All the more reason to get her safely to the brig,' snarled Haddismal. Then he looked down at his fallen soldier. 'You muckin' dullard, Vered! If you'd raised your eyes from her crotch to her blary tattoos you'd still have all your teeth! She's a *sfvantskor!*'

For an amazed moment the sailors even forgot their thirst. *Sfvantskors! It's true! Look at them tattooed necks! They're the enemy, by Rin!*

'Muckin' Sizzies!' bellowed someone. 'Killers! Crazies!'

'Animals, is what they are!' hissed another. 'It's one of them what hacked my old man's arm off in the war!'

'We shouldn't have to share our water—'

'We should gut 'em, here and now—'

'You will place them in the brig!' cried Taliktrum suddenly. 'You above there, come down, unless you would fight the whole ship's company. Girl, I will appoint one of my own lieutenants to watch over you – and besides, that part of the ship is off limits to humans, unless escorted by us. Have no fear! We ixchel determine the course of events on the *Chathrand.*'

'The boy requires a doctor,' said Cayer Vispek, pointing at Jalantri.

Taliktrum studied the moaning figure. 'Let him go to the fore-castle house. Dr Chadfallow is already there. Now yield, *sfvantskor* girl. We are in dangerous waters, and this delay imperils us all.'

Neda tightened her grip on Thasha's neck. She looked quite capable of murder. Through her teeth, and still in Arquali, she spoke: 'No ... Turach ... touching me ... again.'

'Right,' said Haddismal, waving off his men with a sigh. 'I'd say you've made that blary clear.'

But the other Turachs, and especially the friends of the wounded men, studied Neda with hatred, and their eyes seemed to mark her.

5

The Debate in the Manger

—◦∿◦—

At first glance we saw animals in clothes. We recoiled;
it was not proper to look at such things; it was not
right to acknowledge their existence. But we could not
help ourselves. Looking again we saw avenging
demons, straight out of our past. We saw the
bottomless fury of demons, the violence, the hatred
even for themselves, when they slew one another on
the deck of that immense ship, howling in an archaic
language that was almost our own. That is when we
clung to one another in greatest fear. We knew
catastrophe was close; it had befallen nearly everyone
else already. And heaven knows these human beings
had much to avenge.

Masalym Before the Storm: Recollections
by Uluja Thantral

22 Ilbrin 941

'You don't have to do this,' said Pazel.

'Stop saying that,' said Thasha. 'I told you, Neda didn't hurt me.
You're the one covered with bruises.'

Thasha passed under a glass plank, and the afternoon sun
touched her hair – brushed and tied but still brittle; she had not
yet rinsed out the salt. They were in a passage on the main deck,
heading for the Silver Stair. Jorl and Suzyt, Thasha's enormous

blue mastiffs, walked before her like a pair of guardian lions, too proud to tug at their leads. Overhead, boots clomped and clattered; men were laughing, almost giddy. Literally drunk on water. Men had wept at the cool mineral taste. The dogs had lapped two quarts apiece, and looked up hopefully for more.

'It's not bruises I'm worried about,' said Pazel.

Thasha flicked Pazel a glance. 'What is it, then?' she said.

Pazel wished she would slow down. 'Lady Oggosk, for starters,' he said.

Thasha looked baffled. They were about to face some of their worst enemies, but Oggosk would not be among them. The witch remained imprisoned in the forecastle house, along with the captain she so fiercely adored.

'They're plotting something,' said Pazel. 'Oggosk, and Rose, and maybe Ott for that matter. I went to see Neeps the minute the guards took Neda away. All three of them were at the window, talking to Alyash.'

'Well, of course they were,' said Thasha. 'He's the bosun, you dolt. He's Rose's blary right-hand man, now that Uskins is falling apart.'

At the ladderway a fungal stench met their nostrils. They started down into the warm gloom of the lower decks, the big dogs struggling for balance on the stairs. Men and tarboys shrank from the dogs, tipped their hats to Thasha, eyed Pazel with a confused mix of fascination and fear. Some still blamed him for the ship's evil luck; others had heard that he was the only reason the *Chathrand* was still afloat.

Pazel leaned closer to Thasha. 'I heard Oggosk say, "The girl,"' he murmured.

'For Rin's sake,' cried Thasha, 'is that all it takes to rattle you? Oggosk was probably talking about poor Marila. She's the one locked in with them all.'

Beneath the level of the gun decks they had the stairs to themselves. 'Come off it,' said Pazel. 'You know that hag is obsessed with you. And this time she sounded mean. Kind of desperate, like.'

'I'd be desperate too, if I were stuck in that compartment with Sandor Ott.'

Aware that his own desperation was mounting, Pazel thrust his arm across her path.

'It's not just Oggosk, damn it,' he sputtered. 'It's that we're going ... *there*. Where it happened to you. Where the rats went mad, and the Stone – where you ... you—'

'Where I touched it,' she said, touching him.

Pazel flinched, but her fingers on his cheek were just her fingers; no lightning jumped from them but the kind he expected, the thrill and promise that tore him from sleep with thoughts of her. He closed his eyes. *Stop shaking, Pazel, you're not doing anything wrong*. There had been months when her touch, her very nearness, had brought scalding pain, but that spell (laid on him by a murth-girl thousands of miles to the north) was broken or dormant. There had been threats from Lady Oggosk, who harboured some un-fathomable plan for Thasha, a plan that required her to be unloved. But Oggosk had nothing to threaten them with any more. Pazel took her hand, slid his fingers from her palm to her wrist. The blessing-band was still there.

'I thought you'd lost this in the Gulf,' he said.

Thasha lowered her hand from his cheek to the blue silk ribbon, turned it until they could read the words embroidered in gold thread:

YE DEPART FOR A WORLD UNKNOWN, AND LOVE ALONE SHALL KEEP THEE

'I left it behind in the stateroom,' she said, tracing the words with her fingers. 'It's not something I'm willing to lose.'

The silk band was to have played a role in Thasha's wedding back in Simja. Three nights ago, Pazel had at last performed the tiny part of the ceremony allotted to him, and tied it around her wrist. The meaning of the act, of course, had utterly changed, but those ambiguous words troubled him yet. Wasn't she still departing? Not into life with a Mzithrini husband, but into some region of the mind where he could not follow?

Nonsense. Nerves. Thasha was touched by magic, somehow – but not touched in the head. Pazel himself had been living for years under a potent charm and had managed to remain who he was. He put his arm around her, drew her closer, felt her breath tickling his chin.

'You're trembling,' she whispered. 'Why are you afraid?'

Why was he afraid? He had torn a cursed necklace away from her throat, dragged her up flaming stairwells; he had seen her naked and bleeding on a beach. He could kiss her here and now (so far she had planted the kisses, though not always on him) and no disaster would follow.

Presumably.

It was never supposed to happen. You believe me, don't you?

Rin's teeth, he was sweating. And Thasha, impatient, was slipping under his arm and down the staircase, slipping away.

'I'm stronger now,' she said. 'I can face them. They can't make me do anything I don't want to do.'

On they went, past the berth deck with its sound of snoring (some forty victims of the ixchels' sleep-drug remained unconscious) and out into the rear compartment of the orlop deck. The darkness increased, and so did the stench. And flies – more flies with every step, droning like tormented ghosts.

Then Pazel stopped, overcome with sudden disgust. *Pitfire, they've still not cleaned the lower decks.* He was smelling dead men, dead animals – above all, dead rats. Six weeks ago, every last rat on the *Chathrand* had suffered a hideous change, swollen to the size of Thasha's dogs, and rampaged through the ship. Only their mass suicide had prevented the creatures from killing everyone aboard.

'Pathkendle. Thasha.'

Hercól was crossing the dim compartment. As he drew close, the swordsman noticed Pazel's look of revulsion. 'The bodies are gone,' he said, 'but not the blood. Fiffengurt chose to risk disease

73

rather than oblige the men to sweat away the last of their water scrubbing gore out of the planks.'

He and Thasha regarded each other warily. They had exchanged many such looks recently, before and after their arrival at the Cape. Pazel had no idea what those looks were about, but he knew that Thasha's mood darkened whenever the swordsman approached, as though he reminded her of some unwelcome duty or predicament.

'I hoped Pazel would convince you not to attend this council,' he said.

'He failed,' said Thasha, 'and so will you. Enough nonsense, Hercól. I want to get this over with.'

Hercól gripped her shoulder, looking at them each in turn. 'Let them wait a bit longer. Come with me first, won't you?'

He led them across the compartment, around a jagged hole in the floor (there were many such scars on the *Chathrand*, marks of the suicide-fire of the rats) and out through the bulkhead door in the north wall. They stepped into a small square cabin with two other doors, through one of which some light poured down from a shaft in the adjoining corridor. Dominating the room was a round porcelain washtub. This was the 'silk knickers room' (as the tarboys called it): the chamber where first-class servants scrubbed their employers' socks and shirts and petticoats. The big tub had survived the crossing, but it was smeared with dried blood and fur, and the benches and washboards had been reduced to charcoal.

Hercól closed the door by which they had entered. 'Once we join the others we must watch our every word. It is well that we told Taliktrum of the mind-plague, but of the time-skip His Lordship knows nothing, and I do not think we should enlighten him today. Let us not speak of it.'

'Let's not speak to him at all,' said Pazel. 'He's not fit to lead his clan, let alone this ship.'

Hercól looked at him severely, but made no rebuttal. 'Even allies like Mr Fiffengurt may not yet be ready to face the truth of it. One could almost wish that his dear Annabel's final letter had never reached him, telling him that she was with child.'

'*You* could wish it, maybe,' said Thasha. Pazel looked at her in shock. 'I mean,' she added hastily, 'that we can't begin to guess what he feels like. They were going to be married; he's been saving his pay for ten years. I don't think we should *ever* tell him. Let him think they're alive, for as long as he can – Annabel and that little boy or girl. Let him hope. That's not too much to ask, is it?'

She was still watching Hercól with surprising ire. But if her old mentor understood her anger he did not rise to the bait. 'You're right,' he said after a moment. 'In time we may be forced to tell him, or he may find out some other way; but for now it can do little good. Yet *we* must not forget the truth for a minute, however much we long to, if we are to find a way out of this darkness.'

'There is no way out,' said Pazel, and immediately wished he hadn't spoken. The others turned to him, astonished – and then a voice rang out in the darkness.

'I should bite you for that, Pazel Pathkendle! No way out, for shame.'

'Felthrup!' cried Pazel. 'Are you mad? What are you doing here?'

His tiny figure emerged from the gloom: a black rat with half a tail and a mangled forepaw. Thasha's dogs pounced, licking and snuffling; their adoration of Felthrup knew no bounds. With a quick leap the rat was astride Suzyt, balanced between her shoulder blades. His dark eyes glistened, and a sweet, resinous smell wafted from his fur.

'Should I be content to hide for ever behind the stateroom's magic wall?' he asked. 'Ashore they may have condemned all woken beasts, but not on the *Chathrand*. Not yet.'

'The crew will not stop to talk to you,' said Hercól. 'They will see a rat, and they will kill it.'

'Only if they catch it,' said Felthrup. 'But the men of *Chathrand* are not all ignorant brutes. They do not know what is happening – and I agree that you must not tell them, yet – but they know *something* is terribly amiss, and a few may recall that it was I who first said so, when I smelled the emptiness of the village. Surely they will realise the utility – is that the word I want, utility? – of having a rat's olfactory prowess at their disposal. Utility, avail, expedience—'

'No,' said Thasha, 'they won't. They'll be afraid that you're about to turn into a monster before their eyes.'

'They should fear no such thing,' said Felthrup. 'I am safe, thanks to Lady Syrarys.'

'Syrarys?' said Pazel. 'Felthrup, what are you *talking* about?'

Syrarys, the consort of Thasha's father Admiral Isiq, had been revealed to be in league with Sandor Ott. She had worked for Thasha's death, and nearly killed the admiral by poisoning his tea.

'How excitable you are!' said Felthrup. 'I was only speaking of mysorwood oil. The wicked lady used to dab it on her neck, but Mr Bolutu pointed out that it is better even than peppermint oil at deterring fleas. He applied it to my fur, and I am a new rat! Freed, emancipated, delivered from their masticatory assaults – and are we not agreed that those hungry vermin inflicted the mutation upon the rats, and not vice versa? Rats do not, you will allow, bite fleas. But this despair, Pazel! How unlike you, how unbecoming!'

'Unbecoming.' Pazel stared at the rat. 'Do you understand that our families are dead?'

'Your sister is not dead,' said Felthrup. 'And as for my family – it is aboard this ship. My rat-brethren back in Noonfirth cast me out, the very day I woke. They were terrified of my verbosity. They slew my mother's second litter before her eyes, ten blind bleating things not a day old, and chased her off into the streets. When I fled they were trying to determine who had mated with her, so that they could kill or scatter those unlucky males as well.'

Pazel closed his eyes. He was, in fact, intensely grateful for Felthrup's presence, his grounding inanities and madcap wisdom. But you had to have patience, barrels of it, whenever the rat warmed to a theme.

Thasha managed it better than anyone. 'We're late for the council, Felthrup dear,' she said. 'What is it you wanted to tell us?'

'That I have been eavesdropping,' he said. 'Dr Rain has lately been interrogated by several officers concerning one of his patients. Have you heard the rumours surrounding the topman, Mr Duprís?'

'I heard that Rain had quarantined the man,' said Hercól. 'Something about a fever.'

'He has no fever now,' said Felthrup. 'When that serpent neared the *Chathrand*, and every man aboard feared the worst, Mr Duprís fled his post, screaming, "*I won't touch it, I won't, I won't!*" That sort of nonsense. Later his friends dragged him to sickbay. He was in a terrible state, but he grew calmer once they strapped him down: indeed he *thanked* the doctor for strapping him down. But then the surgeon's mate discovered his high temperature. Fearing he might infect the rest of the ward, he persuaded Rain to send the man to an empty cabin. They moved him late at night. But on the way to the cabin, Duprís asked for some fresh air, so Rain and the mate brought him to one of the open gunports and let him bend down. He took a deep breath. Then he looked over his shoulder at them. "He cannot make me do it. I'll never touch that cursed thing." With those words Duprís cast himself into the sea.'

A silence fell. 'Arunis,' said Pazel at last. 'He was talking about Arunis.'

Thasha sighed. 'And the Nilstone, of course.'

'So Arunis has begun to kill,' said Hercól, 'as he always promised he would. It is terrible news that he has grown strong enough to attack our minds in such a way. I always thought that he managed it with Mr Druffle through some prolonged contact with the man – through potions or torture. Now it appears he can do so without ever touching his victim – from hiding, where no one can interfere. During the crossing, when the Turach committed suicide by placing his hand on the Stone, I thought the poor man had simply despaired. Now I wonder.'

'Why isn't the whole ship talking about Duprís?' asked Pazel.

'Mr Alyash feared to start a panic,' said Felthrup, 'and so he ordered Rain and Fulbreech to keep the man's death a secret. But I can tell you something more, friends: I was not alone in listening to their conversation. There were ixchel, somewhere close, for

I heard their whispers. They did not hear me, I think. I have become a better spy on this voyage, if nothing else.'

'What did they say?' asked Thasha.

'Something very curious. They said, "*So it's happening to the giants as well.*"'

A low groan escaped Pazel's chest. 'Arunis must be working on the ixchel too. And why not, since they're in charge? But what in blazes does he *want*? He still needs a crew to sail the ship, doesn't he?'

'We should go to the council,' said Thasha. 'Not that anyone's going to listen to us.'

'Whether they listen or not, we must keep our purpose clear,' said Hercól. 'We swore to place the Stone beyond the reach of evil – and that we *must* do, somehow. Where is that place? I do not know. Even Erithusmé, greatest wizardess since the time of the Amber Kings, did not know. But it exists, or Ramachni would not have set us looking for it. Taking the Nilstone to that place will be impossible, however, so long as the *Chathrand* remains in the grip of evil men. We must break that grip.'

'That could mean killing,' said Thasha.

'I expect it will,' said Hercól. 'Arunis will never relent; Sandor Ott does not know how. If we have truly leaped forwards two centuries, then his Emperor is dead, and the very dynasty of the Magads may well have failed. That at least would be no tragedy. But Ott does not know this, and my heart tells me he would not believe it even if he stood before the tomb of the last Magad to sit on the Ametrine Throne. No, he will fight on, even as a prisoner of the ixchel. Other hearts may change, however. In that possibility we must always have faith.'

'Not all change is for the better,' said Felthrup.

'That's blary true,' said Thasha. 'Those horrid ships – they were flying Bali Adro flags. The whole Empire Bolutu thought would come to our rescue must have turned into something foul.' She looked up at Hercól with sudden dread. 'We can't let them take the *Chathrand*.'

'Now you see it,' said Hercól. 'If Bali Adro is ruled by mass murderers, what greater crime could we commit than to bring them the Nilstone? We are charged with keeping it from evil, not laying it at evil's foot. Once we imagined the South an empty land, where we might persuade the crew to abandon ship in sufficient numbers to strand her, until the villains gave command of her to us. Now the villains may well be everywhere. A sound ship and a willing crew are our only hope of survival.'

Pazel felt anger tightening his chest. 'You want us to go on helping these bastards? Helping Rose and Ott, Alyash and Taliktrum and his gang of crazies?'

'We cannot proceed without them, Pazel. Of course, I don't imagine that they will make it easy. But we must remember the lesson of the fishermen and the crocodile.'

'Ah!' said Felthrup. 'An excellent parable. I have heard it myself. Two fishermen made long war over a favourite spot to cast their nets. Each day they came and bickered, racing each other in their labours. Finally, at the end of one hot, sticky, altogether *infelicitous* day, they came to blows, and one man clubbed the other nearly senseless, and left him crawling on the banks. There Tivali the crocodile found him, and delightedly feasted.'

'Oh joy,' said Pazel.

'I have not finished, Pazel,' said the rat. 'When the other fisherman returned, he was glad to have the spot to himself, and stayed all day, filling his baskets. But in the shadows of evening Tivali crept up and seized his leg. The crocodile was strengthened by his earlier meal, and before he ate again, he remarked through his teeth that he had never dared attack both men together. "You did my work for me," he said. "I knew I could depend on you." You're right, Master Hercól. Rose and Ott may be monstrous, but without them we cannot face the crocodile. And we all know who *that* is.'

'Arunis,' said Pazel, 'of course. But Pitfire, there must be a better choice than that.'

'There will be,' said Hercól, 'when Ramachni returns.'

'"When a darkness comes beyond today's imagining,"' said

Thasha, echoing the mage's parting words. 'Hasn't that time come and gone, Hercól? I don't have any intention of giving up – and neither does Pazel, he just talks rot – but Rin's eyeballs, how dark is dark enough?'

'Ramachni has never failed us,' said Hercól, 'and I cannot believe that he will fail us now, as the battle of his lifetime nears its conclusion. But we must go. The villains await us in the manger.'

'I will be near you, under the floor,' said Felthrup. 'There are passages the ixchel never dared to use, passages that belonged to the rats. They are all mine, now.'

'For a time, perhaps,' said Hercól. 'Go softly, little brother.'

Felthrup scurried off. The humans returned the way they had come, and proceeded to the aftmost passage of the orlop deck. Foul air, sticky floorboards. Pazel knew with a hint of shame that he had not only been worrying for Thasha's sake. He hated the manger like no other part of the ship.

The passage brought them to the looted grainery, and thence to the manger door. Here the stench was astonishing: fur, blood, bile, ashes, rot. Pazel saw the flicker of lamplight, heard the voices of men and ixchel, arguing.

'—can't let one person beyond this room know what's happened to human beings,' Fiffengurt was saying. 'I've seen vessels gripped by plague-panic. They can't be sailed. The men get frightened – of every cough, sneeze, hiccup—'

Thasha and her dogs stepped into the chamber. The mastiffs tensed and growled, and the talking ceased.

'At last,' snapped Taliktrum's voice. 'What took you so long, girl? Do you think we assembled here for the pleasure of each other's company?'

Pazel and Hercól followed her inside. The manger was wide and deep, built to store fodder for two hundred cattle, in the days when the Great Ship had carried whole herds across the Narrow Sea. Their own cattle had all perished: some had broken legs or hips during the Nelluroq storms and had to be slaughtered quickly;

most were savaged by the rats. But no one had yet removed the hay.

Pazel looked at the wall of square bales tied up at the back of the chamber, saw the stain down the front like a dark dried stream. He and Thasha had made their stand on that wall. The rats had seemed endless in number, demonic in their hate. Pazel had fought with every ounce of his strength; Thasha, ten times the fighter he was, had hewn the creatures down like weeds. But the rats had swarmed around them, leaping from behind. They would have perished in minutes without the Nilstone.

It was still there, at the centre of the manger, clenched in the stone hand of the Shaggat Ness, that lifeless maniac, that king become a statue. Pazel could not see the Stone – Fiffengurt had ordered the Shaggat's arm draped with cloth, and the cloth firmly tied about the statue's wrist – but he could feel it all the same. What was he sensing? Not a sound, not a glimmer. The feeling was closest to heat. With every step into the chamber he could feel it grow.

The Shaggat himself was kept upright by a wooden frame, girdling his waist and bolted heavily to the floor. He stared at his upraised hand with a weirdly mixed expression: triumph giving way to terror and shock. He had remained flesh and blood just long enough to see the weapon he'd craved begin to kill him.

On the mad king's shoulder stood tiny Lord Taliktrum. His consort, Myett, crouched beside him, one hand on his calf, tensed for flight or combat as she always was when humans approached. Pazel felt a keen hatred for the pair. *Murderers.* They had not actually slain Diadrelu, Pazel and Thasha's dear friend and the ixchels' former commander. But they might as well have. Steldak, the ixchel man who had jerked the spear through her neck, was deranged, and perished himself in short order. It was Taliktrum and his fanatics who had ambushed Diadrelu, and held her while the deed was done. Pazel would never forgive them.

Around the statue were gathered some twelve or thirteen humans, along with Bolutu and Ibjen. Pazel still marvelled at the dlömic boy's willingness to help them. He had said no more about it since the fire on the beach, never explained who had told him that some on the *Chathrand* were trying to 'redeem the world'. But his courage was being sorely tested. He'd been promised a safe return to the village by nightfall. From the look on his face he was counting the hours.

Six Turachs were present, including Haddismal. And there was Big Skip Sunderling: a welcome surprise, for the carpenter's mate was a trusted friend. Not so the bosun, Mr Alyash, who greeted the newcomers with a scowl: a gruesome expression, owing to the blotchy scars that covered him from mouth to chest. Alyash was a spy in the service of Sandor Ott. The scars, Pazel had heard him claim, were marks of torture with a sarcophagus jellyfish by the followers of the Shaggat Ness.

Mr Uskins was here as well – tall, fair Uskins, the disgraced first mate. The man had loathed Pazel and Neeps from the start – they belonged to inferior races, but failed to cringe before their betters – and the tarboys returned the sentiment. But lately Pazel had begun to feel sorry for Uskins. The man looked like a shipwreck. Once fastidious in the extreme, he had neglected both his beard and his uniform. His blond hair dangled greasy and uncombed. When he looked at Pazel his eyes lit with antipathy, but it was a vague, distracted sort of hate.

The last two figures were even more unexpected. One was Claudius Rain – addled Dr Rain, the worst quack Pazel had ever encountered. Rain had barely stirred from his cabin since the legendary Dr Chadfallow replaced him as ship's surgeon. But here he was, following the flies with his gaze, muttering to himself. And there beside him, damn it all, stood the surgeon's mate, Greysan Fulbreech.

The handsome Simjan youth beamed at Thasha, who returned a brief, uneasy smile. Pazel wanted to smash something. He was visited by the absurd idea that Fulbreech, five or six years older and unbearably decent to everyone, was the true reason Thasha had insisted on attending the meeting. Fulbreech had appeared suddenly one day in the wedding crowd on Simja, bearing a mysterious message for Hercól. Pazel had mistrusted him from that first moment, though he had to admit he had no definite cause. Not for mistrust, anyway; jealousy was another matter. He knew quite well that Thasha had fancied the surgeon's mate – had kissed him once or twice, even, when Oggosk's threats made Pazel treat her with disdain. Of course, that was over now—

Fulbreech gave him a frank, friendly smile. 'Hello, Pathkendle.'

Pazel nodded, failing to bring an answering smile to his lips. *Do I hate him just because Thasha doesn't? What's the matter with me?*

Behind them, Alyash closed the chamber door.

Taliktrum cleared his throat. 'We're alive,' he said. 'That is something. But no one should suppose that we have earned the right to breathe easy. Only giants think in terms of merits and rewards; our people think of survival. That is what we are here to determine: how to survive together, until we can go our separate ways.'

Fiffengurt laughed grimly. 'Did you see that Godsforsaken serpent? Did you hear those drums? We're babes in the wood, Mr Taliktrum. How in Pitfire do you *determine* the best way to survive in a world you know nothing about?'

'You must address him as "commander" or "lord",' hissed Myett.

'You are not equipped to understand,' said Taliktrum, 'but we are. The ixchel have not grown fat in their time of exile; they have not grown soft and selfish. Every house in Etherhorde, every dog-prowled, cat-infested alley, was to us a place of menace and persecution. Do you see how fortunate you are that we seized your drifting helm? Trust me, you are adrift no longer. The *Chathrand* shall move through this great, strange South as the ixchel move through a city: in the shadows, in darting runs and swift concealments, inch by hard-won inch.'

His words tumbled out like an unpractised speech, or a man trying to convince himself of his own consequence. When he finished, he appeared at a loss. Without releasing his leg, Myett looked up and caught his eye, and then subtly directed his attention to Old Gangrüne.

'I have asked our purser,' said Taliktrum at once, 'to remind us of the assets that remain aboard this ship. That is the purser's duty, among other things. Are you prepared, Mr Gangrüne?'

The old, bent fellow nodded sourly. He was fussing with an extremely tattered and dog-eared accounting book.

'Well, proceed,' said Taliktrum.

Gangrüne took a pair of horn-rimmed glasses from his vest pocket, considered the filthy lenses, folded them anew. He opened the logbook and considered it for nearly a minute with the deepest disappointment. At last Haddismal snatched the book, flipped it rightside-up, and placed it again in Gangrüne's hands. The old man glared at the sergeant as though he had been tricked. Then he cleared his throat.

'It is my joy,' he shouted, 'in this, my thirty-seventh year as purser aboard the Imperial Mercantile Ship *Chathrand*, registration four-o-two-seven-nine Etherhorde, to present you with another *exact* and *impeccable* account. To begin with the human assets, gentlemen: our splendid vessel currently boasts three hundred and ninety-one ordinary seamen, one hundred and forty able seamen, twenty-two midshipmen, sixteen lieutenants and sub-lieutenants, two gun captains, six deck officers in full command of their mental faculties, another deck officer, a glorious and decorated captain, a famous and educated sailmaster, a doctor and another who petitions our belief that he is such, a surgeon's mate, two illustrious passengers entitled to partial refunds due to our tardiness in returning to Etherhorde, nine specialists, seven mates, a veterinarian with webbed fingers, a master cook, a tailor, thirty-four tarboys of no distinction or morals, ninety-one Turach marines with full mobility and one who suffers headaches and is prone to falling forwards, a regimental clerk, a foul witch, an experienced whaling-ship commander and his nineteen surviving crewmembers, including four Quezan warriors indecently fond of nakedness, thirty-three steerage passengers, among them twelve women, four boys, three girls and an infant with a cleft lip, eight—'

'Silence!' screamed Taliktrum. 'Mr Gangrüne, what are we to do with such a rubbish heap of detail? I asked you for a summary statement.'

Gangrüne countered that he was presenting a summary, that a full company report would have required him to be 'rather more specific'. He was about to resume his reading, but Taliktrum cut him off.

'That will do, Purser, thank you ever so much. Post your *summary* in the wardroom as I requested. Now then ...' The young lord's eyes swept the room, and at last settled on Thasha again. 'Step forward, girl.'

Thasha hesitated, then moved towards the ixchel and the Shaggat Ness. She regarded Taliktrum coldly.

'We have decided to keep this plague of idiocy a secret from the crew of the *Chathrand*. Have you or your friends spoken of it to anyone?'

'Of course not,' said Thasha.

Nothing about the time-skip, Pazel thought. *Hercól's right. It's safer this way.*

'When we fought the rats in this chamber,' Taliktrum went on, 'I saw a thing I cannot explain. Pathkendle saw it too, and my father, and a handful of my guards. I am not sure whether you saved our lives or inspired the rats to start the bonfire that nearly killed us all. Will you tell us what happened?'

A brief pause, then Thasha shook her head.

'Perhaps you distrust certain persons here?' suggested Taliktrum. 'Will you speak to me privately, to help me better command this vessel?'

Grunts and murmurs escaped the humans. *Command, he says.* One of the Turachs turned aside to spit.

'No,' said Thasha, 'I won't.'

'Do not toy with us,' said Taliktrum, his voice rising. 'By now you of all people must know that we of Ixphir House do not bluff.

We have no desire to see any more of your people killed—'

'What about your own?' muttered Fiffengurt.

'—but if you refuse to face the truth of your situation you will leave us no choice. Look at me when I address you, girl.'

'Her name is Thasha Isiq,' said Hercól.

Every head in the chamber turned. Taliktrum started; Myett's hand went to her bow. Hercól had spoken quietly, but Pazel had rarely heard such depths of hatred in a voice.

Hercól and Diadrelu had been lovers. Pazel did not know what that meant, between a human and an eight-inch-tall ixchel queen. A few months ago he would not have believed it possible: it was the stuff of tarboy jokes. But he had seen Hercól when they found her, hours too late but still beautiful, naked save for her bandaged neck, surrounded by those of her clan who had loved her to the end. Hercól's agony had been like a second death, and Pazel had felt ashamed of his doubt.

That courage, he thought, *and that proud, quiet loneliness. She was perfect for him.*

A sudden rustling from the hay bales. Pazel raised his eyes: eighty or ninety ixchel had materialised there in an eyeblink, ranged like a miniature battalion, armed and silent. Every one of them was focused on Hercól.

Alyash gestured irritably. 'We're all on the same blasted ship, Stanapeth. We've the right to know what her game is.'

The right to know! Pazel was speechless at the bosun's gall. But he wouldn't be speechless, not this time, he—

'Awful, isn't it,' said Fulbreech, his voice dripping sarcasm, 'when people keep secrets?'

Thasha smiled at Fulbreech again.

'You shut your Gods-damned mouth, boy,' said Alyash. 'You've no business here anyway.'

'We were summoned, we were dragged,' Dr Rain protested.

Thasha just shook her head. 'I won't explain because I can't. I simply don't know what happened that day. I touched the Nilstone and it didn't kill me, though it should have. And I told the rats

I was the Angel they worshipped, and they believed me. Of course, I didn't know that the Angel's coming would make them want to go to heaven on a puff of smoke.'

Taliktrum stared at her a moment, then nodded to Myett. Agile as spiders, the two ixchel crawled onto the Shaggat's arm and set about untying the ropes.

The cloth slithered to the ground. 'Behold your ally, men of Arqual,' said Taliktrum.

The hand, etched in stone but withered to a skeleton, was every bit as hideous as Pazel recalled, but now he saw long cracks extending down the arm, nearly to the shoulder. And there, clenched in the fleshless fingers, was the Nilstone. It was no larger than a walnut, but terrifying all the same, for the Nilstone was black beyond seeing. To look at it was like staring at the sun: a black sun, that dazzled without light.

'Oh,' said a man's voice, weak and troubled. 'Oh dear, that is *wrong*.' It was Dr Rain. He was shaking his head and pointing at the Stone. 'Crawlies, Mr Fiffengurt – that is *all wrong*. Do you hear me? Wrong! Wrong!'

Suddenly he was shouting, red-faced, hands in fists, stamping his foot so hard on each *Wrong!* that his body jerked in a kind of circular war dance.

'Get him out of here!' snapped Haddismal, gesturing to his men. But before any of them could move Rain straightened up, drew a great sucking breath and fled the chamber.

'Why in the belching Pits did you summon that fool?' said Alyash.

'He's a doctor,' said Myett, her voice low and feline, 'and your precious Shaggat is disintegrating.'

'From his dead hand down,' said Taliktrum. 'Mr Fulbreech, Mr Bolutu, you're the only medical men left here. What do you see? What would happen to this madman, should the enchantment end?'

Fulbreech and Bolutu approached the Shaggat, flinching when their eyes passed over the Nilstone. Bolutu, among so much else, was a renowned veterinarian. Fulbreech, by contrast, was a mere surgeon's mate, and a new one at that. But his tutor over the past four months of storm and combat had been none other than Ignus Chadfallow, and Pazel well knew what a driven teacher the doctor could be.

'If those cracks become lesions?' mused Fulbreech. 'No question, gentlemen. He will lose the arm.'

'And his life, should the cracks spread greatly,' added Bolutu. 'A tourniquet can stop the bleeding only if it can be fastened to a stump.'

'Then what're you waiting for?' growled Haddismal. 'Patch up his blary arm! Gods of death, Bolutu, the fortunes of our Empire rest on that man!'

'*Your* Empire,' said Bolutu. 'I came north to fight Arunis and the evil he would do to *all* lands. But Arqual has never been my home. Your contempt for my skin assured that, as much as your vile ambition to destroy the Mzithrinis.'

'Why has no one stabilised the arm?' demanded Taliktrum.

'Chadfallow warned 'em off,' said Alyash. He waved a hand imperiously, spoke in a fair imitation of the doctor's stentorian voice. '"Nothing you do will slow the decay. Plasters, splints, bandages – none of these can help. You'll only crumble him the faster, mark my words, mark my words."'

Bolutu and Fulbreech looked at each other and frowned, as though they doubted the verdict. But Alyash pointed irritably at the Shaggat's hand.

'It's that Stone we have to deal with, if we want to save the monster,' he said. 'He'll be dead before you can sing him a fare-thee-well, if he turns back to flesh with that thing in his hand. And if Arunis *is* still aboard—'

'He is,' said Mr Uskins suddenly.

Pazel started; he had almost forgotten that Uskins was in the room.

Alyash, flustered, carried on: '—then we know he's toiling away in a fever, trying to learn how to use it.'

'And failing, so far,' said Haddismal. Turning Thasha a sceptical look, he added, 'You expect us to believe that you did something that mucking sorcerer won't even try?'

'I touched the Stone,' Thasha stated flatly, 'once.'

'Just reached up and gave it a squeeze,' scoffed Haddismal. 'On a whim, like. The deadliest blary thing in Alifros.'

'If I hadn't we'd have died anyway,' said Thasha.

'Do it again,' said Taliktrum.

Uproar, loud and general. Taliktrum and Myett leaped straight up from the Shaggat onto a crossbeam above. Every human voice (and two dlömic) in the chamber cried out against the notion, and Jorl and Suzyt erupted in howls. Pazel squeezed Thasha's elbow. *No, no, no,* his shaking head proclaimed.

'You'll shatter the arm!' shouted Alyash.

'*Be quiet!*' Thasha bellowed, and everyone obeyed. Thasha handed the dog's leashes to Pazel. Then she walked right up to the Shaggat Ness, raised a hand and touched the statue's arm, spreading her fingers wide.

'Thasha, don't!' hissed Pazel.

Thasha closed her eyes, tracing the stone bicep, sliding her fingers around and upwards in what was almost a caress. She reached the elbow, lingered there, then moved her hand slowly higher.

'I could,' she said, and as she spoke Pazel thought the manger darkened, and a cold, prickling sensation swept over his body. The men looked at one another, aghast. Thasha reached higher still, until her fingers rested atop the Shaggat's own, with the throbbing blackness of the Nilstone lancing between them. 'I could take it from his hand, right here and now. But what would be the point?'

She dropped her hand, and a sigh of relief passed through the room. Pazel felt light-headed, as though he had just caught his balance at the edge of a cliff. But Alyash gave a mirthless laugh.

'You're lying through your pretty teeth,' he said to Thasha. 'You know what the point would be. You could send Arunis flying from this ship like a cannonball. The rest of us, too. You could get your friends out of the crawly trap, whisk us home across the Nelluroq and be sittin' down to tea and toast with Daddy by New Year's Day. Pitfire, you could topple Magad the Fifth, and take his place as Emperor of Arqual. The whole blary game's up if someone masters the Nilstone.'

'I never said I could *master* it,' said Thasha. 'I'm no mage. I only told you I could claim it.'

'Do you mean to say that while you can survive the touch of the Stone, you're unable to use it at all?' asked Taliktrum.

'I don't know how long I'd survive, if I took it from him,' said Thasha. 'I have a feeling it would kill me too, just a bit more slowly.'

'You see?' said Taliktrum, glancing quickly around the chamber. 'She is in some sense mightier than Arunis, who fears to touch it at all. Why haven't you applied yourself to its mastery? Have you no desire to help us?'

Thasha gave him a long, poisonous look. 'If I survived the attempt,' she said, 'I still couldn't do anything with the Stone that isn't ugly.'

'Ugly,' said Taliktrum. 'What does that mean? War is ugly, girl. Killing, hunger, disease are ugly. You must risk it. We must be prepared to use every tool in our arsenal.'

Thasha turned and walked back to her friends. 'Not this one,' she said.

'Taliktrum,' said Fiffengurt suddenly, 'you want to play captain? Try acting the part. You said this meeting would be "brief and decisive", as I recall. Well, it ain't been brief, and we've not decided a blessed thing.'

'That's about to change,' said Haddismal.

Drawing his Turach broadsword, he stepped forwards and thrust it at Taliktrum, the blade horizontal, in the ritual challenge of the Arquali military. 'We can have this out right now,' he said. 'You're holdin' hostages, our true captain among them. But there ain't a man on this ship – or a woman either – who hasn't stared down death these past few months. And whether you kill them or not, you'll have doomed yourselves. We'll smoke you out of your holes and deal with you the Arquali way, and your people will die cursing the day they ever heard the name Tliktrum – Talakitrim—'

'*Taliktrum*, you great oaf,' muttered Bolutu.

'Withhold the berries, my lord,' said Myett. 'See how fierce they are when their people feel the claws of the poison ripping at their lungs.'

Alyash drew his sword in turn. 'You think you've got us by the gills, don't you?' he said.

Taliktrum nodded. 'Exactly right, Bosun: we have you by the gills. My father, Lord Talag, is never careless with detail, and he planned this campaign for twelve years.'

'And the Secret Fist planned for forty,' said Haddismal. 'You have no muckin' idea who you're dealin' with. The water emergency's over, crawly, and so's your little game. We'll drop this ship to the seabed before we let ourselves be run by ship lice.'

'Leave bigotry to one side, all of you,' said Hercól. 'It will not achieve the ends you want. We are all thinking creatures, and each of us bears a soul.' His voice was strained, as though he was making a great effort to heed his own words. Facing Taliktrum, he said, 'I will never address you as "captain" or "commander", for you have no right to either title. But your own people count you a lord, and so shall I for the present.

'Lord Taliktrum, your prisoners are in squalor. Thirty days they have been crammed in that space. They are filthy, sore and maddened by inactivity. They sleep poorly and eat little better. You showed a moment's kindness when we first spotted land: you gave a temporary antidote to the captain, and let him walk free for an hour upon the quarterdeck. Will you not extend that kindness to the others? Let one or two out at a time, to breathe the free air, wash themselves, regain their dignity, if only for an hour.'

Shouts of agreement from the humans. Taliktrum crossed his arms and waited for silence.

'Cages are abhorrent to our people,' he said. 'You giants made sure we learned to hate them to our core. And unlike you we are not needlessly cruel. Besides, the antidote is flawless. What have we to lose? Three, yes, three hostages at a time will have their hour's freedom. The women first, and the youngest.'

Pazel felt his heart lift. He caught Thasha's eye and saw the same excitement. The youngest hostages were Neeps and Marila.

Hercól bowed ever so slightly to Taliktrum. 'Now to another matter,' he said. 'We cannot stay here, Lord Taliktrum. The *Chathrand* is hidden behind a rocky islet barely taller than her mainmast, and that is not safety enough. If the armada had passed a few miles closer to the village, we might all be in prison now, or worse.'

'I know that,' said Taliktrum. 'Of course we must sail. The question is, where?'

'And before that, the question's *how*,' said Fiffengurt. 'As in, how far can we get? We have water but precious little food. The rats fouled most of the grain in the hold, devoured everything in the smokehouse, and ate through the tin walls of the bread room. And all the animals are dead.'

'You lie,' shouted a voice from among the ixchel standing on the hay bales. 'I heard a goat bleating on the orlop deck this morning, m'lord, as plain as I hear you now.'

'Can't be,' said Big Skip, shaking his head. 'Teggatz and I did the inventory. There are carcasses we couldn't account for, true enough. But they must have been burned to cinders, or else hurled themselves over the sides. There's no blessed way we missed a goat.'

'Goat or no goat, we'll soon be hungry,' said Pazel.

'That's right, *Muketch*,' said Haddismal, 'and without decent food the men won't be fit to fight, should it come to that.'

'We lack medical supplies as well,' said Fulbreech.

'And the ship needs repairs,' said Fiffengurt. 'That foremast is only a jury-rig – one more hard blow and she'll fall. And probably take the kevels and the chase-beams with her. The gun carriages want attention, too.'

Suddenly Uskins giggled, loud and shrill. 'Fit to fight!' he said. 'Who do you think to fight, Sergeant Haddismal? That armada, maybe? What odds would you give them, eh, crawlies? Let's wager, let's have a little fun—'

Taliktrum's finger stabbed down at Uskins. 'That buffoon should not have been admitted. Who brought him?'

Uskins lowered his voice. 'No one brought me, Lord Taliktrum. I merely followed my friends.'

Now it was Alyash's turn to laugh. 'What blary friends?'

Uskins' mouth twisted, but he made no reply.

'Quarrelling imbeciles!' said Taliktrum. 'Your race truly is a misstep on the part of nature. By the sun and stars, act like men! Where is the sorcerer? When can we expect his next attack?'

The argument exploded again. Haddismal pointed out that Arunis' last attack had only occurred after the ixchel drugged every human aboard. The ixchel fired back that drugged sleep was kinder than what giants had meted out to their people for five hundred years. Jeers and insults flew. When order at last returned, however, it was clear that no one knew where Arunis was hiding.

'I will say this,' said Bolutu. 'He will not wait long. The South is changed, and powers have arisen that were not here before. Arunis will not risk his prize being snatched by some mage or ruler mightier than himself.'

'What can he do, though?' asked Big Skip. 'If he could use the Stone he'd have come for it already, wouldn't he?'

'Let him try,' said Haddismal, and his men rumbled in agreement.

'You speak in ignorance,' said Hercól. 'The mage is three thousand years old. He has survived cataclysms beyond anything we have experienced. Do you think he will let himself be thwarted by a small company of marines? No, it is the Nilstone itself that thwarts him, for the present. And it is these two—' he indicated Pazel and Thasha '—who have best understood his tactics. How does one handle a poker heated in the furnace? With a glove, of course. That simple insight, when Thasha brought it to me, explained so much of the sorcerer's efforts and schemes. This creature—' Hercól gestured at the Shaggat '—is his chosen glove.

Arunis cares nothing for him or his deformed version of the Old Faith. He merely believes the Shaggat will serve his purpose.'

'Arqual's purpose, too,' hissed Myett.

'Now, that just ain't so,' said Haddismal. 'The Emperor wants the downfall of the Mzithrin Kings, and he planned to use the Shaggat against them. That's true, and well deserved, after all their crimes. But His Supremacy knew nothing about the Nilstone, or Arunis for that matter. He never meant things to come to such a pass.'

'Tell that to the survivors.'

Everyone turned. It was Lord Talag, Taliktrum's father. He stood in the midst of the ixchel on the hay bales, leaning on the shoulder of a younger man. His thick grey hair was tied back in the style of elder ixchel, and his eyes blazed with fury. 'Tell them!' he spat again. 'The limbless, the eyeless, the orphaned, the mad. "Don't blame Arqual. We never meant the Shaggat to do so well. We thought he would only sack a few cities, burn a few regions, exterminate a people or two. A brief civil war is all we had in mind – a war to break your will to fight *us*, when our fleets came in turn." Give them comfort, giant. Tell them how much better their lives will be under the Arquali heel.'

Pazel was alarmed. Since his abuse by the rats, Talag had been quiet and withdrawn. But here he was again in all his ferocity, Talag the mastermind, who had swept all his people up in his dream of a homecoming, who had exploited Ott's war conspiracy as deftly as Arunis had. Here was the genius, the human-hater, Diadrelu's brother and her twisted reflection. As much as anyone aboard, Talag had brought them to this moment. Was he recovered enough to lead the clan once more? And which was worse, the clear-eyed hatred of the father, or the hazy delusions of the son?

Talag began to cough; perhaps he was not so recovered after all. When the fit finally ended he shook his head. 'In any case, your plans for the mad king have failed. The soul entombed in that statue will never breathe again, let alone reach his fanatics on Gurishal to lead them in a new holy war. The sorcerer may do all that you fear, if and when he comes for the Stone – but not with the aid of the Shaggat. My son has foreseen this, and much else that he has yet to reveal.'

Thasha looked at Pazel and rolled her eyes.

'Go to your rest, Father,' said Taliktrum. 'Lehdra, Nasonnok, escort him.' Turning to the humans, he drew a deep breath. 'In sum: you cannot locate Arunis, you have no idea what to do with the Nilstone, you do not know the first thing about the surrounding country or the armada that passed us, and you do not have a plan. Am I leaving anything out?'

'We've gold enough to buy a fair-sized realm,' said Haddismal. 'We can hire the best curse-breakers this South has to offer. They'll fix the Shaggat, if he can be fixed. And if we can pop that stone out of his hand without killing him.'

'Or yourselves,' said Taliktrum.

'And meanwhile,' put in Alyash, 'we look for a place called Stath Bálfyr. We have course headings from there, as you probably know. Headings for a safer, western return across the Nelluroq, behind the Mzithrini defences, to the Shaggat's homeland of Gurishal.'

'Y-ess,' said Taliktrum. 'From Stath Bálfyr. So I've been told.'

Pazel saw the sudden alertness in every ixchel's face, and knew its source. Diadrelu had told Hercól everything, a few hours before her death. The ixchel had deceived the deceivers. The course headings were a fiction, the old documents that contained them forgeries. Stath Bálfyr was real, but it was no starting point for a run across the Ruling Sea. It was the ixchel homeland, a country ruled by the little people, the land Talag had sworn they would return to and reclaim.

He's not going to tell them, Pazel realised. *He's no fool: better they should want to find Stath Bálfyr than he should have to drive them there with threats. Of course, it may come to that in the end.*

'Sirs?' said a thin voice from the edge of the chamber.

It was Ibjen, the dlömic boy.

Taliktrum looked at him dubiously. 'You have something to add?'

'The armada, sirs,' said Ibjen, his voice shaking. 'There was talk of it in the village. Just talk, you understand. We are simple folk—'

'You don't have to convince us of that,' said Taliktrum. 'Speak quickly, and be done.'

'Out here we have little to do with the Empire, sir,' said Ibjen, 'and the news we do have comes by way of Masalym. When my father came out to the Sandwall, boats still made the crossing from the city every day or two, and soldiers would be billeted with the townsfolk, and speak of the *Platazcra*, the Infinite Conquest. But that was years ago. For a long time now we have been abandoned – that is why my mother chose to send me here.'

'You ramble, boy.'

Ibjen made an apologetic nod. 'Sir, before your ship we had had no visitors in half a year. And the last visitor died of fever in just three days. We have no doctor, so my father and I tended him as best we could. He was not a man of Masalym. Some guessed that he came from Orbilesc, others from Calambri.'

'These names mean nothing to us,' said Taliktrum. 'If you cannot get to the point—'

'Listen to him!' said Thasha. 'He's doing us a favour, being here.'

'And those words blary well *do* mean something – one of 'em at least,' added Fiffengurt. '"Orbilesc" is engraved on our blary sheet anchors, though the letters are faded now. I always wondered if it referred to her home port.' He gestured at Ibjen. 'You carry on, lad. I say you're mighty brave, to step aboard this ship.'

Ibjen did not look brave at that moment. 'Orbilesc and Calambri are cities far to the west, in the heart of Bali Adro,' he said. 'And it is true that the Empire's greatest shipyards are there.' He looked at Thasha and swallowed. 'My father sent me to the neighbours' house when the stranger began to die. But last night he told me something he had never mentioned before. That the dying man had broken his silence before the end. That he'd said he came from a village on the banks of the River Sundral, near Orbilesc. He said that the whole of the city had been caught up in some huge, secret effort, for years. That Imperial warships turned away all private vessels at a distance of fifty miles, and that a strange glow hung over Orbilesc by night. Later the mountains began to shake, and boulders crashed down upon his village. The fell light grew stronger. And finally the river gushed with boiling water that killed every fish, every frog and snake and wading bird – even the trees whose roots drank from the stream. That, the man had claimed, was when he fled east.'

Ibjen gazed beseechingly at his listeners. 'My father thought it but the ravings of a dying man. Until yesterday, that is. Now he believes that Orbilesc was building ships for the Emperor. The same ships that passed in the Gulf, Thashiziq. The ships of the armada.'

There was a long pause; the men were too unsettled to speak. To Pazel's surprise it was Big Skip who broke the silence.

'Right,' he said. 'Fleet or no fleet, we have to sail before we starve. And it can't be north across the Nelluroq, even if we wished to—'

'Which we do *not*,' said Haddismal, 'until we reach Stath Bálfyr, wherever that may be. This is an Arquali ship, and Magad's word is law, even here on the far side of Alifros.'

'Glory to the Ametrine Throne,' said Alyash dryly, 'and if that ain't motivation enough, there's the small matter of him crucifying us, with our families, if we return to Arqual without completing the mission.'

Pazel kept his face expressionless. *Magad's done all the punishing he's going to do*, he thought.

'So,' said Big Skip, 'turn east and we might catch up with that hellish armada; turn west and we might find the hellish place it came from. And either way we won't get far before we're too hungry to do our jobs. Ain't it simple, then? We head due south – to this Masalym, thirty miles across the bay.'

No one seconded the motion. Big Skip raised his bushy eyebrows. 'It's a city,' he insisted. 'They'll feed us, just as these good village folk gave us water. What about it, mates? Thirty miles to the butcher's shop, says I.'

But Bolutu shook his head. 'The Masalym of my day would have been a good choice,' he said. 'It was a trading city, and so used to visitors – either by sea, or out of the strange mountains of the Efaroc Peninsula at its back. Yet if Masalym today is ruled by the same power that launched those ships, then I for one would rather keep my distance from the butcher's shop.'

'Ha!' blurted Uskins. 'The butcher's shop!'

His laugh was jarring, almost a scream, and nearly everyone looked at him in anger. Uskins flinched, as though expecting a blow. Whether or not his fear was justified Pazel never learned, however, for at that moment the ship's drums erupted in pandemonium.

'Beat to quarters! Beat to quarters!' Already the cries resounded through the ship.

'Damnation, we're still at anchor!' shouted Fiffengurt. 'Alyash, get to the starboard battery! Sunderling, on deck! Set Fegin and his men to bracing that foremast! Go!'

'Are we under attack?' Taliktrum shouted. 'Fiffengurt, how can this be?'

'It can't!' snapped Fiffengurt. 'There's no way in Alifros a ship's crept up on us! But who knows, who knows, in this mad country?' He turned wildly about. 'Pathkendle! Wake the anchor lifters! We can't afford to leave more iron on the sea-floor! Run, by the Sweet Tree, run!'

6

A Hasty Departure

ornament

22 Ilbrin 941

Pazel sprinted from the manger. He heard Thasha shouting his name but did not look back. Foreign-born, mutinous, expelled from the service, sentenced to death – amazing how it all disappeared. In emergencies he was simply a tarboy.

Refeg and Rer, the anchor lifters, slept in a kind of stall behind the portside cable tiers. They almost never moved quickly. Pazel flew across the orlop with all the speed he dared, leaping the broken floor planks, flinging open doors.

He heard their breath, deep organ wheezes, before his eyes discerned their shapes. The brothers slept side by side, curled in beds of straw, their six-foot-long arms folded against their mammoth chests. Their skin was yellow-brown and rough as rhino hide, and festooned here and there with clumps of fur, green-black, like moss on stone. They were augrongs, survivors of a race that had all but disappeared from Alifros, dwellers in an Etherhorde slum when not serving on some Arquali ship. They spent nearly all their time asleep, harbouring their titanic strength, rising for just one meal a week or to perform some labour that would have required scores of men. Their language was so rich in metaphor it seemed almost the language of dreams, and Pazel was the only person aboard who spoke it.

Left to themselves, augrongs could take a quarter-hour to wake, and another quarter-hour to get to their feet. Shouting, pleading, beating on cans did nothing to speed the process, and no one in their right mind would nudge them with pole or pitchfork. But a faster method had occurred to Pazel. Bending close (but not too close) to their sleeping heads, he summoned his memory of the Augronga tongue and boomed in an inhuman voice: *'Music in the forest: tomorrow calls me, I answer with my feet.'*

Two pairs of fist-sized yellow eyes snapped open. The creatures surged upright, grunting like startled elephants. Pazel smiled. It worked every time: he had recited a phrase reserved for the saddest farewells. Each augrong thought that he was hearing the other's voice, and after countless years cut off from their people, the brothers' deepest fear was separation.

When they caught sight of Pazel they heaved irritated sighs. 'Always the same one, the babbler, the noisy goose,' rumbled Rer, his huge eyelids drooping like batwings.

'Noisy till he's plucked,' said Refeg, making a half-hearted swipe at Pazel.

Pazel jumped backwards. 'Emergency, emergency!' he cried, stripping the finesse from his Augronga. 'Beat to quarters! Hear the drums!'

With impressive haste (for augrongs) the brothers stumbled out of their bedding and made for the No. 3 ladderway. They knew where they were wanted: at the main capstan, where each could do the work of fifty men in the arduous job of lifting anchor. Pazel slipped around them carefully, watching those vast flat hands. The augrongs had never hurt him; in fact, he thought they appreciated his occasional service as a translator. But despite his grasp of their language, their minds remained a mystery. And Pazel could never forget that they had helped Arunis extract the Nilstone from the Red Wolf. From that day forward Pazel wondered just what kind of power Arunis had gained over the creatures, and if he could count on it still. But any mention of the sorcerer brought warning growls from the augrongs.

Pazel sprinted ahead, and in short order he was climbing the No. 3 ladderway. Five steep flights of stairs, each more crowded than the last, and the drums still sounding overhead. When he burst onto the topdeck at last he found himself in a crowd of men and tarboys, soldiers and steerage passengers, all making for the starboard rail. It was late afternoon; the sun was low and orange in the west. Pazel ran towards the bow. He could see Mr Fiffengurt ahead, hobble-running, with an ixchel riding his shoulder.

When Pazel caught up with Fiffengurt he found that the ixchel was Ensyl. She was a wispy, earnest young woman with eyes that darted restlessly, until they suddenly fixed on you, and drilled. Catching sight of Pazel, she leaped from Fiffengurt's shoulder to his own, landing lightly as a bird.

'Have you seen them?' she demanded.

'No,' gasped Pazel, still winded from the stairs. 'Who are they? I can't see any ship.'

'There's no ship,' said Fiffengurt. 'That's why we were caught off guard. Damnation, if those villagers betrayed us—'

They reached the tonnage hatch. As he had done many times, Pazel set a foot on the rail and leaped up to catch a mainmast forestay. With one hand on the wire-taut rope he leaned out over the yawning shaft, Ensyl clinging fiercely to his shirt. Now at last he could see over the crowd.

'But I still don't—'

His words died in his throat. He saw them: dlömu, hundreds strong, lining the shore road from the village to the Tower of Narybir. They were still coming, pouring through the gatehouse, leaping down from the wall, even passing over the dunes about the tower's foot. Were they forming ranks, carrying weapons? The land was too distant for him to be sure.

'They look like Mr Bolutu,' said Ensyl. 'Is it true what they're saying in the clan, Pazel – that those beings rule all the South, that there's no one else here at all?'

Pazel leaped to the deck again. He struggled to answer her as he raced to catch up with Fiffengurt, who had almost reached the forecastle. In normal times the commander gave his orders from the quarterdeck, but Fiffengurt was showing great deference to

Captain Rose, who could still communicate by shouting through the window of the forecastle house.

Pazel went straight to that window himself. Alyash and a Besq midshipman were already standing before the dirty glass, yelling to the prisoners within. Framed between them, Captain Rose's huge, choleric, red-bearded form glared out at the deck. 'Stand aside, Pathkendle!' he bellowed, his voice rattling the glass.

Pazel jumped back. On the captain's right stood Sandor Ott, a short man with the most savage face the tarboy had ever beheld. The spymaster's eyes moved ravenously, devouring information. One hand, mottled with age spots and knife scars, the fingernails mangled decades ago by torture, lay flat upon the glass. Behind the two men the other hostages crowded, struggling for a glimpse of the deck.

There was Neeps! The Sollochi boy lit up at the sight of Pazel, and he flashed a tarboy signal (two fingers pinched to the thumb: *Standing by to assist you*) with an ironic grin that Pazel found almost miraculous. *I'd be going mad in there. How's he managing to keep up his spirits?*

There was no sign of Marila, and an instant later Neeps himself was shouldered aside. As he had many times before, Pazel felt the ache of guilt. He had promised to get them out of there, weeks ago, but had made no progress at all.

The lookouts in the crosstrees were flinging down reports. 'Warriors, Mr Fiffengurt! Fish-eyes, every one, and armed to the teeth!'

Fiffengurt snapped open his telescope. 'Conveyance!' he bellowed. 'Where's their blary boat?'

'Not a boat to be seen, sir!' came the answer from the lookouts. 'Not a launch, not a dinghy! They must have *walked* into that town!'

Over the shouting Pazel caught Thasha's voice. She was there at the rail – with Fulbreech, to Pazel's undying irritation. They stood shoulder to shoulder, heads inches apart, taking turns with her father's telescope. Suddenly, as if he could feel Pazel's gaze,

Fulbreech glanced over his shoulder. 'Come and see, Pathkendle! Make room there, Thashula—'

He nudged Thasha over with a familiarity that almost drove Pazel mad. *Thashula?* It was her childhood nickname, but Pazel had thought she hated it; she'd certainly never encouraged *him*—

'Well, come on, man,' said Fulbreech.

Pazel lurched forwards and took the telescope, his face shouting *Fool!* in a banner of scarlet.

No question about it: the dlömu were warriors. They were tall and muscular, though slender like those in the village. All carried weapons – swords, hatchets, flails, glaives, crossbows, clubs – and a variety of other implements, from coiled rope to hammers and picks. They wore no armour, no shirts even, but many sported a kind of dark, round, tight-fitting cap. Some held standards aloft, a white bird against a field of deepest blue. A number of dlömu were inspecting the tower door.

'How did they *get* there?' Thasha asked suddenly. 'Do they have a camp in the woods? If so, they stayed blary quiet yesterday.'

'They could have come from the north side,' said Pazel.

'From the Nelluroq?' said Fulbreech, incredulous. 'How? We sailed for five days along that string of dunes. There's no harbour, no other inlet – just beach after beach, pounded night and day by those lethal waves.'

'They look blary lethal themselves,' mused Fiffengurt. 'However they got there, I'm glad there's three miles of water between us.'

'Under three from the end of that jetty, sir,' put in Mr Fegin.

Pazel glanced at the long, smooth sea wall jutting out into the Gulf from one end of the village. A number of dlömu stood near its base. Like the others they were examining the *Chathrand* with the keenest interest.

'That bunch by the gate must be the officers,' said Thasha. 'Look – they're sending messengers up and down the ranks. And they're pointing telescopes at us as well.'

'Then they know this is a human ship,' said Ensyl. 'That would explain their curiosity.'

'It's *one* explanation,' said Fiffengurt. 'Mr Brule, update the captain. Ah, listen! Your friends Refeg and Rer are on the job, Pathkendle.'

A deep, slow *click . . . click*, like a reluctant grandfather clock: it was the turning of the capstan, as the anchors rose heavily from the seabed. They were harrow anchors, Pazel knew: far lighter than the mammoth mains; still the men would be glad of the augrongs' help before the task was done.

'Good thinking,' said Alyash. 'They might wheel guns out of that village. Just as well we're through with it.'

Thasha turned to him accusingly. 'Ibjen lives in that village,' she said. 'His father's waiting for him.'

'*Ibjen* should've mentioned the army camped out in the bush,' countered Alyash.

'Ten seconds between clicks,' said Fiffengurt, 'and we're at four-teen fathoms. Quickly, now: who's got the calculus for me?'

No tarboy had to ask what *the calculus* meant. Pazel focused instantly: *Ten seconds a click. Six clicks a minute. Four cable-feet per click. Cable length twice the vertical depth.* 'That's about . . . about—'

'Seven minutes,' said Thasha, 'before we could get underway. If we needed to.'

'Admiral's daughter!' said Fulbreech with an approving grin. Absently he passed the telescope to Pazel again, but his eyes remained on Thasha. 'Doesn't she amaze you, Pathkendle?'

Pazel snatched the telescope, calculating the time it would take Fulbreech to strike the water once Pazel pushed him over the rail. Two seconds, maybe. Then a faint voice reached them from the shore.

'Silence on deck!' shouted Fiffengurt.

The voice came from somewhere near the village gate. Pazel squinted and saw a man bellowing into an enormous, funnel-shaped shell, which he held before his face like a voice-trumpet. Try as he might, Pazel could not catch a word.

Then the soldiers parted, and a new figure walked out upon the quay.

He was a massive dlömu, broad in neck and shoulder, and his walk was somehow cruel. The others did not approach him. Something about the man brought the armada itself to mind – something vile, Pazel thought. But whatever it was refused to surface in his memory. The man gestured at the crier, and the latter screamed into the shell-device once again.

'Pathkendle?' said Fiffengurt.

Pazel shook his head. 'Sorry, sir, I can't hear a thing.'

Fiffengurt turned to the midshipman. 'Get some steerage passengers up here on the run, Mr Bravun – some who ain't been deafened by cannon fire.' He twisted, pointing his good eye up at the *Chathrand*'s pennants. 'Wind's on the port beam. We'd have to tack a sight *closer* to those gentlefolk before we could turn and run.'

'We've no cause to run anywhere, till we decide a course,' said Alyash.

'Drogues bow and stern, Mr Coote, if you please,' said Fiffengurt. 'We're close enough without this drift.'

Coote set men running, and in short order Pazel saw an umbrella-like drogue tossed from the forecastle on its chain. In calm waters the drogues would keep the *Chathrand* almost at a standstill, but unlike the anchors they could be jettisoned, and built anew from wood and canvas.

Midshipman Bravun returned with three steerage passengers: a bearded Simjan man, the apple-cheeked Altymiran woman who had lately become Mr Teggatz's galley assistant, and an older, white-haired woman whose husband had perished on the Ruling Sea. Fiffengurt silenced the chatter again. 'Cup your ears and face forward, everybody,' he said. 'Let 'em see we're listening.'

The signal worked: once again the dlömic crier shouted his imperative command. The steerage passengers whispered together, debating what they'd heard. It was clever of Fiffengurt to call on them, Pazel thought: locked in their compartment below the waterline for most of the voyage, the steerage passengers had been buffered from the noise of both battle and typhoon. It was about the only good luck they'd had since stepping aboard the Great Ship.

'We ain't sure, Mr Fiffengurt,' said the bearded Simjan, 'but he *might* be talking about a putative.'

Fiffengurt frowned. 'Come again?'

'"Chin of the putative,"' said the Altymiran woman. 'That's what he said, sir.'

'Madam,' said Fiffengurt, '*putative* ain't a thing, and don't take an article.'

'Does that mean it can't have a chin?'

The white-haired woman merely clung to the rail and stared. When Pazel's turn with the scope came again, he held it up for Ensyl. The ixchel woman steadied it with both hands. 'Focus, Pazel, good. That's strange: the leader is taking off his boots.'

'Most of them are barefoot already,' said Thasha. 'They don't seem to care much for shoes.'

The white-haired woman took a frightened step backwards. 'I think we should go,' she said.

'They're shuffling equipment, too,' said Ensyl. 'Collecting shields, and some of the weapons. But they're strapping other things across their backs. Lighter weapons, maybe, and—'

'Hush!' said Alyash. 'He's calling again!'

The ship held its breath. No use, thought Pazel: he could hear only the tone of anger in the distant voice. It was a bit disturbing to think that the *Chathrand* had stolen part of his hearing for ever.

'I *really* think we should be *leaving*,' begged the old woman, pressing a frail hand to her mouth.

The Altymiran woman smiled. 'Not *Chin*. It's *Give* he's shouting. *Give of the putative* – that's the first bit, and then *stubborn, stubborn*—'

'*Stubborn the consciousness*,' said the Simjan, looking at Mr Fiffengurt for approval. Then his face turned pensive. 'Actually, that doesn't mean a thing.'

'Get rid of these fools,' said Alyash with an irate gesture.

'Where's our dear Brother Bolutu? He should be helping us sort out this gibberish.'

All at once there was turmoil at the village gate. More dlömic warriors were spilling out onto the road. But this time they were bringing villagers with them, at sword-point.

'There's Mr Isul,' said Thasha. 'By the Tree, they're talking hostages! But what do they blary *want*?'

Belowdecks, Refeg and Rer gave a final, satisfied roar. The capstans fell silent: the ship was floating free.

'Captain Fiffengurt,' said the white-haired woman.

'I'm not the captain, my dear lady—'

'*Give up the fugitive.* That's what the creature said. Give him up or *suffer the consequences.*'

Sailors and passengers gaped at her. Then Alyash snapped his fingers. 'The *sfvantskors*! Those lying bastards tangled with the dlömu before you ever laid eyes on 'em, Fiffengurt! They must have killed a few.'

'Nonsense!' said Pazel. 'They told us their whole story, from the moment we sank the *Jistrolloq*. The only dlömu they've seen were dead ones, on a shipwreck.'

'And you believe them Black Rags?' said the midshipman.

Alyash turned and struck the man backhanded across the jaw. '*That's* for your swinish nicknames,' he said. 'I'd give it to you harder, Bravun, but you have a point. A *sfvantskor* will say anything to gain an advantage over a non-believer.'*

'But their words rang true,' Pazel insisted.

---

* Technically true. The Book of the Old Faith contains certain apocryphal material, including the Address of the Vengeful Seraph, who states: 'To defeat the foes of Eternal Truth, lesser truths may be sacrificed, and deception wielded like a knife in the dark.' The materials appear in no copies of the Book before its third century of existence, however, and it appears likely that they were added by a warlike king, precisely to justify the training of a guild of holy assassins. Like the pruning of young oaks, editorship is power over a future one will never see. – EDITOR.

'Especially your sister's, eh?' said Alyash.

Pazel glared at him. *Double agent*, he thought. *Or triple? How can anyone, even Ott, really know which side he's on?*

Fiffengurt rapped his knuckles on the wall of the forecastle house. 'That Jalantri fellow's trapped in here now. But there's no harm in putting the other two on display. Get 'em up here! Let's see who knows their faces.'

Messengers were dispatched to the Turachs. In sight of the dlömic warriors, Fiffengurt raised both hands, palms outwards: *Patience*. A few minutes later a great mob of Turachs climbed the ladderway, escorting Neda and Cayer Vispek, who were chained hand and foot. At the rear came Sergeant Haddismal, dragging Ibjen roughly by the arm.

'We caught this one squeezing through a hawsehole,' he said, 'like he was about to shimmy down the cable into the Gulf.'

'Then *he's* the fugitive,' said Midshipman Bravun.

'Fugitive?' cried Ibjen. 'Fugitive from whom? I just want to get back to my father!'

Ensyl glanced at the distant shore. 'Are you a champion swimmer?' she asked.

'Champion? Of course not! Let me go!'

'Pazel,' said Neda suddenly, in Ormali, 'have you seen Jalantri? Do you know why he's been kept apart from us in this way?'

She was hiding her anxiety – but not well enough to fool a brother. 'It's complicated, Neda,' he said.

Her eyes grew suddenly wide. 'Did they kill him? They did, didn't they? Tell me the truth!'

Pazel was about to assure her that Jalantri was safe when Fiffengurt stepped forwards, waving his arms. 'Quiet, Pathkendle! Listen up, Mr Ibjen, and you *sfvantskors* as well: I'm not handing you over to anybody without a reason. But you might just give me that reason if I find out you're telling lies.'

'Now you insult us,' said Cayer Vispek. 'We surrendered to you in good faith.'

'We'll see,' said Fiffengurt. At his gesture, the *sfvantskor* prisoners and the dlömic boy were dragged to the rail, and stood facing the dlömu host. Once again the two sides fell silent, applying themselves to their telescopes.

'Their leader's waving them off,' said Fulbreech. 'He's not interested in them, that's plain.' He looked the *sfvantskors* over carefully. 'I suppose they were telling the truth.'

'Of course we were,' said Vispek, angrier than ever. 'What have we to do with *them*? Yes, we took some necessities from a ship full of those creatures. But the ship was abandoned, and the crew already dead.' He raised his shackled arms. 'Mr Fiffengurt, where is your shame? You have no reason to treat us like criminals.'

'Reasons, Cayer?' said Neda with quiet bitterness. 'Who needs reasons? Excuses are good enough for Arqualis—' she glanced bitterly at Pazel '—and their pets.'

Pazel could not believe his ears. 'How can you say that, Neda? How can you *think* that?'

'Wait!' cried Thasha suddenly. 'The big man's moving. Ah, look: he's reaching for the shell. Maybe he'll give it a try himself.'

With his naked eye Pazel could just make out the orange shell, as the mighty leader took it from his aide. But rather than shout into the device he tossed it contemptuously to the ground.

Humans and dlömu grew deathly still. Pazel heard the creak of timbers, the piping of shorebirds about the rocky islets, the bumping of a wheelblock against the foremast. And then came a sudden, desperate banging at the window, and Captain Rose's furious, gale-surmounting roar:

'RUN! RUN HER SOUTH! WARE THE SHIP AND BLARY RUN!'

As that very instant the dlömic warriors gave a terrible cry and began sprinting out along the jetty in their hundreds.

'Ware the ship!' howled Fiffengurt. 'Bindhammer, Fegin, aloft your yardmen! Bend them topsails *now*!'

'Gods of death,' said Haddismal, pointing.

The first dlömu were nearing the end of the jetty, some two miles from the *Chathrand*. But they did not stop: they dived with the grace of dolphins into the sea. One after another they dived, in a long coordinated manoeuvre. Dozens, then hundreds: the battalion was taking to the waves.

'Madness!' said Fulbreech. 'Swimmers can't catch a ship! And even if they could, what then? We're sixty feet above the waterline!'

Pazel looked at Thasha: her eyes were wild, darting. All about them swarmed the men of the First Watch, freeing braces, racing up the shrouds, bellowing from the jungle of ropes overhead: 'Let fall! Sheet home! Man the weather halyards!' Already the fore topsail was billowing out the spars. The main topsail followed, and the two vast, cream-coloured rectangles filled and pulled. A tightening energy filled the ship, and slowly her bow swung away from the island.

The dlömu had become a haze of black dots, appearing and disappearing in the waves. Some of the sailors regarded the spectacle with astonished grins; it was as if a herd of cattle had decided to burrow into the earth. But Pazel did not grin. He thought of how Bolutu and Ibjen had brought the wounded Turach so easily ashore. He snatched the telescope from Fulbreech. The warriors' strokes were amazingly fast, and their legs frothed the water behind them. He turned to Ibjen, shouted over the din: 'Will they catch us?'

'How in Hell's Mouth should I know?' Ibjen shot back.

'Could *you* catch us?'

His senses told him the question was ludicrous: the dlömu were swimming; the ship was setting sail. Ibjen hesitated, looking across the water at the black, swimming shapes. 'No,' he said finally, and dropped his eyes.

It should have set Pazel's mind at ease, but it had the opposite effect. Ibjen's reply had been laced with shame.

Rose went on bellowing through the window: 'Let go the topgallant clews! More sheetmen to windward! Brace that foremast or lose it, you creeping slugs!'

Pazel looked up at the windsock fluttering on the jiggermast yard: enough of a breeze for headway, but not for speed. *Doesn't matter*, he told himself. For how fast could they possibly swim? Three knots, four? Fulbreech was right: it *was* madness. But the dlömu came on, swift and arrow-straight, and the *Chathrand* was still turning about.

'Lapwing!' howled Rose suddenly. 'Cut loose those Rinforsaken drogues! Her bow's fighting the turn, can't you *feel* it?'

He was right, Pazel knew at once: the canvas drogues were pulling against the turn like stubborn mules. Pazel shook his head. 'Rose guessed the whole tactical situation from in there,' he said to Ensyl, 'and he couldn't even see what was happening ashore.'

'He saw us seeing it,' Ensyl replied.

A decisive *chop* from the forecastle: Lapwing was taking an axe to the drogue cable. On the third blow the cable parted, and the *Chathrand* leaned into the turn, gaining speed. Now her bowsprit pointed at the red tower (its lock had been broken, its doors flung apart), now at the empty dunes, now at the corner of the village wall.

Fiffengurt twisted aft. A glance and a nod, and the teams at the mainmast began hauling with a will. A sudden thought brought his telescope snapping up: yes, the aft drogue was clear as well. Then up went his gaze, and both arms, and, 'Topgallants, bow to stern!' he thundered, and one after another the higher sails were loosed. They filled faster than the canvas below: more wind at that height. They were turning with a will, now, the ship canting leeward in her eagerness to come about. Fiffengurt put both hands on the rail and heaved a sigh.

'Now we'll be just fine, boys,' he said to no one in particular.

He slid down the forecastle ladder like a younger man and turned to face the captain. Rose's bellows had given way to coughs (the smoky forecastle house was affecting all the prisoners) but he gave Fiffengurt a nod of affirmation. Fiffengurt touched his cap, turned smartly about (chest out, chin high) and then the lookout screamed from the fighting top:

'Sand! Sandbar at half a mile, three points off the starboard bow! No depth! No depth! Sandbar right across our way!'

They had not started their run, and no speed endangered them. But the ridge of submerged sand was disastrously placed. It began at the eastern edge of the island and meandered shorewards for nearly a mile. Fiffengurt howled a course correction. Hundreds of men at the ropes scurried and swore. They could only tack north, right at the village gate, until the sandbar ended.

No one smiled now. The swimmers had gained a tremendous advantage: indeed, the *Chathrand*'s new course was actually bringing it closer to them. Worse still, they could not attain anything like the speed of a straight downwind run. All at once the race looked very tight.

Pazel and Thasha climbed the jiggermast shrouds, just high enough to see the sandbar. 'But it's *huge*,' cried Pazel. 'How did we miss it before?' For they had rounded the little island from the east, right through these waters. 'It must be a lot deeper than it looks, some trick of the light. We sailed right over it.'

'Yes,' Thasha agreed. But even as she spoke he saw her reconsider. 'Pazel, maybe it *wasn't* there.'

'Don't be daft.'

'Look where it begins.' Thasha pointed to the island's eastern tip, a confusion of jagged rocks. 'The serpent. That's where it was smashing about, trying to break free of its bridle. What if it dragged the thing along the sea-floor, too?'

'And ploughed up *all that*?'

'You think your explanation's more likely?'

Pazel shrugged. 'No,' he admitted. Then he actually laughed. 'Thasha, this mucking world wants us dead.'

She didn't laugh, but she smiled at him with black mirth, and that was almost better. It was a look of private understanding. Not one she could share with Greysan Fulbreech.

Warmed, Pazel turned his gaze on the swimmers again: less than a mile off, and closing. They moved as a single body, like a school of dark fish. He shaded his eyes, and felt his dread surge to life again, redoubled.

'Rin's eyes, Thasha – *they're swimming with objects on their backs.*'

'Weapons,' said a voice beneath them. 'Light and curious weapons, but weapons nonetheless. And why, pray, are you without your own?'

It was Hercól, dressed for battle, which in this case meant that he wore little more than breeches, boots and a small steel arm-guard. His longbow was in his hand; his ancient, enchanted sword Ildraquin was strapped sidelong across his back; on his belt hung the white knife of his old master, Sandor Ott. Pazel had last seen that knife in Thasha's hands, during the battle with the rats. He wished now that she had thrown the cruel thing away. Wearing it, even Hercól looked sinister.

'Fetch your swords,' said the Tholjassan.

Pazel sought his eye. 'This is some sort of crazy bluff, isn't it? They were trying to drive us onto the sandbar, maybe, or—'

'Fetch them.'

Thasha swung down to the deck. 'Stay with Fiffengurt, Pazel, he needs you. I'll bring yours from the stateroom.'

She was gone, and Hercól sped forward, shouting to Haddismal, and Pazel was swept into the martial frenzy of a ship preparing for violence. The cargo hatches were sealed with oilskins, the lower gunports were closed (too near the water, Fiffengurt had decided); the wheels of the deck cannon were greased; damp sawdust was flung down for traction; the firing crews assembled and rehearsed their cues. *Arqual!* rang a furious cry from the main deck, as ninety Turachs raised a clatter with sword and shield. Corporal Metharon, the Turach sharpshooter, led his archers to the stern.

The sun began to set. Fiffengurt hobbled for the quarterdeck, bellowing down ladderways, firing orders up the masts. Tarboys streamed up the Holy Stair, lugging cannonballs and buckets of powder; gunners darted about with match-pots like small, fiery lunch pails. Ixchel were everywhere: racing up the shrouds ahead of sailors to warn them of broken ratlines, adjusting the chafing fleece where ropes abraded, diving into guns to scrape the rust out of fuse-holes, retying sailors' bandannas before they could slip.

Humanity was their science: not a task existed on the Great Ship that they had not watched in secret.

As they ran north the sandbar grew taller, closer to the surface. The waves broke over it, choppy and low. Ship and swimmers were converging on the same point: that deeper blue where the bar finally ended, where the ship could jackknife east and run with the wind at her back, every inch of square sail thrusting her faster. Lookouts scanned the Gulf: no boats, no place to hide them. Whatever the attackers were doing, they were doing alone.

Off the starboard bow the water grew shallower yet, the waves collapsing into foam. 'Ease away windward, helmsmen,' shouted Fiffengurt. 'If we shave that bar the game's up. Steady on.'

Pazel arrived just as Fiffengurt was starting up the quarterdeck ladder. He could see that the man was in pain – a rat's jaws had savaged his left foot, and the wound had not yet healed. Pazel tried to steady him from behind, but Fiffengurt shook him off with a twitch.

'Pathkendle, I want you right *there*—' He pointed at the tip of the mizzenmast yard, twenty feet higher than the quarterdeck and about as many out over the Gulf '—with a great blary Turach shield. We'll have to judge depth by eyeball, see? Look straight down from out there. When that point clears the sandbar, you shout, "*Mark!*" Not a second before – and not a second later, lad.'

'Oppo, sir. But our practice shields would be better up there. Hard to handle all that Turach steel.'

Fiffengurt waved consent. 'Just don't fall in the blessed sea.'

Warning cries from the stern: the dlömu force had split in two. One mass of men continued straight at the *Chathrand*; the other broke east, towards the sandbar. Moments later the shouts were renewed, this time mixed with shock: the splinter group was wading. Thigh-deep, knee-deep, and then they were running in mere inches of foam, sprinting along the sandbar's crest. The fastest were drawing level with the *Chathrand*. Pazel stared, transfixed. Their belts jangled with strange hooks and daggers and coiled ropes. Their silver eyes looked the ship up and down.

BOOM.

The first carronade shook the timbers under Pazel's feet. Through the smoke Pazel saw the huge ball's impact, the white spray, and two black figures crushed into the sand as if by a giant stake. The others did not flinch; indeed, they put on a burst of speed. Then Pazel heard Metharon's cry, and the shrill twanging of longbows. Six or eight more dlömu fell.

'*Pathkendle!*' raged Fiffengurt.

Pazel's trance shattered; he swung out to the mizzenmast shrouds. Even as he climbed he felt tiny hands on his shirt, a tiny foot on his shoulder. 'Get down, Ensyl!' he cried. 'You won't be safe out there! I don't need help, I'm just a spotter!'

'Two can spot better than one,' she said.

Pazel argued no further: to judge by that grip, he wouldn't lose her unless he lost his hair.

Four more blasts – and hideous carnage among the runners. The ship had opened up with grapeshot guns from the stern windows. The spray of flying metal ripped bodies to pieces. Yet those behind came on undeterred, through the pink foam, leaping the fallen and the maimed. Pazel felt his body clench with nausea. The gunners reloaded, visibly shocked at their handiwork. Ensyl was retching. Pazel forced himself on.

More arrows now, more death. *What are they doing, what do they want?* Pazel stepped onto the footropes, eased out along the mizzenmast yard. Beneath him, Hercól and Metharon fired their bows with deadly accuracy, bringing down one soldier after another.

In the waning light, Pazel could just make out the end of the sandbar, sixty or eighty yards ahead. He caught Fiffengurt's eye and nodded, laying a finger beside his eye: *I'm watching.* Then someone among the dlömu gave a short, clipped command, and in perfect synchrony the runners dived back into the waves.

There were ragged cheers: some of the men thought they were looking at a retreat. But who could tell? The dlömu had dived deep; Pazel could see no more than shadows in the depths. The archers hesitated; all their targets were gone. For a moment no one was shouting. They had fifty yards to go.

It was Uskins who broke the silence. 'Oil, pour the oil!' he screamed suddenly. Pazel hadn't noticed the first mate until now, and neither, it seemed, had Mr Fiffengurt, who whirled on him in a rage. 'Belay that order! Stukey—'

'Do it! Pour the oil!' shrieked Uskins, more desperate than before.

'Belay!' roared Fiffengurt again. 'Stukey, you guano-eating worm! I ordered you to clear off the quarterdeck!'

For an instant Uskins' eyes flashed with rebellion. He had been cowed after nearly destroying the ship in the Vortex, but his hatred of the quartermaster was stronger than his shame. Livid, he advanced towards Fiffengurt. 'Ordered *me*? You're not the Gods-damned—'

'CAPTAIN FIFFENGURT!' howled a topman. 'THEY'RE BOARDING! THEY'RE BOARDING PORTSIDE AFT!'

All eyes turned to port. At that moment a sailor at the gunwale screamed and twisted. A light, barbed grappling hook had just arced over the rail and snapped back, pinning him by the hand. Other grapples followed.

'Damn it, we can't see *anything* here,' said Pazel.

'Yes we can,' said Ensyl, pointing down at their wake.

Pazel gasped. Half a dozen dlömu were clinging to the rudder. No, not just clinging – *scaling* it. They were swinging those scythe-shaped hooks, embedding them in the wood of the rudder stem, hauling themselves like ice climbers up towards the deck.

Pazel howled a warning – and the climbers heard. Silver eyes snapped onto him: the only person on the *Chathrand* from whom they were not hidden by the ship itself. Two of the dlömu put their hands into small, tight shoulder pouches, tugging something loose. Then the hands flicked violently. Fierce insect whines sounded around Pazel, and near his left hand something struck the yardarm with a *tok!* It was a star of razor-sharp steel.

'Oh *credek.*'

Pazel yanked in his legs and clung sidelong to the spar, hiding as much of himself as he could. He saw Turachs leaning out from the taffrail. They had seen the dlömu on the rudder at last, but could still not get off a decent shot. The dlömu could certainly take shots at Pazel, however, and did: once again he heard the whines, and the *t-t-tok!* of steel striking wood.

'Don't move!' said Ensyl. 'I'll watch the sandbar, you keep us alive.' She had curled herself into a ball, her feet on his neck, holding tight to his shirt and hair as she leaned out over the Gulf, staring straight down. Even in that moment he was stunned by her fearlessness. *This is why Dri wanted her for a disciple.*

'Twenty yards,' she said. 'You must shout to Fiffengurt – he's listening for your voice, not mine. Fifteen—'

Breaking glass. Pazel peeked under the yard. The attackers had smashed a window in the stern. The officers' wardroom, he thought.

'Ten yards, eight—'

Surely the Turachs were already there. Surely someone had dispatched them.

'Now!' hissed Ensyl.

Pazel shouted, '*Mark!*' with all his strength, and heard Fiffengurt respond instantly with commands of his own. Then the creak of the wheel, the groaning of cables and counterweights – and sudden howls of agony from below. The dlömu were being crushed between rudder and sternpost. Pazel looked, wished he hadn't, wished he could spit the images back out of his mind. Their skin was not human; it ruptured like the flesh of some dark, plump fruit. But under the surface there was no difference – the blood, the muscle, the shards of bone . . .

'*Pazel!*'

He wasn't ill. He should have been. Sometimes not to be ill meant you were broken inside. Then a hand gripped his shoulder. Not Ensyl's hand. It was Thasha: she had raced out along the spar; she was begging him to come down while he could.

Trimming the giant sails was harder than spinning a wheel, of course: the *Chathrand*'s turn actually slowed her at first, and that was when the dlömu pounced. Grapples flew over the rails port and starboard, and a second team assaulted the stern, keeping well clear of the rudder. It was all very organised. Those still in the water swam very close to the hull, protected by its curve from any shots from the deck or gunports. The attackers were quiet and purposeful, as if they had done this sort of thing before.

The sailors cut their climbing ropes with a will, and not a single dlömu gained the topdeck by that means. But many climbed twenty or thirty feet on the ropes, and then switched to hand-hooks. Soon there were ladders of these embedded hooks ascending from the waterline, and the *Chathrand* resembled some great prone beast assaulted by columns of ants.

The upper gun deck became a war zone. Dlömu flung themselves in through the gunports, which had been kept open for the cannon. The Turachs met them head-on, and killed many before they even gained their feet. Common sailors, armed with everything from cutlasses to galley knives, backed up the marines. Still a number of the dlömu managed to scatter deeper into the ship.

The unthinkable audacity of such an attack nearly let it succeed. But the sails were trimmed, the canvas did billow and pull, and the bulk of the attacking force was still a stone's throw behind. For all their ferocity, moreover, the exhausted dlömu who entered at the stern fared badly against the Turachs – rested, furious and armoured head to foot. Haddismal fought at the vanguard of his men, laying on in the wreckage of the wardroom with a great double-bladed axe, hacking off limbs that reached through the shattered windows, hurling down chairs and candlesticks and the bodies of the slain at those still climbing.

In the adjoining compartment, a luxury cabin, some twenty dlömu broke through the Turach ranks and sprinted up the Silver Stair. The few men who resisted them were swept away. They were one stairlength from the topdeck, and would have gained it if

Hercól had not stepped into their path. Above the open hatch he stood, the black sword in his left hand and Sandor Ott's white knife in the other, and his face was terrible to behold. Still the dlömu pressed the attack, for they could hear the Turachs storming after them from below. Hercól whirled and struck, his arms two blurs of black and white, and the dlömu began to fall. One after another they came, eyes maddened with the nearness of death, and one after another they died.

The ports were sealed, and the battle for the upper gun deck turned in the *Chathrand*'s favour. But from the quarterdeck, Fiffengurt looked down and cursed. The dlömu had fastened drag lines to the ship, scores of them, and flung them backwards to their swimming comrades. A hundred at least had grabbed hold already, and more were piling on.

Then it came, a desperate warning relayed from below by a living chain of ixchel: the attackers had uncoiled a flexible sawblade, they cried, and were drawing it over the rudder in whiplash strokes. Left to it they would, in a matter of minutes, saw the rudder off at its base.

Fiffengurt closed his eyes and made the sign of the Tree. Then he snatched the rigging axe from its hook on the taffrail and climbed up among the oil drums lashed between the lamps. With a few strokes he broke their seals, and lamp oil gushed in slippery torrents down the *Chathrand*'s stern, sloshing over the windows, soaking Fiffengurt and the dlömu alike, spreading in a great stain among the swimmers.

Fiffengurt looked up at the deck, his eyes full of murder and rage. 'Matches, Stukey, damn you to the Pits!'

Uskins came to life, unlidded the match-pot, churned the live coals with a stub.

'Never mind, give it here!' bellowed Fiffengurt. Seizing the match-pot, he emptied it in a shower of sparks over the side.

There was no explosion, no inferno of flames, no screams of agony. There was only a great *whoosh*, and orange light, and sudden silence from the army below. Everyone stumbled: the *Chathrand* had just leaped forwards, a carthorse cut free of its cart. Fiffengurt toppled between the lamps, staring, and once again it was Thasha who went, unbidden; Thasha who caught him before he could fall, only to stand there swaying, transfixed herself at the sight of the great pillow of fire upon the Gulf, wider than the ship and widening still, falling behind them in little streamers of flame.

'Rin forgive me,' muttered Fiffengurt. He was blind: oil in his good eye, oil on the hand that tried to wipe it away.

'Don't worry,' she told him, 'there's nothing to forgive.'

Beyond the fire, a dark mass trod water. The dlömu had known what was coming: they had dropped from the ship and the trailing lines, dived underwater, surfaced well behind the blaze.

7

The Editor Recommends Other Reading
to the Faint of Heart

To My Thus-Far-Loyal Readers:

Happiness is not nothing. One should embrace it. The world groans under the weight of serious minds bent miserably over their books, over their smithy's bench, their ledger or their laundry or their weevil-withered crops. Happiness may vanish in an eyeblink, never to return. Why should anyone spend the length of a tea-sip on a story that does not guarantee – absolutely guarantee – the emotion's increase?

My purpose here is simply a warning. If you are part of that infinitesimally small (and ever smaller) band of dissidents with the wealth, time and inclination to set your hands on the printed word, I suggest you consider the arguments *against* the current volume. To wit: the tale is morbid, the persons depicted are clumsy when they are not evil, the world is inconvenient to visit and quite changed from what is here described, the plot at this early juncture is already complex beyond all reason, the moral cannot be stated, and the editor is intrusive.*

The story most obviously imperils the young. But certain others should weigh the benefits of persevering. These include the old,

---

* Do not misunderstand me: *The Chathrand Voyage* has merits aplenty. Why else would I dedicate this last effort of my life to its telling? Why else would the lord of this domain have granted me five (young, ambitious, 'promising', petty, cynical, rude) editorial assistants, and a meal allowance? Never mind that Holub's *Curse of the Violet King* is better known. I know Mr Holub. I wish him well and feel no envy, and incidentally he suffers miserably from ringworm.

who after all will perish soon enough; the able-bodied, whose vigour may decline if they make a habit of reading at length; the unmarried, who had best cultivate more sociable pastimes; the married, who find the freedom to read only by neglecting commitments; those whose religious views are policed by employer, priest, king, grandmother or guilt internal; the nearsighted; the nervous; the gleefully patriotic.

But the first criticism – the sheer grey gloom of the tale – is the most damning. To that end, and conscious of my duties as a curator of this splendid archive, I have assembled a list of some 700 titles surpassing *The Chathrand Voyage* in both brevity and good cheer. Among them:

- Bissep, Mother K., *The Good Millipede of Wilber Meadow*
- Tennyson, Virzel, *Kh'iguar Mutis* ('Great Scaly Things Defeated', bilingual edition)
- Lace, Helium, *And Then They Were Married*
- Slabbe, Lord Cuprius, *What I Eat*
- Ungrok, Egar, *Battle for Battle's Sake: An Adventure for Boys*

The complete list is available upon request. It is quite startling how much one has to choose from. I merely implore you to recall that life is fleeting, and that choices must be made.

8

Carried Away

—⁓—

Night fell. The pool of fire dwindled behind them. Without chart or knowledge of the Gulf they fled, east by south-east, pulling gradually away from the Sandwall. Ibjen wept; he had tried a second time to throw himself overboard, and had been seized again by the Turachs. Even when eight miles separated them from the northern shore he begged to be allowed to swim.

'Not on your life,' said Fiffengurt. 'Besides, you told us you have family in the city.'

'I do,' said Ibjen. 'But my father, those soldiers—'

'Would only grab you too, lad. You can't help your father that way.'

'But I thought you were *avoiding* Masalym! Oh, where are you taking me? Why did I come aboard?'

Where indeed? Geography, at least, should not have changed in two centuries. Ibjen was too upset to be consulted, but Mr Bolutu recalled from his schooldays that the city lay due south from Cape Lasung. 'A wonder, they say: Masalym, the city above the falls. I should dearly love to see it.'

'You were the one who warned us *not* to pay 'em a visit,' snapped Fiffengurt. 'Sorry to disappoint you, but we're taking your first piece of advice. We need food, and a calm harbour for repairs. But most of all we need to stay away from bastards like the ones we just escaped.'

An hour later he turned the *Chathrand* hard to the south-west, a tack calculated to bring them in sight of land at least thirty miles west of the city. 'We'll put you ashore wherever it's safe, Master Ibjen,' he assured the boy at last, 'with a purse of gold for services rendered, and hardships endured.'

'Enough to buy a horse?'

'Enough for a blary brood stallion. Now go and eat, before Teggatz licks out the pots.'

It was a chilly night; the old moon absent, the strange little sapphire moon winking low and pale in the south. Far to the east, flashes of light could be seen, and low, deep rumblings followed, like the growls of giant dogs. Traces of a storm, the men told themselves. But Pazel recalled the armada that had sailed that way, and was not sure.

They shortened sail: even in these calm waters it would not do to come suddenly upon a lee shore, or a reef. At first light they would take in their surroundings, Fiffengurt declared: perhaps they would find another village, well away from the city, a humble settlement blessed with cove and croplands, where no army of marauders lay in wait.

Neither Pazel nor Thasha wanted to eat. They helped out in the surgery, cleaning and binding wounds, cutting cloth into bandages, rinsing blood from the floor with buckets of saltwater and doing anything else Rain or Fulbreech asked. Hercól and Bolutu joined in as well: the swordsman knew a great deal of field medicine, and Bolutu was, after all, a veterinary surgeon. All the same, it was like a battle after the battle: they ran, cursed, held the bleeding men down, stabbed sutures into their wounds. If only Dr Chadfallow—! They did not have to say it. He would have made it all look easy. He would have made them into a platoon.

Hours into the work, Pazel looked up from the pan of knives he was washing to see Fulbreech leaning exhausted over a surgical table, trembling; and Thasha supporting him, an arm over his shoulders, her chin against his cheek. Hercól noticed them too, and his eyes narrowed to slits. When he glanced at Pazel it seemed almost a warning.

Later, Pazel, Thasha and Hercól visited the forecastle house. Light from two moons spilled through the window, illuminating huddled sleepers, stacked dishes, Ott's watchful eyes. Pazel's hatred struggled in the chains of his fatigue. Did the man never sleep?

Chadfallow slept near the window, snoring through the nose Pazel had broken on Bramian. Lady Oggosk crouched by the smudge-pot, burning scraps of paper. And there in a corner lay Neeps and Marila, curled up like puppies, dead to the world. Someone might have nudged them awake, for Neeps had wanted to talk no matter the hour. But it wasn't going to happen: Ott was already approaching, stepping over Chadfallow, demanding information. There was no defying him, not with Neeps and Marila there to punish as he liked. The damage? he asked Hercól. The course heading, the winds? And what about the Shaggat's arm?

You've failed, Pazel longed to tell him. *Your Emperor's dead, and the Shaggat's worshippers have been waiting for two hundred years.* But Hercól was right: Ott's mind would only spin new evil from whatever knowledge it gained. The only winning move was to keep him in the dark as long as they could.

It was two in the morning when Pazel, Thasha and Hercól returned to the stateroom. They didn't speak. They fed the dogs their evening ration of biscuit, and ate the same themselves, with a bit of rye porridge (several days old) for dessert. Felthrup ran back and forth upon the table, studying and sniffing them, begging them to eat. Pazel glanced often at Thasha but her look was far away.

Hercól sat mechanically stroking Jorl's blue head, and at last began to tell them of the horrible deeds he had done for years as a servant of the Secret Fist. Kidnappings, betrayals, false letters designed to set prince against prince, fires sparked in the temples where uncooperative monks shielded enemies of the Arquali state.

'I told myself it was for a cause,' he declared, watching them, unblinking. 'What cause? Order in Alifros, the end of war, of fiefdom against small, stupid, tyrannical fiefdom. But that was only Ott's credo, his manic religion. "Arqual, Arqual, just and true."

I was a warrior-priest of that religion, as much as any *sfvantskor* is of the Old Faith. Indeed, I wonder sometimes if Ott did not model us on the *sfvantskor*, even as we fought them in the shadows. When I met your sister and the other two, Pazel, I felt at once that I was meeting kin.'

Seeing their long faces and Felthrup's anxious twitching, he smiled. 'There are the kin we are born to, or find ourselves claimed by, as the Secret Fist claimed me. And then there are the kin we seek out, with clear minds and open hearts. You are the latter. Now go and sleep; tomorrow comes all too soon.'

He left the chamber, to walk the deck as he did each night. Felthrup chattered on awhile, glad of their company, then he too bade them goodnight and crawled away to his basket. Pazel and Thasha drifted about the stateroom, wide awake, not looking at each other.

Somehow (Pazel wondered later exactly who had moved when) they ended up side by side on the bearskin rug, staring up at the fengas chandelier that had not been lit since Uturphe, listening to the moan of the wind. For Pazel the sound raised a sudden memory. He had been sleeping at a friend's house, very long ago when he still had friends, before his family's disgrace. The wind had been cold, but he had been given a pair of sheepskins to sleep between, and felt that nothing could be warmer or more comfortable. In the night a small dust viper (perhaps of the same opinion) had slithered into the room and curled up behind his knee. It had bitten him when he sat up at dawn, and his calf had swollen to the size of a ham. The friend's father had inexplicably beaten his son; the son had never spoken to Pazel again.

Pazel realised he had taken her hand.

It was warm in his own. She held on tightly, but kept her face turned away. 'I read something about you,' she said.

'What?'

'You know what I mean.'

'In ... the *Polylex*? Something about me in the *Merchant's Polylex*?'

'"Pazel Pathkendle, tarboy of Ormael, second child of Gregory and Suthinia Pathkendle." Isn't that funny? Because you're not from Ormael, and you're not a Pathkendle, are you? Pitfire, you're not even a tarboy any more. The mucking author should have known better."*

He raised her hand to his cheek. He considered telling her that he had no idea what she was talking about, but the remark seemed unnecessary.

'It's funny,' she said, 'you're not your father's son. And I'm not my father's daughter. Isn't that strange?'

'Terribly,' he managed to say. She was breathing fast. Her hand moved against his cheek. He wanted to make love to her and thought it was possible, thought the moment was here and would never come again, and yet he was beset by a kind of vertigo. He feared his mind-fit was coming on, but the telltale purring was nowhere to be heard. Thasha was shaking slightly – nervous laughter, he thought. He was aware of every inch of her, every least movement. It was a kind of madness. He imagined the bearskin coming to life and charging from the stateroom, racing to some deep spot in the hold and digging Arunis from his hiding place, like a honeycomb from a stump. It was like that, the way he wanted her. But his thoughts were darting everywhere, uncontrollably. He thought: *Arunis is afraid of this rug. What happened, what does he fear?*

He kissed the back of her hand, felt it trembling. When she exhaled there was a low moan in her voice that went through him

---

* The mucking author did. We must conclude, with the benefit of near-infinite hindsight, that Thasha Isiq is being ironic. Nowhere in the thirteenth edition of the *Polylex* do we encounter an outright falsehood about the person it identifies as 'the *Smythídor*'. And while Thasha quotes her brief passage correctly, she might have spared Pazel no little anxiety had she but continued. The next part of the entry reads: 'Thus, and only thus, was he known in Alifros, and to the people of the ship on which he served.' But it is not Thasha's part to comfort Pazel tonight. – EDITOR.

like lightning. They hadn't started, but it was as if they were already done. Everything was answered. He would be with her for the rest of his life.

'I have to ask you something,' she said.

'I do,' he said. 'Of course I do. Obviously.'

She turned to face him, and suddenly he knew that what he had seen was not laughter, but tears. They were flowing still.

'I have to ask something *of* you,' she said. '*Have* to, not *want* to. I have to ask you to stop. Not just this. Stop everything. Will you do that for me? Oh, my dearest—'

Thasha had just said *my dearest*. The words were so strange on her tomboy tongue that for a moment they shielded him from the meaning of her words. She closed her eyes and bit her lips and snorted and sobbed, and eventually he realised he hadn't misunderstood.

'Everything?'

'I'm sorry,' she said, choking.

'It's Fulbreech, isn't it?'

Thasha nodded, pinching her eyes shut so tightly she might have been trying to make them disappear.

'You love him? Truly?'

Against great resistance, another nod.

Pazel took his hand away. He sat up, and she curled beside him and wept.

'I should have known,' she whispered. 'I did know. When he first came aboard.'

Pazel sat hugging his knees. How many times? How many times could the world change, before there was nothing left that you could recognise?

'I suppose,' he said, trying (failing) to keep the bitterness from his voice, 'that it would be easier if I didn't stay here any more?'

'Yes.'

Pazel swallowed. She had agreed so quickly. She'd thought it all through.

Then a dark notion came to him. 'Hercól knows, doesn't he? All those looks, even tonight in the surgery. When did he figure it out?'

After a pause, Thasha said, 'Before I did.'

'But Thasha, Fulbreech? I don't believe it, I can't. Do you know something about him that I don't?'

Her eyes drifted away from him, shining, and he wished he hadn't asked.

'There's a cabin for you,' she said. 'Bolutu's going to share Hercól's room, and you can take his. You'll be safe there. It's still behind the magic wall.'

Pazel had heard enough. He rose and went to his corner and began putting his clothes into his hammock. Moving like a sleep-walker, like a *tol-chenni*. Bolutu's cabin was far too close; he'd go back to the tarboys' compartment and take his chances. He cast his eyes over the stateroom, thought of the day she'd first tried to bring him here, how some instinct had made him pause at the doorway, thinking, *You don't belong in such a room.*

Not belonging. It was the story of his life.

Thasha was sitting up, motionless, waiting for him to go. He started for the door. But as he passed her she put a hand on his leg. He stiffened. In a cold voice, he said, 'A snake once bit me there.'

Thasha looked up at him slowly. 'It died,' she whispered.

'I beg your pardon?'

'The wind, Pazel. Listen: it's completely dead.'

And so it was. The moaning had stopped. The oilcloth nailed over the broken windows hung limp. They rose and went to an undamaged window and flung it wide. The air was perfectly still. Below them, the *Chathrand* rocked motionless on the waves.

They went topside, and found the sailors gazing with wonder at the empty sails. Moths fluttered about the deck, unmolested by any breeze. The Sandwall was out of sight, and the southern shore, wherever it was, remained invisible as well. The Great Ship sat in darkness, with no points of reference beneath the alien stars. 'Black sorcery,' said a few, whispering.

Ten minutes later the sails began to lift. Another ten, and the breeze was as strong as ever: no great blow, but enough to sail by, and shifted ever so slightly to their advantage. Men shook their heads, chuckling. On the quarterdeck, Mr Bolutu stared into the darkness, his silver eyes wide and watchful.

The watch captain struck two bells; it was an hour before sunrise. Pazel left Thasha standing alone on the topdeck (the thought came unbidden: she would not be alone for long) and descended by the Silver Stair to the berth deck. He moved slowly through the maze of sleeping men and boys. The door still creaked, the tarboy called Frowsy still snored like a bleating goat. He felt his way to the eight copper nails in the ancient stanchion that had always marked his place and began to tie his hammock.

It had all started between these two posts. He and Neeps whispering, becoming friends. His first meeting with Diadrelu, who had laughed when he said he didn't trust her: 'Wise boy. Don't trust.' And his private decision to defy Dr Chadfallow, who had begged him to jump ship before Thasha was even aboard.

Back in Ormael, when his mother's madness reached its worst pitch, when she put spiders in her mouth or made the evening soup with bathwater, he had sometimes fled deep into the plum orchard and bunched his coat up against his face and screamed. It had helped. He had never told anyone. He wished he could scream like that now. His best friend was aboard, and his blary *sister*, and he could not talk to either of them. He shut his eyes.

Five minutes later Mr Coote appeared with his flat, detested bell, rousing the dawn shift. Pazel lay still, trying to summon the old knack for sleeping through bumps and curses, spit and scuffles in the darkness. He sank half into sleep but could go no further. Every part of him ached. In that restless trance he saw them together, Thasha and Fulbreech. *Don't trust. Stop everything. Jump over the side.*

'*Muketch.*'

His eyes snapped open. The tarboy Jervik was standing over him, hands in fists, his hard face clenched in an expression it took Pazel a moment to recognise as concern.

'What happened? Somebody beat you?'

'Worse,' said Pazel, and instantly regretted the reply.

Jervik was crude and violent and very strong; they had once been mortal enemies. But since the rat war everything had changed. Jervik had defected to their side – quietly, announcing it to no one but Pazel himself. He was *their* spy, in a sense: well positioned to learn things, if only because everyone thought him too stupid to be listening. Pazel no longer thought him stupid. He had cunning and courage. And he had come through mental torture by Arunis with his will to fight intact.

Nonetheless, he wished Jervik would go away. The older boy had the wrong idea; he thought someone had beaten Pazel the way he himself used to. Jervik's mouth twisted into a snarl. 'You can't let *no one* do this to you, *Muketch*, you hear? You got to learn that.'

Pazel closed his eyes again. 'I agree,' he said.

'The way you fought them rats, eh? You laid 'em waste. That's how you fight man to man, see?'

'Lay them waste?'

'Tha's right. Never go halfsies. When you're on the dock and they cast off the lines and the bosun shouts, "*All aboard,*" d'ye put just one foot on the mucking boat and stand there? No, you don't. You jump with *both* feet, or you keep 'em both ashore. Same with fighting. You oughta know by now.'

Pazel opened his eyes. 'You're right again,' he said. 'Only this time I can't actually . . . fight him. Them. It's not a fist fight.'

'Easier if it was, eh?'

Pazel was somewhat amazed. 'That's right, Jervik. Easier if it was.'

Jervik stood still, his face all but invisible. 'I thought you were gonna laugh,' he said finally. 'When I told you I wanted to switch sides. I thought you'd laugh and tell me off. "Get stuffed, you thug, you blary halfwit, you fool." Only fancier, o'course.'

Pazel bit his lips. He'd come close to doing just that. 'I'm glad I don't have to fight *you* any more,' he said truthfully.

'You'd do all right,' said Jervik, laughing low. 'Hercól's taught you good – or was it the girlie?'

'Both of them,' said Pazel miserably.

Jervik heard the change in his voice. As though realising he'd overstepped, he turned to go. 'Lay him waste, *Muketch*. And if he's still too much for you—' Jervik's voice dropped low and menacing '—just give the word, and I will kill the son of a whore.'

Pazel slept and dreamed of the Nilstone. It had changed Thasha, transformed her as it did the rats, only the mutation was to her heart. She met him in a corner with a sly and secret grin. She was cradling the Stone, talking to it, caressing the blackness that was too black even for dreams. Then she put it in her pocket and crooked a finger, drawing him close. She lifted her shirt on one side, revealing a line of black stitches, and when her fingers touched it the wound opened like a mouth and let him see into her chest. Her heart was a small armoured ship, secure in the dry dock of her ribcage, bilge pumps fastened to her veins. 'You see?' she said. 'It was for your own good. Your heart grew like an apple, or a shell. Mine was built in Etherhorde. You can't make love to someone who built her own heart—'

'I could,' he protested, though in fact he wished to run.

Thasha winced, in sudden pain. 'You think you know *everything*,' she said, acidly. 'Go ahead, then. Touch it. I bet you don't dare.'

The heart-ship was beating. What could it be but a trap? That was fine, he was ready, he could take iron jaws snapping shut on his wrist. He touched her smooth navel first but the sweetness there was unbearable, so obediently he put his hand into the wound.

Thasha's heart gave a titanic *thump*. And Pazel woke to shouts of alarm from a hundred men and boys. *The keel! The keel! Sweet Rin, we've run aground!*

The ship was heeled over drastically to starboard. There was a dreadful cracking noise from below. Pazel sprang from his hammock to the tilting floor and raced in a crowd of men and boys for the ladderway, everyone slipping and groping. 'She's breaking free again!' cried the tarboy known as Crumb. And so they were: the ship righted herself (more hideous cracking) and Pazel nearly fell as the ladderway once more became vertical. He floundered onto the topdeck, took in sea and ship at a glance. Running feet. Panicked faces. A brilliant morning, strange swallow-tailed birds, flat indigo waters, and—

Land.

There was land off the port bow, ten or fifteen miles ahead. Everyone else was aware of it; he must have slept through the lookout's cry. For a moment Pazel was transfixed: the new world, the Southern mainland. It was purple-brown, with rafts of mist glowing in the morning light. Higher up the sky was clear, and like a ghostly etching, a chain of distant, jagged, silver-grey mountains loomed over the coast—

'Report!' Alyash was bellowing into a speaking-tube. 'Report from the hold! Mr Panyar, are you deaf?'

Shouts aloft: debris was surfacing in the *Chathrand*'s wake. Wood splinters, some of them the size of table legs. Fiffengurt passed Pazel without a glance, running straight to the window of the forecastle house, where Rose waited in a fury, grime and soot coating his face.

'Gods below, Captain,' he said, 'There was simply *nothing* off the bow. The water's clear to eighty feet!'

'No! No!' Rose bellowed. 'Damn it, man, didn't you feel the impact? Whatever it was *crossed* our keel amidships. We didn't run over it – it slammed into us!'

More cries from the lookout: 'Mastwood in the water! Cross-trees, cable ends! We struck a drowned ship, Mr Fiffengurt!'

Rose's expression said he thought he had misheard. When Fiffengurt repeated the lookout's words he adamantly shook his head. 'We just rolled forty degrees! I tell you, that blow came from the side!'

Then Rose grew still. His gaze meandered, as though he were listening to the very walls that enclosed him. 'Unless ... *we* did. Unless we're moving sideways. What's that? What?'

Pazel watched the big man twitch and gape at nothing. *He's finally cracked. He never did have much sanity to spare.* And yet Fiffengurt was quite sane, and ran a tight ship. If his bow lookouts claimed that there had been no obstacles ahead—

'Quartermaster.'

It was Alyash, looking rather stunned. Capping the speaking-tube, he sidled close to Fiffengurt. He spoke quietly, but Pazel watched his lips. It looked like *Two inches*. When Fiffengurt hissed and said, 'Already?' Pazel knew exactly what the men were discussing. Two inches of water taken on. In less than ten minutes. They were leaking, and badly.

Fiffengurt issued a quiet order: six hands to the bilge pumps. Almost in a dream, Pazel moved to the starboard rail. He stood staring at the land, though he could make out little beyond the mountains.

An ixchel voice piped up behind him: a natural ixchel voice, the kind only he could hear. 'A collision, perfect, typical. Can you believe it? We can't trust the giants to operate their own ship. Mother Sky, give me patience.'

'It was the clan who nearly sent the ship into the Vortex.'

That was Ensyl. Pazel smiled a little despite himself.

But the first voice said, 'Do not speak of the clan, traitor. You walk free at the indulgence of He-Who-Sees.'

'You mean Taliktrum?'

'*Lord* Taliktrum, you cur!'

A moment later Ensyl appeared at Pazel's elbow. '"*He-Who-Sees*",' she said acidly. 'I wouldn't have believed things could get this bad. Soon any freedoms left to us will be at his indulgence. But then again, we may not live that long. Are we really sinking?'

'Yes,' said Pazel.

'Fast?'

Pazel shrugged. 'Fast enough to worry about. But the pumps will help.'

Ensyl turned to look back at Taliktrum and his followers. 'I am afraid for my people,' she said. 'Warriors or not, they are terrified, and it's fear that has driven them to this sick worship of Taliktrum. He smelled the opportunity, the weakness in the clan. They're casting about for salvation. They want miracles, and "He-Who-Sees" promises to supply them.' Hesitantly, she touched his arm. 'You are not yourself, Pazel. What troubles you?'

Pazel edged his hand away, irritated by her certainty. Only a handful of women on this ship, but they were so hard, so *impossible* to avoid.

'I can't talk about it,' he said, 'and I doubt you'd understand.'

'I was engaged once.'

'That doesn't mean you'd understand.'

Ensyl shook her head. 'I suppose not.'

Pazel felt churlish, but somehow he could not apologise. *Engaged.* If that was a matter of what you did with your heart, then he had been, too. A one-sided engagement. He could have laughed aloud.

'The land drops away to the east,' said Ensyl. 'How can that be, if we are west of the city?'

'How in Pitfire should I know?' Pazel cried. 'Do I look like I come from the South? Why don't you go talk to Ibjen or Bolutu, and leave me alone?'

Ensyl left him alone. Pazel heard ixchel laughter: *Running a bit short on friends, aren't you, Ensyl?* He felt like pounding his head on the rail. Instead he squeezed it until his knuckles turned white, and blinked at the unknown shore. Then a shadow crossed his face, and he turned his head to look.

Fulbreech.

Their eyes met. The Simjan did not smirk; he did not even wear his usual wry smile. But his eyes told Pazel everything he needed to know. Fulbreech had seen Thasha already. He knew where things stood.

'Morning, Pathkendle,' he said. 'Hope you slept as well as I did.'

Pazel swung at him, hard. Even in his madness of jealousy he knew the blow was skilful: a straight-on jab at the older youth's chin, his free arm jerked backwards for torque, all the strength of his torso behind it. A blow to make his fighting tutors proud. But the blow never connected. Fulbreech jerked his head sideways, dodging by a finger's width, and brought his knee up sharp into Pazel's groin.

Pazel just managed to keep himself from sliding to the deck. He was in searing pain, but he straightened and turned to face the older youth. There was no shouting, no pounding feet. The men on deck had not seen a thing.

Where had Fulbreech learned those reflexes?

Now the older youth did smile, ever so slightly. 'Thasha was just telling me what a hothead you are. I'll have you know that I took your side. I said that losing her could bring out the hothead in anyone.'

'Thasha,' Pazel said between gasps, 'doesn't love you ... idiot.'

'Keep thinking that, if it eases the pain. Just don't lie to yourself *about* yourself. Once you realise that you're nothing, maybe you can start to change that fact.'

'You're using her for something. You planned it all.'

'Planned?' Fulbreech looked amused. 'Now you flatter me. Granted, I don't leave much to chance. Old Chadfallow tells me I'm thorough in the extreme. But I did make one error.' He seized Pazel's arm in mock concern. 'I say, you're a delicate little blossom, aren't you? Can you breathe? Do you need to sit down?'

'Go screw yourself.'

Fulbreech raised an eyebrow. 'That will be your comfort from now on, Pathkendle. Not mine.'

Pazel lashed out again. This time his fist caught Fulbreech squarely in the eye. The Simjan did not strike back; instead he twisted away, disengaging, so that Pazel's next blow went wide. Pazel advanced, but before he could strike again someone grabbed him by the hair and jerked him sideways, off balance. It was Mr Alyash.

'Fiffengurt!' he cried. 'The Ormali's just put a shiner on our surgeon's mate! Right unprovoked, too: I watched the whole thing.

But I suppose you'll let it pass. Different rules for favourites of the commander, eh?'

Fiffengurt gaped at Pazel. 'You didn't, lad. Tell me you didn't.'

Pazel rasped: 'Mr Fiffengurt, it wasn't like—'

'I am the commander!' piped up Taliktrum, standing on the No. 2 hatchcomb. He sprang to the deck and advanced between the men's legs. 'Pathkendle, always Pathkendle! You act as though you were a law unto yourself. What was Fulbreech's offence, pray? Did he steal your shoelaces?'

'Not exactly,' said Alyash with a smirk.

'We cannot have brawls, Fiffengurt. You know that as well as anyone. I want him in the brig for two days.'

'But Taliktrum—' cried Pazel.

'Three,' snapped the ixchel leader. 'And another day for every word that leaves his mouth. See to it, Bosun! And by the Nine Pits, let us return to the matter of the leak.'

Alyash sent for wrist cuffs. Fiffengurt looked on, sorrowful and aghast. Pazel knew he could not intervene, and that Taliktrum's wishes had little to do with it. Fights on the *Chathrand* were like sparks in a hayloft: they had to be squelched at once, or the barn would be in flames.

Pazel stood there, skewered by their looks, boiling with rage and shame. Fulbreech touched the spot where Pazel had hit him. The eye would bruise, all right, and everyone would ask who had done it. Thasha would ask. Fulbreech looked at Pazel and gave him the plainest smile yet. 'Error corrected,' he said.

9

The Fugitive

24 Ilbrin 941
223rd day from Etherhorde

To: The Honourable Captain Nilus Rotheby Rose
Commander and Final Offshore Authority
I.M.S. Chathrand

Nilus,
Victory shall yet be ours. The prison has not been built, nor trap
devised, nor deception plotted, that can snare a man of the lineage of
Rose. Very soon you will walk free, reclaim your rank and powers.
And then, son, I charge you: have no mercy, bar no punishment,
sterilise your ship of doubters. It is yours, after all. Let those who
think otherwise do so on the seabed.

('How does he know she's not just making it up?' murmured the
tarboy Saroo. 'She just scribbles and moans and stares at the ceiling.
She don't even pause to think.'

'Keep silent, fool,' said the Trading Family representative, Mr
Thyne, 'unless you want boils under your tongue, or crocodile
dreams, or some nastier curse. She's the most famous witch in the
Merchant Fleet.'

'She's never done no conjuring in front of *me*,' said Saroo.

'Count your blessings,' grunted Thyne.)

Now to the matter of your 'accomplishments'. You saw the Chathrand *safe across the Nelluroq. What of it? You are not the first to make the crossing. The Great Ship alone has passed over the Ruling Sea thirty times in her six hundred years. I would not shame you with cheap congratulations. Besides, in matters of discipline your conduct is highly questionable.*

('She doesn't even look down at the paper,' whispered Neeps to Marila. 'I can't work out how she writes in straight lines.')

It is all very well to sentence mutineers to death. You will recall that I applauded the decision. But once pronounced, such a sentence cannot be delayed. It shocks me to learn that Pathkendle & Co. yet walk free upon your ship. You suggest that they provide you with certain services: to wit, the containment of the mage through fear, and perhaps the distraction of Sandor Ott from more venal meddling into your affairs. Rubbish. Kill them. Extract the Nilstone from the Shaggat's hand, and hang them within the hour. The bodies must accumulate at some point, if you are to discover the spell-keeper, the one whose death returns the statue to human form.

('I wish she'd apply her witching skills to finding the leak,' said Elkstem, 'or finding out where in Alifros we should be making for.' 'Or getting us out of this stinking trap,' said Kruno Burnscove.)

Your other excuse for clemency is shabbier still. You were chosen, you say, by a 'guardian spirit', resident for an age within the scarlet wolf. Arunis melts the wolf; the molten iron spills and burns you; your burn resembles those of the scoundrel mutineers. And this implies a common destiny? Has it occurred to you, Nilus, that you are playing the fool?

('Mr Fiffengurt told me she gave up casting spells,' whispered Neeps. 'He thinks something must have gone wrong, badly wrong, to make her want to quit. But I wonder if she's not just saving herself for the right moment. She's deadly, I tell you. Just look at her.')

If I brand a bullock with my initials, have I given it some higher purpose? If six such animals roam about within a herd, do they serve as the keepers, the 'conscience' (that weakling's word) for the rest? You have all the destiny you require, being my son. When you are governor of the Quezans, when your children bring you sacks of gold from the manors they supervise, your bastards eliminate your foes, your Imperial soldiers collect taxes and your courtesans compete to give you pleasure – then write to me of destiny. Until that day I forbid it.

As for your mother—

'Undrabust,' drawled Sandor Ott from his corner, 'move away from the witch.'

Neeps slid a wary step back from Lady Oggosk. He had learned weeks ago to obey Ott quickly, instantly in fact, but he still hadn't learned to hide his anger. For that he relied on Marila: the only person he'd ever known who could *always*, it seemed, hide her feelings.

'Come,' she said, rising and leading him away, keeping herself between him and the spymaster.

Without her I'd be dead already, he thought.

They stepped carefully among the sprawled and sleeping men. Rose, crouched behind Oggosk's chair, noticed them with a start, the way a bird notes sudden movement. He was twitchy all the time now, and carried on mumbled conversations with no one, and sometimes lunged at phantoms. Neeps made sure they stayed clear of his fists.

But you could dodge the threats only so well. The cabin was about five paces by six. One window, one yard of translucent skylight, a curtained corner for the chamber pots. One door onto the topdeck: never locked by their ixchel jailors, but latched from within by the prisoners themselves, lest the wind or some unthinking sailor throw it open and plunge them all into agony. And a smudge-pot in the corner, where burned the little berries whose vapour kept them alive.

The gang leaders, Darius Plapp and Kruno Burnscove, sat always against opposite walls. Their hatred of one another was so legendary, and their dedication to doing each other harm so well demonstrated, that Rose had found it necessary to tie their fates together: 'If one of you should die, I will personally kill the other before the body cools. No exceptions. No appeals.' So far this threat had kept the peace. Late at night, when Kruno Burnscove developed a racking cough, Neeps was fairly certain he'd heard Darius Plapp offer him his blanket.

The one most likely to die in the night was the *sfvantskor*, Jalantri. Chadfallow had treated his wounds; the ixchel had dutifully brought everything he required from sickbay. There was no question that the big man was healing. But he was a blood enemy, in a chamber crowded with Arqualis – including the spymaster who had led Arqual's war in the shadows against the Mzithrin for forty years; and the Turachs, whose very corps was created (as they took to mentioning frequently) to counter the *sfvantskors* on the battlefield. And Kruno Burnscove had made it known that he held the Mzithrin responsible for his family's decline, after his great-grandfather's farm was torched in Ipulia.

Of all the prisoners, it was Sandor Ott who enjoyed the most room. His servant Dastu had a bit of coal, and drew a circle around the spymaster wherever he chose to sit or sleep. No one had dared to cross that line; even the two Turachs avoided it with care. But for Neeps, Dastu himself was the greater danger. The older tarboy had been a favourite of both Neeps and Pazel, befriending them the day they boarded in Sorrophran, and standing by them when so many others turned their backs. Naturally they had thought of him first when plotting their rebellion. And it was Dastu who had betrayed them, testified to their mutinous plans, nodded with satisfaction when Rose condemned them all to hang. Neeps had a recurring urge to break something large over Dastu's head. But the older boy was Ott's protégé, and a terrible fighter in his own right. Neeps could outdo him only in rage.

Marila claimed a bit of wall, tried to tug him down beside her.

'I want another story,' she said, 'about Sollochstol, about the salt marsh and your grandmother.'

It was another way she tried to keep him out of trouble. Neeps gently freed his hand. 'Just a minute,' he said, and walked alone to the window.

Chadfallow was there, of course. He spent as much time at the window as Rose and Ott permitted. He stood until he swayed. What did he hope to see? The land? Impossible, until they changed course. The deck? But what had changed? Mr Teggatz, his mouth closed tight as a clamshell and wooden plugs in his nose, bringing their midday meal? But it was only five bells; lunch was still hours away.

You'd do the same if you weren't so lazy, Neeps told himself. *Don't make a virtue of it.*

He stepped up beside Chadfallow. In fact, there was something different on deck: a little conference of ixchel, four of them shouting and gesturing, with Fiffengurt and Alyash crouched beside them, trying to get a word in edgeways. Ludunte and Myett were among the ixchel; the other two were Dawn Soldiers, cold-eyed and tensed. Myett held a bag like a doctor's case against her chest.

Neeps felt murderous at the sight of Ludunte and Myett: betrayers of Diadrelu, both of them. 'What are they doing, the little bilge-rats?' he asked.

'Speaking of us, I think,' said Chadfallow.

'Captain,' said Ott suddenly from the back of the room. 'You know prison etiquette as well as I do. Share and share alike. If one of us gets mail, he lets us all have a taste.'

Oggosk had finished her dream-scribble; Rose was poring over the scrap of dirty parchment, the wet ink smearing on his fingers.

'Have a heart, Captain,' said Kruno Burnscove. 'Give us some news of the outside world. I mean, if that's the appropriate term—'

Rose shot the gang leader a savage look. Ott laughed, delighted. 'Outside, inside, under? Good question, Mr Burnscove. Which world are your parents in, Captain, and where do they go to find a post office? Come, read it aloud.'

Rose snarled. He had done just that twice before, to everyone's amazement: it was not like him to give a damn what anyone wanted of him. Anyone, that is, but Oggosk herself – and the readings enraged Oggosk no end.

Neeps was almost sympathetic. He hated Oggosk, but couldn't deny that she had a strange, beleaguered dignity. This shattered it: making up stories for the distraction of her darling captain, telling him they were messages from the Beyond (which Beyond? The Nine Pits seemed too good for Rose's father). That was bad enough – but to hear them read aloud? Rose apparently wanted to convince his listeners that the letters were real: to prove his sanity, maybe. It was having the opposite effect.

Today he simply refused. 'The letter is of a private nature,' he growled, folding it in two. But a moment later he changed his mind, turned to face Ott with eyes ablaze. 'I will soon walk free. In short order I will resume my command.'

There were smiles, a brief chuckle from one of the Turachs. Neeps shuddered. *Insubordination! On Rose's ship! They're giving up on him – or on everything. Is the same thing happening outside?* The thought chilled his blood.

Then Chadfallow started. Neeps turned back to the window and saw the smuggler, Dollywilliams Druffle, ambling towards them. Mr Druffle had not done well on the Ruling Sea. Already one of the thinnest men on the *Chathrand*, he now had the look of a boiled bone. Fresh water had brought most of the men's faces back to life, but Druffle's skin appeared beyond redemption, like those biscuits that fell and petrified in the back of the galley stove. He had shaved off his greasy hair (lice) and given up entirely on shoes (fungus), but to rum and grog he remained faithful as ever.

He approached with a drunkard's care, watching each step. When he caught sight of Chadfallow he paused, scowling. The two were not on speaking terms.

'The cretin,' hissed Chadfallow.

'Shut up,' said Neeps. 'He's got something to say.'

'Always. And never to any purpose but mischief or slander.'

'Just back off, why don't you? Spare yourself.'

Chadfallow withdrew, and Druffle slouched up to the window. 'Can you hear me?' he bellowed.

'At fifty paces,' said Neeps.

Druffle covered his mouth, deeply contrite. Then he squinted and leaned close to the glass. 'Where's the doctor? He's a muckin' swine. D'ye know we're moving sideways?'

'Sideways?'

Druffle illustrated with a wobbly gesture.

'But that's crazy,' said Neeps. 'A ship can't move sideways, unless you pick her up and carry her.'

'Or the sea does, my heart. We're in a rip tide. Miles wide and infinitely long, or so it seems. It snatched us up in the night sometime – you felt the wind die?'

Neeps was flabbergasted. 'I did,' he said under his breath. 'But Mr Druffle, that means Rose was right. He *said* we were moving sideways.'

Druffle nodded, his eyes red and bleary. 'The going's been smooth as buttercream since that rip tide caught us. You can't even tell, 'cept by fixing on a spot ashore with a telescope. That's what I did, y'see. Then I went to Alyash and made him own up. "Keep it to yourself, Druffle, you boozy arse!" he quips. "We don't want a panic. There's fear enough in the men till we find that leak and plug it. And maybe we can sail right out again, just like we sailed in, and no harm done but a little lost time." That's what the bosun said. But I say, panic. Panic! It's devilry, this ripper, and it's sweepin' us along after that armada, like it wants us to catch up. See here, lad: we were aimin' to make landfall to the west of that all-edges city, ain't that so?'

'All-edges?' said Neeps.

'As in we ain't sure if it's real.'

'The buffoon means *alleged*,' murmured Chadfallow from the room behind.

'Well now we're leagues to the *west* of it, Undrabust,' Druffle continued. 'All night long we've been slippin' backwards. And those flashes ain't lightning, my heart. They're the fires of war. Of course, that ain't what I came here to tell you.'

'There's something else?'

'You should have stayed on Sollochstol. I've been there. You could do worse. You *did* do worse, he he.'

'Mr Druffle,' said Neeps, 'are we sinking?'

'Palm wine and marsh-turtle soup. And the girls in them lily tiaras.'

Neeps sighed. 'Thanks for coming by,' he said.

The smuggler looked up, and his glance was suddenly sly. He leaned forwards until his nose touched the glass. 'It's your mate, Pathkendle. He's in the brig.'

'What?' cried Neeps in dismay. 'The fool, the fool! What's he done *now*?'

'Shh!' admonished Druffle, liberally spraying the window. But it was too late: Chadfallow rushed forwards and demanded that Druffle repeat himself. The smuggler hesitated, swaying and leering at the doctor, and Chadfallow called him a revolting sot. Druffle made an obscene gesture, asked whose wife he'd lately *y'know, y'know*, and then both men began screaming abuse, and the Turachs laughed, and Oggosk shrieked in sudden general loathing, and Rose yanked the doctor away for fear he'd break the window.

It was in this melee that Myett and Ludunte climbed down through the smoke-hole, walked to the room's centre and announced that the prisoners were to enjoy an hour's liberty for good behaviour.

The hubbub vanished. 'Liberty?' said Darius Plapp, his voice barely higher than a whisper.

'*Temporary* liberty,' replied Ludunte. 'You shall enjoy these furloughs once per week, if you try nothing foolish during the given hour.'

Neeps was too astonished for words. For the first time in weeks he saw hope in the prisoners' faces.

'Captain Rose has done this once before,' Ludunte continued. 'The rest of you, take heed.' He pointed to the bag in Myett's hands. 'This is the *temporary* version of the antidote. It lasts an hour only, and it is very precise. Use the hour as you like, but do not be late in returning.'

'Why do you do this now?' said Rose.

The two ixchel said nothing for a moment. 'Our lord Taliktrum is concerned for your comfort,' said Myett at last, in her cold, sibilant voice.

'You must listen for the ship's bell,' said Ludunte. 'It will ring stridently when ten minutes remain. Hurry back when you hear it. Step into this cabin, breathe in the drug. Otherwise you will die, as surely as though you'd taken no pill at all.'

'Remember this, too,' added Myett. 'Below the berth deck the ship is off limits to humans, except by special permission. Do not try our patience. Above all, do not imagine that you have any hope of finding where we hide the drug. The lives of those who remain in this chamber are forfeit if you try.'

The ixchel explained that only three hostages would be released at a time. 'By evening, all of you will have had your turn. We shall begin with the youngest, and the women. Lady Oggosk, Marila, Undrabust: step forwards. The rest of you, prepare to hold your breath when they open the door.'

Marila took Neeps by the arm. She almost never smiled, but he had come to know when she was happy by the wideness of her eyes. They were wide as saucers now.

'This is wrong,' said Dastu suddenly. 'My master should be first, or Captain Rose – not these two traitors and the witch.'

Rose waved a dismissive hand; he would never seek favours from 'crawlies'. Sandor Ott cracked his old, scarred knuckles and smiled wolfishly. 'They won't let me out,' he said with certainty. 'Not for an hour, or a minute. Not first or last. I certainly wouldn't in their place. I'm right, aren't I? Those are your orders?'

Ludunte regarded him nervously. 'I have nothing else to say,' he murmured at last.

'No matter,' said Ott. 'I will free myself, by and by. And then we shall see about Lord Taliktrum's concern for comfort.'

Myett looked at him with loathing, and not a little fear. Then she opened her bag and removed a small cloth package bound with string, which she quickly untied. Within lay three white pills. Side by side, they barely fit on Myett's palm: clearly they had been made for humans.

'You must swallow your pills at the same time, all three of you, and exit together.'

'*Glah*,' said Oggosk, pointing irritably at Rose. 'Give him my dose. I'll go later, when the heat passes. Let the captain see what's become of his ship.'

'Are you certain, Duchess?' said Rose.

'Was I ever otherwise, you fool? Take the offer, and leave me in peace.'

Two minutes later the door flew open with a bang. Rose stormed out and barrelled for the quarterdeck, shouting for Fiffengurt and Alyash, watch captains, duty officers, his steward, his meal. All around him men leaped to attention. Neeps and Marila stepped out more fearfully and shut the door. They clenched each other's hands (for who knew, who knew?), closed their eyes and inhaled.

The drug worked. They were free, if only for an hour. Neeps opened his eyes. A mob was cheering, chasing after Rose. But three figures pushed through it in their direction. The first was running headlong: Thasha. She skidded to a halt and threw her arms around them both and laughed and shouted and kissed their cheeks. Behind her Hercól and Bolutu came striding, wide smiles on their faces.

'Nutter girl!' Neeps laughed, hugging her until it hurt. 'How've you and Pazel managed to stay alive so long without us?'

'It was Hercól who got you out,' said Thasha, her own eyes bright with tears. 'The council was about to explode, but he calmed everyone down and shamed Taliktrum into this furlough idea.'

'Sometimes it takes a fighter to stop a fight,' said Bolutu. 'Come, away! The hour will pass quickly. We have food – of a sort – in the stateroom, and hot water for bathing is on its way, two buckets apiece. And Felthrup is simply going mad.'

'First things first,' said Neeps. 'What in the Nine stinking Pits happened to Pazel?'

There was an awkward silence. Thasha dropped her eyes, and to Neeps' amazement her ears began to redden. Then a voice from behind her called out: 'I'm afraid *I* did, Undrabust.'

Greysan Fulbreech, one eye purple and bloodshot, walked up and extended his hand. Neeps just stared at him. Then to his astonishment he saw Thasha take Fulbreech's other hand, tenderly, like something she cherished.

'I tried so hard, Neeps,' she said, her voice a plea. 'To tell him sooner, to explain. It wasn't anything Pazel did wrong.'

'No one is to blame,' said Hercól.

'Least of all Pathkendle,' said Fulbreech, his fingertips brushing Thasha's arm. 'He was in shock, you know. He really does care for her. Because of that I can't be angry. In fact, I'm hopeful that one day we'll all be friends.'

Neeps hit him. Savagely, in the stomach. He had Fulbreech down on the deck before they tore him away.

'You rabid Rinforsaken slobbering dog.'

Only Marila could deliver insults that cutting in a voice that calm. 'I told you I'm sorry,' said Neeps, pressing clean gauze (provided by Fulbreech) into his nose.

'Brilliant. Just blary brilliant,' Marila continued. 'Thirty minutes left. If we're lucky your nose will stop bleeding for the last three.'

'Why don't you go do something, then?'

'I hate you. I hate you.'

'You're not being fair to him,' said Pazel, hands on the bars of his cell.

'Don't tell *me* about fair,' said Marila, still in that deadpan voice. 'You think I feel sorry for you, locked up for three whole days?' She looked hard at Neeps. 'Taliktrum will never let you out again after this.'

'Listen, Marila,' said Neeps, his head still tilted back, 'Fulbreech is a liar. A fake. He's found a ... weak spot, see? A weak spot in Thasha, and he's exploiting it.'

'Thasha is *not a fool*,' said Marila. 'If she's with him, she has to have a reason. And if you ask me it's because she's taken a fancy, the same way anybody else does.'

'Then *she's* a fake,' said Pazel. 'She doesn't love him. She's pretending.'

'Well she's doing a blary good job.' Then, seeing Pazel cringe at her words, she added in a louder voice: 'I never say things the right way. I know that. If you want somebody to lie and make you feel better, maybe I *should* go.' She paused, breathing deeply. 'But if you ask me you're better off without her, that mucking rich *grugustagral*. You weren't the only one she fooled. I was there when she told you she was done with Fulbreech. I know what you've been through with her. *For* her.'

Neeps whispered, 'What's a *grugu-gu*—'

'Shut up,' said Marila.

'Thasha's a good person,' Pazel insisted miserably. 'And we need her, too. We're supposed to be a team.'

'Exactly,' said Marila. 'Those burn scars mean you're supposed to stick together, you three and Hercól and Bolutu and even Rose, somehow – to stay and fight together to the blary end. Besides, you and Thasha—' She puffed out her round cheeks, angrily. 'It's like magic. You love her despite the invasion of Ormael, despite her father. I think you even managed to *love her father*. And if she wants to throw all that away just because some handsome—'

'Handsome?' cried both boys. 'He's not! He's a goon!'

Marila looked from one to the other. 'Hopeless,' she sighed.

Neeps turned back to Pazel. 'Hercól must be in on it,' he said. 'But why are they doing it, and why won't they tell you? That's what you have to figure out.'

'Right,' said Pazel. But Neeps could see that his heart had gone out of it. Marila's argument had struck home; he was at last considering the possibility that Thasha's change of heart was real.

All at once he seemed to reach a decision. 'Get up, you two,' he said. 'You've wasted almost your whole hour on me. Go and eat something, walk around. And wash off that blood, mate. Go on, right now. I mean it.'

Neeps felt like a heel, but his guilt at keeping Marila from enjoying any of her furlough was gnawing him, and Pazel was unyielding. All three got to their feet. Pazel linked hands with them through the bars.

'Every other time, she trusted me,' he blurted. 'Even when she was scared or ashamed. Why would she start hiding things now?'

Marila looked Pazel in the eye. You had to know her well to realise how much sympathy she felt. 'That's my point, Pazel. She wouldn't, and she's not.'

But as they walked away Pazel was still shaking his head.

The ten-minute bell clanged its strident warning. In the stateroom, Neeps and Marila jumped up from the table, and the little feast their friends had assembled. Hercól and Bolutu rose as well. Neeps looked across the room and stifled a growl.

It just kept getting worse. Thasha and Fulbreech were standing by the windows, close together. She had brought him through the invisible wall. Since its sudden appearance three months ago they had found that Thasha alone controlled access to the stateroom, merely by commanding the wall to admit chosen friends. Uskins had marked it with a red line of paint on the deck; it ran from port to starboard, straight down the middle of a cross-passage twenty feet from the stateroom door. No one but those Thasha named could cross that line. They had no idea where the wall had come from, or why it answered only to Thasha, but they were all glad of its protection. Now without consulting anyone she had added Fulbreech to their circle.

She had tried to make peace between them. Fulbreech had been willing, but Neeps had turned his head with a bitter laugh, and Marila's look made Jorl and Suzyt whimper deep in their throats. After a moment Fulbreech had simply withdrawn to the other end of the stateroom. Thasha had tried to talk to them – about the attack of the dlömic army, the council meeting, the fruitless search for Arunis. Hercól and Bolutu had urged them to eat. Felthrup, in nervous agony, had babbled like a soul possessed, now and then stopping to chew his stumpy tail. At last he had burst into tears and fled into Admiral Isiq's old quarters. Hercól had followed him inside, and emerged minutes later, shaking his head.

'Are you sure it was wise, Thasha, to indulge his request?'

'I'm not sure of much these days,' she responded, her voice suddenly hardening as she glanced at Hercól.

'What are you talking about?' said Marila. 'What request?'

Thasha sighed. 'Felthrup believes that he's accomplishing something vital – in his sleep. You know he used to have those terrible nightmares, the ones he'd wake up from squealing and shaking? Well, they've stopped, thank Rin. But he has an idea that they weren't normal dreams at all. He thinks they were sent by Arunis.'

'What?' said Fulbreech, touching her elbow. 'Your rat friend thinks the sorcerer was attacking him through dreams?'

'That's his suspicion,' said Thasha, 'although he's never been able to remember any details. When the nightmares were happening he was so afraid that he stopped sleeping at all – for *ages*. I think it nearly killed him. And now he's just obsessed. He's been reading about sleep and dreams and trances in the *Polylex* – you know, my *particular* copy—'

'Right,' said Marila quickly, as Fulbreech raised his eyes with sudden interest.

She's cracked! thought Neeps. *She practically just told that slimy bloke that she's got a thirteenth edition! Why doesn't Hercól put a stop to this?*

'He wanted a place to sleep in the daytime,' Thasha continued. 'He asked for a dark nest, and I provided it – found an old hatbox, lined it with scarves, placed it with the open side facing the back of the closet. Then I hung a curtain over the closet door to keep light from leaking in. With all of Father's uniforms and Syrarys' dresses still hanging in there, I guess it's about as dark and quiet as any place on the ship.'

'He retreats to that nest for hours at a time,' said Bolutu, 'and when he emerges, he is strange and preoccupied, but he never tells us why.'

'I don't like this at all,' said Neeps.

'Nor do I,' said Hercól, 'but I have come to trust that rat's intuition almost as much as my own. He often senses far more than he understands. But we must be off, my friends. The hour is ending, and it is a long walk to the forecastle house.'

'Thank you all,' said Neeps. 'You're first rate, I mean it.'

Thasha came forwards, her eyes bright, and took his hand in both of hers. 'We miss you,' she said.

'Yeah,' said Neeps, glancing around, as though for someone who wasn't there.

'We'll go with you, of course,' she said. Then she added awkwardly, 'Greysan's going to stay here.'

A difficult silence. Marila turned to look at the Simjan. 'Alone?' she said.

'Yes, alone,' said Thasha, a bit sharply. 'Why shouldn't he?'

Neeps took a deep breath, and held it. *Because it's insane, that's why. Because you're out of your mind if you let him poke around in the stateroom.* The magical *Polylex* was here, and so was Mr Fiffengurt's secret journal, and the letters he'd written to his unborn child. There were also Bolutu's notebooks, and Thasha's own, and even some jottings Pazel had made in the back of an old logbook.

'We'll go back by ourselves,' said Marila suddenly. 'You can all stay here.'

Neeps quickly agreed: it was as if Marila had read his mind. The others protested, but he and Marila stood firm. Wishing their friends a last hasty goodbye, they bolted from the stateroom.

What occurred next shocked them both. Just beyond the red line that traced the invisible wall they found Rose waiting, terribly tense, fingering something in his pocket. 'What kept you?' he barked. 'Come along, quickly!'

'We have to get back, Captain,' said Neeps. 'I can already feel the pain beginning.'

'Save your breath,' said Rose. 'Come with me, that's an order.'

He plunged across the upper gun deck, not looking back, confident of being obeyed. Neeps and Marila stood rooted to the spot.

'He's going in the right direction,' said Neeps at last. 'We can start off following him, and break for the topdeck if things get strange.'

'Things already are,' said Marila.

Nonetheless they followed the captain as he barrelled past the startled carpenters and gun-repair teams, around the tonnage hatch and into the starboard lateral passage. 'He's still aiming for the forecastle house,' whispered Neeps. 'In fact we'll probably get there sooner this way. No crowds to slow us down. But would it hurt him to—'

Rose stopped dead. Neeps and Marila skidded to a halt behind him, and both cried out in amazement. Just ahead, a passage intersected their own, and at its centre was a huge red cat. It crouched for an instant, startled by their voices, and then with a twitch of serpentine tail it vanished down the right-hand passage.

'That's Sniraga!' said Neeps. 'She survived the blary rats! How did she manage, where has she been?'

'Nothing can kill that animal,' said Rose. 'It will never leave off, never cease to plague me, until I answer for its wounds.'

He was trembling, hoarse with fear. Then he shook himself back to life and pounded on. The Holy Stair was just ahead, and it was with immense relief that they watched Rose enter the ladderway and start to climb. He moved swiftly, raising himself by the handholds as much as the steep steps.

But one flight below the topdeck he stopped again. 'Have a look at these,' he said, bending down.

They leaned around his elbows. Beside the wall, a brass speaking-tube cut through the ladderway, emerging from a hole in a step and vanishing through the ceiling. And on the step beside the pipe sat a small canvas bag. Rose lifted it, and Neeps heard the clink of metal.

'What's that, sir?' he asked warily. 'Coins?'

Rose smiled curiously. 'Not coins. Payment, yes, but not coins.'

Suddenly he grabbed Neeps by the arm. There was a flash of iron, a sharp *click*, and suddenly Neeps found himself handcuffed to the speaking-tube. He shouted and kicked at Rose. Marila screamed and struck at the captain's face. Rose cursed, trying to catch her arms. Marila was quick and slippery: if she had obeyed Neeps (who begged her to *Run, please, run away!*) she might have escaped up the stairs. But she didn't try, and in a moment the captain overpowered her and clipped a second cuff about her slender wrist. He dragged her to the brass pipe and snapped the other cuff in place around it.

Then he stepped back, out of range of their blows.

Neeps screamed at him: 'You mad bastard! What in the Pits are you doing?'

Rose leaned back against the wall. Neeps threw himself downwards, wrenching his arm, but the pipe did not even shake. Marila twisted her arm in the iron cuff, but it was too tight for her hand to slip through. Overhead, the ship's bell began to peal again, urgently.

'You can't kill us!' cried Neeps.

'Can I not?'

'You could lose the Shaggat! You *will* lose him! Marila's the spell-keeper, do you hear me? If she dies—'

'Undrabust,' said Rose, 'you may be gifted at detecting lies, but in telling them you have no skill at all. Lady Oggosk determined weeks ago that no one in the forecastle house carries Ramachni's spell. Given the tension in that chamber, and the presence of Sandor Ott, I decided to keep her discovery to myself.'

'They're calling for us,' said Marila.

And indeed men were shouting overhead: *Where are they? Captain Rose! Undrabust! Miss Marila! Your hour's up! Hurry, hurry, for the love of Rin!* The voices of the ixchel, furious and confused, piped above the rest.

Neeps and Marila pulled together. Rose shook his head. 'Those fittings have lasted centuries. They'll not give way now.'

The youths began to shout for help. Overhead, someone caught their cries and exclaimed, 'The Holy Stair! The Holy Stair!' Boots pounded towards the ladderway.

Then Rose took the strangest step of all. Wading into their blows again, he pulled a third set of handcuffs from the bag and locked himself to the pipe.

'You're insane!' shouted Neeps. 'If you want to die, at least let us go!'

Now they were close enough for Neeps to sense the terror in Rose's flesh. His teeth were locked in a grimace, his fists were clenched. 'Out of time, out of time,' he murmured.

The boots smashed nearer, and then a crowd of sailors, led by Big Skip and the doughy-faced Mr Teggatz, appeared and all but stumbled over them.

'Milk of Heaven's Blessed Tree, shipmates, our captain's a suicide!' cried Teggatz – easily the longest utterance Neeps had ever heard from the cook.

'He's a murderer!' shouted Marila. 'Get these cuffs off, get us *away* from him!'

The sailors tried to do just that. Big Skip put his lumberjack's arms to the task of breaking the pipe, while Swift the tarboy ran for a hacksaw. Teggatz spat on Marila's hand and tried to ease it through the iron cuff, but only managed to bruise and bloody her. Neeps, who had felt the icy stab of the ixchel's poison whenever the door swung open or the fire ebbed, wondered that he was still drawing breath. The hour had passed. They were living on borrowed time.

When Swift returned with the hacksaw, Rose snatched it from his hand and broke the blade over his knee. Big Skip growled in mystified rage. He wrenched at the pipe with all his strength. Other hands shoved in close beside him, and Neeps and Marila joined too. The pipe bowed, and its housing popped loose from the timber.

'Help us, Captain, you crazy old loon!' cried Big Skip.

'I already am,' said Rose.

It was a good eight minutes before the tugging, combined with the work of a second hacksaw (kept well out of the captain's reach) at last succeeded in breaking the pipe. Instantly many hands lifted Marila and Neeps and slid them, cuffs still trailing, to freedom. But even as they made to dash up the Holy Stair, they heard Rose begin to laugh.

'It's permanent, you witless whelps,' he said. 'Haven't you guessed yet? The crawlies blundered. They gave us the same pills they gave Haddismal and Swift. You're cured. Go back in there and you'll start the poison cycle all over again.'

Teggatz, blubbering, tried to push the youths up the stairs. 'He's mad! Oh, misery! Run!'

'Aye, run!' said Big Skip. 'If he ain't mad, he's lying! Get to safety, you two!'

But Neeps didn't move. 'We should have died ten minutes ago. He's not lying. We're free.' He looked at Rose, who was still shaking with mirth. 'But you *are* crazy, and vicious as a snake. Why didn't you *tell* us?'

'First, because you're an irritating brat and a mutineer,' said Rose. 'Second, because you'd never have believed it. You'd have run straight back into the chamber, just to be on the safe side.' He took a small key from his pocket and unlatched the cuff on his wrist. Then he held out the key to Neeps. 'Admit it, Undrabust. You owe me for this. You may even owe me your life.'

Neeps snatched the key from his hand. When he and Marila had shed their cuffs he turned to Big Skip and the others. 'I thank *you*,' he said pointedly. Then he turned to Rose again. He was about to lacerate the man with every choice Sollochi insult he could summon when Marila laid a hand on his arm. Her face was anxious, and Neeps understood at once. Rose was free; he would be taking charge again. There would be consequences for every word that escaped their mouths. And if he really knew that neither he nor Marila was the spell-keeper, he could even carry out the suspended executions.

Marila took his hand and pulled. 'Let's just get out of here,' she whispered.

Neeps let himself be persuaded. But he would not go back to the stateroom: his anger at Thasha burned too bright. *Hercól*, he thought. *Alone.* The swordsman had some answering to do. He knew better than to trust Greysan Fulbreech. How could he have stood by as the older youth swept Thasha off her feet?

He followed Marila to the topdeck. The moment they emerged a great cheer went up from the assembled sailors. Cries and rumours had preceded them. Now here was the proof: two of their number had beaten the ixchel at their own game. Men crowded forwards, clapping their backs and almost hugging them, bellowing good wishes, howling derision at the ineptitude of crawlies. The ixchel on deck merely watched. They were furious, but little had really changed. They still had twelve hostages to bargain with.

Neeps caught a glimpse of the forecastle window. Half a dozen faces were pressed to the glass – Ott, Saroo, Chadfallow, Elkstem – even Lady Oggosk had claimed a spot. *Our good luck is their bad*, he realised. *The ixchel will never hand out any more pills.*

Thasha appeared in the crowd. She was making her way towards him, and her eyes were beseeching. She shouted over the din.

'—tell you something – what you think – believe me—'

Neeps began to turn away, but Marila caught his arm. 'Listen to her,' she shouted in his ear. 'Just once. You owe her that much.'

Thasha reached them. She was alone; there was pain in her eyes. Neeps stood his ground, fuming, gazing furiously at her. 'Well?' he said at last.

Thasha had no time to answer, for at that moment Rose climbed out from the hatch, and the cheering doubled. *Hysteria*, thought Neeps. *Most of them don't even like him.* Rose twitched irritably at the commotion, but no one quite believed he was angry. The men chanted his name, brandishing weapons and tools above their heads. Plapps and Burnscoves cheered shoulder to shoulder. Somewhere the *stomp-stomp-clap, stomp-stomp-hey!* of an Etherhorde flagball game began, and soon nearly everyone on deck had joined in. The men wanted something to celebrate, some victory of will over reason. For the moment Rose was it.

They would have lifted him onto their shoulders if he had not suddenly lurched forwards. His face changed; all at once his outrage was very sincere indeed. Shoving his way through a dozen men, Rose pointed at a figure some thirty yards away by the No. 2 hatch.

'Who in the entrails of the blackest blary fiend is *that*?' he exploded.

'Him, Captain?' laughed a joyful Mr Fegin. 'Why that's just Mr Bolutu, he— Oh, Pitfire!'

It was not Bolutu. The cheers turned to roars of challenge. The figure was quite obviously a dlömu, as tall and strong as any of those who had attacked the ship. He stood straight and proud, although he wore only tattered breeches, a white shirt missing all its buttons and a fortnight's beard. His thick hair hung in tangles to his elbows. He had a lean face and a hawklike nose, and his eyes were full of bright intelligence. As the sailors charged he raised his hands in surrender.

The men were less than calm. They fell on him, howling threats and curses, and dragged him all the way to the gunwale. There they lifted him half over the rail, so that his torso dangled above the sea.

'Hold!' shouted Rose, lumbering forwards.

'On your guard, Captain, there may be more!' cried Alyash.

'There are,' said the strange dlömu.

'Knew it!' said Alyash. 'They're on the lower decks with the crawlies! They must be!'

'Your knife, Mr Fegin.' Rose squeezed in among his men. Burying his hand in the stranger's hair, he pulled downwards, until the man was looking right at the sun. The dlömu winced and closed his eyes. Rose laid the edge of Fegin's knife against his throat.

'How many?' he said.

'Six or eight, I should say.'

'You *should* say exactly. You *should* give me a reason to spare your life.'

'They are not my comrades,' said the stranger. 'Indeed, they wish to kill me. I have been running from them this last month and more.'

'You're the fugitive? The one those madmen attacked us for?'

'I fear so.'

'Aye, you fear it – because for that alone I should slit your throat. How in blazes did you get aboard?'

'You're human beings, aren't you?' said the stranger. 'Amazing. I never thought I'd live to see this day.'

His words sent a ripple of alarm through the sailors: *He's never seen a human, did ye hear? We're alone, marooned with them monsters, alone!*

Taliktrum appeared on the shoulder of a reluctant maintopman. He urged the sailor forwards impatiently. Then Neeps saw Bolutu and Ibjen at the back of the crowd. The young dlömu stared at the newcomer, and Neeps saw recognition in the look.

Bolutu cried out: 'By the Dawn Star, brother, don't provoke him!'

'Provoke him?' said the stranger. 'In this position? Why, I haven't even learned his name. Nor he mine.'

'The captain asked you a question, blacky!' snapped Alyash.

'Did he? Would you kindly repeat it, sir?'

Neeps caught his breath. He had never heard anyone but Lady Oggosk take a tone of levity with Nilus Rose, the man who flogged tarboys for hiccups. The stranger did not know the peril he was in.

Captain Rose slid his hand to the knife blade, pinched it between two fingers and a thumb. A few sailors winced, as if from bitter memory.

'I'll repeat it,' said Rose.

He set the point of the knife on the man's chest, directly over the heart. With a slow and merciless movement, he began to cut, scoring the flesh in a semicircular pattern. The man twisted and writhed in the sailors' grasp. He bit his lips, tears starting from his eyes.

'Stop, stop!' cried Ibjen in distress. 'Captain Rose, you're in Bali Adro! You *can't* draw his blood!'

'You mucking animal!' shouted Neeps at the captain's back. 'Taliktrum, make him stop!'

'Why should I?' said Taliktrum. 'Those savages tried to sink us. Proceed, Rose – go further, if you must.'

Rose glared at Taliktrum over his shoulder: *Give me permission, will you?* Then he turned back to his torture. The cut was now some eight inches long. Suddenly Neeps realised that Rose was carving a symbol in the man's flesh. A question mark. He finished it with a deep prick that made the stranger gasp.

'You nearly took my ship,' he said. 'And in fleeing you, we damaged her, fatally for all I can tell. Now you dare to make sport of her commander. I wish you to understand that to do so again will be fatal.'

'I make no sport of you,' said the stranger, as his blood trickled into the sea. 'It's just that I should have died so long ago that I find humour in my own survival.'

'The joke may have run its course,' said Taliktrum.

'I came aboard in a water cask,' said the stranger. 'I kicked it open just minutes ago, to warn you about the others. I waited on the lower decks until the stair was clear.'

Rose was outraged anew. 'Are you saying we smuggled you aboard *ourselves*?'

'You did, Captain. The villagers were rather clever – I think smuggling is not an infrequent practice in Narybir. They secured stones and water sacks inside the cask with me, so that you should detect no difference by weight or sound.'

'I was pledged to help him, Captain!' shouted Ibjen suddenly. 'To be certain he reached the mainland. I gave my word.'

Taliktrum laughed. 'And then tried to jump ship on two occasions,' he said.

The stranger looked at Ibjen sharply, and the boy dropped his head in shame.

'Why would the villagers help you in this way?' asked Rose.

'Because I was in great need, sir. Your scratch is nothing compared with what the Karysk Expeditionaries would have done, if they had laid hands on me.'

'Karyskans!' cried Bolutu. 'Is it true, then – there is war between the Empires that were once fast friends?'

'War is too glorious a name for it,' said the stranger, 'but there is a great deal of mindless killing. I was in Karysk to warn them of the impending attack.'

'Warn them?' said Rose. 'If you were delivering such a helpful message, why did they pursue you like their most hated enemy?'

'Because,' gasped the stranger, 'I bear a striking resemblance to their most hated enemy – the man who pushed hardest for the attack.'

'Mistaken identity on such a gigantic scale?' said Taliktrum. 'That is hard to credit.'

'We are of the same family, he and I,' said the stranger.' He paused, then added, 'The Karyskans, I think, are hiding among your cattle.'

Rose's hand moved with startling speed. The knife cut a short gash in the stranger's cheek. Ibjen stifled another cry.

Ibjen was wailing: 'Captain Rose! Captain Rose! Make him stop, Thashiziq, for your own sake, for the ship's!'

Thasha started forward, and Neeps and Marila with her, but the mob of frightened sailors stood with Rose now, and held them back. Thasha put a hand on each friend's arm and shook her head: *Not this way.*

'We have no cattle,' said the captain. 'Our livestock are dead. And you will be next, for your mouth is full of lies.'

'No livestock at all?' said the man, sounding genuinely perplexed.

Rose leaned close over his captive. 'We will proceed to fingers,' he said, 'and since your kind can grow back fingers and tongues and other parts, I'll take two for every falsehood.'

'All these years,' sighed the stranger, 'and this is how our races come together again. Captain Rose, I see that I must explain a few points. You are drifting towards the Karysk frontier. You have sailed into an artificial current, summoned to carry the Last Armada of Bali Adro at great speed into enemy waters. If you continue east you will soon reach Nandirag, the first great city of Karysk, and a conflict more horrible than words can express. You must sail out of the current at once, and turn west while the good wind holds. You might find you can repair your ship in Masalym, and I could perhaps do you a favour in that regard.

'But the city of Masalym is part of the Empire of Bali Adro, and so is all the coastline beyond it for a thousand miles. It is cursed, my beloved *Tarum Adrofynd*, and quite possibly dying. But it is not dead yet. And there is one law that shall endure a great while: that no one but my kin may draw the blood of my kin. All other offenders must be executed.'

Rose stood as if turned to stone. Neeps felt cold at the back of his neck. 'Captain,' he said, 'be careful, sir. I think he's telling the truth.'

'Of course he is!' said Ibjen. 'His face—'

'Ah yes, my face,' said the newcomer. 'I can hide my chest under a shirt, but my cheek is another matter.'

'You're speaking of a race law, then?' said Rose. 'Only a dlömu may harm another dlömu, is that it?'

The stranger laughed, wincing as he did so. 'Even in our glory years we were not that kind to one another,' he said. 'No, Captain, by kin I mean my extended family, nothing more.'

As if in explanation, he showed them his left hand. On the thumb shone a rough, heavy ring, like a nugget of solid silver. Rose frowned at it, hesitating, then gestured for the sailors to lower the man to his feet. 'What in the Nine Pits do they call you?' he said at last.

'I am Olik,' said the stranger, wincing as his feet touched the boards.

'Just Olik?'

The stranger probed the wounds on his face and chest. He took a deep breath and straightened to his full height, which was considerable. He gazed steadily at Rose.

'My full name,' he said, 'is Prince Olik Ipandracon Tastandru Bali Adro.'

He raised a hand as if to address them further, but before he could say another word, he collapsed.

10

The Rule of the House

~o00~

24 Ilbrin 941

The thin man in the golden spectacles fled the stateroom in a rush. He was off balance from the first, but there was no turning back. Oh, he had botched things, he was in danger – *he would never again be ruled by fear*. But the ship was not his. He could taste the change. A spectacular dreamer he might be, but not a practised one, like the enemy he faced.

For ten yards the passage was silent, warm, and he sensed the life all around him. Hercól in a meditative trance. Neeps unconscious but restless in his hammock, his dream-self raising head and shoulders to gaze through wooden walls in the direction of the man in glasses. Marila awake, rigid, listening for Thasha and Fulbreech, barely allowing herself to breathe. Thasha herself far behind him in the stateroom, by the windows, hoping there would be no knock on the door. Bolutu asleep and very distant, running through dream-lands of his own.

Then the man stepped over the red line, through the magic wall, and the chaos of his dream engulfed him. The ship tilted – or was it the pull of the earth that changed – and he stumbled against the bulkhead. There was a background rumble, a groaning, in the very air, and the light was fugitive and dim. No matter, he would not be here long. He turned down the portside passage and reached for a doorknob (vaguely aware that it was the entrance to the old first-class powder room) and flung it open to see – the bakery, his own beloved bakery in Noonfirth! The humble shop where he had become a woken animal! He could smell the bread, see the black woman bent over her mixing bowl. Couldn't he go to her for a moment, fall on his knees, inform her of the miracle she had worked? *Madam! I was a thief in your shadows, a rat. You cried one morning, your husband had run away with the butter-churn girl. I heard, and I woke: yours was the spark to the tinder that burns inside me yet.*

No, he could not do that. He was looking not for comfort but for allies, and he had not a moment to spare.

Another turn, another passage. There were ghost sailors fighting in the adjoining rooms. Translucent flashes, limbs and weapons and faces and shields, flowed by at the intersection ahead. Pirates or Volpek mercenaries, battling *Chathrand*'s sailors; a fight to the death among the dead. Echoes of war cries, faint sounds of steel on steel. Was it the past he was seeing? Or the disordered nightmare of another dreamer, just out of sight?

There was the door he sought. No question. He could feel eternities throbbing beyond the fragile wood. Bounding up to it (fear would *not* stop him) he seized the knob, turned it and pulled.

An abyss. A maelstrom. Wind tore at his cloak like a hurricane through tattered trees. All as it should be. He was better at this than he'd thought.

He forced himself to lean forwards until his face crossed the threshold. The wind like a boot to the underside of his chin. He nearly lost his balance; his glasses were torn from his head and flew upwards, out of sight. *No matter. You don't need them. You'll be blind until you will yourself to see.*

But he was blind for now – blind and, yes, afraid. Was it his fault if there was only darkness before him? What should he expect – warm windows, vines, music and laughter spilling onto the terrace? True, he had managed to see all that once before, and to hear a great deal. But that night he had been a stowaway in another's dream, not the architect of his own.

Then he sensed the sorcerer.

It was true: Arunis *was* walking the dream-ship once again, sure enough of himself to call out with his mind, *Ah, Felthrup. I wondered when you'd come back to me. Are you ready to bargain, rat?*

Felthrup turned away from the door, anger crackling through his dream-body. He turned his mind in the mage's direction. *You think nothing has changed. You think you can torture me as before, use me against them, make me your fool.*

I think I would know if Ramachni were guarding you, as he did last time.

Come, then. Come and talk to this rat. He is waiting for you.

He felt his dream-voice betray him. *No control, no control.* Somewhere Arunis was indeed rushing towards him, laughing at his forced bravado.

We have an account to settle, don't we, vermin?

Felthrup closed the door. He turned in the direction of the mage's voice. *We most certainly do, Arunis.*

He felt his slim scholar's body throb with sudden power, hideous and sublime, the strength of a thousand-pound animal, and he spread his jaws and roared through five decks, a bear's furious battle roar, and Arunis stopped dead in his tracks.

That's better.

No taunting reply from the mage. Felthrup was satisfied. Within this ship, within his dream, he was his own master, and would bow to no one again.

Felthrup reopened the door. The black abyss loomed before him, unchanged; the wind made him stagger.

Where can you be going, Felthrup? said the mage, his voice suddenly affable. *Come now, you don't want to step through any ... unusual doors. I know all about them; you'll want to talk to me first.*

He let go of the door frame.

Don't you do it! You have no idea what you're in for, if you stray from this ship!

No more tricks. No more words of poison. He leaped.

As a rat he had once plunged from a moving ship into the sea. This was infinitely worse: the air current blasted him straight upwards, head over heels; the door became a dim rectangle that shrank to nothing in the darkness. He rose like a cannonball fired at a midnight moon – and then the current vanished, and he became weightless, and started to fall—

Only for an instant. The next blast shot him faster, further upwards. *Do not wake. Do not panic.* Now there were windows, and cave mouths, and luminous insects somehow surviving the wind. Felthrup had lost all control of his dream. He perceived the wall of this great black tunnel, ten times the width of any mineshaft, and no sooner had he seen it than he collided, scraping along the wall shaggy with vines, while somewhere within the leaves tiny voices cursed him: *You great oaf, that's my property, you've knocked my mailbox into the River.*

The River of Shadows. That is what the innkeeper called this place. And his name, and his tavern? Think of it, remember. *Orfuin. The Orfuin Club. Anyone whose need is sincere can find his way to my doorstep.*

No sooner had the thought occurred to him than he saw it: the little terrace and the wide stone archway, the scattered tables, the pot-bellied man at his tea. As if he had waited all these weeks for Felthrup to return. But how could he possibly get there? Felthrup spread his arms, the way he had seen Macadra and her horrible companions do, but his cloak only billowed about his head, and like a tossed playing card he flew spinning across the shaft, rising still, leaving the terrace behind. *No control.* He could almost hear Arunis laughing, though he knew the mage could not see or hear him in this place. He flailed, he kicked, he crashed again into a wall. He sank his hands into the vines. They were deep, but not deep enough. Fistfuls of the waxy leaves tore away in his hands as his body tried to lift away once more.

He should not have attempted this journey. *You're failing, rat.* Still just a rat, with a rat's small soul, even if he could dream himself into the body of a man or bear.

Then it came to him, like a gift from some mind beyond his own. *Still a rat!* He had that choice, too. Closing his eyes, he willed the change to happen, and it did. His fur, his half-tail, his dear old claws. All at once the vines closed over his whole body. The wall of the shaft was rough, scabrous; better than the walls he scaled with ease on the *Chathrand*. And the wind sheared past him, deflected by the vines.

He crawled straight down. He veered left and right following the smells of the place, dark beer and gingerbread. Rat, man, bear, *yddek*: he could be any of these. He was Felthrup Stargraven, and for the first time in his curious life he knew with certainty that he was something more. He thought of Arunis, stalking the *Chathrand* like a murderous fog, killing through mind-enslavement and yet afraid to meet him, Felthrup, in dream. *I am*, he thought with a totally unfamiliar pleasure, *a dangerous foe.*

'Do you mean that you had *no* assistance whatsoever?' said the innkeeper, filling a saucer for the rat.

'On the contrary, sir,' said Felthrup, seated on the table beside him. 'I had the assistance of the written word, and an exceptional sort of help it was. The thirteenth *Polylex* often leads one astray, I grant you; and it is certainly biased in favour of the *northern* half of my world. There is no entry whatsoever for "Bali Adro", tragically enough; one proceeds directly from *Balhindar*, a Rekere dish made with green rice and termite larvae, to *Baliacan*, a dance in honour of the Firelords, the poor execution of which was punished – do excuse my redundant vocabulary, sir – with execution.'

'But something in this *Polylex*,' said Orfuin, unruffled by Felthrup's nonstop chatter, 'showed you the way to my door, though you'd never dipped so much as a finger into the River of Shadows?'

'Master Orfuin, I had no inkling that such a River existed.'

A gentle smile spread over the innkeeper's face. 'One day you may long to recover such ignorance. Then again, you may not. For now, let us celebrate your skill. Few dare to leap into that stream who are not born to it, or committed to a lifetime's practice. You, Felthrup, are a natural swimmer.'

'How very ironical,' said Felthrup, beaming. 'All my life – my woken life – I have lived in fear of drowning. But I suppose one cannot drown in a river of air.'

'There is more than one sort of drowning,' said Orfuin. 'But come: tell me how you managed this miracle, and what need brought you to attempt it.'

Felthrup reached to adjust his spectacles, then laughed: they were still gone. 'Cross references, Mr Orfuin,' he said. 'I began with *Dreams*, an entry that ran to some forty-eight pages. Around the thirtieth, I learned of the theory of Occulted Architecture, which states that the objects in a dream-land, like those in any other world, are made of smaller building blocks: atoms, cells, particles too small for any eye to discern – except the mage's, and those of magical creatures. They, being able to perceive the building pattern, can also learn to change it – to turn a rat into a man, candies into worms, a damp tunnel into a castle corridor. Arunis used this ability to torture me for several months, once he discovered my dream of scholarship.

'But the *Polylex* goes on to say that dream-lands are not exactly infinite. Like countries in a waking world, they *do* possess edges: frontiers, borders, watchtowers, walls. Some of the mightiest walls are those erected *between dreamers*. They are invisible even to the dreamer himself, but they are also essential: they prevent us from wandering, by accident or ill design, into the dreams of others.

'Mages, however, can pass through these walls as though they do not exist.'

'If that were not so I'd have fewer customers,' said Orfuin, 'though not everyone who comes here does so in a dream.'

'Well, Mr Orfuin,' continued Felthrup, 'at that point the *Polylex* suggested I consult the entry for *Trespass, Magical*. How fortunate that I did! For that entry described at some length the consequences of dream-invasion for the one so violated. They are mostly horrible. Because Arunis trespassed so often and so aggressively into my dreams, I may eventually come to suffer from insomnia, sleep-walking, fear of intimacy and verbal reticence.'

'Surely not the latter?' said Orfuin with concern.

'Oh, it is likely, sir, and narcolepsy, and excessive familiarity too. But that is all beside the point. What matters is this: that those whose dreams have been invaded sometimes find that they have been bestowed with *an equal but opposite ability*, that is, to enter the dream of the one who invaded them.'

'That is true,' said Orfuin. 'The wall between two dreamers, once transgressed, is never afterwards a perfect barrier.'

'So it proved with me,' said Felthrup. 'My great benefactor Ramachni, wherever his true self has gone, passed into my dream and gave me the power to fight back against Arunis. That act saved my life, for sleep had become such misery that I was performing the most extreme acts of self-torture to keep myself awake. And when at last I had the courage to dream again, I made a shocking discovery: my dreams no longer just *started*, with a bang as it were, in the middle of a fight or dance or bowl of soup. Not at all. Since Ramachni's visit, I *see my dream coming*. Like the doorway to your club, it begins as a tiny square of light in the darkness. Very quickly that square grows into a window, and before I know it, the window crashes against me, and I tumble into the dream. Strange, and useless, I thought: for I was as helpless to control this process as I was tonight, flailing around *out there*.'

Felthrup lifted his head, indicating the rushing blackness beyond the terrace. 'The River of Shadows,' he said, musing. 'What is it, Mr Orfuin? Through which world does it run?'

Orfuin paused for a long sip of tea. 'The River is the dark essence of thought,' he said at last, 'for thought, more than anything else in the universe, has the power to leap between worlds. It belongs therefore to all worlds where conscious life exists. And yet strangely enough, consciousness tends to blind us to its presence. I have even heard it said that the more a world's inhabitants unlock the secret workings of the universe – its occult architecture, its pulleys and gears – the deeper the River of Shadows sinks beneath the earth. Societies of master technicians, those who trap the energy of suns, and grow their food in laboratories, and build machines that carry them on plumes of fire through the void: they cannot find the River at all.

'But we are straying from your tale, Felthrup. You were speaking of these dream-windows. You fall through them helplessly, you say?'

'No longer!' said Felthrup. 'Once again the *Polylex* came to my rescue. In a footnote to the *Dreams* entry – I revere the humble footnote, sir, don't you? – the book provides a list of exercises for taking *conscious control of the unconscious*. And what do you suppose? I mastered those exercises, and found I could slow the approach of my dream-window. Eventually I learned to stop it altogether and examine the dream from the outside, like a wanderer looking in on a firelit home. If I wish to enter, I do so. If not, I simply wave my hand, and the window shatters like a reflection in a pool. But the most astonishing part was yet to come.

'Several nights ago I noticed a second window, a second dream, shining at some distance from the first. It was the sorcerer's, Mr Orfuin: somewhere on the *Chathrand* Arunis was asleep, and sending his dream-self out to prowl the ship. I dared not approach it: suppose my new skills failed me, and I tumbled into the sorcerer's dream? Suppose he sensed me outside the window, and by some magic drew me in? Ramachni gave me the power to master my own dreams, a task I am barely equal to. But should Arunis lay hands on me within his own—'

'You would become his slave, in waking as in dream,' said Orfuin with conviction. 'And when he had finished with you, he could break your mind like a sparrow's egg, between two fingers. Or toy with it, for the rest of your natural life.'

He stood abruptly, as though shaking off a spell, and walked to the edge of his terrace, where the wind of the lightless River tore at his sparse hair.

'To be held in that mage's invisible cell, prey to any torture that occurs to him, for ever. There could hardly be a more awful fate in all the worlds.'

Felthrup said nothing. In the club, someone was tuning a mandolin.

With his back still turned, Orfuin added, 'You knew this in your heart, did you not? Before you leaped willingly into his dream.'

'Ah,' said Felthrup, 'you guessed.'

'Only now,' said Orfuin. 'You were the little *yddek* that hid under my chair. The first such creature I had seen in many months. The one who swam out of the River some twenty minutes after Arunis himself.'

'I was,' said Felthrup, 'though I did not know I would become that strange creature, all tentacles and jointed shell. I only knew that I must learn what he was doing, for even from a distance, gazing fearfully at the window of his dream, I knew he was pre-paring for a decisive step. Maybe *the* decisive step in his struggle with us all. How could I simply watch him take it, and not even try to learn what it was about? So yes: I drew near, and watched him pacing through your club, pretending to be no one in particular at first, but shedding the pretence little by little as his impatience grew. And when his back was turned I summoned all my courage, and jumped.'

The innkeeper turned to face him again. 'You are fortunate that you became an *yddek*. I saw the sorcerer turn in surprise the moment you appeared. He sensed your intrusion into his dream, and raced from door to door, to see if it was Macadra who had come. His glance fell on you, but he has seen many *yddeks* in his time and thought nothing of it. But had you taken this form—'

'He would surely have known me,' said Felthrup, raising his mangled forepaw, and twitching his stumpy tail.

'You were fortunate in another way, too,' said Orfuin. '*Yddeks* have very sharp ears. I assume you heard what they said on this terrace?'

'Much of it, Mr Orfuin,' said Felthrup, 'and all that I heard was terrible. Arunis seeks the complete elimination of human beings from the world! And that woman Macadra seems to share his wish, although she denies it – and something he whispered, something

I did *not* hear, came to her as a brutal shock. Yet I still have no idea who she is. Can you tell me?'

Orfuin took a rag from his pocket and walked to one of windows looking out onto the terrace. He breathed on a small square pane and rubbed it clean.

'Macadra Hyndrascorm,' he said with distaste, 'is a very old sorceress. Like Arunis, a cheater of death. All mages tend to be long-lived, but some are satisfied with nothing less than immortality. None truly attain it. Some, like Macadra and her servants in the Raven Society, deploy all their magical skills in its pursuit. They may indeed live a very long time – but not without becoming sick and bleached and repellent to natural beings. Others, like your master Ramachni, are granted a kind of extended lease: the powers outside of time stretch their lives into hundreds or even thousands of years, but only in pursuit of a very great deed.'

Felthrup jerked upright with a squeak, almost upsetting the little table. 'Do you mean that once Ramachni completes his allotted task he will die?' he cried.

'Death is the standard conclusion, yes,' said Orfuin. 'But Felthrup, you must hasten to tell me what you came here for. I have a roast in the oven. Besides, my dear fellow, you might wake at any time.'

'That is precisely why I have come!' said Felthrup. 'Master Orfuin, my *Polylex* tells me that the wall between two dreamers is not the only sort of wall. There is also, of course, the wall between dream and waking. But by one of the most ancient of laws, most of what we learn, and all that we collect or are given, must be left on the far side of the gate when we return to waking life.'

Orfuin chuckled again. Then, with an air of scholarly formality, he recited:

> *Never night's mysteries are exposed*
> *To the weak mortal eye unclosed.*
> *So wills its King, that hath forbid*
> *The uplifting of the fringèd lid.*

'Or something to that effect. Have you read Poe, Mr Felthrup? A dlömic writer of some interest; there's a book of his in the club.'* Yes, it is a balm to the soul, to travel and converse and gain wisdom in the land of dreams. But only mages can carry that wisdom out into the daylight. The rest of us must leave everything but a few stray memories on the far side of the wall.'

'But master Orfuin, I am denied even those!' cried Felthrup, hopping in place. 'If I saw Arunis' face looming over me, or held on to some brief snatches of his words, then perhaps I could fight him. But he has placed a forgetting-charm upon me. Ramachni told Pazel Pathkendle of this charm, and Pazel told me. But Ramachni cannot dispel it, he said, until he returns in the flesh.

'And that will not do. Here as a dreamer I know all that has happened to me, in waking life and in dreams. But my waking self knows *nothing* of those dreams, and so I cannot warn my friends. I cannot tell them what I overheard, here on your terrace. That this Macadra and her Ravens are sending a replacement crew – isn't that how she put it? – to seize the *Chathrand*. That all the wars, feuds and battles of the North are watched with pleasure, and even encouraged, by forces in the South bent on conquest. I know the most terrible secrets in Alifros! But what good is this knowledge if it vanishes each night at the end of my dream?'

'And you imagine that this old tavern-keeper can help you break what you yourself have just referred to as one of "the most ancient of laws"?' Orfuin sat back in his chair with a sigh. 'Finish your tea, Felthrup. Come inside and eat gingerbread, listen to the music, be my guest. No matter how many years we're allotted, we should never squander life in pursuit of the impossible.'

'Forgive me, sir, but I cannot accept your answer.'

Orfuin's eyes grew wide. Felthrup, however, was possessed of a sudden absolute conviction. 'I *must* take the warning back with me,

---

* Orfuin here slightly amends the original, though not perhaps for the worse. He is also mistaken about the artist's race. Falargrin (in *The Universal Macabre*) presents conclusive evidence that Mr Poe was a transplanted selk. – EDITOR.

somehow. I cannot possibly sit down and enjoy your hospitality if that means pretending I don't know the fate Arunis has in mind for half the people of Alifros. If you will not help me, I must thank you for the tea and the delightful conversation, and go in search of other allies.'

'In your dreams?'

'Where else, sir? Perhaps one of the ghosts aboard *Chathrand* will help me, since you find yourself unable to do so.'

'There is something you must understand,' said Orfuin. 'I am no one's ally, though I try to be everyone's friend. This club survives only because it has, since time unfathomable, stood outside the feuds and factions that plague so many worlds. No one is barred who comes here peaceably. Whether the words they exchange are words of peace or barbarism I rarely know. Wars have been plotted here, no doubt – but how many more have been averted, because leaders of vision and power had a place to sit down together, and talk at their ease? It is my faith that the universe is better off for having a place where no one fears to talk. Arunis was right, Felthrup: when I closed the club and threw them out into the River, I was doing something I had never done before, and will not hasten to do again. I was breaking the promise of this house.'

'Because you heard them plotting the murder of millions of human beings!' said Felthrup. 'What else could you do at such a pass?'

'Oh, many things,' said Orfuin, rising again from his chair. 'I could sell this club, and purchase a home in the Sunken Kingdom, or an apartment in orbit around Cbalu, or an entire island in your world of Alifros, complete with port and palace and villages and farms. I could break my house rule again, and then again, and soon be one more partisan in the endless wars beggaring the universe. Or I could contemplate my tea, and pretend not to have heard anything my guests were discussing.'

Felthrup rubbed his face with his paws. 'I will wake soon; I can feel it. I will forget all of this, and have no way of helping my friends. I should not have come.'

Orfuin stepped close to the table and put his hands under Felthrup's chin, lifting it gently. 'You may sleep a little longer, I think.'

And suddenly Felthrup sensed that it was true: the flickering, stirring feeling, the teasing scent of Admiral Isiq's cigars still clinging to his uniforms, had quite faded away.

'Most visitors to a tavern,' said Orfuin, 'don't come to speak to the barman.'

Felthrup glanced quickly at the inviting doorway. *You cannot help me*, he thought suddenly, *but you spelled it out, didn't you? What your guests speak of is none of your concern.*

'Do you mean, I might yet find—?'

Orfuin released his chin. 'Go inside, Felthrup. You're a talking rat; someone's certain to buy you a drink.'

II

Confessions

'How did it happen, Ludunte?'

The young ixchel man stood with his back to the bulkhead, sweating. 'My Lord Taliktrum,' he said, 'I swear to you I don't know.'

'Three of our prisoners walk free,' Taliktrum continued, pacing back and forth in the lamplight, his Dawn Soldiers lounging behind him, predators at rest. 'Two are allies of my treacherous aunt. The third – tell me, Ludunte, who is the third?'

'C-Captain Rose, my lord,' stammered Ludunte.

'Captain Rose,' echoed Taliktrum furiously. 'The sadist who kept an ixchel locked in his desk for years. In a birdcage. The only man aboard to oversee an actual extermination – did you know he once killed an entire clan of our people, aboard an Auxlei grain ship? We just gave him his freedom on a satin pillow, Ludunte. And the *blanë* antidote was in your keeping.'

From a far corner, Ensyl looked on with unease. It was not going well for Ludunte. Taliktrum wanted someone to fall on his sword, to accept the blame for the disaster quickly and fully, sparing the Visionary Leader (yet another ridiculous title) any further embarrassment. But Ludunte was not playing along. Taliktrum, never one to endure much contradiction, was furious.

They were in the ixchel stronghold on the mercy deck: a series of crates boxed in particularly deep by other cargo, all but unreachable by the crew that had stowed them. Of course, there had always been the danger that the humans would abruptly want something from the crates: ixchel clans lived in perpetual readiness to evacuate their homes. But Taliktrum's decision to seize hostages had changed all that. No humans walked the lower half of the ship unescorted. They were, in a certain respect, safer than most members of the clan had ever been in their lifetime. But that safety had just been shaken to the core.

'You're Treasure Keeper to the clan,' said Taliktrum, glowering at Ludunte. 'You had a key to the strongbox, and changed its location each month, for the sake of security.'

'I do not choose the locations, my lord.'

'*I* choose them,' Taliktrum snapped. 'And you went alone to collect the pills when we decided on this *furlough*, this hour's charity. How could you possibly confuse the temporary antidote with the permanent? It's inexcusable.'

Atop the hunting cabinet that had become his solitary refuge, Lord Talag nodded in agreement. The cabinet was one of some twenty furnishings from the Isiq mansion back in Etherhorde that had passed, in effect, to the ixchel: old Admiral Isiq had never come for his belongings – some whispered that he'd been quietly killed after the fiasco of Thasha's wedding – and Thasha herself had forgotten about the crates, or else never realised that any of her family's goods remained in storage. *Or perhaps*, thought Ensyl, *she knows perfectly well, but wants no reminders of the father she lost in Simja.*

'You'd be wiser to come clean, Ludunte,' said Taliktrum.

'But my good lord! I've done nothing wrong!'

'You cannot keep secrets from me,' said Taliktrum, raising his voice suddenly. 'I have been given a fate. I see further, deeper than you. I see our final triumph as a people – and every selfish, stupid act that impedes that triumph.'

'Then you know I speak the truth,' said Ludunte.

'I know all the truth you speak, and all the falsehood.' Suddenly Taliktrum whirled and seized Ludunte by the jaw. 'I must make you see it as well,' he purred. 'I must hear it from your lips, know that your mind has accepted the truth, if you are to go on serving me – serving the clan, the clan of course, through me its rightful leader.'

Ludunte made a grave error, then. His head could not move, but at the words *rightful leader* his eyes flickered briefly to Lord Talag on his sullen perch. The look did not escape Taliktrum. His mouth twisted with rage. 'I will drown you,' he said. 'I will call on the clan to sanction your punishment, and they will do so.'

Ludunte closed his eyes, trembling. But he said what honour demanded, and with an air of certainty at that. 'If the clan requires my death, I give it gladly. My life is in its keeping.'

'No less than our own,' came ritual response from every mouth. Ensyl spoke too, though the Dawn Soldiers shot her hateful looks. To those fanatics she was as much a traitor as her former mistress. Diadrelu had trusted the giants, and taken one as a lover. Ensyl's sin was loving Diadrelu – adoring her, believing in her to the point of rebellion. She had defied Taliktrum, taken Dri's body from him, delivered it to Hercól. Yes, she was a hypocrite to speak those words. She had broken the clan-bond in favour of her mistress. But Ludunte had also sworn service to Dri for the entire length of his training, and yet he had led her into the trap in which she died. Wasn't that the greater crime? Not by ixchel law, of course. Yet somewhere, surely, there was a law of the heart?

'There are three possibilities,' said Taliktrum. 'One, you confused the pills, mistaking the permanent antidote for the temporary.'

'Never,' said Ludunte.

'Two, you deliberately brought the wrong pills to the forecastle house, because you wished, for some reason, for the giants to be free.'

'My lord – nonsense!'

'Three, you told someone of the location of the pills, and they – or someone they told in turn – tampered with the vials themselves.'

'I told no one!' cried Ludunte, with rising desperation. 'Lord Taliktrum, why don't you trust me? Have I not been your faithful servant in all things?'

Taliktrum looked at him piercingly. 'Leave us,' he said. 'I will speak with my private council, of your faith and other matters.'

He turned, dismissing Ludunte with an imperious toss of his hand. Ludunte's eyes swept the room in great distress, settling at last on Ensyl. She returned him all the sympathy she could manage, which was next to none. Stiffly, Ludunte walked to the door. Taliktrum's Dawn Soldiers hissed and spat at him as he departed.

Taliktrum's gaze fell on Ensyl. 'You,' was all he said.

She rose and followed him past the file of soldiers. They were silenced by the nearness of Taliktrum, but their eyes told her what they would do if given the chance. Some studied her body, others fingered their spears. *He's destroying them, destroying their minds*, Ensyl thought. *They're cut off from every tradition of the clan save obedience and bloodshed.* Dri had always warned her that courage without reason was worse than no courage at all. *Skies above, he's a greater threat to us than Rose.*

They entered what Taliktrum called his 'meditation chamber', where a single lamp burned upon a table fashioned from the lid of a pickle barrel. Myett was there, of course, watching Ensyl like a nervous cat. So was Saturyk: tight-mouthed, quick-fingered, Taliktrum's all-purpose spy. More startling was the presence of the Pachet Ghali, Myett's stern, silver-haired grandfather. The title *Pachet* was given to few: it was the highest state of learning to which an ixchel could aspire. Ghali was a master musician: so great a master that the old, lost lore of ixchel-magic was said to live on in the song of his flute. Diadrelu had seen the proof. The man's playing had called swallows from their nests on a cliff near Bramian, and Taliktrum, wearing one of the clan's two priceless swallow-suits, had been able to command them like a small winged army.

'Close the door behind you, girl.'

Ensyl obeyed, masking her feelings with effort. *I'm the same age as you.*

'A look passed between you and Ludunte just now, did it not?' began Taliktrum, pouring himself a goblet of wine.

'He looked at me,' said Ensyl, 'and I looked back.'

'You will address our leader by his title,' growled Saturyk.

'Which one?' said Ensyl.

'Ludunte was Dri's other *sophister*,' cut in Taliktrum. 'The two of you were closest to her of all the clan. Do you remain close now, you and he?'

'We never were especially close, Lord Taliktrum.'

'How is that possible? She chose the two of you out of many hundreds who wished to study at her knee. You trained together in Etherhorde. You were partners in the Nine Trials, the Midwinter March. You were in the same watch for three years.'

'One can share many things, Lord, and not grow close.'

'Very true,' said Myett in her satiny voice. 'Ixchel blood, for example.'

The two women locked eyes for a moment. Ensyl fought down her anger. *Nothing to be gained by sparring with his mistress.*

'You truly suspect Ludunte of switching the pills?' she said.

'Hold your tongue until His Lordship addresses you!' said Saturyk.

Ensyl bristled. 'Are we slaves, now, to grovel before him? Or am I expelled from Ixphir House? Even then I am no chattel. He has the right as clan leader to call for my silence. You, Saturyk, have no right at all.'

'Careless,' hissed Myett, 'so like another woman who thought herself clever. What became of her, Ensyl of Sorrophran? Tell us that. As you say, you've every right to speak.'

'And I have the right to scold you, daughter's daughter, though it pains my heart,' said the Pachet Ghali. 'Where did you learn such spite?'

'You should be proud of her, Pachet,' said Taliktrum absently. Myett looked at him as though hoping he had more to say. But Taliktrum's thoughts were elsewhere. 'All of you, be still. Ensyl, I do not ask you if Ludunte is innocent or guilty. I merely ask if you think him *capable* of treason.'

A black irony entered Ensyl's voice. 'Of course, my lord. I have seen treason done by his hand. The day he helped you murder Lady Diadrelu.'

She had gone too far. Myett's eyes blazed with outrage; even the Pachet Ghali looked shocked. But Ensyl felt no remorse, only the wound, the outrageous loss, as sharp now as on that horrific night on the Ruling Sea. Taliktrum *had* killed her mistress, even if another hand had delivered the blow.

Saturyk moved forwards, as though to eject her from the room by force, but Taliktrum waved him off. He looked a long time at the slender woman before him.

'I am sorry for you,' he said at last. 'However poorly you were schooled in Sorrophran, there are some childhood maxims you cannot have avoided. *We are the rose that prunes itself*, remember? A clan of ixchel must know when a limb is diseased. And my aunt was diseased, Ensyl. Also gifted, certainly; no one would deny that she was gifted. But her vision was unsound. She loved giants. As a pathology it's nothing new – men and women both have suffered from it, though most grow out of the delusion. Not Dri. She grew worse, and finally obscene.'

'We watched them,' said Myett, as though the memory turned her stomach.

'And saw nothing,' said Ensyl, blinking fast. 'Nothing of the truth, that is. Nothing that mattered.'

Taliktrum's face was carefully blank. 'You revered her, but that does not oblige you to defend what is unnatural. Dri herself would not have done so, before her sickness advanced.'

'She had no sickness!'

Taliktrum dropped his eyes, as though pondering an unwelcome thought. 'I recall a dinner conversation,' he said at last, 'shortly after you arrived in the capital. She hadn't yet decided to take you on. I argued that she should – argued against my father, I'll have you know.' He smiled strangely. 'My aunt called you *the gentlest flower in the field*.' He paused, weighing his words. 'Nytikyn spoke of it too: your gentleness. When the others asked him about you, in the barracks, and on patrol.'

Ensyl's breath grew short. Nytikyn, her fiancé, had been killed a few days before the voyage began.

'The women were fond of him,' said Saturyk. 'He was a handsome lad. He could have had his pick of half a dozen, but he was after you. I gather you took some convincing. You had other things on your mind.'

'What things, Saturyk?' asked Myett.

'Oh, just things. She was very dedicated to her training. And her trainer.'

'A pity that you never arrived at a wedding date,' said Taliktrum.

The Pachet Ghali looked at Taliktrum. His face paled, as though some motive or tactic had just become clear to him. Seeking no one's permission, he rose and left the room.

Myett stared at the door, clearly shocked by her grandfather's act. But Saturyk was smiling wickedly. 'Oh, they set a date, m'lord,' he said. 'A number of them, in fact. Somehow the happy day kept getting postponed. Don't recall the reason.'

'Saturyk, really,' said Taliktrum with mock severity. 'As if such private matters needed to be explained. But let us return to that dinner, Ensyl. Would you like to know what else your future mistress had to say about you?'

'No,' said Ensyl.

'"*Timid, but beautiful.*" That was how she put it. "*When I watched her balance on one hand she took my breath away.*" My father mentioned the childish joy you took in pleasing her. Later, when we had all drunk some wine, Dri spoke of you again: "*If Nytikyn has lost his head over her, I understand it. You can see at a glance she's a heartbreaker. The quiet ones so often are.*" That, of course, brought smiles from everyone. But my aunt said, "*I would do better to reject her as a student. She is too fond of me, and one's sophister must never be distracted by—*" Here now, girl, is something wrong?'

Ensyl's eyes were streaming. He had done it, the monster, he had torn it out of her and held it up for the others to gawk at. She held her ground, enduring it. She would not run from the chamber like the girl they kept calling her. Let them see these tears. Oh, Diadrelu. A time would come.

Saturyk flicked his chin in her direction. 'There's the flaw at the heart of this clan,' he declared. 'Selfish obsession. *My* needs, *my* wants. Never *ours*. The ones your aunt recruited are the worst, m'lord.'

The men went on studying her, cold as doctors facing an autopsy. Myett, however, looked oddly moved by Ensyl's suffering. Her grandfather's departure had left her frightened by the whole affair. 'The clan could have helped you, Ensyl,' she said. 'The clan heals its own, no matter what ails them, but how can it do so unless you tell us? It was your duty to tell us.'

Suddenly Taliktrum swept forwards and seized Ensyl's arm, dragging her to the far side of the chamber. To her surprise he wore no look of triumph. He knew exactly what he was doing, but a part of him was deeply ashamed.

'What if it went further?' he said. 'What if Dri took it *much* further, for her own delight? The clan already has proof that she had strange appetites. What if they knew that she had turned an adoring young student into an instrument of pleasure?'

A madman, thought Ensyl, looking at his sweaty chin.

'You care very much how Dri is remembered,' he said. 'That's why you've fought me at every turn. You have to stop that. I'm the commander and you can't do anything about it, no one can. Not even me.'

'What in Pitfire,' Ensyl managed to say, 'do you want?'

'You switched the pills,' he said. 'We both know it, Ensyl. Because Ludunte isn't the only one with a key to the strongbox. Every clan leader carries a spare.' He put a hand inside his shirt and drew out a brass key on a leather cord. 'Diadrelu carried one identical to this. You used it, didn't you? You were trying in some twisted way to follow her example. Trust the giants. Embrace them, and in time they'll return that embrace. Confess, Ensyl, and I swear on the Great Mother I'll restore her good name.'

For a moment Ensyl could not even breathe. There was the

choice. Lie for Diadrelu, play the part of traitor, give Taliktrum someone to blame for the fiasco. Or refuse, and let Taliktrum cast another stone at Dri's memory, turn her into a predator, a corrupter of the young.

'You won't do it, will you?' said Taliktrum suddenly. 'You won't confess, I can see it in your eyes. It's the right thing to do, but never mind, you'll be obstinate, you'll fight me as she did, no matter the cost. Because you *loved her.* Because you're *keeping the faith.*'

'Yes,' said Ensyl, 'I'm keeping the faith.'

'I did not kill my aunt,' he said, the words spilling out now like something beyond his control. 'Steldak did it, *he* jerked the spear through her windpipe, I gave no such order, there was still time to talk. A waste – I can say that now. She had fine qualities, I know that better than anyone, better than some heartsick girl. Her intuition, for example. She knew I loved music, wanted to *be* a musician, once, before my true responsibilities; she taught me to swim, also, to bend my voice – never mind that – are you going to confess?'

Ensyl stared at him in horror.

'Speak up!' he said.

'What happened to you?' was all she could say.

'Me? Me?' Suddenly Taliktrum was screaming in her face. 'Saturyk, take her out of here. She will tell the truth or face the judgement of the clan. We had to stop that woman, Ensyl. Can't you see how wretched she was inside? Wretched, miserable! Even before we caught her she was destroying herself. We had to act before she doomed us all.'

When the girl was gone Taliktrum threw himself into a chair. Myett came up behind him and began to work his shoulders. He covered his face with his hands.

'She could well be the one,' he said. 'She hates us, hates our leadership.'

'She is twisted and jealous,' said Myett. 'If Hercól is found dead in his cabin some morning, we'll know who cut his throat.'

'No,' said Taliktrum, through trembling fingers. 'They're allies, that girl and the swordsman. I've seen how they talk. We must move to denounce her. We have evidence of her treason already.'

Saturyk frowned. 'It's a trifle risky, m'lord. Oh, the clan would likely endorse your decision. But later, when they're not so afraid, the questions could get awkward.'

'Then keep them afraid,' said Myett, rubbing harder in her fright, trying to make Taliktrum look up at her. 'Ensyl has earned death; there are other ways to deliver it than clan execution. Let her disappear. Two or three of your Dawn Soldiers could do the job.'

'Take your hands from me,' said Taliktrum. As Myett recoiled, wounded, he added, 'Carry on, Saturyk. What awkward questions?'

Saturyk crossed his powerful arms. 'In point of fact, Ensyl was within her rights to stand by her mistress, even against your orders. She may not be certain of that herself, but the House Elders know the law perfectly well – and they know, by the same token, that Ludunte is the oath-breaker, not Ensyl. He vowed to serve the Lady Diadrelu in all things, until released by her consent, or by the will of the clan in full council. Not even a clan leader may sever that bond.'

'But a prophet might,' said a voice from behind him.

It was Lord Talag. The others started; he had come down from his high seat without assistance, and now stood straight and proud in the doorway. Maimed by Sniraga, then held for weeks by the rat-king, Master Mugstur, he had suffered unimaginable abuses. Few had thought that he would live to see the far side of the Nelluroq, let alone the fabled shores of Stath Bálfyr, the beloved Sanctuary he had lived for. But Talag was growing stronger all the time. Clan rumour held that he was in constant pain, but there was little sign of it about his person.

'I would speak to my son alone,' he said, moving to a seat at the table.

Myett and Saturyk left the chamber, the young woman trailing a hand up Taliktrum's arm as she went. When the door closed behind them, Taliktrum rose and poured his father a tall glass of wine.

'How is it with you, sir?'

'You can see that I am healing,' said Talag curtly. 'Taliktrum, you have a traitor in your midst.'

'Apparently,' sighed the young lord.

'What do you mean, "apparently"? You cannot believe this was an accident!'

'No, Father.'

'Well, then a traitor's at work. Have you considered that it may be Myett?'

Taliktrum vehemently shook his head. 'Forgive me, sir, but that makes no sense.'

'To sane men the actions of lunatics are senseless by definition,' said Talag. 'Senseless – not impossible. The girl has a vague and fearful mind. She trails behind you like a shadow. And she shares your bed. She could well have borrowed *your* key to the strongbox.'

'But she has no motive whatsoever. She detests the giants.'

'And worships you – *apparently*. Taliktrum, a perfect cover is reason in itself to be suspicious. Don't exempt her from scrutiny because of the pleasures of her touch. You should devise some way to test her.'

Taliktrum moved away across the room. He stared at a portrait of Alighri Ixphir, third commander of the House that bore his name. 'I will destroy the remaining antidote,' he said. 'Isn't that what you'd do, in my place?'

'And condemn all the prisoners to eventual death?' said Talag. 'You are not thinking clearly. What if the traitor simply informs the humans of your act? What will you bargain with, once their death is assured?'

'Besides, we are not savages. That is what Dri would say, in such a pass.'

Talag glowered. 'Find the traitor. That is what your father says.'

Taliktrum started to pace. 'I will test Myett. I'll take another woman. We'll see what jealousy looks like on *her* pretty face.'

'You're a fool if you do,' said Talag, sniffing his wine. 'It's the jealousy of the clan you'll soon be confronted with – the men's, at any rate.'

'How am I to play the part of a prophet without a prophet's grandeur?'

Talag thumped the table with his hand. 'By not confusing your people's history with the enemy's!' he growled. 'Arquali mystics were epicures, gluttons. Our own knew restraint. How did you ever get the idea that luxury and wealth would inspire awe? These extra rooms, this feasting, this wallowing in bed with your concubine. No one thinks you more powerful for such displays.'

'The younger folk do. They're not the same sort of warriors as your generation, Father – the sort you raised me to be. They've known more safety in your house than any clan in memory. They like comforts. They like to see someone enjoying them.'

Talag allowed himself a wolfish smile. 'Utter rot,' he said. 'They believe in you *despite* your taste for comforts, not because of them. It's their need for a prophet we're exploiting here. Fortunately that need is profound. Be a warrior again, Taliktrum, and they'll follow you to the bottommost Pit.'

Taliktrum smiled in turn. 'Perhaps I don't want to visit the Pits just yet.'

Talag's face darkened. Taliktrum watched him, hands writhing. He drew closer to Talag and lowered his voice to a whisper.

'Skies aflame but it's bad, Father. Rose is the very *last* person we should ever wish to set free. He's maniacal about his command. We don't dare pick a fight with him openly now – he's capable of anything, even sacrificing the other prisoners. All of them. Who does he care for, among them? Oggosk? We know that she adores him for some reason, but is the feeling reciprocated? And even if it is, I think he might sacrifice her, unnatural beast that he is.'

Talag was very still. 'To sacrifice a loved one for a greater cause – you call that unnatural, do you?'

Something in his voice made Taliktrum feel cold in the pit of his stomach. 'Not for us, perhaps,' he said. 'We understand these things differently. But Rose has no clan to fight for. He's demonically selfish, and no more. Yet somehow the crew is elated to have him back. Why do they trust *him*? It proves the giants are halfwits, that's all I can say.'

'You saw how Rose decimated the *Jistrolloq*, twice the fighting ship *Chathrand* is. You saw how he kept us alive through the Nelluroq storms.'

'He's a fine mariner, of course.'

'He is more than that,' said Talag, motionless. 'Some men know exactly what they're capable of, and set out to achieve it. They have no pretence, because they need none. They choose, and they act. Other men detect this quality in them and want to take shelter in its certainty, its safety. Naturally they find themselves following such men, obeying them willingly. It is the same instinct that makes one hurry to leave a bog for solid ground.'

Taliktrum gave him a sharp look. 'Those who believe in me — and it is most of them, you know — believe in me totally. Saturyk has observed them. They stay up late in the night, discussing my chance utterances, trying to catch glimpses of our destiny. It is almost frightening.'

'It is that,' agreed Talag. 'And here is something worse. Those who do *not* believe in you, like Ensyl — they dismiss you utterly, as a weakling and a fraud.'

'I do not like the way they look at me,' said Taliktrum.

'To like or dislike — what is that?' snapped Talag. 'Pay less attention to your likes, and more to the content of those looks. Tell me, prophet, what is behind them?'

Taliktrum looked at his hands. 'Need,' he said at last.

'That is correct,' said Talag, 'need. They believe in He-Who-Sees because they are afraid of their own blindness. Afraid of what may be coming for the clan, in that future they cannot see.'

'Father,' said Taliktrum suddenly, 'the hostages are not our only security, are they?'

Talag had been lifting his glass; now he set it slowly on the table. 'If the worst should happen — if we should lose them all — you have another plan, do you not? Something to fall back on as a last resort?'

The old man looked at his son in silence. At last he said, 'Would you follow any fool this long if he did *not* have such a plan?'

'Then why haven't you shared it with me? You nearly took the secret to your grave!'

Talag just stared at him, unsmiling.

'Do the elders know?' asked Taliktrum.

'Several,' said Talag, nodding, 'and chosen others. Ten in all.'

'But I should know as well!'

'Taliktrum,' said his father, 'has it occurred to you that if we lose the hostages, the first result may well be your torture? Rose will take you to the galley and jam your leg into Teggatz's meat grinder, and ask you questions designed to make it easier to kill us all. There are some answers it is better for a commander to be unable to provide. Do not concern yourself with our move of last resort. Devote your energies to seeing that we never need to make it.'

Taliktrum stared at his father, struggling to be still. At last with an anxious twitch he rushed to Talag and leaned close to him, gripping his chair.

'I would follow *you* again,' he said. 'Resume your command, my lord! You need not go out scouting as before. We can do that. You can lead us from right here, until you're fully yourself again. Just think how the people would rally to you! Their divisions would vanish like a puff of smoke.'

Talag sipped his wine. Then he rose, forcing his son back a step. He stood almost a head taller than Taliktrum. His eyes shone with anger and disgust.

'Would they?' he said. 'After I endorsed this ugly cult you've built around yourself? Though it profanes the creed that has preserved us for centuries, that no one life must ever be exalted above the needs of the clan? I escape the rats and find my house in ruins, my people so frightened and confused that they would believe in anything – would have ended up kneeling before Mugstur himself, if matters had gone much further. You think I can lead, having declared that

I subscribe to this rubbish, that your vision is my own? "Ah, but that was yesterday, men of Ixphir House. Today it is not the prophet's word but Lord Talag's you must accept. Or some muddled combination of the two." No, Taliktrum. You wanted command. You ached for it like a drunkard for his wine. Now it is yours, and you must keep it.'

'I did not always want it,' said Taliktrum, almost pleading. 'There was a time before all this, before you and Dri began my training. My flutes, Father, do you recall how well I—'

Talag dashed wine in the face of his son.

'Find the traitor and punish him,' he said. 'There was a childhood for each of us. It's dead and gone, and I will speak of it no further.'

12

In the Jaws of Masalym

———

Hunger, thirst, loss of blood: such was Dr Rain's diagnosis. Fortunately the bleeding proved easy to control: the prince's wounds were ugly but not deep. A cabin was readied with lightning speed, the bed salvaged from the ample store of first-class wreckage, a new mattress stitched and stuffed, a coal stove mounted on the floor and its chimney pipe routed out through the porthole. 'I'm not cold,' the prince mumbled, waking briefly, but Rose took no more chances. He brought his own feather pillows for the invalid, and plumped them as the prince was carried in. Thasha watched his efforts with grim amusement. The captain didn't mean to be executed at their first port of call.

But was the man truly who he claimed? The other two dlömu certainly thought so. Ibjen said he knew the prince's face from coins, and even Bolutu declared that he recognised the features of the ruling family.

Olik did wake again, heavy-lidded and weak, but only long enough to seize the captain's arm and speak a warning. 'Hug the shore, as tightly as you dare. That will keep you out of the rip tide. And you must also manufacture a flag in great haste – a leopard leaping a red sun, both on black – or the Masalym cliff batteries will rain down enough iron to sink this ship by weight alone.'

'That is your banner ... Sire?' asked Rose.

Olik nodded wearily. 'And when you pass safe under those guns, perhaps you will consider yourself repaid for the Karyskans' assault.

Go to Masalym, Captain. Only there can you safely repair your ship. Now, I think—'

He plummeted again into sleep. This time it was profound, and Rose ordered the cabin off limits to all save Fulbreech and Rain.

About the time of the prince's collapse a great smoke began to rise in the south. It spread quickly (or they were swept quickly towards it), low and black and boiling over land and water. Beneath the lid of smoke, the dark hulks, the weird shimmer of the armada came and went, licked now and then by flashes of fire. Thasha aimed her father's telescope at the melee. It was still too distant – fortunately – for her to make out individual ships, but even blurred and indistinct the scene was terrifying. Wood and stone, steel and serpent-flesh, water and city and ships: they were all in collision, blending and bleeding together in a haze of fire. *Nandirag*: that was what Prince Olik had called the city. What would it be called after today, and who would be left to name it?

By nightfall the *Chathrand* had drawn within a league of the shore. From this distance one could see the effects of the rip tide with the naked eye: a powerful leeway, a slippage, as though the ship were a man walking across a rug while a dozen hands pulled it sideways. *How far did it carry us?* wondered Thasha, studying the shore through her father's telescope. *How long before it sweeps us right into the fray?*

Nearer to the *Chathrand*, the coast was a line of high, rocky hills, silver-grey and crevassed like the hide of an elephant, crowned with shaggy meadowlands. In the last minutes of daylight Thasha saw dark boulders and sharp solitary trees, a wall of field stones that might have marked some pasture's edge, and here and there an immense clinging vine dangling garlands of fire-red flowers over the sea. Among the flowers, winged creatures, tiny birds or great insects or something else altogether, rose and settled in clouds.

Darkness was falling when they cleared the rip tide. It was unmistakable: a line of churning water and disordered waves, a sudden heaving swell to starboard, a rise in the apparent wind. A scramble ensued: Rose actually spread sail, driving them another half-league shorewards in a matter of minutes. Then he brought the ship about to the north and ordered nearly all the canvas taken in. Until dawn they would creep northwards, following a narrow, safe path between the current and the cliffs.

Thasha watched the ship wheel northwards and felt a chill. It was happening. They were doing exactly what they had said they must *never* do: taking the Nilstone straight to evil hands. Was there any doubt that Masalym was evil? It was a part of Bali Adro, the Empire that was even now destroying the city at their backs, that Nandirag. But was there any other choice? The ship was sinking. Without repairs she could neither run nor fight well enough to keep the Nilstone safe much longer. And there was the small matter of food.

Neeps and Marila had gone to sleep on the floor of the brig, next to Pazel's cell. Thasha wanted to go to them, ached to do so, could not. She went to Fulbreech and kissed him long and deep, her arms over his shoulders, her back against the doorway of his cabinette. His hands gripping her hips, two fingers grazing her skin beneath the shirt. He tried to coax her into his chamber but she shook her head, breathless and shivering; it was not yet time. She left him, ran blind across the lower gun deck, pounded up the Silver Stair and through the magic wall. She flung open Hercól's cabin door and flew at him and struck him with both fists in the chest. Hercól kicked the door shut. In the room adjacent Bolutu heard her curses and her sobs, and the warrior's answering voice, low and intimate and stern.

Sergeant Haddismal tossed and turned in his cabin. When he managed to sleep, the same object rose persistently in his dreams. An arm, pulsating, yellow-grey, somehow both dead and alive, groping through the ship on a mission of its own.

It was the Shaggat's arm, and his dream was hardly stranger than the reality that had prompted it. He had inspected the Shaggat that very evening: first with his naked eye, then with a tape measure. Impossibly, the cracks that were threatening the statue had stopped growing, and even – very slightly, but unmistakably, for Haddismal was a meticulous record-keeper – *shortened*. The mad king was not just alive inside his stone curse. He was healing.

Many others shared the Turach's restlessness. All night Lady Oggosk sat awake in the forecastle house, irritating the other prisoners, mumbling Thasha's name. All night Rose paced the quarterdeck, listening to his ship, pretending not to heed the taunts and whispers of the ghosts who walked at his side. All night the chain-pumps clattered, and the men sang songs from the far side of Alifros, pouring out the sea as it poured in through the ship's hidden wound.

The cliffs were higher at daybreak, the vegetation atop them more lush and green. Now Rose took the prince's advice and brought them closer, barely a mile off the rocks. There were grazing animals (not quite goats, not quite sheep) upon a windy hillside, and a dlömic herdsman with two dogs that sprinted in circles around the beasts. When he saw the *Chathrand* the dlömu goaded his animals into a run. They swept over the hill and disappeared.

The day was bright, the water clear to eight fathoms. None-theless, it was tricky sailing, for the winds were erratic, and for all Rose's fury his men were clumsy and slow. They were weakening with hunger, distracted by fear. Rumours passed like foul vapours through the ship: the ixchel were planning executions. Dlömic attackers were still at large in the hold. Arunis was stalking the topdeck by moonlight. Pazel and his friends were fighting because one of them had gone over to the sorcerer's side.

Late morning they came suddenly upon a tiny cove, high-walled and round as a saucer. The remains of a few stone buildings crouched just above the waves, roofless and forlorn. And there were stairs – long, steep flights of them carved into the rock, beginning at the ruins and snaking back and forth up a cleft in the wall. Five hundred feet overhead they reached the sunny clifftops. There the sailors saw with delight the shapes of fruit trees – three fruit trees, their branches laden with bright yellow globes.

'Apples!' declared someone, starting excited chatter.

'I wonder,' said Hercól.

Thasha glanced briefly at her tutor. He was right to be doubtful, she thought. Hercól was *always* right; you could almost hate him for the trait. But Thasha quickly rejected the thought, and flushed with shame.

Bolutu appeared on deck and warned aloud that there were many fruits in Bali Adro, some fit only for wild creatures. But the men were not listening. They had found an orchard, and the trees were groaning with apples. Their days of hunger were at an end.

Rose summoned his officers to his day cabin. Taliktrum, uninvited, joined the conference. The sailors paced, beside themselves, devouring the shore with their eyes. But they did not have long to wait. Ten minutes later the door flew open and the captain strode out among the waiting men. There was a bottle in his hand: fine Quezan rum.

'We will launch the short pinnace,' he said. Then, shouting above their cheers: 'Not for apples – they are secondary, and we may even forgo them, should danger arise. What we seek above all is tactical information. We need a glance at this country before we sail into an unknown harbour on the word of a stowaway, and—'

'We must be very fast,' Taliktrum broke in. 'Who knows how many eyes are watching us from the clifftops, even now?'

The sailors were gasping: no one interrupted the Red Beast. Rose himself looked tempted to smack Taliktrum into the sea. But breathing hard, he continued:

'I need someone who can take those stairs at a run. The apple-pickers will follow at our signal, if that man finds no danger. His will be the first foot to touch the Southern mainland, and there is great honour in such a deed. Tell me now: who is strong, who is bold? Who wants to make history today?'

Many hands went up, including Thasha's and Hercól's, but the captain chose a tall Emledrian sailor named Hastan. Thasha smiled at the choice. She liked Hastan, a quiet topman who was usually too abashed to speak in her presence, but who had danced with her on the topdeck when Mr Druffle played his fiddle.

Rose passed him the bottle of rum. 'Drink deep!' he said. 'That'll give you strength and courage both.'

Hastan took a giddy swallow, smacked his lips. 'You're a gentleman, Captain.'

Rose took the bottle back, glaring at him: 'Chew the apples thoroughly. Don't let me see you gulping food like a hog.'

Minutes later the boat was in the water, with six rowers, two ixchel observers ('I trust our eyes more than theirs,' said Taliktrum) and baskets large as the sailors' hopes. Every eye followed her progress, her glide into the sheltered cove, Hastan's leap into the surf and wallow up the shingle, his running assault on the stairs. Rose had chosen well: Hastan was as nimble as a mountain goat. He had climbed a hundred feet before the others had the pinnace out of the waves.

The five basket-carriers huddled near the ruins, awaiting *Chathrand*'s signal that it was safe to climb. The men with telescopes watched Hastan, still running as he neared the top. Only on the last flight did he pause for breath. Then he marched up the last steps and moved in among the trees.

There he stood, leaning against a trunk, gazing at an unknown world. He was motionless for a surprising time. When at last he turned to look at the *Chathrand* his face was full of wonder. Slowly he waved his raised palm to the sky: the all-clear signal. Then he picked an apple, sniffed it and took a bite.

Breathless anticipation: Hastan chewed, considered, swallowed. Then he tossed the apple in the air, caught it and set about devouring it with a will. The men on the topdeck roared.

'Quiet, you silly apes!' hissed Fiffengurt, though he was as happy as the rest. The signalman waved his flag, and the basket carriers started to climb.

Hastan finished the apple and tossed away the core. 'Glutton,' said Rose.

The men reached the summit and set about stripping the trees.

They worked quickly, and soon had taken all the fruit in easy reach. But there were eight hundred men awaiting apples, so one by one they moved away from the cliff's edge, seeking more. Thasha watched them go through her telescope, thinking, *Perhaps it is an orchard, at that.*

But the men did not return. Five minutes passed, then ten. 'Damn the fools!' cried Taliktrum. 'They're gorging themselves like brats in a sweet shop! You giants can't be trusted with the simplest task!'

Twenty minutes. Not a branch stirred on the clifftop. The men looked at one another with growing alarm. Then Thasha saw Hercól do a startling thing: he touched Rose's elbow, drew the captain back from the rail and whispered in his ear.

At first Rose showed no reaction to Hercól's words. Then he shook the warrior off, walked to the quarterdeck rail and leaned over his crew. 'No shouts, no cheering,' he said in a low and scathing rumble. 'Haddismal, ready your Turachs. Alyash, I want a hundred sailors backing them up. Blades, helmets, shields – empty the armoury if need be. Fiffengurt, clear the eighty-footers for immediate launch. We are going to get our men.'

Instantly the crowd splintered, every man racing to his job. Eager, approving looks passed among them: they were afraid, but waiting helplessly was worse. An assault! Whoever had seized their shipmates had no idea what they were in for.

'Rose is guilty of a million sins,' said Fiffengurt softly to Thasha, 'but leaving crew behind ain't among them.'

The hands swarmed around the longboat and the eighty-foot launch, freeing them to be hoisted into the Gulf. Turachs were assembling, strapping on breastplates and chain collars, feeling their longbows for cracks. They worked in an eerie hush, as Rose had ordered – until the lookout's cry shattered everything.

'*Sail! Three ships from the armada, Captain! Breaking our way!*'

Rose's telescope snapped up to portside. Thasha raised her own and swept the coast. It was true: three frightful vessels had broken away from the warring mass. All three belched fire, and shimmered in that strange, unsettling way. And their bows were clearly aimed at the *Chathrand*.

'Captain,' she said, 'how fast do you think—'

But the captain was already twenty feet up the mizzenmast. Thasha had seen before how Rose handled himself aloft. He moved like a younger man, confidence and fury making up for stiffness and girth. In minutes he had reached the topgallant lookout, snatched the man's bigger telescope and raised it to his eye.

The whole ship was still. Even Taliktrum waited in silence, watching the captain. Rose moved the telescope from the approaching ships to the deserted clifftop and back again. Then he turned his face away and roared – a wordless howl of sheer frustration that echoed all along the coast. He looked down at the quarterdeck. 'Abort!' he bellowed. 'Hard about to starboard! Fiffengurt, get your men to the sheets!'

They were running away. Thasha closed her eyes, fighting the tears that came so suddenly. Tears for Hastan and the others, men who had sailed the ship for her, danced with her, men she hardly knew. And two ixchel. She hoped they'd all tasted the apples. She hoped the fruit was sweet.

Once more the *Chathrand* was fleeing for her life. Some of the men looked daggers at Rose behind his back – so much for loyalty to crew – but it was soon apparent that he had made the right, indeed the only, choice. The things pursuing them (ships, of course, but what kind, and why did the air quake above their decks?) were still distant, but already the gap was shortening. When the *Chathrand* put out topgallants and began her run, the three at once changed course. There could be no doubt: they meant to intercept the Great Ship.

And they were very fast. It was still impossible to say just how large they were, or what sort of weapons lay hidden in their dark, armoured hulls. But one thing was perfectly clear: if nothing changed, they would catch the *Chathrand* in a matter of hours.

Rose tried to wake Prince Olik, but the dlömu only moaned and shivered.

'Toss him out in a lifeboat, Captain,' said Alyash. 'You'll soon learn if it's him they're after.'

'Don't be an animal, Bosun!' said Fiffengurt. 'He could capsize and drown in his sleep.'

'Or be picked up and tortured, or killed,' said Thasha. She gave Alyash a look of loathing. 'How can you speak of such a thing?'

'Because it may have to be done,' said Rose. 'Not yet, however. He's a card up our sleeve – a royal card, for that matter. I'll not toss him away until we're dealt a better hand.'

How noble. Thasha glanced sidelong at Rose. *Just when I was starting to think you might be human.* But then with a flash of bitterness she reflected that she was no different: she kept who she needed, discarded the rest. *Don't think that way. You have a man now, and his name is Greysan Fulbreech.*

When Thasha returned to the stateroom she caught Marila in her private cabin, going through the contents of her sea chest. Books, blouses, shirts, underthings lay about her in heaps. The Tholjassan girl was so flustered she let the lid of the chest fall on her thumb.

'*Buchad!*' she swore, jerking her hand away. Then, glaring at Thasha, she said, 'Fine, I'm snooping. You've given me plenty of reason to, after all.'

'What are you looking for?' asked Thasha, her voice flat and cold.

'Some sign that you haven't gone completely mad. Do you have any idea what you're doing to him?'

'To Greysan?' Thasha asked, startled.

Marila looked as though she couldn't believe her ears. 'I was talking about Pazel. Remember Pazel, our friend? The one who's got another twenty-four hours in the brig?'

'He put himself there,' said Thasha. 'Greysan tried to make peace with him and got a black eye for his trouble.' She looked at a leather folder in Marila's lap, from which trailed the edges of many crumpled papers. 'That's my blary letter satchel,' she said. 'How *dare* you.'

The satchel contained the few letters she cherished – from her father, a few favourite aunts and uncles, and one particularly dear one from Hercól. It was still tied shut, but Marila's intentions were plain. Controlling herself with effort, Thasha rounded her bed and held out her hand. 'You had better leave,' she said.

Marila surrendered the letters. She trained her unreadable eyes on Thasha. 'Listen to me,' she said. 'I know Pazel's been daft around Fulbreech, but *you* haven't shown any sense at all. He could be *anybody*, Thasha. And he's strange. I heard you talking last night.'

'Oh, you heard me, did you?' Thasha raised her voice.

'I couldn't help it, you were ten feet away. Thasha, he was asking you about your *Polylex*, wasn't he? "*How can you be sure the book is safe?*" Why would he ask that, if he's just interested in you?'

'Because I told him how important it was to keep the book away from Arunis,' said Thasha.

Marila gave her a long, steady look. 'You really love him?' she said at last.

'That's my business,' said Thasha.

'What does Hercól say?'

Thasha's hands were in fists. 'He says he trusts me. He's a friend.'

'So am I.'

'Oh, Marila, I know you are, it's just—'

'Pazel hasn't slept or eaten since he went in there. And Neeps is almost as bad. He's worried himself into a blary stomach ache. He won't talk about anything but you.'

Thasha realised suddenly that she was looking at jealousy. *I can't do this any more.* The thought flashed unbidden through her mind; and then, rallying her courage: *Yes, yes you can.* She brought her memories of Fulbreech's face, his soft kisses, to the front of her mind and held them there. 'I thought,' she heard herself say, 'that you of all people might understand.'

Marila began to shove Thasha's clothes back into the chest. 'Understand what?' she said. 'That in the middle of fighting for our lives you suddenly decide you'd rather—'

'Marila,' said Thasha, almost pleading, 'what if it's not like that? What if this is *part* of fighting for our lives?'

'What in the Pits does that mean?'

Too far, Thasha told herself. She hid her face in her hands, stalling, thinking with furious speed. 'For *my* life, then,' she said at last. 'For my chance to live just a little before I die. Is that so unforgivable?'

'Thasha, once he gets what he wants, he's going to—'

'Stop!' Thasha shouted. 'Damn it, he's not some animal, running me down. He hasn't even *tried*.' She bent and hauled Marila to her feet. 'But if he does, I'll make my own choices. Tell *that* to Pazel and Neeps. They put you up to this, didn't they?'

Marila shook her head. 'They don't even know I'm here.'

Thasha laughed in her face. Now that she'd started the words came easier. 'Don't you *ever* lecture me again. I was locked up in the Lorg School. They call it the Academy of Obedient Daughters, but it was just about turning us into wives – rich wives, powerful wives. The kind nobody ever loves, except for fifteen minutes at a time. Those she-devils they call Sisters, they made us dance like whores. They told us to fake pleasure when we didn't feel it, "the first night, and every night". My own father sent me to that place, Marila, to make a suitable present out of me, a plaything for a forty-year-old Black Rag. And then I fell for a boy who's in love with a fish.'

'Pazel's in love with *you*. And Klyst isn't a fish, she's a sea-murth.'

'A fish,' Thasha repeated. 'And don't tell me about fighting for our lives. The Red Wolf didn't mark you, did it? You're not even one of us.' She jabbed a finger into Marila's chest. 'You think you can tell me who I should want, and why? You don't know a Gods-damned thing. You're a peasant.'

Marila stared at her in shock. Thasha wouldn't have been surprised if she had spat in her face. But instead Marila just walked slowly from the cabin. In the doorway she stopped, and looked at Thasha with a frozen blankness.

'I used to feel sorry that you didn't have a mother,' she said, 'but you had one, all right. Her name was Syrarys.'

The winds were spiteful and weak. There was barely room to manoeuvre between the rip tide and the cliffs, and the hunger-weakened men had no rest at all between tacks. The loss of the landing party appalled and frightened them. And to top it all, a great dark vulture came and landed on the Goose-Girl, and defiled her – the worst luck imaginable. Just how their luck could sink lower, however, they did not dare to discuss.

Thasha took a turn at the chain-pumps, battling the hidden leak. It felt good to throw herself into mindless work. But down the row of crankshafts she saw Neeps and Marila, pulling together, drenched in sweat. Their eyes passed over her like the eyes of strangers. Thasha made herself look away.

When she emerged mid-afternoon the land had grown even more rugged and steep, and the mountains that had looked so distant loomed nearer, towering grandly over the cliffs. Thasha could see the rocky point Bolutu had described: one corner of this vast Efaroc Peninsula. Beyond that headland lay the cove called the Jaws of Masalym.

But now their pursuers had closed half the distance. She looked up and saw the new flag the tailor had patched together: the leopard and the rising sun. It clearly made no difference to the ships in pursuit.

The work grew frantic. They tightened backstays and spread more sail. Rose called for topgallants on the spindly foremast, and even stood a team ready to jettison their precious water. The ixchel ran up and down the strained rigging, looking for any sign of failure.

The hunters were within ten miles of their prey when the *Chathrand* cleared the point. Rose saw Alyash and Fiffengurt exchange looks of relief. Once the ship turned the wind would be with her, helping instead of hindering. And there in the west, like a deep bite out of the towering cliffs, was the cove.

'You can hear the falls already,' said Bolutu. Thasha heard them, a far-off thundering. From the mouth of the cove a white mist rose gleaming in the sun.

'They won't catch us now, will they, Mr Fiffengurt?' asked Ibjen.

'No, lad, they won't,' said Fiffengurt, 'especially if the rip tide's where we think it is. They've been sailing on the far side, but they'll have to cross it if they want to get any closer. That should set 'em back another hour at least. We'll make your city, all right.'

'Unless Masalym too has come to hate this Olik and his flag,' said Taliktrum. 'If that's the case, we are dead men.' He pointed: all along the cliffs ran dark windows, out of which the black iron fingers of cannon jabbed down at the Gulf. Other guns sprouted from towers on the clifftops, and still more from steep-walled forts built on rocks to either side of the cove.

'Friend or foe, Olik spoke the truth about Masalym's defences,' said Hercól.

'The guns?' said Ibjen. 'They are not the city's main defence. In fact, you could say they're unnecessary.'

The truth of his statement was soon evident to all. For as they swept west along the shore, the Jaws of Masalym opened to their sight. The great cove was a river mouth, well over a mile wide. The cliffs, twice as high as those where the apple trees blossomed, towered over several miles of sand flats littered with driftwood and fallen rock – and then closed in a staggering array of waterfalls. There was a huge central cataract, where enough water to fill a hundred *Chathrand*s poured each second, churning up the white they had seen from afar. On either side of this mighty curtain towered other falls, great in themselves though small beside the giant. Spray billowing from the deeper crevasses suggested still more falls, but into these places they could not yet see.

Atop the cliffs, great stone walls marched to the very edge of the cataract. Behind them, through the windblown spray, Thasha glimpsed towers and domes. Cliff, wall and water: the folk of Masalym lived behind mighty defences indeed.

'No enemy has ever taken our city,' said Ibjen. 'She is impregnable as the Mountain of the Sky Kings, and her people justly proud.'

'She can't be much of a sea power, though, can she?' said Fiffengurt. 'I don't see a single boat, nor pier to tie it to.'

'There's no port at all!' cried Alyash. 'How in the devil's belly are we supposed to fix the old ship here?'

'You will see,' said a voice behind them. Thasha turned: Prince Olik was emerging from the No. 4 hatch, assisted by Rose and Fulbreech. He blinked at the light, looking rather frail. He leaned heavily on Fulbreech's arm.

'Display me to them, sirs,' he said. 'They would be fools to attack a vessel under my flag, but we can never rule out the presence of a fool. And the sight of humans, after all, is bound to shock.'

Then he noticed that Ibjen was on his knees. The boy's head was bowed, and his arms were crossed over his chest. 'Oh, come, lad, that is very formal,' said the prince.

'I failed you, Sire,' said Ibjen. 'What they said is true. I tried to jump ship and return to my village, not once but twice.'

'Mmm,' said the prince. 'This is a grave matter, of course. For what has a man who has not the honour of his word?'

'Nothing, Sire.'

'In my youth I saw men fight tigers in the circus pits, to atone for broken promises to their lord. How does that strike you?'

Some of the nearest sailors laughed. Ibjen looked even more ashamed. 'I cannot fight, Sire,' he said. 'My mother bade me take the Vow of the Saints-Before-Saints—' he glanced uncomfortably at Thasha '—to carry no weapon, ever, nor to learn the arts of war.'

'And why did she make such a demand of you?' Olik asked.

Ibjen looked down at the deck.

'The press gangs? Did she hope that your vow would make the army pass you by?'

Ibjen, shamefaced, gave an unhappy nod.

'It would not have succeeded,' said Olik. Then he touched Ibjen gently on the forehead. 'A vow given to a mother is more sacred even than one given to a prince,' he said. 'But then again, it was your father who gave you into my service. How could you have faced him, if you had succeeded in abandoning me?'

Miserable, Ibjen lowered his head even further.

'Well, well,' mused the prince, 'stay near me, lad. We will find another way for you to make amends.'

At that very moment there came an explosion. Everyone winced: it was one of the mainland guns. But no cannonball followed. Instead, looking up, Thasha saw a ball of fire sailing from the clifftops. It burst above the cove in a shower of bright-red sparks.

'I've been noticed already, it appears,' said the prince.

'There's the proof you wanted, Captain!' said Bolutu excitedly. 'Fireworks have always greeted the Imperial family when they return from the sea.'

'Yes,' said Olik, 'and a measure of our popularity can be taken by the length and splendour of the display.' He smiled, indicated the now-empty sky. 'I am recognised, as you see, but hardly with boundless joy.'

Rose led Olik to the forecastle, a long walk for the weary prince. Moving beside them, Thasha seethed. *It's all over. For better or worse.* They were at the mercy of this dlömu, this stowaway, this less-than-popular prince. Olik struck her as a good man – but she had been wrong before – disastrously wrong. What if he betrayed them? What if the Karyskans had been hunting him precisely because he was a criminal?

No time to wonder: the ship sailed right in between the soaring cliffs. The shadow of the western rocks fell over them; the roar of the falls grew loud.

'We'll lose the wind if we sail much farther,' said Rose. 'What then?'

'They will send boats with a towline,' said Olik. 'We should bear a little to starboard – that way.' He pointed at the cove's deepest corner, a recess still largely hidden from sight. Rose shouted the course change into a speaking-tube. The helm responded, and with sagging sails they glided on.

A few minutes later they neared the recess. It was an uncanny sight. The cliff walls drew close together here: so close in fact that they formed a cylinder, open only in front, and rising straight from the surface where the *Chathrand* floated to the top of the falls, eight or nine hundred feet above. The walls of the cylinder had been shaped with great precision, with teeth of carved stone to either side of the opening. Thasha did not care for those teeth: they made her think of a wolf trap. Another waterfall, straight as a white braid, thundered down at the back of this stone shaft and flowed out through the narrow opening. Thasha glimpsed huge iron wheels half-hidden in the spray.

'There is the cable now,' said Olik.

A pair of boats emerged from the recess, each rowed by ten dlömu, and each dragging a rope that vanished behind it into the water. They came right for the *Chathrand*, which was now almost motionless. But at the sight of the humans on the deck the rowers all but dropped their oars.

'Carry on, there!' the prince shouted at them. 'Don't be afraid! Be glad, rather – they're woken humans, all right.'

'A miracle, my lord,' one of the rowers managed to croak.

'Very likely. But savour it after you've done your job. Come on, boys, we're hungry.'

The boats drew near; the lines were coiled and tossed to the *Chathrand*'s deck. Following Olik's instructions, sailors began hauling in the lines as quickly as they could. They were light at first, but soon grew much heavier, the cordage twice as thick. Three sailors hauled at each, and then the ropes' thickness doubled again. Now a dozen men worked in unison, running from starboard to portside, lashing the lines to the far gunwale, returning for more. In this way at last they raised the ends of two chains nearly as thick as anchor lines.

'Secure those to your bow, gentlemen, and your work is done,' said the prince.

Rose so ordered. The men awkwardly horsed the great chains to the catheads and made them fast. Then the prince waved to the boatmen, and one raised some manner of bugle to his lips and blew a rising note.

A grinding noise, low and enormous, began somewhere within the stone shaft, and Thasha saw the wheels at the back of the falls turning slowly, like the gears of a mill. At once the chains began to tighten.

'By the Night Gods,' said Rose, 'that is fine engineering.'

'But you've only seen the simplest part, Captain.' Ibjen laughed delightedly from the deck. 'Is it not so, my prince?'

Olik just smiled again. The cables drew taut, and the *Chathrand* moved swiftly, smoothly through the narrow opening.

Inside the shaft it was cooler; the spray misted the deck and soaked into their clothing, and the falls' thunder made it necessary to shout. The area enclosed was about three ships' lengths in diameter. Other dlömu were at work here, rowing in and out of tunnel mouths, blowing whistles, signalling one another with flags. Thasha looked up and saw that the tunnel openings were scattered up the length of the cylinder, like windows in a tower, and that flagmen stood in many of them, relaying signals from below. They had an air of practised efficiency, except when they stopped to gape at the *Chathrand*.

'It may be dark before we reach the city,' said Olik, looking up in turn.

'I dare say,' said Rose. 'Forgive me, Sire, but you hardly seem fit for such a climb.'

The prince turned to look at him. 'Climb?' he said, and broke suddenly into laughter.

There came a sound like the earlier grinding, but far louder and closer. A shout arose from the stern, and Thasha turned to see that a vast piece of the shaft wall was moving, teeth and all: sliding to close the gap by which they had entered. The moving portion appeared to begin at the river bottom and reached some hundred feet over their heads.

'Don't be afraid, Thashiziq,' said Ibjen. 'No harm will befall us. All boats reach the shipyard in this way.'

He pointed up the shaft. Thasha gaped at him. 'The shipyard ... is *up there*?'

The teeth meshed; the moving wall grew still. Instead of a recess in a cove the ship was now in a basin, sealed to nearly a hundred feet. A basin into which a mighty waterfall was still thundering.

'Have your men drop the lines, said Olik. 'Quickly, sir; the shaft will fill in minutes.'

The chains fell from the catheads. Already the lowest tunnel mouths had vanished under the rising flood. Above, a second hundred-foot-high section of wall was rumbling into place above the first.

'All done with water power,' said Ibjen. 'Water, tunnels, locks. In Masalym we have a saying: *No enemy can stand against the Maî*. That is our river, born in the mountains far away.'

'The Maî defends you only from the sea,' said Olik. 'But it is true enough in that sense: even the armada, with its infernal power, sailed by without a second thought.'

'But why would the armada threaten Masalym?' Thasha asked quickly. 'Aren't you all part of Bali Adro?'

The prince looked at her – a sad, lonely look, she thought. 'I am a citizen of no other country, and the Resplendent One, the Emperor Nahundra, is my cousin. But I would be part of no country, no Empire, no faction of any kind that would belch such a killing terror from its ports. As for Masalym's loyalties – well, that is what I am here to determine.'

'Determine?' cried Rose. He advanced furiously on the prince. 'What in Pitfire do you mean, determine? You brought us here without knowing whether they're still part of your mucking Empire or not? They might have cut us to ribbons with those guns!'

Ibjen backed away, horrified by the captain's tone. Olik, however, remained serene. 'They fly the Bali Adro flag,' he said, 'just as many of you, I gather, carry papers of Arquali citizenship. Do those papers tell me your real affections? Whether you will do good or evil, when your last choice is before you? Of course not. We must seek deeper truths than flags, Captain.'

'How do you know about Arqual, damn your eyes?'

The prince gave him a thoughtful smile. 'Eyes are one place to look for truth – maybe the best, when all's said and done. I would say it is our skins that damn us, not our eyes. Indeed, we could do worse than to follow the example of snakes, dragons, eguar, and shed them when they outlive their usefulness.'

Suddenly he seized the captain's forearm. No longer frail, or feigning frailty. Rose was clearly startled by his strength. Only Thasha, and Rose himself, knew that Olik's hand was covering the scar of the Red Wolf.

'It is no easy task, shedding the skin,' he said. 'Let us all remember that in days to come.'

And with that Prince Olik Ipandracon Tastandru Bali Adro ran across the forecastle, leaped with catlike grace onto the rail, caught his balance – and dived, seventy feet straight down into the foam.

The *Chathrand* beat to quarters. Rose sent full gun crews to their stations. For the second time in a week, sailors and Turachs readied themselves for an assault.

Yet this time the frenzy had an air of make-believe. The ship was clearly trapped. The column of water had already lifted them a hundred feet and was still rising, fast. One above another the huge stone sluice-gates proclaimed their helplessness. There would be no fighting their way to freedom.

The small craft fled into the tunnels. Standing on the quarter-deck, mouth agape, Mr Fiffengurt spotted Prince Olik across the basin, treading water, until the shaft filled enough to allow him to reach one of the staircases carved in its side. Then Olik clambered up the stairs and into another open tunnel, where more dlömu met him with bows. At the *Chathrand*'s stern, Mr Alyash jumped at the sound of another splash, found a pair of sandals at his feet. Ibjen too had abandoned ship.

Huge bubbles burst as the tunnels filled. The *Chathrand* turned in a gentle, helpless circle. Somehow the moiling water never moved her anywhere near the fury of the falls themselves.

They rose as smoothly as any cargo pallet from the hold of a ship. But this time the ship itself was the cargo, and the pallet was water, a column of water, growing fast to nine hundred feet. *Imagine the destruction*, Thasha thought with a shudder, *if the gates were all opened at once* ...

It took the better part of an hour to reach the top of the cliffs: an hour during which the men stood like statues, looking upwards, saying very little. The sky above them was darkening. A few torches appeared along the rim of the shaft.

The final gate boomed into place. All at once cries of amazement were heard from the crow's nest, then from the topgallant men, and the archers on the fighting top. And then the water ceased to rise. The topdeck remained some thirty feet below the basin's upper rim.

'What's happening?' said Fiffengurt. 'The falls are still pouring in. Why are we holding still?'

'Since it is still flowing in,' said Hercól, 'we may assume that it is also flowing out.'

'In equal volume,' said Rose. 'Our hosts have opened some other gate. They're keeping us where we are.'

'Which is where, Captain?' asked Neeps. 'Blast it, I want to *see*.'

'Undrabust! Stand down!' boomed Hercól. But the swordsman was no officer, and the officers said not a word. Neeps and Marila leaped onto the foremast shrouds. Thasha was right behind them, climbing with a will. And suddenly she realised that scores of sailors were doing the same. On the other masts they were climbing too, as many men and boys as the lines could support. The wind brought smells of woodsmoke and algae and dry stone streets. The climbers all reached viewing-height at roughly the same time. And held their collective breath.

A vast city surrounded them. It was surely thrice the size of Etherhorde, greatest city of the North. Over rolling hills it spread, a city of stone houses, thatched roofs, dark and still in the gathering night. Narrow, sharp-roofed towers and oblong domes cast shadows over the lower structures. They had risen inside the city's massive, many-turreted wall.

But all that was at a distance. Thasha saw now that the flooded shaft did not truly end where she had supposed: it broadened into a wide basin, like a wine glass atop its stem. There was as yet no water in this upper basin, though it was clearly designed to be filled.

Projecting into the basin was a long bridge, supported by stone arches and ending in a round, railed platform overlooking the shaft where the *Chathrand* floated. Even now, dark figures were running out along this walkway, some bearing torches, their silver eyes glinting in the firelight. They were shouting to one another in high excitement. A great number of dogs loped at their feet.

'There *is* a shipyard!' cried someone. And there it was: indeed, the whole eastern rim of the basin was a dark jumble of ships – ships in dry dock, raised on stilts; ships floating in a sealed-off lock, from which their spars poked out like the limbs of winter trees. Ships wrecked and abandoned in a dry, deserted square.

Thasha looked at the mighty river. Above the falls it rippled down a series of low cascades, like a giant staircase, each step flanked by statues in white stone – animals, horses, dlömu, men – that towered over the modest homes. Away to the south the cliffs rose again. There was another mighty waterfall, and above it, more roofs and towers looking down on the city.

'Night has come,' said Bolutu, who was clinging close beside Neeps. 'Why is the city dark? There should be lamps in the windows – countless lamps, not these scattered few. I don't understand.'

The dlömu reached the platform at the walkway's end. They leaned out over the rails, looking down at the ship, mighty and helpless below. They were pointing, shouting, grasping at one another in shock. There was just enough light for them to know the crew was human.

'Thashiziq!'

Ibjen's voice. Thasha saw him, waving excitedly from a platform. The other dlömu left a little space about him, looking askance. As though in greeting one of them he had become almost a stranger himself.

She waved. Ibjen was chattering, explaining; his countrymen did not appear to be paying attention.

'Pazel should be here,' said Neeps. 'He should be with us right now, seeing this.'

'Yes,' said Thasha with feeling, turning to him. But the distance in Neeps' eyes told her that his words had been meant for Marila alone.

'Are they talking?' someone shouted from above. 'Listen! Listen to them talk!'

Then Bolutu laughed. 'Of course they're talking, brothers! There's not a *tol-chenni* on this ship! Hail! I am Bolutu of Istolym, and it is long – terribly long – since I walked among my people! I want black beer! I want candied fern and river clams! How long before you bring us ashore?'

His question was met with silence. The dlömu on the walkway shuffled, as though all were hoping someone else would speak. Then Ibjen startled everyone by slipping under the rail. Deaf to the shouts of his countrymen, he scrambled out onto the cornice of the last stone pillar. It was as close as one could get to the ship. In a somewhat lower voice he called to them again.

'His Lordship the Issár of Masalym must decide how to welcome you. Don't fear, though. We are a kindly city, and won't leave you long in distress.'

'Just so long as you don't leave us to *sink* in this blary well,' said Marila.

'Ibjen,' called Neeps, 'where's Prince Olik, and why in the Nine Pits did he jump overboard?'

'His Majesty has gone to the Upper City,' said Ibjen, 'to the Palace of the Issár. I am sure he will speak well of you – generally well.'

'Why did *you* abandon us?' shouted the mizzenman, Mr Lapwing, somewhat crossly.

'I was never your prisoner, sir,' shot back the youth, 'and Olik bade me come ashore with him. As you know, I gave him my promise.'

'Your *worthless* promise,' shouted Alyash.

'People of Masalym,' said Bolutu, raising his voice, 'why are your houses unlit?'

'Because we're all out here staring at *you*,' ventured someone, and the dlömu on the walkway laughed. Thasha felt a prickling of her skin: that was a forced and nervous laugh. A laugh like a curtain drawn over a corpse.

'Ibjen,' she shouted, obeying a sudden impulse, 'we're running out of food.'

The crowds above grew quiet, thoughtful. 'I've told them, Thashiziq,' said Ibjen. Then all at once he gave her a sly look. 'There's a saying among us, that even after a hundred wealthy generations, the dlömu would never forget the feeling of hunger. *Barren land and empty sea: from out this womb came I and thee.* In my father's village they still teach us those rhymes. We're old-fashioned out there, you know.'

A new kind of grumbling came from the crowd above. Thasha saw Bolutu turn away, hiding a smile. 'We'll feed them, stupid boy,' called someone. 'What do you take us for?'

There were uneasy nods, but no one moved. The sun-and-leopard flag rippled in the wind. Then a very old dlömic woman cried out in a voice like a shrieking hinge:

'You're human!'

It was an accusation.

'That's right, ma'am,' ventured Fiffengurt.

'Humans! Human beings! Why don't you tell *us* how long?'

Captain Rose, gazing upwards with a malevolent frown, echoed her words. 'How long?'

'Tell us!' cried the old woman again. 'You think we don't know why you've come?'

Now the other dlömu mobbed the woman, hushing her urgently. The woman clung to the rail, shouting, her limp hair tumbling across her face. 'You can't fool us! You're dead! Every one of you is dead! You've come on a ghost ship out of the Ruling Sea, and you're here because it's the end of the world. Go on, tell us how long we have to live!'

13

Faces in the Glass

~~~

There are guests and there are prisoners, and, very rarely, persons whose status in a house is so unusual that no one can assign them a category. Among the latter was an ageing man with a bald, veined head and broad shoulders on the Island of Simja. For three months he had been a secret resident in the North Tower of Simjalla Palace, in a comfortable round room with translucent glass over the window and a fire always crackling in the hearth.

Making his case even more unusual was the fact that his presence, his very existence, was known to just three people on earth. One was his middle-aged nurse, who was quiet and attentive and rubbed brysorwood oil into his leathery heels. The other was a doctor who commended him for his habit of daily callisthenics. The third was King Oshiram, monarch of Simja. The nurse did not have a name for her silent patient. Only the men were aware that he was Thasha's father, Admiral Eberzam Isiq.

It was barely a fortnight since he had recovered his name. It had been cooked out of him during his seven weeks underground, along with most of his memory, all of his pride. Like bricksteak, that detested Navy product he'd choked down for decades, salt beef dried in the ovens against the weevils and the damp, food you had to attack with a chisel. After a week submerged in brine it might soften, might absorb something again – or it might not. So it was with the admiral. He had literally been pulled from an oven.

From a kiln in a forgotten dungeon under Simjalla, where he had barricaded himself against the monster rats.

He was a stout old veteran, well muscled and formidable even in scarlet pyjamas, his new uniform, worn as unselfconsciously as battle fatigues. He stared for hours at his slippers, or his bed. He had survived not only the rats but the agony of deathsmoke, from which addiction the doctor was trying to help him break free.

Insidious doesn't begin to describe it, the physician had told the king. *It's in his blood, his urine, even his sweat. He should have all the visible signs: nosebleeds, wheezing, numb fingertips. He suffers none of these, though his internal pain is classic deathsmoke. She didn't want him guessing – not him or anyone else. But the only way to avoid those telltale signs is to increase a victim's exposure to the drug very slowly – terribly slowly, your highness. The one who did this to him had the patience of a fiend.*

For the doctor, Isiq was a return to form: as a medical student he had worked with veterans of the Second Sea War. For years now he had been the king's own physician, and knew the monarch trusted him. He did not have a relationship of fear with the king, who was almost young enough to be his son. But he had seen the absolute warning in Oshiram's eyes when the monarch swore him to secrecy.

'Not a whisper, not a glance, not a cough, do you hear me? They will kill him. I'm not telling you to deny that you're caring for a patient in the North Tower. I'm telling you *never to need to deny it*. These people are masters of their trade. Imperial masters, *Arquali* masters. Beside them our own spies are imbeciles. They had a bunker inside our walls, under the Mirkitj ruins, and we didn't suspect a thing. You must try not even to think of him, except when you've stepped into his chamber and barred the door.'

The doctor frowned and trembled, but he was no less thorough for his fear. The bloodroot tea he prescribed soothed Isiq's craving for deathsmoke, if only a little. The fresh greens and goat's milk brought colour to his skin.

But memory proved less willing to return. They had given him a mirror; Isiq had turned it to the wall. After he regained his name he had reached for it again, but the moment his fingers touched the frame he felt a warning shock. The face he saw there might be too full of accusation, too aware.

The little tailor bird urged him to be patient. 'Months of winter before us yet, friend Isiq. There's no cause to worry, or to rush. You humans live so blary long.'

He was a woken bird, of course, and small enough to flit through the eye-level hole in the translucent glass of the window. The king had left this tiny aperture so that Isiq might look down upon the palace grounds: the marble amphitheatre, the red leaves swirling on the frog pond, the play of shadows in the Ancestors' Grove. The bird's mate was not woken, and this weighed on his heart. Three clutches of eggs they'd raised, across three years, and not one of the chicks had sparked into thinking before they had fledged and flown away. 'I know the odds, more or less,' he told Isiq, pecking primly at the crumbs of soda bread the admiral saved for him each morning. 'But the truth is, Isiq, that I'm scouting the city. And even beyond it, in the pastureland, although the hawks hunt there. She's very good, my little pale-throat, very quick and devoted. But if a woken bird came along I don't know what I'd do.'

At that he beat his wings suddenly and hard. 'I hate myself! I'm a rogue! But telling you makes it all bearable, somehow. I'd trust you with my life, Isiq.'

The admiral touched the side of the bird's sleek head. 'Secrets,' he mumbled. In his delight the bird scattered all the crumbs to the floor. It was only the third time Isiq had spoken since his arrival at the palace.

Isiq knew that his own debt of gratitude was far larger than the bird's. The tiny creature did not know it, but he had talked him out of his nightmares, chirped and chattered away the rats. Isiq no longer felt them clawing the edges of his blankets, nor heard them gnawing at the door. He longed with all his heart to talk to the bird, and to the king, when the monarch had time for a visit. But his mind still froze, seizing up in a horrid blankness, and the words, like slabs of ice jamming a river, refused to flow.

So modest, his victories. When he had spoken the previous time, only the nurse had been with him. He had stared at her and suddenly barked, 'Puppets!' She had almost screamed, then covered her mouth in terror. She too had been warned to draw no attention to the room.

'Puppets, sir?' she whispered, aghast.

Isiq nodded, hands in fists, mouth working, facial muscles tight with strain. 'All of you,' he managed to wheeze, 'the little people, just puppets, you'll see.'

It was a measure of her kindness that she took no offence.

That was last week. And the first time he had spoken? That had been when Syrarys came back into his mind. Syrarys, his betrayer, his poisoner – even his property, for a year, when the Emperor forced him to accept her as a slave. Appalling to be one of the few men left in Etherhorde to own another human being. A hideous secret, one he prayed would never become known to the bird. Like the fact that his grandfather had survived being stranded in the Tsördons with a broken leg by eating the bodies of his fallen comrades, ambushed and slaughtered by the Mzithrinis. A little thigh-meat each day for four weeks, until the snows melted and a mountain patrol found him, all but frozen beside his dying cookfire.

How he had worshipped her: Syrarys, his legal consort, more arousing when she yawned or coughed than Thasha's mother had been at the height of lovemaking. Syrarys, the only woman whose touch had ever made him weep for joy, though from the first night (her kisses a slave's kisses, her moans of ecstasy indistinguishable from pain) a part of him had suspected that this joy was on loan from devils, and their rate of interest well beyond his means.

She had leaped back into his memory because of a laugh. King Oshiram had taken a new lover, a dancer rescued from some brothel in Ballytween, he'd said. Terribly shy and unearthly beautiful: she was the reason the king now visited him so seldom. The palace was large, and this girl apparently had the run of much of it – though not, of course, the North Tower. Yet one of the king's favourite chambers was just two floors below, and one day he had brought her there, and Isiq had heard her laugh. It had shocked him from months of silence. He had started to his feet and said one word: 'Syrarys.' For it was *her* laughter. How astonishing to hear it again!

Of course it would be anything but wonderful if it were really Syrarys. For despite all the emptiness that remained inside him, despite the lust that accompanied the laugh, Isiq suddenly knew: it was Syrarys who had done it, fed him deathsmoke, conspired with his torturers, wanted him dead.

Fortunately (yes, fortunately; he must keep that clear) Syrarys was the one who had died. But this girl's laugh! Identical, identical. From that day he had listened for it constantly, moving as little as possible lest by making some slight sound he should miss her. Now and then he would kneel and place his ear against the floor.

On his next visit the king spoke of the girl in a state approaching delirium. He wished he could make her queen, though his eventual bride was already chosen. He remarked on how intelligent she was 'in her quiet, listening way'. He was jealous of every man in the castle, he said. Jealous and fearful. Above all he wanted to keep her safe.

One day life changed for the tailor bird. It had befriended a street dog, it told Isiq. A scrappy, short-legged creature, also woken, who slept on a pile of sacks behind the milliner, and begged scraps from the Ulluprid cooks in the tavern across the alley. The dog was sociable and self-assured, though he would not speak to just anyone. Indeed, he had a strict policy, or as he put it, 'a survival plan'. He spoke to humans only in the furthest reaches of the capital, very far from his alley.

'And never in groups. And always at a distance, and with a clear escape path. I don't fancy slavery, getting nabbed and flogged to some travelling carnival, doing tricks or telling fortunes for the rest of my days. You can't be too careful, bird. Just be glad you have wings.'

For all that, the dog was a bit of a gossip, and even more of an eavesdropper. When the mutated rats stormed the city, a number of animals had revealed themselves as woken, screaming for help or howling prayers as the monsters attacked. Some had been killed, others befriended; many had counted on the inability of humans to tell them apart from their unwoken kin (one crow or alley cat looking much like another) and later blended back into their old, hidden patterns of life.

'But the dog and I mean to find our woken kin, Isiq,' said the bird. 'Who knows how many there are? Twenty? Fifty? We can help one another, learn from one another. The dog has thought it all through.'

'C-care—' Isiq squeezed out, with tremendous effort.

'Careful?' Oh, we will be, that I promise. And I'll never abandon *you*, my friend, nor mention you to a soul, human or animal. Oshiram's terribly good to you, and he must have his reasons for keeping you hidden, though what they are I can't begin to guess.'

'Ott.'

'Ought what? Ought to release you? Do you mean he's holding you a *prisoner*?'

Isiq shook his head. Ott was a *who*, not a *what*. A dangerous, deadly *who*. Isiq could summon the face (damaged eye, vile grin) though he could recall nothing specific about the man. *He is far away*, thought the admiral suddenly. But that did not mean, somehow, that he could not strike.

Weeks passed. Sometimes the bird was crestfallen: he had sat on a temple roof and dared to shriek out words in the Simjan tongue, then watched the blackbirds and wrens that flitted from district to district, tree to tree, not one showing the least sign of understanding. But the next day he might be overjoyed, and come to the admiral with tales of some new friendship, or dreams of a future life, when animals and humans no longer had anything to fear from one another, and lived in peace.

One day he and the dog had made the acquaintance of a *fenneg*, one of the giant flightless birds of Simja, ridden by couriers and constables throughout the bustling city. The *fenneg* had been aware of them for some time, but it was only now that he summoned the courage to speak. In their first conversation the *fenneg* shared a secret: he had recently made a delivery to the house of a witch.

She was a dark-haired woman from the mainland who lived alone near the East Gate. She had winked at the *fenneg* in a strangely knowing way, and told the rider that his bird looked unusually clever. The rider was taken aback: he knew the *fenneg* was woken, but never spoke of it to a soul for fear that someone might take his steed away.

'The dog and I are going to have a look at this witch,' the tailor bird said to Isiq. The admiral nodded: that was a fine idea. A few days later the bird had much more to tell.

Her house had a private courtyard and a dilapidated barn. She had spotted the bird watching her from the barn's upper window, and known him for woken at a glance. When the dog padded casually by the courtyard gate she had glanced up sharply and laughed: 'This is turning into a tavern. Well, come in, you filthy thing, your friend's already here.'

The dog did not come in that day – his survival plan forbade such a move. But the courtyard had two gates, and the woman began leaving them ajar, and also pointed out a hole at ground level at the back of the crumbling barn: yet a third means of escape. She set out a plate of dry corn for the bird and saved soup bones for the dog. By week's end they had both concluded that she meant no harm.

'She tells us we're welcome any time,' the bird reported to Isiq.

'Happy,' he replied, meaning that for the bird's sake, he was.

'No,' said the bird, 'I don't believe she's very happy. She talks frequently of war. She waves a hand over the city and says we should expect to see it burn. Don't misunderstand: she's not raving; in fact she's quite presentable – attractive even, when she combs her hair. And she has a pretty name, too: Suthinia.'

Isiq held the name in his mouth: *Suthinia*. It glimmered ever so slightly, in the darkness where his mind could not go.

'I'd started to doubt she was a witch at all,' the bird continued, 'but not after what the dog told me last night. He'd been to see her the day before: I was with my dumb darling, telling stories, weaving twigs. Do you know what he saw that woman do, Isiq? Put her hand through a wall! Right through! Not her fist, not with violence. She simply reached through the solid brick wall beside her mantel-piece and brought out a vial of smoke.'

Isiq raised an eyebrow. 'Smoke.'

'Very good, Isiq! Smoke it was: a pale-blue smoke that shone with a faint light, and swirled like liquid in the glass. A moment later she brought out another, and this smoke was red. The dog asked her what they might be. "Dream-essence," she said. "The purest nectar of intelligence, formed in the soul before a dream begins. When the dream breaks it leaves us for ever, and empties into that dark flood called the River of Shadows. But if you extract it at that precise moment, *before* the dream, you have a connection to the dreamer's mind. You can look into the smoke and see his dream, on that night or any other. And should you have the skill you can give him new dreams, *specific* dreams, the dreams you choose. There are few in Alifros with that skill, but I am one."

'"Whose *dream-essence* do you have there?" the dog asked, start-ing to be frightened of her again. "My children's," said the woman. "Long years ago, I took it. I did not harm them in the taking, but I harmed them in other ways." She was sombre and quiet for a moment, then held up a vial in each hand. "These are the only possessions I care for in all the world. I live in fear of their loss, and have never dared to give my children dreams, lest I make the existence of these vials known to our enemies. They can sniff out magic, even better than you can sniff out a meal. But I cannot wait any longer."

'She asked the dog to lie in the courtyard and bark if anyone drew near. He did so, and heard her whispering within. At one point his curiosity overpowered him, though, so he put his paws up on the windowsill and gazed into the room. The woman was holding the red vial against her cheek. She caressed it, moved it to the other cheek, then closed her eyes and breathed on the glass. Then she set it on the table and knelt as if to pray.

'The dog saw nothing else at first. Then the smoke seemed to pass right through the vial, just as the woman's hand had passed through the wall. It formed a cloud over the table, and within it the dog saw a boy in a coffin – alive, you understand, and battling to escape. The dog was so appalled that he turned away, and lay shivering in the bright sun of the courtyard, until the woman came and told him he could go.'

The next morning the king swept into the chamber, with gifts of walnuts and macaroons.

'Your Highness,' said Isiq. At the sound of Isiq's voice the king put down the gifts and seized his arms.

'Splendid, man, splendid! Try something else!'

Isiq smiled, squirmed, cleared his throat.

'Come on, nothing long-winded. What would you like for breakfast?'

'Your woman.'

'Eh?'

Isiq's mouth worked, and he made a beckoning gesture with both hands. After a moment the king's face relaxed into a smile. He had become quite good at interpreting the admiral.

'Bring her here, to meet you? What a funny idea. She'd do you a world of good, too, with her gentle ways. But you know it can't happen, Admiral. I've explained all that to you.'

Isiq tilted his head. There was a question in his eyes.

'Oh, I trust her,' said the king. 'More than I reasonably should. I'd put a dagger in her hands and sleep like a babe, with her beside me, if you care to know. Yes, I'd even trust her with the secret of *you*. But why burden her? She's had a hard life already. This is her refuge, now, just as it's yours. When both of you have healed a little more, then we'll see.'

He clapped Isiq on the shoulder. 'You're talking. That's exquisite progress, and quite enough for today.'

Isiq's expression was thoughtful, as though he might venture to disagree. Oshiram looked encouraged by the alertness in the face before him.

'It's a real pleasure, watching you heal,' he said. 'By the Tree, I think I *shall* bring her to see you after all. I'll tell her your story this evening. We must tell someone about you, mustn't we, if you're ever to resume a normal life?

'I do hope you take to her, Isiq. She's the best thing to happen to me in years. I was beginning to think my reign was cursed, you know. After your brave Thasha's death and the collapse of the Peace, some of the other lords of the Crownless Lands turned their backs, called me Arqual's fool. Then came the death of Pacu Lapadolma, those furious letters from the Mzithrin Kings, that Gods-awful plague of rats. I should have gone mad without my darling girl. Watching her dance, one can believe that beauty still has a place in Alifros.'

Isiq nodded, smiling to please the king. 'B-beauty,' he made himself say.

'Ha!' laughed Oshiram. 'Carry on, Isiq. Perhaps in a day or two we shall be watching her dance together – or just listening to her sing. Did I mention that she sings?'

An enraptured look came over the king's face. He raised his eyebrows, the corners of his lips, and was suddenly womanish, crooning in soft falsetto:

'Look for me by starlight, lover, seek me in that glade.
I'll bring you all the treasures of the world our love has made—'

He broke off. Isiq was lurching backwards, mouth wide open, flailing. Before the king could reach him the big man fell hard upon the chest of drawers, knocking it back against the mirror, which jumped from its peg and shattered on Isiq's bald head.

'Rin's eyes, Admiral!' The king experienced a rare kind of panic: Isiq was bleeding, the doctor was elsewhere, he could not shout for aid. He went down on his knees and plucked sickles of glass from the admiral's clothes. No danger, no danger, only scratches on that bedknob cranium of his. 'What in Pitfire happened to you?' he demanded. 'Oh, keep still, shut your mouth before you get glass in it.'

Isiq thought his mind would burst. The song was *hers*. She had sung it to him countless times, early in the mornings, in the garden cottage, bringing him his cigar – aboard the *Chathrand*, in bed, with Thasha in the outer stateroom practising her wedding vows. Oshiram had even managed a fair imitation of her voice.

The king was scolding, but Isiq could barely hear. Time slowed to a crawl. There were shards of mirror in his hands and lap. In every sliver, a memory, bright and perfect. There was his daughter, murdered in her bridal dress. There were the four men bearing her body to the *Chathrand*. And Sandor Ott. And the Nilstone, throbbing.

'Don't handle them, you daft old—'

And here in this largest shard, so cruelly, cleverly shaped (the king tried to remove it; the admiral fiercely gripped his hand) was that unequalled beauty, his Syrarys, with her arms around a lover – not Isiq, of course, and not the spymaster, nor even this good, deluded king. Mesmerizing, this clarity, after so much blindness. And yet Isiq was certain. No one else could have made his consort so dangerous. The one in her arms was the one who had always been there, invisibly. The one who'd slain Thasha, and cheated death. The one whose hands moved all the strings—

'Arunis.'

The king froze. *'What did you just say?'*

Isiq's gaze had wandered for months; now it focused sharp as daggers on the king. 'You're in danger, Oshiram,' he whispered.

'A complete sentence!' cried the bird suddenly from the window, forgetting himself entirely.

The king whirled, gaping; the bird was already gone. 'What is happening here, Isiq? Have you been feigning this illness? Where did that bird come from? And why in Rin's name did you mention the sorcerer?'

Isiq stared up at him: glass in his eyebrows, rivulets of blood on his cheeks. 'We must trust each other, Majesty,' he whispered, 'and somehow we must be cleverer than they. By the Night Gods, I remember it all.'

14

Thursday, 26 Ilbrin 941. Where, by the Blessed Tree, to begin? With the dead men? With the blessing of the goat? Or with the fact that Heaven's Tree doesn't even hang over us here, so help me Rin?*

No: I shall start with Pathkendle, since I have just seen him & the lad's misery is fresh in my mind. I had just taken my turn in the rigging, same as nearly everyone aboard. The dlömu were still staring at us, but their numbers were dwindling. Perhaps they were moved by the doomsday-babble of that screaming hag. Perhaps we misspoke, somehow, hurt their feelings. However that may be, we soon concluded that we weren't to be fed, or even greeted with more than fear & superstition, before daybreak. They hemmed us in with cables to stop our drift & placed guards at the ends of the walkway & left us to stew in our own sinking ship.

A few men exploded, cursing them. Others begged loudly for food. The dlömu, however, did not look back & when they were gone from sight even the timid hands joined in until the whole topdeck was bellowing insults: fish-eyes, black bastards, cold-hearted freaks & then someone gave an embarrassed little, 'Ahh,

---

* Scribbled in the margin of this page, Fiffengurt adds: 'This far south, only the tips & branches of the Holy Tree peek over the horizon, in the hour before dawn. Mr Bolutu has ventured the farcical opinion that the Milk Tree is no tree at all, but merely the diffuse light of millions of stars, too faint to be spied one by one. I fear at times that the fellow is delusional. He sometimes speaks of Arqual & the Mzithrin in the past tense, as one might of nations that have ceased to exist.' – EDITOR.

umm,' & we saw that one of the cables was moving like a trawl line & dangling upon it were bundle after canvas bundle. Wisps of steam escaped them & the smell when we hauled them in brought a low moan of ecstasy from the nearest men. Ibjen had shamed them, apparently. Ghosts or no ghosts, we wouldn't be starved.

Inside were warm rolls & slabs of fresh cheese & smoked fish, the river clams Bolutu had gone on about for days, and cloth packages filled with strange little pyramid-shaped confections, a bit smaller than oranges & coated with sugar and hard little seeds. We nibbled: they were salty-sweet & chewy as whale blubber. '*Mül!*' Bolutu cried at the sight of them. 'Ah, Fiffengurt, you'll find nothing more authentically dlömic than *mül*! They've been the salvation of many a sea voyage, or forced march through the mountains.' But what were they? 'Nutritious!' said Bolutu, & quickly changed the subject.

There was dark bread, too, & as I live & breathe, many bundles of what we took for fat white worms. A dozen of these fell to the deck when we tore open the first basket & wriggled away like lightning for fifty feet or so & then lay still. Bolutu snatched one up, peeled off its skin like a blary banana & ate it: the things are fruits – *pirithas*, he calls 'em: 'snake-beans'. They fall from a parent tree & squirm away, seeking new places to grow. 'If it doesn't wriggle it's not worth eating,' he said.

I was about to brave one of these dainties myself (having already wolfed down bread & cheese & fish & clams; the latter stained green whatever they touched & made us all look frightfully murthish about the mouth) when Lady Thasha appeared with a platter heaped with all the aforementioned. 'Will you take this to Pazel?' she asked me.

'We can do better than that,' I told her. 'It's well past midnight, ain't it? That's three days. Let's get 'im out of the brig, my dear! You come along.'

But Thasha shook her head. 'You do it, Mr Fiffengurt. And see that he eats, will you? There's enough food for the *sfvantskors*, too.'

Considerate, that was: the food would be gone in minutes. But the compliment I thought to pay her died on my lips when she turned & walked back to Greysan Fulbreech. Old Smiley fed her a piece of bread & she grinned through the mouthful at him & suddenly I was enraged. A nonsense reaction, of course: young hearts are fickle & Thasha's has clearly left Pathkendle in favour of this youth from Simja. Why does the sight of them fill me with such indignation? Perhaps I merely hoped the girl had better taste.

I ducked down the Holy Stair, bickered with the crawlies at the checkpoint & was finally *escorted* (how the word sticks in my throat) onto the mercy deck & aft to the brig. The four Turachs (two for each *sfvantskor*, none for Pathkendle) were licking clean plates of their own; they turned spiteful when they realised I wasn't bringing second helpings. At the far end of the row of cells, the two *sfvantskor* watched me with bright wolf eyes.

I unlocked Pathkendle's cell; he walked out, slow & dignified & hurt. Some spark in his eye was gone. I might never have become aware of its existence, that lad's blary spark (what do I mean, spark? Here's my old dad's answer: *If you have to ask you ain't never goin' to know*), but for its absence then.

'Chin up, Pathkendle,' says I, much heartier than I feel. 'The ship's out of danger & you're out of jail. Try a wiggler. I happen to know they're fresh.'

'Go on,' said a grinning, green-lipped Turach, 'they only *look* like big maggots.'

Pazel stared insolently at him & bit into a piece of bread. 'I want,' he said, chewing, 'to finish telling Neda my dream.'

Under the soldiers' eyes we took food to the *sfvantskors*. Pazel sat facing them, cross-legged on the floor. They ate. To fill the silence I talked about the waterfalls, the incredible way we rose into the city. Pazel sat there slipping snake-beans into his mouth & gazing at his sister through the iron bars. His sister, a Black Rag priestess: the thought chilled my blood. This was the girl they'd been looking for, those countrymen of mine, during the Ormali siege. They'd beaten Pazel himself into a coma that day, when he refused to guide them to his sister's hiding place. He'd lain there ready to die for her. Could anything – time, training, religion – challenge a bond like that?

'Thasha painted me with mud,' Pathkendle was saying. 'Head to toe. Bright red mud that she'd heated in a pot. It felt—' he glanced at me, colouring a little '—really good. The beach was windy; the mud was smooth & warm. I told you already what happened next.'

'She pushing you,' said Neda. Her attempt at Arquali was for my benefit, I suppose.

'Into a coffin,' said Pazel. 'A fancy coffin, trimmed with gold. She slammed the lid & nailed it shut & I kicked & pounded from the inside. When she was done she dragged the coffin into the surf.'

'And pushed you out to sea,' said the older one, Vispek. He raised his head & looked at me. 'The mud, the gilded coffin in the waves. Those are Arquali funeral rites, are they not?'

'Only for kings & nobles, these days,' I said, startled at his knowledge of us. 'It's a high honour, that sort of burial.'

'And the one who paints the body?'

'The king's favourite girlie. His whatsit, his courtesan.'

'Neda thinks the dream's important,' said Pazel.

Her eyes flickered over me coldly. 'Dreams are warning,' she said. 'We not listen, then we getting die.'

'Is that a fact.'

She said something quick & cross in the Sizzy tongue & her master grunted in agreement. 'The Isiq girl wants to be rid of him,' he said, 'although once she pretended to love him. Like an expensive whore.'

'Now just you shut your mouth,' I said, rising to my feet. But Vispek went right on talking.

'She wished to seem as though she revered him, saw him as her equal. Never mind that she's from one of the most powerful families in Arqual, and the boy is nothing: a peasant from a country her father destroyed. So she honours him, buries him like a king.'

'But is lie,' said Neda, wolfing cheese. 'No honour if he put in water alive. Only after he getting die.'

'The girl's touch was pleasurable, in this dream?' asked Vispek.

Pazel nodded uncomfortably. 'Well then,' said Vispek, 'all the better to catch you off guard in the moment of betrayal.'

'That's enough,' I said. 'You're a slimy beast, Vispek. You're trying to divide us, and using Pazel's sister to do it. By the Tree, you're carrying on the old war, ain't you? Right here in *Chathrand*'s brig, ten thousand miles from home.'

Vispek kept his eyes on Pazel. 'Neda is correct,' he said. 'Dreams *are* warnings, and must not be ignored. The next time you feel that caressing hand, you can be sure a knife will follow. Watch your step.'

'I will, Cayer Vispek,' said Pazel.

'Damn it, Pathkendle!' I sputtered. 'This is Thasha you're talking about!'

The tarboy looked up at me, chewing. 'Thasha,' he said. 'Thasha *Isiq*.' As if the last name changed something for him.

A few minutes later we left the brig, with ixchel scurrying ahead & behind. I was aghast at the whole exchange. What kind of horrid nonsense had Pazel been listening to, in that black cell for three hopeless days? What ideas had those Sizzies stuffed him with? I grew frantic, & as soon as we cleared the checkpoint I dragged him from the ladderway & pressed him up against a wall.

'Flimflam!' I said. 'Mule dung! A man will dream *anything* when his heart's broken. That don't make it true!'

'You don't understand,' he said. 'My sister's special. Wise. They both are, as a matter of fact.'

It was worse than I feared. 'Pathkendle,' I implored. 'My dear, sarcastic, sharp-tongued tarboy. Religion's a fine thing, a truly noble thing – except for the *believing* part. Trust me, please. It's worse than what a girl can do to you.'

'Nothing is.'

I groaned aloud. 'Pitfire, that's true, of course. But so is what

I'm telling you. Listen to me, for the love of Rin—'

He met my eyes at that. 'For the love of *who*, Mr Fiffengurt?'

I stood up straight. 'That's a different matter, the Rinfaith. It's part of society. And it ain't so extreme, like. You know what I'm saying. Barbaric.'

He frowned a little at that. 'I just wanted to talk to my sister,' he said, 'and that Vispek bloke won't let her talk except about grim and serious things.' Then he smiled at me, with his old sly look. 'Maybe he hoped she'd win me over to the Old Faith. Not a chance. Neda's never been able to talk me into anything.' He laughed. 'But it sure kept them talking. And I must have done a good enough job, if I fooled you too.'

I could have smacked the little bastard. Or kissed him. I was that relieved.

'What was all that about her being *special*?' I asked.

'Oh, she is,' he said. 'Mother cast a spell on Neda, too. All these years I thought it hadn't worked, hadn't done anything to her, but it did. It gave her perfect memory. You wouldn't believe it, Mr Fiffengurt. I wrote a six-foot string of numbers in the dust & read them to her aloud. She recited them all back to me in perfect order. She didn't even have to *try*.'

I just stared at him. What could I possibly say? 'You're from a witching family,' I managed at last. 'But does she have mind-fits, like you?'

'Sort of,' he replied. 'She told me her memory can be like a horse that runs away with its rider. It just gallops off & she's trapped, remembering more & more, faster & faster, even if what she's remembering is terrible. I told her that sort of thing happened to me on Bramian, when the eguar made me look into Sandor Ott's mind, and learn about his life. Neda said, "Imagine if at the end of that vision you couldn't escape, because the mind you were looking into was your own."'

The eguar. He'd never spoken to me of it before, but I'd heard him telling Undrabust about the creature. Like a crocodile, but demonic & huge, & surrounded by a burning haze. 'What did that monster do to you, Pathkendle?' I asked him now.

Before he could make any answer, we heard the scream. It came from away aft, one or two decks below. A blood-curdler, if ever I heard one: a great man's howl of pain, a warrior's howl that twisted for an instant into a high womanish screech & was then cut off as if the throat that uttered it had just ceased to exist.

We ran back to the Silver Stair. The ixchel shrilled & threatened but we barrelled past 'em. I already had an idea where we were going. Turach voices were exclaiming, 'Oh no, *no*! Ruthane, you mad mucking—'

Seconds later we were there, in the manger. There was an unspeakable stench. The Turachs were clumped around the Shaggat, moaning; one of them had staggered away & vomited all the food he'd been allotted. But I knew that wasn't what I'd smelled. It had happened again. Someone had touched the Nilstone.

I made myself draw nearer. There he was. Or wasn't. Then I saw the armour, lying in that heap of bone-dust. Sweet Rin above, he was a Turach.

'He cut the sack with his knife,' said another of the marines. 'He just reached up & cut a hole & put in his hand. What for, what for?'

Turachs do not cry, but this one was as close as I ever hope to see. Then he noticed Pathkendle. 'You! Witch-boy! Was this another of your tricks? If you made him do it I'll muckin' break you in half!'

'I didn't,' said Pazel, looking a bit ill himself, 'and I couldn't anyway, I swear it.'

'And he ain't a killer, either,' I said.

'No, he ain't,' said another. 'He's a good lad, even if he is a witch-boy. He's proved that much.'

The soldier who'd snapped at Pazel looked at him now & nodded curtly. But his face was in a crazy rage. He looked down at the jumble of metal, teeth & bones that had been his friend. 'Aw, Ruthane,' he said. Then his hands became fists. 'By the Nine Pits, we *know* who can do this sort of devilry. Arunis! That's right, *Muketch*, ain't it?'

Pazel nodded. 'Yes, sir. I believe it is.'

'Arunis!' howled the Turach at the top of his lungs. He drew his sword & held it on high. 'You're dead! You're a Turach trophy! Can you hear me, you burst boil on the arse of a graveyard bitch? We're going to snap your bones & suck the marrow. We'll pull out your guts with our teeth, do you hear me? You're mucking dead!'

And then, as if a startling thought had just occurred to him, the man spun around & thrust his hand into the hole in the sack his friend Ruthane had opened – and the Nilstone's killing power ran down his body, fast as a flame takes a scrap of paper, and he was gone.

The pandemonium, the terror, the mourning beside those piles of ghastly remains: it went on through the night. I am at last back in my cabin, scribbling, unable to sleep. This is how Thursday begins.

[19 hours later] No further attacks yet – & no sign of the sorcerer, though Rose has ordered the blary vessel torn apart from the berth deck up, & the ixchel swear on their ancestors' souls that he's not to be found on the lower decks. All the same it's been a frightful time. Last night I saw Pathkendle back to Bolutu's vacated cabin, inside the magic wall. I secured his oath not to stir before daylight, no matter what, even if he should be subjected to the misery of hearing Thasha & Fulbreech together in the stateroom. I gave my last report to the duty officer, looked up once more at the crowd on the walkway above (some of the dlömu have not tired of staring yet) & staggered back to my room. I had just closed my eyes when the door swung open, & who should slip into my cabin but Hercól. The Tholjassan raised a hand, warning me to be silent. Then he crouched by my bed & whispered:

'You must not ask me any questions, nor think too long on what I am about to say. I have given you grounds to trust me, have I not?'

'Pitfire, Stanapeth, of course,' I said.

'Then hear me well: you released Pathkendle out of kindness, but in truth he was safer in the brig. A thing may happen soon that will tempt him to interfere – yet he must not. So I must enlist you, though I wished to involve no one else in this matter. If the time comes, you may have to restrain him by force. And Neeps as well. Neither of them will understand.'

'Those prize idiots. What have they got themselves mixed up with this time?'

'This time they are blameless, Graff. But I told you – no questions. Only be ready to take them far from the stateroom, and keep them there, under lock and key if necessary. Be ready to do it the instant you hear from me.'

'Lock and key?'

'Listen to me, you old bungler,' he said, growing fierce. 'You cannot fail in this. Lives are at stake, and not only the tarboys'. When the moment comes it will be too late to think of a story. Choose one now. I would hear you rehearse it before I go.'

'All right,' I said in surrender, thinking frantically. 'The hag's pet, Sniraga. Undrabust saw her last week. I'll tell 'em I've got her trapped – in the bread room, say, and need help catching hold of her. There's just one door, and it's got double deadbolts.'

'Not brilliant,' said he, 'but it should suffice. They trust you entirely.'

'They blary well won't after I pull this trick! Stanapeth, why—'

He clamped his hand over my mouth. 'Be ready, but do not dwell on what we have said. That is crucially important. You will understand when this is over, Graff. Let us hope it will be soon.'

With that he was gone, & I lay back stunned. I groped for my emergency bottle of brandy & nipped a mouthful. Remember, be ready, don't think. How in the Nine Pits did one obey?

It occurred to me that I might yet salvage forty minutes' sleep out of that hellish night. Once more I closed my eyes. Once more, as if the Gods had waited for me to do just that, the door flew open, this time with a bang.

Uskins blundered in, winded, looking even worse than I felt. 'You loafer!' he croaked. 'Still abed, and drinking, and everything falling to pieces!'

'You certainly are,' I said, taking in his wild red eyes & uncombed hair. 'What's happened to you, Stukey? Have you seen the doctor?'

'I've seen the surgeon's mate.'

'What, Fulbreech? *I* know more about illness than that son of a Simjan mule. Go talk to Chadfallow if you're poorly.'

He shook his head. 'Mules have no sons. Nor daughters either.'

'What?'

'And Dr Chadfallow is an enemy of the Crown.' He pointed with an unsteady finger. 'So are you, for that matter.'

'You smell like bad meat, Uskins. Go see him.'

Uskins gave me a derisive smile. 'And shout my troubles through the glass for all to hear. You'd like that, wouldn't you?'

'Why are you here?'

The question recalled him to his purpose with a start. 'Get up, get dressed! They're coming aboard!' With those words he clawed his way out of my chamber & ran thumping away.

I pulled on my clothes & raced after him. Light poured down through the glass planks: it was well past sunrise. I came out topside into a cool crisp wind – & saw the city for the first time by daylight. It was even stranger than the night before: huge but empty-feeling; the numbers of people out on the cobble streets too few for so many homes. Some places looked cared for; most did not. Even as I glanced up, a flock of dark birds flowed like spilled ink from an upper window. Another house stood in a tangle of brush that might have once been plantings, but now half-covered the door. *On its way to becoming a ghost town*, I couldn't help but think.

All this waste & decay, within the splendour of the city wall, the mighty halls & temples & towers, the river winding its grand path among those statues, the lovely bridges, the further cliffs & waterfalls. And above & behind them, huddled giants, the mountains.

But how was I able to see so much? It became obvious the moment I lowered my gaze: we were no longer trapped in the shaft. Some water-gate had been closed in the night; we had risen those last thirty feet, & then some. The upper basin was almost full.

We were hemmed in once more by criss-crossed lines: nudged, I supposed, until we floated where they wanted us, which was alongside the bridgelike walkway jutting out into the basin. Our quarterdeck now floated level with the walkway's rail.

And along that walkway was coming a procession.

It was headed by a small, weird animal. It was probably a goat, but it had tusks instead of horns & slobbery lips & it minced along like a well-trained dog. Behind it came two drummers, & these were even stranger beings: stocky, almost frog-like, nearly as wide as they were tall, with eyes like a bloodhound's & huge fidgeting hands. They wore uniforms of dark-red cloth with blue sequins & their bare feet *flap-flap-flapped* along the walkway. Their drums were big, mournful barrels strapped to their chests & they beat them very slowly, taking turns. The effect was like the ticking of some dismal clock.

Next came twenty or more dlömu. They were soldier types & terrifying to behold: hard of eye & huge of build, with murderous halberds, hatchets, spears. They'd seen battle, too: scars, old burns & gashes & puncture wounds, marked their faces & limbs. Around me, the Turachs grew wary & still.

In the thick of the soldiers, two figures stood out. The first was Olik, frowning & impatient, but dressed now like the prince he was: in a fitted jacket of cream-white leather that stood out smartly against his black skin, a sea-blue cloak, a crimson sash across his chest.

Beside Olik walked an even more extravagant person. Tall & pale for a dlömu, he wore a doublet of green leather & black iron rings, finished with a gold breastplate emblazoned with the Imperial leopard & sun. He was a warrior like the others & scarred to prove it. But what a face! His eyes jerked & darted, his lips were apart: he looked to be suffering permanent amazement. When he walked his head bobbed up & down like a hobby horse's. The man's webbed fingers, sparkling with dark purple jewels, caressed an ornate scroll case tied with a golden thread.

Captain Rose was rushing to assemble his officers. Some stood with him already; others, like myself, had to shove through the mob. We were all there: Alyash, Uskins, Byrd, Lapwing, Fegin, Coote, Tanner, even Old Gangrüne, looking musty & irritable. All of us hurried to Rose's side. Most of the officers were in dress uniform; I felt the captain's wrathful eye take in my dishevelment. At hapless Uskins he did not even glance.

We formed a line behind the captain. I saw Pathkendle & Undrabust & Marila standing nearby, & on the other side, quite apart, Lady Thasha, with pretty-boy Fulbreech at her side. Taliktrum was there too, balanced on the gunwale in his feather cloak, a fair swarm of ixchel around him.

The procession reached the end of the walkway, & the drumming ceased. For a moment we were on display again. Olik looked at his folded hands, wearing a sly little smile. The pale dlömu just stared at us in shock. But a moment later his eyes narrowed, & his mouth tightened to a line. He shouted something, & his soldiers drew apart. Quick as you like, the little tusken-faced goat-creature minced forwards to the walkway's edge. It stopped there & eyed us expectantly, waggling its ears.

Silence. Rose looked around for guidance. So did the goat. Then Bolutu squeezed through the crowd to Rose's side. I didn't catch his words, but the captain's response was plain enough: 'You're joking!' & 'I'll be damned if I will!' & finally, 'No, & no again. You're barking mad—'

Gasps and hisses from the dlömu. Rose shut his mouth. He stared incredulously at Bolutu, who was still whispering, pleading. At last our captain, looking as though he were about to eat something noxious, stepped forwards & bowed to the goat-thing.

The creature blinked, pawed the stone. Then it bent its fore-legs & knelt.

A great sigh went up from the onlookers ashore. One of the guards lifted the animal & bore it quickly away.

'Well done,' said the prince, smiling down at us. 'Old rites must be respected, friends. The *birthig* is the city's liege-animal. When it kneels to visitors, it is granting leave to enter the city. Symbolically, of course.'

Alyash & I traded looks. What if it hadn't blary knelt?

Then the amazed-looking dlömu with the rings stepped forwards. No smiles from this bloke. 'I am Vadu,' he said, 'Commander of the Plazic Battalion of Masalym, & First Counsellor to His Excellency the Issár. It is with regret that His Excellency does not greet you in person, but he looks forward to receiving you in the Upper City at his first opportunity.'

'That is very good of him,' said Rose. 'And we thank His Excellency for his gift of food. Last night my people ate well.'

The dlömu's head gave one of its bobs. He looked a bit put out, & I noticed a sudden unease among the onlookers. They were drawing back, sharing urgent whispers. And all at once I thought to wonder just who had provided our meal.

Vadu held up his scroll case. He gazed at us severely, as if we should know quite well what it contained. Untying the golden thread, he pulled out the parchment & held it at arm's length. One of the drum-wielding creatures waddled over & stood at his elbow.

I am used to odd & cumbersome ceremonies. The Merchant Service has its share. Anni's family too, when it comes to prayer cycles & whatnot. But none of them could touch the strangeness of the next thirty minutes. Vadu began to read in a flowery dlömic, much less like Arquali than anything we'd heard to date. I'm sure I didn't catch more than half of it – & this despite hearing every word twice. For each time Vadu paused, the drum-bearing creature at his side would inflate his deep chest, tilt his head straight upwards, close his eyes & belly-scream the words to the edge of the city. We winced. The creature was shockingly loud; he set dogs barking far away up lonely streets.

What I did grasp of the message was this: that the Issár, something like the mayor or lord of Masalym, was deeply honoured to preside over the city chosen for a visit by *the people of the Magnificent Court of the Lilac* (that phrase I'm sure about: it was too weird to get wrong). The Issár considered this 'Court' a treasure of the world of Alifros, & the arrival of the ship a reason for bound-less civic pride. There was a great deal next about the Emperor Nahundra, away in Bali Adro City, & his 'welcoming embrace' of all people, everywhere. Mixed up with the 'welcoming embrace' talk was quite a bit about the Plazic Legions of Bali Adro, which he also called the Dark Flame, & how their goodness & virtue had made them a fighting force none could stand against.

The proclamation went on to assure us that his people respected the solemnity of our visit, mindful as they were of its 'celestial significance', & that of course we deserved more than just the rite of the *birthig*-beast. For the Court of the Lilac, nothing but 'the full and sacred ceremony' was enough – at this point Vadu gestured for some reason at the drummers. 'Our mizralds will not disappoint you,' he said.

Finally, the Issár (through his scroll) humbly asked us to speak well of our treatment in Masalym should we ever stand before the Resplendent One in Bali Adro, & swore finally that our privacy would at all times be respected.

'Our privacy?' said Rose.

There were uneasy glances among the dlömu above us. The crowd along the basin's rim was muttering, debating the long declaration. They sounded as sceptical as we were ourselves.

Rose had had enough. 'To the Pits with privacy,' he huffed. 'Our ship is damaged, sir. We are taking on water. In a few days there'll be nothing left for you to look at with civic pride but our topmasts. And one meal cannot make us forget our lack of provisions. We're not beggars. We can pay for both – fairly, and in full. But we must request them without further delay. If you would consent to step aboard—'

'DAAAK?'

The voice was like an explosion. It was one of the drum-creatures again, louder even than before. I can't imagine the word was really meant as a question, unless it was addressed to the Gods above, who surely heard it. Rose stared, affronted; he was not used to being shouted down.

'What the blary—'

'HAAAAAAAAAN!' screamed the other creature, who had waddled up beside the first.

'Prince Olik,' sputtered Rose, 'kindly—'

'DAAAK?' repeated the first creature, adding a *boom* on his drum.

'HAAAAAAAAAN!' replied the other, deafeningly.

The soldiers struck the walkway with their halberds. Vadu & Olik bowed low. Then, as the two creatures stood gazing skywards, drumming & shrieking 'DAAAK? … HAAAAAAAAAN!' to wake the dead, the procession turned & marched away.

Rose started forwards, shouting. Olik glanced once over his shoulder, with a certain gleam in his eye, but moved on with the rest. We swarmed along the rail, shouting at their backs. *Food! Repairs! Where are you going?*

'DAAAK?'

'HAAAAAAAAAN!'

They left us with those screaming monstrosities. We could have scrambled somehow up to the walkway & given chase – but what for? We were inside a walled city in an alien land. A moment later the shore gate was sealed, & a heavy guard placed on it, & more soldiers stationed along the rim of the basin.

A great argument erupted. Taliktrum flew into a rage, declaring that we were obviously being punished collectively for Rose's 'barbaric stupidity' in subjecting Prince Olik to the knife 'as your very first act since being freed from confinement'. Rose to be sure had a ready comeback, & his wrath extended well beyond the ixchel. Why hadn't Bolutu intervened, & why hadn't he warned us that the royal family was a hive of lunatics? When were Pathkendle, Thasha, Hercól & 'the rest of you schemers' going to uncover the lair of the sorcerer? Why had Alyash let the Ibjen youth jump overboard, when he might have served as ransom? And so on, while those two oblivious trolls went on screaming DAAAK? HAAAAAAAAAN! until our minds were addled with it.

I saw Bolutu pulling desperately at Rose's sleeve, & drew close enough to catch what he said. But it just made things weirder: the Court of the Lilac, he shouted, was a colony of albinos, possibly mythical, & many thousands of miles to the east if it existed at all.

'Albino *dlömu*?' bellowed Rose over the din.

Bolutu assured him that was the case. For whatever reason, the Issár believed (or had anyway declared) that we were all dlömus. Just weird, colourless dlömu from unthinkably far away.

'But they've *seen us*,' shouted Undrabust. 'Prince Olik's seen us up close, and so has Ibjen.'

'Hundreds of dlömu on that walkway have seen us as well,' said Hercól, 'but that does not mean the masters of this city will hear them. Sometimes those who wield great power come to believe that wishing a thing were true is enough to make it so: that nature must submit to their will, just as men do.'

'And maybe he's keeping us on the ship, Captain,' I added, 'so that we can't make it plain to the whole city that we *are* human. Just a few hundred of them saw us, after all, and half of them thought we were blary ghosts.'

'What of the frog-things?' demanded Rose.

Bolutu said they were mizralds, 'perfectly respectable citizens', found throughout the Empire & employed (no surprise this) as heralds & criers. The horrid bellowing, he added, was probably a *mechine*, a rite of welcome, though Bolutu had never heard of one being carried on & on.

'They are silencing us,' said Rose, 'and at the same time pretending that we're dlömu.'

'But why should they?' asked Pathkendle.

'Think a moment,' said Thasha. 'It was a disaster for the whole Empire when humans became *tol-chenni*. If we suddenly sail into port and start walking the streets, it could mean ... well, *anything*.'

Pathkendle would not look at her.

'You're right, Thasha,' said Fulbreech. 'That old woman last night thought it was the end of the world.'

'Perhaps a ship full of woken humans could make some think it is the dlömus' turn to become *tol-chenni*,' said Hercól. 'And that *would* be the end of the world, for them. At the very least it may seem a threat to rulers of a frightened city in a time of war.'

All this was just speculation. We were trapped. Nor did the folk of Masalym provide us with another bite of food. They watched us, though, as the hours wore on: contingents of well-dressed dlömu arrived & studied us through scopes & field glasses; there was some argument & finger-pointing, too. Rose tried to signal our desperation, with shouts & flags & spoons rattling in empty bowls. He sent Bolutu to the fighting top with orders to beg loud & long in his own tongue. But the trolls' infernal racket made all these efforts nigh impossible, & it occurred to me that this was, perhaps, the whole idea.

The water in the hold reached thirteen feet. Of course, we were pumping like mad, as we'd done for the last three days. But Rose was right: it was not going to be enough. And what if they have no means of beaching us, or no real will to try?

Mid-afternoon, it rained. To our infinite delight the trolls ('mizralds', Bolutu confirms) scurried indoors. But we were still hungry, & the dlömu were still deaf to our pleas. We officers took refuge in our duties. For me that included breaking up a fight between the rival gangs (the issue was a hoarded slab of last night's cheese), & getting the broken-nosed Plapp & split-lipped Burnscove Boy to shake & agree to donate the precious morsel to the steerage passengers. When the lads saw those hopeless faces, I declare they knew a moment's shame. But they were glowering at each other before we parted.

There was walrus oil left in my lamp, so I veered off to check the seams along the starboard hull. Seepage at the waterline, of course. I scratched at the oakum with my knife. *Neglect, neglect*: the word tapped at my thoughts like a luffing sail.

I was on my knees in the carpenter's tool room when I heard the door behind me close.

I spun around. Facing me stood Lord Taliktrum. He was quite alone, & breathing hard from the exertion of shutting the door.

He had his sword drawn & a leather sack tied over his shoulder. He was still wearing his swallow-suit.

Hatred for the little tyrant welled up in me. I could have killed him then & there, merely by straightening my right leg & crushing him between the door & my boot. In another life – a life in which I'd never known Diadrelu – I would have.

'Quartermaster,' he said, grimacing to bend his voice. 'I must speak to you. It has been tremendously difficult to catch you alone.'

'Most folk just barge into my cabin,' I said.

He untied the sack & let it fall. Then he sheathed his sword. 'I did not draw my blade to threaten you,' he said. 'There was a scrabbling noise in the passageway. I am surprised you did not hear it.'

'Mice,' I said. 'The rats are well and truly dead.'

He watched me, dubious. 'Your position is unique on this ship,' he said at last. 'Alone of all the officers, you're an ally of the Pathkendle clan.'

I said nothing. He'd have a reason for naming us a *clan*. I doubted it was a reason I'd care for.

'Among ixchel,' he went on, 'when two clans' territories overlap, it becomes vital that they know each other, lest they compete and cause each other harm. As a first step, the clans send two elders to a safe house, and the elders play a game. We call it duelling with trust.'

'I don't care what you call it,' I told him. 'I don't speak for Pathkendle or Thasha or any of them. And you're sure as snake-eyes no elder.'

'I am more than that,' he said. 'I am the bearer of visions, and of my people's fate.' He spoke gruffly, sticking out his chin, as though desperate that someone believe him. That someone wasn't me, I think.

He untied the sack & spread it open on the floor. It held coins: four coins, which he lifted out in a stack. They were common Arquali tender: two copper whelks, two fine gold cockles. Then he reached into the sack again & brought out two pearls.

I couldn't help it: I whistled. They were the famous blue pearls of Sollochstol, each the size of a cherry. 'You took those from the hoard we're carrying,' I accused.

'We did not,' said Taliktrum. 'The pearls in the hoard are not so fine as ours, though there are crates of them. We carry these, the Tears of Iryg, as a measure of security, for we know what you giants are willing to do for them. We are not above bribery, when cornered. But I have not come here to offer a bribe.

'The game is simple,' he said. 'The elders take turns. One shares a secret of his clan; the other responds with a secret from his own. And if either believes that the other has told a lie, the game is over. The clans remain strangers, and wary. There is no friendship between them, and they may even come to blows.

'The goal is a perfect exchange: I leave with your three gifts, you leave with mine.'

He bent down & rolled one of the pearls towards me across the floor. I pounced on it, afraid it would vanish through a crack. It felt heavy in my hand. Back in Etherhorde, that pearl would be worth a small fortune – worth all the debt Anni's family was in, perhaps. But then I considered the odds of seeing my Annabel again in this life, & felt like tossing the thing away.

Taliktrum slid two coins in my direction as well. 'The copper will stand for a secret of moderate worth. The gold, a more valuable secret. And the pearl – that is the secret that makes the game worth playing. You give the simplest gift first. Then, building on trust, the more valuable. Last of all, the pearl: a secret that it pains you to give. Among us, that might be the password that opens our house to strangers, or the location of unguarded food.'

'When your elders play this daft game, what's to stop them from lying through their teeth?'

'Honour,' said Taliktrum. 'But not honour alone. The key to a successful duel is this: that neither side agrees to play until they have spied on the other clan for a sufficient time. We are excellent spies, Mr Fiffengurt.'

'Hats off to you. But I'm not interested in crawly games. First, because I wouldn't share the secret of a good cup of tea with the man who'd drug a ship's crew in the middle of the Nelluroq. Second, because I don't know anything that could possibly—'

'The prisoners will soon begin to die,' he said.

I drew a shaky breath. 'You cur.'

'This is not blackmail,' he added swiftly. 'Fiffengurt, we are running out of the berries that keep them alive. During the battle with the rats half our stockpile was destroyed. In the forecastle house, we burn two ounces per day: any less and the prisoners will not have enough vapour to breathe. They will crowd around the smudge-pot, fighting each other. Those pushed to the margins will suffocate, after great pain.'

'How much do you have left?' I asked, heart in my throat.

But Taliktrum shook his head. He tossed his copper coin my way.

'Aha,' I said. 'We're playing already, is that it?' Still he did not speak. I thought again about my right foot. But instead of murdering him I asked what he wanted to know.

That caught him off guard. He chewed his lip a moment, then said, 'The old witch, Oggosk. Is she Rose's mother?'

'*What?*' I nearly shouted. 'You're the most twisted nail on this blary ship! Where'd you get that notion?'

'By watching them. We keep the forecastle house under the closest scrutiny, for obvious reasons. The witch doted on him, when they were imprisoned together. She would comb out his beard – in the dark, when they thought no one saw. And she has a superior knowledge of Rose's family, his childhood, although he tries to prevent her from speaking of it. And there are those insane letters he dictates – addressed always to his father, but with a respectful nod to his mother – although everything we learned of Rose before the voyage suggested they were dead.'

I shut my mouth. He knew more than I did. But why did he care what Oggosk was to Rose, or Rose to Oggosk? How could it possibly matter? Unless—

I went suddenly cold. *Unless they're trying to reckon who Rose will fight for, and who he'll allow to die.*

'You've sailed with him before,' Taliktrum was saying. 'You've sat through more meals with him than anyone aboard, except the witch herself. Wasn't she always along on those voyages? Did they *never* reveal the truth?'

I'd quit my gambling years ago as a promise to Annabel – & to stop her dad from quoting Rule Thirty each time we met.* But the old instincts came back to me in a flash. You don't reveal what you know, & even less what you *don't* know. Mind your voice, mind your eyes. Starve the opponent for knowledge any way you can. That was *my* kind of duelling.

'Rose had no use for family stories,' I said, 'no matter how long a voyage we were on. I couldn't rightly say.'

'He found a use for such stories when he was our prisoner,' said Taliktrum. 'Never mind: it is still your turn.'

When I sat there, stone-faced, he added spitefully, 'This was an invitation. No one is forcing your hand. But if you refuse me, or attempt to fob me off with a lie, you are spurning a chance that will not come again. Think, man. Help me help us both.'

'Help you to do *what?*'

'What do you think?' he snapped. 'To save us all from evil. Your people and mine. What else can we hope for, at this stage?'

'You're hoping for a *great* deal more,' I growled. 'You're hoping—'

I stopped myself. I'd almost said, *You're hoping this voyage ends*

---

* Rule Thirty of the Ninety Rules of the Rinfaith: 'What a man cannot afford to lose at dice should not be wagered; what he can should be given to those in need. Thus the man of virtue wallows not in sordid games.' Younger monks of the Rinfaith (starting with Artus in 916) labelled this one of the 'Killjoy Rules', and it is likely that Fiffengurt was aware of this noisy minority. Artus claims further that 'sordid games' is a wilful mistranslation, and indeed the original Ullumaic is closer to 'addiction to risk'. Artus published his suggestions for a gentler, more loving Ninety Rules in a treatise entitled *When Rin Sees Us, Does He Smile?* Days after its publication the man was expelled from the Brotherhood of Serenity; his house was also mysteriously burned down, and his dog pelted with eggs by fellow monks who thought themselves unobserved. – EDITOR.

on Sanctuary, your island; you'll do anything to get there. But that would be breaking my own rules. Besides, I didn't really know. That old yarn, the ixchels' Sanctuary-Beyond-the-Sea, was just a suspicion I'd nursed since I learned his people were aboard. 'You're hoping I'll betray my friends,' I ended vaguely.

He just looked at me. 'Are we finished? Are you so unable to give?'

I closed my eyes. He was right, I *did* want to play. I wanted to take something back to my friends, something they could use. But I wasn't going to get it for free.

'Thasha has a book—' I began.

'The thirteenth *Polylex*,' he interrupted. 'We've been aware of that for months; so has everyone aboard who knows what the thirteenth edition means. That won't do, Fiffengurt. Try again.'

I was on unsafe ground. This was a delicate business, handing knowledge to Taliktrum – a fool & a proven killer. This was the wretch who'd spiked our water with a sleeping drug, after all.

But he'd also fought the sorcerer with commendable courage.

'Pazel,' I heard myself say, very softly, 'has just one Master-Word left, and I don't think it will be any use in a battle. It's a word that *blinds to give new sight*. We haven't a clue what that means, but Ramachni chose the word especially for him, so it must be worth something. Will that do?'

Taliktrum nodded slowly. I tossed him a copper whelk: we were matched again. Then he said, 'We have seen the mage – name him not; he has sharp ears for the sound of his own name! – walking of late on the mercy deck. He appears without warning, and slips quickly away. We have been unable to follow him to his lair – but he has killed five of our guards.'

'You little bastard,' I hissed, furious now. 'You mucking *swore* he wasn't in your part of the ship.'

'Nor is he!' said Taliktrum. 'There is not a chamber, not a crevice or a crate, that we have not explored. He has not made his lair in the lower decks, I say. He has merely passed through them like a shadow, gazing upwards, as though to pierce the floorboards with his eyes.'

'Up at the Nilstone,' I ventured.

'Of course,' he said, & tossed his golden coin my way. 'Your turn again.'

I took a deep breath. 'Hercól's sword—'

'Is called Ildraquin, Earthblood, Breaker of Curses,' he said. 'Put in his hand by Maisa, the deposed Empress of Arqual, whose children Hercól murdered when still in the pay of Sandor Ott.'

His bad news was beginning to feel like a hammer striking my skull. 'Stanapeth?' I said dumbly. 'Hercól Stanapeth killed Maisa's children? *Personally?*'

'Impersonally, I would imagine. Go on, you must find a better secret.'

'It's not my blary fault,' I said. 'You've spied out everything I know.'

'If that were true we would not be playing,' said Taliktrum.

My stomach was in knots. What was I doing? I could betray them all with my urgency to help. Then in a flash it came to me. 'Sniraga's alive,' I said. 'Undrabust and Marila both swear they saw her on the upper gun deck.'

He didn't take the news well. The cat was particularly hated by the ixchel; apparently she had eaten a few. 'We should have fed that creature poison the day Oggosk brought it aboard,' he said. 'My father wanted to. My aunt disagreed. She argued the witch would guess that ixchel had done it. But in truth it was just her softness, again. Dri always blinked when the moment came to kill.'

'If she argued against poisoning a pussycat, it was for a good reason,' I said. 'Your aunt never cared for anything, not even Hercól, as much as she did your clan.'

He snorted: 'What rubbish is that? She chose him – chose all of you, and turned her back on her people.'

'She was ready to kill herself, Taliktrum. She told Stanapeth she'd rather die than see the clan break into factions, some with you, others with her.'

'Anyone can make such a boast,' he replied.

'You'll believe what you want to,' I said, & tossed him my gold coin. 'All the same, it's your turn.'

He set the pearl on the floor & turned his back, hands in fists. This talk of Diadrelu had rattled him. Still burning with guilt, I imagined, as well he should be. When he looked at me again his face was a mask.

He set his foot on the pearl. 'If you take this and depart, sharing nothing, I will be your enemy for ever.'

'I'm no cheat, Taliktrum.'

He kicked the pearl in my direction. Then he said, 'I am leaving.'

'What?'

'Leaving the ship. My people, the clan, everyone. I am going ashore, tonight. I . . . I cannot wait.'

'You don't mean that.'

'After I leave this room, I will return to my people's stronghold one last time. I will write a letter telling them that I have gone ahead of them, to the land we are destined to repossess, and that they must follow Lord Talag once more, until we are all reunited—' he laughed miserably '—in paradise. Then I'll slip ashore. The cables around the ship are many. I'll have no difficulty there.'

'Taliktrum, stop. You're their commander.'

'I am their demigod,' he said, with acid on his tongue. 'My soldiers are carving little statues of me, and carrying them about like idols. Two brothers fought yesterday over which of them I favoured more, and one stabbed the other in the leg. A woman came to me tonight and said that our ancestors had told her she was to have my child. They are insatiable, Fiffengurt. And I am the one who made them that way.' He put his hands in his hair. 'This cult of He-Who-Sees. It should be *He-Who-Is-Seen* – seen, followed, imitated, aped. I live in a prison, a prison of their adoring eyes. You cannot imagine what it took to elude them long enough to come here.'

'But you'll be all alone, man! You don't even know if crawlies – if ixchel *exist* in this part of the world.'

'Unless they have gone the way of human beings, they exist. We came from this side of the Nelluroq, you fool.'

'Ixchel came . . . from the South?'

'Centuries ago. In human ships, human cages.' He paused, suddenly struck. 'Do you mean that Diadrelu did not even tell you why our people boarded *Chathrand*?'

I shook my head. 'There were things she never would talk about. She wasn't a traitor, I tell you.'

He was shocked. It was a long time before he found his voice. 'There is a traitor in our midst today, however,' he said at last. 'The person who switched the antidote pills.'

'Do you have an idea who that person is?' I asked.

'I know who he is with a certainty,' said Taliktrum, 'because that person is me.'

I gaped at him. Taliktrum smiled, but it was a smile of self-loathing. 'Once a person takes the antidote,' he said, 'the least whiff of the poison vapour warns them off. The captain, Undrabust and Marila would have balked at the door of the forecastle house, even if Rose had not guessed that they were cured. I did not release them as a humanitarian act. Hercól's suggestion merely gave me an excuse to thin the ranks of the hostages, thus buying us a few more days. But I was clumsy. I should have foreseen that Oggosk might give her pill to the captain. He and Sandor Ott were never, under any circumstances, to be freed.'

That didn't surprise me. 'So, you've made some mistakes,' I said, 'and now you're running away from them.'

'Now I am accepting the consequences,' he said. 'There is no other path for me. *We are the rose that prunes itself*: so states a motto of my people. And it is the simple truth. When an ixchel knows that his presence in a clan is irredeemably harmful, he must choose exile, or death. But I wanted someone to know the truth about me – that I did this not for the clan, but for myself. I cannot tell anyone of Ixphir House, for like divided leadership, the truth would destroy them.'

'Are you so sure of that?'

He ignored my question. 'My father promised to take them to paradise,' he said, 'to Sanctuary-Beyond-the-Sea. I do not believe they will ever arrive.'

'Not on this boat,' I agreed.

'But if that day should somehow dawn, when the swallows come for my people, tell Lord Talag before he departs. Tell him he was wrong to break my flute across his knee. Can you remember that?'

I nodded slowly. 'I'll remember. But you should tell him that yourself, you coward. Running away's no good.'

'Neither is talking. Some problems can't be solved.'

'What about your woman?'

'Who, Myett?' He looked genuinely surprised. 'That girl was . . . an entertainment. A prophet's plaything, though my father thinks all prophets should be like those of old, chaste and ragged.'

'She's lovely,' I ventured.

At that he glared, as if to say, *Not you as well.* 'She makes a spectacle of her charms – such charms as she possesses. No, Myett was never a suitable match. She is unstable. She took to following me, picking fights with any woman I chanced to look at. My father even thought she might have been the one who switched the antidotes.'

'I'll bet you played along,' I said (his woman problems were intensely irritating). 'You'd probably even accuse her of the crime, although you did it yourself.'

'I would,' he said without hesitation, 'if I determined that to do so was for the good of the clan.'

'If you were my size I'd fight you here and now,' I said. 'It's blary unforgivable. You'd make love to her one day and destroy her the next.'

'Unforgivable?' The familiar, belligerent gleam was back in his eyes. 'The game isn't over, Fiffengurt. You hold both pearls. You must give me a secret to match my own. Do not speak! I will tell you the secret I want.'

He crossed the tool room – & leaped in one swift movement onto a sawhorse, so that our eyes were on the same level. 'Here is what I would know, Fiffengurt: can you choose between life and death?'

'What in the Pits does that mean?'

'We cannot keep all the hostages alive. Some will die. All will die eventually, if they remain in the forecastle house. But I am willing to free two more tonight. Not the spymaster or his protégé, Dastu: they are simply too dangerous. And not the witch. Even if she is not Rose's mother, he loves her. That makes her too precious to give up, now that Rose himself walks free.

'Two more, then. Name your choices, and I will send my Dawn Soldiers to deliver the antidote this evening – my last act as commander. But *you* must decide who is to be saved. Doctor Chadfallow, surely? Or perhaps the two gang leaders, on the condition that they swear a truce? Or Elkstem, your sailmaster, the man whose hand on the wheel has saved the ship more than once already? Or the remaining tarboy, Saroo, with so many years to live?'

I couldn't believe my ears. 'You swine,' I said.

'Of course, an ixchel would never choose the tarboy,' he went on. 'The question of who might *deserve* life the most never occupies our thoughts as deeply as that of who is the most *useful*. If you look at things our way, you might do best to free the pair of soldiers. Their return would improve morale for the entire battalion.'

'You can take a leap off those cliffs,' I said. 'I don't make choices like that.'

'You don't, because you have not had to,' he said. 'Name them, Fiffengurt. Otherwise I will free no one at all.'

I slammed both pearls down beside him. 'Not a chance. You're the monsters who took 'em in the first place.'

'Rose would have killed us if I hadn't. Now I'm willing to reduce our advantage, and you will not even choose?'

'I can't, and I won't. It's inhuman.'

I must have been screaming. In the passage, two or three anxious men called my name, clearly afraid I was in danger. I wrenched open the door & yelled at them to keep their distance. When

I turned back to the room I could not see Taliktrum or his pearls.

'What if you had enough antidote for them all?'

His voice came from near the ceiling. I looked up but could not spot him on any of the shelves or cabinets.

'That's a stupid question, ain't it?' I snapped. 'I'd free every one of them.'

'And guarantee that my people would be hunted down, murdered, exterminated in a matter of hours?'

'Pitfire,' I sputtered. 'Not ... necessarily. I don't hate you – I mean, I haven't blary thought about it!'

'*We* have thought about it, Mr Fiffengurt,' he said. 'Never fear; I gave the order before I came looking for you. The doctor & the sailmaster are already free. Listen, you can hear them shouting.'

And it was true, when I fell silent: high above, & at the other end of the *Chathrand*, I could just catch the cries: *Chadfallow! Elkstem! Hurrah!*

'Then why'd you put me through all this, damn you?' I shouted.

As if in answer, something bounced off a high shelf & fell towards my chest. I caught it: Taliktrum's pearl.

His laughter mocked me from above. '*Not necessarily*, you say. And I'd hoped to hear it straight from a giant's mouth, just this once: either *Yes, I would kill you all*. Or *No, I would fight for your people even against my own*. The way my aunt did, Fiffengurt. But of course, you haven't thought about it. Goodbye.'

There was a slight scraping noise in an upper corner. He's slipping out some rathole or secret door, I thought. On an impulse, I called out, 'Lord Taliktrum?'

The scraping stopped.

'Diadrelu was only going to kill herself if she was *certain it was best for the clan*. Not because something wounded her heart, or pained her personally. Although many things did. You understand?'

Silence. I cleared my throat & went on: 'You're not selfish, you little people. You're better than us in that respect. Don't be selfish about your pain, man. Go, if you have to. Run away from your cult, or from your old man. But don't write any letter swearing you won't be back. Tell them you're off – following a vision or whatnot. Surely it's better for 'em to have someone they can go on believing in? And I'll tell you this as well: I've done some running in my time. All sailors have. But if you live long enough you'll find that most of us are running in circles.'

Taliktrum said nothing & there was no more noise from above. I suppose I'll never know if he heard my advice. But as I sat there, listening to the cheers grow louder, it occurred to me for the very first time that Taliktrum was an Etherhorder, like me.

I am exhausted; the lamp is sputtering out. I wonder where he has gone in this alien city. Rin keep him, the little tyrant, first of us to abandon *Chathrand* of his own free will.

15

Myett Alone

‑‑‑‑‑

27 Ilbrin 941
226th day from Etherhorde

You'd probably even accuse her of the crime, although you did it your-self . . . you'd make love to her one day and destroy her the next.

She lay in a darkness so deep not even ixchel eyes could pierce it. Somewhere in the bilge-well, under the ancient floorboards of the hold. On her back, floating in the filth. It had taken determination even for an ixchel to reach this place.

She is unstable. She took to following me . . .

The water, like the ship, was still: there were no tides or waves in the basin to make it slosh about. Yet it was rising quickly. When her ears slipped underwater she could actually hear the bubbling of displaced air. The water should have been even fouler, here in the rank bottom of the boat, the place all the slop and slime washed down to. But so much of the water was new, fresh from the crystalline Gulf and the cold, gushing river that flowed through Masalym.

Had she lost the wineskin? No, here it was about her neck. She turned her head to the side and drank an ample throatful. *An entertainment. A prophet's plaything.*

Already she could touch the boards above her, when she raised her hand. She imagined the wound in the hull. Poor *Chathrand*, stabbed in the darkness by a fellow ship. Wound a body and it bleeds. Wound a ship and it turns to drink, and never stops.

Yes, she had followed him. But not from jealousy – not that

alone. She had feared for him, feared the demons in his eyes, the agony his father dismissed as mere fatigue. She had been born to fight those demons, protect those eyes. She had been raised with a ravenous addiction, like the children born to deathsmokers, slaves to something heartless before they even learned to speak. All her life she had searched for it, her deathsmoke, the balm for her wound. In Auxlei City, Emledri, Sorrophran, Besq. And one day her grandfather had opened a service door in the Assembly Hall and said, 'Look: that is the young man sent from Etherhorde by his father, seeking crew for an assault on the Great Ship. We will dine with him tonight; so comb your hair, and be pleasant.'

She had thought him strange and severe, bickering with his elders, stabbing at a hull diagram spread out on a table. *We enter here. We will hold this space.* Then the young lord had glanced up and noticed her, and studied her young body frankly, and she had made herself walk away from the door with her chin high and her face indifferent, as though he were the needy one, as though his gaze had not gone through her like a spear, and three weeks later she was his lover on the *Chathrand*.

The water raised her to within a foot of the boards. She drank again, then slid the lanyard of the wineskin over her shoulder and pushed it away. No one had seen her. No one knew that she had not fled with him, had not been invited − had not even been dismissed. He had not thought it necessary to dismiss her before abandoning the ship; one did not dismiss a toy.

But this toy had tracked him last night all the same.

She had tracked him to the secret place, the masterfully hidden door in the ceiling above the scrap-metals storeroom, beyond which the House Treasures were stored in a strongbox bolted to the inner plank. There were ixchel guards within twenty feet, port and starboard, fore and aft, guarding every known approach to this area, but even they did not know precisely where the strongbox stood. And none of them knew about the door.

She had watched him open the box with the key around his

neck, stared in amazement as he set aside the ancient Cyrak Tapestries from the main hall of Ixphir House, the last vials of the *blanë* sleep drug, the sacred swallow-bones with which the flying suits could be repaired. He kissed the urn that held the ashes of his great-grandmother Deijanka, the saint. Then he took out the waxed-cotton bundle that held the antidote pills and broke the seal. Myett held her breath as he extracted two of the big white pills, cradling them in his arm as he sealed the bundle anew. He returned everything but these two pills to the strongbox, locked it – and after a moment's hesitation, slipped the key from around his neck and wedged it securely beneath the box.

That last act had mystified her. Better than anyone (she *hoped* it was better than anyone) Myett knew how he refused to be parted from that key. Night after carnal night it had hung between them, crushed against her breast, striking her chin in time with his soft sounds of ecstasy. Only he and Talag and Ludunte, the clan-appointed Treasurer, had keys to the strongbox. Why in the Pits would Taliktrum leave his behind?

She was bumping the ceiling now. Her nose, her knees. The air that remained was close and stale.

And in her addict's haze she had imagined that he was going to meet a lover. She had thought herself that important: that Lord Taliktrum would take pains to deceive her, to spare her feelings when he hungered for another's touch. But all the same she could not stop following him.

She had tracked him all the way to the tool room. He had heard her only once, and not bothered to investigate, thinking he heard a mouse or beetle. To be so close to him, alone one final time, and be mistaken for vermin.

Then Fiffengurt had stomped and blundered into the room, and the horrible words had spilled out. *Myett was never suitable*. It had been tempting to kill the quartermaster, since she could not kill her lord. Something had to die, of course. After words like that, something always did.

She could no longer float. She was treading water, pressing her lips above the surface, into the last inch of air. Was that the ship's bell, was it morning? No matter. This was the place that morning never touched.

She makes a spectacle of her charms.

No one would find her here.

16

Farewell to a Dream

~~~

The rain was gone and the sun had banished the morning chill when Prince Olik returned to the Masalym shipyard. His arrival, like his departure, was sudden and unceremonious: he fairly ran out along the walkway, fifty feet ahead of his attendants and guards. Even before he came abreast of the midship rail, he was calling loudly for permission to board. Captain Rose was duly notified, and without issuing a response of any kind he marched out to face the prince.

'You may not board,' he said, 'until you are prepared to inform me when my crew is to be fed, and whether or not the city means to help us save the ship.'

The prince stopped short; evidently he had thought the asking of permission no more than a formal ritual. 'I see – well, it doesn't matter,' he said distractedly. 'I'll just – walk.'

He proceeded to do just that, marching back the way he came, waving his entourage into an about-face even as they closed on him. Dumbfounded, Rose and his crew watched him go. 'Mad as a drunkard poet,' was Mr Fiffengurt's verdict. Then the watchman relayed an observation from the quarterdeck: the water in the basin had once more started to rise.

It was true: some further sluice-gate must have been closed, for the river was filling the basin (and lifting the *Chathrand*) at a rate of four inches a minute, as measured against the walkway.

Then the criss-crossed ropes that had kept the ship bobbing in place went slack, and sank under the water. From the north side of the basin, two small rowing craft approached the ship, dragging new cables. These were duly offered by the silent dlömu, who indicated with gestures that they should be attached to the port and starboard catheads. After some hesitation, Rose so ordered.

No sooner were the lines secured than they grew taut, lifting out of the water and turning *Chathrand* gently in place. Slowly and smoothly, they guided her across the basin.

What followed was surprisingly simple. The tow lines, it soon became clear, were guiding the *Chathrand* towards one of the rectangular berths they had spotted the first night, along a part of the basin's rim. These were long, squared-off tongues of water, lined with cargo cranes, loading platforms, watchtowers and buildings that might have been warehouses, or army barracks. The *Chathrand* was moving towards the largest of these berths.

Like a great beast being coaxed into a stable, the ship glided into the enclosure. Now the crew could perceive a pair of enormous capstans revolving on the quay. Dozens of horses, short of stature but muscled like elephants, strained at their harnesses to turn the great devices, while small dogs moved among them with short, precise dashes and darts, yipping, coaxing. The dlömu themselves seemed barely involved. But at the very last, they stepped among the working animals and eased the ship into position with exceeding care. It was a good fit: when she came to rest it was plain that the *Chathrand* was only some forty feet shorter than the berth itself.

More ropes were tossed to the humans, fore and aft. When these were secured the dlömu nudged the ship's bow back and forth, checking her alignment against grooves carved into the stone. At last the *Chathrand* was truly still. Shouts of *Squared off, let fall!* went up from the dlömu. A deep vibration troubled the basin's surface. And then the water level began to drop once more.

It fell far more quickly than it had risen. In twenty minutes, the *Chathrand* descended forty feet. In another twenty, they saw heavy structures of some kind beneath the water. 'Merciful heavens, it's a buildframe!' shouted Mr Fegin, dangling from the futtock shrouds and suddenly boyish with delight. 'Can't ye see what they're doing, Captain? They're lowering us straight into dry dock, by damn!'

The water continued to drop, and beneath them a great V-shaped armature of wood and steel came into view, and the *Chathrand* settled into it with all the dignity of her six hundred years. The outer hull of rock maple groaned as the supporting water drained away from her sides; the long timbers of m'xingu and cloudcore oak strained and shuddered, but held. On the topdeck the crew gave a great, spontaneous cheer. They were on dry land, or over it. For some it had been more than two hundred days.

The pumps clattered on: no one would dream of stepping away from that life-saving chore without permission. But already the water jetting from them was splashing down upon bare stone. Mr Uskins sent word to the captain: barring outside interference, the ship could be pumped empty by midday.

There were staircases cut into the walls of the berth, and the dlömu were already descending, studying the hull, nodding and pointing. But they still said not a word to the humans. *They're under orders*, thought Pazel. *They must think we're terribly dangerous. But we're not, are we?*

In the darkness of the bilge-well, Myett stood dripping and cold. The air reeked, and the wine was still very strong in her blood. She heard the far-off cheering and thought it cruel. Her death had been stolen. Her lord was gone and her love defiled, but she remained. Though she had come here to die an ugly death she stood unharmed, and the whole ship found this amusing. She was here to amuse. She always had been.

She crawled through the nameless, poisonous muck. Out through crevices, rat-gnawed boards, a long pile of stone ballast, algae-slick. When she reached the hold she heard her people's voices in the distance. She moved away from them, silent, un-suspected.

It occurred to her dimly that no one would wonder at her

absence. They would assume she had gone after him. Whenever she chose to let herself be seen, she could tell them that she had done just that. No dishonour, that way, no confinement, chained at wrist and ankle, like others who tried suicide and failed.

Unless he had denounced her.

Suddenly she could almost hear the letter: *Nothing to me. Unsuitable from the start.* Could he have gone so far? How should she know? It was useless to pretend that she could guess, now that she understood how little she had ever known him at all.

To be missing, but not missed ... it was strangely appealing to be answerable to no one (that is the wine, the wine and the chill you took, do not trust it, do not follow your whim). She had no clan duties, for she had no clan. She had no promise to keep to herself. What self? Only her nose and lips had stayed dry. Everything else had been submerged in death.

The Dremland Spirit! That was what she had become. Myett smiled at the thought of the woman from the children's tale (stop thinking, stop crying, go somewhere and sleep) whose people, husband included, had let her die out of cowardice. They had been gathering shellfish at low tide; the woman had fallen and broken her leg. And though they could hear her calling to them in the fog, they told themselves that it was too late, the tide already turning, and they stole away and left her to drown.

But after midnight, back in the safety of the clan house, the woman's cries had resumed, ethereal and cold. *Here I am! Your clan-sister, your wife! I'll not be abandoned again!*

Myett scaled the inner hull, past the catwalks, seeking the ixchel door that gave entrance to the mercy deck. Taliktrum had admitted to a fondness for ghost stories. He had trusted her that much (only briefly, don't start lying now, only in those minutes while you waited for his body's appetite to build). *They chill my blood*, he'd whispered once, sharing a secret grin. *Can you keep that to yourself, my little guardian?*

How did the story end? With the moan growing louder and louder, putting all the clan in danger. First the mice and burrowing creatures heard it, then surface animals, the prowling street dogs, the cats. Finally the giants themselves began to hear the ghost. What could be done? Myett's grandfather would have known the right sort of penance, the act of contrition that a ghost would accept. But in the tale, the foolish clan heaped all the blame on the husband, and threw him into the sea at the place where his wife had perished. Monsters, murdering fools! Couldn't they see that the woman had actually loved him? That she might love him still? They had earned their final punishment; they had begged for it.

The hidden door-latch opened to her fingers. She crawled into the mercy deck and wandered aft, leaving the secret door ajar. Past the empty rice barrels, the swept-out bread room, the brig where guards stood exclaiming to their prisoners: *Them fish-eyes have shipwrights underneath us already! They're going to fix this old boat after all!*

The Mzithrini girl, Neda, looked out through her prison bars and saw her plainly. But that did not matter. All crawlies look the same in the shadows, don't they? And besides, no one listens to the enemy.

Minutes later she was teasing open another door: above the scrap-metals storeroom. The strongbox lay bolted in place, and wedged beneath it, Taliktrum's key. She pried it out and laid it on her palm. How it had hurt, with all his weight pressing down. It had always been between them, a witness to his hunger, her addiction; a painful proof that she would never get closer than his skin.

They had driven him away. With their worship, their torturous need. They had exiled him to a city of dark giants, a city without Houses, without safety. He might already have met his death.

He'd been tender with her. More than once. But their worship had made his love impossible.

She opened the box, set the other treasures aside, took out all the remaining antidote. She would give the clan what it had earned. No one could stop her. No law applied to a woman who had ceased to exist.

The dlömu erected a stone oven on the quayside, and kindled a fire within. Soon a sweet-smelling woodsmoke drifted over the *Chathrand*. Then carts began to arrive, some drawn by stout little horses, others by dogs. Crowds of workers assembled around these carts, making it difficult to see what they contained. Then someone scurried up to the fighting top and gave a shout: 'Food, food! And loads of it, by the Tree! Bless them fish-eyes, they're going to feed us at last!'

It began with sausage, seared to bursting on the open flames, and ample servings of thick-skinned tubers. The hot food was placed in baskets like those of the first night, and the baskets were placed on hooks at the end of long poles and swung gingerly over the chasm to the *Chathrand*'s quarterdeck. Even as they passed out the food, the dlömu kept silent, although the humans and ixchel thanked them with great feeling. Still, as he watched the orderly business unfold, Pazel caught smiles, and even an occasional wink of a silver eye. They were covert, those looks. The dlömu were hiding their kindness, but less from the humans than from one another.

Pazel mentioned the looks to Neeps. 'You see? These blokes aren't unfriendly – at least no more than they were that first night. They're afraid of us, sure. But this not-talking business: it's coming from somewhere else. I'd bet my right foot they've been *ordered* not to speak.'

'Maybe,' said Neeps, watching the baskets collect on the quarterdeck. 'Or maybe it's spreading, that old woman's idea about us bringing the end of the world. Maybe they even think we have a *choice* about it. "Treat us nice, see, or die in storms of fire."'

After the sausage came pies – round, glistening, stuffed with meat and curious vegetables and aromatic herbs. Rose fed his men in reverse order of rank: tarboys and ordinary seamen first, then rated sailors, Turachs, petty officers, lieutenants. The senior officers waited stoically: they had known all along that they would be last. Rose was merely applying the Sailing Code, and most of them knew the wisdom of the old law. Nothing would break a crew's loyalty faster than injustice with food.

But there was no shortage. Fresh bread followed, and olives cured in wine, and small cuts of fish wrapped in aromatic leaves, and a second round of pies stuffed with sweet orange tubers and sprinkled with a spice that tasted like nutmeg and liquorice at once and yet was neither. There was no shortage. They ate and they ate. Mr Bolutu sat with his back to a hatchcomb, using both hands, and Pazel saw tears in his eyes.

Twenty years since he tasted his people's food, he thought. And suddenly he wondered if he would ever again bite into an Ormali plum.

For a time the *Chathrand* was a happy ship. The tarboys sang a tarboy shanty, but collapsed in disarray before the obscene punchline (even this was more than they had ever dared in Rose's presence). The steerage passengers wolfed down everything they were given. The door of the forecastle house was opened just long enough for five baskets to be slid within, and all who stood near heard Lady Oggosk's delighted cackle. When the dlömu sent over boxes of sticky *mül* as a final offering, the sailors even managed to finish a few out of politeness, though no one had yet explained what they were.

Hercól brought Felthrup, Jorl and Suzyt to the topdeck, tied the dogs to a steel deadeye and brought them bread and fish. The dogs ate. Felthrup sat snug by Thasha's knee, and ate. Deep in the ship, someone managed to wake the augrongs; their groans of monstrous satisfaction made the dlömu freeze, and the humans laugh.

Even the ixchel celebrated, in their way. They were in shock over Taliktrum's disappearance (the rumours had escaped already, and sprouted hydra-heads: *He's a runaway, a coward*, some said, and others, *He's off talking with the lord of the dlömu. He and Talag planned it all from the start*) but they still had appetites. They ate well, but in shifts, guarding one another as ixchel always did at mealtimes. Only Ensyl ate alone, not quite joining the humans but shunned by her people.

Pazel, Neeps and Marila sat in a crowd of tarboys near the spankermast. Marila made little chirping sounds of happiness as she chewed her fish. Neeps dipped morsels of bread in the juice from the meat pies, grinning as he popped each one into his mouth. Overhead, the dlömu watched in fascination, murmuring and occasionally pointing.

'Feeding time at the zoo,' said Marila, glancing up at them.

Neeps frowned at her. 'There's a cheery thought. What put that into your head?'

'The way you eat,' said Marila.

The tarboys laughed, and so did Pazel, for there was nothing mean or cutting in the other boys' voices: they appeared ready, for the moment anyway, to let Pazel and Neeps back into their fold. *About blary time*, he thought.

Then he saw Thasha a short distance away, eating olives from Fulbreech's hand. She was turned away and did not see him – but Fulbreech did, and raised an eyebrow in his direction, a wry salute.

Rage went through Pazel, sudden and murderous. He turned away with the remains of his meal. And found himself facing Ignus Chadfallow.

'Hello,' said Pazel, not very warmly.

Captivity had aged the doctor. His craggy face was stained with soot that no amount of washing had yet been able to remove. His deep-set eyes shone with a new, more desperate fervour. The nose Pazel had broken on Bramian had healed with a subtle clockwise twist.

'I've been looking for you since yesterday, Pazel,' he said at last. 'Why have you been avoiding me?'

Pazel shrugged. 'I'm here now,' he said.

They had crossed paths twice since the doctor gained his freedom. Both times Pazel had hurried by, mumbling about his duties. He had no desire to be cornered and questioned by the man.

'You should eat less sausage, more fish and greens,' said the doctor. Neeps slid a whole sausage into his mouth.

Pazel scowled. 'What is it you want, Ignus? Missed trying out drugs on me?'

'May I sit down?'

Neeps and Marila glanced at each other and edged away. Pazel sighed, and Chadfallow lowered himself stiffly to the deck. He was not holding a plate. Instead, he cradled a leather pouch in both hands. It appeared to contain some object no larger than a match-box. Chadfallow held it as one might a fine glass figurine.

'I'm a doctor,' he said. 'I took an oath to defend life.'

Pazel gave him a discouraging look. No philosophy, please.

'Would you like to know what I've been asking myself this morning?' Chadfallow continued.

'Dying to,' said Pazel.

'What if it were you in there? What would I be thinking now? Would I have even stopped to think?'

'What are you talking about?' asked Pazel. 'In where?'

Chadfallow lifted his eyes in the direction of the forecastle house. Pazel grew still.

'Hercól is my oldest friend, after Thasha's father,' said Chadfallow, 'and he loved an ixchel woman, desperately. I honestly don't know what to do.'

'Ignus,' said Pazel, trying to keep his eyes off the pouch, 'what's going on? What *is* that you're carrying?'

'I've just told you,' said Chadfallow, 'the antidote.'

Pazel gasped. 'The *permanent* antidote? What, another pill?'

'Another ten pills. One for every remaining hostage. At least, that is what the note said. When I reached my desk in the sickbay, the pouch was waiting for me.'

'But that's fantastic! You can set them free!'

'Softly, you fool,' hissed Chadfallow.

Glancing about, Pazel quickly understood. There were ixchel all over the deck. And men who had been taught to hate ixchel all their lives. Thasha, he noticed suddenly, was now seated alone; Fulbreech had moved off to starboard. Perhaps they're fighting, thought Pazel, with a vague sense of hope.

'Why can't it always be this way?' said Chadfallow suddenly, his eyes sweeping the deck. 'Peace and cooperation, sanity. There's enough room on this ship for men and ixchel. And Rin knows there's enough room in Alifros. Why do we fight? Why don't we get on with living, while we're alive?'

Now that the doctor pointed it out, the scene did look more harmonious than ever before. Men and ixchel milled about together, not exactly with warmth, but with a sated sort of tolerance, as if the feasting had crowded their mutual animosities to one side. At the starboard rail a Turach was holding an ixchel sword in the palm of his hand, squinting at it, while its owner chattered on about the workmanship. Beyond the circle of tarboys, several topmen actually seemed to be trading jokes with the little people.

Diadrelu, Pazel thought. *You should be here. I'm looking at your dream.*

But of course he wasn't, really. The jokes had a bitter edge. Each side had too many deaths to blame on the other. Rose was an infamous crawly killer, and others – Uskins, Alyash, Haddismal – were almost as bad.

'Tell me about the note, Ignus,' said Pazel quietly.

'It was vile and sarcastic,' said Chadfallow. '*Play God*, it said. *Hand out life and death like sweets to children. The ones who die first may be the luckiest.* It was written by an ixchel hand, I'm certain of that. And the ink was not yet dry.'

Pazel looked away, and for several minutes he and the doctor just studied the deck. No, it was not all good. Taliktrum's Dawn Soldiers were eating in a huddle apart, scowling at those of their brethren who mingled most freely with the humans. A Turach glanced from a pie to a group of ixchel and back again; he frowned, as though concluding that they had touched it.

'You can't just let them out,' whispered Pazel.

'No,' said Chadfallow, 'not yet.'

'You should hide the pills.'

After a moment the doctor nodded. 'Hide them, and negotiate. Once we are certain who speaks for the little people. Is it Talag, now that his son has fled? Or Taliktrum's security chief, the one called Saturyk? In either case, if we are intelligent we may prevent bloodshed altogether.'

Their eyes met. To his own surprise, Pazel actually smiled. 'Diplomacy, Ignus?' he said.

The doctor inclined his head. 'My speciality.'

They both laughed – and it hurt to share a laugh with Chadfallow, after so much betrayal and deceit. But it felt good, too. Ignus had once been like a second father. He had even saved Pazel from slavery. After Pazel's real father, Captain Gregory, abandoned them, Chadfallow had protected the family, and at last revealed his consuming love for Pazel's mother. But halfway across the Nelluroq, Mr Druffle (who had also known Gregory) had told Pazel that the doctor's love for Suthinia had begun years earlier – that it was, in fact, the very thing that had driven Gregory away. Pazel had begged Chadfallow to deny it. The doctor had only replied that things were more complicated than they appeared.

Pazel doubted he could ever forgive Chadfallow for breaking up his family. Still, in the midst of so much waste and ruin and killing, that sort of sin, loving another man's wife, suddenly appeared very small. Of course, Chadfallow had done other things, darker and more suspicious, things that love could not explain.

'You let Arunis board the ship, Ignus,' he said. 'That day in the Straits of Simja. Why in the Pits did you do that?'

'He was about to kill Thasha with that necklace. Wouldn't you have done the same?'

Pazel scowled. He'd asked himself the same question, many times. No answer he could come up with made him feel good.

'You would have done so out of love for the girl,' said the doctor. 'I might have wished to do so out of love for her father, but I would not have. No, I would have let her die, if I had not felt—'

'What?'

Chadfallow drew a slow breath. 'A hunch, nothing more,' he said at last. 'An instinct, that her death would bring a greater disaster than any of us could foresee. I feel it still. In the way Hercól speaks of her; the way Ramachni called her "my champion". They have never trusted me with the whole story of Thasha Isiq. Nor have any of you.'

Pazel averted his eyes. *He thinks I know more than I do. But he's right, I haven't trusted him. How could I, how could I, after—*

'Ignus,' he heard himself say, 'why didn't you warn us of the invasion? You could have saved us then and there. We could have escaped.'

It was the question he had never dared ask, the question that had burned inside him for almost six years. Chadfallow looked as though he had expected it.

'Escape?' he said. 'Do you think Suthinia Sadralin Pathkendle would have been content to escape, to run off into the Highlands with her children? Or—' he hesitated, swallowed; his face was suddenly vulnerable and young '—with me?'

'Definitely not with you,' said Pazel. 'Oh, damn it – that's not what I meant—'

'She would have raised the alarm. She would have stormed out into the city and told everyone the Arqualis were coming.'

'They'd never have listened. They all thought she was crazy.'

'But they did not think *I* was,' said Chadfallow. 'Suthinia would have named me as her source immediately. And I could not afford to lie. I was doing everything I could to negotiate Ormael's peaceful surrender, with guarantees that the city would not be looted, the people enslaved or slaughtered, the women raped.'

Pazel shut his eyes. *Neda*, he thought.

'Admiral Isiq agreed,' said Chadfallow, 'although it meant disobeying his Emperor. We had it all arranged, Pazel. Not a shot was to be fired, not a woman touched. The Turachs hated the plan, but we had them under control. *Tenuous* control, boy. Any friction and we knew they'd riot. It was your own lord, the Suzain of Ormael, who provided that friction. He dug in his heels and swore Ormael would fight to the last man.'

Pazel's head felt rather light. 'Against all those Turach battalions? Against that whole mucking *fleet*?'

'Why do you think the palace was so badly damaged? They had to pry him out like an oyster from a shell. Your fool of a leader could not accept the simple truth, that his days of courtesans and clotted cream were over. He preferred to bask in glory – in the bonfire Arqual made of your city.'

'But for Rin's sake, Ignus! Why didn't Thasha's father just *tell* me all this? Did he think I wouldn't believe him?'

'You had just called him a mass murderer, as I recall,' said Chadfallow.

Pazel squeezed his eyes shut in pure frustration. A peaceful surrender. It wouldn't have been justice, but it wouldn't have been *that*, either: the burning and looting, the blood and death and rape. The terrible words of the eguar rang in his ears: *Acceptance is agony, denial is death.*

Suddenly he realised that he was once more staring at the leather pouch with the antidote inside. He started. 'Pitfire, Ignus, you shouldn't be walking around with that thing!'

'I don't know where to hide it,' said Chadfallow. 'Someone is still doing Ott's work, you know. I find small items moved in my cabin, and in the surgery too.'

'Well put it in your pocket, for Rin's sake. Are you daft?'

Chadfallow glared at him, then sighed and looked down at the pouch.

'Listen,' said Pazel, 'why don't you let me hide them in the stateroom? There's no safer place. Thasha hasn't shut me out, yet, and even if she does, Neeps or Marila could—'

'Hello there, Doctor.'

The voice, loud and abrasively cheerful, belonged to Alyash. He had sidled up to them without a sound. Above the grotesque scars on his throat and chin he was smiling, and his eyes were bright and merry. His hands dangled empty at his sides.

Chadfallow started to get to his feet, but Alyash put a restraining hand on his shoulder. 'Didn't you blary eat? You've got to get your strength back, after all those weeks locked in a cage.'

'Don't answer, he's up to something,' said Pazel in Ormali. Alyash just went on smiling.

Chadfallow looked nervously at the bosun's hand. 'I ate my fill,' he said.

'No discomfort, then? Mr Elkstem had a little discomfort.'

'Of course he did,' said Chadfallow, sounding a bit like a cross professor. 'He ate sausage. He spurned my advice. When one has been confined to a small space for weeks with little to eat, the gut contracts and heavy foods become the enemy, for a while.'

'Ignus,' said Pazel.

'Elkstem should have concentrated on the vegetables,' Chadfallow went on. 'That is what I did. Naturally my stomach is at peace.'

Alyash's grin widened. 'The vegetables, you say?'

'And for my circulation, an ounce of fish.'

'An ounce of fish! Well, that's blary fine.'

Alyash dealt him a vicious backhand blow. The doctor fell sprawling, and Alyash scooped up the leather pouch and ran.

Pazel exploded to his feet. 'Stop him!' he cried, frantically giving chase. 'Oh *credek*, stop him, someone!'

Alyash was making for the bows. To Pazel's great relief he saw Thasha take in the scene and rise with the quickness of her training to join the pursuit. For a moment they ran side by side, leaping over amazed parties of men and ixchel still sprawled upon the deck. Then Thasha, always the stronger, pulled ahead.

Neeps and Marila and even Fulbreech were pounding after the bosun as well, but no one could match Thasha's speed. She was within an arm's length of Alyash when a wall of Turach muscle seemed to rise out of nowhere. Thasha slammed into them, fighting for all she was worth. She actually threw two of the soldiers to the deck as the others piled on – they knew from hard experience what a fighter she was. But Thasha's fall had opened a path. Rolling and sliding, Pazel suddenly found himself beyond the Turachs, and raced on with all his might.

Alyash was past the mainmast now, holding up his prize, shouting to Sandor Ott. From the corner of his eye Pazel saw Fulbreech, sprinting – he too had somehow eluded the Turachs. The youths flailed forward. Alyash rounded the tonnage hatch, the forward guns, the jiggermast. Pazel saw Ott's face at the window. *No*, he thought, *no!* From somewhere he found the strength to run even faster.

And then Alyash tripped.

He rolled almost instantly to his feet – he had his own training with the Secret Fist to draw on – but the stumble made all the difference. Pazel closed the space between them. It was his one chance. He leaped.

The jump did not carry him as far as he hoped, but as he fell, Pazel reached out and caught Alyash by the leg. The bosun crashed to the deck. The leather pouch shot out of his hand and slid forwards. It struck the wall of the forecastle house, just beside the door.

Alyash was kicking Pazel in the head, but he would not let go. 'Fulbreech!' he managed to cry. The youth shot past them, and Pazel heard a door creak open and slam shut. Then Alyash's boot struck him hard in the temple, and for a moment his eyes went dim.

Only seconds had passed. He had let go of Alyash's leg, but the bosun just lay there, gasping – laughing, by Rin, a ragged, evil sound. Pazel raised his head: Fulbreech was slumped by the door, utterly winded. There was nothing in his hands.

'Where is it?' Pazel cried through his throbbing pain. 'What have you done with it, Fulbreech?'

'Done with what?' said Fulbreech, and flashed Pazel a grin.

Turachs hauled Pazel and Fulbreech to their feet. Uskins was there, Rose's daft enforcer, screaming, 'What is happening, Bosun? Did these boys assault you?'

Fulbreech hid his smile away, and glanced expectantly at the door. Alyash turned on his side to look as well. Soon everyone was looking at the door, though few could have said quite why.

The reason soon appeared. Muffled cries came from within, and the sound of a brief struggle. Then the door sprang open and Sandor Ott raced onto the deck, battering sailors out of his path. After some forty feet he stopped dead, closed his eyes, and inhaled.

No collapse. No writhing pain. Slowly, the chief assassin of Arqual turned about where he stood. His cruel, bright eyes took in the crowd, the ship, the dlömu watching from the quay. Then he laughed aloud, raced five steps forwards, sprang into a dizzying roll – and uncurled with his hand around an ixchel. The ixchel drew his knife, but Ott was faster. He dashed the tiny man against the deck so hard it sounded as though he were wielding a club. Then he tossed the limp body over the side.

Horrified, Pazel jumped to his feet. Everywhere he looked, ixchel were running, vanishing. Some over the sides. Many down the ladderways, deeper into the ship.

Ott had now seized a rigging-axe, one of the heavy tools kept on deck for cutting away fallen sheets and canvas in a storm. He lifted the axe above his head and turned to face aft. 'I am free!' he shouted at the top of his lungs. 'Captain Rose! *All of us are free!*'

With that he turned and raced for the Silver Stair, yards behind a clump of ixchel. Pazel could just see Rose, still as a chess piece on the quarterdeck. Ott did not appear to be the focus of his attention. Pazel followed his gaze back to the forecastle house and saw Lady Oggosk framed in the doorway, leaning heavily on her walking stick, gold rings gleaming on her ancient hands. She gave Rose an irascible wave: *Yes, Nilus, here I am.*

'Now we'll see something,' said Alyash, delighted.

The captain howled an order. It was a brief command, just one word in fact, but the crew understood it perfectly. From all parts of the ship men took up the word, repeated it, made it their battle cry, and the word was *Death.*

A waking nightmare: that was how Pazel thought of the next few minutes. As if three-quarters of the crew had been seized by devils. How they ran to their task! Alyash organised the watch captains to take their men to various points belowdecks, saying, 'Kill on the way, kill when you get there, kill as you come back to report!' Haddismal sent his men to secure the gun decks. Mr Bindhammer sent a team to fetch the sulphur barrels, to be used to smoke the ixchel from their hiding places. Uskins climbed to the mainmast fife rail and bellowed encouragement ('Exterminate! Exterminate all the little lice!'). This was revenge: an insane, wild-fire revenge, carried out by men who just minutes ago had been savouring the fullness of their stomachs and the warmth of the sun. From hundreds of mouths came the throbbing refrain: *Death! Death! Death!*

Pazel ran blindly along the topdeck. Ixchel bodies, some horribly mangled, littered his path. The men who had refused the order were faring badly: there was Big Skip Sunderling, being shoved and pummelled by several men. And humans had fallen too: with horror Pazel stumbled over Mr Lapwing, open-eyed beside the tonnage hatch, one hand clutching at his bloody throat. Off to his left, a midshipman was limping, dragging one foot as though the tendon had been slashed. The ixchel would not go down without a fight.

'Stop this lunacy!' someone was shouting. Pazel whirled and saw to his amazement that it was Prince Olik. Alone of all his people he had leaped into the melee. Waving his hands, pleading. 'Listen to me! We can broker a peace between your people! A just peace, an honourable—'

No one harmed him, but they did not listen, either. On the quayside, the dlōmic citizens cried out to their prince. 'Sire! Sire! Get out of that snake pit! Come back!'

Then Pazel saw Thasha, surrounded by a mob of advancing men. She was just holding them off, slashing the air with her knife. *Rin above, she's wounded, she's holding her chest*. No, not wounded, burdened: there were four living ixchel beneath her arm.

Pazel drew his skipper's knife and flew towards her. Whatever had changed inside her, she was still Thasha, still the one he could not live without. He had almost reached her when a terribly familiar voice cut through him like a blade.

He whirled. A few yards to his left, two massive Burnscove Boys were squatting beside the sixteen-foot skiff, raising it and striking (with cries of glee) at something underneath. They had caulking hammers. Pazel swore under his breath and ran at them.

Under the lifeboat he saw Felthrup, backed into a corner, snapping, biting, dodging. Beside him an ixchel woman crawled in a pool of blood.

Pazel attacked so quickly the men never knew what hit them. As the nearer sailor raised his hammer for a killing blow, Pazel snatched it, brought it down sidelong against the face that turned by instinct, threw his body hard against the wounded man and bashed him into the other. With his knife he slashed the far man's ear, then his cheek right at the bone, and atop the two of them he struck with head and hammer and knees and knife-hilt, until he realised that they were not fighting, they were curling into balls.

He scooped up Felthrup, unharmed it seemed, and the ixchel with the bloody scalp. Adept at the move by now, he tucked his shirt firmly under his belt and thrust rat and woman in through his open collar. They clung there, awkward but safe, and Pazel raced to Thasha's side.

The madness of the fight engulfed him. Once again he found everything he had learned from Thasha and Hercól ablaze in his mind. The forward-seeing, the awareness of the blow and its consequences before he landed it, the balance and velocity of his limbs. He was not stabbing, not fighting to kill. He was using the knife to ward and to scratch, its hilt and both fists and his elbows and knees to wound and stun. All the same there was a blade in his hand. One small mistake and he was a killer. Of his own kind. *A killer of someone I don't hate, in defence of those I don't know* . . .

With her back to Pazel's, Thasha fought like a tigress. She did not say a word; she could not spare him the attention. But when the opportunity came, with the nudge of her sweaty shoulder, the bump of her hip, she moved him in the direction of her goal: the Silver Stair.

Of course. She was trying to bring them to the stateroom.

From the ladderway came crashes and thumps and howls of

pain. Out of the corner of his eye Pazel saw Hercól, fighting his way down through a great mob of sailors. They were armed with all manner of swords, knives, hammers, cudgels; Hercól fought bare-handed, disarming one man after another, clearing a path.

Thasha crouched, whirling with one leg extended, and sent the gunner's mate crashing to the deck. Pazel brandished his knife, holding off a Plapp's Pier man and a midshipman. He leaped, and just cleared a capstan bar aimed at his kneecaps. To his dismay he saw that the one who held it was the tarboy Swift. His brother Saroo had been among the final captives. Swift looked at him with rage, and utter incomprehension. He swung a second time, and once more Pazel leaped. Again he and Thasha shuffled closer to the stairs.

Then Alyash himself appeared and charged right at Thasha. His first blow nearly caught her, and she was forced back from the ladderway, dancing just out of his reach, barely escaping one blow after another.

'Hercól!' Pazel cried. But the swordsman was out of sight. Pazel glanced again at Thasha – and this time Swift's blow caught him in the ankles.

He had just enough presence of mind to pivot as he fell, so that Felthrup and Ensyl would not be crushed. He rolled, and Swift struck him across the back. Pazel snarled with pain but still, somehow, managed to gain his feet. He rose, strangely weightless, only to realise that the sensation was due to the fact that four men were lifting him by the arms.

They knew what was under his shirt, and were trying to stick their knives through it without actually killing him. 'Give 'em up, give 'em up, *Muketch*, or you'll bleed!' He lashed out with his legs, but the men caught them too. Thasha, ten feet away, had been reduced to shielding her ixchel from Alyash's non-stop blows.

It all changed with a sound. Or rather, two sounds: the enraged and murderous howls of the mastiffs. Pazel's foes saw them before he did, and dropped him like a red-hot skillet. From the corner of his eye Pazel saw Alyash's face freeze, and then he broke and ran for the nearest rigging. Jorl thundered after him, a dark-blue boulder of a dog, while Suzyt leaped over Pazel and scattered his tormentors.

Pazel felt Thasha hauling him to his feet.

'Go!'

She practically threw him down the Silver Stair. Hercól had cleared a path; Thasha, fighting a rearguard, tumbled behind him, shouting to her dogs. Then she was beside him, studying him, terrified (he knew from one look into her eyes) that he might be bleeding, hiding some wound.

'I'm all right,' he said.

She wanted to speak: he could have sworn to that. But she did not speak; she only turned and dragged him on. Two flights down they ran, stepping on the bodies of the wounded and the stunned, trying not to stare at the ixchel dead. When one of them stumbled, the other's hand was there. Then Jorl and Suzyt caught up with them and led the way.

They reached the upper gun deck, the landing, the money gate. They passed Hercól still fighting in a side passage: 'On, on!' he roared. Thasha whistled, pointed: the dogs sprang to help Hercól, a friend they'd known as long as Thasha herself. But as soon as the dogs were gone a half-dozen Turachs rounded the corner, and the chase was on again. They raced down the long passage towards the stateroom, the marines hurling weapons and curses, and then they reached the intersection with the painted red line on the floor, and they were safe. One of the Turachs shouted to their comrades: '*Look out – that's the mucking magic*—'

Blunt sounds of collisions, groans. Pazel and Thasha ran on, bearing their few survivors. They threw open the elegant carved door and tumbled into the stateroom.

Fulbreech was here already, along with Marila and Neeps and Fiffengurt. All four ran to give their aid. The quartermaster took Felthrup and the wounded ixchel woman from Pazel's bloody shirt; Neeps caught his arm, saying, 'Steady, mate, you did blary good work.' Marila unclenched Thasha's arm, and the battered ixchel let themselves be lifted onto the dining table. Fulbreech ran to Thasha and seized her by the arms. 'Darling!' he said.

Thasha looked up at Fulbreech. She was gasping, red-faced, a terror to behold. *She knows*, Pazel thought, *she must have seen what he did, seen him grin at me, seen him slip the antidote through that door. She's going to kill you, Fulbreech. Right here, right now.*

Thasha lowered her face to his chest.

All told, eleven ixchel had passed through the magic wall – and become hostages themselves, although in better quarters than the forecastle house. As often before, Pazel watched in amazement at the speed with which they began to function as a unit, the strongest tending to the wounded, the designated guard keeping a sharp eye on the humans and the dogs (because who knew, who really knew?) and one more carrying their water bag from mouth to thirsty mouth.

If he had been among the men ordered (and mostly eager) to kill 'the little brutes', he might have been even more impressed. For the carnage of the topdeck – twenty-nine ixchel and four humans slain – was by far the worst that occurred. True, Sandor Ott killed five more ixchel in as many minutes, and Ludunte in an act of madness jumped onto the head of the whaling captain, Magritte, and plunged twin daggers into his eyes. True, eight of the little people were kicked and clubbed to death on the Silver Stair, and another three on the berth deck, and an Uturphan topman was found in a cow stall with the veins in his ankles slit. But the casualties ended there. When Ott raced ahead of everyone down the No. 1 ladderway he was executing a plan. Slight clues, chance remarks by the ixchel to their captives, observations brought to him by Alyash and Haddismal and others – above all, endless hours of maniacally focused thought – had brought him to a certainty. The mercy deck. The ixchel had their stronghold there. Probably forward of the ladderway, in that massive barricade of boxes and crates that were never unloaded in Simja, locked down still by bolts and rings and iron-tight straps, the furnishings for the

Isiq household that was never to be (that he, Ott, had made sure would never be).

Ott was quite correct, and with his usual ruthlessness he slashed the straps and shouldered over crates and axed his way into the heart of the barricade. But when at last he had torn open the hive-like fortress of the ixchel, he found not one of them there to interrogate or kill. They had gone. Some spare clothes remained. A thimble-small teacup was still vaguely warm.

Ott sniffed the cup. He had killed too quickly, he had no one to question. He sniffed again, no conscious idea why he did so, and eighty years of immersion in killing schemes saved his life.

He leaped from the pile of crates, smashed headlong across the compartment, hurled himself down the open shaft of the ladderway – and an explosion tore apart the space where he had been standing.

A black-powder trap. The compartment bloomed with flame. Shards of the Isiqs' antique china flew like deadly spears, silver cutlery embedded itself in walls, a trumpet was forced half through the floorboards into the orlop deck.

Immediately the *Chathrand*'s fire crew sprang for the hoses, and a team raced to start turning the chain-pumps again – but there was no bilge to pump, and certainly no seawater. The men fought the blaze with fresh water and sand. But even with a hundred men battling the fire, Rose kept up the hunt for the ixchel.

He simply did not find any, then or ever.

They were not in the hold. They had not taken to the rigging. Many had been seen going over the sides, but where to then? Only one staircase led from the floor of the berth up into the city, and not an ixchel was seen upon it all day. Fifty, at most sixty, might have made it into the damnably protected stateroom – but not six hundred. They had not crawled between the inner and outer hulls, or into the forepeak, or the light shafts, or windscoops, or into the bottom of the cable tiers. They had not burrowed into the rotting hay of the manger, or massed between the floorboards (Rose gassed these hidden spaces with sulphur, one after another, as day turned to night and the dlömu watch changed again and again).

Witchcraft, said somebody, after the fourth fruitless hour of searching. *They're with Arunis*, said another. But the sorcerer's lair also eluded them. Only his laugh came again in the darkness of the hold, just as a nervous Mr Uskins was watching his lamp go out. He wanted to scream but could not. *The mage is here, I feel it, that is his hand on my shoulder.* Uskins crouched down, a quivering mass, and begged the darkness to spare him.

For those who had always loathed and feared the 'crawlies', the recapture of the vessel should have brought a feeling of triumph. It did not. They would go to their hammocks that night more afraid than ever of being murdered in their sleep.

The humans had chanted *Death, death*. Only some forty-three ixchel proved willing to die that day, however – though it might be assumed, thought Lady Oggosk, picking her slow way through the bodies on the topdeck, that they would all remember the sentiment.

17

Time Regained

230th day from Etherhorde

A warlord pauses on the field
Newly silent, newly taken by his men
There among many corpses shines a face he knows:

They were friends as children
A time like a dream
The heart, once shattered, is open at last.
Sulidaram Bectur, circa 2147

Three days passed. The stone oven was dismantled, and the stones carried away. The dlömu delivered much in the way of raw food-stuffs, and several enormous crates of *mül*. But they brought no more hot meals, and none of the black beer Mr Bolutu had longed for. Masalym had evidently decided that the ship was intoxicated enough.

Pazel had never felt more disheartened. To think of all the hopes they had placed on Bali Adro! An enlightened Empire, Bolutu had said, a place of just laws, peace among the many races, a wise and decent monarch on the throne. A place where good mages of Ramachni's sort would be waiting to deal with Arunis, and take away the Stone. Bolutu had not lied to them: he had simply been describing the Bali Adro of two centuries before.

What would they do with their visitors now? The signs were hard to read. From beneath the hull came the noise of saws and hammers: the repairs, at least, were going forward. Soldiers remained plentiful along the rim of the berth, but the ordinary townsfolk were no more to be seen. Teams of dockworkers, using two of the big cargo-cranes, raised what were unmistakably gangways, and swung the wooden structures into position between the ship's rail and the edge of the berth: lowered, they would have formed wide, railed bridges between ship and shore. But they were not lowered. The workers left them dangling, thirty feet above the topdeck, like a promise deferred.

The 'birdwatchers' – so someone had named the dlömu in the ash-grey coveralls, with their notebooks and field glasses – came each morning, and left only at sundown. They studied the *Chathrand* in shifts, whispering together for a while when one man replaced another. Vadu joined them at the end of each day. He read the watchers' reports, his usual gaping expression often changing to a frown. When he looked at the ship his head bobbed faster.

What had the dlömu really made of the slaughter four days ago? Were they shocked, or was sudden, mindless killing all too familiar to them? In a sense it hardly mattered. They had seen humans at their worst. Any chance of winning the city's trust had surely disappeared.

So, of course, had some five hundred ixchel.

Early morning, the first day of the last month of the year. In the North, winter would have begun in earnest; here each day felt warmer than the last. Pazel woke with sunlight already hot on his face through the single porthole of the cabin he now shared with Neeps. He groaned. Neeps was snoring. He rolled out of his hammock and groped around on the floor for his clothes.

'Such a racket,' mumbled Neeps into his pillow. 'Thought you were Old Jupe, outside my window back home.'

Pazel pulled on his breeches. 'Your neighbour?'

'Our sow.'

Pazel tugged at one of the ropes of Neeps' hammock, untying it, and lowered his friend's head to the floor. Eyes still shut, Neeps oozed like softening butter from his canvas bed. He came to rest among their boots. 'Thanks,' he said, appearing to mean it.

'Get up,' said Pazel, rubbing his eyes. 'Fighting practice, remember? If you want to eat before Thasha and Hercól start whacking us, it's got to be now.'

The scare tactic worked. In short order Neeps too was dressed, after a fashion, and the boys stumbled into the corridor.

'I dreamed of my mother,' said Pazel.

Neeps responded with a yawn.

'She was free. Not a slave or a Mzithrini wife, like Chadfallow's afraid she's become. She was doing something on a tabletop with jars of coloured sand, or smoke maybe, in a little house in a poor quarter of some city – I thought I knew which city when I dreamed it, but I don't remember now. And there was a dog looking in at the window. That's curious, isn't it?'

Neeps might well have been sleepwalking. 'I dreamed you were a sow,' he said.

In the stateroom, Thasha and Marila were finishing a breakfast of Masalym oats, boiled with molasses. Felthrup crouched on the table eating bread and butter, a cloth napkin tied at his neck. The boys looked around carefully for Hercól. The Tholjassan often began their fighting classes by appearing out of nowhere and swinging hard at them with a practice sword.

'Don't worry,' said Thasha, 'he's not hiding anywhere.'

'We're alone, are we?' said Pazel, surly already.

Thasha stared at him. 'Isn't that what I just said? Nobody's lurking in one of the cabins, if that's what you mean.'

'Well *that's* blary good,' said Neeps, yawning again. 'Because you just never know.'

'Come here, you two,' said Marila quickly. 'Be quiet. Eat oats.'

At least Fulbreech hasn't moved in, thought Pazel acidly. *Yet.*

Then, waking further, he shook his head. 'Hold on. The ixchel. Where are the ixchel?'

'One is behind you,' said Ensyl, leaping onto the back of an armchair, startling both boys. But to Pazel's shock, the young ixchel woman proceeded to explain that she was the last. The other ten who had sought refuge in the stateroom had departed at sunrise, not planning to return.

'They asked me to thank you,' she said, 'and to say that you may always count on their help, should your paths cross again. Those are not idle words, either: ixchel do not make promises of aid unless they mean to keep them.'

'But where in blazes did they go?' Neeps demanded. 'The same place as all the others?'

'So I imagine,' said Ensyl. 'They asked if I would hinder their departure, and I said they were guests, not prisoners. Then they offered to take me with them. "Your final chance to stand with your people," they grandly declared. "I might do that, if my people stood for anything," I replied. Then they spat on the backs of their hands and called me a traitor, and left.'

'But everyone knew where to run, that first day,' said Pazel, dropping into an armchair.

Ensyl nodded. 'Every clan has its disaster protocol. They change often, but they are always remembered. If the signal came we were all to fly to different rendezvous points deep in the ship. Elders were to meet us there, and take us to a place of safety.'

'Safe from *Rose*?' said Thasha, incredulous.

'We doubted that ourselves,' said Ensyl. 'But this plan came from Lord Talag, and it was followed without question. I heard the ten who took shelter here discussing it – though they fell silent at my approach. All the rendezvous points were on the orlop deck, between the steerage compartment and the augrongs' den. If they had not been trapped on the upper decks, that is where they would have gone.'

'Orlop, portside, amidships,' said Neeps. 'That's a lonely spot, all right. Especially now that the animals are—' He stopped, looking from one face to another. 'The animals. The live-animals compartment. It's right smack there, isn't it, forward of the augrongs?'

'Yes,' said Thasha, with a glance at Marila. 'And that's where the . . . strangest things have happened, to some of us.'

Marila's round face looked troubled, and Pazel knew why: several months ago, Thasha and Marila had one day found themselves on a very different *Chathrand*. A *Chathrand* sailing a frigid winter sea, a *Chathrand* crewed by pirates. They had barely escaped with their lives.

Of course, men passed through those chambers every day and met with nothing strange. Pazel himself had spent more hours than he cared to recall filling buckets with manure and spoiled hay. Still, it was an odd coincidence. If the ixchel had gone where Thasha and Marila went, they couldn't be much better off. But perhaps the magic didn't work that way. Perhaps one never went to the same place twice.

Suddenly Thasha gasped. She placed a hand on her chest, then started to her feet.

'Someone's just stepped through the wall! It's not Hercól, nor Fiffengurt or Bolutu or Greysan. I didn't let them pass through; they just *came*. Get your weapons! Quick!'

She and the two boys raced for their swords. Marila grabbed Felthrup and backed away. Jorl and Suzyt crouched low, silenced by a warning finger from their mistress, every muscle tensed to spring. Pazel gripped the sword that had been Eberzam Isiq's, wishing he could use it half as well as Thasha used her own. *Hercól was right. He always said the worst thing we could do was to depend on the magic wall.*

Thasha flattened herself against the wall near the door, sword raised to strike whoever entered. Then they heard the footsteps: a single, heavy figure, walking with long strides to the door. When it reached the threshold, someone knocked.

Thasha looked at Pazel: a tender look, gone in half a heartbeat. Then she set her teeth and snarled: 'If that's you, Arunis, come.

Ildraquin is waiting for you. It's here in my hand.'

She was lying; she had only her own fine sword, not Hercól's Curse-Cleaver. Then a voice spoke from beyond the passageway: 'Your pardon, Lady Thasha. It is only me.'

They stared at one another. The voice belonged to Prince Olik. The door opened a few inches, and the man's bright silver eyes and beak-like nose appeared in the gap.

'A splendid morning to you all,' he said.

Thasha opened the door wide. She lowered the sword but did not sheathe it. 'Your Highness,' she said. 'How did you get in here? No one has ever been able to pass through the wall without my permission.'

'Then you must have given it, my lady,' said Olik.

'I did no such thing,' said Thasha.

All at once she leaped back into fighting stance and pointed her sword at Olik's breast. 'Stay where you are!' she shouted. 'We haven't seen Prince Olik in four days – and suddenly here you appear out of nowhere, alone? How do I know you're not Arunis in disguise? Prove that you're you!'

Olik smiled. 'That is just what the Karyskans said. Mistaken identity appears to be my fate. Alas, I'm not sure how to prove myself – but as it happens, I've not come alone.'

'Thasha Isiq!'

Captain Rose's bellow carried down the passage. Olik stepped aside, and they could all see him, toes to the painted line, fists pounding empty air. Behind him, pressing as close as they dared, were four well-armed dlömic warriors.

'Let me pass!' bellowed Rose. 'This is a royal visit: I'm escorting His Highness on a tour of my ship!'

'Your guards I *won't* allow,' said Thasha to the prince.

'I am delighted to hear it,' said Olik. 'They were inflicted on me by Counsellor Vadu.'

'And you yourself, Sire? Not armed?' she asked.

'Certainly I am,' he said. 'Knife in my boot. I've carried one that way since I was a boy. Would you feel better if I surrendered it?'

'Yes,' said Thasha, 'and I'm glad you told me the truth. I spotted that knife straight away.'

Olik passed her the knife. It was broad and well used, the leopard-and-sun design on the sheath nearly worn away. Without turning to the hallway again, Thasha said, 'Come in, Captain Rose.'

Rose's fast, limping gait echoed down the passage, and then he barrelled into the chamber and spread his hands. 'The master stateroom,' he said, rather more loudly than necessary. 'Fifty-four heads of state have travelled in these chambers during the ship's public history alone – her early years being classified, you understand. Note the aromatic woods, the Virabalm crystal in the chandelier. To your left there's a panel that once disguised a dumbwaiter. And the walls are triply insulated, for the warmth and privacy of our guests.'

He slammed the door and fell silent, leaning on the frame, breathing like some winded animal. Then, slowly, almost with fear, he turned his head so that one eye could look at them. Pazel's hand tightened on his sword. Rose's eye swivelled about the room, left to right, floor to ceiling.

'Sweet Rin in his heaven,' he whispered. 'There's not a ghost in this room.'

After a long silence, the prince asked amiably, 'Is that unusual?'

'They can't get in,' said Rose. 'Outside the wall they're thick as flies in a stable, but here—' He turned to look at them directly, standing straight. 'Here a man can breathe.'

An expression came over his features that Pazel knew he had never seen before. It was not satisfaction, or not that alone (he had seen the man satisfied, often for the worst of reasons). The look was closer to contentment. On Rose's face it was stranger than a third eye.

Ignoring the prince, he walked forwards until he stood directly in front of the youths. 'It's as I thought all along,' he said. 'Ghosts avoid you, and that makes you blary useful. Waste not – that's my father's iron law. I told him I shouldn't have you killed.'

Pazel sighed. *That* was the Rose he knew.

'You're not on a tour of the ship,' said Thasha. 'Why have you come here, Captain?'

Rose waved a hand at the prince. 'His Highness—'

'Desired an audience,' Olik interrupted. 'With all of you, who fought so hard to protect the little people. Captain Rose would not agree to it unless I gave my word that he too could be present. I did so, reluctantly. But now that he is here I think it is for the best.'

Thasha opened the door once again, and a moment later Hercól, Bolutu and Fiffengurt entered the room. Hercól stiffened at the sight of Rose.

'Excellent,' said Olik. 'Now everyone I wished to speak to is here.'

'I do not understand your interest in these mutineers,' said Rose. 'You've still not met our spymaster, or Lady Oggosk, my soothsayer hag.'

'I saw quite enough of Mr Ott four days ago,' said the prince with finality. 'As for these people, I wished to see them because their behaviour in that terrible circumstance was the opposite of his – and yours. But I have another reason, and this one includes you, Rose: for you also bear the mark of Erithusmé.'

Thasha whirled. 'Do you mean our scars? What do you know about them, Sire? What do they have to do with Erithusmé?'

'Close the door, Lady Thasha,' said the prince, 'and let us keep away from the windows, too. Counsellor Vadu and his legionnaires know quite enough about me as it is.'

'We, however, do not know much at all,' said Hercól. 'I would ask you to change that, Highness, before asking for our trust.'

'Nothing could be more fair,' said the prince, 'or alas, more difficult. I cannot say all that you might wish, for I don't know how far my words will travel. Oh, I'm not impugning your good faith, my friends. You won't breathe a word if I ask you not to – I'm confident of that. Even in your case, Captain Rose.'

'I've given no such promise,' grumbled Rose.

'But you *will* keep my secrets, all the same,' said Olik with a twinkle in his eye, 'except perhaps from that Lady Oggosk of yours, and she will not breathe a word. But not only words can be spied upon – as you should know, who fight Arunis.'

'You know about Arunis?' asked Pazel.

'Who does not, in the South? You are safe within this splendid chamber, but you cannot always be here. And when you emerge, he probes at you, and feels the outlines of your thoughts.'

'Just a minute,' said Neeps. 'You still haven't told us how you know about our blary scars. Maybe you saw Pazel's hand, and Thasha's, and Rose's arm. But Hercól's scar is under his shirt, and Bolutu's hair covers his. And I was never anywhere near you, until today.'

Thasha sheathed her sword. 'I know the answer to that question,' she said.

'Let us not discuss that now!' said the prince. He went to the table, lowered himself into a chair. 'We may have only minutes,' he said. 'The physicians have nearly made their choice.'

'Physicians?' said Ensyl, who had climbed onto the table.

'The men who watch you from the quay, and report to Vadu – the ones your men have so delightfully labelled "bird-watchers". They are about to choose a few representatives for an audience with the Issár. And I have a strong hunch that you will be among them, for they are tasked with determining who is uncontaminated.'

'Uncontaminated!' thundered Rose. 'That is outrageous! Fewer than twenty of my men have touched dry land this side of the Ruling Sea, and six of those disappeared without a trace. Of the rest, it is precisely these agitators who spent the longest time ashore. Yet you expect them to be chosen to visit the lord of Masalym? What, pray tell, does that Issár think we might be contaminated with?'

'Why, madness,' said the prince. 'Captain Rose, you appear to care about your men. Do you realise the harm you have done them already? The Masalym physicians were on the point of attesting to your crew's sanity when you ordered that killing spree against the little people.'

'So they're admitting we're human after all?' said Fiffengurt.

'My dear quartermaster, everyone in Masalym knows that you are human – the poor of the Lower City, the shipwrights under orders not to speak to your own carpenters, the Issár's scientists and above all Vadu and other servants of Emperor Nahundra. They have known since we sailed into the Jaws of Masalym. They simply hope, with some desperation, to keep the world from learning about it. From their perspective it is convenient that we are at war. This city and its Inner Dominion are effectively quarantined. News does not easily escape by land or sea. I happen to know, however, that letters have already been sent by courier albatross. I can only assume that they repeat the official story.'

'You mean that nonsense about albinos,' said Pazel, 'and the Magnificent Court of the Lilac.'

'Precisely,' said Olik. 'But even as he spreads a nonsense tale, the good Vadu is struggling to determine just what kind of humans you are. With my encouragement, and after days of reports, he was prepared to let you all come ashore. But now that is out of the question.'

'We didn't even catch that many,' Rose objected. 'Crawlies, I mean. As an extermination it was a dismal failure.'

'How dispiriting for you,' said Olik. 'Still, the show you put on was gruesome enough. The rage to kill! It can, in fact, be a sign of the onset of the mental degeneration that turns humans into *tol-chenni*.' He looked at their shocked faces and added, 'That, and a sharp smell of lemon in one's sweat.'

'No one on *Chathrand* smells of lemons,' said Felthrup, from Marila's arms.

Olik shot to his feet. He stared at Felthrup with his mouth agape. 'That creature,' he said at last. 'I saw you with it on the topdeck, but I took it for a pet. Did it speak?'

'Marila is not a ventriloquist, Sire,' said Felthrup. 'I can speak.

I am woken. There are many like me in the North. And if you please, we consider "it" rather derogatory.'

The prince stepped forward, awestruck. He dropped to one knee before Marila and the rat.

'Many?' he said.

'More all the time, Prince,' said Bolutu. 'The rate of wakings has exploded in ... recent years.'

Pazel caught his look of torment. *Recent years.*

'Then perhaps it's true,' whispered Olik. 'Perhaps this *is* the ship of our doom. The council foretold it, and though I was part of their foretelling I could not make myself believe. Have we come to the end? Will I live to see ... *that?* O Watchers Beyond, take pity!'

'Your words are blary strange,' said Fiffengurt. 'Can't you speak more plainly, Sire?'

Olik crept to the window and peered out. 'Yes, I can,' he said at last. 'The poor folk of Masalym are not ignorant, by and large. Not two generations ago, every last dlömu in this city could read and write, and a great many had collections of books in their own homes—'

In Marila's arms, Felthrup kicked and squirmed, overcome with feeling.

'—and that delight in learning has not left them altogether, though it is hard to keep alive in these darkening days. Those who believe that you are hastening the world's end could give you reasons for that belief.'

He came back to the table and sat down. 'There have been foretellings. Prophecies, if you like. For a century at least. The Empire has tried to silence them. They have jailed and killed the augurs, and those who repeat or publish the foretellings. Indeed, the very practice of foretelling has recently become an Imperial crime. And why wouldn't they try to silence us, when what we see ahead is an end to their dynasty, a final disintegration of their power?'

'We?' said Ensyl.

Olik looked up at Thasha. 'You guessed, didn't you? Tell them now, if you will.'

'I didn't guess,' she said. 'I felt it, when you passed through the wall. You're a mage.'

Everyone tensed; Felthrup's fur stood up bristling along his spine.

'I am a mage,' said Olik, 'but I am nothing at all like Arunis. I can cast no spells, work no charms, summon no imp to do my bidding. I am a Spider Teller.'

Bolutu cried out in delight: 'A Spider Teller! What joy, Your Highness! Then they at least have not perished from the South during my absence!'

'Not quite,' said Olik soberly. 'But we are hardly flourishing. I am the first member of the royal family ever to don a Teller's cloak. My cousins in the capital feel quite vindicated, I understand: all along they thought me mad; now I have given them proof.'

Turning to the others, he said, 'We Spider Tellers do only one thing. We search for clues. Clues about the future of Alifros, its destiny, and the secrets hidden in its immensity. A Spider Teller may seek this sort of knowledge by many paths. In my case, I was drawn to the order's few surviving chasmamancers, and in time became one of them. Chasmamancers spend less time behind temple walls than our brethren, for to practise our art we must roam far and wide. We read the future through earthquakes, and volcanic eruptions, and other disasters.'

'My own mentors, Sire,' said Bolutu, 'used to say that such violent events disturbed the universe.'

'Ever so slightly,' agreed Olik. 'No more than a pebble tossed into a lake disturbs the distant shore. The larger the disaster, of course, the greater the effect. The Worldstorm occurred fourteen centuries ago, but the waves it caused are still breaking. These waves are the oracles we try to read.

'For a long time now we have sensed the coming of a terrible event. For decades its shape was too faint to discern. Only this past spring was the vision clearly revealed: a moving palace, gliding out of a storm. Within the palace were beings we could not see, but only sense. In the words of the foretelling, they were *the ones we thought were gone for ever.* My brethren in the Spider Temple long debated who those figures might be. Some said humans, returned to their right minds. Others said *Thinkers,* what you call woken animals. Here on this ship you have both.'

'Not to mention ixchel,' said Ensyl, 'who also came from this side of the Nelluroq originally, though you do not appear to know of us.'

'Many stories mention you,' said Olik to Ensyl, 'but few of us believed them.' He looked up at the others excitedly. 'The last part of the foretelling was this: that the moving palace would appear at the time of the death of Empires, the sundering of nations. That its movement across the world would trace lines along which the world might be broken, snapped, like the lines scored in glass by a diamond blade. And that when all the world was in fragments, a new mosaic would be formed out of the pieces, though how long it would take, and what the mosaic would show, we could not, and cannot, foresee.'

Captain Rose grunted and shook his head. 'Rubbish. Poetry. We're an Arquali ship, on a plain, ugly mission. We have old foes called the Mzithrinis, and we're trying to stab them in the back. We're only in the South because we couldn't possibly find our way to the Mzithrin's western borderlands by dead reckoning. The crawlies and the sorcerer and that blary woken rat – they're unlawful passengers, nothing more.'

'And the Nilstone?' said Olik.

Rose started, glared at him. 'I don't know who you've been talking to, or how much you know about the Stone. But understand this: my crew did not seek that devilish thing, and my mission does not require it. All that matters is the Shaggat Ness. I will go further: after Arunis himself, the Nilstone is our mission's greatest obstacle. It has already turned the Shaggat to stone. If you or your city possess the skill to remove it from the Shaggat's hand without killing the bastard – your pardon, Sire – you may have it, with my blessing.'

'Captain! No!' cried the others, aghast.

'A strange blessing you offer,' said the prince. 'I should rather be blessed with an armful of scorpions than to have the Nilstone placed in my keeping. But others in this city – others in my family, too – would like nothing so much. My cousin the Emperor and his fell advisors will gladly take the Stone off your hands. They will not accept your terms, however. They will pulverise your Shaggat, and kill you all, as eagerly as you killed the ixchel. Ah, Watchers above me! What are we to do?'

He considered the buttered bread Felthrup had nibbled, then snatched it and gobbled it down.

'Six of you bear the wolf scar,' he said, chewing. 'And five of you, along with this young woman—' he nodded at Marila '—fought to save the lives of the ixchel. That, more than Erithusmé's mark itself, made me wish to see you. Of course, the sixth bearer of the mark gave the *order* to kill.'

Rose stiffened. 'Have you come to debate my orders, Sire?'

'No,' said Olik, 'though I find them highly debatable. Still, you must keep the Nilstone, and I must be grateful that it has not yet fallen into the hands of someone worse. At the very least you are not Macadra.'

His last word electrified Felthrup. He squealed, ear-piercing and high, and writhed so violently that he fell from Marila's arms. When he struck the floor he ran in circles, smashing into chairs and tables and people and dogs, all the while shouting, 'Macadra! Macadra! White teeth! White bones!'

At first no one could lay hands on him. Then Suzyt pounced and caught him with loving firmness in her jaws, as she might a hysterical puppy. Felthrup's screams went on for a short while, oddly magnified by the cavernous mouth engulfing his head. Then he fell still, whimpering and muttering. Suzyt disgorged him, and the two dogs curled around him protectively, half-burying him in their folds of flesh.

'Skies above,' said Olik, 'are they *all* like that?'

The others assured him that there was only one Felthrup. But the prince's alarm did not abate. 'How could he know of Macadra?' he asked with dread. 'She *is* white, or at least unnaturally pale. And she is a terrible sorceress – as bad as Arunis, in her way. If she is involved in this matter, things are far worse than they appear.'

'Felthrup's instincts are uncanny,' said Hercól. 'Though often bewildering even to him, they should not be ignored. He is possessed of an exceptional mind.'

'I shouldn't argue with *possessed*, anyway,' said Olik. 'But Macadra is not in the city! Vadu would have told me at once.'

'Unless he has a reason to keep it from you,' said Rose. 'A reason, or an order.'

Olik looked at him. 'You're a disturbing fellow, Captain Rose, but I can't dismiss what you say. Nor can you, my good people, stay in Masalym.'

'We have yet to leave the ship, Your Highness,' said Hercól.

'That will change tomorrow,' said Olik. 'Be glad that I managed to meet with you beforehand. Remember: my powers in Masalym are mostly bluff and bluster. True, the Issár rules the city in the name of my family, and no one in Bali Adro may harm me, on pain of death. But it is the Issár and not Prince Olik who holds the Imperial mandate. When I am obeyed it is more out of habit than duty – and there are ways around any law, even the law that protects my person, if one is willing to sacrifice a few assassins. I too must be careful.'

'My good liege,' Bolutu cried, as though he could contain himself no longer, 'what has happened to Bali Adro? For you speak as though the Ravens themselves have seized the throne.'

Olik looked at Bolutu, and suddenly his eyes were full of concern. Pazel knew vaguely who the Ravens were: Bolutu had described a gang of murderous criminals, some of whom were also sorcerers. It was the Ravens, he had claimed, who first sent Arunis across the Ruling Sea in search of the Nilstone. But the Ravens had been crushed, disbanded, before Bolutu ever set sail.

Rose made a dismissive wave. 'Mr Bolutu asks too large a question. He forgets that he has been twenty years in the North.'

Prince Olik looked dubiously at the captain. 'Twenty?' he asked.

Rose stared back at him, perplexed. Olik turned to Bolutu. 'You have passed through the Red Storm, brother, as have I. Don't you know what it does?'

Bolutu nodded and said, 'I know.'

'What is it you know?' Rose exploded. 'Damn you, what is it you haven't told me? Speak! I'm the captain of this ship!'

'What's this all about, Mr Bolutu?' asked Fiffengurt, cocking his head.

Bolutu looked to the others for support. Hercól nodded. 'It is time we did speak, at that. You had best sit down, Captain Rose. And you as well, Mr Fiffengurt.'

'Sit down?' shouted Rose. 'To the Pits with that! Tell me!'

'This is the little something you wouldn't talk about, ain't it?' said Fiffengurt, angry himself. 'That night by the fire on the Sandwall, when I asked if there was more, and you all played dead-to-the-world. From me, Pathkendle, Undrabust! You kept secrets from me, from old Fiffengurt, your friend through every spot of nastiness since we sailed out of Sorrophran! No I won't sit down either!' Fiffengurt stamped his foot. 'I'm hurt, Miss Thasha, that's what I am.'

'You won't care about that in a moment,' said Thasha.

Her hollow voice scared Mr Fiffengurt sober. He sat down. Rose would not, at least at first, but as Thasha began to speak of the time-skip he groped for a chair. Pazel found that watching the emotions (denial, outrage, terror, wonder, loss) surfacing on Rose's craggy face brought his own agony back to him. Gone, everything gone. It was one thing to imagine death at sea, quite another to survive a terrible ordeal and know that your world – the world that made you, the people you loved – had not. He thought of Maisa, Hercól's beloved deposed Empress, who he had fought for years to restore to the throne. He thought of his mother, who he had dreamed of so strangely for several nights, and of Eberzam Isiq.

Their old age, their final years, their deaths with no family beside them. He thought of Mr Fiffengurt's Annabel, raising their child, never knowing what had become of the father. Mother and child were dead and gone, their very names forgotten, and the *Chathrand* reduced to a few lines in the latest *Polylex*. The Great Ship, the one that vanished two centuries ago.

He could see that Rose did not believe a word.

Fiffengurt, for his part, was turning from one face to the next. Begging someone to laugh. Pazel's eyes grew bright. *Stupid*, he accused himself, *even you don't quite believe it yet. How can you ask them to accept it, if you're too frightened yourself?*

With a great effort he summoned one of Hercól's teachings from fighting class, a phrase from the *Thojmêlê* Code: *You will fail in proportion to your resistance to change. Fluidity is universal, stasis a phantom of the mind.*

'Two centuries,' said the prince. 'That is much worse than my own case. I set sail just after my twenty-seventh birthday, aboard the great *Segral*-class ship *Leurad*. There were five ships in that expedition: all bound for the North, to your own lands. It would have been historic, the rekindling of contact between two worlds, and it might have brought a measure of safety and peace to both, for there were warnings we meant to give, and facts we sought to learn. But the moment our ships entered the Red Storm we lost sight of one another, and when the *Leurad* emerged on the Northern side, she was alone. Worse still, a horrid gale bore down on us not two days later, and we were almost sunk. We limped home again, passing once more through the blaze of light – only to find some eight decades had elapsed. That was twenty years ago. I have become a creature of this latter-day world, but I still mourn the one I lost.'

Rose leaned on his elbows, his hands folded before his face. 'No,' he said, 'this is absurd. This is the stuff of madness, nothing more.'

Pazel had never seen him so shaken. 'It's true, Captain,' he said. 'Everyone we left behind is dead.'

'Oh no,' said the prince, startling him.

The others turned him a mystified look. 'What do you mean, no?' said Thasha.

'I mean,' said Olik, 'that you have misunderstood the Storm. Not surprisingly – I did as well. But I have made a study of the phenomenon since my return, and have established a few points beyond question. First of all, the time-skip occurs only when sailing northwards. Your two centuries vanished, Mr Bolutu, when you *first sailed north*. It is a matter of how totally estranged North and South have become that you were not even aware of it during the twenty further years you dwelled in those lands.'

Pazel felt light-headed. He saw Thasha gripping the edge of the table as though some wild force might try to snatch it, or her, away. She said, 'When we passed through the Storm on the *Chathrand*, then, heading south—'

'No time-skip occurred at all,' said Olik. 'I guarantee it, my dear.'

Everyone but Rose and Fiffengurt cried aloud, their feelings irrepressible. Even Hercól's face was transformed by a sudden, unbearable change in his understanding of the world. Thasha dropped her eyes, and Pazel knew it was taking all her effort not to weep. *Her father's alive. Somewhere, ten thousand miles from here, he's alive and waiting. And my mother, too. And we can never, ever go back.*

Bolutu rose and walked stiffly to the corner by the washroom. Pazel's mind was flooded, the thoughts almost too sharp to bear. *That man just learned that his world died twenty years ago. Twenty years in exile, never dreaming that every friend, cousin, brother, sister was dead and gone. He lived a lie for two decades. Aya Rin.*

'My second observation,' said the prince, speaking over their oaths and laments, 'is that the Red Storm is weakening. It has always fluctuated in intensity – and thus in its power as both a time-interrupter and a barrier to the flow of magic across the hemispheres. But there can be no doubt that it is in swift decline. I would not be surprised if it vanished altogether within another decade or two. Already there are periods when it is very weak.'

'Meaning what?' Pazel demanded, utterly forgetting that he was speaking to royalty. 'Meaning that there are times when it *wouldn't* toss us centuries into the future, even when we're sailing north?'

'That is correct,' said Olik.

Now they were surrounding his chair, mobbing him. 'How many years forward *would* it propel us?' asked Hercól.

Olik shrugged. 'Forty or fifty? Perhaps fewer at the weakest times. My estimates are quite rough. It's a difficult matter to put to the test.'

'And every year,' said Thasha, 'it *weakens*?'

The prince nodded gravely.

'Then,' cried Marila, 'say, in four or five years, even, those fluctuations, if we hit them just right—'

'Could mean that your time-displacement would be small indeed, on your return – *if*, as you say, your timing was perfect.'

Suddenly Hercól lifted Thasha right off her feet and into his arms. They had eyes only for each other, then – streaming eyes, and a look of understanding that left Pazel mystified.

'Did I not say it, girl?' said Hercól, looking almost furious. 'Tell me, did I not *say* it?'

'You did,' she said, embracing him with arms and legs.

'Now say it yourself,' he growled. 'Say it now and believe it for ever. Claim it, Thasha Isiq.'

'*Eyacaulgra*,' she said. And as she kissed him, and Hercól lowered her to her feet, Pazel's bewildered mind did the translating. The language was Hercól's native Tholjassan, but the sentiment was her father's maxim, his signature: *Unvanquished*.

A few minutes later Prince Olik rose to leave. He was glad to have given them new hope, he said, but he warned them that the immediate peril was real.

'I will leave you with three suggestions,' he said. 'First, you should each pack a visiting bag – clothes and toothbrushes, sleepwear and such – to last you several days. Masalym hospitality is a ferocious business, and once he sees for himself that you're not demons or dangerous lunatics, the Issár may very well insist on parading you through all the finer homes of the Upper City. You would cause great offence if you had to come back here for a change of socks.

'Second, ask for nothing in the Upper City. As a rule we dlömu take pride in our generosity, but in Masalym that pride is an obsession, and among the well-to-do of Masalym it must be experienced to be believed. If you want water, you mention in passing that the weather tends to dry one's throat. To make a direct request is to insult your host for not having provided it already.'

'But all we *did* was ask, when we showed up in port,' said Marila. 'Food, food. We practically begged on our knees.'

'Yes,' said Olik, 'and that made it terribly difficult to feed you. Vadu was preparing a grand feast, but when you begged, he was so offended that he ordered the cooks not to deliver it to the port. I was unable to change his mind until the following day.'

'What about that first meal, the one that came by pulleys in the dark?'

'You can thank Ibjen for that,' said the prince. 'He was clever to mention those nursery rhymes about the feeling of hunger. The poor of the Lower City know the feeling well, and it was the poor who fed you. I doubt if the meal seemed excessive to you, starving as you were. But it would have fed ten times as many dlömic mouths. They gave you everything they could put their hands on – even though many of them believed you were ghosts. In our stories even ghosts need to eat.'

'Perfect lunacy,' said Fiffengurt.

'That too is forbidden!' Olik laughed. 'A grave insult it is – a *fighting* insult – to call another mad.'

'Ibjen explained already, Prince,' said Bolutu, 'but even I have trouble remembering.'

'See that you remember tomorrow,' said Olik. 'Well, goodbye, my new friends. Rest today; you will soon need all your strength.'

He rose then and bowed to Thasha and Marila – and then, catching himself, Ensyl. The captain led him to the door and opened it, and the prince was already in the passage when Pazel said, 'Wait, Sire. What about your third suggestion? It wasn't about madness, was it?'

Olik turned in the doorway. He rested both hands on the frame. 'No, it wasn't, Mr Pathkendle,' he said. 'My third suggestion I nearly decided to keep to myself. But now I think I will speak after all.'

His voice had a sudden, utterly chilling edge. 'My third suggestion is that you be far more careful in whom you confide. As you say, you know little about me. I could well be an enemy – perhaps an ally of Arunis, or of Lady Macadra and the Raven Society. But you assumed I was a friend, and lavished information on me. You confirmed that the Nilstone and Arunis are aboard this ship – I was, in fact, guessing about both. You, Undrabust, named those who bear the mark of Erithusmé: I did not know that you and Hercól were among them. You, Master Felthrup, revealed that you're a woken animal – to a prince of the Imperium that labels such creatures *maukslarets*, little demons, and has hunted them to the edge of extinction.'

Heart racing, Pazel moved in front of Felthrup and Marila. Thasha stepped up beside him. The prince's smile was impenetrable. Then he turned and looked coldly at Bolutu.

'And you, brother, you were the worst by far. You barely spoke, but when you did, you revealed your passionate hatred for the Ravens. You let me know that you would consider it a dark day if Bali Adro should ever be ruled by that noble Society, which counts both Arunis and Macadra among its founders. But you have been gone a long time, Bolutu, and that day has come. When I leave here I shall endeavour to forget that you spoke those words. I most earnestly advise you to do the same.'

18

Springing the Trap

Later that morning Arunis killed again.

This time the one who came for the Nilstone was Latzlo, the animal dealer and one of the 'illustrious passengers' referred to in Old Gangrüne's report. He had once been illustrious enough, or at least very rich. To this day he still wore the same broad snakeskin belt, although he had lost so much weight that it could have gone twice around his middle, and the black scales were falling out. The journey had not been kind to Latzlo: he had come aboard to woo Pacu Lapadolma, a young woman who despised him, only to watch her marry the Mzithrini prince in Thasha's stead. After Simja, like many others, he had been kept aboard at spear-point. During the crossing of the Nelluroq he had watched his fortune in exotic animals disappear one by one, sometimes into the galley, and thence the ever-hungrier mouths around Rose's table. A great number had literally disappeared, during the battle with the rats. The animal seller had grown steadily more ill-tempered and withdrawn.

He was not universally despised, however. Mr Thyne, the other 'illustrious passenger' trapped against his will aboard the Great Ship, had kept up a friendship of sorts with Latzlo. When the disaster came the two men, along with a young midshipman by the name of Boone, were playing a fitful game of *spenk* on the topdeck.

They were playing for sugar cubes. Latzlo was winning handily, though his face showed no joy. Thyne was down to six cubes when he executed a particularly daring bluff, and won a round.

'Back in the game, Ernom!' He laughed, slapping Latzlo's knee.

'Ouch,' said Latzlo.

'Never say die!' added Boone, who had a gold earring and a voice that sounded too deep for his skinny frame. 'Bet you thought you had him, didn't you, Mr Latzlo?'

Latzlo rubbed his knee, scowling. 'I quit,' he said.

'Oh, come now, that isn't sporting,' said Thyne. 'You've still got three-quarters of the cubes.'

'Do you think it tickles, when you slap a man?'

Startled, Thyne glanced at Latzlo's knee. 'What, have you got a rash there? I didn't know.'

Latzlo rose to his feet. 'Keep the sugar,' he said. 'I know where there's something sweeter by half.'

'Do you now?' said Thyne, as Boone began to scoop up Latzlo's cubes. 'Where's that, I should like to know?'

'Where it's always been,' said Latzlo. 'Right there in his hand.'

He turned to portside and walked quickly away, like a man with an urgent errand to perform. Thyne watched him a moment, frowning. Then he noticed Boone's sugar-grab, and forgot Latzlo for a moment. The men scuffled, scattering cards and sugar, until Thyne froze with horror in his eyes.

'Rin's Angel, he's talking about the Shaggat Ness!'

They bolted after the animal seller. By now Latzlo was halfway down the No. 4 ladderway. When he heard them coming he too began to run. They caught up with him only as he reached the doors to the manger – unlocked, by the strangest coincidence, for the changing of the Turach guard.

'Stop him, stop him! He's going for the blary stone!'

The replacement guards were due any minute. Of course, the men of the earlier shift were still at their posts. Never for one minute would the Shaggat be left unattended.

'Don't hurt him!' cried Thyne.

There were six Turachs in all, wielding maces and clubs. They had waited for such a moment since the deaths of their comrades, and they formed a deadly line in front of the Shaggat. Latzlo went into a frenzy. He lunged for the Shaggat – and the soldiers slammed him to the ground. He had never been strong, and not even possession by Arunis could give him the strength to overpower half a dozen marines. Still, he writhed and kicked and spat and howled. He bit his tongue; blood oozed from his lips. Then suddenly he began to scream: 'Thyne! Thyne! Help! My knee!'

The soldiers dragged him to a corner. 'His blary knee again,' said Boone. 'Look, he's hurting something awful!'

A Turach poked Latzlo's knee. The animal seller howled in agony: 'Get it off, Thyne! Cut it off! It's burning straight through my leg!'

'That snakeskin belt's all in knots,' said a Turach.

'Cut it away, then, something's wrong!' shouted Thyne. 'Hurry, you louts! It's killing him!'

'Nothing to cut with,' said the Turach in command. 'No blades allowed in the same room with the Nilstone, after—'

'I have one! Take mine!' said Boone, unfolding his stockman's knife.

Latzlo twisted, screaming louder than ever. 'Just cut the mucking trousers!' shouted Thyne.

Boone leaned in and slashed. The knife was sharp; the cloth parted, and a soldier ripped the trouser leg open to Latzlo's hip.

There was no visible wound. But there was something. Words, in fact, scrawled in ink above the knee. Thyne leaned closer, morbidly curious, and read aloud:

'All . . . of . . . you . . . in . . . time.'

Latzlo stopped screaming. The chilling words hung in the air. Then came a dull thump: an object falling to the deck from a height of some six feet. It was the midshipman's knife.

Boone himself was nowhere to be seen. Once again, however, there was a small incision in the canvas hiding the Nilstone. And beneath the Shaggat's upraised arm, several buttons, a gold earring and a few withered ounces of mortal remains.

*

'It's almost as though he planned it that way,' said Neeps.

'Arunis, you mean?' said Pazel, blowing the sawdust from his sanding-stone.

Neeps shook his head. 'Olik. As though he'd warned us that he was with Arunis, and then had to prove it by nudging him to kill again.'

They were on a scaffold over the tonnage hatch, along with Thasha, Marila and Hercól. They were sanding a part of the enormous pine trunk that would replace the makeshift foremast. The pine was their one spare mast-trunk, the other having been lost to fire. It was propped at a diagonal, one end jutting out over the quay, the other six decks below, where men were still ripping away the bark with drawknives, tackling knots with chisels and planes. The dlömu had taken charge of the *Chathrand*'s exterior – their own scaffolding rose on either side of her damaged hull – but they had so far left all other repairs to the crew.

'He didn't quite say he was *with* Arunis,' said Thasha. 'I mean, yes, he said Arunis was with the Ravens, and he called them a "noble Society". But he never claimed to be part of that Society himself. And even when he stopped pretending to like us – stopped saying "my friends" and all that, and told us how reckless we'd been – even then he never praised Arunis. It would have been easy to say "the Great Mage" or "my master" or anything of that kind. But he wasn't gloating, the way Arunis does himself. He really did seem to be warning us.'

'To judge by Bolutu's despair,' said Hercól, 'all such warnings must be in vain if the Ravens have truly seized control of Bali Adro. They were, you recall, the very "gang of criminals" who opposed the old, just regime he so proudly served – the gang who sent Arunis to the North in the first place, to seek the Nilstone.'

'If Olik *is* with the Ravens,' said Neeps, 'then we can't trust what he said about the Red Storm, either. He may just have wanted to keep us off balance, by giving us hope that we might return to our own time one day, or something close to it. So that we'd spend our time pondering that, instead of ways to fight him.'

Hercól shook his head. 'I think he spoke the truth about the Red Storm, at least. Think of Arunis. If we cannot return to the North without leaping centuries into the future, what sense is there in his plans? Either he has always been ignorant of the Storm's nature, or he is counting on the Shaggat cult remaining powerful enough to trigger open warfare hundreds of years after his first rise to power. Neither is likely. Therefore Arunis, too, must be counting on a weakened Storm.'

Neeps gave them a stubborn look. 'I still say Olik's lying big about something,' he said. 'You know I can tell when people lie.'

'Oh please,' said Marila.

'There was something wrong about his whole visit,' said Pazel. 'Neeps is right, it doesn't add up. And every other time a mystery like this has surfaced, we've eventually traced it back to Arunis. *Credek*, we may have just let one of his servants walk around in the stateroom.'

'Why is Arunis doing all this killing lately, anyway?' said Thasha. 'Obviously he's not afraid any more of what will happen if he kills the spell-keeper, and the Shaggat comes back to life.'

'Or rather,' said Hercól, 'he is no longer constrained by the fear of *chancing* upon the spell-keeper, when he kills. And that can only mean that he has found a way to rule certain people out. And that can only be because he has learned who the spell-keeper is. Either that, or he has despaired of the Shaggat altogether, and no longer minds the risk. He had his own copy of the thirteenth *Polylex* for a short time, before Pazel destroyed it. Perhaps in that time he glimpsed some other method of using the Nilstone. Some more remote chance, but one that he never forgot. Maybe he is groping towards it even now.'

'You think he's doing some kind of experiment?' said Neeps. 'Sending one person after another to touch the Nilstone, and watching what happens?'

'But the same thing happens with each of them,' said Pazel. 'They shrivel up and die. And anyway he's not there watching, unless he's turned into an ant or a flea.'

'Maybe he's watching their minds, not their bodies,' said Thasha.

They worked in silence for several minutes, and then Pazel spoke again. 'I'm going to have a fit.'

All the others stopped work and looked at him. They knew what 'a fit' meant in Pazel's case. Thasha reached out as if to touch his arm, but hesitated. 'Soon?' she said.

Pazel shrugged, applying his sanding-stone with force. 'Maybe two days from now. Four at the most. The taste in my mouth started this morning. And the purring sound.'

'No fear, mate,' said Neeps. 'We know what to do. You just run for the stateroom, bury your head in pillows. You won't hear much in— Well, in the admiral's old room.'

The last time Pazel's fits had come, he had fled to the reading cabin – that tiny, beautiful, glassed-in chamber off the stateroom. But the reading cabin was adjacent to Thasha's own. For days now she and Fulbreech had passed an hour or two each evening in her cabin, laughing and murmuring. They kept their voices low, but it pierced the walls nonetheless. During his fits any voices at all were a torture to Pazel. Thasha and Fulbreech's would be unbearable.

'Those signs, the purring and the evil taste,' said Hercól, 'mean that your Gift is at work even now?'

'This very minute,' said Pazel, 'for all the good *that* does us.'

'And your hearing's sharper too?' asked Marila.

'I don't know yet,' said Pazel. 'It used to work only with translated voices – as if my mind was *reaching* for them, you understand? But the last time, when Chadfallow gave me that drug, I could hear most everything. Birds, breathing, whispers fifty feet away. That was on Bramian. A lot of things changed on Bramian.'

Thasha was looking at him, pensive. 'That thing you spoke with. The eguar.'

Pazel's encounter with the deadly, magic-steeped eguar was one of the worst moments of his life. 'What about it?' he said.

'It mentioned the South, didn't it?'

'Yes,' said Pazel. 'I told you. It called the South *the world my brethren made.*'

Thasha nodded. 'Last night I was reading—'

Pazel bit his lips. *With your darling Fulbreech.*

'—and I learned something about eguar. Not under "eguar" of course; the *Polylex* doesn't make anything that easy. But there was a little paragraph under "longevity". It says that eguar live an extraordinarily long time – longer than the oldest trees. Some of the oldest were born before the Dawn War, in the time when demons ruled Alifros. They can spend a year without moving, a decade between meals. And the book said, "*This near-immortality, along with the terrible black magic concentrated in their blood and bone, has long fascinated the wizarding folk of the South.*"'

'Ah! That is telling,' said Hercól. 'Bolutu studied magic at Ramachni's knee, though he says he never succeeded in becoming a mage. And he reacted strongly when you mentioned the eguar, I believe.'

'Strongly!' said Pazel. 'He acted as though I'd met the prince of all devils, and caught the talking fever to boot. And Chadfallow wasn't much better. He said Ramachni had spoken to him about eguar. He made us bathe in the first river we came to. When we got back to the camp he burned all our clothes, and made Ott's men scrub the horses down with gloves on.'

'Well then,' said Neeps, 'those Ravens wanted the Nilstone, but they haven't got it. Maybe they found some other way to make themselves mighty – something involving the eguar.'

'Gods,' said Pazel, suddenly shaken, 'that's right, I'm sure it is. That shimmer over the armada – that weird, bright haze, you remember? It was how the air looked around the eguar, from a distance, when we first saw it basking in the sun. And the leader of the swimmers who attacked us – there was something of it around him as well. Just a touch. I could barely see it through the telescope.'

'I will speak to Bolutu about these eguar,' said Hercól. 'In any case, Pazel, I am glad the creature never touched you.'

'It didn't have to touch me,' said Pazel, flinching at the memory. He began to sand again, quickly, needing to move. Once more

Thasha reached for him, and once more she stopped her hand.

'When you came back,' she said, 'you were so different, for a while. So strange.'

'Must have been hard for you,' said Marila, 'Pazel changing like that.'

Thasha turned to her as if she'd been slapped. Marila picked up her stone and began to work again. But she added quietly, 'You let Fulbreech see the book whenever he wants. Handle it, too. He knows you have a thirteenth *Polylex*.'

'You're a damned little spy.'

'Thasha,' said Marila, 'you came out of your cabin last night with the *Polylex* under your arm. He took it before he ... greeted you.'

Pazel sanded harder, faster.

Then Hercól straightened his back and glanced at the darkening sky. 'We should leave off until the morning. Teggatz will be calling us to our meal.'

'Think I'll work a little longer,' said Neeps, his voice as cold as Marila's.

Thasha laughed bitterly. 'I'll go,' she said. 'Then you'll *all* be happier.'

She pushed past them, walked to the end of the scaffold and stepped over the rail onto the topdeck. Then she turned and looked back at them.

'I'm ending this tonight,' she said. 'Do you hear me? I won't play your game any more.'

'For some of us it never was a game,' said Neeps.

But Pazel thought, *Who is she talking to?*

Thasha marched to the Holy Stair and descended. Towards sickbay, Pazel realised, where Fulbreech worked.

'She's right,' said Neeps. 'I *do* feel better.'

Hercól looked at him with quiet regret. 'You speak proudly, both of you,' he said. 'Well and good, but if shame should follow, remember what you said to that girl.'

Then he departed as well. Pazel, Neeps and Marila sanded

wordlessly in the gathering dark. But despite the shadows Pazel saw his two friends exchanging glances. 'All right,' he said at last, 'spill it. What is it you want to tell me?'

'Listen,' said Marila. 'You know I tried to take her side at first. I was wrong. She's lost her mind over him, and it's ruining everything, and it has to stop. We should push him down a hatch.'

'Marila!' cried both boys.

'I mean it. Something terrible is going to happen – and Thasha's *helping* it happen, damn it. We bumped into each other last night – really bumped, in the stateroom, it was pitch dark. I started to fall and she caught me, helped me up. But then she wouldn't let go of my arm. "Let me do what I have to do," she said, "with him."'

'Thasha said *that*?'

'There's worse, Pazel. I said she was becoming another person, and she said, yes, she was. Then I said I liked the old one better, and she said, "What you like makes no difference. Just stay out of my way." Then I said what we're all thinking. "Arunis. He's gotten hold of you, hasn't he?" And Thasha laughed and said, "Arunis is scared to death of me. He always has been. And you should be too." Then she shoved me aside and I *did* fall, blary hard, and she walked right out of the room.'

Marila blew away more sawdust, felt the smoothness of the pine with her fingertips.

'She's going bad, I tell you. I don't want to believe it, but all you have to do is look at her when he walks in the room. She forgets everything else, and goes all dreamy and warm. I think she's going to end up – you know – knitting little boots.'

Pazel dropped his sanding stone.

He swore, and they all screamed warnings down the tonnage shaft, where men were still working by lamplight. There came a loud *thud* and a barrage of curses. *You careless Gods-damned tarboy dog! That was two feet from my head!*

Time to quit, they decided. Fleeing guiltily along the starboard rail, they saw the 'birdwatchers' gathered together on the quay. They were arguing, waving their hands, now and then gesturing at the *Chathrand* as if to emphasise a point. *Tomorrow*, Pazel thought. *What's going to happen to us tomorrow?*

'She's probably in the stateroom with him right now,' said Marila. 'He likes to see her right after his shift.'

'There's the dinner bell,' said Neeps.

'And Hercól,' added Marila furiously, 'does *nothing* but defend her.'

Pazel stopped walking. *Defend her.* That was what he had promised himself he would always do. No matter what it took. No matter what Thasha said or did. How could he ever have allowed himself to be confused on that point? He turned and looked at his friends.

'Is there any doubt at all,' he said, 'that Fulbreech is a liar?'

'No,' said Neeps.

Both boys looked at Marila. She closed her eyes a moment, thoughtful. 'No,' she said at last. 'Not if he really said "error corrected" after you punched him in the eye.'

'I'm going to see her,' said Pazel.

'Oh, stop it, mate,' said Neeps. 'You've tried. She doesn't want to hear you. She doesn't want to believe.'

'I don't care.'

He would make her hear. He would explain word for word, and Thasha would see at last that he wasn't simply jealous. And he would explain about the antidote, how even though Fulbreech had appeared to be chasing Alyash, as they were, he was really on the bosun's side. No one else could have slipped the antidote through the doorway at the bitter end. It was Fulbreech who had freed the hostages, paving the way for Rose's bloodbath.

He reached the Silver Stair and plunged down, among the crowd of hungry sailors making for the dining compartment.

'You can't just walk in on them!' Marila shouted.

'Bet I can,' he shot back.

The sailors grinned and winked. Pazel could not have cared less. Walking in on Thasha and Fulbreech was exactly what he planned to do. Let her choose who to believe, once and for all, face to face with both of them. At least she wouldn't be able to feign a need to be elsewhere.

Neeps' hand closed on his elbow. 'At least let Marila go first, Pazel. She'll tell you if it's all right to go in there.'

'Damn it all, leave me alone!'

Pazel wrenched his arm away. But as he turned he found the passage blocked by Mr Fiffengurt. 'Pathkendle!' he said. 'And Undrabust too. What luck. I have a little job I need your help with.'

'Now?' said Pazel.

'Right now,' said Fiffengurt, strangely anxious. He bent closer, and spoke in an ominous whisper. 'Urgent business. The hag's cat, Sniraga. She's alive.'

'I've heard. I'm sorry.' Pazel began to slip by, but Fiffengurt lurched in front of him.

'You don't understand. She's in the bread room. She's slipped inside, the little monster.'

'So what?' said Neeps, briefly forgetting his own efforts to stop Pazel cold. 'Best place to put her if you ask me. That's no blary emergency.'

'We don't even have any *bread*,' said Pazel.

Fiffengurt turned his gaze from one to the other. He looked confounded by their response. 'Why! Anyone could tell you – a cat, loose in the— Oh, blast you both, come along! That's an order!'

Fulbreech sat in the chair by Thasha's writing desk, hands on his knees, his pale face troubled. 'All of them,' he said, 'believe that my intentions towards you are . . . dishonourable?'

'Yes,' said Thasha, 'entirely.'

She sat cross-legged on her bed, in an old pair of red trousers and a loose white shirt of Admiral Isiq's. 'I don't care, Greysan. I don't care *what* they imagine.'

He shook his head. 'You should care. They love you dearly, Thasha.'

They were sharing a glass of water and some dlömic biscuits. They had not touched since she led him into the room. The desk was cluttered: jewellery, creams, pencils, knives, a whetstone, the admiral's flask, the *Merchant's Polylex*. Behind all these, the softly ticking mariner's clock, Ramachni's doorway from his own world into Alifros.

The wind had risen. The night would be cool. Against the hanging oil lamp a weird Southern moth tapped hairy antennae; its huge shadow wriggled on the bedspread. Thasha was looking down at her hands.

'Not like this,' she whispered.

They were both very still. 'Of course,' he said, 'what I feel for you is different.'

Thasha smiled.

'But I have been blind – blind and selfish. These evenings with you, learning of your life, hearing your dreams: Thasha, I've been drunk on them. But now I fear your friends are talking about us, and not just among themselves.'

'Let them.'

'No,' he said, 'that won't help, making enemies. Your good name is priceless, even though our society is reduced to one mad ship, hung out to dry in an alien port.'

'You say all that because you think you *have* to.' Thasha touched a hole in her trouser knee. 'But I know what you're feeling.'

'Do you really think so?'

Thasha nodded. 'I know you're ... impatient.' She laughed, trying to make a joke of it, then blushed and had to look away. He smiled too, generously.

'Are you afraid of something, Thasha?' he asked.

She looked at him shyly, then glanced at the *Polylex*. 'In Etherhorde, in Dr Chadfallow's house – you know he was a family friend – there was a book about Mzithrini art. Did you know that the Old Faith has nothing against showing ... men and women?'

'Lovers, you mean?' Fulbreech squirmed a little. 'I may have heard something about that.'

Thasha paused as if to steady her nerves. 'I used to take out that book whenever we visited. There was a painting of a sculpture in a Babqri square. Three women on their knees, reaching desperately for a man being lifted away by angels. He's beautiful, naked of course ... and he's forgotten the women; his eyes are on the place the angels are taking him, some other world, I suppose. But when you look closer you see that the three women are really just one, at three moments in life. Young, and older, and very old, shrivelled. And the name of the sculpture is *If You Wait He Will Escape You*.'

Thasha looked at him, blinking nervously. 'I've been dreaming of their faces. Greysan, you must think I'm crazy—'

'Nonsense.'

'I'm afraid you'll escape me.'

She sat there, trembling, and then his hand closed over hers. Neither of them speaking. His fingers rough and warm between her own.

'Impatient.' Fulbreech gave her an awkward smile. 'Perhaps that is your delicate way of saying *vulgar*. Listen, darling: I would sooner die than insult you. Only it seems I can hide nothing in your presence. Not my dreams for our future, certainly. And not even—' he took a deep breath '—dreams of another kind.'

He flinched; surely he had gone too far. But Thasha's gaze only softened, as though she had known this was coming and was glad the wait was over. She reached out and gently touched his face.

In the torchlight from the quay she saw struggle in his eyes. They were travelling her body, but now and then they stopped, uncertain. Some idea, some duty maybe, giving him pause.

'Later the others will be here,' he said.

Thasha stood in one smooth motion. She raised the water glass and drank it dry. Then she set the glass beside the *Polylex* and blew out the lantern.

'Later we'll have to be quiet,' she said, and sat astride him.

She used her mouth as she never had in any previous kiss. She heard him gasping, felt his hands on her thighs, his legs moving beneath her. She sat back trembling. The struggle was almost over.

'You don't know who you're dealing with,' she said.

'No?'

'I was raised by Syrarys as much as my father. She came out of the slave school on Nurth. She was trained in love. I spied on them for years. How she moved, what she said. I saw how she ... made him happy.'

'You can't have known what you were seeing.'

'I was at the Lorg School, too.'

'Learning to be a wife?'

Thasha didn't answer. Slowly, watching him, she unbuttoned her shirt.

Fulbreech was motionless. Thasha's lips were parted, her face almost stern. When his own hands moved at last she put her head back and closed her eyes. Do not think. That is crucial. Do not let it be real.

He was atop her; she lay back and put a hand in his hair. When his kisses became more urgent she squeezed her left hand into a fist. The wolf scar on her palm, self-inflicted years ago, felt suddenly raw and unhealed.

Voices in the outer stateroom. Greysan froze, catlike, his chin an inch above her breast. 'It's Hercól,' she whispered. 'Damn him, damn him. Why can't he just stay away?'

'Bolutu as well,' he said, frustration in his voice. 'Thasha darling, we can be careful—'

'No!' she whispered. 'I can't, I'm sorry, if they heard me, I'd—'

Fulbreech could not catch his breath. He began again, and she stopped him instantly, her hand tight on his wrist.

'They don't know you're in here,' she said. 'Just stay with me, Greysan, stay right here and hold me. And later, when they're asleep—'

He looked at her. For a moment she thought he'd gone beyond the reach of words. Then a sigh of anticipation passed through him, and he settled by her side.

*

In the bread room, Neeps was pounding on the door. 'Fiffengurt! You've blown your gaskets! Open this blary door!'

'Not possible, Undrabust,' came Fiffengurt's voice. From the sound of it he was seated with his back to the sturdy, tin-plated door. They had already heard him telling puzzled sailors to mind their own business.

'What in Pitfire did we do?' shouted Neeps.

'You didn't do anything. Just calm down, now, save your breath. And speaking of breath, you'd better snuff those lanterns. That's an airtight room.'

Neeps turned his back and began mule-kicking the door. 'Why – why – why – *why?*'

'Ouch! Stop that! Screaming will do you no good.'

Pazel sat in the centre of the chamber, in the flour and the dust. The entire room – walls, floor, door, ceiling – was lined with tin, as a protection against nibbling mice. Their lantern-light reflected dimly from the walls.

Fiffengurt had caught them easily: told them to clear away the stacked and empty bread racks, since 'that red monster's got to be lurking in one of the corners', then slipped out as soon as the work began to throw the deadbolts. Neeps had exploded, but Pazel had not said a word. Everything that had happened since Thasha stalked away from the tonnage hatch was suspicious. But he could not for an instant believe that Fiffengurt would betray them. Nor would Thasha, for that matter. Something else was going on.

'Liar!' spat Neeps at the door. 'You made all that up, about Sniraga!'

''Course I did,' said Fiffengurt. 'Now just sit tight like Pazel's doing, there's a good lad. I'm not doing this for fun, you know.'

Neeps was working himself into a lather. 'You're a lunatic! Let us out! Pazel, why don't you mucking *do* something?'

'I am doing something,' said Pazel. 'Be quiet. Let me think.'

'You're a daft, white-whiskered fat old pig, Fiffengurt!' bellowed Neeps. 'What have you done with Marila?'

'Oh come off it, Undrabust,' said Fiffengurt. 'How should I know where Marila went? Back to the stateroom, I imagine. Ah no – fancy that! – here she is in the flesh.'

'Hello, Mr Fiffengurt. Hello, Neeps.'

Marila's voice was oddly circumspect, but Neeps paid no heed to her tone. 'About time!' he shouted. 'Get around that old pig, Marila, and slide those bolts!'

'I can't, Neeps.'

'Then run and tell Hercól that Fiffengurt's a lying, sneaky, sell-'im-cheap-to-the-sausage-grinder fat old pig.'

'Neeps,' said Marila, 'try to be like Pazel for once.'

'Listen to your lady, Undrabust,' said Fiffengurt. 'Sit down and relax.'

Neeps threw his body against the door. He staggered, bruised, and backed up for another run. Pazel shook his head. It was never a good idea to tell Neeps to relax.

Thasha, for her part, was already unconscious. She lay holding Fulbreech, her long hair pooled around them, her breath deep and even. Fulbreech touched her with his fingertips. He, of course, remained wide awake. Sandor Ott would murder him if he fell asleep on the job.

Bolutu was gone at last, but Hercól remained in the outer stateroom, reading; Fulbreech could hear the scratch of turning pages. The girl was right, sound carried; it would have been madness to pleasure himself on her until the Tholjassan retired. She had saved him from a grave mistake. A *human* mistake, as his master would have said with scorn.

But his hunger for this girl: that was human too. He saw no reason why he should not have her when the man departed. He could allow himself that much. So many months of waiting, performing, drawing her in but never seeming to, never arousing her suspicion. Even Ott would agree that the timing was right. And yet he'd held back, let her own hunger flourish, her curiosity. Let her worry in her girl's foolishness about him 'escaping her'. Yes, it was very well done. If she was ready to give her body she'd give anything. The *Polylex*, whenever he wished to take it. The truth about Pathkendle's Gift, the whereabouts of Ramachni, the secrets of that lovely clock.

But how close he had come to ruin, merely through the weakness of the flesh! Ah, but you *didn't*, Fulbreech, and hasn't your whole life been a gamble for the highest of stakes? For that was what he was: a gambler, possessed of exceptional instincts, and addicted to the dare. Some gamblers played with caution, and hoarded what they feared to lose; others raised their bluffs without a backward glance.

Thasha Isiq, of course, was a trifle. His master might arrange for him to keep her, but if not – well, for a chancellor of a new world power, there would be as many women as nights to fill them. And for the moment, in any case, the girl was his. Fulbreech lay there, savouring the image of her fingers freeing buttons, her brief abandon, that foretaste of the meal to come.

Then Bolutu returned. The youth's anger flared: did they plan to come and go all night? But the dlömu was now in a very different state of mind. His boots pounded across the floor, and quite audibly, he said, 'It's happening! They're taking him! Tomorrow at dawn!'

Fulbreech held his breath.

'Tomorrow?' said Hercól, incredulous. 'Are you certain?'

'Prince Olik himself will lead the team,' said Bolutu, 'with sixty hand-picked warriors at his side. His man just handed me a note over the gunwale. I went straight to Rose, of course, and the captain promised once again to cooperate. What else can we do, he said to me, with that sorcerer killing left and right?'

'Those may be the sanest words Rose ever uttered,' said Hercól.

'Haddismal was present as well, and he concurs: "Let them have it," he said, "the sooner the better." He was quite relieved, I think: the Nilstone is not an enemy he knows how to fight.'

'But they could *kill* the Shaggat trying to extract the Stone from his grip,' said Hercól. 'Haddismal must not understand the risk.'

'He understands perfectly,' said Bolutu. 'He's simply come to see what we always hoped he would: that armed with the Nilstone, the sorcerer threatens Arqual itself. "My oath is to the Ametrine Throne," he said, "not any one order that comes down from it. His Supremacy didn't know about the Nilstone when he sent us off to deliver the Shaggat. If he orders me to prune his garden and I see killers climbing over the wall, do I go on snipping roses? Is that how I prove I'm a loyal subject?"' Bolutu laughed. 'For all his talk, though, I think he holds out hope that they will manage to take the Stone without destroying the Shaggat altogether. The prince, apparently, told Rose that they would spare no effort to do just that.'

Fulbreech lay petrified. Rose, Haddismal and these traitors, collaborating? The Shaggat and the Nilstone, removed? This was all wrong. His master had assured him nothing would happen for a week.

Hercól too sounded suspicious. 'How did Olik convince the Issár to go along with this plan?' he demanded.

'I know nothing of that,' said Bolutu. 'I am only glad that he succeeded. Think of it: six hours from now, that accursed Stone will be off the *Chathrand*.'

'And beyond the mage's grasp,' said Hercól. 'Belesar, can it really be true?'

'It is true, friend. Our oath will be fulfilled at last – for neither Arunis nor any other power will be able to wrest the Nilstone from *that* guardianship. With the sunrise, Erithusmé's long task will be over – and the worst part of ours as well.'

What were they doing, embracing? Yes, by the sound of it they were hugging each other and laughing. 'Over,' said Hercól, as though savouring the word. 'The horror, the decades of treachery, the slow strangulation of two Empires.'

'Three,' said Bolutu. 'You cannot forget what Arunis did to these lands of mine.'

'I will never forget his crimes,' said the swordsman, 'and his ultimate punishment I will deliver with this sword, Rin willing.

But first things first. Ah, Belesar! Tomorrow will be a bright day for Alifros – for the world as a whole, not these splintered tribes we call nations, which greed and villainy have made mad. Come, let us go to Oggosk at once.'

Oggosk! Fulbreech's amazement boiled over into a twitch. He froze: Thasha mumbled in her sleep, pressing closer to his side.

'The duchess awaits us even now,' Bolutu was saying. 'But where are Pazel and Neeps? For that matter, where are the young ladies?'

'All abed,' said Hercól. 'Come, snuff that lamp for me; we shall go at once. I'll wake Thasha and the tarboys when I return. They will want to be up and watching, when this nightmare comes to an end.'

Moments later the outer door closed behind them. Fulbreech found that he was drenched in sweat. His master had been deceived! The youth was outraged, and very frightened. The wondrous future that had opened before him was about to be snatched away.

But his training under Sandor Ott had never failed him, and it did not fail him now. *Terror manifests in a sphere of inaction; make your choice and it falls away, mud from the runner's feet.* Calm returned. Dawn was still hours off. With consummate patience, Fulbreech slid from Thasha's embrace, untangling one limb and then another, soothing her with kisses when she stirred, for to this girl his presence was safety and his kisses a drug; and because he would never have her now (uncoerced, at any rate) he bent to graze her breast with the lips that had lied to her since Treaty Day, and then he was out of her bed and easing open the cabin door.

The dogs watched him emerge. They had never taken to him, never licked his hand; indeed, their eyes chilled him slightly, as though the brutes knew better than their mistress what he was about. Still, he had Thasha's protection, and he passed unhindered between their hulking shapes. Like a mother hen, Suzyt crouched atop what could only have been Felthrup, precocious little dreamer, another whose death could not come soon enough.*

He pressed his ear to the stateroom door. Not a sound from the corridor. He smiled, turned the handle and stepped out into the hall. No light in the passage: better still. He moved down it, soundless, congratulating himself already. Even after this night she might trust him, he realised suddenly. Why not? *They came and went for hours, darling; surely it was best that I stole away?*

But what was he thinking? After tonight there would be no more games with Thasha Isiq. His master would have other tasks for his clever, his irreplaceable aide.

Seconds later Fulbreech passed through the magic wall. He felt nothing, but Thasha did. Her eyes snapped open. She pressed a hand against her mouth. She rose and groped beneath the bed for the wide bowl she'd placed there for such a moment.

Somewhere in Etherhorde the Mother Prohibitor was smiling: *So you were paying attention after all, child? Never forget who taught you, who made you what you are.* Thasha's stomach heaved. The food they'd shared burst out of her, an acrid pulp. It was the first good feeling in days.

Of course, she'd not slept an instant – but feigning sleep had been, by far, the easiest part of the act. She buttoned her shirt. It was her father's but all the same she would burn it. She ran to the washroom and plunged her face into a bucket of salt water. *Don't blame us, Thasha Isiq. You hated us, spat on our tutelage, pretended you'd never need such skills. We gave them to you anyway. Are you still too proud to thank us?*

A growl, murderous, bestial, wanted to tear itself from her throat. No time for that. Back in the stateroom she donned her sword,

---

* What Fulbreech glimpsed was not Felthrup, who by that time slept only in his closet. In all likelihood it was Bolutu's veterinary bag. If he had taken it, the youth would have been startled to find inside a notebook with the very words the dlömu and Hercól had just spoken – 'a bright day for Alifros', etc. – written out like a playscript in Bolutu's hand. – EDITOR.

knife, gauntlets. She called her dogs: they rose like dark lions, eager to hunt. Out through the stateroom door they went, then down the passage, through the magic wall and the money gate.

'They're waiting for you, Thasha,' came a voice from the wall.

'Thank you,' she said. 'And remember, Ensyl – you promised.'

'When we give our word, Thasha, we do not forget. Listen for me; I will come.'

Thasha raced up the ladderway, swift and soundless. *Let it be me, Rin, only me who deals with Fulbreech. I've earned that much, haven't I?*

On the topdeck the night shift was still at repairs. It was very windy; the lanterns sputtered, and the torches of the dlömic guard writhed fitful and low. Thasha's bare feet were cold on the dew-spattered planks. But just ahead of her the door to Rose's cabin beneath the quarterdeck creaked open an inch, and there was Rose himself, scowling, beckoning. 'What took you so long?' he whispered, tugging her in.

Pazel stared at the lamp before him. Fiffengurt was right: it would have to be extinguished. Already the bread room was filling up with fumes.

Outside the door there was an ominous silence. Marila had not spoken again, and Fiffengurt had stopped answering questions. But there were new sounds, creaks and cleared throats and footfalls, and they didn't belong to the quartermaster and Marila alone.

Neeps was still pacing, raging, coughing on the smoke. In time he heard the new voices as well. Staggering over to Pazel, he whispered, 'They've brought reinforcements. Good show, mate, sitting there like that. When things get rough, drop on your bum and brood, I always say.'

Pazel caught him by the arm. 'Be quiet. Please.'

'Quiet? *Quiet?* You'll be saying that when Arunis grabs the Stone and fries us like a skillet of clams!'

Pazel closed his eyes. In the depths of his brain an idea was fighting for air (as he himself was, with growing difficulty). No matter how he struggled it slipped away, just out of reach. Neeps went back to the door, coughing and shouting for Marila.

At last Pazel had it. He opened his eyes and turned to face a cluttered corner. The very corner where he had briefly crouched, looking for Sniraga. He crawled forwards, shouldering the bread boxes to one side.

Neeps saw him and hurried back to his side. 'What is it? You have a scheme, don't you? Tell me!'

'The floor,' whispered Pazel. 'Look at it, right there.' He pointed at a spot some three feet out from the wall. Neeps stepped closer, squinting: almost imperceptibly, the tin floor sagged.

'My knee did that,' said Pazel. 'I put my weight there, and felt it bend. I'd nearly forgotten – it happened just as Fiffengurt was locking us in.'

'A weak spot?' said Neeps.

'Something even better,' said Pazel. 'A *bare* spot is what I'm guessing: a place with no planks beneath the tin.'

'What on earth makes you say that?'

'Think about it,' said Pazel. 'This is the orlop, and we're two compartments forward of the Holy Stair.'

'So?'

'Neeps, that's damned near dead centre above the spot where the ixchel set their trap.'

'The charge, you mean? The black-powder charge that nearly blew Ott to pieces?'

'Right,' said Pazel. 'Uskins was talking about it only yesterday – in the middle of his rant about finding and killing the remaining "crawlies", remember?'

Neeps' eyes gleamed suddenly. 'Pazel, you're a wonder! He said the blast *tore up the ceiling*, didn't he?'

'Right again,' said Pazel. 'Now give me a hand.'

He turned and began shoving the bread boxes closer to the door. Neeps pitched in at once, asking no further questions. The fumes were by now very strong; when they stood up they could hardly breathe at all. Somehow they managed to push the majority of the boxes close to the door; then they hurried back to the corner.

'Hold this,' said Pazel, passing Neeps the lamp.

By its dim light Pazel crawled towards the low spot in the floor, pounding experimentally with the heel of his hand. At first the tin rang dully against solid wood: the low solid planks of the underlying floor. But as he neared the spot, it changed. It sounded hollow, and his blows caused the metal to shake. He rose to his feet and jumped. From beneath him, faintly, came the sound of falling debris. 'We're getting out of here,' he said.

'Don't be ... too sure,' Neeps replied between coughs. 'The metal's nothing sturdy, I know. But we'd still need ... tin shears, or a hacksaw maybe. I'm sorry ... you know I want out of here as badly as— Pitfire, watch it! What do you think you're doing?'

Pazel had kept one of the bread boxes near at hand. Now he was raising it with difficulty above his head. He pointed one sharp metal corner at the floor. 'Stay back,' he said, and brought it down with all his might.

The resulting crash was very loud. Outside the room, voices exploded: 'Pathkendle! Undrabust! What in the sweet Tree's shade are you doing?'

The box had dented the floor, but not pierced it as he'd hoped. He raised it again, and slammed it down once more.

'*Muketch!* Stop it, damn you!'

This time the box gouged a pinhole through the tin. Pazel struck a third time, and the hole became a matchstick-length tear.

'Blow out the lamp, Neeps,' he said.

'Now? You'll be blind as a mole!'

'Hurry!'

Neeps blew out the lamp, and darkness swallowed them. Pazel struck out blind, again and again. His lungs were burning, his mind in a haze. Then the door flew open and someone leaped into the room.

'*Muketch!* Undrabust!'

It was Sergeant Haddismal. The Turach waved his hands before his face, choking on the fumes, and began to thrash among the bread boxes.

Pazel struck once more. Haddismal spotted them and lunged. He swatted Neeps from his path with one hand. On an impulse Pazel tossed his box aside, leaped in the air and came down hard on both heels.

The floor split like an awning stabbed by a knife. Pazel scraped through, bloodied, and was running before his feet touched the floor of the deck below.

Fulbreech glided past the gunports, the dormant cannon, the heaps of rigging struck down for repairs. Not hiding: he was the surgeon's mate, after all, and this was the way to sickbay. No one would ask where he was bound, at this or any hour. Still, it was a pleasant surprise to find the ship so quiet. Hardly anyone about, save a few tarboys scrubbing pots in the galley, and the night shift on the main deck, shaping crosstrees for the mizzenmast. *As if they were going to take her anywhere*, he thought with a moment's unease. But then he reminded himself that it no longer mattered. Once his master heard what was coming he would have no choice but to act.

I could take it now, he had told Fulbreech. *Just as surely as she did, ages past, from that cavern in the Northern ice. But she was weaker than I, weaker by far. The Stone marked her, burned her hand, and from that first tiny incision the great Erithusmé began to die. I have been more careful, Fulbreech — her fate will not be mine. All the same I will wait a little longer, if I can.*

Thus had Arunis spoken at their last clandestine meeting, just hours after Thasha had come to Fulbreech in tears, and said, *I told Pazel, Greysan. About us. He didn't want to believe me, but he did at last. There's no one between us any more.*

His master had smiled at that.

But Fulbreech knew there would be no smiles tonight. His master forbade any visit to his hiding place, his lair, between their scheduled meetings. Had threatened to skewer him alive if he did so, in fact — unless disaster threatened them, or threatened the

Nilstone. *In that case, you must come to me instantly. Decide nothing for yourself beyond the practical. You understand? While you are in my service you may entertain no philosophy, no questions of motive or end. You could never grasp the answers. Concern yourself with how, not why. You are my puppet, Fulbreech. You are my eyes, ears, hands.* That would all change, his master had promised, in the life to come. But for now there was a disaster to avert.

Fulbreech quickened his pace. Just this once he was tempted to abandon the guise of the young medical apprentice. But could he bypass sickbay altogether? No, that *would* draw attention; he must walk through the ward at least. There was time. He'd been quick. Twenty minutes ago he'd still been fondling that girl.

He entered sickbay, with its reek of iodine and sweat, and to his unspeakable rage found Ignus Chadfallow on duty. The man was indefatigable. After midnight, and here he was, bothering patients, kneading their scalps, taking notes on the discharge from their eyeballs, poking that thermometer in whatever orifice was nearest to hand.

'Fulbreech! I've been looking for you, lad. Would you like to observe a nearly flawless vestibular spasm?'

'Nothing would please me more, Doctor,' said Fulbreech, 'but I must beg your indulgence for ten minutes; I haven't come for my regular rounds, you see.'

'Quite right,' said Chadfallow. 'You're here for Tarsel, naturally.'

'Tarsel?' said Fulbreech, eyes darting.

'You have a surgeon's passion, Fulbreech. At noon I give you Lognom's *Joints and Their Injuries*, and twelve hours later here you are, ready to set a man's thumb.'

'As it happens, sir, I'm not entirely ready.'

'Good!' replied Chadfallow. 'Overconfidence is a plague in our line of work. And such manipulations cause agony, nearly every time.'

Fulbreech gave a deferential nod. He had not even glanced at *Joints and Their Injuries*. 'I hope you won't hold this against me, sir.'

'Not at all, my boy.' Chadfallow stood and led him down the row. 'Why, I too needed help restraining the patient the first time I wrenched a thumb.'

The man in question, Tarsel the blacksmith, lay with his right hand floating in a tub of some aromatic broth of Chadfallow's. The thumb, pointing backwards, was swollen up like the thumb of a drowned man. Tarsel lay shaking. His good hand was clamped on the edge of his cot.

'Doctor,' he said, 'I can't wait no more.'

Chadfallow put his own hand in the tub. 'Still warm,' he said. 'The ligaments should be pliant enough. Go ahead, Mr Fulbreech.'

'What, him?' cried Tarsel, raising himself in the bed. 'Nay, Doctor, nay!'

'Silence!' said Chadfallow. 'You've no cause for alarm. This is a simple procedure.'

'Simple for *you*,' said the blacksmith, 'but this lad here, he's just a clerk. And he's nervous as a maid on her wedding day!'

Fulbreech was staring at the hideous thumb. How hard, he asked himself, could it be?

'Mr Tarsel,' said Chadfallow, 'you will kindly lower your voice. Men are sleeping. Besides, you risk distracting the surgeon, to your own inconvenience.'

'My inconvenience!' screamed Tarsel. 'Look at him, he's set to soil his breeches! Keep him away from me!'

'Shall we proceed, Mr Fulbreech?' said the doctor.

Fulbreech never knew how he got through that wrestling match with the blacksmith, whose arm was muscled like the haunch of a bull, and whose screams must have woken men far beyond sickbay. He was not really aware, or much interested, in his own efforts to *wrench the thumb*. His mind was on the story he would have to tell to escape the doctor's clutches. He finished piecing it together just as the blacksmith fainted dead away.

'Low pain tolerance,' said Chadfallow, placing two fingers on the man's neck. 'Ah well, finish up. You'll have no trouble now.'

Somehow, brutally, Fulbreech snapped the thumb back into

place, with a *pop* that made him fear he might be ill. Chadfallow's praise was restrained: he might be blind to other matters, but in medicine little escaped him. Then Fulbreech explained that he would have to forgo the pleasure of the vestibular spasm, as he had actually been sent for headache tablets. 'The captain's own request, sir: he's lying in the dark, quite unable to sleep.'

It was a perfect fib: even if the captain later denied asking for the pills, Chadfallow would attribute the contradiction to Rose's lunacy. Chadfallow took a small vial out of a cabinet and tossed it to Fulbreech. Then he looked the youth squarely in the eye.

'You may wish to consult Lognom again,' he said.

'Before I sleep, sir,' promised Fulbreech, and slipped out.

All this time Ensyl had waited in the ceiling of the darkened passage. Her people had once had a spyhole beneath a cot in sickbay, but it had been deemed too risky: Chadfallow liked to rearrange the furniture, and to inspect the walls for fungus with a magnifying glass. She kept watch now above a spring-loaded trapdoor. Fortunately there was no other entrance to sickbay.

What were they doing, stalking Greysan Fulbreech? A fool's watch, a fool's errand – or the most vital task on Alifros? Ensyl had no way of knowing which of these she had undertaken. But Dri had died believing in Hercól as well as loving him. And who was she, Ensyl, if not the guardian of her mistress' beliefs?

It had grown harder, though. Hercól explained so little. Worse, he had become morbidly obsessed with Thasha: her moods, fancies, above all her romance with the surgeon's mate. Was he another Dastu, another spy for Sandor Ott? Ensyl had demanded. Hercól had begged her not to ask, and more strangely, not even to *think* overmuch about what they were doing.

It weighed on her, that last request. Don't think? Blind obedience? That was part of what Dri called 'the madness of Ixphir House', the disorder she feared would ruin the clan. And what if Hercól was wrong about Fulbreech? What if he was no more than he seemed? A fuse was burning, Dri had whispered once: a fuse that will end in a blast to set the world on fire. The Nilstone, she'd believed, was the explosive at the fuse's end, only waiting for its spark. How much time did they have? How many more mistakes could they survive?

Then Fulbreech stepped back into the passage, and Ensyl forgot her doubts. The youth's eyes were desperate, his mouth tight and strained. Those were not the eyes of one whose work was done. He slid to the left of the door and stood there, back to the wall, like a hunted thing. Seeing no one in the corridor, he suddenly darted across it and threw open the door opposite the sickbay.

Ensyl swore. *Hercól was right all along.* For the place Fulbreech had entered was a tiny pump room, a service cabin for the machinery that lifted water from the bilge or the open sea, for dousing shipboard fires. It was probably the least-visited cabin on the deck. No other door led into the chamber. Nothing stored there was used in sickbay.

She pulled the trapdoor open wide. The passage was deserted all the way to the bend at the foremast. But just around that bend, she knew, waited her accomplice. Dangling upside-down, she spread her lips, tightened the muscles in her throat and produced a high, soft *cheeet*: very much like a cricket's song. An answering shadow flickered at the bend in the passage. Ensyl nodded to herself, jerked her head back inside and sealed the door.

On soundless feet she ran to the space above the pump room. Four large bilge pipes rose through the ceiling and continued to the upper gun deck. Like all handiwork on the *Chathrand* they were tight-fitted, built to allow no seepage of wind or moisture from one deck to another. But what luck – there had been damage here as well: a seam between board and pipe had opened, by warping or trauma to the ship. It was no more than the width of two fingers – two ixchel fingers – but it allowed Ensyl a view of half the chamber.

Fulbreech had struck a match and was now lighting a candle stub. Ensyl watched as he glued it with its own wax to the top of a cabinet. Then he pulled something else from his pocket: a brass jar, very small, no larger than a cherry. Lifting the lid, Fulbreech inserted a finger and scooped out a tiny amount of white cream. This he proceeded to rub into his palm. He rubbed thoroughly, entirely focused on his task. Then he put the jar back in his pocket and turned to face the door.

That's it? thought Ensyl, for already Fulbreech was reaching out (with the cream-coated hand) for the knob. But no, he wasn't exactly. The hand was aiming for a space *above* the doorknob. He moved slowly, and with trepidation, as though reaching into a darkened burrow. Then suddenly the hand stopped. The fingers probed, gripped, tightened. Fulbreech inhaled sharply. He stood as though holding a second doorknob, mounted above the first, but Ensyl could see plainly that he was holding only air.

Until, suddenly, he wasn't. She gasped, and thanked Mother Sky that her voice was an ixchel's and could not be overheard. Fulbreech *was* holding a second doorknob. She had seen no flash or puff of smoke. The knob was simply, suddenly there.

Fulbreech was shaking with fright. His free hand seized a pipe and held it rigidly, like a backstay in a gale. Slowly, with his eyes tightly closed, he turned the knob.

Something terrible happened. The door flew wide, Fulbreech stumbled, Ensyl drew back her head. The candle was extinguished – and strangely, no light at all came from the passage beyond. But in the last instant of light, Ensyl thought she had seen through the open door – but not into the passageway. Instead she had glimpsed a strange, dark space, not framed with wood but carved from solid rock. Ensyl had sensed some great bulky shape lunging forwards, but then the light had died.

Mother Sky, what's happening?

A low sound, half-slither, half-shuffle, rose from darkness. Ensyl felt like running; she felt like a child in a darkened bedroom in the clan house, frightened by the echo of human footfalls. But there was nothing human about the sound coming from the darkness beyond the door.

Fulbreech's voice came out hoarse and aghast. 'M-master?' he said.

He was answered, if answer it was, by an assortment of foul vocalisations. They were mouth sounds, maybe, but they formed no words. The sounds were sucking, gurgling, the licking of foul slobbery lips. Suddenly Fulbreech moaned, as though he had touched something unspeakably loathsome, or been touched by it. He stumbled backwards; she heard his body collide with the pipes. The door creaked shut again, and clicked.

For almost a full minute there was silence. Then a voice said, 'Have you brought another match?'

The voice belonged to Arunis.

'Y-y—'

'Relight the candle, Fulbreech, and tell me why you have disturbed my rest.'

Pazel knew the Turachs were on his heels. Their pounding boots sounded right above him; they could probably hear his own progress through the sleepy ship almost as well as he heard theirs. But they would never catch him. The ship's four great ladderways all ended on the orlop deck: there were of course other staircases, but you had to know where to find them. It kept pirates from racing straight to the hold – and a few weeks ago, mutant rats from swarming straight to the topdeck. The Turachs would have to run all the way to the tonnage hatch, where they could swing down, if catching Pazel was worth such acrobatics. Otherwise they would press on to the midship scuttle. Pazel was running for that narrow stair himself: it was the fastest way *up* from the mercy deck as well.

But already his heart was sinking. He had escaped the bread room, but the Turachs knew the layout of the ship as well as he did, and they were larger and faster. They'd be waiting for him at the scuttle. They'd be waiting on *every* Gods-damned stair.

He stopped. It was hopeless. A weird alliance of his friends and enemies was determined to keep him from getting anywhere near Thasha. And maybe that was sign enough that he ought to sit still, just as Marila had told Neeps to do. Something that could make Fiffengurt and Haddismal work together was surely a matter of life and death.

Unless ...

He laughed at a sudden, ridiculous idea. Could Rose be *marrying* them? Could that be how Thasha meant to 'end it'? Were they keeping him away out of pity, for fear he'd attack Fulbreech on the spot?

Impossible. A ship's captain could marry anyone, it was true ... but Thasha couldn't be that far gone. Could she?

He thought suddenly of Neda and Cayer Vispek, and his unsettling dream about the burial at sea. *The Isiq girl wants to be rid of him.* He felt ill. Maybe his mind-fit was coming early. Or maybe Thasha wanted to be married before the dlömu came to take them off for their visit to the Issár.

But hold on: the dlömu. Perhaps there *was* another way off this deck. He turned on his heel and ran straight back the way he had come. When he passed by the wreckage of the ixchel's fortress he saw lamplight shining down through the hole in the bread-room floor. Fiffengurt's voice sounded hoarsely, calling his name. He didn't answer. Straight on he ran, and minutes later reached the forward scuttle: a tiny, neglected laundry-chute of a staircase dropping sharply down to the hold.

He descended. *Rin's eyes, the smell.* The flooding had washed out some of the cinders, blood and rat-filth, but what remained was exposed to the air now, and rotting. He shut his mind to such thoughts and groped into the darkness ahead. He had one chance, and if it came he would have to seize it instantly.

The scuttleway let onto a flying catwalk: a kind of bridge some twenty inches wide and eighty feet long, spanning the cavernous hold. No rail, and no way of telling if the boards were intact. Pazel set out across it, utterly blind, restraining a suicidal urge to run. The catwalk felt sound. He walked with arms stretched before him, but in fact he had no idea of his distance from the hull. And what then? How on earth would he get down to—

The catwalk ended. His foot met with empty space. He fell like a stone and, almost before he had time to be afraid, struck the curving wall of the hull, and rolled and spun and crashed to the bottom of the hold.

First, a moment of stunned stillness; then the pain rushed in, and he cursed in a cascade of languages. But he was not dead, so he'd keep moving. He could still make everything all right. He crawled through a blackness of soaked and stinking wreckage. Bags of spoiled grain, ends of cables, shards of broken amphorae and scraps of wood. At times he was almost swimming in it. He doubted that he was moving in a straight line, but when he could touch the solid hull he corrected his path.

And suddenly there it was: moonlight. Not from any window above him, of course, but from below, reflected in a puddle on the stone quay beneath the *Chathrand*, through the hole in her flank. The shipwrights had not yet closed the wound: two enormous planks, or wales, remained to be fitted in place. Pazel dragged himself through the sawdust (fresh sweet smells) and looked out through the belly of the ship. He was at the very bottom of her, just yards from the keel, and about fifteen feet off the ground.

Thasha. Love and fury blended hopelessly inside him. He had been too timid in protecting her, too selfish and slow. *Aya Rin, let me get there in time*.

He dangled from the bottommost wale, and let go. Pain shot up his legs where they struck the stone, but he managed a clumsy take on the straight-drop-and-roll manoeuvre Thasha herself had tried so hard to teach him. Landfall at last, he thought absurdly, struggling to his feet. Then he ducked under the keel, dashed to the opposite scaffold and began to climb.

The cool air brought flashes of hope. Sometimes bad luck was a whale that devoured you. Sometimes you crawled out of its belly and fought on.

The dlömu ashore did not notice Pazel at first, and by the time they did, they could think of nothing to do about him. Humans were not to leave the ship, but this youth's only wish seemed to be to get back inside. They might have scolded him, but they were under orders not to speak to the crew except in emergencies, and so held their tongues. The decision, as it happened, cost lives.

Pazel had climbed about eighty feet when, on the lower gun deck, Fulbreech stepped out of the pump room and quickly closed the door behind him. For the last time in his life he put on his old, false face. He was ready with a laugh and a self-effacing story about ducking into the chamber to collect himself, after some ugly work in sickbay – but no one had seen him, the passage was still deserted. Once again he opened the pump-room door.

Arunis swept into the passage, his great mace raised before him. Fulbreech thought again how ghastly he had become. Once the mage had been stout; today he was a skeletal, staring creature, large of build but wasted within his dark, enveloping coat, the old white scarf twined about a dry and scrawny neck. And yet there was power in those hands that gripped the cruel weapon like a plaything, and his eyes still gleamed with appetite.

He was marching aft at a swift pace. 'The Stone is in the manger yet,' he said, more to himself than to Fulbreech, who was half-running to keep up. 'I will not have to touch it. I will take it, of course. No one will dare to cross me. The Turachs will flee their posts, and those who do not flee I will burn. I will claim the Stone tonight, and it will know me for its master, the shaper of worlds, the next ascendant to the Vault of the Skies. The Stone brings death only to weaker souls. All the same I will not touch it. Why should I touch it, before I know that I can?'

'You should cross the ship by the orlop deck, Master,' said Fulbreech, touching his sleeve.

'We cross here,' said Arunis.

'On the lower gun deck? As you will, Master. You may be lucky here as well.'

Sorcerer and servant hurried on, past the gunners' cabins and the armoury. Finally the passage ended and they stepped out into the central compartment. Moonlight filtered dimly through the gunports, and the glass planks overhead. The long rows of cannon gleamed blue-black in the shadows. Arunis hesitated, glaring.

'Empty,' he said.

'As I say, Master, you're fortunate tonight. Stanapeth and Bolutu may be huddled with Lady Oggosk, but in general the ship is asleep.'

'It is *not* asleep,' snapped Arunis, shooting him a furious look. 'Scores of men are awake, whether they dare to stir from their chambers or not. I can feel them, crouched and frightened. Why should they be frightened? What has been happening this last hour, Fulbreech?'

'This last hour? Nothing, Master. I told you, I was with the girl. Pathkendle and his friends retired early. Bolutu spoke with someone dispatched by Prince Olik, who delivered the awful news.'

Arunis began to walk quickly down the row of cannon. 'Delivered it to *him*, not the entire crew. I begin to wonder if you've kept up appearances, Fulbreech. Does Sandor Ott still consider you his agent, or has he seen through your mask?'

'He relies on me utterly, sir,' said Fulbreech, with a hint of pride. 'It was he who sent me in pursuit of Thasha to begin with, as you know.'

'Then what is the great Arquali spy telling you?'

'Master, he knows nothing of Olik's plan to take the Nilstone.'

'Sandor Ott is awake, fool! Rose is awake! I smelled their nervous brains the moment I stepped from my chambers! Why are they nervous, Fulbreech? What are they waiting for?'

'Your death, sorcerer. These many years – but no longer.'

It was Hercól. The swordsman rose from a crouch between two gun carriages. With a gliding step he moved to block their way, Ildraquin loose in his hand, murder in his eyes.

The sorcerer's face convulsed with rage. '*My* death,' he managed to scoff, but there was fear in the spiteful voice.

'I think,' said Hercól, 'that you have taken an interest in this blade, since last we met. Certainly your creature here saw fit to question Thasha about it – in the most unassuming way, of course.'

'You must satisfy his curiosity, Stanapeth,' said a second voice.

Arunis and Fulbreech whirled. Sandor Ott had appeared behind them, a Turach sword in hand, wearing his savage smile.

Arunis turned and seized Fulbreech by the throat. 'Maggot! Your death shall be the first of many!'

'Snap his neck and you're doing him a mercy,' laughed Ott. 'My own punishment for traitors would take several minutes just to describe. But you've got it wrong, Arunis. I was the one he betrayed, not you.'

Arunis turned Ott a look of hateful suspicion. All the same he let go of Fulbreech. The youth fell to the floor, wheezing in agony. Arunis kicked him flat, then held him still beneath his boot.

From the corner of a bruised eye, Fulbreech saw Ott draw something from his belt: a short, cylindrical device of wood and iron. The old spy raised an eyebrow at him. 'Remember this, do you, lad?'

Fulbreech did remember. The thing was a pistol: a sort of hand-held cannon, the first of its kind in all the world. It was clumsy, inaccurate, fragile and useless without a match. But on Simja, Ott had shown him how the device could fire a lead sphere through an armoured chest. Fulbreech had thought: *The Empire that could build such a thing cannot be opposed. That's the winning side, my side.* And until he'd met Arunis, he'd been right.

Ott began to circle the pair, slowly, casually. 'Well, Stanapeth,' he said, gesturing at Fulbreech, 'you promised this would be worth my time, and I'm happy to admit you spoke the truth. A traitor in the Secret Fist! If we were in Etherhorde I'd be submitting my resignation at Magad's knee. But why didn't you tell me sooner?'

'For the same reason I told almost no one,' said Hercól, starting to circle as well. 'Because this mage has been listening to our thoughts. He cannot probe below the surface, maybe, but when our minds turn to killing and betrayal, the surface is enough. It was all I could do to keep *myself* from brooding on Fulbreech, and thus giving everything away. And of course there were appearances to maintain in front of the Simjan himself.'

Arunis turned where he stood. He looked suddenly like a cornered animal, his gaunt lips drawn back from his teeth.

'Deceiving the deceivers,' said Ott. 'You always were the best in your class.'

'We had a strong incentive to succeed,' said Hercól.

'We?' said Ott.

'Yes,' said another voice in the shadows, 'we.'

It was Bolutu. He walked up quickly in the moonlight on Hercól's left. He looked at Arunis, and his face, usually so placid, was transformed by rage. 'Twenty years have I given to your downfall. Twenty years – and two hundred. I lost my family, my whole world. The only friends left to me were my shipmates, those who had sailed North with me, and them too I watched you hunt down and kill. You are depravity incarnate, mage. But you have not managed to kill us all.'

'Then let us amend that,' said Arunis, and leaped at him.

'Ah-ah-*ah*!'

The voice was Lady Oggosk's. Arunis was suddenly floundering, as though he had collided with an invisible curtain, or a net. There was the old woman, hobbling around the edge of the tonnage hatch, leaning heavily on her walking stick. At her feet slithered the Red River cat, Sniraga, all her fur on end.

'I warned you, sorcerer,' she said, 'that if you boarded the *Chathrand* she would be your tomb. Do you remember that day, in the Straits of Simja? Do you remember how you laughed?'

'I am laughing still,' said Arunis.

'Liar,' she cackled, 'you're scared to death, and well you should be. I have done little witchcraft since we met – very little these past forty years, truth be told, and I'll do little more in the time I've left. But I saved my strength for tonight, and that's more than you can say. Your power's been squandered of late, hasn't it? Dream journeys, thought-spying, healing the cracks in the Shaggat's arm.

Above all, burrowing like a ferret into weakened minds, and then throwing them at the Nilstone to see how fast it would kill them. What did those experiments teach you, eh? Were you going to claim the Stone at last?'

Arunis let the mace fall from his hands. He struggled: it was as if cottony walls enclosed him, tightening the more he fought. 'The witch's web,' he sneered. 'A charm for island pranksters, for tripping the town drunk when he steals eggs from your henhouse. The most primitive magic in Alifros!'

'So primitive I doubt you've bothered to learn a counter-spell,' said Oggosk.

'Witless hag. This charm will not hold me.'

Oggosk kept her blue eyes fixed on the sorcerer. 'Not for long, no,' she said. 'But long enough. And when I wish to—'

She pinched two fingers together. Arunis ducked his head and hissed, as though the walls had just closed tighter.

'—I'll bind your arms to your sides, for just half a minute, maybe: plenty of time for one of these men to step forwards and harvest your head. Fight on, bastard! Give me a reason to do it now! Do you really need proof that I can?'

'Old woman,' growled Arunis through clenched teeth, 'I am going to roast you to slow death, over a pit of coals and fire-weirds. Release me. You do not know whom you are toying with.'

'Neither do you.'

This time the voice was Thasha's, from the ladderway behind the spymaster. Out she stepped, armed and armoured, and the hatred in her eyes made Ott himself look up with respect. Ensyl rode upon her shoulder. Behind her came Captain Rose.

Fulbreech lifted his head to gaze at Thasha. A small sound of terror escaped him.

'Yes, Greysan,' said Thasha, 'I know who you are.'

'But you're wrong, girl,' said Arunis. For the first time a gleam of craftiness returned to his eye. 'You see, *I* know all of you, quite well. But you still do not know one another.'

He kicked at Fulbreech. 'You, for instance, may have known

what this worm had in mind for you from the start. But do you know what he did to your father?'

Thasha's hand tightened on her sword hilt. She looked at Lady Oggosk. *Now*, her eyes seemed to say.

'Do you know that your suitor here delivered him *personally* to Sandor Ott? And that this diseased old spy, this abomination, tortured your father to madness in a dungeon under Simjalla City?'

'Kill him, Hercól,' said Thasha quietly.

'And the noble Tholjassan!' cried Arunis. 'The one you've always trusted, worshipped, adored. The first man whose touch you ever dreamed of, isn't that so?'

'Bind his tongue, witch!' said Rose. Oggosk glared at him sidelong, as if to say, *How much do you think I can manage?*

'He told you how he served Ott for years, but did he ever elaborate? Did he mention how he doted on your father's torturer, like every lackey in the Secret Fist, like Dastu and Fulbreech himself? Did he name the deeds that made him Ott's right-hand man? Did he confess who really killed the children of Empress Maisa?'

Rose, Bolutu and even Ensyl looked shocked. Hercól's face was grim. Thasha's, however, did not change. She merely stepped close to her old mentor and touched his arm. 'Yes,' she said, 'he told me. And I love him. Will you end this now, Hercól?'

'Arunis,' said Hercól, his voice tight but steady, 'you are defeated, and in seconds you will be dead. Once before I urged you to turn back to your true path – the path you swore to follow when your Gifts were bestowed. You responded by trying to kill us, yet again. Now there is but one thing you can do to save your life, and only if you do it this very moment, without delay or deceit.' Hercól looked at Bolutu. 'Tell him,' he said.

'You must cast the Spell of Abdication,' said Bolutu.

'Ha!' cried Arunis. 'To save my life! That is very droll. Cast the Final Charm, the Last Command, the spell that reduces mage to mortal, with no possibility of ever using magic again. Cripple myself, and then surrender! A kindly offer from a failed dlömic mage and a reformed assassin. How can I refuse?'

'Very well. Madam,' said Hercól.

Oggosk threw her scrawny arms upward. '*Saikra!*' she shrieked. The spell-word crackled through the deck. Arunis twisted backwards one painful step towards the gunports. There he froze, arms flat against his chest, writhing only in face and fingertips. He appeared to be trying to speak, but his lips were clumsy, quivering. Oggosk, straining, gestured with one clawlike hand at Hercól.

'Do it!' she snapped. 'A swift, clean stroke!'

Hercól raised Ildraquin and started forwards.

Arunis' eyes swivelled to stare at Thasha. With immense effort, he said, 'Y-your mother lives.'

Thasha showed no response for an instant; then her calm shattered like a vase hurled at a wall. 'Stop! Please!' she cried, leaping forwards to grab Hercól's arm.

'Do *not* stop!' bellowed Rose. 'The duchess is tiring! Kill him!'

'Clorisuela is dead, Thasha Isiq,' said Ott. 'I can guarantee that. I'm sorry.'

'Clorisuela was b-barren,' said Arunis, leering now. 'Ask Ch-Ch-Chadfallow.'

'Chadfallow?' said Thasha.

If Arunis was breaking free of Oggosk's spell it was happening from the head down: already he spoke more easily. 'The d-doctor c-couldn't help her. Isiq gave up, and w-went looking elsewhere. Can you guess who he found?'

'Thasha,' said Hercól, 'your mother's name was Clorisuela Isiq.' But Thasha still held his sword-arm.

'Your mother's name is Syrarys,' said the mage. 'Isiq began to bed her years before his wife was killed. Ott arranged everything. He needed Isiq to have a daughter, after all. For Treaty purposes.'

'Lies, Thasha, lies,' said Hercól.

'Isiq paid for her rooms in the banking district. He had her two or three times a week – as often as Ott himself could stay out of her bed.'

Thasha was weeping. Ott shouted at Hercól: 'Do it now,

Stanapeth, or step aside.' He had pulled a box of matches from his coat.

Hercól freed his sword-arm from Thasha's grasp.

'The whore was your mother, that's a certainty,' said Arunis. 'The question is, who was your father?'

Then came a madman's shout from beyond the ship. Like an apparition, Pazel flung himself in through the gunport. He knocked the sorcerer from his feet, landed on his chest and struck him a blow to the face that might have broken a weaker man's jaw.

'No! No! Idiot!' screamed Oggosk.

Pain flashed through the mage's contorted features – and then he gasped, and his limbs moved naturally, free from Oggosk's spell.

His first act was to shout a spell of his own: a terrible spell. The black mace rose and flew at Thasha. At the same time, two cannon swivelled on their frames like batons. The first blocked Hercól's killing blow with Ildraquin. The second flailed at Sandor Ott. But the old spy was too quick: he leaped over the gun, pistol in one hand, a burning match in the other, and as he came down there was a deafening noise (a cannon, raised three octaves), and Arunis screamed aloud.

But the mage was far from slain. His second act was to throw Pazel upwards, with such violence that nails popped in the ceiling planks where he struck. Pazel thought his back must be broken, yet somehow he did not lose consciousness: his determination to kill Arunis, before he could strike again, with hands or spells or lies, was simply too great. But as he crashed to the floor Arunis shouted again, and darkness engulfed them all.

It was a tangible darkness, like ink poured in water. Pazel vanished into it, and found himself in a bedlam of howling, whirling bodies. Fists and feet struck at random. He heard Rose shout, 'I have him!' and felt several thunderous blows shake the deck. Then the captain roared in agony, and a body lunged near Pazel, and something crashed onto the boards of the scaffold outside. Even as Pazel groped in the direction of the noise there came two similar crashes. Then Pazel found the edge of the gunport and thrust his head out.

The mage-darkness stopped at the window: beyond it, plain moonlight resumed. Pazel saw Hercól and Sandor Ott hurling themselves down the scaffolding like a pair of acrobats. Thirty feet below, something dangled over a rail: a body, it appeared, kicking feebly, perhaps even dying. When Pazel looked back into the ship, the magical darkness was gone. Rose was supporting Oggosk; one of them was bleeding fast. But where was Thasha?

'No!' cried Hercól suddenly. Pazel looked and saw him holding Arunis' empty black coat. 'Trickery, illusion! Find him before he escapes!'

Pazel dived back into the ship. Rose, leaning heavily on a cannon, waved a bloody arm towards the centre of the compartment. 'That way! They're chasing him! Run, run, damn your soul!'

Pazel ran. In a moment he caught sight of Bolutu, rounding the capstan, sprinting with his sword drawn. Up ahead it was brighter: moonlight was flooding down the tonnage shaft. The great foremast timber still lay there, propped at an angle – and suddenly, as his eyes travelled its length, Pazel saw Thasha, scaling the timber as fast as she could. Above her, much higher, climbed Arunis.

'Bolutu, this way!'

Pazel put on a burst of speed. He reached the tonnage hatch and climbed out onto the scaffold and then the mast. Up he went, much faster than Thasha: climbing was perhaps the only physical activity in which he outdid her.

Past the upper gun deck, the main deck, the topdeck where they had all stood and worked together a few short hours ago. Then cries rang out from the shore. Pazel glanced up – and thanked the Gods.

Fifty or sixty dlömu, mostly fighting men in uniform, had just stormed onto the quay. They were arguing, some quite heatedly. Several were fitting arrows to bows.

From the topdeck, Bolutu cried out: 'Shoot him down, brothers!

Shoot him, for the love of Alifros!' Seconds later Fiffengurt's voice joined Bolutu's, urging much the same.

Then came a general shout of alarm. Pazel looked up and saw Arunis jump from the mast. He had reached a height where it extended well past the *Chathrand*'s rail towards the quay. The distance looked impossibly great: Arunis, he thought, was going to fall short of the quay, plummet some one hundred and fifty feet and strike hard stone, close to where Pazel had crawled out through the hull.

But it did not happen. Arunis cleared the gap with ease. The soldiers caught him, supported him – and then (Pazel felt a sudden, powerful urge to leap himself) stood back from him and raised their weapons in salute.

The mage's voice came from below, faint but clear: 'Bring a horse, and send another rider ahead to announce me. I have business in the Upper City, and I do not wish to be stopped and questioned at the gates.'

Someone darted away through the crowd. Arunis staggered over to one of the broken lamp posts and leaned against it, while the soldiers milled about him, offering him water, bread, someone's coat. Arunis touched his leg, and the gaunt hand came away bloody. Then he felt his jaw, and winced. As if remembering, he turned and looked up at the mast where Pazel clung. Youth and sorcerer locked eyes for a moment. Then Arunis smiled, nodded to him almost cordially, and turned his back on the *Chathrand*.

'Shameless, interfering, cow-headed dullard!'

Lady Oggosk cracked her walking stick over Pazel's back. Pazel, climbing over the tonnage hatch rail, took the pain as his due. Facing Hercól and Fiffengurt, as he did when he stood upright, hurt considerably more.

'I'm sorry,' he said.

'You sure as five-week fishcakes are,' said the quartermaster. 'Why couldn't you do as you were told, just *once*?'

'That would not be Pazel Pathkendle, would it?' said Sandor

Ott, who was studying his cracked-open pistol with some disappointment.

'He didn't know what was happening,' said Thasha, climbing over the rail in turn.

'Be silent, you impious girl,' shrieked Oggosk. 'Many who played their part did not know what was happening. The captain did not know, Sandor Ott did not know, Fiffengurt remained ignorant as a stump.'

'That's a tad overstated, Duchess,' said Fiffengurt.

'Shut your mouth, you walking salt-dried carcass of a toad! Arunis escaped death because this boy defied you, and leaped on him before Stanapeth could strike. It's true, my spell *was* a weakling's charm. I held him not with iron but with thread, and I only managed that because I'd been spooling and hoarding my thread for *thirteen years*. Even so, I knew the spell would break the instant anyone touched the mage. If not for this lovesick tarboy, Stanapeth would have killed him with ease! We'd be standing around his corpse now, toasting our victory! Oh, damn you, damn your low Ormali blood—'

'*Leave him alone*,' said Thasha, her voice suddenly dangerous. Oggosk, to general amazement, obeyed.

Hercól turned to Sandor Ott. 'I keep my promises,' he said, 'even when no good can come of them.' With that he unbuckled Ott's white knife from his belt and held it out, sheathed, to the spymaster.

Ott's eyes were locked on Hercól's. He took the blade without looking down. 'You did well to ferret out that snake,' he said. 'He was a greater threat than I ever understood. But we've learned this much: he still has cause to fear a blade. At least, certain blades.'

'And yet he bested us all,' said Hercól. 'Rose had a good grip on his arm, but he lost two fingers when the mage produced a knife of his own. Lady Oggosk herself suffered blows—'

'Pah,' spat the old woman.

'And you, Thasha: let me see what that mace accomplished. Right away, if you please.'

Thasha reluctantly lifted the edge of her shirt. On her ribs were a wide, blackening bruise and two gashes, left by the teeth of the sorcerer's mace.

'Fool!' said Hercól. 'You climbed a spar with *that*? You might have lost consciousness and fallen to your death!'

'But I didn't, did I?' said Thasha.

'Go to the surgery at once. Pathkendle, take her there, drag her. Chadfallow is already at work on the captain. Have him examine you, too, when he's finished with Thasha. You may have a hard head—'

'A gargoyle would envy it!' said Lady Oggosk.

'—but I saw you strike those ceiling planks. And there's your fall into the hold as well. Go on.'

'Hercól,' said Thasha, 'was Arunis telling the truth? Did my father know Syrarys . . . years before?'

'Nonsense!'

'You weren't in Etherhorde when I was born,' said Thasha. 'You were still in hiding with Empress Maisa. You never saw Clorisuela with child.'

'What of it? Go to surgery, I say, before you collapse.'

'Is Syrarys my mother, Hercól?'

'Thasha Isiq: as your martial tutor, I command you to seek treatment for that wound.'

'Come on,' said Pazel, touching her arm.

Thasha pulled her arm viciously away. She looked at Hercól for a long moment, and then moved slowly towards the hatch.

Pazel walked at her side. They did not speak as they descended to the orlop. Thasha marched aft with hands in fists. Ahead in surgery, Rose gave a howl of pain. All at once Thasha stopped and turned to face Pazel, her eyes enraged and wet. A lock of her golden hair was pasted to her shoulder with someone's blood.

Pazel stammered: 'You know, to me— I mean, I don't care whose daughter you—'

'Shut up.'

He waited. Thasha steadied herself against the wall. It would take hours to spit all the curses from that mouth, and she was not speaking, not saying a word. He wondered how much blood she'd already lost.

'I've ruined everything, haven't I?' said Pazel.

Thasha clamped a hand over his mouth. With that gesture they both grew still. Her hand tightened; she swayed closer to him. Then, not weeping but shaking from head to toe, and sighing with all that she had not said to him in weeks and could find no words for now, she was in his arms.

19

They are, of course, too young.

You know of what I speak. With the exposure of Greysan Fulbreech there can be no remaining (logical) impediment to a carnal encounter between Lady Thasha and Pazel Pathkendle. In dramatic terms, such an encounter is almost obligatory. Neither youth is hormonally defective. Both have considered the possibility for months – and with unseemly specificity, in the case of Mr Pathkendle. They show no signs of disease or contagion. And they have been supplied with a preposterous array of opportunities: a magic wall, no less, deflects all rival suitors from intruding on their presumably impending bliss.

But I repeat: it cannot happen. Said bliss cannot, and therefore does not, impend. They are too young.

My own status as philosopher and moral paragon is beside the point. Anyone, from the lowliest fishwife to the most venerated saint, can grasp the fundamental wrongness of such a liaison. We need not elaborate. The Great Designer unquestionably decreed that human beings should reach bodily maturity at a certain age precisely that they might refrain from expressing that maturity for another five to ten years. In ancient Senadria the legal age was thirty-three (although we now know that in its declining years the republic collected a third of its income from the sale of special permits to younger citizens); in fair Elynon it was thirty (twice the age at which boys were forced onto the battlefield, and girls into factories to stitch their boots). Truly enlightened cultures, such as the Elari in their frigid fishing townships, aspire to eliminating the behaviour completely. A few no doubt succeeded.

Yearn then, Pazel and Thasha, but yearn alone. We do not wish you joy, indeed far from it. The matter is not open to debate.

Except, of course, in the fugitive territories of their minds. However trivial the latter (it is not *their* inclination, after all, that concerns us) we should note in passing that neither Mr P. nor Lady T. views the matter with our own precise and perfect clarity. This is where the moral lesson resides.

You may encounter persons who should not mate. Be ready to explain things. If, as with Pazel, they feel that to do so is no more than the natural expression of a love that is beyond question and well proved, urge them to doubt the very notion of 'natural'. If, as with Lady Thasha, they feel the desire to give what is most intimately their own to the one of their choosing, remind them that there is nothing sacred in that choice. Magic may surround them (one may say *I love you* in twenty-five tongues, another be strong enough to hold death's orb in her hand) but magic does not inhabit the sordid act of love.

If they protest that an overwhelming mutual tenderness draws them together, observe that virtually all cases of first love end in separation and tears, and that consequently they should do better to skip the experience. If they reply that *some* love has to be one's first, unless one would go through life playing come-not-hither, tell them not to split hairs.

If, finally, they live in fear that at any day it may be too late: that the death stalking fleets, cities, empires must surely catch up with them; or that some morning soon they will wake up and find themselves asleep – that is, mindless, insensate *tol-chenni* with no possibility of experiencing love – well, that changes nothing. Virtue is virtue, and no one should face death without its comforts. Tell them this, if ever you have the chance.

20

A Broken Blade

2 Modobrin 941
231st day from Etherhorde

She swayed, and he steadied them both. When he kissed her, Pazel realised how hard she was labouring simply to breathe. Her embrace began as something hungry and sorrowful, and in seconds was reduced to an effort not to collapse upon the deck.

'Let's go, Thasha,' he said.

She shook her head. Tears were crowding out the fury. He told her he understood what she'd been doing, using Fulbreech to get to Arunis, shielding her thoughts to keep everyone safe. He said he loved her for it, that she hadn't done anything to him that she could have avoided. The words just made her weep. So in desperation he lifted her chin and kissed her once more, fiercely.

'You care what I think?'

Thasha nodded through her tears.

'Then don't fight me, for Rin's sake. You're bleeding into your boots.'

In the surgery, they found Captain Rose kneeling before one of the heavy slate tables, head tipped back, drinking deeply from a flask. His left arm was strapped down firmly on the table's surface, the hand swaddled tightly in bandages. Chadfallow was laying out instruments behind him.

'The fiend returns,' said Rose, looking at Pazel.

'I'm sorry, Captain,' said Pazel. 'I was trying to help. I didn't know about Oggosk's spell.'

'Go rot in the Pits,' said Rose, and drank again. Smacking his lips, he added, 'I'll find a way to collect on what you owe me, Pathkendle. At a time and place of my choosing. Better keep one eye peeled, lad. The Rose family always settles accounts.'

Chadfallow ordered Pazel to wash Thasha's wound, and to hold clean cotton gauze over the incision. Pazel did as he was told, thinking of his dream about her wooden heart. Thasha did not speak or even look at him.

The door opened, and Swift rushed in with a small, smoking cauldron. 'Hot coals from the galley, sir,' he piped, 'just as you wanted.'

'Our new surgeon's mate,' said Chadfallow, nestling an odd tool like a blunt iron spike into the cauldron. 'A waste of my efforts, training Fulbreech. Is he in custody, then?'

'Excellent custody,' said Rose, and laughed. Despite himself, Pazel shuddered. He could guess who had taken charge of the Simjan youth.

'I am glad to hear it,' said Chadfallow, bustling over to Thasha in turn. 'I will have some words for that boy myself. He very nearly cost Tarsel the use of his thumb.'

He moved Pazel aside, began to scissor away part of Thasha's bloodied shirt.

'Was my mother barren?' asked Thasha suddenly.

Chadfallow's hand stopped cutting, but only briefly. 'A non-sensical question,' he replied. 'She could not very well have been your mother if she *was*, now could she?'

'Are you going to tell me, Doctor?'

Chadfallow frowned and fixed his eyes on the wound, as though her head were an unwelcome intruder on the scene. Watching him stitch up Thasha's skin with deft, swift draws of his needle, Pazel could almost forgive him the evasiveness. But as he tied off the stitches, Chadfallow said, 'This is most inappropriate, Thasha Isiq. I have a difficult operation to perform on the captain. And not even for Magad the Fifth would I disregard the privacy of my patients.'

'She was my mother,' said Thasha.

'Well, ain't that the question?' put in Rose, and cackled.

Chadfallow looked at him with loathing. He walked to the cauldron, donned a padded glove and lifted the spike. The last inch glowed cherry-red.

'Fresh cotton over the wound, Pazel,' he said, 'then a wide wrap about her torso, to secure it. Come here, Swift, and restrain his other arm.'

Pazel did as he was told. He tried to resist the weird temptation to steal a glance at Rose and Chadfallow, but eventually succumbed just as the doctor was applying the tip of the red-hot spike to the captain's mutilated hand. Rose's screams were like nothing Pazel had ever heard. He looked away, hoping Thasha would show better sense than he had. The reek of cauterised flesh made him think of a pig roast he'd attended as a boy.

Rose became hysterical. 'Dog! Hatchet man! Mutilator! I'll cut out your stomach, Chadfallow! Do you hear me, you pitchforker, you barb-wielding devil? I'll have your stomach, your stomach and your licence too!'

'Keep him still, Mr Swift!'

'He's too strong, sir! He's pulled the blary screws from the floor!'

'Pazel,' said Thasha, 'you look awful. You had better lie down.'

'I'm fine,' he said.

'Stop looking at Rose. Was it your *head* that struck the ceiling?'

A moment later they had traded places: Thasha was on her feet, making him sit on the table, raising his legs. When he lay flat on his back Pazel felt the chamber start to spin. Rose had begun to rave about his father, and Lady Oggosk, and her cat. Thasha told him to close his eyes, and when he hesitated, bent down to kiss them shut.

'You should have done as Ignus wanted,' she said.

'About your bandages?'

'About jumping ship back in Etherhorde. You poor dear fool.'

He really had taken some blows. Thasha pressed a cool wet cloth to his forehead, and his eyes. The noises in the chamber began to recede.

When her hand touched him again he caught it, drew it to his lips. There was a grunt of surprise. From under the cloth Pazel saw that the hand was black, and webbed to the first knuckle. He pulled the cloth away and looked into the startled eyes of Counsellor Vadu. The pale dlömu's head bobbed up and down.

'*Jathod*, I thought he was a corpse! What were you doing, boy, trying to kiss my ring?'

The surgery was full of armed dlömu. Thasha, Swift and Chadfallow were surrounded; Captain Rose stood gagged with surgical gauze, spears pointed at his neck. The hand with the missing fingers was in a bucket of water; the other still held his open flask. Pazel tried to spring to his feet, but Vadu's hand clamped roughly on his shoulder.

'Calm yourself. No one is going to do you harm. We heard screaming from this deck, but it was only a veterinary— That is, a medical procedure. Are you Undrabust?'

'Pathkendle,' said Pazel. 'What's happening, why are you here?'

Vadu turned his perpetually amazed face in Thasha's direction. 'And that is the girl called Thashiziq. Very good, very good.'

'See here, Counsellor,' said Chadfallow, 'you may have good intentions, though gagging the captain is an outrage. But whatever you're about, this is a surgery, and these are my patients.'

'I was hoping you would admit as much,' said Vadu, his head bobbing faster. 'Do you consider yourself qualified to describe their condition? And would you be willing to do so in the presence of witnesses?'

'Of course I'm qualified,' said Chadfallow, 'but medical knowledge is private, sir, at least in our culture—'

'His *culture*, did you hear?' laughed one of the dlömic troops.

'You must all leave the surgery at once, Counsellor. You're disturbing the wounded.'

'They are already disturbed,' said Vadu. 'And so are you …

Doctor. That is the verdict of the best minds of Masalym, who have watched you from the shore these many days.'

Chadfallow was incensed. He pushed forwards through the crowd until stopped firmly by Vadu's guards. 'Counsellor Vadu, I am Imperial Surgeon to His Supremacy Magad the Fifth of Arqual. You have nothing to teach *me* about derangement.'

'No,' said Vadu, almost with regret, 'it did not occur to me that you could be taught.' He made an abrupt little wave. 'All of them but the captain. You know what to do with him.'

'We're not insane,' said Thasha. 'Your people have simply made a mistake.'

Vadu turned to her, impatience showing in his staring eyes. 'When I came into this room, your captain looked up at me and screamed, "My mother is a cat."'

Rose snarled.

'Damn it, man, I just cauterised the stumps of his fingers!' cried Chadfallow. 'I dare say *you* might rave a bit yourself, if I held a red-hot iron to your open wounds.'

'You don't have the right to judge our sanity anyway,' said Pazel. 'This ship is sovereign territory, and we're all citizens of Arqual.' That was not entirely true, but at that moment subtleties hardly seemed called for.

'You are delusional,' said Vadu. 'You speak of places that do not exist. It is a sad thing to witness, and I doubt you can be cured. Still, since the Empire's leading facility is right here in Masalym, why not try?'

Chadfallow narrowed his eyes. 'What do you mean? What facility?'

'All in good time,' said Vadu.

'Where's Prince Olik gone?' Thasha demanded. 'He said we were to meet with the Issár.'

'Prince Olik has been ... called away,' said Vadu. Then, raising his voice, he said, 'Enough! Will you come quietly, you five? Yes or no?'

'No!' cried Swift, clinging to a table leg.

'No,' said Thasha, loosening her hands for a fight.

'Why,' said Pazel, controlling his fury with great effort, 'won't you even *consider* that we might be sane? Isn't that a bit crazy in itself?'

Vadu looked suddenly angry. His eyes shifted, as though Pazel had said something to embarrass him in front of his men. 'I did not think that they would prove so vulgar,' he said. 'I like them better without speech.'

'You can plainly hear that I'm being reasonable,' said Pazel. 'I'm not even raising my voice. I don't mean to insult you, Counsellor Vadu. I'm just pointing out how wrong you *aarrgwhaaa* oh Rin, please not no*lufnarrrrrr*—'

He covered his ears. The mind-fit, the assault of unbearable noises, dropped him shuddering to his knees. The soldiers backed against the walls; most looked ready to flee. Vadu screamed orders, waving his many-ringed hands at the humans. And before the fit blotted out his thoughts altogether, it occurred to Pazel that the argument had just been decided.

The gangways had been quietly lowered: halberd-wielding dlömic soldiers had swarmed onto the *Chathrand*. The show of strength was overwhelming. Wagons had been swiftly pulled up along both sides of the quay, and scores of barbarous cannon were revealed when their canopies were dropped. Archers with huge tripod-mounted crossbows, each one a bouquet of steel-tipped bolts, had raced into position between the wagons. Foot soldiers poured over the gangway, and with them came riders on beasts that filled the humans with terror. They were more like cats than anything else, but their backs beneath the saddles were broad and flat, and they stood as tall as horses. They growled at first sight of the humans, and their dlömu had to shout reassurances, swearing that the *sicuñas*, as they were called, would not harm a soul without their riders' permission.

Sergeant Haddismal saw the choice before him at a glance: surrender, or death and defeat. He cursed, but in truth he had expected this from the moment he saw that first stone wall rumble into place, sealing in the ship. He bared his teeth at the victors, but that was as far as his defiance went: martyrdom (this martyrdom at least) was no way to serve the Empire. He ordered his men to lay down their arms. In a matter of minutes the Great Ship was taken.

The dlömic forces were civil but firm. The ban on speaking to humans having been at least slightly relaxed, they demanded all weapons 'larger than folding knives and smaller than cannon'. They also confiscated all sources of flame or combustion, from Mr Teggatz's stove-lighting matches to the explosives in the powder room. The humans themselves they split into groups: officers and soldiers on the topdeck, sailors, tarboys and steerage passengers below.

Counsellor Vadu, pleased to have met with no resistance, climbed back to the topdeck and addressed the officers. 'Your captain has been invited to assist the Plazic Battalion with certain inquiries. He will be returned to you shortly, if all goes well. Meanwhile, I charge you with maintaining discipline among your people. They will not be harmed; indeed, we have prepared extensively for their comfort and relaxation, in the pavilion at the Masalym Tournament Grounds. There you will, I think, have few complaints. You will cook your own meals. Women and children will have private quarters, with beds. You officers will be provided the same, but the rest of the crew must bring hammocks. Take whatever clothes and cherished belongings you may desire. It will be some time before we return you to this ship.'

The officers protested loudly. 'What are you up to with her?' said Fiffengurt. 'You're fixing that crack in her hull, and we thank you for it. But that ship's our home – our *only* home, now that we've crossed the Ruling Sea. You've got no right to poke around in her like something washed up on the beach.'

Vadu replied that Masalym reserved the right to inspect *any* vessel that entered its waters, let alone its walls. But he had clearly not come to debate.

'This is a time of war. I require you to bear that in mind. Chaos and disorder cannot be tolerated in a time of war. Your removal begins in ten minutes.' With those words he turned his back on the outraged officers, passed over the gangway, and descended into the city.

The debarkation was an orderly affair. The humans were marched in single file over the gangways, checked for weapons a second time on the quayside, then led away in groups of forty and fifty, each contingent surrounded by twice as many dlömic soldiers. Their path led down a wide, windy, lightless avenue. From the platforms, the sailors still disembarking could see their shipmates moving away in dark masses, surrounded by the torch-bearing dlömu. More like pilgrims setting off into a wilderness, thought Mr Fiffengurt, than men at the start of shore leave.

The steerage passengers were offered assistance; the women handed woollen shawls against the wind, the oldest placed in litters, like royalty, and carried out on dlömic shoulders. Of all the humans, Neda came closest to provoking violence. She emerged onto the topdeck struggling and shouting, first in Mzithrini, then Arquali: 'Where take my brother? He would be here, would be seeing me! You have him prisoner apart, yes? Where is my brother, monsters?'

There were few other incidents. One of the Quezan tribals from the whaling ship had yet to see a dlömu, and panicked at the sight of what he took for demons of the Underworld. He was held at bay in the officer's mess until he saw by their faces that demons too could grow bored; then he grinned, shrugged and joined the exodus. A midshipman tried to smuggle a dagger ashore inside his bedroll. He was taken aside, made to kneel, beaten thrice with a cane and helped to his feet.

Outside the stateroom, Counsellor Vadu's expression reached a new extreme of shock as he leaned his hands against the magic wall. The utter surprise of encountering such magic was startling enough, although he knew quite well that charms and sorcery were leaking out everywhere these days: bleeding from the open sores of the South. And the largest sore of all was Bali Adro City, the capital he served (heretical thoughts, thoughts that could hang him; how fortunate that one's mind was off limits to investigators and spies).

A door stood open at the end of the passage beyond the magic wall. He could see a corner of an elegant cabin or stateroom. But he was far more taken with the sword. A great black weapon, battered and stained but radiating (he thought) a subtle power, an authority. It lay just inside the wall, as though flung in great haste – or carried there, by someone with the power to pass through.

He ordered the wall attacked with hammers, chisels, fire. He lowered men to the stateroom windows and tried to break them, but the glass when they struck it proved harder than any stone. The once-luxurious chamber could only be pierced with lamplight: inside, the dlömu saw a bearskin, a samovar, a table with the remains of a meal.

Some hours later Vadu returned to the passage outside the stateroom. Half a dozen men were still attacking the wall. 'Sir, it's no good, we can't even scratch it,' confessed his captain-at-arms.

Vadu nodded. 'I will try myself,' he said. And then, noting his men's distress: 'Yes, yes, you may all leave the compartment. Seal it behind you, in fact.'

His soldiers fled with unseemly haste. Vadu filled his lungs, squared his shoulders and put his hand on the pommel of his knife.

To draw the weapon required the whole strength of his arm. In the darkened passage a fell glow surrounded him, and the air began to shimmer. But in Vadu's grip was little more than the handle of a knife: a hilt, and an inch-long, corroded stump of a blade. Yet all the disturbance in the air flowed from this tiny splinter.

Vadu felt as he always did when he drew the Plazic Blade: impervious and ruined, a titan of steel, ripped by dragons' jaws. Above the hilt, a ghostly outline of a knife was forming, like a pale candleflame. He staggered forwards and plunged it into the wall.

(Two miles away, in a wagon clattering through the Middle City, Thasha Isiq cried out in pain. She shot to her feet, eyes wide, furious with the sudden violation.)

The counsellor felt the knife begin to cut. But the spell he was fighting was no simple one. After a moment, it became clear that it was the work of a greater wizard than he had ever faced. With a grunt of effort he managed to carve down through four inches of wall. Then he turned the knife to the left.

(Thasha was thrashing. The guards marching to either side of the wagon looked in terror at a girl possessed. On the floor of the wagon, bound and weeping in the torments of his own fit, Pazel heard her screams and thought his mind would break.)

Vadu cut a square out of the magic wall. He pulled the knife free, almost dropping it in the agony of lightning that danced up his arm. Then he sheathed it and put his arm through the gap. His fingers groped towards Ildraquin.

(Thasha's stitches tore; her side once more began to bleed. Hercól, Neeps and Marila begged her to say what was happening, but she did not hear them. 'No,' she said, pressing fists against her temples, 'no, I won't let you. I *won't*.')

Vadu screamed suddenly and wrenched his arm from the hole. His tunic was smoking, the sleeve burned through. He ripped the cloth away and saw a band of red skin around his upper arm, blistering already. 'Hmm! That's a pity,' he thought. 'Still, it could have been much worse.'

(Thasha whirled, flailed among her companions. When Hercól tried to seize her she knocked him aside like a doll. Then a voice came from her throat: a woman's voice, but not her own: '*Bihidra Maukslar*! Bile of Droth! He is going to steal it, steal it and loose the Swarm! What are you waiting for? When will you let me strike?')

Vadu stumbled out of the compartment. 'Never mind,' he told his men. 'The sword can stay where it is; tomorrow we will try our luck with rod and reel, or something of the kind. Now show me to the manger.'

They descended, passing among the few remaining humans, Vadu's lieutenant supporting his arm. By the time they reached the manger he was recovered.

'That Stone is not to be touched,' he told his captain-at-arms, pointing at the Nilstone. 'Tomorrow you will reinforce this door with iron bands, and install a new lock, and deliver the key to my person. For tonight you must secure the door with padlocks and thirty-weight chain.'

It was three in the morning when the last group of humans set off for the Tournament Grounds. The soldiers moved through the *Chathrand* in a dragnet, lanterns ablaze. They found two cobalt-blue dogs of great size on the lower gun deck, searching frantically for their mistress. They caught Lady Oggosk's cat and nailed the beast up in a crate ('Take it to her before she deafens the whole pavilion,' said Vadu). They captured the augrongs after a hideous struggle and the deaths of six men, and led the beasts off together wrapped in anchor chains. They heard the lowing of cattle but could not locate a single animal, nor the source of the noise. They saw two ixchel darting across a passage on the mercy deck, pounded after them, found no trace.

The wind rose, and thunder growled in the mountains. Vadu cursed, and ordered his men off the ship until morning, when the complete inventory would begin. Large detachments were left on both gangways, more around the perimeter of the berth. Before the counsellor made it to his carriage a lashing rain had begun to fall.

He slammed the door and slicked back his hair. 'They are safe,' he said, 'and tomorrow you may examine them. Are they really so precious to you?'

On the seat beside him, Arunis shrugged. 'They are but symbols. Not important in themselves, and quite worthless to anyone this side of the Nelluroq.'

'I should say so. A hideous statue, and a magic bauble that one cannot even look at directly.'

'Think of them like the *birthig*, your liege-animal. Outsiders see a grotesque little creature with tusks. But the honour of the city hinges on the *birthig*, does it not, when strangers come to call? So it is with that bauble, Counsellor. The humans covet it, as they do so many things, but in truth they can do nothing with it at all. They might even hurt themselves.'

'Are you saying it is dangerous?'

'Not very. Let us say rather that it is best left to mages.' Arunis laughed. 'Do you know, the humans played a joke on me tonight? They said Prince Olik was coming to seize that Stone, and the statue, too. They woke me from a pleasant slumber on that pretence.'

'How irritating,' said Vadu. 'Is that why you persuaded the Issár to send us in tonight? To turn the joke back on them?'

'In a sense. They were ... complicating my work. And they would only have been in the way, when my replacement crew arrives from the capital. So will Prince Olik, if he is not managed with skill. He seemed rather to warm to the humans, even after they took knives to his flesh. You do understand that he must learn nothing of our intentions, until the replacement crew is actually aboard the *Chathrand*?'

'You made that quite clear, sorcerer. You expect them in a week's time, you say?'

'Perhaps sooner, if the winds are favourable. Where *is* Olik, incidentally?'

'Never mind him,' said Vadu. 'He is a dilettante, a lesser son of noble sires. You will find him meditating with his Spider Tellers, in a temple in the humblest corner of the Lower City.'

'Olik, a Spider Teller?' said Arunis, his eyes wide with disbelief. 'A prince of the ruling family, and *that* is the extent of his ambition?'

'His blood is his licence for eccentricity,' said the counsellor. 'But yes, he is a true philosopher, which is to say a buffoon. You think him fond of these ... freaks? I thought him supremely indifferent. Yes, Rose appears guilty of drawing Bali Adro blood – and must therefore die, unless Emperor Nahundra himself issues a pardon. But the humans also saved the man from the Karyskans. They nearly lost the ship, protecting him. And yet he could not wait to abandon them – *did* not wait; he literally took to the stevedores' tunnels as the ship was being raised. I shouldn't wonder if he has forgotten all about them by now.'

'You must forget them too, Counsellor,' said Arunis. 'I know you are not fond of killing – who is? But believe what I tell you: they are incurable. In short order they will all become *tol-chenni*. As will every human north of the Ruling Sea. Their time in Alifros is over; soon they will take their place alongside the fantastic creatures whose bones grace your museums.'

'The doctor insisted that not one of them had yet been affected,' said Vadu.

'Denial has always been part of the plague,' said Arunis. 'Here, whole cities maintained that they were clean, lest the Emperor place them in quarantine. Householders swore up and down that all was well, even as they kept a gibbering ape or two locked in the cellar. Read your history, man.'

'But there were no gibbering apes found on the *Chathrand*.'

'Rose is no fool,' said Arunis. 'He tossed them into the Gulf before we came within sight of Masalym. Pity them, if you will. I certainly do. But don't share in their illusions.'

Vadu fell silent a moment. 'If that is how things truly stand,' he sighed, 'then I begin to grasp the terrible command that came tonight from my Emperor. You might as well know. We're to select fifty specimens, in addition to the few in the Conservatory, and chain them in the hold for transport to Bali Adro. For study, I assume. The rest will be marched into the emptied basin, sealed inside. The floodgate lifts, the basin quickly fills. It was done before with *tol-chenni*. I do read history, sir – at least when it pertains to my job.'

'I am relieved to hear it,' said the sorcerer.

'All told, it is a merciful system,' said Vadu. 'When they are drowned we simply open the lower gate, and their bodies are carried over the falls and into the Gulf.' The counsellor glanced upwards. 'What about your servant?'

'Fulbreech?' said Arunis. 'I shall keep him, while his mind is whole.'

'Of course you will. I only ask if you wish to bring him into the cab, since the rain has turned so cruel.'

'By no means,' said Arunis. 'He has worse ahead of him than a little soaking. And the wound he took in the battle tonight is nothing. I examined it because it was made with Ildraquin, that sword you failed to obtain.'

'So it is a special blade?'

Arunis nodded.

'But not as special as my own.'

'The difference, Vadu,' said Arunis, 'is that Ildraquin has an owner, whereas the Plazic Arsenal, despite the conquering power it has granted Bali Adro, has slaves.'

Vadu laughed, but when Arunis did not even smile, he checked himself. 'I am a proud servant of the House of the Leopard, and ever shall be,' he said. 'The Emperor knows my loyalty, and I know how he trusts in the Raven Society. Yet I myself am often baffled by your council's ways.'

Arunis raised a warning eyebrow.

'Macadra,' said Vadu, 'never setting foot outside the palace, though they say her word is law. Stoman the Builder, obsessed with growing the Navy, when already we are the sea's unchallenged masters. Ivrea, who would send her own mother to the gallows if she suspected her of disloyal thoughts.'

'In a heartbeat,' said the mage.

Vadu's head gave a twitching bob. 'And now you, Arunis Wytterscorm, returning like a legend aboard a ship of *tol-chenni* freaks.'

'They are human, Vadu,' said Arunis. 'Don't make me repeat it. The North is rife with them.'

Vadu looked thoughtful. 'How many are there, really?'

'They are more numerous than the crickets in the *chúun*-grass,' said Arunis. Then he raised his head and looked Vadu in the eye. 'Before the burning season, that is.'

The driver flicked the reins, and the horses trotted off. Lightning flashed; the mountains appeared in looming silhouette, and vanished again. On the bench beside the driver, Greysan Fulbreech shivered. Not with cold, but with a sort of intoxicated wonder. His changes of luck that night had been breathtaking. He had been duped by the Isiq girl, tasted her body, faced a hideous, gelatinous devil guarding his master's door. He had nearly been strangled by Arunis, and saved only by Ott's wish to torture him at leisure; then he had been saved from Ott by his true master's swift instigation of the raid. Yes, a night of dangerous gambles. But as always his hand was a little stronger than the day before. The ship was doomed; he would not stay with it. And it was clear that in all the world there was no greater patron than Arunis.

Unless this Macadra was *his* master, perhaps? Fulbreech was unclear on this point, but no matter. Time would tell him what to do. A flood was rising in the world, and he would do as he had always done, scramble from rock to higher rock, and who could fault his strategy? What harm, after all, had come to him during these months of violence and death? A black eye from Pathkendle, tonight a little scratch on the chin. He touched it gingerly: the bleeding had stopped already, yet for some reason he found it difficult to ignore.

The carriage left. The Great Ship sat in darkness. Rain poured down the tonnage shaft; the wind prowled as indifferently as it did the hulks and wrecks that littered shores from one end of Alifros to the other. Here and there a sound echoed in the lightless corridors: a mouse, a cricket, the ghost of a laugh. And in the stateroom, in Admiral Isiq's former cabin, in the back of the closet, in a box turned to the wall, Felthrup Stargraven lay twitching, unconscious, dreaming with a will.

21

Under Observation

4 Modobrin 941
233rd day from Etherhorde

'Prisoners,' said Neeps. 'We've crossed the entire world to become prisoners who stare at the walls.'

'It is certainly better than the forecastle house,' said Dr Chadfallow, biting into a silver pear.

'This is more room than *I've* ever had in my life,' said Dr Rain. 'Not all of us had mansions back in Etherhorde, or crossed the Nelluroq in the Imperial Stateroom.'

'We're being examined,' said Uskins, crouched in the weeds, his eyes on a large antlered beetle near his foot. 'They're spying on us. I can feel their fishy eyes.'

'We're just monkeys, as far as they're concerned,' said Mr Druffle, rising to Uskins' gloomy bait (he was suffering greatly from lack of rum). 'The experiments will come later: the injections, the probes.'

'And then they'll turn us into frogs and eat our legs,' said Marila, whose opinion of Druffle was even lower than Dr Chadfallow's.

Pazel turned his face to the sky. 'At least the sun is out,' he said.

He was seated on the steps near the glass wall, eyes closed, basking. Thasha was leaning against his shoulder. They had clung together quietly since his mind-fit, and her own brief spell of strangeness. It was Thasha who had held him through his last raving hour, Thasha who had washed his bloodstained face, cradled his shivering body while he slept. Thasha who had explained, when he woke in the dawn chill, that they were in a place called the Imperial Human Conservatory, and that the hoots and squeals and grunts that woke him were the *tol-chenni*, in some other part of the compound, screaming for their morning food.

Now she rose and looked at their prison again.

You could call it a garden, or the remains of one. It was about fifty feet long and half as wide. Ragged shrubs and flowers, unpruned trees, a fountain that had not flowed in years. Benches and tables of stone, a little wood-burning grill and stocky chimney, a fenced-in patch that might once have been used for vegetables (this was where Uskins sat). Five tiny bedchambers, with no doors in the frames.

The main courtyard was roofless, but the walls were nearly forty feet high. Set into the wall across from the bedchambers was an immense pane of glass, thirty feet long, six inches thick, and without a scratch on its gigantic surface. Hercól thought it might be the same crystal used in the *Chathrand*'s own glass planks, a substance lost to the knowledge of the Northern world. There were small boreholes in the glass, possibly for speaking through. To one side, tucked into the corner, was a solid steel door.

It was through this glass wall that the birdwatchers came to stare at them, to take notes and whisper together. From the corridor, the birdwatchers could see the whole space within, and even much of the bedchambers. You could sleep out of sight, but the moment you got to your feet you were on display. So of course were the birdwatchers themselves. Close up, they had revealed themselves as rather careworn, older dlömu, grubbing for handkerchiefs in the pockets of their grey uniforms, squinting at their notebooks. But they were earnest in their study of the prisoners. On the second day they had brought a painter, who set up his easel in the corridor and worked for many hours, filling a number of canvases.

The birdwatchers paid unusual attention to Marila and Neeps. Once, when Neeps stood close to the glass, a dlömic woman had lowered her nose to the borehole and sniffed. Then she had backed away, eyes widening, and fled the corridor, calling to her fellows.

The intense scrutiny had abated, however. On this third day their keepers had so far appeared only at mealtimes. But they had not abandoned the watch altogether: a dog had been left on duty. The musty brown creature sat upon a wooden crate carried in for the purpose, watching them through mournful eyes. Thasha had tried speaking to the dog, as she would to Jorl or Suzyt. The animal had turned its eyes her way, but it never made a sound.

The birdwatchers never spoke to them either, but they were as generous with food as everyone else in Masalym. Twice a day, under heavy guard, the steel door was unlocked and a cart rolled inside, heaped with fruit, vegetables cooked and raw, snake-beans, cheese and of course the small, chewy pyramids of *mül*. They never ran out of *mül*. Druffle was morbidly chewing one left over from breakfast.

'You know what we have to do, shipmates,' he said to no one in particular. 'We have to show 'em we're sane.'

'Ingenious,' said Chadfallow.

'You leave him alone,' said Neeps. 'If the two of you start fighting they'll throw away the key. Anyway, he could be right. It might be the only way out of here. We *are* sane, after all.'

'Did you hear that bird?' said Uskins, brightening. 'It sounded like a falcon. Or a goose.'

The south wall was lined with cabinets and shelves. There were some books, mould-blackened, nibbled by mice, and cabinets with cups and plates and old bent spoons, a tin bread box. The north wall was a grille of irons bars, at the centre of which hung a rusted sign:

TREAT YOUR BROTHERS WITH COMPASSION
REMEMBER THAT THEY BITE

Beyond the iron bars stood further enclosures, which were larger and wilder, with ponds and sheds and stands of trees, all neglected, all walled off from the city. Now and then, between the trees and outbuildings, she saw the *tol-chenni*, squatting naked, raking hay into piles and scattering it again, picking things from the dirt and eating them, or trying to. They seemed quite afraid of the newcomers. Neeps had tossed a hard dlömic roll over the gate: it had lain there in the sun all day, untouched. But by this morning it had disappeared.

This, surely, was the place Ibjen's father had spoken of, where Bali Adro had tried and failed to cure the degenerating humans. But what was its purpose today? Were they locked in a prison, a hospital? A zoo?

'The dlömu are moving in the next wing,' said Hercól, from his listening post near the glass wall. 'Be ready – our chance may come at any time.'

Thasha sighed. He had been talking that way since their imprisonment began. She drifted into the chamber she shared with Marila and looked down from the barred window at the world outside their prison. She had spent hours here, entranced.

The Conservatory was built on a bluff over the river, near the cliff that divided one part of Masalym from the next. They were in the Middle City, but a stone's throw from the window the land fell away into Lower Masalym, vast and largely abandoned. Oh, there were people – two thousand, she guessed, or maybe three. But the homes! There must have been fifty thousand or more. The Lower City by itself was the size of Etherhorde, and yet it was very nearly a ghost town. Countless streets lay empty. Yesterday smoke had risen in the distance: a blaze had consumed three houses, unmolested by any fire brigade. The ruins were smouldering yet.

And there were stranger things: hulking buildings of iron and glass, and monstrous stone temples that looked as old as the surrounding peaks. But like the tower of Narybir, these giant structures lay closed and dark.

By daylight she saw the dlömu scurrying about their lives, carting vegetables, mending windows and fences, gathering scrap wood into bundles. They met at street corners, talked briefly, anxiously, scanning the empty streets. A mother marched her child down a sunlit avenue, clearly afraid. A face appeared at an upper window, through mouldering curtains, vanished again. Four times a day, a dlömu in a white robe climbed the steps of a half-ruined tower to strike a brass gong, and the lonely noise lingered in the air. His coal-black face, framed by the white hood, turned sometimes in her direction, thoughtfully. At dusk, animals crept from the abandoned homes: foxes, feral dogs, a shambling creature the size of a small bear but quilled like a porcupine.

There were also soldiers, of course, servants of the Issár. She could pick them out here and there. At the port, they surrounded the *Chathrand*: the Great Ship was plainly visible from her window. Along the road they had followed two nights before, a few troops came and went. And on the outer wall there were soldiers, milling, marching, tending the great cannon that pointed down into the Jaws of Masalym.

But for all the busy movement along the wall, the number of men there was not very large. There were far more guns than men to use them. By night, they lit lamps at sentry posts where no actual sentries stood guard. By day they appeared at pains to keep every man on duty out of the turrets and walking the battlements in plain sight. *It's a façade*, she thought. *They're hiding behind those cannon, these cliffs. They're mounting a guard around an empty shell.*

All this was strange enough. But even stranger, beside the wind-swept emptiness below was the bustle and noise of this higher part of Masalym, this Middle City. Thasha could see only a few blocks of it, but the curve of the cliff told her that the Middle City was a fraction of the size of the Lower. And yet the Middle City was alive. Its streets were crowded, its shops abuzz by early morning and aglow half the night. There were musicians playing somewhere; there were dlömic men with water-pipes seated on rugs outside doorways; there was a fruit market that appeared as if by magic at dawn and disappeared by noon; there were dlömic children walking to school in daisy chains.

'It's two cities, isn't it?'

Pazel had stepped into the chamber. She reached for his hand and drew him near.

'Three, probably,' she said. 'There's the Upper City, somewhere. But I don't know if we'll be going there after all.'

'Not if the Issár's as afraid of madness as everyone else.'

'And not if Arunis is as tight with him as he seems,' she said.

They stood in silence a moment. A bird cried shrilly. They looked at each other and smiled. 'Uskins wasn't dreaming,' she said. 'That's an eagle, or some other bird of prey.'

'Look,' he said, 'the crew's out exercising again.'

He pointed to the Tournament Grounds, three miles away in the Lower City, at the end of the broad avenue that led to the port. Thasha could just see the pale humans in the courtyard of the pavilion, a huge and crumbling mansion that might once have been rather splendid.

'I wonder,' she said, 'if any of those people are going home.'

'Well, we blary are,' said Neeps. He and Marila had stepped into the room. Marila threw herself down on the straw-stuffed bed. 'I said I wanted a nap. Tell me you're not going to start babbling about *plans* again.'

'Not exactly,' said Neeps. He was looking strangely at Thasha. 'I want to talk to you,' he said. 'By yourself, maybe. If you don't mind.'

His request turned heads. 'By herself?' said Pazel, knitting his eyebrows. 'What do you have to tell her that you can't tell us?'

'It's not like that, mate,' said Neeps, 'it's just something I need to . . . bring up.'

'Something about what happened to her in the wagon?' Pazel demanded.

'What do you know about that?' asked Neeps, startled. 'You couldn't understand her words; you were in the middle of your own fit. You were screaming and covering your ears.'

'I haven't forgotten, believe it or not,' said Pazel. 'But I could still *see*. I know she was in trouble. What did she say?'

'Was it something awful, Neeps?' asked Thasha, studying him. 'Is that what you want to tell me?'

Neeps glanced at Marila. 'What does *awful* mean, really? You heard her. Would you call that awful?' When Marila only rolled onto her stomach and sighed, he turned back helplessly to Thasha. 'Maybe,' he said, 'we could forget the whole thing?'

Thasha closed her eyes. 'You sound like a *perfect* fool.'

'Half-right,' said Marila. 'He's far from perfect. And he won't quit until he gets his way. Go and listen to him. Then you can tell us yourself, if you want to.'

But Thasha shook her head firmly. 'No more secrets,' she said. 'Not from you three. Not ever.'

She looked at Pazel, hoping he understood. What she'd had to do with Fulbreech, what she'd had to do to *him*: that had been the last straw. She turned to Neeps and snatched his hand. 'You come here, and listen. I was there the night you talked about your brother. The night you almost killed me. I was on the same mucking divan with the two of you.'

Marila blushed; Neeps looked mortified. Pazel felt himself ambushed by a smirk.

'You've seen Pazel go crazy with fits,' Thasha went on. 'You saw me pretending to be Fulbreech's little ... *whore*. And you heard what Arunis said. It might be true, even though he said it to hurt me. Syrarys might really be my mother and ... Sandor Ott—'

She could not get the words out. Pazel stepped behind her and held her shoulders, and Thasha felt some measure of calm returning.

'We've shared all that,' she said, 'and a lot more besides. So don't tell me to start keeping secrets from you *now*. I don't want any. I want friends who know who I am.'

All four youths were quiet. Suddenly Marila leaned forwards and put her arms around Thasha's waist, hugging her tightly. Thasha was speechless, but a moment later Marila released her with a mumbled apology and quickly wiped her eyes.

Everyone looked at Neeps, waiting. The small boy sat down, ran his hands through his dusty hair, puffed out his cheeks.

'Right. Now don't yell, anybody, unless you feel like sharing secrets with the rest of 'em out there. I don't think your mother was Syrarys *or* Clorisuela. I think she was Erithusmé, Thasha. I think they're hiding the fact that you're the daughter of a mage.'

Even with his warning, the other three struggled to contain themselves. 'Where in the sweet Tree's shade did you get *that* daft idea?' said Pazel.

'From Felthrup, that's where. He helped you read the *Polylex*, Thasha – for weeks and weeks, when touching the book used to make you so ill.'

'He saved me a lot of pain,' said Thasha.

'He was also delirious,' said Marila.

'Only because he was afraid to close his eyes,' said Pazel. 'Arunis was attacking him in his dreams.'

'I know all that.' Neeps waved a hand dismissively. 'The point is, he talked a lot. To us, the dogs, the blary curtains. And you two must have read a lot about Erithusmé.'

'We did, when we could find anything in that book.'

'One night,' Neeps continued, 'I woke up late and heard him talking to you, Thasha. I think you must have been asleep, because you never answered. "If you inherit her power, will you be any different, dear one?" he said. "Will her burden pass to you as well? To run with the Stone eternally, from land to land, hounded by evil, seeking a resting place that does not exist? Or will you grow into something mightier than the seed from which you came?"'

Thasha grew pale.

'He chattered on for a while,' said Neeps, 'about a "plan" for you, and how Ramachni was essential to it, and the Lorg School as well.'

'The Lorg!' hissed Thasha.

'But Thasha,' said Neeps, 'Felthrup didn't make it sound as though Ramachni had *made* the plan. The way Felthrup talked, he was just there to help. The plan was hers.'

'Erithusmé's?'

Neeps nodded. 'I think so, yes.'

'Well, I think you're cracked,' said Pazel. 'All this because Felthrup babbled to himself one night? He wasn't just being attacked by Arunis then, you know. He was suffering from the fleas that the Nilstone had cursed. You're putting a lot of faith in one hysterical rat.'

'But it fits, don't you understand?' said Neeps. 'Why else would she be the only one in this blary world who can put her hand on the Nilstone and live? And what about the other night in the wagon?'

Thasha blinked at him, frightened now. 'You still haven't told us what I said.'

'It wasn't your voice,' said Neeps.

'Tell me,' said Thasha. 'I'm ready.'

Neeps and Marila looked at each other. 'You shouted a few curses,' said Marila, 'with words like *Maukslar* and *Droth* in them, words I've never heard before. But then you said, *He is going to steal it and loose the Swarm. What are you waiting for? When will you let me strike?* That was all. You howled a bit after that, and then you dropped back into your chair and slept until we got here, soaked with rain. You broke the wagon cover.'

'And you tossed Hercól aside with one hand,' put in Neeps. 'You know what I think, Thasha? I think Erithusmé was speaking through you for a moment. I think, somewhere, your mother is still alive.'

'Of course she is.'

They all whirled. Straight across the enclosure, gazing in through the wall of crystal, stood Arunis, laughing. Counsellor Vadu stood beside him, along with half a dozen birdwatchers – and Greysan Fulbreech. How Arunis had managed to hear them from such a distance was unclear, but he had replied by shouting at the top of his lungs.

The four youths rushed from the sleeping chamber. The others were on their feet, facing the glass: all save Mr Uskins, who shrank down into the shrubbery and wrapped his arms about his head.

'Yes, Thasha, your mother Syrarys is very much alive,' said the mage. 'She's in the house of King Oshiram even now – his house, and his bed – making certain the upstart does not cause any trouble in the Crownless Lands, before our glorious return. Another safety precaution on the part of Sandor Ott. And Syrarys herself? Why, she is another tool the spymaster thinks he owns, like Fulbreech here. When in fact I had only loaned them to him, for as long as it profited me to do so. Listen, Thasha: Isiq's wife was barren. She could no more have children than she could walk through walls. Syrarys gave birth to you, and tolerated you with effort, for ten long years. She told me a great deal about that effort. She dreamed of the day it would be over: with Admiral Isiq handed to Ott for torture, and you in the Mzithrinis' hands, awaiting death.'

'Your own death grows more certain with every word you speak,' said Hercól.

Arunis turned to Vadu and raised his hands, as if presenting evidence of something they had already discussed. Vadu frowned at Hercól, and his head bobbed up and down. 'That was an unwise remark,' he said. 'I cannot release anyone whose stated intention is to commit murder. Especially when the declared victim is a guest of the city.'

'I thought *we* were guests of the city,' said Chadfallow.

'You're here because you're ill, Doctor,' said Fulbreech, smiling his handsome smile.

'Correct,' said Vadu. 'I suggest you all work in good faith with our specialists. If anyone can help you, it is they. Be glad you were brought here. Your shipmates—' he faltered, looking troubled, '—may well come to envy you.'

'Counsellor,' said Hercól, 'you are deceived. This sorcerer is the enemy not only of all the men of the *Chathrand*, but all men, all people in Alifros. Help him no more – for however it may seem, he is not helping you. Very soon he will attempt to steal the Nilstone. You must prevent that at all costs.'

'Steal the Nilstone!' laughed Fulbreech. 'Do you know why he says that, Counsellor Vadu? Because that girl went mad and screamed it, on the way to this asylum. Steal that little bauble, the Shaggat's toy—'

Arunis shot an angry glance at Fulbreech. The youth drew back a step, clearly frightened.

'He has no need to resort to theft,' said Vadu. 'We have an understanding, Arunis and I. Come, sorcerer, you can see that they are well looked after. Let us go.'

'Not without my idiot,' said the mage.

Even as he spoke a door opened at the end of the hall, and several more birdwatchers appeared, this time leading a docile figure in chains. Thasha gasped: the figure was human. He was dressed, and of a rough, solid build like a farm labourer. He was also quite clearly deranged. His eyes fixed on nothing; his lips flexed and squirmed aimlessly. Both arms dangled at his sides, but his left hand twitched repeatedly, a sharp motion like the leap of a frog.

'Are you certain you want it?' said Vadu. 'Look at it, mage. It's useless.'

'Oh, I want him – *it*,' said Arunis. 'If *it* is truly as they describe.'

'We told you the truth,' said one of the birdwatchers, frightened and angry at once. 'This one's a special case, and needs special handling to keep it from harm. It walks upright, and lets itself be dressed. But it's blind to danger. You'll find it a burden, sir, you should leave it with us. It will swallow rocks, nails even. And it doesn't see what's in front of its nose. It sees something else. It would walk off a cliff, or into a fireplace. It lives in the mist, in the fog – and we're attached to it, you see. It's been here so long.'

'Perfect,' said Arunis.

'Twenty-eight years,' said another of the birdwatchers, his voice sour and upset. He was the only one of the dlömu who struck Thasha as cruel: a look somehow heightened by the bright gold tooth in his upper jaw. He gestured at the tarboys. 'It was younger than them when we caught it. We *raised* it.'

'With loving care, no doubt.' Fulbreech snickered.

'It's not fair to prance in here and snatch it,' the dlömu went on. 'We've written *books* about this *tol-chenni*, Counsellor. Why doesn't he take one of the newer ones, they're just as healthy, and—'

'I will have this one, Vadu,' said Arunis. 'Rid me of its handlers. Quickly.'

As Vadu ushered the unhappy technicians from the corridor, Arunis stepped close to the glass. He glanced briefly at Druffle, his former slave, and at Uskins, who cowered deeper into the bushes when the mage caught his eye. His gaze rested longer on Hercól, and longer still on Pazel and Thasha. His eyes did not gloat. Despite the hunger that was always part of him, he appeared almost serene.

'We haven't really talked,' he said, 'for months. Since that day on the bowsprit, Pathkendle – you recall? After that there were so few opportunities. I admit I wanted for conversation. I had Felthrup, of course – and you too, Uskins, after the captain assigned you to wait on me, and keep me under observation. You're not likely to forget those chats, are you, Stukey?'

'I didn't do anything,' said Uskins in a whimper. 'I was good.'

'You may be here a long time,' said Arunis to the others. 'For as long as Bali Adro continues to pay for this institution, this relic of its former glory. I do not think that we shall meet again; not in any form that you would recognise. So I wish to thank you. Of course, you will not understand it when I say so, but you were ... necessary. This long, long struggle was necessary.'

'You say that,' said Chadfallow, 'and you mean necessary to some end you have dreamed up. Something violent and fantastically selfish.'

'Yes,' said Arunis, clearly pleased. 'So you do understand, a little. You think you have been fighting me, but it is not so. You have been fighting *for* me, as slaves fight in the ring for the glory of the gladiator. And so it has always been. These centuries of battle, of searching for the way the task could be done, of racing the others to the finishing line. Battling you and your ancestors, battling

Duñarad and Suric Roquin, the Amber Kings, the Becturians, the selk. Battling Ramachni and Erithusmé the Great. All for my benefit, my distinction. And now the final step is come, and I am grateful.'

The nine humans could only stare. Thasha knew that the driving lunacy of the being before her had reached some new and hideous threshold. He wasn't lying, wasn't playing a trick. He really was saying goodbye to something – to them, and something he had decided they stood for.

'It's not going to happen,' she said. 'Do you hear me? What you think is going to happen – it won't. No one is with you, except out of fear. You can't turn your back without fear that someone will stab it. But we're stronger. We have each other. You're alone.'

If Arunis heard her, he showed no sign. He raised his hands before his face as though framing a picture.

'I will reward you,' he said. 'When all else is gone, burned beyond ashes, burned back to heat and light, I will retain the image of your faces as I see them now. My enemies, who almost killed me. My final collaborators. I will remember you in the life to come.'

'And I will help you remember, Master, if you wish,' said Fulbreech suddenly. His voice was soft, but anxious nonetheless. 'I will be there with you, just as you told me. I will keep helping you, with my cleverness, my skills. Won't I, Master? I'll help you all the way *there*, and beyond. Won't I?'

Arunis passed his eyes over Fulbreech, and said not a word. Taking the chain from Vadu, he led the *tol-chenni* down the corridor and out of sight. Fulbreech hurried after him. A door opened and closed.

Vadu looked at the human prisoners. His head bobbed in agitation.

'I should like to know why he insists on the company of lunatics,' he said.

The sorcerer's visit left them quiet. For Thasha the word *collaborators* had stirred some buried feeling, a blend of guilt and terror that her conscious mind could not explain. She had assumed that the mage and Syrarys were in league from the day her mother's necklace, so long in Syrarys' hands, had come to life and nearly strangled her. But it sickened and terrified her to think that both might have been involved with her family since before her birth.

She was still mulling over these dismal thoughts when the dog sat up with a startled *yip*, the first sound it had made since its arrival. Voices followed: loud, angry dlömic voices, drawing nearer. Mr Uskins squealed and darted for the bushes.

Some argument or stand-off was occurring within the Institute. Then all at once a crowd, almost a mob, burst into the corridor. The old birdwatchers were shoved aside as thirty or forty newcomers pressed up to the glass.

They were rough-looking dlömu. Some carried clubs or staves; a few wore swords on their belts and one carried a burning torch. They stared and the humans stared back.

'Very well, you've seen them,' said the leader of the birdwatchers, trying to reassert his authority. 'Quite harmless, and under our care. It's the Emperor's will that this facility exists. You know that, citizens.'

'The Emperor,' said one of the newcomers, 'has no idea that *they* are here.'

'And better that he never finds out,' said another. 'We'd be pariahs, and you know it. They'd quarantine the city.'

'Why should anyone wish to do that?' asked Hercól loudly.

The dlömu showed extreme discomfort at the sound of his words. They drew back from the glass and fingered their weapons.

'Men of Masalym,' said Chadfallow, 'in my own country I have been an ambassador of sorts. I know how strange we seem to you, but you need not fear us. We are not *tol-chenni*. There are no *tol-chenni* where we come from – no dlömu either.' At this the mob grumbled in surprise and doubt. Chadfallow pressed on. 'We're simply people, like you. We've come from across the Ruling Sea, but we mean you no harm. All we wish is to go on our way again.'

As on most every occasion since the night of their arrival, his words were met with stony silence. But the frowns deepened. Some of the dlömu were looking at the iron door, as if to see how well it was secured.

'Creatures!' shouted one of them suddenly, as if addressing very distant, or very stupid, listeners. 'We know you do not come from the Court of the Lilac. We read history, and we read signs in the earthquakes. Tell us now: what is the price of forgiveness? Name it and be done.'

'Forgiveness?' said Pazel. 'For what?'

'Name it I say,' the dlömu went on. 'We will pay if we can. We are not a selfish people, and we do not deny the Old Sins, like some. You come when the world is dying, as we knew you would. But you cannot simply taunt us – we will not stand for that. We will send you back to the dark place; we will burn you and scatter you on the wind. Name the price of expiation. Name it, or beware.'

Chadfallow moistened his lips. 'Good people—'

'A pay increase!' shouted Rain suddenly. 'Fourteen per cent is what I'm owed, I can prove it, I have records on the ship!' Druffle pulled the doctor away, whispering imprecations.

The mob was not pleased by Rain's outburst. The one who had spoken before pointed a finger through the glass. 'Creatures!' he exclaimed again. 'We will defend Masalym from all who come with curses. Think on that before you jest with us again.'

Uskins popped up suddenly from the bushes, pointing at Dr Rain. 'Ignore him! Ignore him! He's mad!' Then he bit his lips and squatted again.

'We will come back and kill you,' said the dlömu quietly.

They did not kill then and there, however: in fact, a dozen Masalym soldiers appeared moments later and drove them out, more cajoling than threatening. The birdwatchers stood in a nervous group, comparing notes and shaking their heads; then they too filed out, locking the outer door behind them. Only the dog remained.

Thasha was terribly frustrated. If only they would talk – really talk, not just threaten and shout. Old sins? Whose sins, and why should they ask the first woken humans to come along in generations for forgiveness? The mysteries were too many, the answers too few.

But there was one mystery she was not powerless to explore. She called her friends back into the sleeping chamber, and this time brought Hercól as well. Crowded as it was, she made them all sit on the beds. Once again she wished she had a door to close.

'I told you I wanted no more secrets, and I meant it,' she said. 'Hercól, you were friends for so long with my father. With the admiral, I mean.'

'Admiral Isiq *is* your father, Thasha,' said Hercól, 'and Clorisuela was your mother. Why would we lie about this?'

Thasha considered him for a moment. 'I don't expect Chadfallow to level with me,' she said at last, 'but I expect it of you, Hercól. I was born before you came to Etherhorde. I know that. But later, when you and Daddy became friends, did he ever say anything about Clorisuela ... not being able to have children?'

Hercól glared at Thasha. He looked tempted to stand and walk out of the room. But slowly his gaze softened, and at last he gave a heavy sigh. 'Yes,' he said. 'For several years they tried for children in vain. Clorisuela would lose them quite early, along with a great deal of blood. Your father said it happened four times.'

Thasha closed her eyes. 'And then?'

'They stopped trying, stopped daring to live as husband and wife.' Hercól drew a deep breath. 'And yes, that was when he ... obtained Syrarys.'

'Bought her,' said Thasha.

Hercól shook his head. 'She was, as you were told, the Emperor's gift. But that is not the end of the story, Thasha. Your mother knew nothing of Syrarys. But Clorisuela did come to Isiq once more, strangely hopeful. And even though the midwives had told her it would be dangerous, they tried again. You were the result.'

'After four failures?' said Thasha, her eyes moist. 'You believed him, when he told you that?'

'I believe it to this day,' said Hercól.

Everyone was still. Once again, Marila's round cheeks were streaked with tears. Thasha swallowed. *Finish this*, she thought. *Make him say it, while you can.*

'You told me what happened in the wagon. But there's another moment I don't remember. What did I say when we first stepped into that village? When we saw the *tol-chenni*, and learned what had happened to human beings?'

'We were all in shock,' said Hercól quickly, 'and we all said foolish things. I expect none of us recalls exactly what came out of your mouth.'

'What does your nose tell you about *that*, Neeps?' said Thasha, smiling ruefully.

Neeps fidgeted. 'Sometimes I can't tell.'

'Well I can,' said Thasha. 'You're lying, Hercól. I think you remember exactly what I said.' She turned to Pazel. 'And I'm *certain* you do. The last clear memory I have is how you stared at me. As if I'd just told you I'd killed a baby. I couldn't very well demand honesty when we were all playing charades with Arunis and Fulbreech. But that's over, and I want to hear the truth.'

'Thasha—'

'Now.'

The others exchanged glances. They had all discussed it; she could see the awareness in their eyes. At last Hercól cleared his throat.

'Let me,' said Pazel suddenly. He stood up from the bed and rubbed his face with one hand. She thought suddenly how old he looked, how loss and danger had bled the child out of him, out of them all. He was young and old at once. He took her hands.

'You said, "*I didn't mean to. It was never supposed to happen.*" And then you asked if I believed you. That was all.'

Thasha felt a coldness settle over her like sudden nightfall. She felt Pazel's grip tighten, but the sensation was far away. *Air*, they were saying, *give her air, take her to the window*. She stumbled forwards and leaned on the sill.

For a moment she felt better – good enough to speak one of her father's salty naval curses, and to hear them laugh with relief. Then she raised her eyes and looked out through the window.

Masalym shimmered before her in the midday heat. But it was not the same place. The Lower City was bustling with life – humans, dlömu, smaller numbers of other beings she could not identify. Thousands went about their business, and the homes were solid and cheerful, flower boxes in the windows, fruit trees in the yards, carts pulled by dogs or donkeys rattling down the streets. Human children, dlömic children, milled together in a schoolyard. An old dlömic man sat by his old human wife, feeding birds in a square.

Thasha blinked, and the shadows grew longer. Now the humans were pulling the carts: were chained to the carts, chained in work teams, chained to wooden posts in the square where the couple had sat a moment before. The dlömus' faces were as hard as the leather whips they swung. A few humans were still well dressed: the ones carrying dlömic babies, or holding parasols over dlömic heads.

Another blink, and it was midnight. The city was on fire. The dlömu ranged the streets in rival bands, charging one another, stabbing, slashing, cutting throats. Mobs raced from broken doorways with armfuls of stolen goods, prisoners at swordpoint, dlömic girls in nightdresses, wailing. The humans scurried in terror, bent low to the earth. They wore rags, when they wore anything at all.

Once more the scene changed. It was a bleak, ashen dawn. Masalym was a city nearly abandoned. The few dlömu to be seen were rebuilding as best they could. The human faces were gone entirely.

'Never to return,' said Thasha aloud.

'We might yet,' said Pazel, embracing her. 'The ship's nearly repaired. We might find a way.'

'Never,' Thasha repeated. 'I won't let her. She had her chance, and look what she did with it. Look at that city, by the Blessed Tree. Are you looking?'

'We see it,' said Hercól. 'We've been looking at it for days.'

'I won't let her, Pazel,' said Thasha, trying hard to feel his arms around her. 'I want you to stay with me. She can try whatever she wants, but this is me, this is my life, and I will never, ever let her come back.'

22

Strange Couriers

5 Modobrin 941
234th day from Etherhorde

Professor J. L. Garapat
Odesh Hened Hülai

Entreats Your Participation in a Gathering of
Extraordinary Consequence
for the Several Worlds

Guest of Honour: FELTHRUP STARGRAVEN of Pöl Warren,
Noonfirth, NW Alifros

TOMORROW NIGHTFALL
THE OLD TAP ROOM • THE ORFUIN CLUB

Admission by This Card Only
Your Absolute Discretion is Assumed

The historians passed the card from hand to hand. They were sharp-eyed and earnest, and ready for a confrontation. It was not right for them to have been stopped at the door. 'Extraordinary consequence be damned,' muttered the first of them. 'How consequential can it be, Garapat, if your guest of honour never bothered to show?'

'But of course Mr Stargraven is here!' said Garapat, a tall, frail human with a serious voice and colossally thick glasses in bone frames dangling from his nose. He waved at the round table, which was cluttered with pipe-stands, cakes, gingerbread, mugs of cider and ale, someone's fiddle, countless books, one black rat. The old leather chairs outnumbered their occupants, but the half-dozen seated guests had the look of determined squatters, prepared to resist their eviction.

'Where?' said the historians, jostling. 'That animal, that rat? Felthrup Stargraven is the rat?'

'Hello,' said Felthrup miserably.

The historians wanted to squeeze into the room, but could not manage to do so without overtly shoving the old professor from the doorway. Most of the newcomers were humans or dlömu, but there was also a translucent Flikkerman; the first historian, their leader, had the dusky olive skin and feathered eyes of a selk. It was to the latter that Garapat addressed himself.

'He's come with a ghastly dilemma,' whispered the professor, indicating Felthrup. 'Night after night he's braved the River of Shadows. He's no mage, and has no travel allowance. He's just leaped in and dreamed his way here, by grit and courage. And he's up against—' The professor leaned close, and whispered in the first historian's ear. The listener started, jerking his head back to look the professor in the eye.

'A little rat,' he said, 'has pitted himself against *them*?'

'There are worlds at stake,' said Garapat. 'Someone has to help him.'

'And naturally that someone is you,' said another historian, who had blue ink-stains on the hand that gripped the doorframe. 'What's the matter with you, Garapat? Why do you spend so much time in this club, picking up strays?'

'Garapat's a fool,' said someone at the back of the crowd.

'He's from a hell-planet,' said another. 'It's called Argentina. He leaves every chance he gets.'

'Listen,' said Garapat, unperturbed by their slander, 'this was terribly hard for me to arrange, and it's been a washout, and the poor rat's spirits are so low. Cibranath couldn't travel, Ramachni's nowhere to be found. And Felthrup can't keep making this journey – indeed, he doubts he will ever be able to come here again. Leave us a while longer, won't you?'

'You were supposed to vacate an hour ago,' said the first historian. He had managed to wedge his foot into the meeting room. 'And you know perfectly well we can't work in the common chamber. The tables are far too small. Besides, this is the only summoning room in the Orfuin Club. We can't finish our work without Ziad, and we can only summon him here. Now, if you please—'

Garapat made one more attempt, reminding them that Alifros was a magnificent world, that a number of their mutual friends called it home, and asking if they were truly willing to contribute to its destruction merely for the sake of a prearranged meeting to discuss the editing of a history text? But the last question doomed his case. Was the study of history some esoteric pastime, rather than a vital tool for understanding the present? The historians bristled at the notion. 'I'm going to fetch the innkeeper,' said someone. 'Rules are rules.'

Garapat sighed and looked back towards the table. Felthrup had overheard the debate.

'Let them in!' he squeaked, waving his paws. 'You've done everything I could have hoped for, dear professor. The failure is mine. Enter, sirs, the room is yours, of course. Do not trouble Master Orfuin. We will vacate now, and I will return to the ship in disgrace.'

With a shake of his head, Garapat stepped aside, and the crowded room grew quickly more so. The professor's invited guests – a hypnotist from Cbalu, the high priestess of Rapopolni, a world-skipping baron who had misplaced his physical body decades ago only to become far more contented as a shade, a radical Mzithrini philosopher – cursed and grumbled, and looked at Felthrup shamefaced. 'We have done you no service,' said the priestess. 'We have wasted your time.'

'And ours,' said the historian with the ink-stains, dropping his own stack of books onto the table.

'You are worse off than before,' the baron agreed sadly. 'I felt certain more people would come tonight, Garapat. Mr Stargraven's cause is the best you've ever championed.'

'They may *still* be trying to get here,' said the Mzithrini. 'The astral paths are dark tonight, and the River turbulent.'

'*We* managed, somehow,' said the first historian.

'No squabbling!' Felthrup turned in circles on the table. 'Scholars, friends. If I reduced you noble souls to fractiousness I should never forgive myself. I will go. I am beaten. I must serve my friends in this small rat's body, since my mind has done them no good.'

'Now he tries to play on our sympathies,' said the ink-stained man. 'Very good: you have them, like the Kidnapped Souls' Collective that was in here last month. Tragic, but the room's still ours. Ask Orfuin to send a boy to clean the table, will you?'

'That's enough, Rusar,' said the selk. 'Mr Stargraven, if it is not safe for you to linger in the common room—'

'It is *not* safe,' broke in Garapat. 'The Raven Society sends members here almost nightly.'

'—then you must trust these new friends of yours to carry on with the effort.'

'Just so, kind stranger.' Felthrup sniffed as Garapat prepared to lift him from the table. 'And may I say in passing that it is an honour to meet with members of the Tribe of Odesh, however briefly.'

'You know something of Odesh, do you?' said the Flikkerman dubiously, as he settled into his chair.

'I know you are pledged to defend knowledge above all else,' said Felthrup, 'and that you have paid a great price for that dedication through the centuries – not least when the Emerald King burned the archive at Valkenreed, and threw the librarians into the flames. I know how heroically you have laboured since then – laboured against forgetting, as your motto proclaims. It is a mission to which I aspire in my dreams, though I know full well that I am unsuitable. Why, I cannot even grasp a pen.'

The bustling scholars had grown still as Felthrup spoke. Now all eyes were on him. 'You've been telling him about us, then, Garapat?' said the selk.

'Not a word,' said the professor.

'Then where, Mr Stargraven, did you learn about the Tribe of Odesh?'

'By reading, sir,' said Felthrup. 'I have no library of my own, but in the course of my journey I have read certain small selections from a book by Pazel Doldur.'

'Pazel Doldur!' shouted all the scholars at once.

Suddenly the lamplight flickered. Paintings on the walls rattled in their frames, and a number of the items on the table danced in place for an instant.

'There, now we've gone and summoned him by accident!' said the first historian. 'Welcome to an increasingly chaotic evening, Doldur. No, we didn't mean to bring you here. We're with Ziad, if you care to know. We're your competition.'

'Felthrup,' said Professor Garapat, 'are we to understand that when you spoke of the *Merchant's Polylex* you meant the *thirteenth edition*? Are you really in possession of a copy?'

'Of course,' said Felthrup. 'But who were you speaking to?'

All at once he squealed, and jumped three feet straight up from the table. Something had stroked his back, though no one in the chamber had moved.

'They were speaking to the editor-in-chief of your *Polylex*, Felthrup,' said Garapat, 'and a man whose second great work, *Dafvniana: A Critical History*, is, dare I say, nearing completion?'

'All in good time, Jorge Luis,' said an old man's rasping voice. The rat's fur stood on end: the voice was coming from an empty chair. Felthrup backed away in instinctive terror, until he stepped onto a fork and scared himself anew.

Garapat nodded at the chair. 'Mr Doldur has not gone to his final rest. He is a dweller in Agaroth, death's twilight borderland, while he waits for his own subeditors to finish their work.'

'I want to have a look at the last book that will ever bear my name,' said the voice. 'Is that so very odd?'

'Most understandable, I should say,' continued Garapat, 'especially as *A Critical History* will serve as the cornerstone of Dafvni studies for decades to come.'

The other scholars hissed: 'Not true! Our book will do so. Ours will be finished first.'

'These gentlemen are writing a similar book,' said Garapat, 'but both teams were hobbled, tragically, by the early deaths of their editors. The difference is that Ziad would happily retire to his grave, and leave these worthies to complete the book alone. But they still long for, indeed demand, his help. Consequently they have ... delayed the natural course of things.'

'What is "natural"?' scoffed one historian. '"Natural" is an abstraction, a will-o'-the-wisp. Besides, he signed a contract.'

'I will be off,' said the voice from the chair. 'My compliments to Ziad. And I will thank you to be more careful what you chant in Orfuin's summoning room, henceforth. Next time you bring me here in error I shall scatter your documents, and your ale.'

'But Doldur!' said the time-skipping baron, who appeared to be the only one who could see him, 'you simply must meet Stargraven before you go.'

'I am dead, sir. And a full professor, too. I *must* do very little.'

'He knows your protégée's son, your namesake.'

The chair squeaked, and a pile of books slid sideways. Felthrup had the impression that someone was leaning towards him over the table. 'You know Pathkendle? Pazel Pathkendle, Suthinia's boy?'

'Of course,' said Felthrup. 'We are allies, and fond friends. Shipmates, too – or so we have been.' Felthrup's cheek began to twitch. 'But Arunis and Macadra are going to steal our ship, steal it and sail away. What they will do with the human beings I cannot imagine. But the Nilstone! It will pass into their hands, and that will bring disaster on us all. Macadra's Ravens are already the power behind the Bali Adro throne; I heard that much in this club, before Prince Olik said a word. Her dream is to bind all Alifros within that Empire, with her at its ugly centre. And that plan is sweet – tender, modest, benevolently restrained – compared with Arunis' own. He would use the Stone not to rule Alifros, but to destroy it. He told Macadra how it was to be done, and it even shocked *her*. Orfuin heard them and closed the club!'

'He didn't,' said Doldur.

'He did, in fact,' said Garapat, as heads nodded around the table.

'He did! Oh, he did!' Felthrup was rubbing his paws together before his face. 'I was hiding under the stool in the form of a small wriggly thing, an *yddek*, and Orfuin called them devils and announced that the bar was closing, that they could not plot holocausts here, and Macadra's servants were so angry that one of them stomped a little sweeper to death, and would have done the same to me if I had moved from hiding. Then vines closed over the doors and the terrace vanished, and the River of Shadows took us all. But Master Doldur! I cannot warn my friends! Arunis has placed a lock on my dream memories! I thought someone here might carry the message for me, but all these nights of asking, pleading, have been in vain. No one goes to Masalym, or comes from there.'

'It is a dark place on dreamers' maps,' said the baron. 'No roads lead there. One could take to the River, of course. There was an entrance under the pool in the Temple of Vasparhaven, but no one speaks of it any more. I think it has been sealed.'

'I beg your pardon,' said the selk historian, 'but the very source of the River of Shadows in Alifros is not far from Masalym.'

'And it's *our* research site, not theirs,' grumbled the ink-stained man.

'Not far on the scale of the world,' said the baron, nodding. 'The River does indeed surface deep in the Efaroc Peninsula. But it would be no swift journey after that: out of the Infernal Forest, up the winding river, across the lava fields with their horrid guardians, over the glacier lake. Then down again, by a long path to the city of waterfalls. Many days it would take, even if no storms impede the passage of the mountains.'

'We have no time for such adventures,' said Felthrup. 'Oh why, why does he want to *do* it? Ramachni says that Arunis is a native of Alifros, that he belongs there. Where does he mean to live when it is gone?'

'You mustn't grow hysterical,' said Doldur.

'I mustn't,' Felthrup agreed, dropping violently into a squat.

'They may hear you in the common room,' said Garapat.

'Worse,' said Felthrup. 'If I grow hysterical I shall wake, and it will be over, finished. I am alone on the *Chathrand* already! The dlömu have evacuated the ship, and a new crew is coming. I fear I will soon wake no matter how I behave. It is not easy to sleep so long. My stomach is empty and growling like a wildcat.'

'Eat some cake,' said the ink-stained scholar.

'It won't help, he's a dreamer, you're not listening!' hissed the others.

'Do you mean,' said the voice of Pazel Doldur, now hushed and astonished, 'that the Nilstone, Droth's Eye, the Scourge of Erithusmé, is back aboard the *Chathrand*?'

'Back?' said Felthrup.

'Of course, back. The great wizardess herself conveyed the Stone through Alifros upon that ship, in her quest to banish it from the world. She had a hidden safe built right into the wall of her cabin, lined with all the spell-dampening materials she could lay her hands on, and yet the Nilstone still caused terrible things to happen aboard the *Chathrand* – altered it, too, by drawing ghosts and spell-shards and residue of old charms into that vessel like iron filings to the lodestone. Felthrup, sir: you must tell me more of this. I am very fond of Suthinia, you know. She named her son after me.'

Then the scholars, and Professor Garapat, and his five invited guests, began to talk in great excitement, spouting names, grabbing books, completing one another's sentences. Felthrup twisted and turned, his stumpy tail knocking against the tankards and plates.

Then the Flikkerman raised his arms and flashed so brightly that everyone was briefly dazzled.

'We're going to wake him ourselves at this rate,' he said.

'Quite right,' said Doldur. 'Now do tell your story, Felthrup – but briefly and calmly, pray.'

Felthrup did not manage to respect either condition. His nerves were all but destroyed, and the gleam of hope in this eleventh hour had gone straight to his heart. But with the aid of Garapat and the other invited guests, who had heard it once already, he got the essence of the tale across. 'I can't imagine what will happen to the human crew,' he said in closing. 'Will they be killed, or taken away as curiosities to Bali Adro City? Will they be enslaved?'

'It will not long matter what becomes of them if you lose the Nilstone,' said Doldur. 'No, this is truly frightful. To think that my book has done so little good! That it has even come close to informing Arunis how to master the Nilstone! And this travesty involving the Shaggat! It seems that Arqual has only sunk deeper into corruption since my death.'

'There is hope for Arqual,' said Felthrup, 'if Empress Maisa should somehow regain her throne. As for your book, it had little chance to do good, for the Magad dynasty has sought out and destroyed nearly every copy – along with their owners. When mere possession of a book can see one burned at the stake or tossed into the sea, the natural inclination is surely to get rid of it.

'But Master Doldur, there is something I do not understand at all. The thirteenth *Polylex* was written a century before my time. How is it possible that you know Suthinia Pathkendle? Is she ancient? Did she marry Captain Gregory and give birth to Pazel as an old, old witch?'

'Nothing of the kind,' laughed Doldur. 'Indeed, I believe in your time she is barely fifty. It is a long story, Felthrup. The creation of the thirteenth *Polylex* was an adventure in its own right. But here is an answer to your question, in brief: I was orphaned by Magad the Second. His wars of greed and conquest took my father and my elder brother – soldiers, both of them. And his royal cousins, flatterers, bootlicks – they took the life of my mother. Not with a spear but with a disease of the bedchamber. She'd given herself into their foul hands for years, in exchange for my school money. Right there in Etherhorde, right under my nose. Astonishing what a love of books can blind one to. You know the revenge I sought, don't you?'

'To expose his crimes,' said Felthrup.

'His crimes, and all the crimes, lies, venality of Arqual. In pursuit of that end I was a driven soul, a maniac. But only a mortal maniac, and an impoverished one at that. I needed help, and in good time I found help, from the one being in Alifros who could make my impossible dream a reality. I mean, of course, the wizardess Erithusmé.'

'Aha!' said the rival historians. 'Magical help from the start! That's cheating!'

'I earned my reputation as a historian with no aid from any charm,' Doldur continued, 'but Erithusmé saw the kernel of a mage within me, too. She warned me of the consequences if it should germinate – no normal existence, no wife or family, no rest – and I accepted them, dreaming only of my book, my book of revenge. So it was with her help that the *Polylex* came to be. I poured all the spell-craft I learned into research, research. I plucked secrets from the Empire like grapes from the vine, and gave them in bushel-baskets to my assistants. The book grew like a vine as well: mad, unruly, heavy with forbidden fruit.

'One warning, however, Erithusmé never gave me – that Magad would tear all Alifros apart in his desire to find and punish me. I became the most wanted man north of the Nelluroq. The wizardess could protect me only so well: she had other, grander fights than mine, and was breaking under the strain. Nor was there any place to hide me in the North. Arqual was impossible; the Crownless Lands were thick with Magad's forces and spies; the Mzithrin was closed to non-believers. So the wizardess did what she could: she smuggled me away, to a distant time and place.

'It was a fair city called Istolym, part of the Empire of Bali Adro.

A gentle and a wisely governed land, then. In time I learned that I was on the far side of the Nelluroq, living in the century previous to my own. Why she chose that place, I suppose I'll never know. But I think now that she sent me back in time in case I should ever make the journey home – in the rough hope that the Red Storm would bring me forwards about as far as I'd been sent back, so that I might return to an Arqual I recognised.

'I never heard from the wizardess again. But I dwelled in Istolym happily enough, growing as a mage, though lonely for my own time and country, and anxious about the fate of my book. Nine good years I spent there, until the day when another mage, Ramachni Fremken, came to me and said that Erithusmé was lost and feared dead. He told me also that a foul sorcerer had gone north to steal the Nilstone, and that an expedition was being launched to track him down.'

'Mr Bolutu's expedition?' said Felthrup.

'Yes, Belesar came with us,' said Doldur. 'And so did a student of mine, a human woman of no great magical promise, truth be told – but such intensity, such a will to work for others! She had studied with me for one year, and we did not yet know if she would ever develop the powers of a mage. But she would not give up. She'd come from a hard, cold place in the Fastness of Ihaban, lost her family to an avalanche; she was as ready as anyone could be to leave the world she knew behind. Her name was Suthinia Sadralin. In time she would marry a Northerner, one Captain Gregory Pathkendle, and give up magecraft for years.'

'Pazel's mother! Then she was not from the Chereste Highlands at all?'

'No, Felthrup. She was a Bali Adro citizen, and proud of it. She went north like a volunteer soldier, to fight a threat to her homeland.'

'And when you sailed north, the Red Storm caught you,' said Felthrup, 'and propelled you *forwards* again in time.'

'Yes,' said Doldur, 'but we had ill luck with the storm, and it hurled us two centuries forwards. Arunis had decades to himself in the North – and when we arrived he was waiting for us. An ambush. We were massacred. The survivors scattered, lived for years in hiding, wanting to fulfil our mission but reduced to the effort of staying alive. Suthinia and Bolutu were the only ones who managed it, in the end. And all that protected them, truth be told, was their failure to blossom into mages. We learned later that Arunis could follow the scent of our Southern magic, like a hound follows blood.'

'But Suthinia did at last become a mage, didn't she?' said Garapat.

'Years later. When the scent had grown cold. And when Captain Gregory abandoned her. She knew, you see, that she could not have both a family and a mage's calling. The two simply cannot be combined. I think she was torn for years. When he ran away it must have become easier for her – though not necessarily for her children.'

'And see here, Doldur, wasn't she rather good with dreams herself?'

'A fair hand, yes,' said Doldur.

'And if I recall, her favourite experimental subjects were her children?'

'That's rather a brutal way to put it,' said the ghost. 'What are you driving at, Professor?'

'Well, it's plain as day,' said Garapat. 'Felthrup can't warn anyone back in Masalym, because he forgets everything the moment he wakes. But he's told you, here and now. And you might just be able to tell Suthinia—'

'Ah!' said Doldur. 'You startle me sometimes, Jorge Luis. Yes, yes, I could do that.'

Felthrup ran to the edge of the table. 'Could you? Could you truly?'

'I don't see why not. I did it once before, after the Arquali invasion. She heard me perfectly – though I was not able to offer her much comfort. She had just lost her children. This time, perhaps, I'll be able to do more than wish her well.'

'O splendid man!' squealed Felthrup. 'Greatest of dead scholars! Oh, brilliance, brilliance, joy and song!'

'Least I can do for someone who's dared to read the thirteenth *Polylex*.' The ghost chuckled. 'Of course, we don't know if our efforts will go any further than that. It would be far better if I could visit young Pathkendle directly – but it is far harder for the dead to visit one they never knew in life. I would spend weeks merely trying to claw my way to Masalym in the darkness: your light is our darkness, you know, and the Little Moon in Southern Alifros is particularly hostile to the restless dead. I say, rat-friend, whatever's the matter?'

Felthrup had gone suddenly rigid, head to toe. 'The hatbox,' he said, through clamped teeth.

'Hatbox! What hatbox?'

'I am asleep within a hatbox. And I have become aware of it. My head is pressed against the wall of the box; I can feel the pressure. I am waking, waking. I cannot fight it much longer.'

The inky man stared at Felthrup as though tempted to poke him.

'Don't you *dare*,' said Pazel Doldur. 'Listen to me, Felthrup my boy. I think it's high time I paid my old apprentice a call. So tell me quickly: is there anything else you would like me to say to her, besides the fact that forces are coming from Bali Adro's capital to seize your ship?'

'And the Nilstone, Master Doldur,' said Felthrup, not moving a whisker.

'Of course, of course.'

'And tell her that her son, your namesake – please, could you tell her that he is brave and kind-hearted, and that the tongues he speaks number twenty-five at least? Oh, and that Dr Chadfallow is aboard as well. Oh! And this is desperately important – that the destination of the ship is Gurishal, the island of Gurishal. Is this too much to remember, sir?'

'My dear boy, I'm a historian. Come, what else?'

'Wise, quick-witted, mentally capacious ghost! Nothing else, unless ... yes, oh yes!'

Felthrup forgot himself, turned his head, knocked it against something no one else in the room could see. It was done: the black rat faded like a mirage. His last words seemed to hang in the air when he himself was gone:

'Tell her that Pazel is in love.'

One hour later, at an unthinkable distance from the cluttered room in the lively tavern, Suthinia Pathkendle awoke with a start, in her hard bed in the rented cottage on the poor side of Simjalla City. The voice that had begun in her dream was still speaking, though she knew she was awake. It was a beloved voice, her old master's; it filled her with the near-irresistible urge to put her hand out and grasp his own. But she could see no hand. And the message, when she fully woke and understood it, terrified her with the certainty that she had waited too long.

That remains to be seen, I think.

'Master?'

He was gone. A normal person would already be deciding that he'd never been there, that the voice was only the wind's, moaning under the eaves, sighing through the cracks she'd never bothered to fill. But Suthinia would never again be normal. She'd become herself at last, a true mage, and she knew a spectre's voice when she heard it.

After midnight the fire always died; the house grew bitterly cold. Suthinia lit a candle, pulled her tattered coat over her nightgown. She crossed the freezing floor into the main room. Yes, the curtains were drawn; the night patrols, the tramps and prostitutes, would see nothing. She took the vials of dream-essence from their hiding place within the brick wall. She studied them, red smoke, blue smoke, cherished links to two souls. Then she held them to her cheeks. The blue vial was cold. It usually was. Neda's training as a *sfvantskor* had raised walls inside her; only in the deepest sleep did they come down.

But there was an answering warmth from the red vial. She moved it from her cheek to her neck, wrapped her coat over it, and her arms over the coat. As the vial warmed she could sense his nearness, the soft sound of his breathing, the beat of his heart. For the thousandth time in the last six years, she found herself aching with the need to touch him, hold him as she was holding this hard thing of glass. She felt a violent tearing, a rending inside her and she knew the feeling was guilt. *Son of mine, son of mine. How did my fight become yours?*

'It wasn't your fault,' said Pazel to the woman who walked at his side. 'It was Chadfallow's, wasn't it?'

They were in the tall grass over the headlands in Ormael. Below stretched the Nelu Peren, sparkling at midday, threshing against the rocks. Gulls cried, and curlews. The sea-wind moved over the grass like the bellies of invisible ships, racing one after another into the plum orchard beyond. The woman was holding his hand.

'The more I learn of what has happened,' she said, 'the less I dare to speak of *fault*. Except my own, that is. I know well enough what I might have done, had I thought more of you and Neda, and less of myself.'

The plum trees were suddenly all around them. The white blossoms had opened; bees moved from branch to branch, pollen-dusted. It was spring.

'Yourself?' said Pazel. 'Come on, Mother. You thought of yourself even *less*.'

She looked at him sharply.

'I always knew you had *something* on your mind,' Pazel went on, 'but I never for a minute thought it was anything selfish. Neither did Neda. We could tell, you know. You had awful tasks, awful secrets you didn't want to burden us with. But you *should* have told us. We were jealous of those secrets. That's why Neda was angry all those years. Because she missed you so badly, wanted you back.'

They were leaving the orchard for the ragged woods beyond, looking up at the Highlands, the land he had always thought she came from. He knew better now. His mother had come from the South; he himself was but half-Ormali; he had cousins in Istolym – *tol-chenni* cousins, if any were still alive. She hadn't told him in words, exactly; she had simply decided it was time he knew.

'I could have handled the truth,' he said.

'Yes,' she said, 'you could have. You always had *idrolos*, that special courage that let you look at things squarely. Neda had far less of it, and so did I. Don't you understand, Pazel? I couldn't tell you the truth without facing it myself. And the truth was that I'd failed everyone – Doldur, Ramachni, my murdered friends. I'd failed Bali Adro, failed Alifros itself.'

'The fight wasn't over, Mother. Arunis still didn't have the Nilstone.'

'It was over for me. I gave it up the day I married Gregory. My friends from the expedition had all been found and slain, by Arunis or the men he hired for the job. One was poisoned at a meal I was late for. I'd have died that evening if I hadn't got lost in the back streets of Ormael. Another was killed in Eberzam Isiq's garden. He travelled all the way from the Mzithrin to the heart of Arqual, a miracle, and only managed to croak a few words of warning to Isiq's daughter. She's the one, isn't she? The one your rat-friend believes you care for.'

Pazel looked down, suddenly shy. 'Why did he mention that?' he asked.

'I wonder if he knew why himself?' said his mother. 'The rat is not a mage, by any chance?'

'No,' said Pazel, worried now. His mother looked so grave. 'You're upset because she's Admiral Isiq's daughter, aren't you?'

Suthinia shook her head. 'That sort of thing doesn't matter now. Pazel, does she love you too?'

'Yes. I mean, Rin's eyes, I think so. She's . . . alluded to it. Mother, why do you look so blary *morbid*?'

'I wish you happiness,' said Suthinia. 'You know I always have.'

'Well,' he said uncertainly, 'thanks.'

'We should not love,' she said with sudden fierceness. 'The

dlömu do a better job of it, or used to. Ask them about dlömic love, if you find someone who remembers the old days. But our own kind, human love: we never can make that work. It's like the milk I used to send you for, from the Brickpath Dairy. Always souring, sometimes even before you reached home. Souring into fear, or dumb greed, or shame. It was shame that kept me silent, Pazel. I wanted to live, to love Gregory, sail with him maybe, raise children at his side. What could I have said to you? "I come from a proud, fine kingdom. They sent me here to fight a monster, but I stopped fighting him, I fled." How could I have looked you in the eye? People always say that our children want our approval, but what about the reverse?'

'You told Captain Gregory.'

'And lost him. Forget what they said in Ormael, Pazel. Gregory was never a traitor.'

'I know that,' he said. 'I've always known that. He was honourable.'

The woman laughed. 'So honourable he couldn't bear to stand in my way. I swore that he was doing nothing of the kind, that I'd made my choice freely, with no regrets. But he was too clever. He listened close, the few times Doldur or Machal or one of the other survivors stayed under our roof. He put the pieces together. "You've shaped your life around this, Suthee," he said at last. "You studied magic, crossed the blary Ruling Sea, tossed away your world. Not to keep house for a sailing man. To fight for your people. *All* people. And we both know why you're not doing it."

'That was the last real talk we ever had. He was outbound the next morning, on a voyage of less than a month. The voyage he never returned from.'

They had reached the black oaks beyond the orchard. Pazel looked at his mother. Deep sadness in her eyes. But something was missing; she was leaving the best part out. It was a familiar tactic. This time he wouldn't stand for it.

'Go on,' he said, 'tell me the rest.'

When he upset her the landscape shimmered, quaked. It was

quaking now. 'I'll tell you this,' she said. 'I've guarded your dream-essence all these years, and haven't dared use it, because I knew it would hurt you when I did. You've changed, you know. You've developed an oversensitive mind.'

'I can't imagine why,' he said.

'The language spell made it harder, yes,' she said. 'But tell me the truth, will you, please? Hasn't it been worth it, after all? Worth the fits, the pain, even the danger?'

No hiding here: whether he said it or not she was going to know. Which meant he too had to face the question, choose an answer, once and for all.

'Yes,' he said at last, 'barely. I don't know who I'd have been without the Gift. Happier, maybe, or just as likely dead. It's all right. I like who I am.'

Suthinia touched his cheek. 'My son,' she said, 'who has sparred with eguar and Leopard People, and chatted with the murths of the sea.'

Her smile contained a hint of triumph. He did not much care for it. 'What else?' he demanded, for he could sense that a great deal remained to be said.

'I've been taking out the dream-vials for two months now,' she said, 'and I've looked a little into your dreams. Not because I wanted to spy on you. It was simply the only way to make contact.'

So that was how she knew about Thasha. 'What else?' he said again, impatient.

'You . . . react, each time I look,' she told him. 'That's probably why your fits have come more often. And now that I've finally stepped into your dream I expect it will be even worse. You might have another fit any time.'

Pazel took a deep breath. 'All right,' he forced himself to say. 'I understand, and I'm not angry. But you have to stop. Maybe I could put up with more fits, to be able to talk with you now and then, even in this strange way – but not until all this is over. It's too mucking dangerous. The last fit I had is part of why they locked us up. The dlömu are weird about madness; it scares them silly.

Promise, Mother. Promise you won't look into my dreams any more, unless it's a matter of life and death.'

Suthinia tossed her hair, resentful. 'Fine,' she said. 'I promise. Of course.'

She was angry, biting something back. He took her hand, hoping to soothe her, and they walked on for a time. He tried to find a way out of the silence, but every path seemed choked with thorns.

'So that's why Papa left us?' he said at last. 'So that you'd be less bound to Ormael? To help you return to the fight you came for?'

'Yes,' she said, 'that's why.'

'Then it wasn't about Chadfallow?'

Suthinia jerked her hand away. Suddenly the world was fluid, a blur. The sunlight lanced through the oak limbs, blinding; down was up, and though his mother remained close by he somehow could not look at her directly.

'Ignus?' she said. 'Ignus. Yes, he may have had something to do with it.'

'You weren't going to tell me, were you?'

'I've tried to respect his wishes,' she said.

'Whose wishes? My father's? Chadfallow's? Rin's eyes, Mother, why are you still hiding things? What did Papa carve in that tree?'

For they had come to the very oak his father had climbed to impress him, the one he had carved a message in at eighty feet. The one Pazel had been too young to climb, and later hadn't bothered to go looking for again.

'What tree?' she said. 'Pazel, you're wool-gathering.' She grabbed his elbow, started marching away. 'Listen, I've been waiting to tell you what's most important. Waiting until I knew you were all here, so that you'd remember it when you woke. It's a warning, Pazel, a warning from your rat-friend. But you distracted me with questions. *Credek*, did I wait too long again?'

'I'm already awake,' he said.

'Oh, skies! You're not. Listen close, Pazel. I'm not fooling any more.'

No, she was just avoiding his questions, ordering him about like a child. Suddenly he knew what he wanted, broke free, ran back to the oak with the lightning swiftness of dream-legs. He could climb that tree today, all right. It would be as easy as a flight of stairs beside the masts he'd climbed in Nelluroq storms.

Except, of course, that Mother had to try and stop him. Screaming, howling for an audience, demanding that he hear. She hadn't changed that much. 'Go away, I'm not listening,' he shouted. He was already halfway up the tree.

But so was Suthinia. Like a weasel, she sank her nails into the bark, and his trouser leg, begging, weeping, threatening, so very familiar. He climbed on. He was going to reach that branch, read his father's message, find out whatever it was she didn't want him to know. Meanwhile, Suthinia was throwing everything she could at him. Felthrup. Arunis. Isiq in a tower, historians in a bar.

'Not listening!' he shouted. 'Ya ya *ya!*'

It's not for my sake, she was saying (YA YA GO AWAY) listen for your own, for Alifros (I HAD A DOG AND HER NAME WAS JILL) for that oath you swore in Simja (WHEN SHE RAN SHE DIDN'T STAND STILL) blame me all you want, but after you hear what I (SHE RAN AWAY) they're coming, Pazel (ONE DAY) sending a ship to take the *Chathrand* (AND ALSO I RAN WITH HER) and the mucking Gods-damned Stone, they've never given up, Arunis, Macadra, all those carrion birds, they're flocking towards you, don't make my mistake, darling, don't hide when the world needs you most.

'Shhhhh.'

He tried to kick his mother's hand. But the claws had retracted, or vanished; her touch was light, her voice a gentle whisper. 'Easy, easy. You're going to wake up Neeps.'

He was hugging the tree; it was hugging him back, and kissing him, begging him for silence.

'Mother?'

The lips froze against his cheek. Then came a voiceless, delicious laugh. It was Thasha, lying in the darkness beside him, while Neeps (five feet away) snored on like a mooring line chafing against a dock. Her laughter faded back into kisses, dry quick kisses that barely required her to move.

'Rin's eyes,' he said, 'I'm half-Bali Adron.'

'Uh-huh.'

'I wonder if I have citizenship.'

She paused, and he reached for her. She was fully dressed, indeed she had on her boots. 'Goodbye,' she mumbled, kissing his hand, 'I came to say goodbye.'

'Goodbye?'

'Hercól and I are going over the wall. Shhh!' Thasha touched his lips with a finger. 'We're *all* going to break out of here, Pazel. But it's going to take some time to do it right.'

'No,' he murmured, 'wait.'

'Listen before you say no. We're not going to live here, are we? But what good will it do us to break out into a city where we're the only humans? We can't do *anything* by day. Our only chance is to learn as much as we can about the city after sundown – on the darkest nights, like this one, cloudy nights with no moon – and then get *out*, somehow, to the mountains, or in a smaller boat.'

'How are you getting out of the building?'

'Don't ask me that. Hercól wants you to be able to say you have no idea, in case anything goes wrong. It won't, though. His plan's a good one. It may take a few nights of doing this before we find a safe place to hide.'

'Don't go,' he said.

She sighed deeply, and nuzzled against his cheek, and he knew she'd misunderstood. 'No,' he said, 'Thasha, something's happened. I talked to my mother.'

'You were dreaming.'

'Yes, yes, of course I was dreaming. Oh, Gods, it's still coming back. Felthrup, the Ravens, Pitfire! Thasha, we don't have a few nights. We've got to get out of here *now*.'

Suddenly Neeps woke with a start. 'Thasha! Pazel! What's the matter?' he whispered.

'Everything, that's what,' said Pazel. 'Thasha, I need to talk to Hercól before you go anywhere.'

Thasha was in no position to refuse, trying as she was to keep from waking still more sleepers. The three youths groped as quietly as they could from the bedchamber to the dining area, where Hercól was crouched in silence. He was not happy to see the tarboys emerge. But he listened as Pazel whispered the fantastic story of his dream.

'It's so weird that it *has* to be true,' he said. 'Felthrup trailing Arunis to some sort of tavern, overhearing his plans, going back night after night, telling his story to a blary ghost, who tells my mother, who tells me? I couldn't dream that up.'

'It does have a certain mad air of truth,' said Hercól. 'Something, after all, drove Felthrup to spend so long in that closet. But if it is a true message, then all the more reason for us to go as planned, Thasha. We cannot leave the others here to rot in this asylum, but we cannot just set them loose in a city of unknown dangers. Come, girl, it is barely two hours before dawn. Pazel, Neeps, go back to your beds and do not watch what happens next.'

'Ha!' scoffed Neeps. 'You take us with you.'

'I will do nothing of the kind,' said Hercól, 'and if you think a moment, you will realise how right I am to refuse. If something should happen to me and Thasha, who else stands any chance of finding a way forward? Chadfallow? Possibly, but we all know his limits. No, the burden will fall on you two, and Marila.'

Suddenly Thasha started. 'I heard wings, wings flapping!' she said. 'Didn't you hear them?'

'No,' said the Tholjassan firmly.

'What exactly are you looking for?' said Pazel to Hercól. 'A way out of the city? And just for us, or for the whole crew?'

'If we don't go now,' said Hercól, 'it won't matter *what* I'm looking for.'

'You're lying,' said Neeps.

Pazel heard the ring of conviction in his voice, and something inside him clicked. Neeps wasn't always right when he thought he smelled a fib, but he was better at it than anyone else Pazel knew.

'The Stone,' he said, looking at Hercól. 'You're going to try to sneak aboard, and take the Nilstone yourselves, tonight. Break it out of the Shaggat's hand before someone else does. Hide it somewhere. Take it ... take it—'

'Beyond the reach of evil,' said Thasha, looking at her mentor. 'He's right, isn't he? That's what all this is about.'

Hercól stared hard at Pazel. 'Of all the *irksome, interfering* tar-boys,' he whispered at last. 'Yes, I mean to fulfil the oath I took upon the wolf-scar, and that means taking the Nilstone. But I had never meant to do so tonight. First I meant to scout the Lower City, and especially the quay: a failed attempt would only signal to Counsellor Vadu that the Stone is worth guarding to the hilt. Of course, he may already be doing so, but Fulbreech's slip of the tongue suggests that Arunis has lied about the Stone, convinced Vadu that it is no more than a trifle. In such tiny errors lies our hope. We must pray that there is more jealousy among our foes: between Arunis and the sorceress, Macadra; among those who call themselves Ravens; among the warlords who appear to rule this once-great land.'

'So what do you mean to do now?' asked Neeps.

'Throttle you to start with, Undrabust, if you can't lower your voice! Be silent, let me think!' Hercól shut his eyes, frowning with concentration. 'In light of this ... message,' he said at last, 'I *will* seek the Stone tonight. But you, Thasha, will not be going any-where near the ship. You are to do exactly as we discussed: locate the safest, surest exit from Masalym. If we must run with the Stone to fulfil our oath, so be it.'

'What sort of rubbishy plan is that?' hissed Pazel. 'You're going to send her off into this blary city *alone*? And try to storm the manger, unarmed, steal the Nilstone and make off with it by yourself?'

'I will not be unarmed for long,' said Hercól. 'Ildraquin lies just inside the magic wall, waiting for me. And neither of us will be going alone. Vadu's seizure of the *Chathrand* did not catch quite everyone unprepared. It did not, for example, catch me. Or those with my training.'

'What are you talking about?' asked Thasha.

Hercól looked up sharply. Pazel followed his gaze: twenty feet above them, on the roof of the main building, a figure crouched, one arm held out straight before him. A large, powerful bird was just lifting from his arm.

'Oh, Pazel!' said Thasha. 'That's him! That's Niriviel!'

So it was: Niriviel, the beautiful, woken moon falcon, who had disappeared on the eve of the *Chathrand*'s plunge into the Nelluroq. A miracle, Pazel thought: that the bird had survived, and that it had found them. For a moment he did not care that the bird was a fanatical Arquali, and had always called them traitors.

The falcon was gone in an instant. On the roof, the figure moved with catlike silence to the corner. Suddenly its arm snapped towards them, and Hercól, standing straight, caught the end of a rope.

'Time to kill,' whispered Sandor Ott from above.

23

Stealing the Nilstone

Ensyl leaned back against the scabbard of Ildraquin, winded. The dust was going to make her sneeze. With a bit of string she'd found under Thasha's bed she had just hoisted the weapon to the top of the cupboard in the stateroom. Not much of a hiding place, but it would be out of sight from the floor, and as long as the ship was on dry land there was no danger of it shifting. In any case, it was better than leaving it inside the straw mattress in Bolutu's cabin, where she had stashed it three nights ago, in desperate haste, just to keep Vadu from fishing it through the tiny hole he'd cut in Thasha's wall.

She had watched that deed from the inside, watched him slide his arm towards Hercól's blade. She had charged, ready to hack the fingers from that hand, but then the wall itself had attacked Vadu, burned him, and she had danced sidelong into the shadows again, still unseen. When Vadu retreated she had dragged the sword to Bolutu's chamber, then raced back by the ixchels' secret paths to a vantage point on the quarterdeck.

Like so many heads of cattle, the humans were being herded ashore. Far down the lightless avenue she could see them trudging in the chilly rain, soldiers on *sicuñas* pacing between them, dogs to either side watching for strays. Where were the tarboys, the young women, Hercól? She had not caught sight of any of her friends since well before the dlömic charge.

But then Fiffengurt had appeared across the quay, supporting

Lady Oggosk as he might his own mother. His true eye glanced back at his beloved *Chathrand*, searching for any sign of hope. Ensyl wanted to go to him, show herself, prove that the fight was not lost. *If only*, she thought, *I had a swallow-suit*. Pointless yearning. She would never again be trusted anywhere near such a treasure of the clan.

Now, dust-coated, she sat atop the cupboard, elbows on knees, looking down at the chamber of her allies. Vast, safe, deserted. Alone at last. She didn't dare laugh at the thought; laughter could too easily slide into tears.

What had she just accomplished, wrestling his sword up here? What would she do next, clean the windows? The thought pounced on her suddenly: they were defeated, utterly crushed, stripped of their vessel and their freedom and any chance to determine their own fates.

They? Who do you mean by they, *Ensyl?*

I don't mean they. I mean us.

Your clan despised you, abandoned you—

Not the clan, forget the clan, count me out of it, that broken thing, that lie.

You just mean her.

And what if she did? What if it had all been for Dri – for her beautiful, murdered mistress? Dri, who understood the life inside the ritual, who knew what *clan* could mean, ought to mean, the deeper *us*, the source in the heart, that chance of kinship no matter the bodies or the histories involved.

Dri, killed because she loved out of turn.

You hate Hercól Stanapeth, don't you? The noblest soul on this ship, maybe, and you hate him. You think of them together and you could stab him through the heart.

Ensyl tried desperately to still her mind. The guilty conscience exaggerates: that was something Dri herself used to say. *When guilt would claim you, be cold. Accept the whole truth, but no more than that, or you will wander among phantoms alone.*

But wasn't that exactly what she was doing? Her mistress had died. Her clan-brethren had fled, and not trusted her with the secret of where they had gone. Her human allies had been marched off down a dark road through the Lower City. All her pride in her choice of loyalties, and what was she left with for company? A bearskin rug. A black, stained sword.

Then a door creaked, and Ensyl was herself again. Flat against the cabinet-top, hidden, one hand reaching for her knife.

A slight scrabbling from below, and then a shrill, worried voice called out timidly, 'Thasha? Hercól? Where is everyone?'

Ensyl shouted with joy. 'Felthrup, why, Felthrup, you – rat!'

She was down to the floor in seconds, embracing the startled beast. He was glad to see her, too, but frightened and disorientated, and very thirsty. He knew nothing of the fight with Arunis or the seizure of the ship. He had been asleep, as they both soon realised, for three days.

'Three days! How did you manage that?'

'It was hard work,' he said, 'but worth it. Oh, I *pray* it was worth it. Somehow I feel as though I've accomplished a great deed, only I cannot remember anything about it. But where are the others, Ensyl? Why is the ship so still?'

Ensyl told him about the events he had slept through, and Felthrup ran in circles about her, in a paroxysm of remorse. 'Fulbreech! I hate him! I will give him the sort of bite he can't recover from! I knew it, I *always* knew – and yet when Lady Thasha needed me most I lay asleep in a closet, not twenty feet from that – that – *androsuccubus*, is that the word?'

'I'm sure it is,' said Ensyl. 'But you could not have helped her then. Let us go to work now, and perhaps we will find our revenge.'

Then they both heard it: a faint cry, from beyond the doorway. 'That's an ixchel voice!' said Ensyl, and flew to the door. Reaching the knob was an easy leap; turning it, a whole-body effort. But she managed, and Felthrup nosed open the door, and both of them tumbled through.

Counsellor Vadu had made his men paint around the hole he had cut in the magic wall. Now a splotch of white enamel hung in the air at the centre of the crossed passages, outlining the jagged rectangle. And beneath the hole, cradling her hand, stood Myett.

They raced towards her; she watched them come. 'The edges are sharp, like broken glass,' she said, displaying a long cut on her hand.

'You dare not try to pass through it,' said Ensyl. 'Counsellor Vadu was branded by it, like a mule. What are you doing here, Myett? Did you not go after Taliktrum, as the clan supposed?'

Myett just looked at her, wary and mistrustful, and Ensyl wished she hadn't spoken.

'Is there food in the stateroom?' asked Myett.

Ensyl told her to wait in Bolutu's chamber while she ran and gathered bread and biscuit crumbs and the last dlömic peach into a bundle. Then she ran back to where Felthrup waited, and the two of them stepped out through the wall and went to the veterinarian's cabin. Myett ate and ate; Ensyl had rarely seen one of her people so famished. 'The humans are gone,' she said between mouthfuls. 'They're being treated like kings, though – captive kings. Fattened up, in a great pavilion across the city. And given new clothes, and baths, and nurses to scrub them and kill their fleas.'

'You went there?'

'I rode there, in a wagon with the invalids who could not walk. And back upon a dog-drawn coach. I could see them eating through a window in the pavilion, but I couldn't get a bite. The dlömic giants don't waste food like humans; they don't drop it and throw it about. They're giving heaps of it to their prisoners, but all the same—' She looked up, puzzled, at Ensyl and the rat. 'I don't think they have that much.'

'We're trapped, then,' said Felthrup, eating alongside Myett. 'Unless they bring the crew back, and set us afloat upon the Gulf.'

'We're trapped,' Ensyl agreed. 'There are a hundred dlömu on the topdeck, at least five times that number surrounding the port. And by day there are the shipwrights, the dockworkers, inspectors going through every compartment and cabin. There will be no fighting our way out of the Jaws of Masalym, even if all the humans fought at our side. I doubt we could master the river-machines, the gates and shafts and spillways, without destroying the ship in our trial and error. No, there's no escape by sea. If we leave this city, we do so without the *Chathrand*.'

Myett did not look at her. Sullenly, she asked, 'What does Lord Talag say?'

Ensyl hesitated, and then Myett did look at her, with a certain gleam of understanding. 'You missed the rendezvous on the orlop,' she said. 'You were in the stateroom with your true friends. Of course.'

'I was fighting the sorcerer,' said Ensyl. 'Do you know where they went?'

She nodded. 'A safe place indeed. Even the dogs will not sniff them out. But Ensyl: I will not go there with you, nor tell you how to find it.'

Ensyl was taken aback. 'Sister,' she said, 'everything has changed now. Perhaps you did not see them? Arunis is allied with the rulers of the city. They do his bidding, or much of it. We cannot quarrel among ourselves. Your lover accused me of treason, and it is true that I disobeyed him. But that is all beside the point. Doom is coming for us like a great wave, Myett. We must help one another to higher ground or be washed away.'

'Everything *has* changed,' said Myett, nodding, 'and I have changed with it. Your treason is nothing to me, nor is your standing, or mine, or all the old stale points of honour. Let our fellow crawlies help one another to escape the wave, if they can find the will to do so. I want no part of that struggle. I am alone.'

For an ixchel, the last statement was close to heresy. Ensyl struggled to keep her voice even and low. 'Sanctuary awaits us, sister,' she said.

'We will never reach it,' said Myett, 'and *they* – they do not deserve it.'

Her look was adamant, and Ensyl's heart sank. Myett the worshipful had become Myett the indifferent. She had not run off, like

Taliktrum, but she had exiled herself all the same. The clan was crumbling; foolishness and self-deceit would be their epitaph.

'But, sister—'

'I am no one's sister any more.'

Ensyl could not summon the strength to argue. But Felthrup, who had been gaping at Myett, shook himself and stood up from his meal. 'Now see here,' he squeaked. 'You owe your life to Ixphir House.'

'Don't lecture me, rodent,' said Myett with a caustic laugh. 'I know my debts, all right.'

'Be quiet, you know very little,' said Felthrup, his mouth twitching so hard that crumbs flew from his whiskers. 'You have a grievance with Taliktrum. That is plain as a bruise on your face. Be quiet, be quiet! You have *no* grievance with Ensyl, who has only shown you kindness. And you have no right to destroy the clan that raised you. No right by your people's laws, nor by the moral constant that unites all woken souls.'

'You read too much,' said Myett.

'A clan, a crew, a colony of rats: they are neither blessed nor damned, neither chosen nor cast out. But they are your family. Some have mistreated you. What of it? The rest need your strength, and more wisdom than you've shown.'

What had happened to Felthrup in his sleep? Ensyl wondered. He was shaking and nervous as ever, but at the same time he was speaking in a rapture of certainty, not breaking eye contact with Myett.

'They need you,' he said, 'and that matters more than your damage and pain. You must *let* it matter more.'

'They despise me,' said Myett. 'They have taken decades of my life and given back only scorn.'

'And did they take nothing from me?' Felthrup displayed his mangled forepaw. 'They sealed me in a bilge-pipe to suffocate. But they rescued me, too – from *my* family, my diseased and mutant kin, the ones who bit three inches off my tail. I gnawed at that stump, Myett – gnawed it back to bleeding each time it started to heal. Oh, how I pitied myself! I dreamed of drowning, and I did not care who drowned with me.'

At the word *drowning*, Myett's face changed. 'That was you, scrabbling in the dark!' she cried. 'You little vermin. You followed me, you watched. You watched me and said nothing!'

'I watched you rush into the hold as the water rose,' said Felthrup, 'and wondered what you sought there. I never dreamed it was death.'

Ensyl turned her back, so as not to shame the young woman before her. *Aya Rin, Myett. Was it love of Taliktrum that drove you to this?*

'I will not tell you again,' said Myett, breathing hard, 'to leave me in peace.'

'That is what I mean to do,' said Felthrup. 'I will go to the manger, to have a look at the Nilstone. And you, friend Myett: you will do the right thing, and be strong. Take Ensyl to warn your people. The water spared you for a reason, as that pipe spared me. It is up to us to discover those reasons, I think – and if we cannot, then to find reasons, create them if necessary. Yes, I mean it. Sometimes we must fabricate reasons to live.'

Ensyl looked at Myett once more, and saw a broken agony in her face, a desperation. Myett lifted a hand towards her knife, and Ensyl froze. *Don't make me fight you, Myett. Don't make one of us die. We're both victims of our love for that family.*

Myett's hand hovered over the knife. Then it rose, slowly, as though she would touch Felthrup on the muzzle. She did not complete the gesture, but something in her own face changed, and she turned swiftly to the wall. She could not face them, maybe, but Ensyl thought she stood a little straighter than before.

'Damn you, Stanapeth! We're not ready to tackle the ship!'

Alyash was fuming. Neither Sandor Ott nor Hercól responded to his whispered outburst. They were moving as only trained assassins could, shadow to shadow, crouch to crouch. Alert to the tiniest noises, wearing dark clothes swapped with or stripped from other crewmembers, faces and hands and bare feet blackened from a pouch of soot. Boots would have been safer: glass and splinters and rusty nails littered the streets. But they had no proper, soft-soled footwear, and one accidental thump could make the difference between life and death.

'Do you hear me? Nabbing the Stone tonight is blary impossible! We'll be lucky to get aboard her at all.'

Ott did not like sudden changes to careful plans any more than Alyash. But Hercól's reasoning was sound. *Take the Nilstone tonight or lose it to enemies tomorrow. Lose it to enemies, and you will never defeat them.*

But Alyash had a point as well. The ship was under heavy guard, and they had not yet cased her fully. Blind terrain! How he hated it! Ott himself had already been attacked: a dozen creatures, like small monkeys but for their hairlessness and fangs, had exploded from the window of a gutted house. All on him, coordinated as a wolf pack, and Ott wondered if they had somehow decided that he was the weakest of the three. He had responded with a frenzy of killing, and sent the few survivors screeching into the night.

In fact, the ruined state of the Lower City was mostly to their advantage. Only near the cliff where the Middle City began did the streets come to life. Descending that cliff had been a moderate challenge. It had been more difficult to persuade Thasha Isiq to go with Dastu, seeking an exit to the mountains, a place they might flee to, a hideout.

They were halfway to the port.

Right now the greatest danger was the dogs. Killing them was too dangerous: they had only six arrows and one bow, of strange dlömic design, taken off a man Ott had personally authorised Dastu to kill. A foot soldier, sent back to the barracks for a cough, and quite unaware of the falcon gliding soundlessly overhead, guiding Dastu through the darkened city. The cough, at least, would bother him no more.

But they could not waste those precious arrows on dogs. And a wounded dog might howl. That wouldn't do. They had to mount to the rooftops whenever the creatures stirred. Luckily the houses were low and ramshackle, and often abandoned. Four or five empty streets for every one where citizens clung together, fearful and poor, nightwatchmen armed with no more than sticks to keep the feral dogs and other, stranger animals at bay. Given a month, Ott could have learned to mimic the sounds of these animals, and thus moved through Masalym with far greater ease. But they had only tonight. Had they been spotted already, though? Taken for dlömic criminals? Surely there were many such parasites, feasting on this carcass of a city.

Most of the houses were slate-roofed – easy to climb, hazardous to cross – but eventually Hercól beckoned, and sprinted to a flat-roofed building. It was the drainpipe he'd spotted: a solid iron thing. It bore his weight as he pulled himself up, hand over hand. Despite himself, Ott had to smile as he watched Hercól's fluid movements. Alyash had strength and utter fearlessness, and a mind like a steel trap. But Hercól had something more: blazing intuition, a welding together of thought and deed that was swifter even than Ott's own. Such a masterful tool. And yet Hercól was not his to wield, ever again, for Arqual or any other cause. *He's wielding you, if anything, old man. Your hunting days are numbered.*

When he crawled forwards to the roof's edge, Ott saw why Hercól had chosen it. Before them stretched a wide, dark road: the avenue up which the captives had been marched. Half a mile to the south the *Chathrand* towered over the quay. The lamps of the dlömic guard blazed on her topdeck.

'They've mounted the new foremast,' said Alyash. 'There's rigging on it too, by the hairy devil. They work fast.'

'The breach in the hull is surely repaired as well,' said Hercól. 'No boarding her from below, then. And if we climb the scaffold they will spot us for certain. We will have to enter by one of the starboard hawse-holes.'

'Like rats,' said Ott, and smiled.

'I just hope your knife's good and sharp,' muttered Alyash. 'The splash-guard on the inside of those holes is made of walrus hide.

You're going to have a dandy job cutting through it while dangling from the cable.'

'My knife is sharp,' said Hercól, 'and your plan is sound, of course, Master Ott. A direct approach would be suicide. But this way we have a chance.'

He calls me master! By the Night Gods, I taught him respect! He was not deceived, of course: there was hateful irony when Hercól spoke the word, even if he had never found another to replace it.

Sudden wings overhead. Ott rolled onto his back: Niriviel swept over them, cutting a turn that meant *No enemies moving.* 'All clear,' said Ott. 'Let's get on with it, gentlemen.'

They climbed down, rounded the building, broke across the road. At once a door slammed off to their right. Well, Pitfire, they'd been seen. But recognised? Not likely. You open a door, you see figures running in deadly earnest, you slam it. Nine men in ten will hold their breath and hope the danger passes. Of course, these were not exactly men.

Keep running, keep cold. In the lead, Hercól reached the far side of the avenue and dived into a side street, ducked left at the first alley, then right into the next. This one was straight and long and amazingly narrow, three- and four-storey row houses so close together that you could, at times, touch both walls at once. Mounds of refuse, scent of just-burned garbage, rodents squeaking and popping out of their way, fitful candlelight in scattered windows. They ran.

One block, two. No incidents. Then disaster – a dlömic woman's shriek, half a dozen answering voices, rage and fear and shouted names. A cacophony of dogs' howls, objects shattering near their heads. They flew into the fast sprint they had not yet asked of themselves, saw the vicious monkey-squirrels leaping across the alley through open windows ahead of them, then all around them, like crossfire, and then they were at the end of the alley, dashing over a ring road paved with old cobbles, and vaulting onto the eight-foot wall at the rim of the basin.

'The floor below is curved,' cried Hercól. 'Drop! Drop and run!'

Cries from behind them; stones whizzing past their ears. They dropped, struck ground, rolled onto their feet. They were in the mile-wide basin into which the *Chathrand* had been lifted when she entered Masalym. It was a great stone bowl, half-empty, with a disc of water at the centre. They made for that disc, racing down the side of the bowl, then crouching and sliding, clowns and not killing machines when they hit the slippery slime-layer near the water's edge. Once submerged they dived deep, so no ripple would betray them above. They rose together, breathed together, dived at the same time. *Like my lads crossing the border at the River Narth, to kill the Sizzies in their sleep,* thought the spymaster. *We're strong swimmers, and we know what we're about. But beside the dlömu we're slow as cows. If they catch us in the water we're dead men. Stay deep, my boys, stay with me.*

Stones and arrows fell around them. But they did swim deep, and none of the arrows found its mark, and Ott heard no sound of pursuit. With long, swift strokes they crossed the basin, until at last the curved floor met their feet once more. Out they crawled into the slime, three crocodiles, belly-sliding right to the foot of the stone gate across the *Chathrand*'s berth.

'Not here,' said Ott. 'Too many eyes. We should climb out at the third berth, the abandoned one. Good cover there: it's full of derelicts and weeds.'

Hercól nodded. The three men bent low and ran along the wall for some five hundred yards. No guard here, no lights. And the makeshift grappling hook bit on the third throw, bit and held tight: such splendid luck. Right up the wall Hercól climbed, forty feet, hand over fist. Alyash followed. When Ott's turn came he found the two men hauling him up.

Red fury engulfed him. He glowered as he hooked a leg over the rim.

'I need no man's help up a wall,' he said. 'Do you think I'd be out here tonight if I doubted for my readiness to— Eh?'

The others were staring, transfixed. Ott sprang to his feet and looked in the same direction.

They were at the edge of the abandoned berth, some five hundred yards from the *Chathrand*. At their feet, three boats sat in dry dock in various stages of decay. Upon the largest, which was draped like some ghastly burial chamber with the mouldered remains of her sails, dark figures were moving towards the bows.

Ott pulled the other men down into the weeds. The figures numbered ten. Eight of them wore black clothes, rather like the men watching ashore. They were dlömu, of course: the slight gleam of silver about the eyes proved that. All had light, thin swords, and three carried bows as well, with arrows already nocked.

The last two figures were bound at the wrists. One was a youth in a ragged shirt and trousers; the other wore a soldier's mail. Both had dark leather sacks pulled over their heads.

The archers took up positions on the boat's perimeter, studying the darkness. The others led the prisoners to one of the few remaining sections of rail and forced them to their knees.

'Bandits,' said Alyash, 'settling scores. Come on, they're the last ones we need to worry about.'

'Look again,' said Ott.

The archer at the stern of the vessel, having raised a hand to his neck, was holding oddly still. Hercól's mouth fell open in surprise. 'Dead,' he declared with certainty, and even as he spoke the man pitched forwards and toppled without a cry upon the stone below.

'What in the bottomless black Pits!' hissed Alyash.

The wheelhouse obstructed the others' view; they had not missed their companion yet.

'Did you see an arrow?' Ott demanded.

'No, Master,' said Hercól. 'But look at the prisoners now.'

The youth was being held with his forehead to the deck, but the sack on the other's head had been pulled off. Ott could make out none of his features, but somehow, even on his knees, there was pride in his bearing. He twisted about to look up at his captors. Suddenly he cried aloud:

'Don't you know the law? It is death to touch me.'

'That is no soldier!' hissed Hercól as one of the captors kicked the kneeling figure in the stomach. 'That is Prince Olik!'

'By damn, it is!' said Alyash. 'Well, well – he did say he wasn't popular. But it's not our problem, Stanapeth. You wanted to go for the Nilstone tonight. You can't play hero-to-the-fish-eyes as well.'

'Alyash! We are looking at regicide!'

'You are – I'm looking at dawn in the east. Think a moment, you soft-hearted fool. Dastu and your little girly will be waiting outside that blary nuthouse before long. Are you going to just leave 'em there? Oh, devil's arse!'

A second bowman was down. This one crumpled forwards onto his knees and remained that way, chin to chest. Still the executioners at the bow saw nothing – they were bending the struggling prince over the rail, holding him by his arms and his hair, and one was testing the sharpness of a knife – but this time Ott caught a glimpse of something tiny and airborne lifting away from the fallen bowman.

Alyash was ready to burst. 'Do you know what that was? It was a crawly in one of their wing-suits! That prince has crawlies working for him! But it's a bit late all the same.'

The dlömu was lowering his knife to Olik's throat.

'A good, quick death,' said Alyash. 'That prince will hardly feel a—'

Ott's bow sang. The dlömu with the knife staggered backwards, with a surprisingly low cry of pain considering that the arrow had passed through his leg above the knee.

Hercól was already sprinting for the boat. Ott rose and followed. 'You mucking bastards!' Alyash roared behind them, but he came on too. Ott was his commander, and he knew just how far insubordination could go.

The dlömu had seen them, were scattering, drawing their weapons. The deck was some ten feet forward and thirty feet below the rim of the berth. Hercól flung himself into space, and Ott followed, and wanted to scream with the joy of it, free fall, the longest since his leap through the palace window in Ormael, and slaughter at the end of it, beside the best man he'd ever trained.

He made it as far as the rigging – of course he did, a given – brought down bushels of the rotten canvas, turned as he fell, and had a yard of sound rope pulled taut between his hands to catch the first blow aimed at him. The dlömu was crushed under his knees; the sword was gone. Ott whipped the rope around his neck in a blur and *jerked* and that was one of them, still kicking but dead. Then almost wondering why he did it, Ott rolled and took the body with him, held tight by the twisted rope, and felt the prick of his next foe's blade pass through the man and half an inch, no more, into his own chest. He kicked. The dlömu tumbled. They were trained but not sufficiently; Hercól had slain two at least. Ott's next kick disarmed his opponent. He felt a webbed hand claw at his face, seized it, wrenched himself atop the dlömu. As his elbow crushed the other's heart, Ott found himself saddened at the thought of an Empire forced to rely on such mediocre assassins. *Give me a year with them. They'd never be the same.*

His sadness did not last long, however. Their final opponent was fleeing. Ott assumed he'd try to break over the plank onto solid ground, and the dlömu at first seemed intent on doing just that. But something overcame him as he ran, and oddly, he veered away from the plank around the starboard side of the wheelhouse, like a runner circling a very small track. And when he emerged to portside the spymaster thought for an instant that he'd been replaced by someone else. The dlömu was singing – a weird, wordless noise – and what had been a clumsy fighter was suddenly—

Great Gods!

They clashed. The man was his equal: Ott was forced backwards, his moves defensive; the keening dlömu was suddenly imbued with a speed and grace that would be the envy of any fighter alive. He wasn't thinking; he was possessed. When Alyash came at him with his cutlass, the dlömu spun away from Ott, his thin sword whistling, falling short of the bosun's jugular by a quarter-inch. Hercól was in the fight as well, now, but *the three of them*, for Rin's sake, were barely holding the man at bay. Ott danced backwards and nocked an arrow. The man sensed it somehow, pressed after him; Ott had to twist the bow around to save his own neck from that damnable, flimsy-looking sword. Another spin; Hercól leaped backwards, sucking in his chest. Ott twisted, and felt the sword's tip graze his jaw.

Rage, and the certainty of time running out, awoke something long dormant in Ott. He leaped straight up, mouthing a bitten-off curse from campaigns long ago. His foot lashed out; the singing ceased. The dlömu fell with a broken neck upon the boards.

'Great flames, what a fighter!' said Alyash, gasping for breath.

'What happened to that man?' said Hercól. 'He was the weakest of them all. He was hanging back, terrified, only darting with his sword.'

'Don't you know?' said a voice behind them. 'It was the *nuhzat*, gentlemen. You could see it in his eyes. Here now, won't you help that boy, before he falls?'

The hooded youth was bent over, trying to pull the sack over his head by pinching it between his knees. Hercól steadied him, then wrenched the sack away. It was the village boy, Ibjen. He was nearly hysterical with fear, and jumped away from the bodies on the deck. 'The *nuhzat*!' he cried.

'You needn't speak the word as if it means *plague*,' said Olik. Then, turning to the others, he said, 'You saved our lives. May the Watchers shower you with favour.'

'The *nuhzat*!' cried the boy again.

'Silence, you fool!' hissed Alyash. But of course it was too late: the dead man's singing had been as loud as a scream. Ott looked up at the *Chathrand* and saw the row of lanterns, the mob of dlömic soldiers, gazing at them over the empty berth. They were repeating the same strange word, *nuhzat*, *nuhzat*, murmuring it in fear and doubt.

'But Ibjen, it is perfectly natural,' the prince was saying as Hercól cut their wrist-bonds. 'Dlömu have had the *nuhzat* since the dawn of our race.'

'Natural, my prince? Natural as death, perhaps. We must get away from these bodies, wash ourselves, wash and pray.'

The soldiers on the *Chathrand* were growing louder, more frantic.

'You realise,' said Alyash, 'that we're not taking another step towards the Great Ship? We'll be lucky to get out of here with our skins.'

Hercól turned to Olik. 'What is this *nuhzat* you speak of?' he demanded.

'Why, a state of mind,' said the prince (at this Ibjen broke into a sobbing sort of laughter). 'It is a place we go inside ourselves, in times of the most intense feeling. Or used to: it has almost disappeared today. A pity, for it offers much. It is the door to poetry and genius, and many other things. Very rarely it manifests as fighting prowess. But there's an old saying: *In the* nuhzat *you may meet with anything save that which you expect*. Usually only dlömu can experience the state, but in the old days a small number of humans were able to learn it as well.'

'*Learn* it? Learn it!' Ibjen threw up his hands.

'If they counted dlömu among their loved ones,' added the prince. 'And strangely enough, those humans were the last to become *tol-chenni*.'

Another voice began to sing. This time it was a soldier on the *Chathrand*'s quarterdeck. His song was slower, deeper, but still eerie, like a voice that comes echoing from somewhere very far away. Not unpleasant, thought Ott, and yet it produced only terror on the Great Ship. Most of the dlömu ran, leaping from the quarterdeck, dropping lanterns, shoving and jostling. The singer's nearest comrade shook him by the arms, then slapped him. The man paused briefly, then raised his arms to the sky and resumed the song. His comrade darted into the wheelhouse and returned with a rigging axe. He clubbed his friend down with the flat of the axe-head. Only then did the singing cease.

'Now do you understand, at last?' cried Ibjen. 'Now do you see why madness is not something we joke about?'

Dlömic officers were screaming: 'Hold your ground! Stay at your posts!' A few soldiers obeyed, but the bulk simply fled, over the gangways, down the scaffolding, away from the fallen man and the scene on the derelict. All around the port, lamps were appearing, swinging wildly as their bearers ran here and there. Cries of panic echoed through the streets.

'Gentlemen,' said Olik, 'the Nilstone is gone.'

'What?' shouted Hercól. 'How do you know this? Tell me quickly, Sire, I beg you!'

'I was aboard the *Chathrand* not thirty minutes ago,' said the prince. 'Vadu caught me, demanded to know what I had done with the Stone, made oblique references to my death. He drew the tiny shard of the Plazic Blade he carries and showed it to me. "This," he said, "is eguar bone. I could use it to dry the blood in your veins, or to stop your heart – without touching you, without breaking the law." Then he told me that the Issár had just received a message from Bali Adro City, by courier osprey. Absolutely no one was to meddle with "the little sphere of darkness" in the statue's hand, until further notice. On pain of death. Vadu said he had rushed to the ship to redouble the guard, but had found his men slain in the doorway to the manger, and the door unlocked, and the statue empty-handed, with two broken fingers lying in the hay.

'Then Vadu raised his blade, and I felt a sudden cold grip my heart. I had a last, desperate card to play, and I did so. "The Imperial family is defended by more than laws, Counsellor," I said. "Ours is a destiny as old and certain as the stars. No one who draws my blood shall escape the wrath of the Unseen." I could see that he was not wholly convinced. "The Nilstone has vanished," he said, "and you alone are here at the moment of its vanishing. You would do better to confess what you know than to threaten me with superstitions." I assured him that the Stone was a deadly weapon – deadlier by far than his Plazic Blade – and that only Arunis could have stolen it. Vadu replied that he had the Great Ship surrounded, and that no one had been in or out of the ship save his guards – and me.'

The shouting now was like the mayhem of a town besieged by pirates. Children and parents all screaming, dogs howling, maddened; everyone running away. The exodus from the *Chathrand* was almost complete: only a score of guards remained on the topdeck.

'What *were* you doing aboard?' demanded Ott.

'Looking for gold,' said the prince, 'to bribe the Issár on your behalf. I do not know what he intends to do with you, gentlemen, but despite the repairs to your vessel I doubt strongly that he means to let you go on your way. Ibjen and I have spoken often of your plight since we jumped ship. You made a deep impression on the boy, Mr Stanapeth – you, and Fiffengurt, and your three younger allies. Ibjen has the idea that there are riches aboard, and Mr Bolutu, whom I visited this morning (he remains locked up with your shipmates, incidentally), confirmed it, though he has no idea where they might be hidden. It occurred to me that they might be in the stateroom, for where else could they be safer than behind the wall? But I found nothing: only your rat-friend, Felthrup. He is in a curious state of mind himself.'

'You took a grave risk for us,' said Hercól, but his voice was still uncertain.

'And nearly died for it,' said Ibjen. 'Counsellor Vadu is a traitor! He has raised his hand against the royal family!'

'Strange, isn't it?' said Ott. 'A man in his position will have thought hard about that law, and especially the words *on pain of death*. All the same, he decided it was time to kill you. Though he feared to wield the knife himself.'

'And so hired assassins,' said Olik, nodding, 'and presumably meant to have them killed in turn. But it was still an astonishing move. I wonder what else was in that message? Does the Emperor himself wish me killed? And if death is to be my fate, what can they mean to do with you?'

'*I* know what Bali Adro means to do with us,' said Hercól. 'I have learned it this very night.'

'You have?' snapped Sandor Ott. 'From whom? When were you going to tell us, damn your eyes?'

'As soon as we found a moment's safety,' said Hercól. 'But I will not tell *you*, prince. I am glad we saved you, but I cannot give you my trust: not after your words in the doorway of the stateroom.'

'Hercól Stanapeth,' said the prince, 'that is exactly why I spoke them. I dared not leave you thinking well of me. Arunis was spying on your thoughts – crudely, but persistently. If trust and warmth had been uppermost in your minds, he would have known at once that I was his enemy, and turned Vadu against me that much sooner. But he has fled now. He has betrayed Vadu and the Issár, and stolen the Nilstone, and disappeared. And now I may stand before you and speak the simple truth. I am one of your number, swordsman: a foe of Arunis and the Raven Society, and a friend of Ramachni. I would be your friend also.'

'Well that's blary scrumptious,' said Alyash, 'but what are we to do about the Nilstone?'

Hercól turned to Olik. 'You say that Vadu told you he'd searched the ship?'

'Deck by deck,' said the prince. 'There was no sign of Arunis. Vadu was convinced the mage had taken refuge behind the magic wall. I tried to explain the impossibility of that, but I am not sure he believed me.'

Hercól looked from the prince to Ott, and back again. 'I may yet regret this choice,' he said, 'but I think you are exactly what you claim. Prince Olik Bali Adro, here is what I know: Arunis has made magical contact with a sorceress almost as powerful as himself. Someone close to your Emperor by the name of Macadra.'

'Macadra!' The prince started forwards in terror. 'The White Raven! Are you sure?'

'Let me finish,' said Hercól. 'She has dispatched a ship for Masalym; it is to arrive any day. And when it does, the crew of that ship is to take possession of the *Chathrand* and sail with it, and the Nilstone, back to where she waits in your capital.'

'Flames of the Pit!' shouted Ott, enraged. 'How long have you known this, Stanapeth?'

'Not two hours,' said Hercól. 'But there is yet a little more. Rivalry may well exist between Arunis and Macadra, but they both intend to see the Nilstone used to dominate or destroy the lands we come from. Not Arqual alone, Master Ott. I mean *all* lands north of the Ruling Sea. And Arunis, perhaps, does not mean for it to end even there.'

'By the eyes of heaven,' said the prince, 'you *do* come at the time of the world's ending! You have brought both the devil and his tool into our midst, and now our own devils are joining the game.'

He checked himself with a sigh. 'No, that is not fair. Arunis is our devil as much as anyone's, and the Nilstone has plagued both sides of the Ruling Sea, and the *Chathrand* was built in Bali Adro herself. How small the world becomes, when we contemplate its doom.'

'I don't understand,' said Ibjen. 'Why would Arunis steal the Nilstone if he is a friend to those who are coming from Bali Adro City?'

'A fine question,' said Olik. 'Arunis and Macadra founded the Raven Society together, and have long worked side by side. But if it is true that jealousy has arisen between them – well, that at least could be called good fortune.'

'It would have been better fortune,' said Alyash, gazing up at the *Chathrand*, 'if that nutter on the quarterdeck had started to crow a little sooner. Have a look at the Grey Lady now, will you?' He gestured at the *Chathrand*. 'Nine guards, maybe ten. We could blary *walk* aboard unchallenged.'

Hercól grew suddenly still. 'Or ... walk off,' he said.

He glanced sharply at Ott, and the spymaster felt his heart quicken again. 'The pump room,' he said. 'The hidden chamber. If Arunis slipped back in there, right after snatching the stone—'

'Alyash,' said Hercól, 'stay with the prince.'

'I'll be Pit-pickled if I will, you mucking—'

'Do it,' said Ott, and then they were racing, flying for the plank that led ashore, leaving behind the two dlömu and the swearing bosun. The weird alien port flashed by as in a dream, and the dlömu on the deck saw them coming and cried out, and fired arrows that splintered on the stones beside their feet, and the joy of it, the joy of the horror, came back to Ott as his old, old body strained to keep up with his protégé, and just managed, though the price was fire in his chest and a throat so raw it felt torn by fangs.

But when they gained the topdeck, ready to fight any dlömu that braved their onslaught, a death-scream rose above the general mayhem. It came from the far side of the *Chathrand*'s berth. Ott saw a terrible suspicion bloom in Hercól's eyes. They raced the hundred yards from port to starboard and looked down.

Arunis was there on the quayside, mounted, a freshly murdered soldier by the horse's hooves. Their sprint to the *Chathrand* had distracted the only guards brave enough to remain aboard. They had made it possible for Arunis to escape.

Hercól spun around in search of a bow to fire, but the sorcerer was already galloping away, galloping into the dark sprawl of the Lower City, a small round bundle held tight to his chest.

24

Masters and Slaves

'Gone out?' said Ignus Chadfallow. 'What under Heaven's Tree do you mean?'

'Be quiet,' said Pazel, 'you'll wake the others.'

It was still very dark, though a pale husk of morning light wrapped the sky to the east. 'Gone out,' repeated the doctor. 'For a stroll, is it? Did the birdwatchers lend them a key?'

'They went over the wall. Ott escaped the pavilion some time ago, or maybe he hid and was never captured at all.'

'And Hercól and Thasha went off with that monster? Just like that?'

'They didn't *want* to, Ignus,' said Pazel. 'But Pitfire, how else are we going to get out of here? And they made Ott leave the rope behind.' He gestured at the corner of the wall, then waved desperately at the doctor. 'Quiet! The blary birdwatchers are going to learn all about it if you can't keep your voice down.'

Chadfallow said no more, but he could not stop himself from pacing, and his footsteps rang out clearly on the stones around the ruined fountain. Marila was awake now, too; standing silent and fearful, hugging herself against the chill.

Neeps looked at Pazel and whispered, 'The sun's coming up. Twenty minutes, thirty at the most, and there won't be any darkness left to hide in.'

'You think we should go over the wall?' Pazel gazed at it, desperate. 'Just climb out and run, all of us?'

'I think that's better than waiting for them to notice that two of us disappeared in the night. But I'm worried about the dog.'

The guard animal lay curled on its platform, looking rather cold. Pazel could not tell if it was awake or asleep.

There came a soft noise from above. *Thank the Gods*, thought Pazel. It was Thasha, sliding down the rope. And after her, a far less welcome sight, came Dastu. They rushed across the courtyard, and Thasha squeezed Pazel's hand.

'No sign of Hercól?' she asked.

'Haven't you seen him?'

'They missed the rendezvous,' said Dastu. 'Blast! Some turmoil has erupted near the shipyard – and it's spreading faster than fire. Even here in the Middle City the streets are waking. Something is very wrong. And I'd swear Arunis is behind it.'

'Ott's other little helper turned out to be working for Arunis,' said Pazel coldly. 'How do we know you're not?'

'Judge for yourself, *Muketch*,' said Dastu with equal venom. 'As for me, I'd gladly leave you here. But alas, Sandor Ott *is* my master, and he commands otherwise.'

'For now,' said Thasha, 'all we need to think about is getting out of here. We didn't find a way out of Masalym, but we learned one thing: if we don't want to be captured again immediately, we have to make for the Lower City. It's dangerous, but at least there are hiding places. Here in the Middle City there are dlömu everywhere.' She stiffened. '*Aya Rin*, he's seen us.'

The dog was sitting up and watching them. Its eyes fixed on Dastu, as though quite aware that he didn't belong. But it did not make a sound.

Suddenly Pazel noticed how well he could see the dog's face. Night was over, and daylight was growing by the minute. 'Right,' he said, 'if we're going, we have to go *now*. But let's not wake Uskins and Rain until some of us are up on that wall. They're too unpredictable. They might make any sort of commotion.'

'There's plenty of flat roof to stand on,' said Thasha. 'We can get everyone up, then choose our moment to slip down to the street and make a run for it.'

'Whatever you do, make it fast,' said Dastu. He walked to the dangling rope, planted his feet against the wall and pulled himself swiftly to the rooftop. The others glanced apprehensively at the dog, but the animal sat silent on its platform, alert but motionless. 'Something strange about that animal,' muttered Chadfallow.

Thasha climbed next. Crouching beside Dastu on the roof, she beckoned Marila. 'Come on, you're light, you can help us pull from up here.'

Marila seized the rope, and Thasha and Dastu hauled her upwards. Again Thasha tossed down the rope. Pazel caught it, passed it to Neeps. 'Same reasoning, mate,' he said. 'For Rin's sake, don't argue with me.'

'I won't,' said Neeps, 'but you'd better start waking the others now.'

As Neeps climbed and Chadfallow steadied the rope, Pazel went to rouse the three remaining men. Uskins had bedded down in his patch of weeds; he gave a bewildered snort when Pazel shook him, and his eyes seemed reluctant to open. Druffle was instantly alert, and rose to his feet as though he had been waiting all night for a signal. *That's a smuggler for you*, Pazel thought. Dr Rain muttered to himself, frail and disorientated.

'I'll hurry the doctor along,' said Druffle. 'Get old Chadfallow up that wall if you can manage it.'

But 'old Chadfallow', as Pazel knew, was strapping for his age, and climbed with ease. The trouble came from Uskins, who looked frightened by the whole procedure. As Pazel steadied the rope for Chadfallow, the first mate stared at him, lips a-tremble. '*Muketch*,' he said at last, 'I have no desire to return to the ship.'

Pazel turned his head, astonished. 'Mr Uskins,' he said, 'we don't know where we're going yet. The important thing is to get out of here, while we can.'

Softly, the dog began to whine.

'Not important to me,' said Uskins. 'I'll follow orders, thank you very much.'

'Orders? Who ordered you to sit in a blary asylum?'

'Sir,' corrected Uskins.

'Sir,' repeated Pazel, increasingly confused. 'Listen, you don't want to stay here. They could lock you up for ever, or experiment on you, bury you alive – anything. Don't you realise who's in charge in this city? Arunis and his gang, that's who.'

At the mention of the sorcerer, Uskins recoiled, as though Pazel had struck him in the face. 'You scoundrel!' he exploded. 'You've had it in for me from the start! I told Rose to put you off the ship back in Etherhorde, that day you tormented the augrongs. And now you've provoked the sorcerer!'

'Mr Uskins—'

'You're insolent and clever, and you won't stop until we're dead. This is what Arqual's coming to – you, you're the face of the future. I can't bear it. To think that you've served on *Chathrand* herself. In my grandfather's day you'd not have been allowed to speak to a gentleman sailor, let alone serve under him.'

The dog whined louder, and even began to paw at the glass. 'A gentleman sailor,' said Pazel, seething now. 'Mr Uskins— Pitfire, that's not even your real name. You're Stukey Somebody, or Somebody Stukey, from a guano-scraping village west of Etherhorde, and the only reason I'm trying to save your damned pig-ignorant hide is because I think you're ill, actually ill, and I feel a bit— Oh *credek*, never mind, just *get up the blary wall*, for the love of Rin. *Now*, sir.'

Uskins froze, clearly shocked by the tarboy's vehemence. Pazel thrust the rope into his hand. Slowly a look of understanding crept into Uskins' eyes, and with it came a new, sharper fear. He put his feet against the wall and began to climb.

The dog gave an anxious yip. Pazel look at it: the creature was dancing on its pedestal, turning in circles. On an impulse, Pazel dashed across the courtyard to stand before it. 'Hush!' he whispered. The dog glanced down the corridor and cocked its head. Then it looked Pazel in the eye, whining pitifully. Its breath clouded the glass.

'Shhhh,' said Pazel, 'good dog, *good* dog.'

Suddenly the dog pressed its nose to the fogged-over glass between them. It moved sideways, dragging its nose, struggling for balance. 'Mr Druffle,' said Pazel aloud, 'I think this dog is awake. I mean woken. Because, Gods below, it's ... *writing*.'

The dog was writing. With its nose. One scrawled and desperate word.

RUN.

Pazel jumped. And then he heard it, soft but certain: the rumble of angry voices. Many voices, shouting, and growing nearer by the second.

He backed away. The dog wiped out the word with its forehead. Mystified, Pazel raised his hand, a gesture of thanks.

'Deserters! Faithless deserters!'

Pazel whirled about again. It was Dr Rain, in the doorway of the bedchamber. He was staring at the figures on the rooftop, his shouting like crockery hurled at a wall. 'Leave your shipmates, leave an old man behind in this human zoo! Villains! Backstabbers! Cold, mean, monstrous—'

Pazel had to hand it to Mr Druffle: the freebooter did exactly what was called for. He silenced the doctor with one humane, swift *thump* to the stomach, then lifted him and ran to where Pazel stood clutching the rope.

'Under the arms, lad! Tie him quickly!'

Shouts echoed from somewhere down the corridor – many voices, loud and even menacing. *They're in the north wing! Get that door open! Which of you has the key?*

The dog raced back and forth. 'Haul him up!' begged Pazel, and the others complied. Rain kicked and struggled; the poor man simply had no idea what was being done to him.

The next two minutes were agonising, as Thasha tore at the knot around Rain's chest, and the doctor batted her in confusion. At last she gave up, seized Dastu's knife and slashed off the rope above the knot. She hurled the shortened rope down to Pazel and Druffle. There were a few awful moments of paralysis, as each begged the other to climb first, and the voices grew louder, nearer. At last Druffle relented, and scurried up the wall like a monkey.

'Tell them to lie down!' said Pazel, 'flat and quiet, and away from the edge. Hurry, Mr Druffle, please!' He looked back anxiously at the glass wall and the doorway. The dog had vanished; from some distance away he heard it barking. He heard Druffle grunt as he rolled over the edge. Thasha tossed him the end of the rope. Even as he caught hold of it a door smashed open. Pazel climbed, wishing he had Thasha's strength, as the others hauled him upwards. 'Faster!' hissed Thasha through her teeth. Pazel gasped, pulling, swaying as feet pounded down the corridor. He hooked a leg over the roof, and Chadfallow seized his shirt and wrenched him up with one great effort. Pazel caught a glimpse of torchlight through the glass. He rolled away from the edge, and those still standing threw themselves down. No one moved.

Angry voices, men's and women's both, sounded from just outside the glass wall. 'They're in the bedchambers! Open the door, open the door!' Keys jangled, hinges gave a rusty shriek, and a mob forced its way in, shouting, raging. 'Don't let them bite you,' a male dlömu cried. 'And don't get their blood on you, either. Turn your faces away before you cut them down.'

Pazel felt the hair rise on the back of his neck. It was the voice of the man who had led the mob the day before. The one who had promised to come back and kill them.

The cries changed abruptly: 'Not here, Kudan! The place is empty! This brainless dog's guarding an empty cage!'

'But I heard something.'

'They *were* here, it's been lived in. Maybe they were moved to the south wing.'

'Spoons, cups, plates. Earth's blood, they were treated just like men. And so much food!'

'Some of it's mine,' said Rain aloud. Neeps pounced on him, covering his mouth. Fortunately the old doctor was still catching his breath, and his voice did not reach the dlömu.

'We'll have to burn all the food,' one of them was saying, 'and the mattresses too. Just the same as their bodies. Fire for the cursed, as they say.'

'Best do it well outside the city. Somewhere too far away for the curse to come back. The Black Tongue, maybe.'

'The Black Tongue! Surely we don't need to go *that* far, Kudan.'

'We still have to catch the humans,' said their leader. 'Come, it's time to talk with those physicians again.' Some nervous laughter, then: 'Get along there, dog! No treat for the likes of you.'

The voices faded. For several minutes no one moved. Pazel found himself shaking from head to foot. 'Don't move, anybody,' he whispered. 'They're still looking for us, remember.'

For nearly ten minutes they lay silent; even Dr Rain seemed to have comprehended the situation at last. Pazel gazed past his own feet: above them rose more mountains, more city, more waterfalls. He had the strange sensation of looking at the same picture through a smaller window: Masalym was *still* looming above them, as it had from the deck of the *Chathrand*, but now he was inside the Middle City, peering between its domes and towers and solitary trees, at what was surely the Upper City, the highest level, where the mountains came close to one another, and the river squeezed through to fall over one more cliff, in one more white mass of foam.

Cautiously, they sat up. 'What now?' whispered Thasha.

No one appeared to have an answer. Pazel turned his gaze left and right. The Conservatory was a larger complex than he'd realised: eight or nine whitewashed buildings, connected by arches and covered breezeways. There were three other spacious courtyards like the one they had just escaped, and a grand approach with white marble stairs and flowers blazing red and yellow. The whole place might have been mistaken for the mansion of some eccentric lord, except for the walled-in enclosures on the eastern side, where the *tol-chenni* huddled in frightened packs.

'We know what we have to do,' said Neeps. He pointed north

to the cliff. 'Sneak over there, climb that fence, tie off the rope and slip down into the Lower City. Right?'

'Impossible,' said Dastu. He gestured at a squat stone building half a mile away, constructed right up against the cliff. 'That's a barracks. It's full of men keeping watch on the Lower City. See, there's another beyond it. They're all along the cliff.'

'The Middle City's on guard against the Lower?' said Neeps.

'Don't you understand?' said Dastu. 'The Middle City is for richer sorts. The ones down there are nearly starving. These people don't want them swarming up here, making life difficult, begging for work or food. Anyway, we don't stand a chance of slipping down the cliff by daylight. Besides, the rope is too short. Even dangling from the end of it we'd have a forty-foot drop.'

'How did you and Thasha get down?' asked Pazel.

'We ran a mile nearer the mountain, where the cliff's not so high,' Thasha answered. 'But Dastu's right, we'd never get away with it by daylight.'

Mr Druffle, who had moved nearer to the street, crawled back to them on his belly, scowling. 'It's even worse than you think,' he said. 'Those ruffians are all over the streets, looking for us. And there's more of them than before. A few hundred, I'd say.'

'Well, that decides it,' said Pazel. 'We're not going anywhere soon. Maybe they'll give up by nightfall.'

'Nightfall,' scoffed Uskins. 'We will never make it to nightfall! All those towers. Someone is going to notice us, and then we'll die. You were a fool to bring us up here, *Muketch*.'

'Call *him* a fool,' said Marila. 'We'd be dead already if we'd stayed down there, like you wanted to. And the only tower near us is that giant thing straight ahead, and it looks abandoned to me.'

The first mate sniffed. 'Twenty minutes, at the very outside. That's how long I give us. Assuming that quack can keep from howling again.'

They lay down, as far from the edges of the roof as they could, as the Middle City went about its bustling, grumbling, early morning routine. Now and then they heard dlömic men in the street, asking about them, sometimes with open suspicion. Once a nearby voice erupted in rage: 'Harmless? *Harmless?* Sister, they're devils! Haven't you heard what went on at the port? They've brought the *nuhzat* back among us! They're reviving old curses, inventing new ones. We went to them humbly, we asked how we could make amends. They wouldn't answer.'

'Maybe they *couldn't*,' replied a dlömic woman, 'because they didn't know what you were asking.'

'They knew!' shouted the man. 'It's not justice they want, sister, it's revenge! This day was foreseen!'

After the two dlömu moved on, the angry voices sounded less frequently, and with more discouragement. But when the humans peeked down from the roof they saw that the streets were still crowded. There was no means of escape.

Twenty minutes passed, then twenty more. Pazel, Thasha, Neeps and Marila lay on their backs, a bit apart from the others, with their heads close together and their legs sticking out like the spokes of a wheel. Pazel realised, almost with shock, that he was comfortable. The sun was bright, the roof warm against his back. He looked at Thasha and thought he had never seen a more beautiful face, but what he said was, 'You could use a good scrub.'

Thasha gave him a pained sort of grin. She needed to laugh, he thought, but how could she, after those terrible hints and guesses about where she came from? Hercól might believe what Admiral Isiq had claimed: that his wife Clorisuela had finally succeeded in bearing a child, after four miscarriages. But Thasha didn't. And Pazel could find little reason why she should.

It was not that he believed a word Arunis had spoken. But Neeps' ideas were another matter. Thasha had done some extraordinary things, in the Red Storm, and in the battle with the rats. She controlled the invisible wall. She'd been watched over her whole life by Ramachni. And who else could Thasha have meant when she said, *I'll never let her come back*?

But old Isiq, making secret love to a mage? That was unthinkable. Pazel had witnessed the admiral's shock at everything that had happened to Thasha. No, Isiq was no insider, with a hand in these intrigues. He was just another tool.

Pazel smiled back at her, to hide the blackness of his thoughts. Even a tool could father a girl on his concubine, and then feel shame, and invent a lie about his wife's miraculous pregnancy. *She really might be the child of Syrarys. Aya Rin, don't let that be true.*

Thasha returned her gaze to the sky. 'What do you three want to do when this is over?' she whispered. 'I mean, when it's *all* over, and we're back in the North, safe and sound?'

She wasn't fooling herself; Pazel could tell she knew just how unlikely it was that they'd ever face such a choice. No one answered at first. Then Marila said, 'I want to go to school. And then, when I know something, I want to start one. A school for deaf people. Half the sponge divers in Tholjassa lose their hearing sooner or later.'

Neeps turned over and planted an awkward kiss on her cheek.

'You can't come,' Marila told him.

'What do you want to do, Neeps?' Pazel asked quickly, before they could start to argue.

Neeps shook his head. 'Get away from the blary ocean, that's what. I know we islanders are supposed to love it, and sometimes I do. But *credek*, enough is enough. I've been at sea since I was nine. I'm tired of imagining all the ways I could drown.'

After a brief pause, he added, 'I've never been atop a mountain in my life. Not one. And I've never touched snow. I want to pick up a handful, and learn what that feels like. Maybe it's foolish, but I dream about these things.'

Thasha touched Pazel's leg. 'Your turn.'

Pazel hesitated. Why was it such an unsettling question? Thasha was not even looking at him, and yet he felt as though she had backed him into a corner. He tried to picture the two of them, married, settled in the Orch'dury or her mansion in Etherhorde. Thirty years from now. Fifty. He recalled the vision he'd had at Bramian, he and Thasha joining some forest tribe, retreating from the world into the heart of that giant island. What was he thinking?

What did fantasies, or love for that matter, have to do with saving this world from a beast like Arunis? He touched the shell that Klyst had placed beneath his skin at the collarbone. It used to burn him when Klyst was jealous; now it was just an ordinary shell. The thought left him briefly desolate.

'Well?' said Neeps.

Pazel groped for a truthful answer. He thought, *I don't want to want anything. I couldn't stand it, if Ormael was dead, or dying, or two hundred years older. To go there, dreaming of something that will never come back . . .*

'I can't seem to decide,' he said, pathetically.

Suddenly there was a great commotion from the others. Pazel thought for a moment that they'd been eavesdropping, and were leaping up to vent their disgust at his indecision. But then he saw something that made him forget all that: Ibjen and Prince Olik, walking across the roof towards them, both smiling. And emerging last from the trapdoor that none of them had seen beneath the leaf-litter, Hercól. He was also smiling broadly.

'Eight lizards, basking in the sun,' he said. 'Come down before you burn.'

'So that is how things stand,' said the prince, stalking almost at a run down the corridor. 'He has the Stone, and we must get it back before that ship arrives – and more importantly, before he manages to do something hideous, irreparable.'

The humans were bunched around him, keeping pace. 'How do we know he hasn't mastered the Stone already, Sire?' asked Neeps.

'By the fact that we yet breathe, Mr Undrabust,' said the prince.

He reached the end of the corridor. Without stopping, he leaned into a pair of big double-doors, spreading them wide, and charged into the main entrance hall of the Conservatory. His personal servants and guards were waiting there, along with most of the birdwatchers, who seemed caught between relief and disappointment at the sight of the departing humans. One tried to hand a sheet of parchment to Mr Druffle.

'A simple questionnaire, it will take just a minute—'

'It'll take less than that,' snarled Druffle, crushing the sheet in his fist.

They passed through the outer doors and found themselves in dazzling sunshine. They were on the portico, facing the marble stairs and wide gardens that fronted the Conservatory. Thasha gave a cry of joy: Jorl and Suzyt were waiting there, untethered. They leaped on her, ecstatic and squealing. 'They are clever dogs,' said the prince. 'You have trained them almost to dlömic standards, and that is high praise.'

'How did you get them to obey you?' said Thasha, hugging both mastiffs at once.

'They did nothing of the kind,' laughed the prince. 'But they listened to Felthrup, right enough. And he convinced them I was a friend. Hurry, now, let's be gone from here.'

'Yes!' shouted Dr Rain, shuffling quickly down the stairs. 'Out, out, out!'

'The doctor disapproves of our facility,' said Olik, 'but in fact you were lucky to have been locked up here. There are not many flat-roofed buildings in the Middle City, although there are plenty of flat heads. One or the other kept your would-be executioners from seeking you in the most obvious of hiding places.'

'How did you get rid of them?' asked Uskins, who was having a lucid moment.

'I left that to Vadu,' said the prince. 'He was rather startled to find me alive, and rather terrified to imagine how many people might already have learned what he put me through last night. Suffice it to say that our relations are off to a fresh start.'

Beyond the gardens that fronted the Conservatory waited three fine, gilded coaches. Their teams were not made up of horses but dogs: twelve massive, square-shouldered dogs apiece, waiting silently but with eager eyes. There were no drivers that Pazel could see. But a crowd of onlookers had appeared, held at a distance by well-armed Masalym soldiers.

'Prince Olik! Prince Olik!' cried the onlookers. 'What happened at the shipyard? Was it really the *nuhzat*?'

'It was,' said the prince. 'I saw the man's darkened eyes. But you must trust your grandfathers when they tell you that the *nuhzat* is not madness. At its worst it is a trance, at its best transcendence. If it comes back to us as a people we must call ourselves blessed.'*

'Your cousin the Emperor – will *he* think us blessed?' shouted an old woman.

The prince smiled ruefully. 'No, he will not.'

The mob grumbled as Olik ushered the humans into the coaches. 'I can give you honesty, my people, as I always have – or I can give you words to make you smile. Sometimes one cannot do both. Step lively, Dr Chadfallow, in you go. Jorl and Suzyt can run alongside the pack.'

'They have names,' said someone.

'Of course they do,' said Pazel. 'Don't you name *your* dogs?'

His reply caused an uneasy stir – and Pazel realised suddenly that the speaker had not been referring to the dogs. A tall dlömic man pointed at them between the soldiers. 'What are they *really*, prince?' he cried. 'Demons sent to punish us? *Tol-chenni* cured by magecraft?'

'Don't you know?' said Olik, swinging into the coach. 'They're our albino brothers, of course. From the Magnificent Court of the Lilac.' He closed the door with a bang.

Each coach had seating for six. Pazel was squeezed in between Thasha and the prince, facing Ibjen, Hercól and Chadfallow.

---

* Olik's assertion has mythological undertones. Dlömic legend identifies the *nuhzat* (literally, 'night path') as one of the Four Gifts chosen for the race when they descended from the stars (perhaps in proto-dlömic form?). The gifts, from certain obscure supernatural beings, were meant to help the newcomers become native to the world of Alifros, and hence survive there. Two other gifts were the 'friendship of water' and the seed of the *loloda* tree. The fourth gift was capriciously withheld, by a spiteful being who did not welcome the arrival of the race. Its identity remains a mystery, and many dramas and moral parables refer to this possibly fatal hollow in the dlömic character. – EDITOR.

'Home!' shouted one of the prince's aides. The dogs yipped and whined; the carriage jerked once, then started to roll. Thasha called to Jorl and Suzyt, who fell in beside them, barking. The open space around the Conservatory gave way to narrow streets. Brightly painted homes, shops, taverns closed them in.

'You're surprised by the dog teams,' said Olik. 'They have always been preferred in the Middle City. The distances are not great here, and the beasts are versatile. A full pack like this one can be broken up into smaller teams, for smaller coaches, or even sent on errands alone, following routes they learn by heart. The city would be lost without its dogs, I assure you.'

'Are we going back to the *Chathrand*, Sire?' Thasha asked him.

'I certainly hope that *some* of you are,' said the prince. 'But ride with me to the Upper City first. At the moment there is no safer place.'

They rattled across a bridge over the foaming Maî, then up a winding hill. Dlömic faces turned their way, staring. Flower vendors, holding out bouquets and calling prices, dropped their arms and gaped at the sight of human faces.

Life was clearly better in the Middle City. The roads were less potholed, the gardens less choked with weeds. No abandoned homes met Pazel's eye, though here and there a broken window gazed forlorn upon the street, or a crumbling wall looked more patched than repaired. But such blemishes were slight after the wreckage of the Lower City.

'It truly is another world,' said Chadfallow, stooping to peer through the window. 'I see almost no malnutrition – but would I recognise it in a dlömu's face, I wonder?'

The prince gazed wistfully at Chadfallow. 'A hungry child looks quite the same, whether human or dlömu,' he said. 'As for the Middle City: yes, it is another world. This is the core that Masalym has shrunk to – but I fear it will shrink further still. There is food here, just enough. And there is safety from outside attack, so long as the river flows, and the guards keep up appearances on the wall. But there is no contentment anywhere in Masalym, no peace. Most dwellers in the Middle City have but one ambition: to gain a foothold in the Upper, to join its small, rich ranks. Events like a sudden outbreak of *nuhzat* only make them want it more desperately. And the ambition of those who *already* dwell in the Upper City is to forget the lower levels.'

'Forget them, Sire?' said Hercól.

'They would forget the Middle City except as a place the cook is sent for cabbages, or the butler for a wet nurse,' said Olik. 'The Lower City they would forget altogether. It is not considered quite proper even to mention it, especially in front of children, or during a meal.'

'I don't understand,' said Thasha. 'They can't *not* think about it. It's sitting on their laps.'

'Their laps are hidden under a table of plenty,' said Olik.

Ibjen looked away, embarrassed.

Dr Chadfallow frowned. 'How can such an arrangement possibly continue?' he asked.

'How indeed,' said the prince. He drew the curtains over the carriage window. 'Felthrup has done a great deed, in warning us about that ship,' he said. 'If we live through the next few days we have him to thank.' He smiled at Pazel. 'Along with all the others in that nocturnal chain.'

'Your Highness,' said Pazel, 'how is it that everyone is obeying you now? It can't be just Vadu's fear of the law that protects your family.'

'Quite right,' said Olik. 'The Family Law should keep Vadu to heel – I have a witness to his attempt on my life, after all – but there is a deeper reason, too. It is very simple: when the Ravens arrive in Masalym, they will have either the Nilstone or the heads of everyone who was guarding it. For Vadu there is no choice: he must catch Arunis, or spend the rest of his days in flight from Macadra.

'There is also the danger of panic. The city is afraid of you, and of the *nuhzat*, and behind both of these lurks madness, our people's ultimate fear. I confronted the Issár this morning, and he needed all my help to overcome his own terror enough to look facts in the face. When at last he did, he named me Defender of the Walls, which is to say that I am now Vadu's superior officer. I promptly removed him and his senior officers from the shipyard. I also demanded a look at those orders from the capital. They came last night, by courier osprey, and they confirm Felthrup's warning: the *Kirisang* is en route to Masalym.'

'The *Kirisang*,' said Thasha, eyes lighting with recognition. 'I read about her. She's a Segral-class ship like the *Chathrand*. She's one of the Great Ships that crossed the Nelluroq and never returned.'

'She is twice the age of the *Chathrand*,' said Olik, 'but make no mistake: she is both sound and formidable. And she has been part of the *Platazcra*, Bali Adro's great orgy of conquest, and will be outfitted for war in a most terrible fashion. But there is worse: *Macadra herself is aboard that ship*. Macadra, who has not left Bali Adro City in thirty years, except on astral journeys – Macadra who detests the sea. There can be but one reason for the journey: she intends to claim the Nilstone for herself. That would also explain why Arunis moved when he did. Better to abandon the *Chathrand* and the Shaggat Ness than to lose the Nilstone for ever.

'Only one part of the message did I welcome: the fact that the bird was released, apparently, from Fanduerel Edge, which would mean that the *Kirisang* is still six days from here.'

'Thank the Watchers above,' said Ibjen.

But Olik raised a warning hand. 'The sorceress may well have lied – especially if she hopes to catch Arunis off his guard. Moreover, the enchanted current may still be flowing, and speed them faster than any wind. And what if both are true? To be sure of escape, I fear you must leave by dusk tomorrow.'

'Tomorrow!' cried the others.

'But that is amazing!' said Chadfallow. 'How did you convince the Issár to agree to our departure at all? Why would he compound his loss of the Nilstone with the loss of the Great Ship?'

'Because he is cornered,' said Olik. 'To displease Macadra even in a small matter is quite enough to seal his fate. I have offered him one hope of survival, and he is jumping at the chance. As for the ship, her repairs are essentially complete. The larger problem is supplies. Vadu's men had not begun to lay in food or water, cordage or cloth. Except for the casks from Narybir, her hold is largely empty. Nor will we have time to load her properly, or to assemble enough preserved food for months at sea. It will be hard enough to get your crew marched back from the Tournament Grounds to the ship, and set them to work on the rigging. You will have to balance the cargo while underway, I fear.'

'But we can't just sail off and leave the Nilstone with Arunis!' said Thasha.

'I very much hope that you will not have to,' said Olik. 'We have already begun a house-to-house search of the Lower City. It is a daunting task: Masalym's army is small, and the panic caused by the *nuhzat* has led to desertions. Nonetheless, if Arunis remains in the Lower City, we will find him.'

'We'll help you, Sire,' said Pazel.

'Don't be a fool,' said Chadfallow. 'You heard what Hercól said about the terror at the port. Our faces would only add to the chaos, and make it that much easier for Arunis to know we were coming.'

'The doctor is quite correct,' said Olik. 'But once we have Arunis cornered it will be another matter. I would welcome your help if it comes to a fight.'

'It will come to a fight,' said Hercól, 'now or later. But Sire: both search and fight could be more easily won if I had Ildraquin. You must question Vadu again. I told you how I raced ahead of his men before we were imprisoned, and placed the sword just inside the magic wall. But this morning it is gone, and as you know, there is a jagged hole in the wall.'

'Vadu makes no secret of having carved that hole with his own blade,' said Olik. 'He is proud of the deed.'

'As well he should be, if he has plucked Ildraquin through the wounded wall,' said Hercól. 'I saw no sign of it about the stateroom, or in any of the cabins. Felthrup never saw the sword at all, and

447

though he spoke with Ensyl and another ixchel woman, I saw neither them nor any of their people. Whatever the truth, I must regain Ildraquin, for it was entrusted to me by Maisa, rightful Empress of Arqual.'

'And yet it was forged here, in Dafvni-Under-the-Earth,' said the prince. 'Yet another sign that the sundering of our two worlds is nearing its end.'

'Why would Ildraquin make the search any easier?' asked Thasha.

'The sword will make it *effortless*,' said Hercól, 'so long as Arunis keeps Fulbreech at his side. I never managed to wound the mage, but I did cut Fulbreech on his chin. And here is something I have never told you, Thasha: Ildraquin leads me, like a compass needle, towards any foe whose blood it has drawn.'

'Ah,' said the prince, 'then it is a *seeking* sword as well. I did not know any were left, after the burning of the Ibon forge. We must find it, clearly.'

'And pray that Arunis has kept Fulbreech at his side,' said Chadfallow. 'What a shame that you did not at least nick the sorcerer's little finger, Hercól.'

Pazel thought of the fight on the lower gun deck, how he had set Arunis free by attacking him, and felt himself burning with shame. *All of this because of me. People may die because of me.*

Suddenly he realised that they were nearing a waterfall: its deep thunder had in fact been growing for some time. Olik spread the curtains and whistled once. The carriage rumbled to a halt.

They climbed out, and Pazel saw that they had reached the base of yet another cliff. It was narrower than the others, and only some eighty feet high. The Maî poured down in a torrent just beside them. A gust of wind bathed them in cool, delicious spray.

The cascade fell into a lake edged with chiselled stone and surrounded by gnarled fir trees; to their left the Maî flowed out of the lake to continue its winding descent to the sea. Pazel's heart skipped a beat when he saw a dlömic boy no taller than his knee fling himself into the churning water. Then he thought: *The boy can swim, of course he can*, and saw that the lake was full of boys, and girls too, and that none of them feared the river in the least.

But when they saw the humans the children began to scream.

'No time for a swim, Mr Pathkendle,' said Olik. 'This way, if you please.'

The street entered a tunnel in the cliff wall, heavily guarded and sealed with an iron gate. But the prince was marching towards the pool, and now Pazel saw that a narrow walkway ran between it and the cliff, very close to the waterfall itself. One of the guards ran ahead of Olik and unlocked a small door set into the cliff.

The guard opened the door and held it wide. 'Plenty of lift today, Sire.'

Olik nodded and led them (mastiffs and humans alike) into the passage. It was short, and not as dark as Pazel expected, for there were light shafts cut into the stone. At the end of the passage were two round steel platforms, each about the size of a small patio. These platforms were attached to the passage wall at two points by thick beams that vanished into slots, and before each was a large metal wheel mounted on the stone. The prince stepped quickly onto one of these, and beckoned his companions to do the same. When they had all crowded onto the platform, Olik nodded to the waiting guard. The man spun the wheel, and a clattering and jangling of chains began somewhere above. Pazel looked up: a straight shaft rose through the stone, cut to the exact shape of the platform.

'Mind the dogs' feet, Thasha,' said the prince, and then the platform began to rise.

'Water, again,' said Hercól.

'Of course,' said the prince. 'Ratchets, pulleys, a wheel behind the falls. Most citizens use the tunnel; these lifts are for royalty and other invalids.'

The ascent was rapid; before Pazel knew it, daylight struck him full in the face. The platform was rising straight out of the ground. When their feet cleared the top of the shaft it stopped with a clang.

'Welcome to the Upper City,' said the prince.

Under the bright sun Pazel felt himself shiver with awe. They were in a gazebo-like structure at the centre of a grand plaza, built around a curve in the Maî. Slender trees with feathery crowns swayed in the wind. Beds of white and purple flowers surrounded them, bees and hummingbirds competing for their nectar.

Beyond the gardens, the Upper City spread before them like a box of jewels. Pazel had never seen Maj Hill, the famous Etherhorde district where Thasha grew up, but he wondered if even its fabulous wealth could compare. Every building here was tall, with slender windows that glittered like sugar frosting and spires that reached for the sky. There were four- and even five-storey mansions, with great marble columns and imposing gates. There were soaring crystal temples, and bridges over the surging Maî, and other bridges that leaped from one building to the next. Right at their feet began a splendid boulevard, paved with ceramic tiles of a deep russet-red. Straight through the Upper City it ran, like a carpet – and ended, some three miles from where they stood, at a breathtaking building. It was a pyramid, but flat at the summit, as though the apex had been cut away with a knife. Except for the long rows of windows at various levels, the whole building appeared to be made of brass. The side that faced the sun was nearly blinding.

'Masalym Palace,' said Prince Olik, 'where I hoped you would be received with dignity by the Issár. Very little, alas, has gone as I hoped. But that may change today.'

Another set of carriages awaited them at the edge of the gardens. A crowd stood about them: wealthy dlömu with servants and children in tow, watching the lift with frank curiosity. But already a strange reaction was spreading among the watchers. At first sight of the humans' pale skin (and Thasha's golden hair) they were turning away, and soon all of them were rushing from the plaza. Pazel saw one or two begin to glance back and check themselves, as if to preserve the appearance of having seen nothing at all.

'They are even more fearful than those below,' said Chadfallow.

'They are better educated, after a fashion,' said the prince. 'They know what it means to be associated with anything to which the

Ravens might object. And they know full well that my power in Masalym is a fleeting thing, no matter how I work to help them while it lasts.'

'The pyramid is raised!' said Hercól suddenly. Pazel looked again. It was true: the huge building rested on low, thick columns of stone.

'Family tradition,' said Olik. '"Your kings are not bound to earth like other men," we tell our subjects. "The winds pass under us; we are creatures of the sky." Even our country homes are raised a little off the ground. It makes for cold floors.'

They boarded the carriages, and soon they were moving down the red road at a fast clip, the dogs pulling eagerly, the mansions flashing by.

'Sire,' said Thasha, 'suppose you track down Arunis – what then? Do you think that you can defeat him?'

'You know full well what a terrible opponent he is,' said the prince, 'and yet we do stand a chance. He may be more vulnerable now than ever, for until he masters the Stone it will be more weight than weapon. And though he has great powers of his own, he is still reliant on that human body of his – that mortal shell. He will not be able to defy the warriors of Masalym, and all the enemies he has made on the *Chathrand* – and his newest enemy, Vadu, bearer of a Plazic Blade.'

'Fashioned from the bone of an eguar,' said Hercól, looking at Pazel and Thasha. 'You were right.'

'So you guessed, did you?' said Olik. 'Ah, but then you, Pazel, have confronted an eguar in the flesh. I doubt, however, that you can have imagined anything so terrible as what actually befell us. We reached for power, and attained it; but that power has been a curse. Should we recover from it – and that is not certain at all – it will be as a chastened country, wounded and poor, and certainly no longer an Empire.'

'Did the eguar themselves curse you, Sire?' asked Chadfallow.

'In a sense,' said Olik. 'As you know, they live for thousands of years, and when death finally approaches they make a last pilgrimage, to one of the deep and terrible Grave-Pits of their ancestors. In such pits they end their lives, so that their flesh may decay atop the bones of past generations. They shed their skins in these places as well, once every five or six centuries. If anything these are acts of kindness on the monsters' part, for the remains of an eguar, steeped in poison and black magic, are as dangerous as the living beast.

'There were many Grave-Pits in the youth of Alifros, but today we know of just one: deep in the hills of central Chaldryl, forty days from the coast. Despite its remoteness there were some who made the journey and explored the Pit, for the place fairly reeked of ancient magic, and the lure of power was great.'

He looked out at the bright mansions, the stately trees. 'I was your age, Pazel and Thasha, when my father remarked over breakfast that certain alchemists in a far corner of the Empire had devised a method for carving eguar bones into tools. I said, "How interesting, Father," and wished that he would hurry and carve the cake. I was an eager youth: in those days no shadow lay upon my heart.

'But the rumour proved true. Already the alchemists had placed seven eguar blades at the feet of the Emperor. He kept one, and gave the rest to his generals. At first they seemed mere curiosities, but later something woke in the blades, and they began to whisper: *Let me in, let me into your soul and I will perfect it.* That at least is how the Emperor recounted the sensation to my father, on his deathbed.

'The blades gave our generals power in battle such as had not been seen since the time of the Fell Princes. But that taste of power awoke an insatiable hunger in the blade-keepers. The Emperor demanded further weapons, darker tools. Of course, he was not all-powerful, then. The Great Assembly of the Dlömu opposed him, as did the Council of Bali Adro Mages. Even his own family sensed the danger, and urged him to stop. But he did not stop. Instead he found secret partners, criminal partners, with the riches and the will to work in the shadows. I mean the Ravens, of course.'

Pazel sat back with a sigh. 'The Ravens. Is *that* how they came to power?'

Olik nodded. 'They were all but defeated, after sending Arunis away to seek the Nilstone. But they rose to the Emperor's task. More blades were delivered, more power seized, and soon our lust for power swept all cautions aside. The Grave-Pit was quarried out. The bones and teeth of the eguar were carried by the ton to the War Forges, where the foulest blades of all were smithed. Plazic Blades, we called them: conquering blades. They made us invincible, for a time. Our armies spread over neighbouring lands in a flood. *Platazcra*, Infinite Conquest, became both our motto and our aim.

'Is it any wonder that we failed to notice how we ourselves were being conquered? The Ravens, and above all Macadra, had become indispensable to the Crown. Little by little they came out into the light. Murder by stealthy murder, they removed those who stood in their way.'

'But that is not the worst of it,' said Ibjen. 'Sire, you must tell them about human beings.'

'Yes,' said Hercól, 'I should like to know what part we played in this tale.'

'A great one, as it happens,' said Olik. 'The human mind-plague was only beginning, in tiny outbreaks we chose to ignore. But no humans, Nemmocians, atrungs or selk were ever trusted with Plazic Blades. Only dlömu. And because dlömic hands alone grasped the power, it was easy, and tempting, to push the races further apart. We were the mighty, the feared. They were leaner and shabbier, and their famished eyes made it hard to enjoy our plunder.

'Because humans were the most numerous, they made us the most uneasy. We began to live apart, more and more, and to restrict humans to the labour we disdained: the hard labour, that is. We compelled them to build our ships, forge our armour, march behind us as vassals in our war-trains. It was not long before this servitude decayed into outright slavery.'

'So we were slaves before we were animals,' said Chadfallow. 'Is that what our would-be killers meant by the Old Sins?'

'They go by that name, yes,' said the prince. 'Slavery, and later the denial of the plague. For all this time the *tol-chenni* affliction was spreading: a blighted village here, a swirl of panic there. And we dlömu, drunk on conquest as we were, could not make ourselves pay attention.

'But human beings did, of course. The first uprisings were on the borders of the slave-lands, and they were brutally repressed – townships razed, prisoners driven over cliffs at spear-point. And still we were afraid. We imagined that all humans wished us death, even those who swore their loyalty. This terror was magnified by new losses on the battlefield. The Plazic Blades had begun to disintegrate, to rot away. Their owners became irrationally suspicious, accusing one another of tricks, curses, theft. They slew one another over the blades, one man coveting another's, especially if it seemed less corrupted. A few even fell to our enemies: the commander of the Karyskans who attacked your ship had a Plazic Knife. I expect he used it to strengthen his men.'

'How many were there, the keepers of these blades?' asked Pazel.

'A few hundred in all the Empire,' said Olik. 'Some were minor figures, like Counsellor Vadu. Others really did walk the earth like Gods – mad Gods, blinded and diseased. They could not rest. They bled the Imperial coffers dry. The War Forges blazed day and night; some were consumed by their own flames or exploded, and whole regions of Bali Adro were laid waste.

'Then, very suddenly it seemed, we woke to find our slaves stolen from us. It took but three decades for the plague to destroy every human mind in Bali Adro. And without them our Empire was crippled. The Blades gave us the power to destroy, not to build or nurture. Without human labour, we were titans of straw. We could not even feed ourselves.

'We lashed out. Karysk and Nemmoc remained to be conquered, as did some mountain regions, like the interior of this great peninsula. Enemies surrounded us, we thought, and if they were not killed, we would be. In growing delirium, our generals drove their armies to superhuman feats: marching them six hundred miles in as many days – only to see them collapse on the eve of battle, victims of a starvation the magic had disguised. Such blindness! All our worst wounds have been self-inflicted. The armada may destroy the realm of Karysk, but it will do nothing to save Bali Adro from itself.'

'You sound as though you've lost all hope,' said Thasha.

'Do I?' said Olik. 'Then I must beg your pardon. I have not lost hope. Perhaps that is because I did not have to witness all these horrors unfolding. Ten years after that breakfast with my father I sailed into the Nelluroq on my doomed expedition, and the time-shift robbed me of eight decades. When I left Bali Adro I was still a thoughtless young man. The *Platazcra* was well underway, but our fortunes had not yet turned. I had a son of nine years and had wearied of raising him – and of his mother, truth be told. I thought a year or two away might help me tolerate them better. And though troubled by the Empire's wars, I still accepted the verdict of my elders, who gave the name of Glory to all that murder, greed and gobbling.

'When I returned, our nation's back was broken. Human beings were almost extinct; the other races were scattered; woken animals were no more to be seen. Laughter was cruel, poets mad or silent, temples were converted to armouries and barracks, schools to prisons, and the old world, my world, was a thing forgotten. *That* was despair, Lady Thasha, and I barely survived it. Yet from that blackest pit strange gifts have come to me. Like Mr Bolutu, I am a window on a vanished world, a spokesman of sorts for Alifros-that-was. When I accepted that bitter truth, I found my life's purpose. I became a Spider Teller, and in time a chasmamancer, and there has been more joy in the fellowship of those impoverished wizards than ever I knew in palace or keep. I fell in love with learning, and out of love with the family cult. I met Ramachni, and his wisdom strengthened me in my resolve. "You are a fine mage, Olik," he said at our last meeting, "but you are also a warrior. You will fight less often with your hands than with your mind and heart, but you will fight *ceaselessly*, I think. A wiser path for all Alifros – that shall be what you fight for. That, and the extinction of madness and greed." Thus he spoke, and thus it has proved to this day.'

Thasha's whole face had brightened at the mention of Ramachni. Suddenly she gripped the prince's hand, startling him. 'I'd hoped from the beginning that you were allies,' she said. 'I've been praying you'd help us find him, or help him return to us. Now I'm certain you're going to do just that.'

Olik gazed at Thasha: a humble glance, such as Pazel would scarcely have thought possible on the face of royalty. *Just like Bolutu*, he thought. *They hang on her every word. They know, blast it. They know the truth about her.* And he resolved to corner Bolutu at the next opportunity, to wring it out of him. Arunis was gone; no one was spying on his thoughts. What possible excuse for secrets was there now?

Suddenly all the dogs barked in unison: the signal, said Olik, that they were nearing the palace. Rows of soldiers flashed by. Olik signalled them with a wave, then looked at Thasha again.

'Yes, I still hope, lady,' said Olik, 'but that hope has been sorely tested. One reason is personal. Do you recall what I told you of the Karyskans, and why they pursued me?'

'You said they mistook you for someone else in the royal family,' said Thasha, 'for the one who wanted to attack them.'

'Yes,' said Olik, 'and I cannot blame them for the mistake. I sailed openly into their waters, and at first they welcomed me. But Karysk has certain spies in Bali Adro, and as I was making ready to depart these spies returned, and declared that they had seen my face in Orbilesc, pressing rabidly for the launch of the armada. Today the Issár's message has confirmed my worst suspicion: that rabid warmonger is my grandson. We are alike as two peas in a pod.'

The others stared a moment. Then Pazel gasped. 'The Red Storm,' he said. 'You sailed away and left a son, and he—'

'Bore a son as well, in time. When I returned I found my own son a frail old man, and *his* child grown to manhood. We have the same features, the same name – and thanks to the Red Storm, very nearly the same age. But Olik the Ninth hates this Olik the Seventh. He is a Plazic warlord; like Vadu he carries the stump of a Blade. I am sure he thinks of me as some sort of *maukslarín*, a demon made in his image, sent from Elsewhere to oppose him. There are days when I fancy he's correct.

'The other blow to my hope is more serious – but only because the hope itself burned so brightly. For at long last, the horror of the Plazic Blades is ending. They are corroding, melting into nothingness. It seems the very act of removing the bones from the Grave-Pits began the process of decay, and in our greed we removed them all. In another year or two the Blades will have entirely decayed, and perhaps my people will be free of the *Platazcra* madness for ever.'

'And now you bring the Nilstone!' said Ibjen.

'Yes,' said Olik, 'the Nilstone. A thing more powerful and ruinous than all the Plazic Blades together. And who should come with it – and steal it before one week is out – but Arunis himself, old ally of the fiends who fashioned the Blades, and perhaps the vilest mind in Alifros? I do not despair, Lady Thasha, but I fear greatly for this world.'

'We'll get it back,' said Thasha.

At that moment the sunlight disappeared. All about them were massive columns of red stone: they had driven right under the palace. There were shouts and echoes, the roars of *sicuñas*, the rumble of gates. The carriages ground to a halt.

Before they could alight someone threw the door wide. It was a servant, but he had not opened it for them. A dlömic man of middle years, round-stomached, with a nervous pucker to his lips, was scurrying in their direction. A plain grey cloak was tied around his ample form; it appeared to have been hastily thrown over finer clothing. Servants bearing chests and sacks followed in his wake.

'Step down, get out!' he said. 'Won't you hurry, Sire? Do you know how long I have waited for a coach?'

The riders in both carriages descended. 'Your pardon, Tayathu,' said Olik. 'We had some difficulty locating the city's . . . guests.'

'That's enough about *that*!' snapped the man, bounding into the coach. When he was seated he leaned out again, facing Olik. To Pazel's amazement he cupped his hands around his eyes, as though protecting himself from the sight of the humans. 'My lord and prince,' he said, with some slight derision, 'you have given me your word, you know. You absolutely *must* be gone before they . . . you understand the importance, surely?'

For the first time since Pazel laid eyes on the prince, he looked angry. 'When Olik gives his word he keeps it, Tayathu, son of Tay.'

The man recoiled, waving his hand in agitation. 'All so terrible, so ghastly! I wish you had never come to Masalym, and I hope we never, ever meet again! Of course we will not! You're going to be jailed, or hunted, penniless, shoeless— Oh, get in, you creeping sloths, do you want to be left behind?'

The servants hoisted the last of their burdens onto the carriages' roofs and crawled inside. The man in the grey robe slammed the door with a little shudder of nervousness. Olik whistled; the dogs rose and bore the carriages away.

'Who was that blary bounder?' said Druffle, walking forwards.

'That,' said Olik, 'was His Excellency the Issár.'

25

The Choice

~~~

The Honourable Captain Theimat Rose
Northbeck Abbey
Mereldin Isle, South Quezans

Dear Sir,

*I will not be astonished, Father, if this proves our last communiqué.
You have always made plain your intention to disown any son who
failed the test of obedience, no matter at what stage of life. I hardly
think that death will have altered your opinion; nothing alters your
opinion. But there are those on this ship (those you pressed me to slay,
for their own disobedience) who hold that the possibility of change is
not for us to deny. We must believe it can happen in the heart of the
basest wretch, they would say, no matter to what epic depravity he
has pledged his life.*

*You will observe that I do not choose to continue our long charade
with Lady Oggosk. I know full well that you are dead. This very
evening I went to the witch and demanded the truth, and she had no
choice but to provide it. 'Dead' may technically be inaccurate for one
who dwells in the twilight of Agaroth. But you are in sight of the
Last Domain, and it is long since fitting that you be released from
the Border Kingdom and allowed to go your way. You, and the one
who dwells there at your side, the one I have called Mother hitherto.*

*All I ask before I release you is the truth. You won the three sisters
at cards: I know this. You kept them as servants and concubines, and*

you did not care how many brats you sired on them. Such trifling issues were easily resolved, no doubt, once the Flikkermen developed a market for infants, and the Slave School on Nurth realised what returns were possible on an investment of eight or nine years. How many of my brothers and sisters (half-brothers, half-sisters) did you scatter to the winds? Are any of them known to you by name?

Those are the first questions I should like addressed. But there is another, more vital by far: which sister gave birth to me? Is it the one who followed you to the Border Kingdom? Or the one who simply vanished from our household, one evening of my fourteenth year? Or the third sister, Oggosk herself? All my life I have taken your side against her: never would I recognise her as family, and only in these letters have I named her Aunt. But is she my mother's sister, or my mother? You could always strike a bargain, sir, so let us bargain away this inefficiency: tell me the truth about myself, and I will hold you and your companion in Agaroth no longer.

As ever, I shall bargain in good faith. You have always demanded a full accounting of my captaincy, and this I am willing to provide. I am back aboard the Chathrand now, and my crew is for the most part reassembled – only some twenty fools broke out of the Masalym Tournament Grounds, and are hiding yet in the vast warren of the Lower City. They may end up dwelling permanently among these black-skinned, coin-eyed creatures, for we are preparing for an emergency launch, and nothing whatsoever may delay it. Not even prudence: I have given my most reluctant consent to a launch at dusk tomorrow, before the wares we are taking aboard can be secured or balanced, knowing full well (you need not remind me, sir) the great peril involved. Any sizeable swell may roll us, sink us, but such odds are better than the certainty of seizure if we remain here an hour too long. In any case, we shall have thirty miles in the Gulf to prepare for the open sea.

Except for those few deserters, the men all but stampeded back to the Chathrand when the gate was opened at the Tournament Grounds. Days of rest and feasting had given way to fear about the dlömus' intentions. Now they are relieved (and amazed) to have *been restored to their ship, even though we sail once more into danger. They have not yet grasped the nature of the Red Storm that lies between us and home, and though rumours circulate, they are considered too outlandish to be true. I have forbidden the officers, and Pathkendle's gang, to speak of the Red Storm to anyone. The men feel lost enough as it is, without the terror of becoming lost in time.*

For the moment their good spirits hold, and they are labouring with a will. So, for that matter, are the dlömu, whose orders now are clearly to see us gone with all possible haste. But they will no longer step aboard the ship, or even pass supplies directly into our hands. What is not loaded by cargo-crane they carry to the centre of the gangway. We must wait for them to withdraw onto the quay before retrieving it ourselves. All of this because one of them went mad and began to sing upon the quarterdeck.

When we set sail at nightfall tomorrow, there are yet a few others who will not be among us. You may think it good fortune, and for most of this voyage I have wished for nothing more ardently. Now I think their absence may prove disastrous. Or perhaps I misstate the case: perhaps it is my own absence from their number that haunts me now as a looming, possibly fatal, mistake. I know of course what you will say, Father, but do restrain yourself. I will welcome no advice at this juncture; the shades of Chathrand's *old skippers inflict quite enough as it is.*

Thasha raised her eyes from the scribbled vellum. Crowded around her, Pazel, Neeps and Marila continued to read. Oggosk was leaning on her stick by the palace window in the bright evening sun, watching them. She had appeared suddenly in the palace, and been escorted to their waiting chambers by a pair of dlömic chamber maids. 'What do you want us to do with this?' Thasha asked.

The old woman walked stiffly to them and snatched the page back. 'I want you to bear it in mind,' she said. 'Nilus faces a terrible decision – probably the greatest in his life. And how you speak to him next may make all the difference.'

461

'What's this about "a few others not among us"? asked Pazel. 'Who's he talking about?'

'You're about to find out,' said Oggosk, glancing at the door.

'Where's the rest of the letter?' asked Marila.

'Right here,' said the witch, pulling two more sheets from inside her cloak. Placing the three sheets together, she ripped them in quarters. Then, walking to the hearth – it was chilly in the palace, despite the warmth outside – she tossed the pieces onto the bed of glowing coals.

'Again!' cried Neeps. 'I've never understood why you *do* that. Such a blary waste of time.'

Oggosk looked at him over her shoulder, contemptuous. 'Scrawny little ape. When did you ever understand a thing?' She crouched before the fire and blew. The vellum smouldered, then burst suddenly into flames. Oggosk stood with a groan and turned to face the youths.

'The letters I burn, *he* watches forming in a fireplace, beneath the dying coals. When the last ember goes out he brushes off the ash and there they are, waiting to be read. I speak of Theimat, of course, the captain's father. He is a prisoner in Agaroth, on the doorstep of death, a shade without the rest that every shade must long for. Until Nilus chooses to let him go.'

'And Rose keeps him there,' said Pazel, 'because he wants to know which of you is his real mother?'

'You can see that much plainly,' snapped the witch. 'Now listen to *me*: you will keep the family matters to yourselves, am I clear? Nilus will go mad if he learns I've made you privy to the worst secret of his childhood.'

'Why did you?' asked Thasha.

Oggosk hesitated, and the wrinkles tightened around her milk-blue eyes. 'Perhaps for no good reason,' she said. 'In any case we will know in a matter of hours.'

The door of the chamber banged open. It was Prince Olik's footman. 'His Highness asks his honoured guests to join him on the Dais of Masalym.'

'He's back!' cried Pazel. 'Is Hercól with him? Is there any sign of Arunis?'

The man did not answer at first; like most of the dlömu he seemed caught between wonder and fear when in their presence. 'I am to take you quickly,' he said at last.

They followed him, Thasha's dogs padding at her side; Oggosk struggling irritably, leaning on both her stick and Pazel's arm. Out of the splendid drawing room they walked, through a portrait gallery where they had tried to glean clues about Bali Adro history (and where Druffle now stood transfixed before a dlömic nude), across the dining chamber where Rain and Uskins sat earnestly masticating *mül*. How could they possibly be hungry, Thasha wondered, when two hours ago they had all been treated to such a staggering meal?

What they had not been treated to was information. They had climbed a broad stair from beneath the pillar to these chambers, where Alyash, Dastu and Sandor Ott were waiting already, and twenty servants (and twice as many guards) attended them, in that same abashed and fearful style. Olik and Bolutu had returned at once to the Lower City, and the frantic search. Ibjen had stayed to dote on them — carrying tea trays, measuring their feet for new shoes when the tailor's hands shook too much for the task. It was good luck, Thasha realised, that they had landed first in a village too small and isolated to trade in the fanciful, terrifying gossip that had swept Masalym. Ibjen had had time to realise they were simply people, before anyone declared them something else.

From the dining chamber they walked down a short corridor, then climbed a steep and narrow staircase. Then another, and another. Only after the fifth staircase did the footman speak again, announcing, 'The Dais of Masalym,' and throwing open a door.

Sunlight and wind: the door let onto a small, roofless space with another staircase, very short, leading up to what Thasha saw instantly must be the roof of the entire palace, the cut-off apex of the pyramid.

'There you are! Come, hurry!' came the prince's voice, faintly.

Up they climbed, into the last hour of daylight. The roof was flat, featureless, immense, a great courtyard thrust up into the sky, with no railing, no shelter of any kind. Here at the centre they could see nothing of the city, only the snowy peaks in the south and west, and on the other side the spire of Narybir Tower, hazy across the Gulf. Olik and Hercól stood close to this edge – and beside them, tiny in that enormous space, were two figures that made Thasha's heart leap with joy.

'Ensyl! Felthrup!'

The dogs bounded forwards, skidding to a halt before their beloved rat. Thasha saw that Hercól was holding Ildraquin naked in his hand. 'You found it!' she cried.

'It was never lost,' said Ensyl, 'though in removing it from Vadu's reach I made it appear so, alas. Dear friends! I wondered if I should ever see you again.'

'Felthrup, you're a hero,' said Thasha, dropping to her knees beside him.

The black rat scurried into her arms, shivering with pleasure. 'I am nothing of the kind,' he said. 'What sort of hero sleeps through a fight, and awakens when it has ended?'

'It has not ended,' said Oggosk, wrapping her cloak tighter against the wind.

'Quite right, Duchess,' said Prince Olik. 'Listen well, you four. A great deal has changed since this morning.'

'You know where Fulbreech is, don't you?' said Marila to Hercól.

The Tholjassan drew a deep breath. 'I know,' he said. 'Ildraquin has told me.' He stepped back, closing his eyes and straightening his sword-arm. At first he appeared to be pointing down at some place in the city, but then his arm swung slowly to the right, and upwards, until it was pointing south-west, at a place in the mountains between two peaks. It was a saddle, a pass, but still a very high and distant spot. The mountain peaks were white all around it; the slopes looked harsh and dry.

'*There?*' asked Neeps, disbelieving.

'At the Chalice of the Maî,' said Prince Olik, 'where the river that flows past our feet has its source in cold Ilvaspar, the glacier lake. Yet I must doubt you, friend Hercól. Arunis stood in this very spot just twenty hours ago, with Fulbreech at his side, and the *tol-chenni* he took from the Conservatory, too – his "idiot", as he calls the creature. Many servants, and the Issár as well, confirmed that they were here. And even on the swiftest steed, they could not yet have reached the Chalice. It takes that long to cross our Inner Dominion, the high country that begins here, at the Upper Gate of the Upper City, and runs to the mountain's foot. And another twelve to climb to the Chalice, and Ilvaspar's frigid shores.'

'Yet Fulbreech is there all the same,' said Hercól. 'Alone or with the sorcerer? That I cannot guess. But Ildraquin has never led me astray when we follow a blood scent.'

Olik sighed. 'Then perhaps they did not use the highway at all, but some magic that let them ride the very wind. As you say, however, we have no proof that Arunis has kept the boy by his side.'

'It could well be a trick,' said Ensyl. 'Arunis might have sent him to the mountains alone, to throw us off.'

'That is true,' said Hercól, 'for I cannot be certain what he knows of Ildraquin's powers.'

'You've got to make Ott send Niriviel,' said Thasha. 'He could reach the summit by midnight, and be back here by dawn. He can tell us if Arunis is with Fulbreech or not.'

'If they are not indoors,' said the prince.

But Hercól shook his head. 'You have not seen Niriviel by daylight, Thasha. He nearly died of exhaustion on the Ruling Sea, and when he made it across, he did not rest, but began weeks of searching for the *Chathrand*, and his master. He needs days of rest and feasting. He stole the ropes and grapples we used last night, and did some scouting for us over the Lower City, but even those efforts taxed him. If Ott sent him racing to that mountain he would go – but I fear the poor, deluded creature would fly until his heart broke, and he fell dead from the sky. No, we are blind to the sorcerer's movements. We can only hope that he is also blind – to the danger of keeping Fulbreech near him.'

'And that we cannot know,' cried Felthrup, beside himself. 'What a miserable fix!'

'You should not run in circles on a rooftop, little brother,' said Hercól. 'But we may be glad that for his part, Fulbreech is holding still. He has not moved these two hours since I regained Ildraquin. Of course, that could change in an instant.'

'We should assume that it will,' said Ensyl, 'unless the youth has died.'

'He has not died,' said Hercól. 'That too I can sense.'

A flash of shame passed over Thasha. *I'm disappointed*, she thought. *I wanted Hercól to say he might be dead.*

'Yes, Mr Stargraven, a fix,' said the prince, 'and that is precisely why I summoned you.'

Beckoning, he led them forwards, closer to the pyramid's sharp edge. All three levels of Masalym were spread before them, looking something like an irregular layer cake, except that the decrepit first layer dwarfed the upper two. There in the raised shipyard stood the *Chathrand*, a dark crowd about her on the quay, paler forms on her topdeck, all of them busy as ants.

'There is a choice before you,' said Olik. 'I wish you did not have to face it so quickly, but with the *Kirisang* approaching you dare not delay. Arunis may still be hiding in the great maze of the Lower City – or he may be on that mountain, and about to escape us further. Regardless, the *Chathrand* must flee, across the Gulf and into hiding. Will you be upon her? That is what you must decide.'

Thasha felt a sudden dread creeping over her. She looked from the city to the mountain pass and back again. 'What's beyond the mountain?' she asked Olik. 'A lake, you say?'

'Ilvaspar, which is *Snowborn* in the tongue of the mountain folk. An enormous, frigid lake, closed in wholly by the mountains except at its two narrow ends. One is there at the Maîtar, the Chalice. The fisher-folk who dwell there may agree to row you down Ilvaspar's length, for a fee, but no gold will persuade them to venture further. The southern end of Ilvaspar is a place of many perils. The lake flows out in a second river, the Ansyndra, far greater than the Maî, but for the first twenty miles that river blasts through gorges and cataracts and canyons, and descent along its banks is impossible. The only way down is upon the Black Tongue, a cursed place, created in the early days of the *Platazcra* by a warlord with an eguar blade, to terrify the mountain folk into surrender. He called up magma from the depths of the earth and sent it gushing down the mountain, with his forces marching behind upon the cooling rock, a sight terrible to behold. They conquered the mountain folk, of course. But the Black Tongue kept spreading, and when the warlord tried to melt it back into the earth, he only succeeded in opening many cracks and tunnels into the roots of the mountain. On warm days, flame-trolls may issue from those cracks, and they are awful foes.

'Beyond the Black Tongue the Ansyndra flows more gently, and may even be navigable in places. The danger, however, merely changes form.' He looked at them each in turn, and at last his eyes settled on Felthrup. 'You do not remember, Mr Stargraven, but you have already faced the danger I speak of, which we call the River of Shadows.'

'The River of Shadows!' said Felthrup, his hair suddenly bristling. 'Yes, yes, I know that place, certainly! No, I don't. Oh dear. What is it?'

'It is a tunnel between worlds, and a flood that never abates,' said the prince. 'The channel cut by the wild pulse of life through a hostile universe, the thought that flees on waking, the pure stuff from which souls are distilled. If I speak in riddles, Mr Stargraven, it is only because riddles are what one meets with there. Like the *nuhzat*, the River of Shadows must be experienced to be understood. One way is through dream-travel, as you have done; another is by astral journey. That is high magic, for one can bring back objects, creatures even, when one returns. Lord Ramachni showed me the River that way, once.'

'But there is a third way,' said Oggosk.

'Yes,' said the prince, 'a third way. As I said, the River of Shadows winds through many worlds – and travellers tell us that those it does *not* enter are unthinkably grim, soulless realms where men live like machines. In each world the River touches, it has a source and an exit. Between these points it usually runs deep under the earth, in the living heart of the world, so that we feel its presence beneath us only when we are very still. But here and there it comes close to the surface. In Alifros, more than a dozen such places are known to exist. After the Dawn War, the victorious Auru found most of these places and built great watchtowers beside them, for they knew that the demons they had just defeated had crept into Alifros by way of the River.'

'This is all strange and wonderful,' said Ensyl, 'but why are you telling us about it, Sire?'

'Because you are looking at the place where the River of Shadows enters this world,' said the prince, pointing again at the mountains. 'Somewhere under those peaks it rises, perhaps entering the deep depths of Ilvaspar, but certainly – and uniquely, in all Alifros – joining for a time with a natural river. That river is the Ansyndra. For nearly a hundred miles, it and the River of Shadows follow the same course. This has made our Efaroc Peninsula one of the strangest parts of Alifros. Beings from other times, other worlds – other versions of *this* world – have washed or crawled up from the River over the centuries. Many perish, but some dwell on in the pockets and folds of those mountains. Bali Adro claims the peninsula, but in truth it is a land apart, beautiful and ghastly by turns.

'Ghastly wins out at last, however, in a place where no sensible person ever sets foot: the *Bauracloj*, the Infernal Forest. I can tell you little of that place, for I have never been near it. But it is said that a whole city of the Auru was swallowed up by that forest, and the first watchtower on the River of Shadows thrown down in pieces.'

'Great Mother!' said Ensyl. 'Could Arunis possibly mean to go *there*?'

'Who can tell?' said the prince. 'It is a place of dark magic, certainly. Many Spider Tellers believe that the Nilstone entered the world right there, carried upwards by the bubbling force of the River. But none of us knows for certain.'

He stopped speaking, and gazed out over Masalym again. 'At dawn tomorrow,' he said, 'unless Arunis be found first, an expedition made up of those who still revere me will ride out towards the Chalice of the Maî. I will not be with them, for while there is a chance that he remains here I must ensure that the hunt in the city does not fall to pieces. You would all be welcome on the expedition. But I do not ask it of you. The *Chathrand* will be far from Masalym before any return is possible, and no one can predict what sort of city will await those who descend from the peaks. This much is certain: I will no longer be ordering its affairs. By then I may indeed be a prisoner in the bowels of the *Kirisang*, waiting for transport back to Bali Adro City, and the judgement of the Ravens.'

'Well, don't blary wait for that to happen,' said Neeps.

Olik gestured over the city. 'I hold the lives of these people in trust,' he said, 'and I promised them I would remain here, until all the dangers I brought with me were removed. I will not depart until I am sure that Arunis has done so.' He smiled broadly. 'Then I will depart very quickly.'

Thasha swallowed. *If you still can.*

'I am sending you back to your ship tonight,' said the prince. 'But an hour before sunrise the carriages will again be on the quay, for any who wish to join the expedition. You will have tonight to decide.'

'And to prepare,' said Oggosk, 'for either choice will have its costs.'

The four youths looked at one another. They were shaken. This was something none of them had foreseen.

'Nothing to decide, is there?' said Pazel, his voice less certain than his words. 'We swore an oath. That settles it.'

'Right you are,' said Neeps. But his expression was haunted. The tarboys looked anxiously at their friends. Thasha found she couldn't speak. Marila's face was a mask.

'It may be less simple than you think,' said Hercól. 'Grant me this much, boys: that we sit with our choices in silence awhile, until we are all back on the *Chathrand*, at least.'

'But Hercól,' said Pazel, 'we already—'

'Heed his words!' croaked Oggosk with sudden vehemence. The tarboys started; Ensyl stared up at her with great unease. Felthrup looked from Oggosk to Thasha and back again. He rubbed his paws together, a blur before his face.

Mr Teggatz cooked a vat of pork and snake-bean stew. It was a surprising success in taste, but some kind of gelatine leaked from the bean pods and turned the whole cauldron into a translucent solid. His tarboy aides served it like a jiggling, messy pudding, and the crew devoured it without comment. They were well beyond shock.

The cook kept a few servings aside for the youths and Hercól, but none of them was hungry. They sat quietly in the stateroom, which was unchanged but for the mould in the pantry area, while everywhere else on the ship men laboured in their hundreds, shouting, thumping, dragging crates, coaxing animals and once more cursing 'the fish-eyed freaks'. The dlömus' fear had infected them. Every man aboard knew that they were running from some mortal threat.

Captain Rose would keep them at it all night, and all the next day, Thasha knew. Even after they launched the work would continue: below the waterline, the crew would keep on shifting and securing the wares by lamplight, all the way across the Gulf. And if that work was ever done, there were the forty miles of ropes to double- and triple-check, and paint with tar against the damp; seams to caulk, chains and wheelblocks and pump-gears to oil, extra sails to cut and stitch, hatchcovers to mend, stanchions to shore up; some fifty new animals to fuss over, two surly augrongs to scrub, delouse and copiously feed.

Hercól was right, but so was Pazel. It had been better not to talk any more, there atop the city with nothing to lay their hands on, no mould to wipe away, no little tasks to hide behind. Still, they all knew what the morning would bring. Neeps was putting his clothes in sacks. Hercól was seated on the bearskin, sharpening weapons. Pazel was rubbing oil into the creases on Thasha's boots.

Everyone was on edge. Neeps and Marila bickered when they spoke at all, though they never seemed to be more than an arm's length apart. The dogs lay in deep mourning, unable to bear the sight of the bags and bundles collecting near the door. Felthrup crouched on the window seat, gazing out at the night.

It fell to Mr Fiffengurt to break the silence, roughly at midnight, when he staggered in from a long work shift and collapsed in the admiral's chair. Pazel silently brought him a mug of dlömic beer – frothy, fruity, black. They had spent the evening developing a taste for it.

The quartermaster drank deeply. 'Rose has just let me in on the plan,' he said. 'It's the damndest bit of hide-and-seek nonsense I've ever heard. And I can't for the life of me think of a better idea.'

The *Chathrand* was to speed by night across the Gulf, he explained, and land a tiny force, just three or four men, not far from where their little boat had been capsized by the emerald serpent. Those men would hide their boat, hide themselves deep in the dunes 'and live off Rinforsaken *mül*' while the *Chathrand* sped out through the inlet, tacked west and raced along the outside of the Sandwall for a good sixty or eighty miles. There were rocky islets there, like those at Cape Lasung. A hiding place. Every sixth day the men on the Sandwall would climb the tallest dune and look for mirror-signals from Masalym, giving them the all-clear. On the same day, the *Chathrand* would venture carefully out of hiding and creep back along the Sandwall, hoping for a corresponding signal from the landing party.

'What then?' said Thasha.

'Then?' said Fiffengurt, startled. 'Why, then we come and get you, m'lady.'

'Is that the captain's plan?'

Fiffengurt gazed at her for a long time, his fingers caressing the chair's felt arms. 'If Rose tries to sail off and leave you here,' he said, 'I will put a knife into his heart. D'ye understand me, Lady?'

As if there could be two ways of understanding a statement like that. Fiffengurt drained his mug and pushed to his feet. 'Time to check the watch lists,' he grumbled. 'The off-duty lads won't sleep unless I order 'em to, their heads are so twisted with worry. The damned fools. Won't be any blessed use tomorrow if they *don't* sleep, will they?'

When he was gone, Hercól shook his head. 'Do not mind Fiffengurt. He is angry at himself for that game leg: he knows it would make him useless on an overland journey. I fear he's in more pain than he cares to admit, both from the leg and the thought of Anni and their child, and the slim chance that he will ever seen them again. But he thinks his own suffering too small a thing to share with anyone, just now.'

'Dear old Fiffengurt,' said Neeps. 'But he's assuming a lot, isn't he? I mean, we still haven't decided to go.'

'Haven't we, mate?' said Pazel.

No one answered. Hercól rose and left the stateroom; the others went on with their work.

They were still drinking the black beer when a shout came from beyond the stateroom. Pazel at once felt a tightness in his chest: the voice was Ignus Chadfallow's. He went to the door and opened it. The doctor was crouched by the invisible wall, his lips near the hole Counselor Vadu had made.

'Pazel,' he said, 'come out here, will you? There is something you should see.'

Pazel glanced back at the others. 'Go on,' said Thasha. He went, but he dragged his feet. He had a strong sense of having wronged the doctor. He had said nothing to Chadfallow about his dream-encounter with his mother; in fact, they had barely spoken since their escape from the Conservatory. And Suthinia hadn't admitted everything, to be sure. But clearly Captain Gregory had more than one thing on his mind when he abandoned his family.

He stopped a few feet from the wall.

'It's not the best time, Ignus,' he said.

The doctor rose to his feet, watching Pazel gravely. 'It is the only time,' he said.

Pazel drew a deep breath, summoning all his reserves of patience. Then he stepped through the wall. 'Make it quick, will you?' he said. 'I'm blary exhausted.'

Chadfallow nodded and turned, beckoning Pazel to follow. They descended the Silver Stair to the lower gun deck and set off briskly towards the bows. Even at this late hour the deck was swarming with men. Some were inspecting the gun carriages; other were guiding freight down the tonnage shaft or muscling crates across the floor. There were a few dlömu working among them, and Pazel saw with amazement that they were in uniform – Arquali uniform. *Olik's found dlömu willing to sail with us. To run away with the humans, to be hunted by their own people. Rin's eyes, some of them must still love that prince.*

Chadfallow begged a lamp from one of the work crews and led Pazel down a side passage into forward first-class: a ravaged corner of the ship, burned in the rat battle, and unoccupied since their landfall at Ormael. The once-luxurious cabins gaped in a line, like five missing teeth. Rose had ordered the doors removed, to prevent the ship's deathsmokers from creeping in and lighting cigarettes – one fire per voyage was more than enough.

Chadfallow sniffed. 'The drug is still in the air,' he said. 'Bring an addict here and he will go feverish before your eyes.' Then he froze. 'Look, there it is.'

Across from the first of the gutted cabins was a waist-high green door. Pazel was startled: he had seen that door before, but not on the lower gun deck. They approached it. The door was untouched by fire, although the wall around it was black with soot. Yet the portal was clearly ancient: warped and cracked, with peeling paint and an iron handle that had rusted to an irregular lump.

'It's exactly like the door on the berth deck,' said Pazel. 'The one Thasha showed me, the night she fell into a trance.'

'Where on the berth deck?' asked Chadfallow.

'Starboard aft, I think,' said Pazel. 'The odd thing is that I never could find it again.'

'Then it *is* the same,' said Chadfallow. He pointed down the corridor. Twenty feet from where they stood, someone had drawn a rectangle in chalk upon a bare stretch of wall. The shape was roughly the same size as the little green door.

'I drew that not an hour ago,' he said, 'around this very door. It moves, Pazel. It slides, and melts away, and reappears on other decks.'

'A vanishing compartment?'

Chadfallow nodded. 'They are quite real. And they lead to other places, other *Chathrands*, lost in both space and time. Some are reached through doors like this one, others merely by walking passages in a prescribed order. Some flare to life when a mage is near, or a powerful spell troubles the firmament. Others flicker in and out of existence like an erratic flame, as though the well of their enchantment is running dry.'

Pazel looked again at the door. Suddenly it felt menacing, like a trap waiting to break the leg of an unlucky dog. 'How do you know all this?' he asked.

'I made it my business to know,' said Chadfallow, 'and I would have told you myself ere now, if you had not tried so hard to avoid me. There are benefits to a life spent in diplomatic circles. One is the chance to collect on favours. I have a friend inside the Trading Company – a record-keeper, and a man obsessed with the magical architecture of this ship. Not long after I received my orders to report to *Chathrand* I paid him a visit.'

Chadfallow looked at the green door. 'He told me about that one. It is unlike any other magical portal on this ship. It is part of a relic spell, I think, laid down even before Erithusmé's time, by the mage-shipwrights who built this ship for war.'

'Ramachni warned Thasha not to open that door,' said Pazel.

'Hercól informed me,' said Chadfallow, 'but I am not Thasha, am I?'

He put his hand on the corroded knob. And Pazel was suddenly flooded with apprehension, with outright fear. 'Don't do it!' he shouted, seizing the doctor's arm.

Chadfallow gave him an unpleasant smile. 'What awful thing do you imagine lying in wait?'

'Pitfire, Ignus, do we have to find out? If Ramachni said to avoid it, that's blary well good enough!'

'Normally, yes,' said Chadfallow, 'but I have an equally valid reason to want to proceed. I was told that finding this door might prove the key to our success. To ridding the world of the Nilstone, that is, and perhaps Arunis as well.'

'Told, were you? By whom?'

'By Ramachni,' said Chadfallow. When Pazel gaped at him, he added, 'It was a dream, some months back, as we drew close to Bramian.'

Pazel quickly averted his gaze. 'You can't trust dreams,' he said.

'Ah, but can we afford to ignore them?'

'You're absolutely cracked,' Pazel heard himself say. 'That dream could have come from Arunis. We know he's been getting inside people's minds.'

'The minds of the weak and the ill,' said Chadfallow, 'or do you count me as one of those?'

Pazel turned away, a string of florid Ormali curses on the tip of his tongue. 'Damn it all, I don't feel like arguing,' he said at last. 'Just stay away from that door, wherever it turns up. Ramachni didn't warn Thasha through any blary dream.'

'True,' said Chadfallow thoughtfully, 'it was a message in an onion skin, wasn't it?'

Not waiting for an answer, he walked on. After a minute, Pazel hurried after him. Soon they reached the entrance to sickbay. Pazel could hear someone groaning within.

The doctor opened the door but did not enter. Pazel looked in and saw that the beds were almost full. Men and tarboys glanced up miserably, holding their stomachs, leaning over buckets and pans. Two or three called out to Chadfallow.

'I will attend you presently,' said the doctor to the room at large.

Then he closed the door and looked at Pazel. 'Thirty patients,' he said. 'The water at the Tournament Grounds was unclean. Some sort of parasite, I expect.'

'I'm sorry to hear that,' said Pazel, wondering if they were finished.

Chadfallow leaned against the passage wall. He looked at Pazel with great melancholy. 'I am still a hostage, you see: this time to the well-being of the ship. Rain is no use. I am the only reliable doctor this side of the Ruling Sea. The only *human* doctor, I mean.'

'And you sure are reliable,' said Pazel, looking away.

Chadfallow's voice grew hard. 'I know what you're thinking: that unless Arunis is stopped and the Nilstone recovered, it will not make any difference whether or not these people live or die. That is true. But my own choice is not between defeating Arunis and saving these souls. It is between the certainty of saving lives here, and the small chance that I will be of decisive use on the expedition.'

'Glad to know how carefully you've weighed all this.'

A spasm of irritation passed over Chadfallow's face; then his look became resigned. 'You will believe what you wish of me,' he said. 'I could change your mind, perhaps – but I would prefer you reached your own conclusions. That has always been my aim: to give you the freedom to think for yourself, and all the tools I could to make that thinking fine.'

'Ignus,' said Pazel. 'We're not going on that expedition, either.'

The doctor stared at him, taken aback. 'None of you?'

'How could we, damn it?' said Pazel. 'We cause a panic every-where we go. It will be a hundred times better if the dlömu go by themselves.'

'You were chosen by the Red Wolf.'

'So was Diadrelu,' said Pazel, 'and look where that got her. And *credek*, you just finished talking about choosing for oneself. Did you mean a single word? Because it seems to me I do just fine when I make choices alone. The trouble is when all of you try to choose for me. If it's not the Wolf it's Ramachni, or Ott, or Captain Rose. Or you.' Then Pazel added wildly, 'Neeps and Thasha feel the same way I do. We're humans. We belong on this ship. It's not as if we brought the Nilstone into this world.'

'What does Hercól say to this?'

'You'd better ask him.'

Chadfallow straightened his back. He looked down at Pazel and nodded. 'I understand your reasoning perfectly,' he said. 'Your decision mirrors my own, after all.'

No words could have been less welcome to Pazel's ear. 'I think I'll go back to the stateroom now,' he said.

'May I walk with you?' asked the doctor.

Pazel shrugged. He set off, retracing their steps, and Chadfallow walked at his side. Pazel had the grating feeling that he'd just been outmanoeuvred once more by a man who'd made a lifetime game of needling him. Had someone told the doctor about his own dream of Suthinia? Was this his way of gloating over how wrong Pazel had been?

'Ignus,' he said through his teeth, 'I'm going to ask you a question. And if you answer with anything but *yes* or *no*, I'm not sure I'll ever speak to you again.'

'Mercy me,' said Chadfallow.

'Are you the reason my father abandoned us?'

Chadfallow stopped in his tracks. He looked like a man who has suddenly been hurled a great distance, and is surprised to find himself on his feet. He opened his mouth and closed it again, never breaking eye contact with Pazel.

Then he said, 'Yes, I am.'

Something exploded in Pazel at those words. He flew at the doctor, aiming for the nose he had broken once before. Chadfallow jerked back his head just in time.

'Son of a whore!' Pazel shouted, lunging again. 'He never mucking *spoke* to me again! Did you do it in his Gods-damned bed? Did he think I was your brat, your bastard child? Did he? Am I?'

'No.'

'No to *what*, you blary pig?'

'No, you're not my son.'

Pazel stood frozen, his hands still in fists. He had seen Chadfallow enraged, pompous, indignant, even suicidal. But he had never heard such sadness in his voice.

'You're sure?' he said. 'How can you be sure?'

Chadfallow blinked at him slowly. 'Your father,' he said, 'is Captain Gregory Pathkendle.'

Men were staring. Pazel looked at them until they turned back to their work. Chadfallow stepped forward and placed a nervous hand on his shoulder.

'Captain Gregory doesn't give a damn about me,' said Pazel.

Words he'd never meant to speak. Words too plain and factual, a truth too obvious to bear.

'Some men are not born to be fathers,' said Chadfallow. 'Very few rise to all the challenges of the task.'

'Some men try.'

Pazel felt hot tears on his face. Now that they had started what could ever make them stop?

'Why . . . do you say you're the reason he left?'

Chadfallow gazed into their sputtering lamp. 'Because I shamed him, once. Before your mother, whom he revered even more than he loved. You know what your mother is now, Pazel: a warrior in the fight for the soul of Alifros. That is what made me fall in love with her, by the way – not her beauty, not at first. I was swept off my feet by her goodness, the mission that had brought her over the sea. It was all I could think about. It exposed my diplomatic charades for the petty game they were. And there she was, giving it up for a commoner, a sailing captain! What was worse, she *wanted* Gregory, and he her. So I shamed him, purposefully. It was the lowest act of my life.'

'Tell me,' said Pazel, nails biting into his palms.

The doctor's hand trembled on his shoulder. 'I thought the three of us were alone. You were at school. Gregory was perhaps a little tipsy – he was not above a glass of wine at midday, when he was home in Ormael. And on that day he told his wife that he wished her to have no more to do with Ramachni or Bolutu, or the other survivors of the expedition, the ones Arunis had not yet killed. That he would shred their letters if they came, and stop her from attending their clandestine meetings. He was merely letting off steam, I think – and voicing a most reasonable fear for her safety. Suthinia just laughed at him. No man alive has ever ordered her about, or ever will.

'But I chose to take his words seriously. Out of spite and jealousy. I said he was a fool to stand in her way. That his wife had been chosen for the greatest task imaginable and should not be thwarted by a man whose highest ambition was to corner the barley trade with Sorhn. He rose in a fury, and soon we were shouting at each other like Plapps and Burnscovers. I called him a small-minded smuggler. He answered that it was high time I stopped sticking my great Etherhorde nose into his family's affairs.'

Chadfallow drew a sharp breath. 'Things might have gone differently if Neda had not been listening at the top of the stairs. She chose that moment to remark that my nose wasn't all I was sticking in.'

Pazel's mouth fell open, but Chadfallow gave a dismissive wave. 'It was nonsense, girlish babble. And looking back I think Neda meant only to take her father's side, to drive the interfering Arquali from your home. Even if she had to lie.'

Pazel felt hollow inside, and cold. 'She didn't manage to drive *you* out,' said Pazel. 'She drove Gregory away. Oh, Neda.'

'I told him it was rubbish,' said the doctor, 'and he professed to take my word. We shook hands that day, affirmed our friendship. But it was never the same – and two months later, he was gone. Yes, I think he must have believed Neda in his heart. As for Suthinia, I doubt if he ever dared ask her. They are perfectly matched in one way, your parents. They are both quite terribly proud.'

Pazel slid down against the wall. He dragged a grimy arm across his eyes. 'He *wanted* it to be true that you were sleeping with her. He was looking for an excuse to leave us. That's what I think.'

Chadfallow sat down next to him, shaking his head. 'I can't tell you, Pazel. But I hope you won't torture yourself with *what-if*'s, as I have done these many years. The past is gone; the future is wailing for its breakfast. That is what *my* father used to say.'

Pazel stared at him blankly. 'Ignus,' he said, 'we can't go hunting Arunis. We can't.'

'I will question you no further about the expedition.'

'But if we did,' said Pazel, 'I'd understand you having to stay here. I'd ... be proud of you. For seeing clearly. For knowing how to choose.'

Chadfallow dropped his eyes. He was struggling for composure, and then the struggle ended, and his shoulders shook. Pazel embraced him for the first time in more than six years, and the Imperial Surgeon wept and said, 'My lad, my excellent boy,' and the sailors passing in the corridor had the grace to look away.

Thasha entered her father's cabin with a tin of sweetpine and placed a little in the pocket of each of his coats, to keep the moths at bay. She took down the portrait of some nameless uncle holding a cat and wrapped it in a sheet.*

'I despise those creatures,' said Felthrup, startling her from behind. 'Oggosk's monster Sniraga has already been sniffing at the hole in the magic wall. Can you not repair it, Thasha?'

'Don't you think I'd have done so by now?' answered Thasha. 'For some reason I was given the power to decide who passes through the wall, and who doesn't – but that's as far as it goes.'

'Of course, of course.' With a sigh Felthrup leaped onto the bed, where he gazed deeply into Syrarys' dressing mirror. When he caught Thasha looking at him, he gave a small, embarrassed squeak. 'I am not vain,' he said. 'There is something odd about that mirror. Whenever I look into it, I see only myself, and yet always – for no reason I can discover – I expect to see someone else.'

---

* Admiral Isiq's letters refer to the dour gentleman with the cat as 'Great-Uncle Torindan, the war hero'. – EDITOR.

'Someone in particular?' asked Thasha.

'Yes,' said Felthrup. 'Ramachni. I expect to see Ramachni, looking out at me. And I feel his presence in other places, Lady: standing before the magic wall, or napping on the bearskin.'

Startled anew, Thasha gazed into the mirror herself. She saw nothing strange, except her own face: eyes that were hers, but not quite hers, eyes more wary and knowing than the last time she'd studied herself in a glass. She did not much like that look of hers, and wondered how long she had worn it.

'My lady,' said Felthrup, 'I will go with you to the mountains.'

Thasha turned to him, overwhelmed. The courage of the little creature, the loyalty. '*If* we go,' she said, 'you must stay behind, darling rat.'

'No!' Felthrup whirled in a circle. 'I don't want to stay here alone! I can't face it, this great mean ship, without you and the others beside me!'

'You wouldn't be alone,' said Thasha. 'You'd have Fiffengurt, and Jorl and Suzyt. And whether we go or stay you'll have work to do. Someone has to find the ixchel, and make peace. And there's something else, too: you have to dream for us, Felthrup. That is how you'll do your travelling, from now on. Who knows? Maybe you'll find Ramachni that way, and bring him to us.'

'Ramachni has always done the finding,' said Felthrup.

'You found Pazel Doldur,' said Thasha.

A light shone in Felthrup's black eyes. 'It was wonderful there, in the Orfuin Club, among the scholars. I felt at home with them, somehow, even the one who told me to go away and eat cake.'

Suddenly the floor heaved. The *Chathrand* was tilting over: a slow, scraping list to portside, accompanied by groaning timbers, creaking screws, curses from above and below. Thasha and Felthrup scrambled into the outer stateroom.

'We're afloat,' said Neeps, mopping beer from the floor. '*Credek*, they've got a lot of rebalancing to do.'

'Let's go up there,' said Marila.

The three youths left the stateroom. They met Pazel on the

Silver Stair, and together they climbed to the topdeck. It was very dark, but even by the dim lamplight they could see how much had changed. The inner wall of the berth had been retracted, and the locks opened wide. The river had been allowed to pour back into the great basin, and the *Chathrand*, as Pazel said, was at last afloat. The mooring lines creaked, the gangways rocked on their hinges.

Suddenly Thasha stifled a cry. Two beings were sweeping towards them from amidships. They were dressed in rags, which they clutched tight against the evening wind; their hands were bone-thin and colourless. One was hooded, the other wore an ancient Merchant Service cap. But neither figure possessed a face. It was appalling: the fronts of their heads simply blurred to nothingness. She grabbed Pazel by the arm.

'You don't see them, do you?'

'See what, Thasha?'

She knew quite well that they were ghosts. She had seen them by daylight, these shades of the former captains of the Great Ship. But by daylight they looked human – old, strange, crazed maybe, but human. Only drugged with *blanë*, close to death herself, had she seen them in this form. A vision she had tried for months to forget.

The two figures came right for her. Thasha stepped backwards, feeling the cold in them from yards away. 'Duchess!' sighed the figure in the cap.

'I'm not,' said Thasha.

'Blind fool,' hissed the hooded figure to its companion. 'The hag is in the cabin with her child. You're standing before our mistress now, so keep a civil tongue.'

Her friends were talking, their voices far away. 'I'm not your mistress, either,' she said. Then, a bit more bravely: 'I don't want you near me. Go to your rest, or wherever you belong.'

'We belong in the stomach of the night,' said the hooded spirit, thrusting its non-face closer to hers. 'We are the bread of the unborn, the milk they will drink in their first hours. *You* keep us here, Mistress – you and the Red Beast. How can you order us hence, while you hold our chains in your hand?'

'Go to him!' cried the figure in the cap. 'Go to Rose and help him face his doom! Go now, girl, before it's too late!'

The hooded figure turned on its companion, outraged that it had taken such a tone with 'our mistress'. They began to bicker, a sound like driving rain. Thasha turned and fled to starboard, dragging her friends with her. Suddenly another ghost rose through a glass plank on their left and began shuffling towards her purposefully. She was not going to be able to ignore them. And perhaps she shouldn't: Oggosk too had been trying to tell them something about Rose, when she shared that letter.

'Come with me,' said Thasha to the others, and headed straight for the captain's door beneath the quarterdeck. But as they neared it Sergeant Haddismal emerged, frowning at some inner thought. At the sight of them he was at once suspicious. He stopped in the doorway, blocking their path.

'Where d'ye imagine you're going?' he said. 'The captain's too busy to breathe. He don't need to hear from four lunatics on top of everything else.'

'Haven't you learned how *insulting* that is?' said Marila, with such vehemence that even her friends looked at her in surprise.

'Insulting?' said Haddismal. 'You taking after the fish-eyes, now?'

'Could be worse folk to take after,' said Neeps. 'Right, Marila?'

'Just be quiet,' she said.

'Sergeant,' said Thasha with rising impatience, 'we were *told* to see the captain, right now.'

'Told, eh? By whom?'

Thasha said nothing, and Haddismal's mouth curled in anger. 'Don't muck around with me,' he said. 'You know what strange fancy's grabbed hold of him, don't you? You're here to take advantage. Do you know that he's been marked for execution, just because he bled that fishy prince a little? I suppose you want him to go back ashore and walk among them. Throw himself on their mercy. Not likely, girl.'

'What in Pitfire are you talking about?' said Thasha. 'What fancy's come over him?'

Before Haddismal could reply they heard Rose himself, bellowing from behind him. 'Stand clear, you tin-shirt bastard! Let me out before I choke!'

Haddismal jumped aside, and Rose barrelled into the doorway. For the second time in five minutes, Thasha had to contain the urge to cry out. The others did cry out, and even Haddismal made an appalled noise in his throat.

'*Aya*, Captain, you should leave that behind in your chambers! Don't let the lads see you with it, sir.'

Rose was clutching the entire carcass of a leopard. It was dry and shrivelled and hard as wood, but quite real. Its glass eyes were open; a waxy tongue lay rippling between huge yellow fangs. Rose was holding it against his chest with one arm. Like the Turach, he stopped dead at the sight of Thasha and her companions. His face paled; his eyes moved from one youth to another.

'You devils,' he said. 'I curse the day you came aboard.'

'Beg your pardon, sir,' said Haddismal. 'I was about to send them away.'

'Not till dawn! Not till dawn!'

'I meant away from your door, sir.'

'I'll do it,' said Rose, but his eyes were drifting, and it seemed he spoke neither to the Turach nor to the youths. 'Do you hear me? I'll do it! What more do you want?'

'Do *what*, for Rin's sake?' asked Pazel. 'What's the matter with you? What's that leopard for?'

Rose gave the leopard a convulsive squeeze. Then, noticing that Haddismal too was staring at the creature, he barked, 'Get on with your preparations! You're fifteen hours from launch, and I'm still captain while I walk this ship!'

Haddismal stalked off, perplexed and affronted. Rose was still looking past them – at the ghosts, of course. He had always been able to see them, those shades of his predecessors. They hounded him, jeered and poked. Thasha wondered how he managed to hold on to the least hint of sanity under such conditions. But had the ghosts' torments made him crazy, or was he able to sense them because he was already mad? Either way, it chilled her to know that the only other person aboard who saw the figures was herself.

'I never requested the *Chathrand*,' he said. 'Has the witch not told you? I was running inland when the Flikkermen tracked me down.'

Like everyone aboard, Thasha had heard the rumour, though not from Lady Oggosk. But with Rose it was always better not to tip one's hand. 'Why are you telling us this, Captain?' she asked.

'*Say it!*'

Rose flinched. It was another ghost, just above them on the quarterdeck. Thasha recognised the figure as Captain Kurlstaff: no other commander of the Great Ship dabbed pink paint on his fingernails. Thasha and Rose both looked at Kurlstaff: his tattered dress, his ancient pearls. He pointed a long white fingerbone at Rose.

'Say it!' hissed the shade again. 'Raise your sleeve and swear!'

Rose professed to despise Kurlstaff, called him pansy and tarboy-tickler, among uglier names. But Thasha knew he also put more stock in Kurlstaff's opinions than those of any of the other spirits.

'I am responsible for the well-being of this ship,' said Rose.

'Swear, you hairy red dog!' cried Kurlstaff.

Most reluctantly, Rose tugged his right sleeve up above the wrist. They all knew he bore the wolf-scar there: a burn identical to those carried by Pazel, Neeps, Thasha, Hercól, Bolutu – and Diadrelu, though hers they had only seen after her death. Rose held his arm up like a talisman.

'I didn't ask for *this* either, by the Night Gods,' he said, 'but it's burned too deep ever to heal. I'm stuck with it, stuck with you, to the last tack and beyond.' He was still looking at Kurlstaff. 'If a hopeless quest is to be the fate of Nilus Rose – why not? I'll swear. You'll see and be amazed, for I'll give the oath, live by it, and die by it if necessary. And it *will* be necessary – just look at these circus clowns. But I'll swear. You don't believe me, do you?'

'What's the leopard for?' asked Neeps.

'Shut up about the leopard! I hate the leopard!' Rose lunged forwards and swung the animal like a club. The youths jumped back. Rose dropped to his knees and smashed the leopard against the deck so violently that one of the glass eyes popped out and rolled away. 'I hate it! I hate it! And you ghouls also, you dead swindlers, transvestites, whoremongers, cheats! Why should I swear anything to you? After tonight I'll never see you again, unless we meet in the Pits!'

From within his cabin, Lady Oggosk gave a peremptory shriek: 'Nilus! That is undignified! Come here, I haven't finished with your shirt.'

The captain grew still. He hugged the leopard once more to his chest, staring at the astonished youths. 'Don't you dare be late,' he said.

When the door closed the others drifted forward along the portside rail, through the mad scramble of departure-less-fifteen-hours. The ghosts were still visible to Thasha but they kept a respectful distance. If she faced one of them directly, it bowed.

'Do you realise what he was telling us?' said Neeps. 'He wants to come along! Rose! And he didn't even stop to ask whether or not we're going through with it.'

'He should have asked,' said Pazel, 'because there's no mucking way we can. We'd never see the ship again. We'd never see other *humans* again. Besides, we'd draw all sorts of attention on that highway, just as we've done here. I'll bet Arunis has paid someone to keep watch for anything outlandish coming his way – human beings, for instance.'

Pazel's argument was met with silence. He was trying to convince himself as much as anyone, Thasha mused. They walked on towards the bow, dodging the busiest work areas. Neeps tried to take Marila's hand but she would not let him. Then out of nowhere, Bolutu rushed up and pointed excitedly at the quay.

'A snow heron! A snow heron has flown right into the city! It is a sacred bird, a blessing that comes in times of change. Look there to starboard; you will see it.'

A play of shadows in the lantern-light: then a huge, long-legged bird swept over the quay, its eight-foot wings beating slow and fragile. It was pure white, and by the lanterns' soft glow its unruly feathers were ghostly. With a raucous croak it alighted on the *Chathrand*'s forecastle, a few yards from the Goose-Girl figurehead. On the quay the dlömu stood staring, their work forgotten. The heron folded its wings and stood motionless, its back to the ship, as though it knew somehow that the eight hundred humans would do it no harm.

The bird's stillness was monumental. Thasha wanted to ask why the dlömu revered it so, but a part of her seemed to understand already. If it was an omen of change, then its stillness was the perfect opposite of what was to come. *Cherish this*, it might have said, *for when you move again it will be gone; you will have lost it for ever.*

'I have seen but one other snow heron in my life,' said Bolutu. 'It stood on the harbour wall as I sailed out of Masalym to cross the Nelluroq. They were rare even then, two centuries ago. Now I understand that years go by without a single sighting anywhere in the South.'

Thasha closed her eyes. An image had burst into her mind, sudden and unsought. A sky above a marsh, full of blowing confetti, living snow. *Thousands*, she thought, as the image sharpened, and the roar of their mingled calls echoed inside her. *I've walked among these birds in their thousands.*

Pazel's hand on her elbow brought her back. She opened her eyes, the vision gone. She gave him a frightened smile.

Pazel turned to Bolutu. 'Someone gave Rose a stuffed cat,' he said.

'A leopard,' said Bolutu, smiling. 'Of course. It was a gift from the Naval Commander of Masalym – an old fellow with a cere-monial post; he commands a fleet of sixteen hulks and derelicts. But it was a grand gesture all the same. By tradition a departing captain must hold the leopard until the last mooring line is cast off. Then he throws it ashore, and the well-wishers catch it, being most careful not to let it touch the earth. Good luck follows any who observe the rite; but if the creature so much as brushes the cobbles – disaster. And if the captain lets it be held for even an instant by another man aboard – well, that man will be his death.' He shrugged. 'Dlömic seafarers are as superstitious as any.'

'No wonder he barked at Haddismal,' said Neeps. 'But why is he so upset about the leopard?'

'I guess you haven't noticed,' said Marila, 'that he's terrified of cats.'

'All his life,' said Bolutu, nodding. 'That much I have gleaned from his exchanges with Lady Oggosk. It goes beyond Sniraga; he cannot abide cats of any sort. The *sicuñas* must have struck him as horrors from the Pits.'

Thasha glanced at Bolutu. 'You've lost your monk's hat,' she observed.

'It is only put away,' said Bolutu, a bit sadly. 'One day I may wear it again, if we indeed sail north together. But there is no Rinfaith here, Lady Thasha. Not south of the Ruling Sea, and not in my heart.'

A few sailors stopped their work and looked at him. 'That's a funny sort of faith, Brother Bolutu,' said Mr Fegin.

'I don't disagree,' said Bolutu, 'and yet I am bound to respect the Ninety Rules, and the second of these is the call to honesty. For twenty years my body was human. Now it has reverted to its old form, and I find my old, ancestral faith contending with my adopted one.'

'But the Gods are the Gods, all the same.'

'Are they?' asked Bolutu. 'We have no Gods here, Mr Fegin. And yet we know we are observed. The Watchers, we call them: those who do not intervene, do not speak, do not instruct. One day they will be our judges. But until then, they tell us absolutely nothing.'

'Well, that just beats everything,' said another sailor. 'What kind of Gods – or Watchers or what have you – refuse to tell you how to worship 'em?'

'The best kind,' said Bolutu, smiling, 'or so we are taught as children. There is no divine law given us, no rules, no scripture. What we are given is here, and here.' Bolutu tapped his forehead, then his heart. 'Wisdom, and an instinct for the good. It is to those things we must strive to be true. As for worship, what good has it ever done? In the Last Reckoning the Watchers will judge our deeds, not our praise of them, our flattery.'

'Deeds, eh?' said Fegin, turning back to his work. 'D'ye suppose they'll like what they see?'

Mr Bolutu looked down sadly, as if the same question had occurred to him. He walked away from the youths, trying for a closer view of the heron. The bird had not moved a feather. Thasha wondered if it would see them off at sunrise.

She drew a deep breath. 'We're really going, aren't we?' she said.

Pazel drew her close, rested his chin on her shoulder. 'Love you,' he whispered, so softly she could barely hear. Thasha wished suddenly to pull them all close, to tell them they mattered to her more than anything, more than their quest. She turned and kissed Pazel, felt his urgency, his hammering heart, and wondered just how long they had before dawn, and then Marila said, 'I'm with child,' and they all looked at her, speechless. The heron lifted off, as though it had come for just this information, and Neeps covered his face with his hands.

26

Trust

—◦◦◦—

In the dead of a moonless night in North-west Alifros, in the midst of the coldest spell of weather the Crownless Lands had seen in fifty years, two boats ran afoul of the same reef in the Straits of Simja. They were light, swift vessels; they had been shadowing each other with lamps extinguished; they were under orders to avoid a firefight. One was an Arquali Kestrel-class frigate, the other a Mzithrini *tirmel*. Neither boat could break free of the reef, and with the first light of dawn they became visible to one another. There was shockingly little distance between them.

On the Arquali boat, a certain ageing weapons officer found himself in possession of a full gun team, a fair shooting angle and a lit cigar, but rather less tranquillity of mind than the moment called for. His cigar served as a match; his cannon boomed; a 32-pound ball skipped over the water and shattered on a knob of exposed reef, just in front of the enemy ship. Coral exploded in fist-sized chunks; a Mzithrini sailor dropped, senseless, half over the forecastle rail. Before anyone could reach him the boat lurched on the incoming wave. The dazed man fell upon the reef; the weight of forty sailors rushing to portside shifted the boat's centre of gravity; on the next wave the boat pitched lethally in the man's direction, and with it the Third Sea War of Alifros began.

King Oshiram of Simja received the news in the wood behind the Winter Keep, a day's ride from the capital. The message, dashed off in a panic by his chancellor and delivered by a rider whose exhausted horse stood steaming beside him, flooded the king's mind like a swiftly darkening dream. Sudden and immense hostilities. The two Empires' fleets exchanging fire in the Narrow Sea. The Arqualis demanding access to Simja Harbour; Mzithrini battalions spotted on the beach at Cape Córistel. A plea for aid from Urnsfich, Simja's neighbour-island to the south, overrun by land forces already.

Whose forces? The king turned the parchment over, as though something might be scrawled on the back. Who were they being asked to help Urnsfich repel?

Aya Rin, what did it matter? He stepped back into the tent and drew the frost-stiffened flaps closed behind him. For a moment he succeeded in believing none of it, reducing the world to this canvas cocoon, where the loveliest woman who ever drew breath lay sleeping, naked, among furs and satins disordered by their lovemaking. Syrarys. The king fixed his eyes on one pale, perfect hand. The palm he had kissed and tasted rose water, the fingers that had enslaved him with a touch. Never again, never again, unless he went to her this minute – but that was out of the question. War had come. He crept forwards, ashamed of his trembling, and began to pull on his clothes.

Isiq had foreseen it: general war before the year was out. Day by day the old admiral's mind had grown sharper, his torn memories knitting together like muscle to bone, as though the tactical news Oshiram had been providing were a food for which he'd been starved. 'We no longer have months, Sire. We may not even have weeks. Sandor Ott wants panic in the Mzithrin: he wants them to look like superstitious fools. Scared of the Shaggat's return, accusing Arqual of treachery they cannot prove, striking at shadows. But Arunis only wants war, the sooner and fouler the better.'

'And my Kantri—'

'Her name is not Kantri, Sire. It is Syrarys, and she is no more yours than she ever was mine, or Sandor Ott's for that matter, though perhaps he trusts her still. It was Ott's wish that she poison me, but it was never Ott's wish that my Thasha die before she could marry.'

'You blame *her* for Thasha's death?' the king had cried, incredulous still.

Isiq had replied with devastating logic. Syrarys alone had handled the necklace that had strangled his girl. She had polished it with a salve from Arunis himself, before he cast away his disguise. And she had insisted that Thasha Isiq wear the necklace every day of her life. 'She is a servant of the sorcerer, Your Majesty,' said the admiral, 'and like him she has made fools of us all.'

The king stepped into his trousers, struggling not to make a sound. Her beauty like something flung at him. Like that high, crystal note at the end of the opera, the one you waited out before breathing. He had told Isiq he could not go through with it. Oh, the plan was good enough. Syrarys had to be removed from the capital, and quietly, without revealing to Ott's other spies that her true identity was known. And only with the king and his retinue gone from Simjalla Palace could Isiq himself hope to slip away into the city. *If the Arqualis find him now, if they learn that I have harboured their rogue admiral, a war hero prepared to denounce their treachery . . .*

Too late for regrets. He must do all he could to help Isiq escape, and certainly that meant drawing attention away from the palace. But to bring the woman here, to their special hideaway, to dine and hunt and carry on as if nothing had changed, to make love to her—

Isiq had cut him off with a gesture. 'Do it,' he'd said, turning away, and of course he'd been right. She had only to step out of her riding clothes and her king was there, ready for her, calling her darling, dearest one, travelling her body with the same tongue that would condemn her, surrendering to her hands. Pretending was easy; facing the truth might be lethal yet. He had (the king saw now with perfect clarity) never before been in love.

One by one he donned his rings. They'd made a game of this for weeks, her lips moistening his fingers, slowly, languorously, until the rings slid free. But where was his coronation ring, with its ruby the size of a grape? Somewhere among the bedclothes, or under the nightstand. Well, let it stay there. He flexed his fingers, and it occurred to him that a few hard blows with these jewelled hands would disfigure her for ever. Hideous thought! He had never struck a woman, nor even a man since his early youth. Better to do it through others, isn't it, Oshiram? *Drag that torturer out of retirement; it seems we haven't outgrown him. Do the sort of job my father used to ask of you, Mr Ghastly-whatever-you're-called, and don't limit yourself to her face. See that she's no longer a temptation for anyone, for me.*

Of course, he would give no such order. He was soft; he was a peacetime king. Gently, he drew the sheet over her breasts.

A moment later he stood outside, surrounded by his captains, the servants, the eager dogs. 'Ready me a horse,' he said, 'and a small escort, whoever's at hand. I ride for Simjalla at once.'

He gulped his tea, stole a flap of chewy lamb from the provisions tent. Wolfing the meat before his men like a savage, he heard her call to him. Then her face appeared between the folds of the tent.

'My lord, I was frightened,' she said, in that voice like a rain of music. 'I woke and didn't know where I was.'

The outline of a shoulder, through the rough canvas. She had not dressed. Her lips formed a fragile smile.

'Lady,' he said, 'that is one thing you have always known.'

Her smile grew. 'You tease me, my lord. And you are most unkind to leave me shivering.'

'I'll send someone to build you a fire. There must be coals in the brazier.'

'Won't you come back inside?'

'I cannot,' he said, swiftly turning his back. 'Go, now, cover yourself.'

'You are not hunting today, my lord?'

There it was in her voice: the first suspicion, the first hint of a change.

'I must go,' he said. 'You will be staying at the Winter Keep for a time.'

A silence, then: 'My Lord Oshiram, have you tired of me?'

Tired of her! The king's nails bit into his palms. 'Where is my mount, damn it all?' he shouted.

Syrarys forced out a laugh. 'I don't understand, my lord.'

'Don't you?'

A long silence. He would not look at her again, not ever. Then, as a guard barked a warning, something small and hard struck his back. He winced, knowing instantly what she had thrown. He stepped backwards until he saw it lying there, that gaudy ruby and golden band. His coronation ring.

He bent down stiffly. Was she watching? Were those eyes still on him, those lips still trembling with hope?

He put out his hand and touched the ring. But as he did so, a vision rose within his mind: Isiq's girl, gasping, writhing on the dais in that tarboy's arms, tearing at the necklace that was killing her.

The king withdrew his hand, leaving the ring where it lay. Then he stood and looked at her. No spell transformed her features, and yet she changed. The mask of love fell in pieces, hatred took hold. And as his boot ground the ring into the mud, he found himself looking at the ugliest face he had ever beheld.

'Feed her breakfast,' he said to his captains, 'and put her in chains.'

In Simjalla Palace, no one could speak of anything but war. The island was so far untouched, but few doubted that an attack would come. Warships of Arqual and the Mzithrin plied the Straits where the last war had ended; cannon fire lit up the night. Simja's own little navy was boxed into the bay, except for the half-dozen ships patrolling the coastlines, and who could say what had become of them?

Fear trickled into the palace by many paths. The cooks heard stories in the market: great Mzithrini Blodmels racing east over the Nelu Gila, bodies washed up on the Chereste beaches, a merchant vessel in flames. The blacksmith's cousin had heard that the

Arqualis were executing spies in Ormael, mounting heads on stakes. A vicious rumour spread that the king and his consort had not gone to the Winter Keep but into exile, abandoning Simja to its fate.

In the midst of this upheaval came a tragedy so small that it nearly passed unnoticed: the death of a schoolmaster. The old man had lived as a ward of the palace for thirty years, since the talking fever left him mute. He was polite but solitary, keeping mainly to his tiny room beside the library, and he died after dinner, in his sleep. As he had outlived his few friends, no particular ceremony was forthcoming. The king's own doctor, who had stopped in by chance with a bottle of cactus spirits for the king's lumbago, offered to prepare the corpse for burial at the Templar Clinic, where the poor of the city went to die.

A page was sent running; a coffin procured. At nine o'clock that evening, six palace guards bore the pine box into the shadowy courtyard and placed it on a donkey cart, driven by the doctor himself. The schoolmaster's departure from the palace drew the attention of no one but a tailor bird, flitting excitedly about the ramparts.

The road to the clinic was in poor repair. The doctor leaned back and put a hand on the coffin, as though to steady it. His fingers drummed briefly on the planks, unconsciously it appeared. His face was studiously blank.

Three blocks from the clinic he turned the animals down a narrow side street. It was one of the harder moments of his life. The doctor had seen Arquali torture first-hand, and with that tug of the reins he had become Arqual's enemy. He suppressed an urge to whip the donkeys into a trot.

The street ran south, into a decrepit quarter of the city near the port. Eventually it passed through a tunnel beneath a wider boulevard. It was a damp, shadowy stone tube, reeking of urine and mould. At its very centre the doctor glanced quickly around, stopped the cart, whispered a prayer. He reached back and freed the coffin's single latch.

The lid flew open, and Eberzam Isiq bolted upright. He wore a dark oilskin coat and black woollen cap: the outfit of a Simjan fisherman. Before the doctor could speak, he squirmed free of the coffin and leaped to the ground. When his feet struck the cobbles he snarled in pain.

'Careful, man!' hissed the doctor.

'Damn it all, my knee – never mind, never mind.' Isiq limped forwards and shook the doctor's hand. 'I owe my survival to you as much as to Oshiram,' he said. 'If we both live long enough I'll try to repay that debt. Now be gone, my friend.'

'I knew you'd recover,' said the doctor. 'I saw the fighter in your eyes. But Isiq, the gold—'

'Here,' said Isiq, patting a heavy pouch beneath his coat.

'And your medicine? The bloodroot tea?'

'I have everything. Go, go, Rin keep you.'

This time the man did whip the donkeys into a trot. Eberzam Isiq flattened himself against the slimy wall, watching them disappear. Two minutes, he told himself. Then the walk to the port, head down, eyes fixed. Neither too fast nor too slow. He felt for his weapons. Steel knuckles, hidden blades. This fight he would win for his murdered girl.

He rubbed his face and found it unfamiliar. Thick beard, no sideburns. Another layer of disguise. Oshiram was a good man, Isiq thought. He had done his best to grasp the danger to his island. But he was still an innocent, a civilian to his marrow. He could not imagine the extent to which the Secret Fist already controlled the streets of his capital. Ott's men had been at work in Simja for forty years. They had surely bought everyone who could be bought, killed many who could not be. And any spy trained in Etherhorde would have known Isiq at a glance.

He thought of the old schoolmaster, old but very much alive, spirited away last night to the same tower chamber where Isiq himself had convalesced. How long would they have to keep the poor fellow there?

He left the tunnel, wetting his boots in puddles he couldn't see.

His knee still hurt, and he wondered if the jump had done it lasting harm. *No more dramatics. You're an old man, you fool.*

Then the breeze struck his face, cold and clean off the harbour, and he smiled grimly. *Not as old as they took me for.*

He had memorised the route to the witch's house. Two blocks south to Vinegar Street. Four blocks east to the abandoned theatre, the Salty Lass, if one could believe it. Dismal, derelict streets, odours of bad wine and rancid cooking oil. Broken streetlamps, one still audibly leaking gas, loomed over him like the feelers of monstrous insects.

There were poor folk in the streets, but they barely spared him a glance. They rushed from door to door, bearing bundles, frowning and nodding to one another, exchanging a few whispered words. All so familiar. The Pellurids, before the Sugar War. The doomed settlers on Cape Córistel. Rukmast, before the Arquali retreat. The quiet of a people who have learned that disaster is coming, that they will not be spared.

It was because of this fugitive memory that he spotted the killer. A big fellow leaning in a doorway, too relaxed for the circumstances, and far too focused in the look he trained on Isiq. Twenty or twenty-five, and ox-strong to boot. Not one of Ott's men – he was far too obvious, too large and surly – but that did not mean he was harmless.

The man stepped out of the doorway, grinning a whiplash grin. Oh no, he was not harmless. He took a last long drag on a cigarette, flicked the butt into the street. Deathsmoke! Isiq could smell it ten yards off. He felt the ghost of his own addiction, like jaws closing on his brain. The big man stepped into his path.

'Sir—' began Isiq.

'You shout, and I'll cut a hole in you big enough to slide in a skillet,' said the man. 'What's in that pouch, eh? Nah, don't tell: just give it to me, give it here.'

Isiq put a hand on the pouch. A cry for help would make him the centre of attention, and that could prove as deadly as anything this man had in mind. The steel knuckles, he thought. Use them.

Right now. But what he said was, 'You're bigger than me.'

'Bigger? Mucking right I am, you rotten-arsed old dog.' The man took a firm hold on Isiq's shirt. 'You're about to bleed,' he said.

The reek of deathsmoke on the man! Isiq could almost taste it. He felt his blood responding, the sick happiness rising in his soul. 'Let go of my shirt,' he said.

The man must have heard the intended threat. He backhanded Isiq with casual brutality, looking almost bored. Then he put a hand on his own belt. A glint of metal there, below a well-worn handle.

Isiq squirmed, an old man's feeble struggle against the certainty of death. Then his elbow slashed up at the man's neck and the stiletto did its work, burying itself to the hilt in the soft flesh below the jaw, and the man fell forwards, eyes staring, lifeless. He kicked the corpse away, furious beyond reason. 'You bastard, you bastard. You didn't have to die.'

Then, like a bursting boil, the thought: *He might have more cigarettes.*

Isiq ran, fleeing the temptation more than the evidence of his deed. His elbow warm and sticky, his fingers cut trying to close the stiletto, his knee wrenched anew. Behind him, someone began to scream.

Go back. There's still time. Go back and search his pockets.

Where was that mucking theatre? Had they taken down the sign? He blundered on, limping, trying to keep to the shadows. People everywhere. The nearest recoiled, murmuring at his back. Already winded, he forced himself to run on. A second turn, a third. Why were there no empty streets?

Deathsmoke.

Put it out of your—

Deathsmoke.

He stopped, weak and wheezing, soaked with frigid sweat. If another addict passed him he would fight for the drug. Eyes on him everywhere. A shadow in a window, a mongrel dog across the street.

Isiq shuffled backwards, collided with a rubbish bin. There were rats, probably, rats before him and behind. They would remember him from the dungeon. They would smell the blood.

Look, look! the street was sighing. The decorated soldier! The leader of men! The one who thinks he can stop the war!

'Admiral?'

The voice was soft and circumspect.

'This way, sir, quickly.'

Precious Pitfire, it was the dog.

Isiq stumbled across the street. 'Don't stare, please,' said the dirty, shaggy creature.

'You're real?'

'Very much so. And we have a mutual friend.'

'I know you. Of course. You're the dog.'

'I suppose I can't argue with that.' The dog was looking left and right. 'The bird lost you in that tunnel; someone should have told him what to expect. Well, we can't stay here. Follow now, but not too close. And whatever you do, don't stare. It's your eyes that give us away to other men.'

He darted off down the street. The admiral drew a deep breath. Somehow the craving was gone. Strange allies, he thought. A street dog, a little tailor bird, a king. And one other, the strangest of all, perhaps, if only he made it to her door.

The dog, fortunately, had no wish to be discovered. He led Isiq through abandoned buildings, gaps in fences, grassy lots. The admiral's knee was on fire, but he kept moving, and the woken animal never left his sight. The row houses gave way to old, careworn cottages, and the sea-smell grew. Then suddenly they were passing through a gate into a dusty garden. Facing him was a little shoebox of a cottage with peeling paint. The door was shut and the window curtained, but from between them a spear of lamplight stabbed at the yard.

'Eberzam Isiq.'

The witch! He hadn't seen her, standing there in the darkness by the garden wall. Now she came towards him, until the spear of light touched her face. The bird was perfectly right: she was not ugly, not bent and shrivelled like Lady Oggosk. She was tall, and her eyes were dark and wild, and her voice had a resonance that tickled the ear. Dark hair cascaded to her elbows. A pretty witch: imagine that. All the same, he knew the moment was terribly fragile. She had spoken his name with fury.

'If we have met before you must forgive me,' he said. 'I have been ill. My memories were lost for months, and they are only slowly returning.'

'You would remember me,' said the woman. 'And never, ever tell me what I *must forgive*.'

'Very well,' said Isiq, standing his ground. 'All the same, I've heard the name "Suthinia" before, somewhere. And your face is vaguely familiar.'

The woman stared at him, unblinking. He could feel her rage like a flameless fire, a pit of live coals. Then she moved closer and he saw that she too carried a knife. It was naked in her hand.

'The face you know is my son's,' she said.

'Your son, madam? Did he serve in the Navy?'

She took another step, and now he knew she was in striking range. 'He served your bloodsucking Empire,' she said, 'after your marines burned our city to the ground. My son's an Ormali. So was I, for two decades.'

'No you weren't, my dear.'

Isiq whirled. A man ten years his junior stood behind him, just inside the gate. His face in shadow. His hand twirling a club.

'You tried, Suthee. Rin knows, you did try. Pitfire, one year you even canned fruit with the neighbours! But they never did let you forget you were foreign.'

'It wasn't the neighbours who ruined us,' said the woman. 'It was this one. Because of him, and his damned Doctor Chadfallow, my boy and my daughter are on the far side of the world. They're doing my job, hunting the sorcerer I was sent here to kill. They've gone to my home, and I'm stranded here in what's left of theirs. My name is Suthinia Sadralin Pathkendle.'

'Oh, come now, darlin'.' The man laughed softly. 'You don't have to keep the family name for *my* sake.'

'Gods below,' said Isiq. 'Pathkendle! It's you! Captain Gregory Path—'

The club moved so fast he never saw it. Isiq was down, flat, deafened in one ear. And the woman was kneeling, pinning his head between her knees, pressing the knife-point to his chest.

The dog gave a furious bark. 'Stop, stop!' it cried. 'You didn't mucking tell me you planned to kill him!'

'War's a dirty business, dog,' said Captain Gregory Pathkendle.

'You cut him, witch, and I'll bring every spy in Simjalla to your door. I'm not a killer, damn you!'

'I understand,' said the woman to the admiral, 'that you had Pazel flogged for his cheekiness. For calling the invasion an invasion, to your face. I hear his back was torn to ribbons.'

'Yes,' said Isiq.

'He admits it,' said Captain Gregory. 'Incredible.'

'I didn't order the flogging,' said Isiq. 'You're wrong about that. But I could have stopped it, yes. Rose would have done me that favour.'

'And Pazel's ejection from the ship?'

'My fault. My fault.'

'You sat in your stateroom, and let him be sold to the Flikker-men.'

'That's right.'

'You never thought about it.'

'My best friend was dying. And I was drugged.'

'Oh, drugged,' laughed Captain Gregory. 'With what, old man? Platinum brandy from the Westfirth?'

'With deathsmoke!' said the dog, padding in circles around the three of them. 'The Syrarys woman put it in his tea. The bird told me all about it.'

'Deathsmoke, is it?' said Gregory. He marched out of Isiq's sight and returned bearing a lamp, which he placed painfully close to Isiq's face. Then he took hold of Isiq's lower lip and pinched it outwards, beneath a calloused thumb. He squinted; then his face grew very still.

'He's an addict, Suthee, it's no lie.' He released Isiq's lip and stood up. 'The note said so, too. Perhaps it really did come from King Oshiram.'

'Of course it did, you clown,' snapped the woman. But the knife was still pressed to Isiq's chest. 'We are safer without him, no matter what he means to the monarch of Simja.'

'Safer, but weaker,' said Captain Gregory. 'We need him on that boat tomorrow. You know that.'

'How many Arquali betrayals do you have to see?' hissed Suthinia. 'Why wouldn't they use Isiq? How else could they ever dream of getting close to her?'

'To whom?' said Isiq.

'Shut up,' said the witch. 'Trust Admiral Isiq? Six years after the invasion, and still dripping blood? He could doom us in a heartbeat. He could be working for Sandor Ott.'

At the sound of Ott's name Isiq lost all control. He lashed out, one steel-knuckled hand smacking the knife away from his chest, the other catching Gregory Pathkendle in the jaw. The woman fought him but he was not to be stopped. Before he knew it he was on his feet again, standing over them, his own knife drawn and raised.

'You dare,' he said, 'after that man killed my two angels, my darling Thasha, my wife.'

Suthinia and Gregory looked up at him sharply.

'I know it was Arunis!' roared Isiq. 'But it was Ott who built the trap called the Great Peace – built it around them, required them to die! And you *dare* suggest I serve him! I would sooner serve the maggot-haired hags in the Ninth Pit of Damnation! As for you two—'

'Isiq, Isiq!' cried Captain Gregory, his tone suddenly changed. They were both gesturing, pleading. 'We had to know,' said Suthinia.

'Know what, damn you? That I did not serve that fiend of a

spymaster, that creature who calls himself a patriot?'

'You were a patriot, too,' said Gregory, 'a famous one, same as I used to be. That's right, man, we *had* to be sure, before we told you they're alive.'

Isiq looked from one to the other. 'Who?' he whispered. 'Who are *they*?'

Suddenly the tailor bird appeared. He whirled about them, shrilling: 'Get inside, inside! A posse of men is approaching! They're at the corner of the street!'

Seconds later, Isiq found himself crouched in the cottage, the door barred and the lamp extinguished, the bird hopping ecstatically about on his shoulders, the dog still as stone beside his boots. Footsteps rang in the alley; gruff voices murmured. Isiq's knee was in agony but he did not make a sound.

Then he felt the witch's hand. Gently, it found his throbbing knee and remained there, cool and almost weightless. And to Isiq's amazement the pain began to subside.

The footsteps faded, the voices trailed away. Finally a match flared in the darkness. Captain Gregory was lighting a pipe.

'Have a pull, Admiral?'

Isiq shook his head firmly.

'Relax, man, it's only tobacco. Etherhorde greenleaf, the smuggler's friend.'

'Do be quiet, Gregory,' said Suthinia. Isiq looked up and met her great dark eyes.

'*They*,' she said, 'are two women who will change this world. The first is your Empress, Maisa of Arqual, the one to whom you swore allegiance long before Ott put the usurper Magad the Fifth upon the throne. We will go to her tomorrow, and together we will try to stop this idiot's war.'

'Maisa? Maisa *lives*? Gods below, where is she?'

'A place no Empress should be caught dead in,' chuckled Gregory.

'The other woman,' said Suthinia, 'is the one I've been waiting for, all these years. When she came at last I did not know her, but

I know her now. She is the hope of Alifros, and the one my boy, it seems, can't live without. I'm speaking of your daughter, Admiral. Thasha Isiq is alive.'

The tears struck faster than Gregory's club. He choked, and sat down hard, and the witch's arm went around his shoulders. They were arguing (husband, wife, dog) about how Suthinia had broken the news, how she might have done it better. Isiq scarcely noticed. Before his eyes the tailor bird was flitting in the darkness, Don't cry Isiq, she'll find you, she'll fly home somehow, the young are very strong. He wept, and felt the call to arms within him, and the warmth of a woman's touch, and the swish, swish of angels' wings against his face.

27

On the Hunt

6 Modobrin 941
235th day from Etherhorde

The terrible choice, stay or go, haunted many in what remained of the night. For some, deciding was the whole struggle; others reached a decision but had to argue, plead, even fight with their fists to defend it. There were the needs of the *Chathrand* to consider, the calculations of her officers and spies, the doubt as to whether anyone who left the ship would ever see her again and the ability of a panicked Masalym to find steeds, saddles, boots. Against all of that, a mystery: the threat to the world posed by one mage and one small black sphere. When the Upper Gate of the city opened at last and the party rode out upon the still-dark plain, its composition was a surprise to just about everyone.

Lord Taliktrum was no exception. From atop the gate's stone arch he watched them emerging: three Turachs, eight dlömic warriors, the latter on the catlike *sicuñas* rather than horses. Lean, swift dogs spilling about them, visibly eager for the hunt to begin. Next came the allies: Pazel and Neeps sharing one horse, Thasha and Hercól on mounts of their own. The youths looked exhausted already, as though they had never gone to sleep. Big Skip Sunderling bounced along awkwardly behind them, a sailor on horseback. The shock on his face made it clear that no one had foreseen his inclusion less than Big Skip himself.

Two pack horses, then Ibjen and Bolutu. And what was this? The *sfvantskors*, Pazel's sister and her two comrades – prisoners no longer, but still under the Arqualis' watchful gaze.

The young lord tasted bile at the sight of the next rider: Alyash. He wore a look of foul displeasure. Sandor Ott's curious weapon, the thing called a pistol, was strapped to his leg. Beside him rode the elder tarboy, Dastu. *Ott's servants, both*, mused Taliktrum. *He didn't dare leave the* Chathrand, *but he's wise enough to realise that the Nilstone, even from here, could threaten his beloved Arqual. He's forced them to go in his stead. They'll hate him for that, if they've any wisdom of their own.*

There were yet two more in the party, though they might easily have been overlooked. They rode on the withers of the pack animals, holding tight, facing forwards: Ensyl – Taliktrum should have expected to see her among the giants, but also—

'Skies of fire!'

Myett. Taliktrum's hands tightened to fists. What possible excuse? Had *she* been hounded out by worshippers, by vicious expectation?

An outrage, that's what it was. Ride away with the humans, to the Pits with the clan. And he could only watch them go. The woman who had loved his aunt, and the woman who had loved him. Indeed, the *only* such woman, apart from the mother who had died in his infancy – and the aunt herself.

They were forty feet gone, then sixty, then as far as a giant could throw a stone. Something overcame him, and he dived on his swallow-wings and flew with all his strength, needing to touch her, command her, speak some word of fury or desire.

With five yards to go he swerved away. Coward, weakling! Who was he to question Myett? On what authority? Moral, rational, the law of the clan? He was nothing, he was far less than nothing. He was an ixchel alone.

'No sign of the great Captain Rose,' grumbled Neeps. 'After all his rage and noise and don't-you-be-lates. I wonder if he meant a single word.'

Pazel answered with stuporous grunt.

'Even this morning he acted like he was getting ready to come with us,' Neeps went on. 'And it didn't seem like a lie. Maybe he couldn't bear to leave Oggosk, in the end. Do you think she really could be his mother?'

Pazel shrugged.

'You're not going to speak to me all the way to the mountain, are you?' said Neeps.

'Doubt it,' muttered Pazel.

They were still in darkness, though the tops of the mountains had begun to glow. The 'highway' that ran through Masalym's Inner Dominion, from the city to the mountain pass, was really no more than a wide footpath, hugging the left bank of the meandering Maî. Fog blanketed the river, snagged on the reeds where birds were chattering, spilled here and there over the path, so that the horse's legs became stirring spoons. Already the city lay an hour behind.

'You heard what I told Marila,' said Neeps. 'I said I'd stay behind. *Credek*, Pazel, I tried all night to convince her.'

Pazel waved a beetle from the horse's neck. He was glad he was riding in front, where there was no need to look Neeps in the eye.

'She wouldn't let me stay,' Neeps pleaded.

'Did you ever make her believe you *wanted* to?'

That shut him up. Pazel felt a twinge of guilt for not wanting to hear Neeps talk any more. But why should he, after a whole night lying awake, suffering for both of them, furious that they'd let it happen *now*.

'When was it, Neeps?' he said at last, trying and failing to keep the bitterness from his voice. 'That night you almost killed Thasha, while I was on Bramian?'

'Yes,' said Neeps. 'That was the first time.'

'The first time. Pitfire. Were there many?'

'We tried to be careful,' said Neeps.

Pazel bit his tongue. He was thinking how easily a jab with either elbow would knock his friend to the ground.

'Those storms on the Ruling Sea,' Neeps was saying. 'We really thought we were going to die. And the mutiny, the rats … and then we woke up in the ixchels' blary pen.'

'Why didn't you just tell me?'

'What, from in there? Shouting through the window? Or afterwards, you mean? "Listen, mate, I'm sorry Thasha's taken up with that grinning bastard Fulbreech, but you'll be glad to know that I'm—" No, we couldn't have done that to you. And by then it was too late. Probably.'

'But Gods *damn* it, you're stupid! Both of you.'

He'd spoken too loudly; Thasha's glance shamed them both into silence. For at least half a minute.

'You know what I think?' said Neeps.

'I never have yet.'

'I think it could have happened to you and Thasha.'

Half a dozen retorts occurred to Pazel instantly – and melted on his tongue, one after another. 'Let's say that were true,' he managed at last. 'So what?'

'So try thanking your stars,' said Neeps, 'instead of going on like Mother Modesty about the two of us.'

This time the silence lasted a good mile as they trotted down the dusty trail, past the fisher-folk's mud huts, the trees with their limbs dangling low over the water. Pazel thought he smelled lemon trees. But he had yet to see a lemon or anything like it in the South.

'Neeps,' he said at last, 'I'm sorry. You're right.'

After a moment, Neeps said, 'So are you.'

'What did you say to Marila, just before we left the ship? When you took her hand and ran off towards the Silver Stair?'

'You mean Thasha hasn't told you?'

'Told me what?'

Neeps actually managed a laugh. 'Pazel, Marila and I had already talked right through the blary night. We didn't leave the stateroom to talk. We went straight to Captain Rose and asked him to marry us. And he did.'

*

An hour later the whole western range was bathed in sunlight. There were vineyards here, and pear trees, and herds of sheep and goats and *birthigs* that scattered at their approach. Lamps passed from window to window in the waking farmhouses. Dogs appeared out of nowhere, challenged the hunting dogs briefly, changed their minds. The land was as peaceful as Masalym had been chaotic.

Suddenly Cayer Vispek cried out a warning: dust clouds behind them, and faintly, the pounding of hooves. Someone was giving chase.

The soldiers raised spears and halberds. Pazel's hand went instinctively to the sword at his belt, though he knew nothing about fighting on horseback. Ensyl stood up on her horse and studied the road through the monocular scope that had belonged to her dead mistress. 'It is just one rider,' she said. 'A dlömu, coming fast.' Then she lowered the scope and looked at them, amazed. 'It's Counsellor Vadu,' she said.

He was dressed in the same fine armour he had worn at the welcome ceremony, the gold breastplate gleaming in the early sun. He rode with a great battle axe lashed sidelong across his back, and on his belt hung the shattered Plazic Blade. He galloped right up to the travellers, then reined in his horse.

'If you think to turn us back,' said Hercól by way of greeting, 'you have made a worthless trip. Unless it be that the sorcerer is found.'

Vadu glared at Hercól as he caught his breath. 'The mage is not found,' he said at last, 'but the city is calming under Olik's stewardship. And I ... I will not sit and wait for death at the hands of the White Raven.'

'She will forgive nothing short of the Nilstone's return,' said Bolutu, 'and that you cannot provide. We are not setting out to wrest the Stone from one sorcerer only to hand it over to his ally. Go your own way, Vadu. Or ride with us to Garal Crossing, and then turn east on the Coast Road and follow the Issár into exile. But do not seek to thwart our mission.'

The soldiers began to grumble ominously: whatever the chaos

in Masalym, Vadu had been their commander for years, and now this strange dlömu, who had come on the ship with the mutant *tol-chenni*, was trying to dismiss him like a page.

'I say he's *more* than just welcome,' said one *sicuña*-rider. 'I say that if anyone's to lead this expedition, it's Counsellor Vadu.'

The other soldiers shouted, 'Hear, hear! Vadu!'

A sword whistled from its sheath. Hercól raised Ildraquin before him, sidelong, and the men stopped their cheering at the sight of the black blade. 'Olik entrusted this mission to me,' said Hercól, 'and my oath binds me to the cause as well. I cannot follow this man, who ordered regicide, and helped Arunis gain the Nilstone to begin with.'

Everyone went sharply rigid. The Turachs nudged their mounts away from the dlömu; the *sfvantskors* watched the others like wolves tensed to spring. But the dlömic soldiers were all looking at Vadu's Plazic knife, still sheathed upon his belt. 'You *can't* fight him,' muttered one. 'Don't try, if this mission means anything to you at all.'

'Counsellor,' said Hercól, 'will you depart in peace?'

Vadu's face contorted. His head began to bob, more violently than Pazel had ever seen, and suddenly he realised that it was not a mere habit but an affliction, involuntary, perhaps even painful. The counsellor's eyes filled with rage; his limbs shook, and his hand went slowly to the Plazic Blade. Muscles straining, he drew the blade a fraction of an inch from its sheath. The *sicuñas* crouched, hissing, and the horses of several warriors bolted in fear, deaf to their riders' cries. Pazel gasped and clutched at his chest. That poisonous feeling. That black energy that poured like heat from the body of the demonic reptile, the eguar: it was there, alive in Vadu's blade. He could almost hear the creature's agonising language, which his Gift had forced him to learn.

With a smooth motion Hercól dismounted, never lowering Ildraquin, and walked towards Vadu's prancing steed. The counsellor drew his weapon fully, and Pazel saw that it was no more than a stump upon the hilt. But was there something else there? A pale ghost of a knife, maybe, where the old blade had been?

'I can kill you with a word,' snarled Vadu, his head bobbing, snapping, his face twitching like an addict deprived of his death-smoke.

Hercól stood at his knee. Slowly he lowered Ildraquin towards the man – and then, with blinding speed, turned the blade about and offered its hilt to the counsellor.

'*No!*' shouted the youths together. But it was done: Vadu snatched the sword from Hercól with his free hand. And cried aloud.

It was a different sort of cry: not tortured, but rather the cry of one suddenly released from torture. He sheathed the ghostly knife and took his hand from the hilt. Then he pressed the blade of Ildraquin to his forehead and held it there, eyes closed. Slowly his jerking and twitching ceased. The sword slipped from his grasp, and Hercól caught it as it fell.

Vadu looked down at him, and his face was serene, almost aglow, like the face of one clinging to a marvellous dream. But even as they watched him the glow faded, and something of his strained, proud look came back to him.

'Mercy of the stars,' he said. 'I was rid of it. For a moment I was free. That is a sword from Kingdom Dafvniana.'

Hercól polished the blade on his arm. 'The smiths who made her named her Ildraquin, Earthblood, for it is said that she was forged in a cavern deep in the heart of the world. But King Bectur, delivered from enchantment by her touch, called her Curse-Cleaver, and that name too is well deserved.'

'My curse is too strong, however,' said Vadu. 'The sword cannot free me from the curse of my own Plazic Blade – but time will, if only I can remain alive. Listen to me, before the knife seals my tongue again! The Blades have made monsters of us, and a night-mare of Bali Adro. Through all my life I've watched them poison us with power. Olik told you that they are rotting away. Did he tell you that we who carry them rejoice in our hearts? For we *are* slaves to them, though they make us masters of other men. They whisper to our savage minds, even as they break our bodies. What happens to the Blades, you see, happens also to those who carry them. When they wither, we scream in pain. When they shatter, we die. Many have died this way already: my commander in Orbilesc swept an army of Thüls over a cliff with a sweep of his arm, and we all heard the knife break, and he fell down dead. That is how the knife came to me – a last, loathsome inch. I am a small man to own such a thing, or be owned by it. But I mean to survive it. When only the hilt remains, I shall be able to toss it away. Until then I must resist the urge to use it, for any but the smallest deeds.'

'Better no deeds at all,' said Cayer Vispek. 'That is a devil's tool.'

Vadu's eyes flashed at the elder *sfvantskor*. But there was struggle in them still, and when they turned to Hercól they were beseeching.

'Pazel,' said Neda in Mzithrini, 'tell the Tholjassan to drive this man away. He will bring us all to grief.'

'I can see by the woman's face what she wishes,' said Vadu. 'Do not send me off! I tell you I mean to survive, but there is more: I wish to see my people, my country, survive. Do you understand what I have witnessed, what I have done? And in another year or two the horror must end, for all the Blades will have melted. Our insanity will lift, and Bali Adro can start to heal the world it has profaned. I live for that day. I cannot bear to see the harm renewed by something even worse. I rode out to help, not hinder you.'

Hercól studied him carefully. 'Then ride, and be welcome,' he said at last, 'but guard your soul, man of Masalym. It is not free yet.'

As the track moved away from the river it grew into something like a proper road, running between fields neatly laid out, and sturdy brick farmhouses with smoke rising from their chimneys. They rode faster here; the smallest of the hunting dogs had to be picked up and carried. At midday they did not pause for a meal but ate riding; Olik had advised them to cross the open farmland as swiftly as possible, and to rest where the track entered the riverbank forest called the Ragwood, where the trees would hide them. Pazel found it hard to imagine anyone watching from the

Chalice of the Maî. But there were nearer peaks and, for all he knew, villages scattered among them, watching the curious procession along the valley floor.

In the hottest hour of the day they rode through a plain of tall red grass, dotted by great solitary trees and swarming with a kind of hopping insect that rose in clouds at their approach with a sound like sizzling meat. The horses shied and the *sicuñas* growled. Pazel did not understand their distress until one of the insects landed on his arm. It jumped away instantly, but as it did so he felt a shock, like the kind the ironwork on the *Chathrand* could give you during an electrical storm.

'*Chúun*-crickets,' said Bolutu. 'We have them in Istolym as well. By autumn there will be millions, and they will have sucked all the sap from the *chúun*-grass, and those little shocks you feel will set it all ablaze.'

'What happens then?' asked Pazel.

'They all die,' said Bolutu, 'and the plain burns down to stubble – only those great oaks can live through the blaze. Then there are no more crickets until their eggs hatch underground the next summer. It is the way of things. They flourish, they perish, they return.'

The company rode on, and the little shocks were many before they left the *chúun*-grass behind. An hour later they reached Garal Crossing, where the Coast Road bisected their own. The surface of the Coast Road was heavily rutted and dusty, as though some great host had passed over it, but on their own road the signs of passage were few. By the time they reached the Ragwood the horses were winded, and the *sicuñas* lifted their paws and licked at them unhappily. Pazel saw Jalantri dismount quickly and hurry to Neda's horse before she could do the same. 'Your blisters,' he said, reaching for her boot.

'They are nothing,' said Neda quickly, drawing her foot away.

'Not so. I saw them when you dressed. Come, I'll treat them before you—'

'Jalantri,' said Vispek softly, 'your sister will ask for aid when she requires it.'

Jalantri looked at the ground, abashed. Then he noticed Pazel watching and swept past him, tugging his horse by the bit.

'These animals need water,' said Vadu to Hercól. 'We will take them down to the Maî and let them wade. Come, my *Masalyndar*.'

The dlömic soldiers went eagerly with Vadu. Caycr Vispek watched them carefully, then turned to Hercól. 'They think much of him,' he said. 'He must have had some merit as a commander, once. But I fear they may scheme in private.'

Hercól nodded slowly. 'That is likely, Cayer. But not, I think, if you go with them.'

Vispek looked rather amused. 'Come, Jalantri,' he said at last. The two men rose and started down to the river's edge.

'Are we to warm no food before nightfall?' asked Ibjen.

'My lad,' said Hercól, smiling in turn, 'we may warm no food before we reach the shores of Ilvaspar. Go with the *sfvantskors*, Ibjen – that will make their errand less obvious to Vadu.'

A short distance away, Neda sat and pulled off her boots. She gestured at the departing dlömu. 'He is just boy,' she said. 'Not fighter, no good for anything. Why he coming?'

'Because Prince Olik wants him to,' said Thasha, bending low to comb the dust from her hair, 'and Ibjen's sworn to do whatever the prince asks, to regain his trust. Everything short of fighting, I mean. Anyway, Ibjen's not useless. He's an excellent swimmer.'

Neda looked at her wryly. 'Good. Swimming on mountaintop. Very helpful.'

'There's a lake up there,' said Thasha, 'and another river beyond it.'

Neda said nothing. Pazel sat down close to her. So familiar, and so strange: Neda rubbing her sore feet. Huge, hard feet, but still hers, still his sister's. In their native tongue, Pazel said, 'Olik trusts him. That's the real reason he's along.'

Neda answered in Mzithrini. 'More than he trusts the soldiers, you mean? Well, that is something. If they desert us, we'll still need a dlömu to talk to the villagers.'

'Tell me something,' said Pazel. 'Why did you join this hunt? The three of you, I mean?'

'That should be obvious,' said Neda. 'The prince gave us our liberty, and we didn't want to lose it again. We thought of staying in the Masalym, but it is no place for human beings. And we still could not take the *Chathrand*.'

'Is that the only reason? Your only reason?'

Neda looked at him, and he knew she would admit to nothing more.

'Why won't you talk to me in Ormali?' he said.

Neda's face was clouded. 'The language of Ormael is Arquali, now,' she said. 'You know what happens when the Empire takes a prize. It's been almost six years since the invasion. Give it twelve, and everything will be in Arquali. Laws, trade, schoolbooks. Children will be whipped by their teachers if they speak the old tongue.'

'It won't go that far,' said Pazel.

'Says the boy from the Arquali ship, with the Arquali friends, the Arquali girl he worships, even though her father—' Neda broke off, her eyes blazing at him. 'I don't live in the past,' she said.

The Ragwood was long and somewhat empty, the underbrush thinned out by grazing animals. They passed through it swiftly, grateful for the shade and the cover. They saw a few dlömu cutting lumber in a clearing, a herd of milk-white buffalo wallowing in a pond. Then Big Skip gave a start that nearly toppled him from his horse. He pointed: naked figures, human figures, were running crouched through the trees. The dogs raced towards them, baying. Wild with terror, the figures made for the deeper woods. A few of the soldiers laughed, but fell silent when they glanced at Vadu.

'Yes,' said the counsellor, 'there are still *tol-chenni* in our Inner Dominion. They raid crops, steal chickens. But they are dying fast.'

'Your dogs look mighty used to chasing 'em,' said Big Skip.

Vadu shrugged. 'A dog will chase any animal that runs.'

They did not stop again in the Ragwood, but the sun was setting nonetheless before they reached its far end. Just beyond the last trees a smaller river poured into the Maî, cutting straight across their path. It was spanned by a battered wooden bridge. A stone fortress rose on the near side, and as they drew close, soldiers with torches began to emerge. They were known to their comrades and greeted with some affection. But like all dlömu they could not help but stare at the humans.

'His Highness sent a scout ahead of you,' said their commanding officer. 'We know you ride in haste. We have no *sicuñas* here, but you're to leave any horse that's lagging and take one of ours in its stead.'

'My own suffers,' said Vadu. 'I had ground to make up, and rode him hard. But I count nearly twenty of you – why so many, Captain, here at the Maîbranch? Half should be guarding Thistle Chase.'

'Counsellor, where have you been?' said the other. 'Thistle was abandoned before Midwinter's Day. The farmers had had enough of raids.'

'*Tol-chenni* raids?' asked Ibjen.

The soldiers laughed uneasily. '*Tol-chenni!*' said their captain. 'You think our countrymen would take fright at *them*? No, boy, I'm speaking of hrathmog warriors. Barrel-chested, long-limbed brutes, sleek-furred, teeth like knives. They're getting bold, Counsellor Vadu. They've been seen walking right out in the open, on this plain. They've slaughtered animals, poisoned wells. And they killed old Standru and burned his house and holdings, away there across the Maî. His kin had moved closer to Masalym already; they'd heard the night drums and the caterwauling. But Standru wouldn't go. He said his land was part of the Dominion and he'd been born there, and wouldn't leave it to hrathmogs.'

'They put his head on a stake,' said another soldier. 'And when they saw it, the last families south of the Maîbranch locked up their homes and fled.'

Vadu looked from one soldier to the next. 'Do you mean that Masalym's Dominion ... ends *here*?'

'Unless the city can spare enough men to hold the Chase,' said the officer, 'but even then I doubt the farmers would return.'

'Captain,' said Hercól, 'did no other riders – other human beings – pass over this bridge?'

The officer looked doubtfully at Hercól.

'Answer him!' snapped Vadu. 'He is a natural being like yourself.'

'No one has passed this way,' said the captain. 'No one crosses the bridge any more, save the brave few who still ride out hunting, and they do not go far. I do not think the hrathmogs will challenge a group of your size, but you must post watches all the same.'

They brought Vadu a fresh horse, and the company continued. Vadu was clearly shaken by the news. Pazel wondered if it was the cursed Blade or the countless problems in Masalym itself that had kept him from knowing what had befallen his city's territories.

Ensyl, who was riding for a spell with the tarboys, looked up at the mountain ahead. 'If they didn't use the road, how did they get up there?' she asked. 'But of course, we don't even know who *is* there. If Arunis somehow learned what Ildraquin can do—'

'Then he'll have sent Fulbreech alone,' said Pazel, 'and we'll have played right into his hands, and probably won't ever catch him. But I don't think that's what's happening. If Arunis wanted us to chase after Fulbreech, he wouldn't have sent him that far away.'

'Why not?' said Neeps.

'Because we might not have believed he could have travelled so far,' said Pazel. 'Olik himself said it couldn't be done. No, if Arunis wanted us to chase after Fulbreech, he'd have sent the rotter just far enough away to entice us, and given him a fast horse so he could stay ahead.'

'Then why in Pitfire are they just sitting up there?' Neeps asked.

'If luck's with us?' said Pazel. 'Because Arunis thinks he's safe, and has crept into some shack or cave to keep up his experiments with the Nilstone.'

Ensyl laughed grimly. 'If luck is with us,' she said.

They rode on. Ensyl wanted to know about their time in the Conservatory, and the tarboys related a version of the tale, interrupting and correcting one another, and succeeded in becoming irritable again. But as they grumbled to a conclusion, a thought struck Pazel with an electric jolt.

'Pitfire,' he said, 'I've got it, I understand. Neeps, what's *wrong* with us?' He spurred the horse faster, catching up with Thasha and Hercól. 'The idiot,' he said. 'Arunis' *tol-chenni*, the one he took from the lab. He's going to use the idiot to control the Stone.'

They all looked at him, startled. 'Why do you say so?' asked Myett, who was riding on Hercól's shoulder.

'The birdwatchers – the physicians in the asylum – they were upset when he took that particular *tol-chenni*. They said he was special—'

'By the Night Gods!' Hercól exploded. '*I* am the fool in question! I should wear motley in a circus tent! The technicians said he was *blind to danger*. That he would swallow nails, walk off a cliff or into a fireplace.'

Thasha raised a hand to her cheek. '*Aya Rin*. He's fearless. Unnaturally fearless.'

'And the Nilstone kills through fear,' said Pazel, 'but it won't kill that *tol-chenni*, will it? Arunis doesn't have to control the Nilstone any more. He's found a puppet to do it for him. That's what he was trying to do all along, with those men he drove to suicide. Once he gets control of the idiot's mind—'

'He's won,' said Ensyl.

Hercól's face darkened. 'He will have won only when all those who oppose him lie dead and cold.'

And Pazel thought: *Arunis would agree with you there.*

On they went into the darkness – slowly, with no lamps lit. Then the moon began to shine over the eastern hills, and by its light they quickened their pace. They moved through smaller woods, crossed other streams, passed the wreckage of country homes looted and abandoned. The night remained warm and hazy at first, but some three hours beyond the Ragwood they climbed the first foothill onto a plateau of leathery grass and small wizened conifers, and here a chill wind was blowing. They broke out heavier coats. Off to their left the Maî rumbled softly in its gorge.

'There's shelter ahead, Stanapeth,' said Alyash, drawing up beside Hercól. He was pointing to a spot a few miles above them: a bluff where three buildings shone in the moonlight. Two were ruined, but the third, a barn maybe, appeared intact.

Hercól nodded. 'If they are empty, we might sleep there,' he said. 'Let us go and find out.'

Up they climbed, the horses stumbling over the ruts and stones. The buildings were all that was left of yet another farm: the buildings, and many acres of hacked-off stumps the remains of an orchard or a woodlot. The soldiers fanned cautiously through the farmyard, stalked through the ruined home and storehouse with halberds levelled. They met with no worse than bats and a pair of foxes, but they posted watches at the perimeter all the same.

The floor of the barn was dry, and its doors were still on their hinges. It was an ample structure, and the beams were solid enough to serve as hitching posts for the animals. The horses applied themselves to their feedbags, but the *sicuñas* were turned out into the night and slunk away noiselessly, looking more like giant cats than ever.

'It's cold already,' said Big Skip. 'Let's sweep a spot clear in the barn and have a fire. In that old shell the smoke won't bother us. And some hot food would see us quicker up that mountain tomorrow.'

Hercól looked uneasy. 'A small fire, then,' he said at last, 'but well inside, away from the doors and windows.'

There was plenty to burn scattered about the farmyard, and soon a cheerful blaze was crackling on the earthen floor. They cooked yams and onions and salted beef, a hasty stew. The dlömu wanted to add dried *pori* fish to the pot but Vadu forbade it. 'You men know as well as I that the smell of *pori*, fresh or dried, can carry twenty miles,' he said sternly. 'And hrathmogs have sharp noses, and sharper teeth.'

Pazel found himself caught between hunger and exhaustion.

Hunger prevailed, barely, but he was nodding over his bowl before he could empty it. Thasha put a finger under his chin and lifted.

'When we find Fulbreech,' she said, 'don't attack him. Don't do anything.'

'I can't promise that,' mumbled Pazel.

'You mean you won't,' she said. 'For Rin's sake, he was Ott's man, and Ott doesn't use anyone who isn't trained. Fulbreech could cut you wide open, and you'd never see the knife. He let you hit him on the quarterdeck because he thought a black eye would make me take his side against you.' She put her hand on his ankle. 'Promise me you won't be a fool.'

When Pazel shrugged, her hand squeezed like a tourniquet. 'I'm not joking,' she said.

'What about you?' he said, pretending his foot wasn't going numb. 'What will you do when you see him?'

Thasha looked at him steadily. 'I don't care about Fulbreech any more. But when we find Arunis, I'm going to be the one.'

'The one?'

'To kill him. Don't try to stop me.'

'I'm blary fortunate,' he said, 'that you're around to keep me from being a fool.'

Thasha's eyes were wild in the firelight, and her face grew hard and angry. Pazel met her gaze, hoping his own face looked merely bemused. Then all at once Thasha laughed and relaxed her grip. 'You're insufferable,' she said.

But they both knew he'd won again. Not the argument, but the struggle to keep her from vanishing into that transformed state, that furious intensity where her visions came and he ceased to know her. Late in the night he woke to find her snuggled against him, feet icy, lips warm, the blanket that had felt too small for him alone somehow stretched to encompass them both.

It felt like mere minutes later when someone began prodding his stomach. 'Get up, get up now, we're leaving.'

Pazel started; Thasha was still in his arms. 'Leaving?' he said. 'It's pitch dark.'

Thasha groaned and clung to him. Then an oil lamp sputtered to life, and he snapped fully awake.

'Sorry, turtle doves,' said Neda, turning her back.

Pazel and Thasha sat up, blinking. From across the barn Pazel caught Jalantri staring at them with a strange look of outrage. Then he and Neda moved out of the barn.

Pazel and Thasha followed, and found the others already outside. At the edge of the yard some commotion was underway. Pazel heard a soft *clink-clink*. Moving closer, Pazel saw that everyone was looking at one of the *sicuñas*, twenty feet away beside a mound of dry brush, eating something. When Neda took a step in the creature's direction, it growled.

Then Vadu took the lamp and approached the *sicuña*, whispering to it softly. When the light reached it Pazel's stomach lurched. The *sicuña* was devouring a manlike creature. It was fur-covered and enormously muscled; its face was broad and flat like a bulldog's, and a shield still hung from one limp arm. The *sicuña* had clearly caught it by the neck, which was torn wide open. The sound Pazel had heard was the creature's shirt of mail, lifting as the *sicuña* ate.

'Hrathmog,' said Vadu. 'That fire was a mistake, and we must leave at once. *Sicuñas* kill in silence, but the creature will be missed by the rest of its band, and then they will come in force.'

'Even without this danger I should have been obliged to wake you,' said Hercól. 'Ildraquin has just spoken to me: Fulbreech is moving. Indeed, he is rushing away, more quickly than we can climb the mountain, at least until dawn.'

They packed swiftly, fumbling with bags and bridles. No one talked, everyone was cold, dawn was still far off. All the while Pazel's ears strained for the first sound of attackers swarming out of the night.

The next hours were miserable. Summer might be at her peak in the city they had left behind but here frost slicked the trail, and the cold wind gnawed at them. The horses were skittish but could move no faster than a walk. The *sicuñas* fared better, gliding on their broad, soft feet, growling low as their great cat eyes probed the darkness. Jackals, or wild dogs perhaps, bayed in the north, and from somewhere on the black ridges Pazel caught the echo of drums.

The narrowed Maî gushed close at hand, invisibly. At one switchback they had to pass very near a waterfall, and the horse Pazel and Neeps rode lost its footing, dashing both boys into the frigid spray. They shed their wet coats for dry blankets, but Pazel's teeth chattered for the rest of the night.

With the first glimmer of morning, Neeps suddenly whispered, 'Ouch! *Credek*, Pazel, I keep meaning to ask you: what's that thing in your pocket? Every time we hit a bump it whacks me like a piece of lead.'

'Oh, that,' said Pazel, 'it *is* lead. Sorry, mate.' He reached back with one hand and pulled out a two-inch metal disc, sewn into a soft tube of buckskin leather. Carefully he passed it to Neeps.

'Fiffengurt's blackjack,' said Neeps, amazed.

'He gave it to me while you and Marila were off getting married,' said Pazel. '"Saved my life a dozen times, that wicked thing," he told me. "Clip a man smartly with it, and you can bring him down no matter what sort of brute he is. And you can hide it better than any knife. Never let it out of your reach, Pathkendle. It's worth the headache, you'll see." And do you know what he did, to be sure I obeyed? He sat down and *stitched*, by Rin. An extra pocket, just this size, in my two best breeches. How do you like that?'

'Fiffengurt's our man,' said Neeps, returning the weapon, 'but I'll thank you to put it in your blary coat until we're back on our feet.'

With sunrise came a little warmth. Their destination, that notch in the mountains where the river began, was suddenly much closer. All the same, Hercól quickened the pace. There was no longer any hope of remaining hidden, should anyone be watching from above: near dawn they had cleared the treeline, and the wind-tortured scrub around them now barely reached their stirrups. Cables of ice braided the rocks along the river. Higher and higher they climbed, the road deserted, and all the land empty but for small, scurrying creatures in the underbrush, and here and there a ruined keep or watchtower, older than anything in the valley below.

'The thin air may go to your head,' warned Vadu. 'Take care above all near a precipice.' And there were many of these: sheer falls of hundreds of feet, with the road narrowed and crumbling, and at times great rocks to weave around. Pazel had thought that nothing could compare to the terror of being aloft in a Nelluroq storm. But this fear was sharpened by helplessness: no matter how true his grip, one false step by the horse and they would die.

The horse clearly appreciated this fact as well. But alone of their animals, the poor creature seemed unused to mountains, and stamped and skittered and threw its head about, eyes wide with fear. At last the boys could stand it no longer. When the chance came they slid to the ground and led the horse by the reins.

'He's loads better now that we're off his back,' said Neeps.

'So am I,' said Pazel. The path was bad enough on foot, however, and around the next bend chuckled one more ice-fringed stream. The riders crossed easily, but their horse balked at the water's edge, backing and snorting.

'Silly ass.' Pazel moved behind the horse, clapping and nudging its rump, while Neeps, already across, tugged the reins with all his might. At last the beast lunged forwards. Pazel gritted his teeth and waded in himself, using his hands for balance on the rocks.

'*Aya!*'

Something had stabbed his arm. He jerked it from the water, then shouted again in amazement. Among the stones where his hand had rested, a huge spider was wriggling away. It was nearly the size of his head, and more amazing still, perfectly transparent. Indeed, he had taken it for a lump of ice, and its folded legs for icicles. The spider vanished among the rocks, and Pazel, clutching his arm, stumbled out of the water.

The pain, as it happened, was not as bad as the shock. By the time Hercól reached him, the bite on his arm felt no worse than a scratch. 'But did you *see* it?' he said. 'It was *huge*. It must have just nicked me, or I'd be a goner.'

The path was far too narrow for the others to approach, though Neda and Thasha looked back in alarm. Hercól studied his arm, frowning. 'There is a bruise already,' he said. 'I wish I had seen the creature.'

'It was a *medet*,' said Vadu. 'A glass spider – if the boy is telling the truth, that is.'

'Of course I am!' Pazel shot back. 'Do you think I could make up something like that?'

'The spiders are kept in temples across the Empire,' said Vadu, 'and Spider Tellers handle them daily. I have never heard of them biting anyone.'

'That is true, Pazel,' said Bolutu. 'Some new mothers even visit the temples and allow the glass spiders to crawl on their newborns. It brings good luck, and they're never bitten, never.'

'This one bites,' said Pazel, 'but it can't have been very deep, because it doesn't hurt much.'

Neda, turning her horse, gave Thasha an accusing look. 'Can't you make him be more careful?' she said. Thasha just stared at her, too amazed to reply.

Hercól wound a bandage about Pazel's arm. 'We will keep an eye on you,' he said. 'Some poisons are quick, and others slow.'

On they stumbled, Neeps and Pazel still leading the frightened horse, and the wind stronger and colder by the minute. Pazel's heart was racing. Hercól's warning had unsettled him, though at the moment his arm felt almost normal.

Then they turned a final switchback and found themselves at the pass. Smoke was rising from a point just out of sight beyond the ridge; bells or windchimes sounded somewhere; and a rooster, of all things, was crowing above the wind.

A last scramble brought them to the top of the ridge. Pazel caught his breath. Straight ahead of them ran file upon file of mountain peaks, towering over the pass, their sharp summits wrapped in capes of snow. These were the mountains that had loomed like distant ghosts, that first day he'd glimpsed the mainland. They were cold and forbidding. And winding among them was an immense, dark lake.

It was crescent-shaped; they stood near one tip of the crescent, and the other, presumably, was hidden somewhere far off among the mountains. The lake was the heavy blue of a calf's tongue. Waves tossed on its surface, breaking against the sides of the mountains, which appeared to descend into its depths; and on the narrow, pebbly shores between. Scattered along these shores were humble dwellings of mud and thatch, and docks so frail they might have been made out of the wingbones of birds. Miles offshore, boats with strange ribbed sails plied the lake.

Almost at their feet, the lake narrowed into a deep defile that looked as if it had been cut by a plough. Of course, that plough was the Maî, shrunken here to a swift stream, but still managing to pierce the wall of the lake to start its journey to the sea.

'Ilvaspar, the lifeblood of Masalym,' said Vadu. 'It is more than a decade since I beheld her shores.'

'It's mucking enormous,' said Alyash.

'Twenty miles to the south-west point, where the great Ansyndra is born,' said Vadu. Some say that a demon prince lies chained in its depths, others that it was cut by the fang of Suovala the Elderdrake. I know not. But I am glad to see that Vasparhaven survives.'

He pointed, and looking up Pazel saw an extraordinary sight. Built into the side of the cliff on the lake's southern shore, at least a hundred feet above the surface, hung a stunning mansion. It was all of wood, painted a dark, weathered green, and there was no foundation beneath it; the whole structure rested on five massive beams jutting out from sockets in the cliff wall. One could almost imagine that it was *half* a mansion, and that the other half lay within the cliff: the tiled roof slanted upwards to meet the stone, and ended there. Many balconies and scores of windows looked out upon the lake. From its chimneys rose the smoke Pazel had seen from below.

'They're the ones to ask about that bite of yours,' said Vadu.

'Who are *they*?' asked Pazel.

'Didn't Olik tell you?' said Ibjen. 'They're Spider Tellers, like the prince himself. Vasparhaven is the oldest temple in the peninsula.'

Hercól was gazing across the lake. 'Fulbreech has reached the far shore,' he said, 'and begun to descend the other side of the mountain. But he has not gone far; something has impeded his progress.' He turned to the soldiers. 'Gather brush here and set it aside – enough for a large bonfire. Tonight I must signal Prince Olik.'

'What will you tell him?' asked Ibjen.

'That will depend on what we learn here, and what we choose to do about it. Lead on, Counsellor; another day is waning.'

They rode along the southern shore, past boulders fallen from the slopes and chunks of ice ten feet thick: shards, perhaps, of the lid that sealed the lake in winter. As Vasparhaven loomed nearer, Pazel saw a pair of massive green doors at ground level, just beneath the temple.

More bells began to ring. Pazel saw faces leaning down from the balconies. Strange faces, belonging to many peoples: dlömu, mizralds, Nemmocians ... and then a face peered down at him that set his mind suddenly awhirl. It was a girl's face, thrust through the rail of the balcony, staring right at him with joy and fascination. But that mouth, those eyes! All at once he could not stand it, and cried out, 'I'm here! It's me!'

He succeeded in drawing her attention – and everyone else's. Three horses shied, including his own, and the rooster they had heard before launched itself from one balcony to another, and came near to falling to its death. Pazel had not shouted, *I'm here*, at least not in any familiar tongue. The sound he made was a wailed, inhuman *skrreeee*, followed by four emphatic clicks of his tongue.

'Rin's mercy,' said Neeps, shaken. 'Pazel, you've got to stop that *right now*.'

'I know,' said Pazel, heart thumping. He had shouted in Sea-Murthic, a tongue no human should be able to pronounce, but one his Gift had forced on him. The face that had looked down at him was that of the murth-girl, Klyst.

Only it wasn't, of course; it couldn't be. The girl in any case had disappeared from the balcony, and those who had not withdrawn stared down in fright. Some of the soldiers in his own party were doing the same.

'Well done, Pathkendle,' said Hercól with a sigh. 'Humans – animals on horseback, to them – appear suddenly on their doorstep, and you treat them to a murthic howl.'

'He sounded like a stabbed monkey,' said one of the soldiers. 'What's wrong with him? The prince said he was safe.'

'Oh, he's far from that,' said Neeps.

'Undrabust!' snapped Hercól. 'Listen, all of you: Pazel has fancies, but they are harmless. The only danger that should concern us is the one we chase. All else is foolishness.' He shot a hard glance at Pazel. 'We have no time to spare for foolishness.'

A chain dangled from a small hole in the wall beside green doors. Vadu pulled it, and somewhere deep in the cliff another bell sounded faintly. But thanks to Pazel's outburst, perhaps, they stood a long time waiting for an answer, colder by the minute.

'Neeps,' whispered Pazel, 'didn't you *see* her?'

'Which her?'

'The girl on the balcony. It was Klyst, mate. She looked right at me.'

'A sea-murth,' said Neeps, looking up at the hanging mansion, with its icicles and frost. 'You're barking mad, you know that?'

'That's insulting,' said Pazel. 'I tell you, it was *Klyst*.'

Through the crowd of men, horses and *sicuñas*, Thasha's eyes found him suddenly. Amusement shone in them, but also a wariness that was nearly accusing. She knew about the murth-girl too.

At last the doors groaned open. In the doorway stood an ancient dlömic man, straight-backed and very thin. Like all dlömu he was without wrinkles, his old skin tight and smooth, but his neatly combed beard was white as chalk and hung almost to his knees.

'I am the Master Teller, father to the people of Vasparhaven,' he said. 'I regret that I cannot permit you within our walls.'

The soldiers glared at Pazel; Neeps' look was only slightly more benign. But what the old dlömu said next made them forget their irritation. They were not, he declared, the first humans to appear at the temple door. Two days earlier, others had presented themselves, seeking shelter. One was a youth, dirty, frightened, but clever with his words. Another was an abandoned creature who stared at nothing, whose left hand twitched constantly and whose lips formed words it did not speak: a *tol-chenni* dressed up like a thinking being, and able to walk erect. 'A freak of nature, I thought,' said the Master Teller. 'The youth held him by a rope about the neck, as one might a donkey, or a dog.'

The third figure, he said, was a terror to behold: tall, gaunt, with eyes that looked famished and cruel, and a tattered white scarf at the neck. 'He was their leader, but he was cruel to the youth, who seemed to have no value to him except as the keeper of the *tol-chenni*. He required the youth to keep the creature warm, to make it eat and drink.'

'We seek those three, Spider Father,' said Vadu. 'Did they depart in the night?'

'Yes,' said the old man. 'The tall one was anxious to be gone, and tried to demand our help to cross Ilvaspar. But what could we do? There is no commerce beyond the lake – not in fifty years, since the Plazic general summoned the accursed Black Tongue. The three waited long upon the shore, the tall one pacing and cursing, until at last a fisherman returned and was persuaded – or bullied, perhaps – into taking them where they wished to go. You must seek passage with the fisher-folk as well, if you really want to pursue those three.'

'It is the last thing we want, good Father,' said Hercól, 'and yet pursue them we must. How did they come here, though? For they made the journey from Masalym faster than seems possible for man or beast.'

The old man frowned, and closed the doors. At first they

wondered if they had given some offence, but soon the doors creaked open again and a younger dlömic man dressed like the Master Teller stepped out nervously. The old man stood behind him, a hand on his shoulder.

'Have no fear, they are courteous folk,' he said. 'Tell them what you saw.'

The young man struggled to find his voice. 'A *gandryl*,' he whispered. 'A winged steed. They rode upon its back, all three of them, and it put them down beside the Chalice of the Maî. I saw it. I was checking my rabbit snares.'

The soldiers murmured, wonder-struck: 'A *gandryl*! The mage rides a *gandryl*!'

'They are not all gone,' said the Master Teller. 'More goatish than horse-like, as befits life in the peaks, but the size of war stallions. They are woken creatures, long-lived and crafty. We never see them today, only their footprints on the lake isles, where no goats live. I was not sure I believed our young novice here, until you spoke.'

'Why didn't the creature fly them on, past the lake?' asked Thasha.

Stumbling over his words, the novice explained that Arunis had tried to demand just that. But the *gandryl* had replied that he had bargained for a flight to the shores of Ilvaspar, and that his payment was barely worth that much trouble, and certainly no more. It had left them right at the Chalice, and the mage had cursed it as it flew away.

'He may have set out on horseback from Masalym, and called the creature down from the sky,' said Vadu. 'The great mages of old were said to do that, upon the plain of the Inner Kingdom.'

'At least he no longer has the creature's service,' said Hercól. 'He has gained an advantage, but not escaped us altogether.'

'You should sleep here tonight,' said the Master Teller. 'I cannot let you enter Vasparhaven, but there is a *llyrette*, a way-cave, not far from here, and it is safe, and sheltered from the wind. In happier days it was a place where travellers rested often, before crossing the lake, or descending to the plain. I will send food from our kitchens, and bedding too.'

'Both would be welcome,' said Hercól, 'though we will only nap on the bedding, I fear. The one we chase is bent on the worst sort of malice, and if he escapes, not even your refuge here will long be spared. Take our animals in payment, Father – or if you need them not, take them as a favour to us.'

'We have stables,' said the old man, 'and will care for your beasts until you return.'

'I cannot say when that will be,' said Hercól. 'But there is a final matter we must raise. Come here, Pazel, and tell him what happened to you.'

As Hercól unwound the bandage on his arm, Pazel told the old dlömu about the spider. 'It was as big as a coconut, Father. And transparent. I thought it was a piece of ice, until it jumped and bit me.'

The novice, clearly shocked, turned in agitation to his master. The old dlömu for his part showed no reaction at all. He studied the mark on Pazel's arm. 'They do bite, sometimes, the wild *medet* spiders,' he said, 'and some who suffer the bite know great pain. With others, however, there is no pain at all. You may feel a little cold in the arm, but it will pass.'

'Then with your leave, Father, we will go to our brief rest,' said Hercól.

'You may have more time than you think,' said the priest. 'The lake is vast, and the fishermen go deep into coves and streams, and rarely return before midnight. I will make enquiries, but do not hope for much.'

The travellers bowed and offered their thanks, and the Master Teller sent the novice to show them the way. A few minutes' walk brought them to another cliff door, smaller and simpler than the doors of the temple. Inside was a dry cave of several rooms. There were tables, chairs, rough beds of a sort. Just minutes later the food arrived: cauldrons of thin stew balanced on either end of a staff across broad dlömic shoulders, hot bread, flat cakes made with onion and some sort of corn. It was all delicious, and so was the jug of black beer that washed it down.

By the time they finished eating it was nearly dark. Hercól asked Thasha, Pazel and Neeps to help him with the signal fire. Bearing a heavy woollen blanket, lamp oil and a telescope, they set off back along the lake, watching the first stars appear over the teeth of the mountains. In Vasparhaven shadowy figures were moving, placing candles in the windows. The stars were igniting too, and by the time they reached the ridge and looked down on Masalym's Inner Dominion the sun was gone.

Hercól dashed oil on the brush pile. Then he bent to strike a match, and soon the dry scrub was roaring with flame. Next he reached into his coat and removed a sheet of folded paper, glanced at it briefly and replaced it. 'Very well,' he said. 'Take a corner of the blanket, Thasha, and step back.'

Hercól and Thasha stretched the blanket between the fire and the sweep of the plain. 'Hold it higher – we must block as much light as we can. That's the way. Now flatten it to the ground – and raise it again – very good.'

They moved precisely, hiding and revealing the fire by turns. Each time they bent down Hercól looked pointedly across the Inner Dominion. At last it came: a pale and distant light. Hercól raised the telescope to his eye. 'That is Olik, upon the Dais of Masalym,' he said. 'He is answering with the code we agreed. Now to tell him that Arunis is here.'

Five times they stretched the blanket, and five times lowered it. Then Hercól, studying the valley again, nodded his satisfaction. 'The prince has understood . . . two, three, four – five! Well, there is something you'll want to know. Five flashes means that the *Chathrand* is safely away.'

The relief was so great Pazel almost cried aloud.

'Wait! He is signalling again,' said Hercól. ' . . . four, five, six, seven—' He lowered the telescope and looked at them. 'Eight. Macadra's ship is entering the Jaws of Masalym, even now.'

'Then he's got to get out right now!' said Thasha.

'Can we tell him that?' said Pazel. 'Do you have some way to tell him?'

Hercól shook his head. 'Olik knows the danger better than we do,' he said. 'But feed the fire all the same, boys. We must inform him that we ourselves mean to go on. And then hope that he flees instantly, now that there is no reason to keep searching the city. A noble prince! He kept his word to the folk of Masalym, despite the peril to himself.'

They raised and lowered the blanket several times more, and the light below them flickered twice, and Hercól said that it was the signal that Olik had understood. Then they sat down on the stony earth, waiting for their fire to die. The wind tossed Thasha's hair about like a tattered flag. The light in the valley abruptly disappeared, as though snuffed, but the friends sat a while longer in silence.

'I'm a mucking fool,' said Neeps suddenly.

'You are that,' said Thasha.

Neeps did not even look at her. 'I've got nothing,' he said. 'How am I supposed to take care of them? I should be hanged, is what.'

'Not every act of yours was foolish,' said Hercól. 'You chose a Tholjassan for a mate: that counts for something. Tame your fear, Undrabust. Your child will find its way in the world.'

'My child,' said Neeps, as though the notion shocked him yet. 'Do you know, there are times when my mind just seems to vanish? To go out like that fire down there. I can't even think about what I'll do when this is over. What the *three* of us will do.'

'See first that your future is not stolen from you,' said a voice from the darkness.

The humans started. It was the Master Teller. The old dlömu seemed to have just appeared there, conjured by the night, his cloak billowing about him. They could not see his face; only the silver eyes shone from beneath the hood.

'I warn you,' he said, 'it is being stolen even now. We who read the signs have never beheld such a conjunction of ills. Alifros is bleeding; soon it will haemorrhage. And the wounding hand – it belongs to that mage who came before you. Who is he? Will you tell me his name?'

The others hesitated, and the Master Teller said, 'I shall name him, then. He is the murderer of Ullimar, Ullum's son. He is the Traitor of Idharin and the author of the White Curse. He is the father of the Ravens: Arunis.'

'You knew all along!' said Pazel.

'I did,' said the old man, 'but you were quite unknown to me, and though you claimed friendship with our brother Prince Olik, I could not be sure. I feared you might in truth be part of the sorcerer's company – especially as one among you bears a Plazic Blade. Now that that cursed thing is elsewhere I can better sense your goodness. Yes, I recognised Arunis Wytterscorm. Long have I traced the arc of his journeys, in the tremors of the earth, the grinding of her bones against one another. He has come back across the Ruling Sea to plague us again, this time bearing some horrible tool.'

'It is the Nilstone, Spider Father,' said Hercól.

The old man was very still. 'That I did not know,' he said after a pause, 'and worse tidings I cannot imagine. Arunis, with Erithusmé's orb! The death of this world has been his long, his passionate ambition. Now he has the power to bring that prize within reach.'

'He has aimed a cannon at Alifros,' said Hercól, 'but we think he is still struggling with the match. Should he gain full control of the *tol-chenni*'s mind he will become invincible. That is why we are in such need of haste.'

'When the fishermen return you may bid them in my name to take you swiftly across the lake. But come, your fire is out, and this wind is too chilly for an old man.'

Pazel was glad to move; the night would be icy, and he too was growing cold. They walked back along the lakeshore. At Vasparhaven the green doors opened as they neared, and two novices came forward to assist the Master Teller.

The old man halted them with a wave, then looked sharply at Pazel. 'You are quite sure that your arm is not in pain?' he asked.

Pazel, who had almost forgotten the spider bite, shook his head. 'It wasn't bad even at the time, to be honest. And there's no pain at all now.' When the Teller continued to stare at him, he added nervously, 'That's good, isn't it?'

'No,' said the dlömu, 'I would not call it good, exactly. There are two sorts of reactions to the bite of the *medet*. One, as I said, is great pain; and that is usually to be preferred, for it passes after several hours. Those who suffer no pain feel cold instead. This begins about a day after the bite, and lasts for three.'

'Cold?' said Pazel, feeling chilled by the discussion alone. 'And then?'

'Then the eyes shrivel, and the victim goes blind.'

The humans cried aloud, but the Teller quickly raised a hand. 'There is a treatment, and I have asked my people to prepare it. But it must be given to you in Vasparhaven, Mr Pathkendle. Are you willing to ascend?'

'Willing? I wish you'd told me hours ago! I don't want to go blind!'

'I had to be certain that you were in no pain,' said the Teller, 'and the cure must be given in three stages, over as many hours. It is just as well that you are delayed in crossing Ilvaspar.'

'Let us go with him, then, can't you?' cried Neeps, who was if anything more distraught than Pazel himself.

The Master Teller shook his head. 'Your friend must face this challenge alone. And even if that were not so, I would still be forced to turn away the bearer of Ildraquin. Yes, Hercól Stanapeth, I know your sword as well. It is not cursed, like the Plazic knife your companion bears. Yet it is powerful, and would throw the quiet music of Vasparhaven into discord.' He looked at Thasha. 'For the same reason, I cannot permit you to enter, young mage.'

'Mage?' said Thasha. 'Father, I'm nothing of the kind! Some

mage is … meddling with me, that's all. I don't know why she's doing it, or how—'

'She?'

Thasha grew flustered. 'Or … he, I suppose. The point is, I don't have any magic of my own.'

'Be that as it may, the power within you is great,' said the Teller.

'Well, do get on with it, Father,' sputtered Neeps. 'And please, please make sure he takes his medicine. Don't turn your back until he drinks it all, and don't let him spit it up again—'

'Neeps, for Rin's sake!' cried Pazel. 'Father, listen to me, please: if outside magic can do you harm, I should explain—'

'That you carry a Master-Word?' said the dlömu. 'I know that, child. It would do great harm indeed, should you speak it within our walls. And I know too that you and your sister have been burdened with augmentation spells.'

He knows that Neda's my sister, thought Pazel, his mind awhirl. *We didn't even glance at each other in front of him.*

'I trust you will not speak that Word,' the old dlömu continued, 'and the language-charm you carry presents no danger, for its power does not extend beyond your mind.'

'Father,' said Thasha, 'have you used this cure on human beings?'

The Master Teller looked at her with compassion. 'I am old, daughter of the North, but not that old. The last human residents of Vasparhaven succumbed to the plague before I ever set foot in these mountains. Still, our ancient records describe the process clearly.' He put a hand on Pazel's shoulder. 'You must leave your knife and sword outside our walls, Mr Pathkendle, common blades though they be. Let us go, now.'

Pazel took a shaky breath. His friends' eyes were wide with concern, but he forced himself to smile. 'Don't cross that lake without me,' he said, and passed them his knife and sword.

He followed the Master Teller inside, and the novices began to close the heavy doors. Once more the old man stopped them. Looking back at the humans outside, he said, 'You may not understand, but this is an auspicious event. The *medet* is the creature at the heart of our ceremonies and our mystic arts. It is a rare distinction.'

'Getting bitten,' asked Thasha, looking anything but hopeful, 'or going blind?'

'Either one,' said the Teller, drawing Pazel away.

28

Spider Telling

236th day from Etherhorde

Inside it was cold and dark, but the Master Teller was already climbing the wide staircase before them, and as Pazel and the novices followed him up the air began to warm. They passed several floors, with dark hallways tunnelling off into the stone. Pazel saw lamplight at the distant ends of some of these halls, and heard the ring of hammers, the rasp of lathes and saws. 'Our workshops,' said the old man, gesturing, 'and our warehouses, our mill. In its younger days, Vasparhaven was a stronghold where scholars took refuge in times of war or other catastrophe, and kept their learning alive for those who would come after. We are preparing to serve that function again.'

Pazel was distressed by his statement. How much could the old man sense about the world to come? Then, from above, he heard the sound of many voices raised in song – a low, lovely music, and the dread in his heart melted away.

'It is the hour of Evensong,' said the Master Teller. 'The hour when we often welcomed guests, in happier years.'

The climb ended on a landing before two large and ornate doors, finished with padded leather of a deep, lustrous red. The novices stepped forwards and pulled. Hinges groaned, and the doors swung slowly outwards.

A blaze of candlelight met Pazel's eyes, and a wave of sweet smells – apple blossom, cedar, cinnamon, fresh bread – flooded his nostrils. They were stepping into a grand hall: not vaulted and soaring like that of a Northern palace, but deep and intricate, with several levels to the floor, and pillars carved from the living rock, and many alcoves and niches filled with candles in iron stands. Tapestries adorned the walls, and censers burned on iron stands, grey cat-tails of smoke rising from them to mingle at the ceiling. The hall was full of people. They were dressed humbly, and busy with a variety of tasks, but as the Master and his guest came forwards they stopped and bowed as one. Not all were dlömu. The other races of the South were all represented here, in greater proportions than in Masalym. And there were new beings, too, like nothing Pazel had seen before. A hulking figure nearly the size of an augrong, with a barrel under each arm. A pair of lean, wolfish beings who rose from all fours when they bowed. A grey fox watching them from a corner, its tail twitching like a snake. 'Welcome, human,' it said in a voice like satin.

'Where is Kirishgán?' said the Master Teller. 'I would that he meet our visitor.'

'I will find him, Father,' said the fox, and darted away into the chamber.

They walked deeper into the room. A young novice handed Pazel a cup and bade him drink. It was wine, pale but very strong, and when Pazel swallowed he felt warmer still. 'We dlömu drink more beer than wine,' said the Master, smiling. 'But humans always preferred our wine, in the old days when we lived as brothers. Drink it all, child: it is the first part of your cure.'

Pazel finished the wine. As he lowered the cup he wondered if the drink could already be going to his head: for coming towards them was a manlike figure with olive skin and fine black feathers where his eyebrows should have been. They jutted out to either side of his temples, as if a pair of black wings were about to emerge from the skin of his forehead. The eyes beneath these oddest of brows were youthful, but the man himself was not exactly young. He was tall and straight-backed, but there was a subtle, knowing quality to his expression that made Pazel think of the wisdom of great age. The figure greeted him with a bow.

'Welcome, spider's favourite,' he said.

'I'm glad you're not afraid of humans,' said Pazel. 'In Masalym no one wanted to speak to us.'

'Your murth-cry gave us a start,' said the newcomer, as the corners of his lips curled wryly, 'but as for human beings – well, there are stranger things within these walls.'

'Vasparhaven is home to many beings, not all of them native to this world,' said the Teller. 'Some were castaways on the River of Shadows, who, unable to return to their own world, climbed to the temple and dwell here yet. Others, especially dlömu, come as war refugees, fleeing the *Platazcra*. There are woken animals, whom we shelter until their persecution ends. And a few, like Kirishgán here, come as pilgrims did for centuries, before the current darkness: to learn, to study, to bring us new wisdom and carry something of us away with them to distant lands.'

'By his face, Spider Father, I guess that he has never met with a selk.' The olive-skinned figure smiled warmly. 'Of course, that is no surprise. We are rare enough on this side of the Ruling Sea. In the North we are rare as lilies on a glacier.'

'And yet older than glaciers – old as the mountains themselves,' said the dlömu. 'I am glad of this encounter: the young and the ancient of Alifros, met here at the crossroads of our common fate.'

'A crossroads surely,' said the other, 'but which road is the world about to choose, I should like to know?'

'So should we all,' said the Master Teller, 'for one is sunlit yet, but the other descends into shadow and fear: to what depths none can say.' He took the empty cup from Pazel's hand. 'Our guest would be welcome for a year, Kirishgán, but he has only hours. You know what the second part of the cure entails. The third and final will be given on the Floor of Echoes.' His old eyes focused on the selk. 'You will visit the Floor yourself on the morrow, I think.'

'Spider Father!' exclaimed the other, suddenly excited.

'Stay here in the Great Hall for now,' said the Teller, 'and when Evensong concludes, be so good as to show him to the door. I will alert the Actors myself.' The old dlömu moved away without another word, flanked by his two attendants.

'So the day has come!' said the one called Kirishgán. 'I thought it might have, as soon as I saw your face.'

'What do you mean?' said Pazel. 'I thought all I needed to do was drink three gulps of that wine, over three hours.'

'There is a bit more to it than that,' said Kirishgán, smiling again. 'Come, and I will try to explain.'

He threaded a path through the Great Hall. The people watched, quietly fascinated, and some murmured soft words of welcome. Tapestries gave way to windows, and Pazel realised that they were no longer within the mountain but in the part of the temple that projected over the lakeshore, suspended on those titanic beams. They climbed a short stair, passed a fire dancing in a brass vessel and sat upon a rug in a little glassed-in alcove, with the stormy lake spread beneath them. The wind moaned and rattled the windows, and despite the fire the glass was rimmed with frost.

'The bite of the *medet* is rare,' said the selk abruptly, 'because it never occurs by accident. There are two possibilities. The spider bit you that you might go blind, and stay among us for the rest of your days. Or the spider bit you that you might visit us, and be cured, and perhaps gain something else in the bargain.

'Vasparhaven is larger than it appears from outside, and while most of its halls are open to the whole community, some are closed and sacrosanct. Of these, the most sacred of all is the Floor of Echoes. None go there save the Master Teller, and a special group we call the Actors – and very rarely, travellers in need. The Actors dwell on the Floor for nine months – never exiting, never even speaking to their brethren outside. For those pledged to the Order it is a privilege extended only once in a lifetime.'

'And your Master is sending me *there*?' Pazel exclaimed. 'Whatever for?'

'I cannot tell you,' said the selk, 'but I am glad you have come.

Three years have I dwelled in Vasparhaven. When I came, weary and cold, I thought only to spend the night, but the Master bade me remain until the deeper purpose of my visit should reveal itself.'

'Has it, then?'

'We shall see,' said Kirishgán. 'There is an old rule concerning the Floor of Echoes: that anyone who sets foot on it must leave it by a passage that exits Vasparhaven, and not return for nine years at the earliest. I am to visit the Floor myself, the Master has declared; therefore my time here is at an end.'

A novice brought a tray with a steaming kettle and two cups, and Kirishgán served them each a cup of fragrant tea. Pazel seized it gladly: it was good to have something to warm his hands. 'Don't you mind being sent away?' he asked.

'Mind?' laughed Kirishgán. 'On the contrary. Life is rich here, in ways I cannot hope to describe. But I have grown restless. Friends await me far across the Empire, and beyond it too. I doubt I shall ever again know the peace I have found in Vasparhaven. Yet I came here to heal and to learn, not to escape. The arts I have studied here tell me of the doom that is building over Alifros, gathering like a second Worldstorm. I would fight that storm, and those who are brewing it with their hate. I am anxious to resume my journeys.'

'And we're not eager at all,' said Pazel, 'but we have to go, as quickly as we can.'

'You are close to the heart of that doom,' said Kirishgán. 'You, and your party, and those ill-favoured three who came before. And above all the one you call Thasha. I have never felt a stronger tremor from a passing soul! Who is she, Pazel?'

Pazel looked at him uneasily. He had taken an immediate liking to this Kirishgán, but what of it? They'd been betrayed so many times, and the circumstances of his visit to this temple were odd to say the least.

He was groping for some evasive reply when he noticed with a start that his right arm was colder than the rest of him. He placed his hand on the kettle, but only dimly sensed its warmth. 'Please,' he said, 'what about the cure?'

'The second part will be given to you soon,' said Kirishgán. 'The third you must seek on the Floor of Echoes. But it is no good counting the minutes, Pazel. Tell me of yourself! For sixty summers have come and gone since last I met a woken human – and ten times that since I met a human from the North. Let us share what we can while the music lasts.'

Pazel sighed: there was clearly no way to hurry anyone here along. Kirishgán for his part was insatiably curious. Pazel told him of the Northern Empires, the cities he'd visited on the *Chathrand* and his earlier ships. He described the great market on Opalt, the splendid mansions of Etherhorde, the jungles of Bramian and the warm white sands of the Outer Isles. But when he spoke of Ormael and the life he had lost there, he felt a strange emptiness, almost an indifference, in himself. And that was a new sort of loss. *I could tell him anything. I could say that Ormalis worship ducks. It's unreal to him and always will be.* And what if they never caught up with the *Chathrand*, never found a way home? Would the North become just a story for them as well – a yarn that unravelled with each telling, a fable about the lives of people they no longer knew?

'Tell me of the crossing,' said Kirishgán.

Pazel spoke of the awful storms, the lives lost on the Ruling Sea, the Vortex that had almost swallowed the ship. He moved on to their landfall at Narybir, the attack of the Karyskan swimmers, their confused reception in Masalym. Kirishgán listened in silence, but when Pazel mentioned Prince Olik he looked up sharply.

'You are friends of Olik?' he said, his feathered eyebrows knitting. 'How close? Did the prince give you no token of that friendship to prove your claim?'

Pazel could only shake his head. 'Nothing, as far as I know,' he said.

'Then you are his friend indeed,' said Kirishagán, delighted. 'Olik hands gems to those he wishes others to be wary of. Had you produced one I should have told you nothing more. But this changes matters. Olik Ipandracon! Years have passed since I saw his noble face. Where does he wander now?'

Pazel told him what he understood of Olik's fight against the Ravens and Arunis. Kirishgán was dismayed. 'Let him not fall into the hands of Macadra!' he said. 'She would find a way to kill even a Bali Adro prince, if it suited her. But more likely she would alter his face by magic or mutilation, and hide him in one of the royal "hospitals" in the west, where those she fears to kill outright are locked away.'

'Your Empire seems fond of such places,' said Pazel. 'We were locked in one ourselves. Oh, Pitfire, we should have *begged* Olik to come with us.'

'Do not despair for him yet,' said the selk. 'The prince has a knack for survival, as any must who fall afoul of the Ravens. But Bali Adro is not *my* Empire, Pazel. Indeed, we selk refuse all citizenship save that of Alifros itself. When I first woke into life, Bali Adro was a little territory on the Nemmocian frontier, and this temple was yet to be built, and the waters of Ilvaspar remained frozen even in summer. Lake and mountain claim no citizenship, nor do the eagles drifting above them. So it is with the selk. By ancient practice most countries grant us freedom of movement, and we joke with border guards that we permit them the same. In any case, there are few who could prevent our coming and going.'

'But don't you have a home?' asked Pazel. 'The place you were born, a place you dream of going back to?'

Kirishgán's eyes grew briefly wary. 'That is one secret I am sworn to keep,' he said.

There was an awkward silence. Then Kirishgán seemed to reach some decision, and gestured for Pazel to lean close. In a softer voice, he said, 'Hear me, lad. For as long as the Ravens have existed there have been those who fought them. I am one of that number: I resolved long ago to resist them until the day I breathe no more. Olik has made a similar choice, and so have many across Bali Adro and even beyond it. Once, the dlömic Emperors stood with us. But for well over a century now the throne of Bali Adro has been merely a tool of the Ravens, the figurehead behind which they marshalled the *Platazcra*.'

'I thought those Blades were the whole cause of this *Platazcra*,' said Pazel.

'By no means,' said Kirishgán. 'The Blades and their power are an awful drug, but more awful still is the idea. The hideous idea! *Dlömu Irrimatak!* Dlömu atop the hill, all others at their feet! It is the founding lie of the *Platazcra* that such is the natural order, the right path for the universe. How else to sustain a cult of infinite conquest? Without a belief that dlömic supremacy was ordained by heaven, there would be no *Platazcra*, only frenzied warfare among the various keepers of the Blades. The Ravens rule the South, Pazel, because they gave the dlömu a sick, sweet lie to believe in. And now, through that lie, the dlömu are destroying themselves.'

'Everyone believes in that lie,' said Pazel.

Kirishgán sat back, startled.

'I mean, it's no different in the North,' Pazel went on. 'The Shaggat's cult on Gurishal – that's infinite conquest, too. And the Secret Fist, Arqual's network of spies – why, they're selling the same blary story to the Arquali people: that they should rule everyone, everywhere, because they're naturally better and Rin wants it that way.'

His voice tightened. 'Do you know how many Arqualis have told me I ought to feel *grateful*, Kirishgán? Told me how *lucky* I am that Arqual came along and noticed me, lifted me up? Rin's eyes, half the Arqualis I've met think they ought to be in charge of the world. Not consciously, I don't mean that. It's half-buried, but it's there.'

The selk's eyes were suddenly far away. For a moment Pazel was afraid that he had given offence. Then Kirishgán blinked and looked at him again, and his gentle smile returned.

'Your words touch me,' he said. 'The old prejudices, the cleaving to the tribe: *half-buried*, you call them. But if you were a selk you might take hope from that assertion. To bury them halfway is a great achievement. When at last they are fully buried, they can decay into the primal soil from whence they came.'

Pazel looked down at his tea. Years of insults, abuses, slurs flowed like a phantom river through his mind. 'I understand your words,' he said at last, 'but I don't think you'd see it that way if you were in my shoes.'

'Perhaps not,' said Kirishgán. 'But I am not in your shoes. And when I looked at your party from the balcony I saw a miracle: humans and dlömu riding out together, side by side. That is something I have not witnessed since before the days of slavery and plague.'

Pazel was abashed. He was sharing tea with a being whose memory spanned centuries. And lecturing him, with the deep wisdom of his years.

'Kirishgán,' he said, 'my hand's getting colder.'

'That is expected,' said the other.

'Am I really going to go blind?'

The selk was quiet a moment, and closed his feathered eyes. 'There is darkness ahead of you,' he said at last, 'but of what sort I cannot fathom. Despite my great age I am new to Spider Telling. And even the Master has his limits. "We pan for gold, like peasants along the Maî," he says, "but the river is dark, and the sun shrouded, and the gold we call the future is more often dust than bright stones."'

'I've been scared so many times,' said Pazel. 'From the first few days on the *Chathrand*. Out of my wits, if you care to know. But *blindness*?' He drew a shuddering breath. 'I don't think I can face that, Kirishgán.'

The selk looked at Pazel a moment longer, then drank off his tea abruptly, and rose. 'The time approaches,' he said. 'Let us go.'

Pazel got to his feet, and Kirishgán took a candle from the window and led him quickly through the chambers of wood and glass, the varied people of Vasparhaven bowing and smiling as they went. Finally they reached a spiral stair and began to climb. Three floors they ascended, emerging at last into a small, unlit chamber.

It was cold here; the walls were ancient, moss-covered stone. There was a single door, and a round stone table of about elbow height in the centre of the room, on which rested a box.

Kirishgán set the candle on the table. Opening the box, he withdrew a small square of parchment, a writing quill and a bottle of ink. Pazel looked upwards: he could not make out the ceiling. 'What is this place, Kirishgán?' he asked.

'A *medetoman*, a spider-telling chamber,' said the selk. 'Now, let me think—'

He primed the quill with ink, gazed distractedly at the crumbling walls for a moment and then wrote a few neat, swift words on the parchment scrap. He raised the scrap close to the candle flame, drying the ink. As he did so he looked up thoughtfully at Pazel.

'Your country was seized and savaged. It is true that I cannot know what that is like, having no country to lose. Still, I do know something of loss, Pazel Pathkendle. The selk have been killed in great numbers by the *Platazcra*. We are loath to bow before those we do not love, and our failure to grovel at the bloodstained feet of the Emperor has made us suspect. This was bad enough when the Plazic Blades granted Bali Adro victory after victory. Now that triumph has turned to chaos and defeat it has grown much worse. Among other things, we are blamed for the decay of the Blades themselves. We talk to eguar, you see.'

'You *talk* to those monsters?' said Pazel, with a violent start. 'Why?'

'Only the elder creatures of this world possess memories to match our own,' said Kirishgán. 'We talk to them as we would our peers – as I dare say you would wish to speak to a fellow Ormali, even a dangerous one, if he were to step into this room. But the Ravens imagined that we were plotting their downfall. They could do little against the eguar, but us they have tried to exterminate. They did not quite succeed, but the damage done to our people may never be repaired: not in Alifros at any rate.'

Pazel did not know what to say. He was ashamed of his earlier words to Kirishgán, and his assumptions. At the same time he felt glad that the other had been willing to tell him of such terrible loss.

Then he saw the spider.

It was descending on a bright thread, directly over the candle on the table: a creature of living glass and ruby eyes, twice as large as the one that had bitten him. Kirishgán watched it descend, walking in a slow circle about the table, both hands raised as though in greeting. He was murmuring a chant: '*Medet ... amir medet ... amir kelada medet ...*' The spider dropped to within a foot of the flame, and its crystalline legs scattered rainbows on the stone.

'Come here, Pazel!' said Kirishgán in an urgent whisper. 'Hold out your hand!'

Nervously, Pazel approached. He trusted Kirishgán, but did not relish the thought of a second bite. With some trepidation he raised his hand. Kirishgán took his wrist and tugged him closer, and Pazel's breath caught in his throat. The spider's head was inches from his fingertips.

The creature grew quite still. Pazel had the strong feeling that those red eyes were studying him. Two mandibles like slivers of glass reached out cautiously towards his hand. Kirishgán tightened his grip. 'Don't pull away,' he hissed.

It took a great effort not to do so, but Pazel held still, and felt the brush of those strange organs against his fingers. They were barbed; it would have been easy for the spider to grab him with those mandibles and sink its fangs, hidden in that glass knob of a head, into finger or palm.

But this time the spider did not bite him. The mandibles withdrew, and Kirishgán released his wrist.

'Excellent,' he said. 'The second stage of your cure has begun.'

'Has it?' said Pazel, starting. 'But nothing happened, it barely touched me.'

'Only a touch is required. Now watch.'

The spider turned about on its strand of web, so that its head pointed upwards. It remained directly above the candle. As Pazel stared, transfixed, a drop of clear liquid the size of a quail's egg emerged from its abdomen and descended towards the flame. Though clear, it was thick, and hung suspended like a teardrop. In that moment, Kirishgán reached out and pressed the little square of parchment into the liquid. It passed inside, and the bubble of liquid separated from the spider, and Kirishgán caught it with great care. The spider retreated up its strand and was soon out of sight.

Kirishgán rolled the droplet from hand to hand, inches above the candle flame. It had become a perfect sphere. It was also expanding, and Pazel realised it was hollow. And very light now, too, for it moved with the slowness of a feather. Then Kirishgán withdrew his hands. The sphere floated above the candle, motionless, glistening in the yellow light.

'This is *not* part of your cure,' he said, 'only a gift, from one traveller to another.'

Kirishgán blew. The sphere drifted towards Pazel, and once away from the candle flame it began a slow descent. 'Catch it, it is yours,' said the selk. 'But be gentle! The shell is delicate as a prayer.'

Pazel let the tiny sphere settle onto his palm. It was light as a dragonfly, and its surface was an iridescent marvel: every colour he could imagine danced in its curves, only to vanish when he looked directly. 'It's beautiful,' he whispered. 'Kirishgán, I don't know that you should give it to me. How can I keep from breaking it?'

'You cannot,' said the selk, 'but surely you knew that already? We can possess a thing, but not its loveliness – that always escapes. Close your fist, lock your door, imprison the cherished thing in your home or heart. It makes no difference. When next you look, a part of what you cherished will be gone.'

'I'd like to give it to Thasha,' said Pazel on an impulse.

'A fine idea,' said Kirishgán. 'I will send it to her, while your cure progresses. The message within is for all of you.'

Pazel carefully rolled the sphere back into his hands. 'Thank you,' he said with feeling. 'But Kirishgán, I still don't understand what that spider had to do with my cure.'

'A great deal,' said Kirishgán. 'Pazel, the *medets* exist in this world the way murths and spirits do: here and elsewhere at once, and detecting us as much by our spirits as our bodies. There was a reason for that bite, and you must seek it on the Floor of Echoes, or there can be no cure. The Actors will help you if they can – but the help of the *medets* is more important. They are expecting you, though you may not see them.'

He gestured at the door. 'You may enter as soon as you like. Leave your boots; they will be returned to you when you exit Vasparhaven. And do not speak on the Floor of Echoes unless bidden to do so: that is essential.'

Pazel looked at him steadily. 'This is a sort of test, isn't it?'

'What isn't, Pazel?'

'And does everyone who visits the Floor of Echoes take this test?'

Kirishgán nodded. 'In one form or another. Tomorrow it will be my turn.' He gripped Pazel's arm. 'I must bid you farewell, sudden friend. Do not forget the heavens: that is what my people say. We are all young beneath the watchful stars. They will wait out our ignorance and errors, and perhaps even forgive them.'

Cradling the glass orb, he descended the stair. Pazel listened to his footsteps fade. It felt strange to be alone in this temple, inside a mountain, on the far side of the world from Ormael. Strange, and eerily peaceful. But he could not linger, he knew. Lifting the candle from the table, he walked to the door and swung it wide.

Another staircase rose before him. It was steep and built of ancient stone, and candles burned in puddles of wax on the crumbling steps, dwindling into the darkness above. Pazel tugged off his boots and set them outside the door.

The stones were wet and cold against his feet. The staircase curved and twisted, and soon Pazel knew that he had climbed the height of several additional floors. He glanced back, and saw to his great surprise that every candle he had passed was extinguished. He cupped his hand protectively around the one he bore.

The staircase ended, as it had begun, with a door, but this one stood open a few inches, and a brighter light was shining through the gap. Pazel crept forwards and glimpsed a small fire crackling in a ring of stones. Figures crouched around it, and through their shoulders Pazel caught the flash of a crystal abdomen, the flicker of a ruby eye. Then the door creaked, and the figures leaped up and scattered into the darkness.

All but one. A young dlömic woman remained by the fire, wearing a pale peach-coloured wrap that left her black arms bare to the shoulders, and a dark mask on the upper part of her face. She was holding a wide stone bowl over the flames. Of the spider Pazel saw no trace.

The woman beckoned him in, her silver eyes gleaming. Pazel stepped through the doorway, and found that he could see neither the ceiling nor any wall save that behind him. A strong draught, almost a wind, blew about them, making the fire dance and flare and shrink by turns. If he had not known better, Pazel would have thought that they were meeting not underground but on some desolate plain.

His candle went out. The woman held the bowl in one hand and with the other took his own, drawing him down to kneel across from her. As he did so a flute began to play in the darkness: a melancholy tune, full of loss and yearning, but somehow thankful all the same, as though there were gifts the music remembered. Pazel closed his eyes, and it seemed to him that the song drained some of the road-weariness from his body. There were other sounds from the shadows, now: a voice softly matching the flute, a repeated note from the quietest imaginable drum. The woman moved the bowl close to his chin.

'Breathe,' she said.

The bowl held a colourless liquid. He gave it an uncertain sniff, and the woman shook her head. She drew a deep breath, demonstrating, and rather stiffly Pazel imitated her. Whatever was in the bowl had no scent.

'Again,' said the woman, and, 'Again,' once more. Still Pazel could not smell a thing, but all at once he realised that his eyes were watering – streaming, in fact. The woman leaned closer, her masked face glowing; Pazel blinked and scattered tears.

It was then that her eyes changed. Silver darkened suddenly to glossy black, and the pupils vanished altogether. The woman's mouth opened, as though she were as startled as Pazel himself. '*Nuhzat!*' she said, and emptied the bowl into the fire.

The sudden steam burned Pazel's eyes. He surged to his feet. It was pitch black, and hands were gripping him on all sides. The dlömic woman was standing before him, her bare feet atop his own. Then a hand daubed something cold and sticky on his eyelids, and Pazel found he could not open them. He wanted to shout aloud, tell them to stop – but Kirishgán had warned him to be silent, and he knew somehow that he must obey.

The woman removed her feet from atop his own; the hands abruptly withdrew. Pazel reached out, trying to find what had become of them. His hands met with nothing at all.

He groped forwards, one step, then another. The stone floor pitched like a boat in a gale, and wild thoughts raced through his head. *Nuhzat.* The dlömic dream-state, the trance. Pazel was frightened, and furious – what was being done to him this time? Why didn't anyone, ever, ask his consent?

I did, Pazel.

He whirled. That voice! Didn't he know it? Had it really spoken aloud, or was it an echo in his mind? Whatever it was, it suffused him instantly with an almost unbearable mixture of sadness and hope. He walked forwards, blind. *Ramachni!* he wanted to scream. *Where are you?*

Afterwards it felt as if he wandered for an age on the Floor of Echoes. The mage's voice called to him again, but now it was one among many: some kind, some desperate, some chuckling with hate. There were heady scents, frigid drafts. There were rough rock walls that ended suddenly in yawning spaces, and tight little rooms with strange objects that he explored with his fingers: tables, statues, a mute piano, an unstrung harp. He found a wooden box with hinges and a padlock, and from within it came a desperate thumping. He brought it close to his ear, and to his horror it was

Chadfallow, Ignus Chadfallow, crying from within: *Let me out! Let me out!*

Time became slippery. One moment he would be creeping along with moss beneath his feet; the next he would find himself rushing headlong, with the sound of a panting animal close on his heels. He was often frightened. And yet in the worst moments, when he was close to falling or giving way to panic, he found the webbed hand of the dlömic woman in his own, and a little peace returned to him, and he went on.

Then all at once a different hand touched his shoulder, and his head was suddenly, perfectly clear. The hand moved to his face, and a warm, wet cloth rubbed his eyes. The sticky resin melted away. Pazel blinked, and found himself facing the Master Teller.

'Welcome back from blindness,' said the old dlömu. 'Now I know that I was right to send you here, for the purpose I could not see before is revealed. You needed practice with the dark.'

Pazel shook his head.

'You don't understand, of course,' said the Teller, smiling. 'Never mind: you will.'

They were in a large, lavish, forbidding chamber, like the hall of some subterranean king. There was a stone table, a barren hearth, some hulking cabinets stuffed with books and scrolls. But dominating the chamber was a round pool. It was about a dozen feet wide, with a ring of stairs descending some five or six feet to the bottom, and the palest imaginable blue light that seemed to come from the water itself.

'You stand in the *Ara Nyth*, the ancient heart of Vasparhaven, and its most sacred chamber,' said the Master. 'It is with the water of this pool that I bathed your eyes, and drew the last of the *medet*'s serum. The pool is fed by a spring deep beneath the lake: a spring fed in turn by the Nythrung, which some call the River of Shadows. Through blindness you have come here, protected by our Actors, but guided by your spirit alone. Therefore you may drink from the pool if you like, and become the first human to do so in a great many years. Or you may depart: turn your back, walk directly away, and leave Vasparhaven by the stairway ahead. Do you know your wish? You may speak now, but softly.'

Pazel realised he was blinking over and over. *Nuhzat*. The dream that was not a dream. He was trapped in it; he did not know whether to be honoured or appalled. 'Did it work, Father?' he asked. 'Am I cured?'

'You are cured,' said the old dlömu, 'but do not imagine that you are leaving the darkness behind. Not yet, at any rate.'

'What happens if I drink from the pool?'

The Master Teller looked at him piercingly. 'I can read the possible fates of Alifros, in a tremor, or the twisting of a spider's thread. But I do not know what the pool would offer you. And I would not tell you, even if I did: that would be to spoil the wine before you drank it.'

'The glass spiders come from here, don't they?'

The Teller looked pleased. 'That was shrewd, my boy. Yes, they enter Vasparhaven by this pool, and it is said that when they no longer come we must abandon the temple for ever. That day will certainly come, for I see it in every version of our future. A few years from now, it may be, or when my novices grow old, or perhaps when Alifros itself falls to ruin. But of that darkest future you know more than I do myself. You have borne the agent of that future, the black orb you call the Nilstone. And you have seen the Swarm of Night.'

Pazel shuddered. He did not want to think about the Swarm. 'Father, how can I be in *nuhzat*? I'm not a dlömu.' He looked up at the old seer, pondering. 'Unless ... Prince Olik said that some humans could go into *nuhzat*, if they'd been close to dlömu, in the old days before the plague. And my mother came from that time. And Rin knows she has a lot of fits. Could she have been with a dlömu, Father, before she crossed the Ruling Sea? Was she slipping into *nuhzat*, all those times we thought she was mad?'

The old Teller smiled inscrutably. 'Knowledge, Pazel Path-kendle. Hasn't that been your desire from the start?'

Pazel leaned over the edge of the pool. The bottom was a mosaic of fine blue tiles. 'I'm not going to drink,' he said. 'Don't take it the wrong way, Father, but I've had quite enough of—'

He stopped. The Master Teller was gone without a trace. He stood alone in the chamber, facing the dimly glowing pool.

Alarmed, he turned in a circle. Behind him was a dark doorway, and a staircase leading down. He felt the temptation sharply ... but there lay the pool. He bent down and dipped his hand into the water. It was icy cold.

Knowledge. What good did it do? Was he happier for knowing the mind-bruising languages of murths and eguar? The tortured life of Sandor Ott? The fact that something as ghastly as the Swarm lurked just outside Alifros, pressing in, like an ogre's face at the window? What would he learn this time? Something even more terrible, probably.

He cupped some water in his hand, and winced: even that little puddle on his palm burned with cold. He brought it close to his mouth. No, by the Pits. He did not want any more visions. He deserved not to see.

He drank.

At first the cold all but scalded his lips, but when he swallowed it was mere water he tasted, cool but pleasant. He dipped his hand and drank again, his fear abruptly gone. It was too late anyway, and despite the earlier wine and tea, he was thirsty.

After his fourth drink something made him look up. Directly across the pool a figure crouched, in almost the same posture as Pazel himself. A woman. She was no more than a silhouette above the pale-blue light.

Was she the one who had met him in the first chamber, the one whose hand had always been there to catch him? He blinked. Something was still wrong with his eyes, or his mind. For although there was enough light to see her, he could not decide if she were young or old, human or dlömu. 'Who are you?' he whispered.

The woman shook her head: speaking, apparently, was once more forbidden. Her very silence, however, woke a sudden and almost overpowering desire in Pazel: a desire to see her clearly, to know her, touch her. More than anything, to speak her name.

He rose and started around the pool – and the woman, quick and agile, jumped up and moved in the opposite direction, keeping the water between them. Pazel changed directions: she did the same. Heart hammering, he feinted one way, then dashed another. She mirrored him perfectly. She could not be fooled.

He stopped dead. Their eyes met; he had a vague idea that she was teasing him. *Fine*, he thought obstinately, *you win*. He stepped down into the pool, and the cold closed like teeth upon his ankles.

The woman gazed at him, standing very still. Pazel gritted his teeth and stepped down again, and then again. The water was now above his waist, and the cold was a shout of pain that would not stop. Two more steps to the bottom. There were deep cracks in the floor, some wide enough to put his foot in, and an idea came to him that the cracks led down infinitely far, into a dark turbulence beyond the bounds of Alifros. He descended another step, and then the woman put out her hand.

Stop. The command was as plain as if she had spoken aloud. She crouched again, lowering both hands into the pool, and when she lifted them he saw that they held something beautiful.

It was a transparent sphere, very much like the one Kirishgán had formed with the spider's liquid, but this one was as wide as a bushel basket, and growing even as he watched. Like the other sphere it seemed light in her hands, and very fragile. Colours and whorls and tiny translucent shapes danced over its surface, racing like clouds. Like a soap bubble, it rested on the surface of the pool, and very soon it had grown so large that Pazel had to retreat one step, and then another, until he was back upon the pool's rim, watching her distorted features through that sleek, uncanny shape.

Pazel knew now what he must do. Watching her, he raised his hands and laid them very carefully upon the sphere.

It trembled at his touch. The woman stared at him, cautious as a deer, and Pazel found he could barely breathe. He had been missing her before he knew she existed. Or had been a part of her before he ever fully became himself.

Mother?

He moved towards her slowly, keeping his hands upon the sphere. He knew somehow that she was alarmed, but this time she did not step away. The sphere so unthinkably delicate. Perhaps she did not dare to move.

Neda?

Islands formed between his fingers; continents turned before his eyes. Their hands were on the surface of the world. They were lifting countries, moving seas. She was frightened, yet she laughed silently, and so did he.

Thasha?

He could feel the world's winds across his knuckles; the ocean currents tickling his palms. It was like the best moments of his Gift, when the joy of an exquisite language, a language not of suffering but of song, burst open like a rose in his mind. He could look wide across the sphere and see whole coastlines; he could peer close and see the smallest details. A crumbling glacier, a forest draped with sleeping butterflies, a tiny houseboat in a river delta, a diving bell abandoned on a beach.

Klyst?

There was Etherhorde, smoking, bustling; there were her fleets on the prowl. And *Aya Rin*, there was Ormael, her flat little houses, her cobbled streets, her rubbishy port. The orchard settlements, his house-row, his house. The very window of the room he'd crawled out of years before, clutching a knife and an ivory whale.

Pazel blinked, startled, and found his gaze had flown westwards thousands of miles. Now he was following a real whale as it hurled itself, suicidally, upon a beach. It wallowed in the surf, exhausted, possibly dying. Then an armed mob rushed down the beach and surrounded it. One of them, the bravest, put his hand in the whale's mouth and extracted a golden sceptre, and when he held it high the other men fell to their knees in prayer. And suddenly the whale was no longer a whale but a young man, or possibly the corpse of one.

But that sceptre: solid gold, but crowned with a black shard of crystal. It was Sathek's Sceptre, the Mzithrini relic, and that meant the island must be—

Pazel blinked again: the scene was gone. He was only an arm's length from the woman, and more desperate than ever to know who she was. But now upon the world-sphere there moved a teeming darkness, a boiling cloud. It passed over towns and cities and left them blackened; it moved over the land and left blight. The woman saw it too, and he felt her calling to him silently: *Fight it, stop it, stop the Swarm!* The Swarm! How could she expect him to fight it? How could anyone fight for a world plagued by *that*?

And yet (Pazel met the woman's eyes again) it was no greater than what they shared, the bond between them, the growing trust. He felt suddenly that this was the knowledge he had taken with those gulps of water: the absurdly simple gift of trust and peacefulness. For a moment he did not care if she were human or dlömu or something drastically different. He knew the joy of being close to her, and that was enough.

The darkness began to retreat. Light shone again from the sphere, and once more the winds flowed clean over his hands. They stood like twin statues, and Pazel sensed the woman's fear ebbing away. Such peace! Could you still want conquests, power over others, worship and dominion and treasure, once you'd felt such peace?

To notice peace when you had it. That was treasure. That was what *waking* was for.

Through the glass he saw her wide adoring smile. She closed her eyes, and in repose she was so lovely that he could not help it, he lifted a hand and reached to touch her, and the glass sphere burst and rained in a million shards into the pool.

He was alone.

Pazel whirled: one small glass spider crawled from the water and vanished across the floor. He raced around the pool. Gone, gone: he should have been howling with loss. But he could not. He had loved her (loved what?), but her loss was suddenly distant and elusive, as though they had parted years ago.

No, not years. Centuries.

He stared at the empty chamber, shaking, convulsing. There was no source of warmth; he had to move or die. He groped for the exit, dripping, sensing already the deeper cold that lay ahead.

The stairway spat him out upon the lakeshore, half a mile from Vasparhaven, among tall rocks sheathed in ice. The first thing he saw was Hercól and Alyash and Counsellor Vadu, talking to a squat figure beside a long wooden boat.

Pazel staggered from the doorway, and the wind went through him like knives. But a bit further on a great fire blazed, and Ibjen stood warming his shoes. Thasha and Neeps were there as well. They raced to his side, and Thasha wrapped a woollen towel about his shoulders and dragged him to the fire, swearing like a Volpek.

He watched her gruffly as she dried his hair. 'You *lunatic*,' she said, her voice shrill with concern. 'You're cold as a blary fish. How did you get soaked like that?'

Pazel closed his eyes.

'Get nearer to the fire. Take off that mucking shirt!'

He obeyed. Neeps made a joke about him needing a bath anyway, but fell silent when he glared. Thasha was looking at him strangely.

'A novice came from the temple,' she said. 'He gave me something gorgeous, in a tiny wooden box. He said it came from you.'

Pazel wished she would just stop talking. He was clutching at memories, like fragments of a story heard once in childhood, and never again. A strange woman, a shining globe.

'We're crossing the lake tonight,' said Thasha, drying him vigorously, 'in three boats. If Hercól can make himself understood, that is. You should go and talk to the fisher-folk, Pazel. They're mizralds, and we just can't tell what they're trying to say. I think they're afraid of the north shore, but Hercól—'

'Ouch!' he snapped. 'Not so hard, damn it!'

Thasha lowered the towel. 'Baby.'

'Savage.'

Their eyes met. He touched his scalp, brought away a bloody

finger. He was quite annoyed with her, and wondered at the months of agony he'd let her cause. Then Thasha reached into his hair, and brought away something small and hard. It gleamed in the firelight: a shard of crystal, which even as he reached out a finger melted like ice and was gone.

29

The Black Tongue

8 Modobrin 941
237th day from Etherhorde

When the keel of the fishing boat dug into the sandy shore, Ibjen was first out: the journey had turned his stomach. And it had been bad, Pazel thought: the open boat with its one spindly mast and weird ribbed sail flapping about like a fin, no lamps on it anywhere, cutting through all that darkness with the wind howling over the peaks, the bright stars wheeling as they pitched and heaved, ice floes looming up suddenly, sometimes even grinding against their sides ... He shuddered, and leaped out himself, and winced as his feet sank to the ankles in the watery sand. *Freezing, even at midsummer.* How did they manage, those fisher-folk, year after ice-bound year?

At least the moon had sailed above the peaks: a full moon, by which the snowcaps dimly glowed. The second boat drew up beside the first, and the fisherman's uncle leaped barefoot into the water and pulled it in.

'And to think I'd hoped to *sleep* a little,' growled Big Skip, wading ashore as the dogs leaped out around him. He cursed as the nearest one shook its wet fur vigorously, then opened the front of his coat. 'Are you well, my ladies?' he asked.

'Alive, anyway,' said Ensyl, as she and Myett crawled groggily to his shoulders.

The mizralds kept looking at the shore, as though anxious to be gone from it. Hercól counted coins into the fisherman's hand. The

560

man's wife took one and studied the strange Arquali designs. 'It's a fake,' she announced. 'There's a *tol-chenni* on this coin.'

'It's real gold, I bit one,' said the fisherman's brother.

'That's the face of His Supremacy Magad the Fifth you just gnashed,' said Dastu coldly. 'You understand? He's our Emperor, our king.'

The fisherman's son laughed. 'King of the *tol-chenni*. King of the monkeys, the beasts!' He hooted and beat his chest. His uncle laughed, but his father scowled at him, embarrassed. Pazel looked at the wrinkled, wind-chapped creature. Was he, like Ibjen's father, just old enough to recall the days before the plague?

Soon all the chilly passengers were ashore. Hercól placed the twentieth coin in the man's palm, then smiled and added another fistful. 'Ask them not to speak of us to strangers, Pazel,' he said. 'There is still a chance we might be pursued.'

The family waved goodbye, delight beginning to show on their faces as they realised there was no trick.

'Come,' urged Hercól. 'We have gained a few miles on Arunis, I think. Let us gain a few more.'

He started at once up the grey, wind-sculpted beach. As the others straggled after him, Pazel heard a shout from the old fisherman. He turned: the mizrald was splashing up to him.

'You will go down the Ansyndra, and across the burn? What you call *Black Tongue*?'

'Well, yes,' said Pazel. 'There's no other way, is there?'

The mizrald shook his head. 'No other way. No other way except with wings.'

'Wings would be dandy,' said Pazel.

The fisherman nodded solemnly.

'Well,' said Pazel, 'goodbye.'

'You go at night, eh? Only at night across the burn. Darkly, quietly: that's how it's done. Tell your friends. Because by daylight – no, no.'

'No?'

The mizrald drew his finger across his throat. 'No, no and no.'

He stared at Pazel with concern, and looked as though he wished to say more. Then (as his family howled in protest) he pulled the youth down and planted a kiss upon his forehead. Then he turned and pushed his boat offshore.

Stunned, Pazel hurried after the others. They were trudging west along the rim of the lake, towards the spot the mizralds had said was the only way down. Pazel could hear a rushing of water, and the now very familiar, slushing roar of a waterfall. He ran, catching up with Neeps and Thasha. Neeps was gazing back across the lake.

'How are we supposed to return?' he said. 'The fisherwoman herself said they almost never come down here. And half the time there's no shore to walk along, just blary cliffs. How are we supposed to get back?'

'There must be trails through the mountains,' said Pazel, trying to sound as though he believed it. 'Hercól and Olik must have thought about it, mate. Don't worry.'

Thasha's gaze swept darkly over the peaks. 'They thought about it, all right,' she said.

Their destination, as it happened, was similar to the Chalice of the Maî: a river outlet above a sharp descent. But then Pazel swayed and stepped back, dizzied by what he saw. Where the Maî had begun as no more than a stream, this was a thrashing watercourse, descending almost vertically within a deep, twisting crack down the mountainside. In many spots the water vanished under boulders; in others it surged forth in a chaos of white spray. There were outright cliffs beneath them too, where the river became falls. And very close to the river, bolted fast to the rock, was a heavy iron ladder. It descended some forty feet and met up with a wet, steep trail that snaked back and forth down the mountain to another ladder, which in turn met another trail, and so on for some distance. Even by moonlight Pazel could see how far and fast the Ansyndra descended, falls beneath falls beneath falls ...

'The ladders will take us only so far,' Vadu was explaining.

'There, at that widest shelf, you can see where the Black Tongue begins.'

Pazel could not see it, in fact, for the men were all crowding hazardously for a view. Quickly he told the others what the mizrald had said.

'By night alone,' mused Hercól. 'Prince Olik too had heard rumours to that effect.'

'Nonsense,' said Vadu. 'Day or night makes no difference. Look there: you will see what does.'

This time Pazel managed to catch a glimpse. Far down the black ridge a faint light shone. Something was burning, with flames that danced and guttered in the wind, throwing sparks into the night. Then all at once it was gone. Utter darkness wrapped the slopes again.

'A fumarole,' said Vadu, 'a tunnel into the depths, formed as the lava cooled. The gases that erupt from those horrid pipes are flammable, and sudden in their emergence. But something worse dwells in them: the flame-trolls. Idlers who never leave the Upper City will tell you that they are mere legends, but we who carry the Plazic Blades know better. They are real, and deadly. When they emerge no living thing can cross the Tongue.'

'And when is that, Counsellor?' asked Myett, from Big Skip's shoulder.

'When they hear footsteps on their roof,' he said. 'Or loud voices, possibly. Many parts of the Tongue are but a hollow crust.'

'How did ye learn so much about the place?' asked Alyash.

Vadu gave him a rather hostile glance.

'The answer to that can wait,' said Cayer Vispek. 'The crossing cannot, if we are to go by night as Pathkendle says.'

'I tell you silence is all that matters,' said Vadu.

Nonetheless, they began the descent without delay. It was not the longest leg of their journey but certainly the most terrifying. Some of the ladders shifted on the rusted iron pins that held them to the cliffs; one had been reduced to a single bolt and three wooden splints. The rungs were corroded, and bit into their hands. But to

Pazel the spaces between the ladders were worse: slick ledges, barely flat enough to balance on even when motionless, too narrow for crawling (which would have been far safer than walking upright) and devoid of any handholds whatsoever.

Only the ixchel were at ease, and even they crouched low when the wind surged suddenly. Pazel, at home on masts and rigging, had to fight down panic at every turn. They crept down the cliffs, barely speaking. The four hunting dogs, slung in harnesses on the backs of the Masalym soldiers, held absolutely still. One particularly long ladder spanned a pair of rocks jutting well out from the cliff, so that for a good seventy feet there was no cliff to see or touch, just rung after iron rung, lost in the clawing wind.

How many more? thought Pazel desperately, after the eighth or ninth descent. He glimpsed his sister in the moonlight and was amazed at her poise. The other *sfvantskors* were the same, and so was Hercól: masterfully aware. Did such awareness free one from terror or increase it, he wondered, when each step might be your last?

At last, after fourteen ladders, they reached a broad, rocky shelf. Pazel was shaking, and feared he might be sick. But the air was warm: they had dropped right out of the icy wastes of Ilvaspar, and into a gentler place. But there was also a strange, biting smell that for some reason made Pazel think of rats.

It was very dark. He moved away from the ladders and at once bumped into Neda – and Neeps. The small boy was holding his sister, rigid with indignation, in a tight embrace.

'Is all right,' said Neda, squirming, her Arquali rougher than usual. 'Let go now! You do same for me, same situation.'

Neeps did not seem able to let go. Pazel touched his shoulder; he started, and abruptly dropped his arms. There was mud on his face but he did not seem aware of it.

'I should be dead,' he whispered, staring at Pazel. 'I mucking *fell*, mate. On that path with the ice underfoot, that terrible spot. Your sister caught me by the belt and dragged me back. She could have fallen herself. I should be dead.'

Neda looked at Pazel. Switching tongues, she said, 'Your friend is in shock. But when he's able to listen, tell him I'll break his arms if he tries to grab me again.'

'I don't think it's likely,' said Pazel. 'He's a married man.'

Neda's face was blank. She looked the small tarboy up and down, and when her eye flicked back to Pazel she began suddenly to laugh. She turned away, fighting it, but Neeps' baffled look made matters worse, and she spun back helplessly to Pazel and pressed her face hard against his shoulder. Reckless, wondering if she would break *his* arms, Pazel held her a moment and gave way to silent laughter. That old, choked guffaw. She still existed, she was still Neda somewhere inside. He could have held her for an hour, but when she lurched away he let her go.

Cayer Vispek looked stern, and Jalantri glared at him with something like fury. But Pazel found he no longer cared what they thought. Something *had* changed in Vasparhaven. He was older; he knew something that they did not. Rin's eyes, he thought, sometimes even a blary *sfvantskor* needs to let go.

As if he'd just given the idea to the mountain, there came a deafening *clang* that reverberated in the rocks, and for the first time ever, a yelp from one of the dogs. An entire ladder had parted from the cliff, fallen soundless, and shattered just inches from the animal. The stone cracked; bits of iron flew among them; the bulk of the ladder pinwheeled over a big boulder and lay still.

The dog crept whimpering among them, pleading innocence with its eyes. Hercól glanced up at the cliff. 'One bolt,' he said, 'and three wooden splints.'

For a time the night grew even brighter: the old moon still shone down on them, and the Polar Candle, its small blue sister, joined it in the sky. By this double illumination they saw the strange new place they had reached.

The shelf was the size of an ample courtyard. On the right-hand side the Ansyndra poured into a kind of natural funnel in the rock and disappeared, bubbling and gurgling. Behind them and to their left rose the high cliff wall, up which they would never climb again. Straight ahead, growing from cliff to cliff, there rose a stand of willows, straight and lovely, and utterly startling after so much barren rock. Ferns grew among them, and streamers of moss dangled from their limbs. A long-disused trail led away through the trees.

They gathered their belongings and followed it. For a gentle mile it ran, only gradually descending. The gorge did not widen much, and they were never more than a stone's throw from one cliff or the other. Then, like something lopped off with an axe, the forest ended, and they saw the Black Tongue.

It was old lava: a deep, smooth expanse of it, like a hardened river of mud. It began at their feet and swept down a long, gradual decline, widening ever, for several miles or more. Nothing grew upon its surface; nothing could. There were smooth, mouthlike holes in the lava, some no bigger than peaches, others wide as caves. There were cracks and fissures, and small puffs of fire like the one they had seen from atop the mountain.

'Not a troll to be had,' said Alyash. 'Pity.'

'Keep your voices low,' replied Hercól.

The smell Pazel had noticed before was far stronger here, and now he recognised it: sulphur.

'That's why I thought of rats,' he said to Thasha. 'We almost used sulphur on the rats, to smoke them out of the hold, remember? And we used it all the time back on the *Anju*.'

'It must work like a charm,' she said, grimacing.

'Oh, it does,' said Myett suddenly, 'and on *crawlies* as well.'

'Blary right it does,' said Alyash.

'Enough of that!' said Hercól, who had not taken his eyes from the scene before them. Then he growled low in his throat. 'The descent took longer than I hoped. There is not enough darkness left for us to make it safely across that dismal field. We shall retreat into the forest until this evening.'

'That is sheer folly!' said Vadu. 'Weren't you listening to me above?'

'I listened to you,' said Hercól, 'but also to what Pazel heard from the fisherman, and to what Olik knew, and to my own counsel above all. You may be sure that I am making no light choices. We have abandoned our ship for this cause. And our people.'

'Then let it be worth your sacrifice!' said Vadu, his head starting to bob. 'You are said to be a warrior, but this tactic is more suited to a counting clerk. Show some courage. Let us go now, and quickly – and if we must run the last mile, so be it. Come, our goal is the same.'

'It is,' said Hercól, 'but we are not agreed on how to reach it. For I *am* thinking like a counting clerk. I am counting every person in this expedition, and intending to send none of them heedlessly to their deaths.'

'Heedless?' The counsellor's voice rose in anger. 'You claim that death awaits all of us, if Arunis masters the Nilstone. Do you not understand where he is going? The River of Shadows. The River of Shadows enters Alifros just downstream from the Tongue, in the heart of the Infernal Forest. Throughout the ages of this world it has been a pilgrimage site for wizards good and evil. Whatever advantage Arunis thinks to find is surely there. He does not have far to go, Stanapeth, and neither do we.'

'I have heard you out,' said Hercól, 'and you, Vadu, have sworn to abide by my decisions. I gave you a warning then, and I repeat it now.'

'I am no child, and need no warnings,' said Vadu.

'No?' said Hercól. 'Did you place your hand on the knife-hilt, Counsellor? Or did the knife call it there, as it has called the tune before?'

Vadu started, and jerked his hand away from the Plazic Blade, wincing as he did so as if the gesture caused him pain. He was breathing hard, and his men backed a little away from him. 'Do as you will, then,' he said, 'but I am not responsible.'

'Only for yourself,' said Hercól, watching him steadily.

The party retreated into the trees and found a level spot to rest. 'I think we must light no fire,' said Jalantri.

'How about a candle?' said Big Skip. 'The ixchel are cold and wet.'

Ensyl and Myett protested, but Hercól at once gathered stones into a ring and thrust four candles into the ground within them. Pazel looked at the two women, warming themselves amply by the little flames, shaking their short hair dry. *We're finally in the same boat*, he thought, *cut off from our own kind, in a world that knows nothing about us.* But it wasn't the same, not really. The humans numbered thirteen, not two, and they had not been raised in a clan that honoured the whole above the parts, the House above the self. And they were not eight inches tall.

The humans and the dogs settled down to wait out the day, posting watches on the Black Tongue. Pazel fell asleep almost instantly, and dreamed of Chadfallow. He was lecturing Pazel in his old professorial way, but the subject, oddly, was how to trim a foresail braceline. 'Up, in, down to the pin!' Chadfallow kept repeating, watching Pazel struggle with rope and cleat. And as his frustration grew, Pazel realised that Chadfallow wore a captain's uniform. 'No good, boy, no good,' he said. 'It's that hand of yours. Too fishy by far.' Pazel looked at his left hand and saw nothing unusual, just the leathery scar he'd borne for months. 'Not *that* one,' said Ignus crossly, and raised Pazel's other hand by force. It was black and half-webbed.

Dawn came, and with it Pazel's watch. He was paired with Ibjen; they lay low at the edge of the trees, listening to the chatter of unseen birds, and watching the flames spout and sputter on the Tongue. The nearest fumarole was only about a hundred yards from where they lay, but the big ones – wide enough for something man-sized to crawl from them – were much farther down the lava flow. Sounds issued from them: soft piping like stone flutes, low surging moans. With every noise Pazel half-expected to see a troll crawl out into the daylight. Ibjen, however, seemed more worried about Vadu and his Plazic Blade. Hercól, he said, should have driven the man off while he could.

'I thought so too,' Pazel admitted. 'But Hercól's thought carefully about it, and I trust him.'

'He hardly sleeps,' said Ibjen. 'That cannot continue, you know. Unless he too draws his strength from some unnatural source.'

'Ildraquin isn't cursed,' said Pazel, 'and Hercól is strong without help from any blade.'

'Pazel,' said Ibjen, 'is it true that you can cast spells?'

'What?' said Pazel, startled. 'No, it isn't. Or … just one. And Ramachni says it's not even right to call it a spell. It's a Master-Word. He gave me three of them, but I've spoken the other two, used them, and that erases them from my mind.'

'How are they different from spells?'

Pazel thought back. 'He said that a Master-Word is like black powder – gunpowder, you understand? – without the cannon to control the explosion. He said the key thing about spells is that control. Otherwise you can't stop them from doing what you *don't* want to do.'

'Like turning men into dumb animals,' said Ibjen, 'when your goal is to make animals think like men.'

Pazel sighed. 'I suppose Erithusmé didn't have much control either, when she cast the Waking Spell. But that spell drew its power from the Nilstone, and it ruins everything it touches, I think. And I wonder, Ibjen: what's going to happen to woken animals, if we succeed? I'm afraid for Felthrup. For all of them, really.'

He gazed out at the Tongue, the sudden plumes of flame that came and went like harbour-signals. Ibjen was quiet so long that Pazel glanced at him, wondering if he'd nodded off. But the silver eyes were wide, and staring at him with concern.

'I must add to your fears, Pazel,' he said. 'I'm sorry. It's Neeps.'

Pazel gave a violent start. 'Neeps? What about him? What's the blary fool done this time?'

'I wasn't sure at first, because the stench from the Black Tongue was so strong. But it's there, all right.'

'What's there?'

'The smell of lemons. I know that smell, Pazel: my father tamed *tol-chenni* on the Sandwall, you know. Once you're used to it there's no mistaking it for anything else.'

When he finally understood, Pazel felt as though his own death had just been handed to him, as if he'd thrown back a drink only to learn it was poison. 'No,' he muttered, shaking his head, looking away from the dlömic boy.

'Father always claimed it was the sure sign,' said Ibjen gently, 'back in the days when humans were changing.'

'It isn't true, Ibjen, it's not happening, you're crazy.'

But even as he spoke Pazel remembered Olik's words in the stateroom. Rage was one warning sign, he'd told them, along with *a sharp smell of lemon in one's sweat.* And what had Neeps said, when they were sitting beside the signal fire? *There are times when my mind just seems to vanish.* Panic, deep terror, welled up inside him. Ibjen's hand was on his arm. 'How long does it take?' Pazel heard himself ask.

'Five or six weeks,' said Ibjen. 'I think that's what father used to say. Pazel, are you crying?'

Pazel pinched his eyes shut. Images from the Conservatory assaulted him. The mindlessness, the filth. He would not let Neeps become a *tol-chenni.* He turned to Ibjen and gripped his hand in turn. 'Don't say a word about this,' he begged. 'The plague doesn't spread from person to person anyway. Your father told us that.'

'I know,' said Ibjen, 'and I won't tell anyone. You're right, it would only make things worse. The others might drive him away.'

'We're going to stop it,' whispered Pazel, 'before he changes. We will, Ibjen. We have to.'

Ibjen said nothing for a time. Then he asked, 'What does it do, your Master-Word? The one you haven't spoken yet?'

'I don't know,' said Pazel. 'Ramachni told me it would *blind to give new sight.* What that means even he couldn't guess.'

'Blindness?' said Ibjen. 'Blindness, from a kind of magic that you say runs out of control?' The dlömic boy looked terrified. 'You must never speak that word, Pazel. Try to forget it, and soon, before you utter it one day in your sleep.'

Pazel shook his head. He trusted Ramachni. His two previous words had shaken the fabric of the world around him, but done no lasting damage. Ramachni had assured him of that, just before repeating his promise to return. But in his mind Pazel still heard Arunis back at Bramian, gloating, saying that the mage had abandoned them, vanished into the safety of his own world. And now Neeps—

'Look there!' whispered Ibjen, pointing. 'Something does live on the Tongue. Or dares to crawl on it, anyway.' Far down the black slope, Pazel caught a glimpse of reddish fur, vanishing behind a bulge in the lava. 'A marmot, or a weasel,' said Ibjen. 'I suppose trolls don't bother with weasels.'

Their hour was over. They crept away from the edge of the lava flow, then stood and walked back towards the clearing. But as they drew near Pazel felt a sudden, horrible sensation in his mind: the same sensation, in fact, as two days before. The power of the eguar was being summoned again.

He dashed to the clearing. Everyone was awake, afoot, rigid with alarm. Counsellor Vadu had drawn his knife. His head was twitching almost uncontrollably; his soldiers had massed behind him, steeled for a fight. Ildraquin in hand, Hercól glared at the counsellor. Vadu's own face was screwed up in a strange mixture of bravado and pain.

Floating in the air before him were Ensyl and Myett. The two women's backs were together; they revolved slowly as though hanging from a thread. Vadu's free hand was raised, his fingers cupped as though squeezing something tight between them.

'No!' Pazel cried.

Vadu whirled and the women cried out in pain, in the ixchel voices only Pazel himself could hear. 'Stay where you are, Pathkendle!' cried the counsellor. 'And you, Hercól Stanapeth: where are your lectures now? Have you realised that you should have left them on the far side of the Nelluroq? Or will you try again to order us about in our own country?'

Hercól gestured for Pazel to be still.

'You should have taken this Blade when you mastered me on the plain,' said Vadu, his voice made staccato by the twitches of his head. 'It called out to you; it would have abandoned me, and served you in my stead.'

'That Blade serves no one,' said Hercól, 'except perhaps the beast from whose corpse it was fashioned.'

'Be that as it may, I am now in command,' said Vadu, 'and I will not let this mission fail through cowardice. Don't you realise that I can fight off the trolls, if they should come?'

'Are you sure?' asked Cayer Vispek. 'There is almost nothing left of that knife. Look at it, Counsellor: it has shrunk in a matter of days.'

'We will cross the Black Tongue now,' said Vadu, as though the other had not said a word, 'and overtake the mage before he reaches his goal, and slay him, and then the Nilstone shall be ours.'

'Ours,' said Bolutu, 'or yours? Vadu, Vadu, you are not the man who came to us on the plain! That man understood the very dangers you are surrendering to!'

'The only danger is inaction,' said Vadu. 'We will go, in prudent silence. These two I will hold until we reach the shores of the Ansyndra; and then we shall see.'

'Fight him!'

The voice was Ensyl's, and it was torn from her throat. Vadu bared his teeth and the ixchel women cried out again. Pazel saw that Neda was looking Hercól in the eye.

'We can kill this fool,' she said in Mzithrini. 'We have him on three sides, and those little seizures will not help his fighting. Whatever his power, we will be too quick for him to stop.'

'Do nothing, I beg you,' replied Hercól in the same tongue. 'We could kill him, yes, but not before he kills his prisoners.'

'There's no other way,' said Jalantri. 'They're warriors. They're prepared.'

'*I* am not prepared!' shouted Hercól. And looking at his tortured face Pazel knew he was remembering another moment, another ixchel woman facing death and urging him not to give in.

Staring hard at Vadu, Hercól sheathed his sword. 'I would pity you, if you would but speak the truth, as you did when I briefly set you free. Indeed, I should have taken the knife – for your sake. Lead on, man of the *Platazcra*. But harm those women and no blade will protect you.'

'They will be harmed only if you are foolish,' said Vadu.

Fighting his twitches, he reached out and closed his hand around the waists of the ixchel women. Quietly the party moved down the path. At length they came to the edge of the black, smooth lava flow. Hercól stopped and pointed to the right.

In a low murmur, he said, 'The eastern part of the Tongue is still shadowed by the mountain. Will you at least permit us to walk there, and not in the bright sun?'

Vadu nodded impatiently. 'Yes, yes, if it will strengthen your spine. Only say nothing, and plant your feet lightly, and make no sound until we are well among the trees on the far side.'

Hercól looked at the others. 'Check all that you carry. You soldiers especially: do not let your scabbards knock against the ground.'

'I was about to say as much,' said Vadu.

'If we should have to run,' asked Hercól, 'what will happen to Ensyl and Myett?'

'I will not run,' said Vadu.

Hercól's look was withering. Then he stepped out onto the lava. Vadu came second, his prisoners against his chest. The rest of the party followed gingerly. Within the first few steps Pazel knew that the going would be harder than he had supposed. Though smooth, the surface was anything but even. It was like a candle melted down the side of a jug, one liquid trail hardened atop another. And twisting through them all were the shafts of the fumaroles. Was it better to walk, or crouch down and creep? Many times he was tempted to jump, as he would from stone to stone at a river crossing. But he dared not risk making a noise.

The flames were sudden and unpredictable: one moment there would be a black, dark fumarole, the next a geyser of twisting flames. Gas, searingly hot and reeking of sulphur, issued from others in bursts and wheezes. There was absolutely nothing one might call a trail.

Yet the going grew easier the further they went. It did help to be able to see, Pazel reflected, although he supposed Hercól would have waited for the moonlight. So far no one had made a sound. Even the dogs, marvels of perception that they were, understood what was required, and crept along with mincing steps.

The sky was beautiful, cloudless. Far overhead, a few vultures drifted. On the lava bed they were the only things that moved.

The shadow of the mountain was shrinking towards them, but they could always, Pazel supposed, move closer to the mountain.

Thasha and Neeps were descending on his left; Neda and her brother *sfvantskors* on his right. All of them watching the ground; it was the only safe way to proceed. And yet, Pazel thought, and yet—

He raised his eyes – and fought down the urge to cry aloud. About three yards from Neeps, a tiny face was watching them from a hole in the lava. It was hideous, part-human, buck-toothed, squinting, red. The face was attached to a hairy body about the size and shape of a gopher. The creature had hair everywhere except on that face, and the hands – they were *hands*, not paws – that gripped the edges of the scalding rock.

It vanished down the tube. Pazel was so shocked that he nearly missed a step. The others looked at him in alarm. No one else had seen the creature. He pointed at the hole, then gestured wildly (squinting eyes, fingers for teeth). Was it the same sort of creature he and Ibjen had glimpsed? Was it dangerous, or did its silence mean that it, too, had learned to remain unnoticed by the trolls?

There were more vultures now, and they circled lower over the Tongue. The others in the party glanced at them, frowning. Pazel realised that they had quickened their pace.

Less than a mile to go. The dogs gazed ahead, clearly wishing they could run. Each man and woman moving precisely, silently. A Masalym soldier lost his balance, and a Turach caught his arm.

The dlömu mouthed a silent *thank you*; the Turach smiled, and then everyone stopped dead.

Hercól had flung his arms wide, a violent gesture. At first Pazel did not understand. Then someone gasped and, turning, he saw that they were surrounded. From inside every hole and behind every bulge and hardened bubble, the red-faced creatures stared at them with their strange squinting faces, like old men who had lost their glasses. A hundred, perhaps many more. Yards deep they stood, eight or ten together in the larger tunnels. Not one of them moved a muscle.

Vadu's mouth was agape. The dogs' hair stood on end, but they did not growl.

'Warriors,' said Hercól with monumental slowness. 'Be ready with your weapons, but do not attack first. We are going on.' And with Ildraquin's tip hovering just before his knees, he stepped forwards.

The creatures bristled, and bared their white rodents' teeth. Hercól took another step. The creatures directly before him hissed, and shrank into their holes. But those on the sides only tensed and twitched, as though ready to spring.

Then Vadu laughed. He held his knife at arm's length, and over the tiny nub of bone the ghost-blade flickered. Suddenly a great shrieking hiss went up from all the creatures, and they whirled about and disappeared into their holes. A brief sound of scurrying rose from the depths. Then nothing more. The travellers looked at one another in shock.

'I told you I had power to keep us safe,' said Vadu.

'Let us go on,' said Hercól.

'Counsellor Vadu?' said Pazel suddenly. He startled everyone, beginning with himself, but he knew what he was doing. 'Let the ixchel go. We've come too far to turn back anyway.'

Vadu glanced down at Myett and Ensyl, clutched against his chest. He laughed again. 'It is not enough that I obeyed a human, for a time. Now I am to take orders from a human underling, a servant boy!'

Pazel swallowed. 'I think—'

'That is open to question.'

'—you're going to need that knife for something else.'

Vadu started. His head wobbled as he looked at the holes, the massing vultures, the distance yet to walk. Then, with a jerky motion, he thrust the two ixchel into Pazel's hands. 'I release them,' he said. The women gasped suddenly.

'Quiet!' said Pazel, in their own language. 'Don't shout! You were enchanted. You're free now, but we're not safe.'

Both ixchel began to shake. Through closed eyes, Myett whispered, 'Who did this to us?'

Pazel was about to answer when he noticed that Vadu was still staring at his knife. The look of rapture on his face made Pazel think suddenly of the Shaggat, gazing with adoration at the Nilstone that had almost killed him. Vadu raised the knife above his head, and as he did so his hand cleared the shadow of the mountain. Sunlight touched the last, minuscule bone shard upon the hilt – and with a slight quaking of the air, the shard was gone.

Vadu lowered his arm. 'It is over,' he said. 'I released them, and the Blade released me. That was its final act. The end was closer than I dared hope.' He rubbed his face, his neck: the twitching had finally ceased. Joy welled suddenly in the counsellor's eyes. Before anyone realised his intention he turned and flung the hilt across the lava flow with all his might. 'I am free!' he cried, and with that all bedlam erupted.

Fire burst from holes far and near. A roaring filled the earth. A dog howled, and from the larger tunnels the flame-trolls began to emerge: first their long fingers, ash-white and clawed; then their mighty arms; then their heads, large and powerful as the heads of horses, but with the spreading jaws of wolves. They were hairless, and the flames of the depths licked over them, as though their very pores exuded some combustible oil. Their eyes wept fire; the spittle in their mouths was fire. The first to emerge was nearly nine feet tall.

It made to leap but Hercól moved first, and before Pazel knew what had happened the troll was waving the stumps of its hacked-off limbs, and its foul blood was spattering them all.

'Run!' thundered Hercól. 'Turachs, *sfvantskors*, to the vanguard! Men of Masalym, stand with me behind!'

No one questioned his orders now. The party charged for the forest with weapons drawn. Pazel ran with Thasha at his side, and Neeps just behind. He bore his sword in one hand, Myett and Ensyl in the other, curled to his chest. They were ahead of the trolls, that was clear. The creatures were bursting forth in greater numbers, but always a step or two behind. As though their footfalls were guiding them, waking them. And he remembered suddenly running along a hollow log back in Ormael: a log that housed a great, drowsy hive of bees. He had felt them stirring under his feet, but had gotten away without a sting.

Then he saw the red-faced creatures, swarming out of the fumaroles dead ahead. They squealed piercingly, and the trolls rose in answer, cutting off the party from the trees.

The *sfvantskors* met them first, slashing at the flaming arms, the spitting heads. The Turachs did their part as well, hacking and stabbing alongside their old enemies. Three or four trolls died before they could escape the tunnels.

But right and left the creatures were gaining their feet and leaping to the attack. Suddenly all was carnage, terrible and blindingly swift. Cayer Vispek jumped over a troll's groping hand, then killed it – *killed* it – with a savage kick to the head. A Turach drove his blade straight into flaming jaws. The dogs killed the rodent-beasts with swift efficiency, shaking them, flinging the carcasses away. But their muzzles were burning; Big Skip's shirt was burning; a dying troll spat flame in Vadu's face. On Pazel's right a dlömic soldier beheaded a troll just rising from the earth, and a second troll caught his arm and wrenched him, head first, into the fumarole. He never managed a scream.

'On! On! Stop for nothing!' Hercól was bellowing. And somehow they did go on, right through the fire, over the twitching bodies, the arms still reaching from the earth. They ran with the red-faced creatures dragging from their ankles; they ran not knowing which of them, what part of them, was burning.

'Pazel, stay with us! Protect them!' Thasha shouted, waving at the ixchel. He ran with her on one side, Neeps on the other. Together, as though maddened by danger, they charged a huge troll with broken fangs. The beast lunged at Thasha; she parried with her sword and stabbed it through the hand with her knife, and turned her head before its fire-spittle could scald her in the face. Neeps managed only to graze the creature before it raked him with the claws of its free hand, sending him sprawling. The troll snapped at him, tore out a mouthful of hair. Then Pazel and Thasha lunged together. His sword pierced its chest; Thasha's tore its belly open. It toppled sideways, dying; the three of them were past it – and then Pazel felt it sink those teeth into his calf.

He fell flat atop the ixchel; the troll's claws were shredding his pack and clothes, seeking his flesh. Then from the corner of his eye he saw Neeps make a desperate upward thrust, and blood from the troll's severed throat washed down his leg.

The corpse fell burning atop him; Thasha and Neeps somehow moved it in a matter of seconds, and to their clear amazement Pazel leaped up and ran at their side. But the burning followed him, enveloped him, and still more trolls slavered at their heels. He felt that his run was an extended fall down a black cliff, faster and faster, his feet somehow staying under him just enough to fend him off the lava, and then suddenly he was on thinner lava, crumbled lava, then earth, then leaves, and the hooting, howling pursuit went on into the forest, and he smashed through vines and palms and thorns and flowers and brush, his arm over the ixchels' faces, his own flesh torn, and then *Praise Rin and His host* there was the river, a blessed short muddy bank and then in, down, the fire in his clothes hissing out, the ixchel coughing and choking as he lifted them clear, trod water, kicked out into the water among the other survivors, while on the banks behind them twenty or thirty flame trolls stood screaming their hate, and fighting over the corpses already roasting in their grasp.

The Ansyndra here was wide and shallow; they bobbed along with it gently, the dlömu helping the humans stay afloat, until they rounded a long bend and left the creatures behind. Then they dragged themselves ashore. Three of the eight Masalym soldiers were gone, and one Turach also. Two dogs limped onto the sand, and a third, nearly hairless, came whimpering from the forest.

'Sit down!' said Thasha to Pazel, catching him by the arm. 'We've got to take care of that leg. Damn it all, the packs, our medicine kit, our food—'

'How did we do it?' Pazel gasped. 'How did we get away?'

'Hercól,' she said, 'and Vadu. I know it looked like there were trolls everywhere, but most of them were behind us. They held them all back. Vadu can fight, by Rin.'

'Hush, Thasha,' said Neeps, looking past her shoulder.

The surviving dlömic warriors were laying Vadu in the grass. He was hideously burned, his face unrecognizable, the lids barely moving over the silver eyes. His hands were so blistered and torn it was hard to tell where one finger ended and the next began. 'I don't think he can move,' whispered Neeps. 'They floated him downstream like a log.'

But Vadu could move, for he was raising one hand, weakly beckoning. It was Hercól he wanted. The swordsman drew close and knelt at his shoulder.

'Now I pay,' said Vadu, his voice faint and rasping. 'For all my folly, and a life of borrowed strength.'

'You have been paying for years, son of Masalym,' said Hercól.

Vadu shook his ruined head. 'Not everyone who touched a Blade surrendered to it. I gave myself to the eguar, and lost my sanity, my soul. You alone had no fear to say so, to my face. Human, warrior human. I look at you and see the man I should have been.'

'You are that man,' said Hercól. 'You have outlived the curse you carried.'

'I have done that,' said Vadu. 'Yes. That is something. Farewell, strange friend.'

Vadu said no more. He lay still, and though Pazel knew he might be imagining it, he thought that peace stole over the counsellor's body; and Bolutu, no longer a monk of the Rinfaith but practised in such moments nonetheless, gently closed his eyes.

30

The Infernal Forest

Thasha's hair was half the length it had been an hour before; her locks ended in singed, black strands. Kneeling beside Pazel, she cut away the shreds of his trouser leg, and winced at what she saw. But Pazel knew he was lucky. His calf had been pierced in four places, but the broken fangs had not gone deep; the troll had meant to hold him while its claws did the killing. Still, something was wrong. The wound throbbed, and ugly green-purple blotches were rising around the broken skin. Thasha looked around helplessly. 'Blary wonderful place to be without a doctor,' she said.

Pazel thought of Neeps, and cringed inside. What doctor could help him, though? In Arqual, Chadfallow had cured the talking fever, but that was not a magical plague. And all the doctors of the South had obviously failed. So much horror, he thought, watching a Turach wrap wet bandages about a burned dlömic forehead.

'The trick will be to keep those holes from getting infected,' said Ensyl, studying his leg.

No, he thought, the trick was to keep moving. To keep moving, and not to let his thoughts wander anywhere he couldn't stand to look. With that goal in mind he glanced up at the trees. There were fifty shades of green straight overhead. Tiny butterflies were descending like a fall of orange snowflakes. 'This doesn't look very infernal to me,' he said.

'No,' said Thasha, 'I don't suppose we're there yet.'

The survivors dressed their wounds, and those of the three remaining dogs. Then they carried Vadu into the forest, and built a cairn of stones over his body, and held their breath to the count of one hundred for the dead, as their people had done for so many generations that no one could say how the custom began.

As they returned Pazel looked over the remaining soldiers. Two Turachs: an older warrior, with a scar on his forehead like an extra eyebrow; and a younger man with a sullen, boyish face. Five dlömic warriors, including a tall and capable woman who appeared to be taking charge of her comrades.

Ibjen walked knee-deep into the river, staring intently at something offshore.

'What is it, lad?' asked Cayer Vispek. But instead of answering, Ibjen suddenly dived.

He surfaced many yards away, swimming with a power no champion human swimmer could hope to match. As Pazel watched he closed on some jagged rocks at mid-river, where sticks and other debris had collected. Carefully he plucked something from the detritus, then turned and swam back to the shore.

'This is yours, Thashiziq,' he said as he emerged. On his palm rested an ornate wooden box, soaked and battered but intact.

'The box from Vasparhaven!' said Thasha, taking it. 'The one the novice said came from you, Pazel. I thought for sure it was lost. But that lovely crystal – it can't possibly have survived.'

She sprang the latch, raised the lid. Unfortunately she was quite correct: nothing but a fine dust remained of Kirishgán's exquisite sphere. The parchment was damp, but not soaked. As the others gathered, watching, Thasha took out the little scrap and unfolded it with great care. The selk's writing had begun to blur, but it could still be read.

A sworn secret must be kept – but in like measure, a fateful meeting must be honoured. Therefore in deepest trust I tell you: there is hope downriver, between the mountains and the sea.

Alyash turned away, sneering. 'That's profound, that is. I'm all aquiver.'

'You're a fool,' said Pazel. 'He's telling us something important. As clearly as he can without breaking an oath.'

'The message is surely important,' said Hercól, 'but we cannot debate it now. Rest a little more, all of you, and see that your wounds are dressed properly. We have our own oaths to keep, and they will soon spur us onwards.'

Pazel lay down with his head on a stone, watching the butterflies, trying not to think of the trolls. He closed his eyes and saw their faces, their flame-slobber, their claws. He heard Dastu say something about 'Pathkendle's nurse' and realised that Thasha was still fussing over his leg. Once again he felt a surge of annoyance with her, although he knew the response was foolish. What was he resisting, exactly? Her touch, his need for it? Whatever it was, Thasha sensed his impatience, and her fingers grew clumsy on his bandages.

Very soon Hercól called the party together. 'It is best that you know the truth,' he said. 'We have lost all our supplies, save the weapons we managed to swim with, and what Alyash and I carried on our backs. We have some half-dozen *mül*, but nothing else to eat. We have no spare clothes, no oilskins against the rain, no telescope, or rope, or compass. There are torches, and a box of matches that may dry out eventually. Between the twenty-one of us we have nine swords and two knives.'

'And one pistol,' said Alyash.

'One soaked pistol,' said Hercól. 'This is what I would tell you now: we may perish in this quest. But if you are with me still, I can promise you that ours will not be a thoughtless or an empty death. We will stand together, and if need be fall together, but we will yet do all that we can to prevail.'

'But of course we'll follow you,' said Thasha.

Hercól's fondness for her shone in his eyes. 'You are my right hand, Thasha – or perhaps I am your left. It is to others I speak.'

'As for the three of us,' said Cayer Vispek, 'you need not waste your breath. The scriptures tell us that it is a blessing to discover one's fight, to see the devil by the plain light of day, and take after him with a blade. Most are denied this; most lunge at false devils – even at their brothers. We have taken enough false lunges. I think now that you were sent to show us our true fight – even if that is a fight from which we do not return. So lead on, Tholjassan. I say again, if we did not follow you, where would we go?'

'This is no debate we need to have,' added the dlömic woman. 'Any doubts we harboured, we left behind in Masalym. Even Counsellor Vadu knew in his heart that you must lead. We will go forward, and if fate permits we will kill this sorcerer before it is too late.'

The other dlömic soldiers nodded. 'The Otter speaks for us all,' said one.

'Otter?' said Hercól.

The dlömic woman looked slightly embarrassed. 'I am Lunja, a sergeant of the Masalym Watch. My name means *Otter* in the old tongue of Chaldryl. So to my men I am the Otter.'

Hercól nodded to her. 'I thank you for your trust, Sergeant Lunja.' He looked at the remaining faces, one by one. His gaze fell last on Alyash, who was something of an apparition. His hair had burned off completely; his shirt was torn open, revealing his old, extensive scars, and blisters like embedded pearls graced his ears and forehead.

'What are you staring at?' said the bosun. 'Yes, I'll blary follow you. Not as if anyone here's going to take orders from *me*.'

'Then prepare to march,' said Hercól, strapping Ildraquin over his shoulder. 'Fulbreech is still moving away. We will rest at dusk, whether he pauses or not. But since we have crossed the Black Tongue by daylight, let us at least do as Vadu wished and use these hours well.'

He set off at an unforgiving pace, and the others, in their burned boots (and in Vispek's case, no boots at all) struggled to keep up. They walked under the trees, out of the dense underbrush at the margin of the forest, but near enough its edge to keep the river in sight. Thasha, who carried nothing except her sword, began to help Pazel hobble along on his wounded leg. After a few minutes she gave the task to Neeps. 'You're the right height,' she said, sliding Pazel's arm over his shoulder. Neeps flashed her an awkward smile, and so did Pazel. But when he smelled lemons he turned away, pretending that his leg hurt him awfully, so that neither would see the truth on his face.

An hour later Pazel felt stronger, and told Neeps he could manage on his own. The forest began to thin by mid-afternoon, and in time they marched out of it altogether, onto a narrow plain of low, feathery grasses, bounded on the right by jagged cliffs and the scree of old landslides, and on the left by the crumbling banks of the Ansyndra, along which grew scattered pines and cedars and the occasional oak. It was strange country, very warm and windless, and yet enclosed on all sides by those enfortressed mountains, looming over them with vast shoulders of snow. The Ansyndra became deeper, narrower, more violent and swift. They had no other guide but Ildraquin's whispers to Hercól, but he drove them on, nearly running, saying that their quarry lay ahead, always downriver and ahead.

So the day ended, and at dusk as promised Hercól let them rest. They chose a spot with many cedars near the river. The mountain's shadow brought swift darkness, but they had good luck with the matches and soon a fire was burning. It cheered them some and dried their boots, but its heat made their burns ache. Alyash disassembled Ott's pistol, drying the components on a stone. Pazel gazed blearily at the little wood-and-steel mechanism. Hard to believe that it could kill a man.

Famished, the twenty-one travellers and three dogs shared half their stock of *mül*, which came to about a teaspoon each. Pazel was battling sleep even as he chewed. He drifted off with Thasha once more examining his leg, and a dog licking his *mül*-sticky fingers with equal concentration.

At dawn they were chilled and soaked with dew. Hercól had

them up and marching before they were properly awake, and certainly before they could commiserate about their injuries, their fallen comrades, the lack of food, the impossibility of return. The plain widened as the river (unreachable now, sunk deep in its rocky gorge) cut longer serpentines. Hercól maintained his savage pace, cutting off any protests with a lancing stare. When they crossed a stream he ordered them to bend and drink deep, and while they did so he wrenched off his own boots and handed them without a word to Cayer Vispek. In the heat of the afternoon the scalded dog began to limp and drop behind, calling after them with a mournful yelp. Hercól turned back and lifted it over his shoulders, and carried it that way like a sack of grain. 'If its foot does not improve by morning we will eat it,' he declared.

They ate the last of the *mül* that night, and Bolutu extracted a long thorn from the dog's paw. Hercól would not permit a fire. 'We have closed the gap,' he said. 'I think the sorcerer is within five miles, and I would not lose him now.'

Just beyond their camp the land rose in a stony bluff, leaning out over the river gorge. While the others prepared to sleep, Hercól climbed the bluff with Ensyl on his shoulder. They crouched among rocks at the summit, hidden from the sight of anyone beyond, staring through small gaps. They remained there a long time, motionless.

'What are they looking at?' said Neeps finally.

Thasha got to her feet. 'Let's go find out,' she said. She and Neeps climbed the bluff and stood beside Hercól. At once they grew still, gazing beyond the rocks, transfixed.

When Neda too noticed their fascination, Pazel held out his hand. 'Help me up,' he said. 'We'll go and see for ourselves.'

At that Jalantri leaped to his feet and caught Neda by the arm. 'You're not thinking, sister! You're badly bruised and there is fighting ahead. Let him waste his strength if he will. We know better, Phoenix-Flame.'

Neda seemed at a loss for words. She looked at Jalantri's hand on her arm until he dropped it, chastened. Then she glanced quickly at Pazel and started up the hill.

They walked in silence (so weirdly normal, climbing a hill beside his sister; they might have been back in Ormael) until Neda said, 'The way of the *sfvantskor* is perfection.'

'Okay,' said Pazel.

'If you are distracted by the personal,' she said, 'you will fail when your people most need their champion. That is certain, proven. That is why we are chaste. We turn our passions to the needs of the people, to the Grand Family. That is the Mzithrin way, and the *sfvantskor* must be the example.'

Pazel looked back: Jalantri was still watching them. 'You don't have to explain, Neda,' he said.

She smiled, as though amused that Pazel thought he understood. Then she said, 'The dogs keep sniffing at Neeps. They look at him strangely, too.'

Pazel glanced at her, aghast. He could have kicked himself for not noticing. *They're hunting dogs*, he thought. *Were they trained to hunt* tol-chenni? *Is that what Neeps smells like to them?* Fear for Neeps surged through him once more. But when they reached the hilltop, where the others were still crouched and staring, what he saw drove everything else from his mind.

A gargantuan lake spread before them, far greater than Ilvaspar, almost as large as the Gulf of Masal itself. Or was it a lake? It was almost perfectly round, and its shores were sheer, rocky cliffs. But there was no water that he could see. Instead, across the whole expanse, some twenty or thirty feet below the rim, spread a layer of dark, murky green. A flat surface, but not entirely smooth. It appeared to be composed of one round patch atop another, like overlapping lily pads choking a pond, except that these pads were all fused at the edges into one solid mass. Pazel could see no gaps at all, except very close to them, where the Ansyndra tumbled into the crater.

'Hercól says Fulbreech is down there,' said Thasha. 'Inside it. Moving around.'

'But what is it?' said Neda. 'A lake, covered in waterweed?'

'I think,' said Hercól, 'that we are looking at the Infernal Forest.'

'That's no forest,' said Pazel. 'I mean . . . could it be?'

'We have seen many strange things on this side of the Nelluroq,' said Ensyl, 'but that is the strangest. I do not like it. I fear it will not go well for us there.'

'Then let us rest,' said Hercól, 'for Fulbreech *is* there below, somewhere. And Arunis must surely be with him, for who would enter such a place if not compelled?'

That night, for the first time since Masalym, the air stayed warm. Pazel lay down next to Thasha and held her near. The others lay all around them; a dog curled up and leaned into his back. He tried to nudge the creature but it only groaned.

Thasha's eyes were still open. He leaned close and whispered, 'What are you thinking about?'

'Marila,' she said.

He felt a tightness in his throat. He wanted to tell Thasha about Neeps, but the words would not come.

'We're going to know their child,' said Thasha. 'If we live, I mean. If we live and we win.'

A shudder flashed through his body. He pulled her tight. Then Thasha turned and pressed her lips to his ear.

'Half-Bali Adron,' she said, tapping his chest.

He nodded.

'What did you find there, Pazel? In the temple, in Vasparhaven? Are you allowed to tell me?'

Pazel said nothing. He could hear the bursting of the globe, see the empty space where the woman had been, feel the stab of what he'd known was love. Such a distant memory. Such a terrifying force.

'Crystal,' he said.

'Hmm?'

'Everything there was made of crystal, Thasha. The spiders and the people and the music and the stones. And everything outside the temple's the same, isn't it? You want to hold it because it's so beautiful. And you can't, really. Not for long. It will break if you're bad and selfish and it will break if you're good. It snaps or it shatters, or it melts in your hand. And the more beautiful it is the less time you get to have it. And you don't know what I'm talking about, do you?'

Thasha didn't answer. She turned her back, thoughtful, and then lay still beneath his arm. In minutes they were both asleep.

Well past midnight he felt her guide his hand under her tattered clothing, and hold it tight against her breast. So quiet when it finally happened. So unlike the way he'd dreamed. He raised his head, kissed her silently from shoulder to ear, tasting ashes, feeling her tremble. Then he lowered his head beside her, nuzzling, and tumbled back into sleep.

But later still he woke more fully beneath her kisses, and without a word they rose, and tiptoed barefoot into the grass. They neared the river gorge, felt the breeze over the water, stepped cautiously along the rim. Beneath one of the cedars, they turned to face each other, and Pazel lowered himself onto a stone, mindful of his leg. Thasha undressed before him, and she was no more than a blue-white silhouette by the light of the little Polar Candle (the old moon had set; it was almost dawn) but at the same time she was everything that mattered, Thasha Isiq, his lover, naked and frightened and magnificent and strong. And when he carefully removed his own clothes and embraced her there was no more fear in his heart, no room for it; she was the place in the world where fear ended, and she backed into the tree and said she loved him, and her hands reached up for a sturdy branch, and for a few seconds he was inside her, just barely. She had raised herself almost out of his reach, and knowing he shouldn't he tried to stand higher, to scramble up onto a root, rock, anything, it was like trying to mate with the tree, and then she pushed him out altogether and lowered herself to her feet and clasped him tight in her hand, frantic, hips straining against the side of his leg. She was closer than his own skin, closer than he was to himself.

The moment they fell still another sound reached their ears. The dog had followed them, and was scratching urgently with a hind foot just a few feet away. He felt her heart drum against his chest, the laughter shaking her from forehead to thighs. It was nonsense, what they said about dying of happiness. Happiness made you want to live.

They walked a bit farther along the edge of the gorge. He tried talking to her but she only murmured; she was suddenly far away and thoughtful. He was teased by the notion that they had done something dangerous, perhaps mortally so. Was it the magic inside her, Erithusmé's strange, destructive gifts? Or his, maybe: the language spell working to decode her silence, her yearning; trying to translate her wordless needs into his own? He could not make himself care. They clasped hands, scarred palm to scarred palm. He felt that whatever befell her must happen to him as well, and already he longed to touch her again.

Thasha said she wanted to bathe in the Ansyndra. He tried to dissuade her and got nowhere; she told him it might be their last chance for days. They found a descent, but not an easy one. Thasha looked at his leg and shook her head. 'That's all we need,' she laughed. 'You at the bottom, shouting in pain, and our clothes up here by that tree.'

So he sat beside the dog and watched her creep down the broad rocks, spider-like, moving in and out of shadow. The river was a braid of murmuring darkness, and it was hard to tell when she reached it, until he realised that she had slowed, and was splashing palmfuls of icy water against her legs. The simple gesture enough to drive him mad. She moved a step deeper, staring fixedly at the opposite shore. Another step, and she was gone.

Pazel surged to his feet, terrified. Why in Pitfire had he let her go? Into that water out of Ilvaspar, a river that mixed with the River of Shadows?

His fright grew by the second. How could he have been such a fool? Thasha was gone, gone into the black turbulence he had sensed at the bottom of the temple pool. And suddenly he knew that she had been drawn to the river by more than a desire to bathe.

Then she rose and clambered for shore. Her eyes sought him, found him, and she hugged herself, and Pazel was so relieved that he never did ask, then or later, if the gesture meant that the water was freezing or that he was loved.

When dawn came the party rose and set off at once, for there was no breakfast to linger over, no tea to warm. They rounded the bluff and came back to the side of the Ansyndra, and soon the vast green crater was sprawling before them. Pazel had hoped the mystery of its nature would be resolved as they approached; on the contrary, the place only became more alien and strange. The scrub and feathery grasses of the plain grew right up to its edge. Then the side of the hole fell straight down some thirty feet, to where the green surface began. The latter pressed tight against the rock, leaving barely a finger's width of empty space, and often not even that.

What was it made of? How strong was it, how thick? Alyash tossed a rock onto the surface: it bounced and skittered and lay there in the sun. Not a liquid, then, and not flimsy either.

'It looks like elephant hide,' said Big Skip. 'I'll bet you could walk on it.'

Hercól stepped close to the riverbank. They could hear the sound of a waterfall as the Ansyndra plummeted into the dark depths, but even at its very edge they could not see much, for the green tissue stretched to within a few feet of the spray. But they could at least see the edge of the substance: it was some three inches thick.

'There's a second layer below,' said Ibjen. And so there was: a second layer, slightly less green, about twenty feet beneath the first. And below that, a third? Pazel could not see it, but the dlömu (whose eyes could pierce the darkness better than human eyes) said that yes, there was a third; and the ixchel (whose eyes were better still) detected even a fourth, cracked and withered, about sixty feet below.

'And something else,' said Ensyl. 'Struts, or rafters, on the underside of each layer, propping it up, maybe. But they are very irregular and thin.'

Myett peered down into the rushing void. 'Those are not rafters,' she said. 'They're branches.'

There were grumbles of disbelief. 'Branches,' Myett repeated. 'And I would wager that those—' she swept her hand over the miles and miles of olive surface '—are leaves.'

'Oh, come now,' said the older Turach. 'Leaves? All flattened, crushed together like a griddle cake?'

'Can you think of a simpler explanation?' asked the dlömic woman, Lunja.

'Pitfire, it's true,' said Neeps, crouching. 'The surface is dusty, like, but you can see veins if you look close. Those are treetops, by Rin.'

'Then we're in the right place,' said Pazel.

'And so is Arunis,' said Bolutu. 'The Infernal Forest. And he has taken the Nilstone deep within.'

'Then let us go and take it back,' said Cayer Vispek. 'But there is no entrance here. We might aim for those rocks, but to my eye that is a two-day march, and who knows if the ... *leaves* are as solid everywhere as here.'

'Something is different far off along the rim,' said Hercól, pointing east. 'Perhaps the leaf is torn or folded; I cannot tell. But that too is miles off.'

'We could try to shimmy down the cliff beside the river here,' said Alyash, 'but that's a tricky wall. Very sheer, and wet with spray.'

'And dark, too, it must be, further down,' said Dastu.

'Let's make for that torn spot, if that's what it is,' said Thasha. 'Maybe we'll find something along the way.'

Having no better option, they set out. The day was bright, and the dark-green surface warmed quickly in the sun, and soon the heat was rolling off it with each puff of wind. For several miles there was almost no change in the surface. Here and there they could see a frayed edge, where two leaves were not quite perfectly joined. But they always overlapped, so that one could never catch a glimpse down into the crater. Pazel reflected morbidly that they still had no idea of its depth.

Slowly the thing Hercól had spotted came into view. There did appear to be a hole, but also something white protruding from it. When they arrived at last, they found themselves standing above a semicircular gap some twelve feet in diameter, opening right against the cliff wall. The edges were not torn but smooth and rounded, as though the opening was intentional.

The white shapes turned out to be flowers: enormous, fleshy blooms with dark stamens the size of bottle brushes. They had a rich perfume, a mixture of honey and spirits. The flowers were not part of the leaf structure, but grew instead upon a woody vine reaching up out of the darkness. The vine was massive, and tightly grafted to leaf and stone. Its angle of descent was gradual, no more than a steep staircase, and indeed with its corkscrew pattern and elbow-turns it somewhat resembled a staircase, leading down to the next level.

'We could manage well enough on that, I dare say,' said Alyash.

'Look there!' said a dlömic soldier, pointing downwards. 'There's another opening on the level below. And what's that? Fruit? Am I seeing *fruit* on that blessed vine?'

It did look very much that way: five or six purple fruits, about fist-sized, dangling in a bunch near a second opening in the leaves.

'Beware your hopes, and your appetite,' said Hercól. 'If ever I saw the makings of a trap, it is here.'

'Agreed,' said Jalantri, 'but what if the entire forest is a trap? It must have done something to earn its name.'

Hercól looked gravely into the depths. 'Let us descend one level,' he said. 'We will collect those fruits but not taste them, for now. If we are starving – well, then we shall eat, and hope to live. But this is all too convenient.'

He went first, scrambling down the mighty vine, passing through the highest layer and stepping out gingerly onto the leaf platform below. Pazel and Neeps went next, and couldn't help but smile at each other: this was far easier than climbing the shrouds on the *Chathrand*, and a thousand times preferable to the iron ladders. Still, Pazel's leg was throbbing again, and the wound felt itchy and inflamed.

When they reached Hercól, Neeps shouted to those above: 'You can all come at once. That vine won't break, it's thick as a hawser!'

'Like your head, Undrabust, more's the pity!' hissed Hercól. 'Do you want to announce us to the sorcerer, and whatever else may dwell here? The next time you shout, I expect to find you menaced by something at least as deadly as a flame-troll.'

The tarboy glowered, abashed. The others descended without incident. Even the dogs managed well enough, scrambling down almost on their bellies. Pazel bent and touched the leaf surface: it was spongy, like the inside of a gourd.

When they were all on the lower level, Hercól picked the dark fruits: six in all, very juicy and soft. He placed them carefully in the pack Alyash wore. 'They certainly smell delicious,' he said, 'as they would, if they were meant to lure us down here.'

'Call me lured, then,' said Big Skip. 'Your *mül* lasts a fair spell in the stomach, I'll admit. But not this long.'

'You can see the branches, farther in,' said Ensyl. 'And there in the distance: that may be a trunk.'

Pazel could make out a few of the pale, slender branches, piercing the leaf on which they stood and dividing overhead, to prop up the uppermost level like the beams of a roof. But he could not see any trunk. It was too dark already: about as dark as the berth deck at twilight. *And this*, he thought, *is just the first level down*. He glanced back up along the vine and saw a sliver of blue sky, and wondered what on earth they were getting themselves into.

'The vine keeps going down,' said Neda, crouching, 'and there's another hole like this one, but smaller. And more fruit, too, I think.'

Down they went. The third gap was indeed smaller, and there

were but three fruits. And now it was truly dark. Since the holes were so far apart, no direct sunlight could reach them, only a dull, reflected glow, and small pinpricks of light along the cliff wall.

Pazel bent over the third gap. A mix of pungent smells, earth and mould and rotting flowers, issued from it. He looked up at Hercól. 'Time we lit one of those torches, don't you think?'

Hercól considered. 'We have but six,' he said, 'and each will burn but an hour – or less, if our swim in the Ansyndra has damaged them. But yes, we should light one now. We cannot go on blind.'

'We dlömu are not blind, yet,' said Bolutu.

'And we ixchel,' said Ensyl, 'will not be blind until the darkness is nearly perfect. But if you light that torch it will dazzle us, and we will see no better than you.'

'Let us go first, and report what we see,' said Myett.

The others protested. 'You can't be serious,' said Thasha. 'You don't have any idea what's down there.'

'But we know a great deal about not getting caught,' said Ensyl. 'More than any of you, in fact.'

'Go then,' said Hercól, 'but do not go far. Take a swift glance and return to us.'

The two women started down, with the matchless agility of ixchel. They were lost to Pazel's sight almost at once, but at his shoulder Ibjen whispered: 'They are halfway to the next level. They are pausing, gazing at the space between. Now they are descending farther. They are upon the fourth level, and walking about. But what are they doing? They are going on! Hercól, they are leaving my sight!'

'Fools!' whispered Hercól. Stepping onto the vine, he began to rush down after them. But then Ibjen hissed, 'Wait! They're returning.' And minutes later the ixchel were back beside them, unharmed.

'We saw nothing threatening at all,' said Ensyl. 'But we had two surprises. First, it is very hot, and hotter as you descend. Hot and wet.'

'And the other surprise?' asked Neeps.

The ixchel glanced at each other. 'We reached the fourth level,' said Myett at last. 'There is no fifth. The vine merely continues into the darkness. We crawled down it a short distance, but never caught sight of the floor.'

'It can't be much further,' said Big Skip. 'We're down some seventy feet already from the rim. Drop a torch, I say. That's how we'd explore the old silver mines at Octray, when I was a lad.'

'You would only soak the torch,' said Ensyl, 'and announce us to anyone or anything waiting below. Better to let us lead the way, and light it when we reach the bottom.'

Now even the dlömu grumbled about 'climbing blind'. Myett looked at them and laughed. 'They don't trust us, Ensyl,' she said in their own speech. 'Not even the black giants want to put their lives in crawly hands.'

She was forgetting Pazel's Gift, or not caring that he heard. Impulsively, he said, 'This is rubbish. They can see, we can't. Let's get on with it.'

No one liked the plan, but no one had a better one. They descended. After the fourth level Pazel could not even see the vine he clung to. He trod on Neda's fingers, and Dastu trod on his. The silence was oppressive, and the heat more so. There was no breeze whatsoever, and the moist air felt like syrup in his lungs. 'It goes deeper!' the ixchel kept saying, amazed.

The sickly sweet odours grew alongside the heat. Pazel's hands became slippery. He could not judge how far they had descended (even looking up he saw nothing, now), but a point came when he knew that it was much further than the four leaf-levels combined, and still they went down and down.

Finally Ensyl said what they had all been waiting for: 'The bottom, at last! Watch your step, now! Great Mother, what are we standing in?'

Pazel heard those below him exclaiming softly, and a squelching sound as they left the vine. He reached the ground himself: it felt like a heap of fishing nets, moist, fibrous, very strong.

'Hot as midsummer in the marshes,' whispered the younger Turach.

'Now is the time for that torch,' whispered Myett. 'We are almost blind ourselves. This is not the darkness of a forest; it is the darkness of a tomb.'

A scraping sound: Hercól was struggling with a match. Finally it caught, and Pazel watched the tiny flame lick the end of the oil torch. The match sputtered, nearly dying, then all at once the torch burst into light.

Pazel gasped. They were in a forest of jewels, or feathers, or cloaks of coloured stars. His eyes for several moments simply could not sort out all the hues and shapes and textures.

'Plants, are they?' whispered Jalantri, wild-eyed, tensed like a cat.

'Obviously,' hissed Dastu.

The things grew all around them, some just inches tall, others towering overhead. The colours! They were hypnotic, dazzling. But the shapes were even stranger: branching sponges, serpentine trunks ending in mouths like sucker fish, bloated knobs, delicate orange fans. Bouquets of fingers. Clusters of long, flexing spoons.

'They feel fleshy,' said Ibjen.

'Don't touch them, you daft babe!' said Alyash, smacking his hand.

It was hard not to touch them, the things grew so thick and close. Pazel tried to look through the mass of petals, bulges, braided tentacles, feathery limbs, flaring blue, purple, green in the torch-light. They were even *shedding* colour: rainbow droplets were falling and splattering everywhere, as though the things were exuding brilliant nectar or pollen from their pores.

'Fireflies!' said Bolutu suddenly, and Pazel turned just in time to see them: a trail of blue sparks, whirling around Bolutu's upraised hand, then speeding off to a cluster of growths beyond the torch-light, where they all winked out together. There were other insects, too: flying, crawling, wriggling, with bright reflective spots on wings or feelers. Only the fireflies, however, glowed with their own light, and they were already gone.

Pazel wiped his forehead. The hot air wrapped him in a smothering embrace. Then he felt Ensyl scramble nimbly to his shoulder. 'The ground is alive,' she said. 'Have a look at your boots.'

Muffled cries and curses: their feet were being embraced by pale, probing tendrils, wriggling up from the ground on all sides. They were easily broken, but relentless in their work. The scene might have been comic, if anyone had the heart to laugh: twenty figures shuffling in place, lifting one foot and then the other. 'Pitfire, we can't stay here,' said the older Turach.

'Keep close to me,' said Hercól. Raising the torch, he set off in a straight line, forcing a path through the rubbery growths. The others fairly stampeded after him. They had not gone twenty steps when Pazel realised that they were no longer pushing through so many of the weird living things. Hercól stopped and turned to look back, and Pazel did the same.

They had been standing in a thicket formed by the great vine. The growths surrounded it, grew atop it, buried it in their flesh. The vine snaked away across the forest floor, every inch of it covered with growths.

'Like a reef back home,' said Neeps, 'except that it's so blary hot.'

'It *feels* like the bottom of the sea,' said Pazel. 'And this is just a clearing. Those growing things are still all around us.'

'Other things, too,' said Big Skip. He pointed away from the cliff: white, ropelike strands were dangling there, from somewhere far above. They were thick as broom handles and segmented like worms, and they ended in coils a few feet above the ground. 'There must be hundreds,' said Ensyl. 'They go on and on into the forest.'

'The plants seem hardly of this world,' said Neda, gaping.

'Maybe they're not plants at all,' said Pazel.

'Well, naturally they're plants, *Muketch*,' said the younger Turach. 'What else, by Rin?'

'Mushrooms,' said Thasha.

'Mushrooms?' Bolutu looked startled. 'That could well be so.

Fungus, moulds, slimes – they all thrive in darkness. And moisture too, for that matter.'

'And heat,' said Cayer Vispek. 'But great devils, a whole forest of fungi?'

'Not the trees,' said Thasha. 'They're plants, all right. That vine is a plant too, and there must be others. But most of these things – yes, I'm sure they're mushrooms.'

'Come here often, do you?' asked Alyash. 'Summer picnics and such?'

Thasha turned away, indifferent to his taunts. But Pazel touched her arm, trying in vain to get her attention. The familiar, faraway look was creeping back into her eyes.

Neeps pointed off to the left. There the growths, though tall as apple trees, were the same parasol shapes as any mushrooms of the North. 'I guess that settles it,' he said.

Hercól put his hand on Ildraquin. 'Our quarry is motionless, but still far away. Let us form ranks and be off. Ibjen, bear the torch as you would bear no weapon. Stand in the centre and hold it high. And to all of you, need I say that Alyash is right? You must touch nothing, if you can avoid it, and be ever on your guard.' He glanced back to where they had started. 'The vine heads towards the centre, and that is where we are bound. Let us follow it – safely to one side, of course – for as long as we may.'

They left the cliff wall and started out over the spongy ground. The vine grew thicker still, and its load of outlandish growths even heavier. Soon it was less a vine they followed than a twisting, scaly wall, each section flaring brilliantly in the torchlight as they neared. It was very quiet. Nothing moved save a few tiny insects, and the root-tentacles snatching weakly at their boots. Pazel was soon gasping with heat. His leg began to hurt, but when Thasha came to his aid he shook his head and whispered, 'Not yet.'

'Don't ignore it,' she said, and gave his hand a squeeze. She marched ahead, fierce in her readiness for whatever was to come. As she had been just hours ago, in that so-much-gentler darkness, walking with him to the cedar tree. For an instant the wonder of their lovemaking came back to him, and he felt a wild need for her, a contempt for everything but the desire to be with her, far from these troubles, far even from their friends. The feeling appalled him with its selfishness.

An hour passed. With every step they saw new beauties, new horrors. The crown of one mushroom was a miniature flower garden, each blossom smaller than a grapeseed. Another mushroom was as large as a haystack, and twisted as they passed, aiming a hideous, hairy mouth in their direction. The great dangling worm-tendrils moved also, reaching slowly for an outstretched hand. When Ibjen brought the torch near, the tendril coiled like a snake into the darkness above. In some places the tendrils had reached the ground and taken root, so that one looked through them as through prison bars.

Other vine-reefs descended from the unseen trees. Some they passed under; others lay upon the ground like the one they followed. Climbing them was an awkward business, for it was hard to find the solid vine beneath the fungal mass. And some of the mushrooms burned like nettles to the touch.

Atop one of these reefs they suddenly came face-to-face with a pair of enormous, four-legged creatures, grazing placidly on the far side. Elephant-tall and milky white, they resembled giant sloths, but their backs were hidden under jointed shells. They had great lower mandibles with which they scooped up mushrooms, and gigantic eyes, which they pinched shut against the torchlight. Flapping their soft ears in vexation, they shuffled away from the vine.

As the journey continued they met other creatures: graceful deerlike animals with serpentine necks; a waddling turtle that hissed at the dogs; and far more alarming, a swarm of bats the size of pumas that blasted like a storm through their midst, at eye level, and never brushed them with a wing tip. The bats settled on a gargantuan loop of vine and feasted on its melon-like fungi, before racing off into the perpetual night.

'Fungivores, all of them!' said Bolutu. 'They must rarely go hungry. I wonder if anything in this forest lives off meat?'

'I do,' said Big Skip, 'but I'll settle for one of those fruits. How about it, Hercól? They smelled like blary ambrosia.'

'Hold out a little longer,' said the swordsman, 'we may find something better, after all. I was a fool not to kill that turtle.'

A bit later they heard running water, but saw none. The sound grew louder, closer, and at last Neda bent to the ground and said, 'It is under us. It is flowing beneath the roots.'

After that they realised that they were often mere feet over a rushing stream. Once or twice the gap in the roots was wide enough for them to reach a hand inside. There they found the running water deliciously cool, and bathed their faces. But Hercól warned them not to dip their arms too deep, or to taste even a drop of the water. As soon as they left these gaps the heat swallowed them anew.

They were on their second torch when they reached the base of one of the gigantic trees. It was a straight pillar, twelve or fourteen feet thick. Though painted with lichens its bark was paper-smooth, with no knobs or branchings as high as they could see.

'We will not easily climb such a trunk,' said Cayer Vispek.

'Myett and I could manage,' said Ensyl. 'Those lichens will bear our weight.'

Then they saw it: the vine they had followed from the start took root here, right at the base of the tree. Beyond it there was no clear path to follow.

Hercól was unperturbed. 'We will blaze a new trail,' he said. 'Step up here, Neda, and count paces, and speak each time you reach twenty.'

Sweating and stumbling, they moved on. Each time Neda spoke Ildraquin cut a deep slash at breast height in the nearest fungus. 'What if we miss one, Stanapeth?' Alyash called out. 'What if something eats them? This is lunacy, I say.'

'The bosun's right,' Pazel heard Myett say to Ensyl. 'We should not have descended to the forest floor! We should be walking above, in the sunlight!'

'And then?' asked Ensyl. 'The sorcerer is not up in the sunlight. What if we had marched all day across the surface, only to find no way down?'

'I do not want to die in this place, sister, on this giants' quest. A reunion awaits me in Masalym.'

'I do not want to die at all,' said Ensyl. 'But Myett, be truthful with yourself: Taliktrum surely returned to the *Chathrand*, ere the ship departed?'

'You do not know him as I do,' said Myett, 'and you did not hear his words to Fiffengurt. Nothing will persuade him to return to the clan.'

'Love might,' said Ensyl, 'and I think you will have your reunion, however unlikely that appears. We are not defeated yet.'

'Ensyl, you amaze me. Do you truly have such faith in them?'

'In the humans?' said Ensyl, surprised. 'Not all of them, of course. But in Hercól, and the tarboys and Thasha – yes, in them I have faith aplenty. They have earned it. And besides that, I would honour . . . whatever made us unite. Even as we honour the founders of Ixphir House, what they lived and died for.'

She knows I'm listening, thought Pazel, smiling. *It was Diadrelu who brought us together, Ensyl. Your teacher, Hercól's lover, my friend. Diadrelu who showed us the meaning of trust.*

Someone screamed.

It was Alyash, Pazel realised a moment later. He was holding his head, reeling, smashing into the others. Then Pazel saw that there was something in the air, like a fine sawdust, trailing from his hands and head. Some of it drifted into the torch's flame and crackled; some of it touched those nearest Alyash, and they too cried out.

Alyash crashed away into the darkness, blind with pain, sweeping through the white ropes like curtains. The others charged in pursuit. Cayer Vispek and Neda managed to grab him after thirty feet or so, but it took the whole party to calm him down. 'He was cutting extra notches,' said the older Turach. 'He was afraid you weren't marking the trail well enough. I was about to say something when he slashed one of them fat yellow globs, and it exploded! *Credek*, I breathed that powder in myself, it burns like thunder-snuff!'

'I breathed it too,' said Ibjen. 'What is thundersnuff?'

'Something not to be toyed with,' said Hercól, 'like the things that grow in this place. You are a fool, Alyash. Were you hacking any fungus in your path, or did you choose that one because it resembled a sack fit to burst?'

Alyash's eyes were streaming. 'It stings, damn it—'

'You'll be lucky if the spores do only that,' said Bolutu.

Alyash screamed at him: 'What's that supposed to mean, you damned bookish fish-eyed doctor to pigs?'

With rare fury, Bolutu retorted: 'These *fish eyes* see more than the little oysters in your face! I know! I had to use them for twenty years!'

They were still bickering when Lunja gave a cry. 'Indryth! Indryth is gone!' She was speaking of one of her comrades, a Masalym soldier.

'He was right beside me!' shouted another. 'He can't have gone far!'

'Fan out,' said Hercól. 'Watch each other, not the forest alone. And do not take a single step beyond the torchlight!' Then he whirled. 'Gods, no! Where is Sunderling? Where is Big Skip?'

'Myett!' cried Ensyl. 'She was with him, on his shoulder! *Spiraké!* Myett, Myett!'

Three of their number had suddenly, silently vanished. The others turned in circles, casting about for foes. But there was nothing to be seen but the brilliant spots and stripes and whorls on the fungus.

Then came a sickening sound of impact, not five feet from Pazel. A fungus like a glowing brain had suddenly been crushed, splattering all of them with slime. Out of the remains of the mushroom rolled Big Skip, both hands at his neck, barely able to breathe. Clinging desperately to his hair was Myett.

Big Skip's hand came away from his neck holding six feet of

slippery white tendril, writhing like a snake. With a tortured gasp he hurled it away.

'A worm,' gagged Myett. 'One of those dangling tendrils. It snatched him up by the throat. I was pinned against his neck, but my sword-arm was free, and I managed to saw through the thing. It was lifting us higher and higher.' Her eyes found the dlömu. 'Your clan-brother is dead. Many worms seized his limbs; they were fighting over him. I am sorry. They tore him to pieces before my eyes.'

The dlömic soldiers cursed, their faces numb with shock. Big Skip drew an agonised breath. He did not look badly hurt, but he was frightened almost out of his wits. 'Lost my knife, my knife—'

'You're safe now, Sunderling,' said Hercól. At these words Jalantri actually giggled, earning him a furious stare from his master. Jalantri dropped his eyes, chastened, but a smile kept twitching on his face. *What's wrong with him?* thought Pazel. *Is that all the discipline they're taught?*

But Jalantri wasn't alone in looking strange. The younger Turach kept glancing to the right, as though catching something with the corner of his eye. And Ibjen was staring at an insect on a frond, as though he had never seen anything more fascinating.

'Never mind your knife, Sunderling,' said Hercól. 'We'll find you a club. You showed us what you can do with one, when we fought the rats.'

Big Skip stared up into the darkness. 'The rats were easy, Hercól.'

They marched on. The gigantic trees were more numerous now. Pazel had barely cleared the slime from his face when the next torch died.

'Stanapeth!' hissed Alyash. 'How much further have we got to march into this hellish hole?'

Hercól did not answer, but Pazel heard him searching carefully for the matches. Pazel realised that his heart was still racing exceptionally fast. It was not just the heat – the darkness, the darkness was worse. It had begun to affect him like something tangible, like a smothering substance in which they could drown. Suddenly he thought of the Master Teller's strange words to him in Vasparhaven: *You need practice with the dark.* Surely this was what the old dlömu had meant. But the Floor of Echoes had done him no harm, and the last encounter had even been wonderful.

Perhaps that was the point: that the darkness could hide joyful things as well as danger, love as well as hate and death. Yet when he had reached for that woman with love she had vanished, and the world they'd supported between them had been destroyed.

The third torch lit. Hercól looked at Alyash. 'We should arrive within the hour, to answer your question. That will leave us three torches to return by, if our work goes swiftly.'

'Our work is the killing of a deadly foe,' said Cayer Vispek. 'It may not be swift at all.'

'Then we will find which of these mushrooms best holds a flame,' said Hercól.

Off they started again. The ground descended, slowly; the water gurgling underfoot sounded nearer the surface. The heat, if possible, grew more intense; Pazel felt as if he were entangled in steaming rags. His leg throbbed worse than ever, and now he let Thasha support him, though walking together was hard on such treacherous ground.

'We have to stop and clean that wound,' she said.

'Not when we're this close,' he replied.

'Stubborn fool,' she whispered. 'All right, then, tell me something: your Master-Word. The one that *blinds to give new sight.* Could it help us, when the torches run out? Could that be the sort of thing it was meant for?'

Pazel had expected the question. 'No,' he said. 'I'm sorry, Thasha, but I'm sure it's not. Ramachni said I'd have a feeling, when the time was right. And it feels completely wrong, here – like it would be a disaster, in fact. I don't think it's about *literal* blindness.'

'Ah,' she said. 'I see.'

He could hear the effort she was making, trying not to sound crushed by his answer. She was desperate. The thought jabbed him like a splinter, much harder to ignore than the pain in his leg. And that was love, surely: when you could stand your own suffering but not another's.

Neeps fell into step beside them. 'Listen,' he said, 'there's something wrong with me.'

Pazel turned to him, alarmed. 'What's the matter, Neeps? How do you feel?'

'Easy, mate,' murmured Neeps. 'It's probably nothing, just ... well, damn it! I keep hearing *her*.'

'Her?' said Thasha. 'Do you mean ... *Marila*?'

'Blary right,' said Neeps, shaken. 'And someone else, too, with her. Some man. He's laughing at her, or at me.'

Thasha touched his forehead. 'You're not feverish. You're just worked up, probably.'

'I think it's Raffa,' whispered Neeps, almost inaudibly.

Raffa was the person Neeps hated most in Alifros: his older brother, who had let him be taken away into servitude by the Arquali Navy rather than pay the cost they demanded for his release. 'I know it isn't real,' he said, 'but it *sounds* so real. Pazel, Thasha – what's happening to me? Am I losing my mind?'

'No!' said Thasha. 'You're exhausted, and hungry, and sick of the dark.' She slapped his cheek lightly. 'You stay awake, and calm, do you hear me? Pretend we're in fighting class back in the stateroom. And what's the rule in class, Neeps? Tell me.'

'I obey you,' said Neeps, 'like you obey Hercól.'

'That's right. So obey me, and stop listening to voices you know are just in your head.' She leaned close to him, and sniffed. 'And if we get another chance, wash your face. You smell *sour*. You must have got into something different from the rest of us.'

Neeps sniffed at his arm. 'You're cracked,' he said. 'We stink like blary convicts, sure, but there's nothing special about me.' He looked at Pazel hopefully. 'Is there, mate?'

Pazel avoided his gaze. 'You smell like a bunch of roses,' he said, feeling cruel and false. Even through the general reek of the forest and their bodies, Neeps' lemon smell reached him faintly. When was he going to say something? What was he going to do?

'Here!' shouted Alyash suddenly, just ahead of them. 'What did you go and do that for?'

The bosun was sopping wet, and glaring at the younger Turach. The group had stopped by the base of one of the great trees. When Pazel rounded the trunk he saw a weird growth attached to it: a kind of bladder-shaped mushroom five or six feet wide, which the Turach had evidently stabbed. The thing had burst open like a ripened fruit, and water – plain water, as far as Pazel could tell – was gushing from the wound.

Alyash, soaked to the skin, was still glaring at the Turach. 'I asked you a question,' he said.

'It was sneaking up on me,' said the Turach, still gazing suspiciously at the fungus.

'Sneaking?' cried Alyash. 'That blary thing can't sneak any more than one of Teggatz's meat pies! You're out of your head.'

'If he is, your own foolishness is to blame,' said Neda. 'Taking your sword to an exploding fungus, coating all of us with spores.'

'That's right, sister,' said Jalantri, drawing near her. 'His stupidity could have killed us all.'

'Stupidity?' Alyash looked ready to explode himself. 'You ignorant little groveller. I was smart enough to fool the Shaggat's horde on Gurishal. I spied on 'em for *five years*, while you lot ran about saying it can't be done, they'll catch him tomorrow, they'll roast him, eat him. And all the while I managed to get letters out to Arqual. Your shoddy spying guild never caught a whiff.'

'Devils grant the power of deception to their servants,' said Jalantri.

Neda, clearly annoyed at Jalantri's interference, stepped away from him. To Alyash, who spoke perfect Mzithrini, she said, 'I seek no feud with you. I only meant that you and the Turach made the same mistake.'

'Except that *his* may have done real harm,' put in Jalantri.

'I should blary stab *you*, and see what harm it does!' said Alyash.

'You should sheathe your weapon, and empty your boots,' said Hercól. 'If we turn on each other the mage's victory is assured.

Now be *silent*, everyone.' He drew Ildraquin and pointed off into the darkness. 'Fulbreech is but half a mile away, perhaps less. And he has not moved in hours.'

'Then Arunis must have found what he seeks,' said Cayer Vispek.

'I fear so,' said Hercól, 'but that does not mean he has managed to use it yet. Regardless, the time to strike is now. We cannot go on without the torch, but we can stop it from shining forwards, until we are nearly atop the sorcerer, and then attack him at a run. Come here, Jalantri, and you too, marine. Grasp each other's shoulders, that's it.'

He made the two enemies stand together, as if partnered in a three-legged race. 'Why us?' snarled Jalantri.

For a moment Hercól actually looked amused. 'For the sake of the Great Peace, of course. And also because you have the widest chests.'

Removing his own tattered coat, he draped it over both their shoulders. Then he passed the torch to Neda and made her hold it low behind the men. He looked at the others, grave once more.

'Stay low until I give the signal to run. Then there must be no hesitation, no turning. Arunis is very great, but with Ildraquin I stand a chance of slaying him. I will take that chance, but you must help me drive through his defences, no matter how many, or how fell. Think of what you hold most sacred; think of what you love. You fight for that. Let us go now and finish it.'

They drew what weapons they had and crept forwards. Pazel thought the heat had never been so intense. The very trees felt hot to the touch. Off to their left something enormous loomed in the torchlight: another of the bladder-fungi, Pazel saw, but this one was the size of a house, and wedged high above the ground between two trees. What were they for? Water storage? Could there possibly be a dry season here?

He let go of Thasha and pressed her forwards, shaking his head when she objected. He feared he would be no use in the fight. But Thasha would be, if he let her. He hobbled, gritting his teeth against the pain.

Neeps looked back at him over his shoulder, his face utterly filthy. Neda glanced back at him too. Pazel nodded to them: *I'm managing.* And to his great surprise he felt a kind of happiness. His best friend, his sister and his lover: all here with him, even if here was hell. They cared for him; it seemed somehow miraculous. He thought: *I'm going to fight you, Arunis, on one leg or two.*

Then he went mad.

He was sure of it, for a horror beyond anything he had ever dreamed had enveloped him, a horror you could not look at and stay sane. They were walking on babies. Mounded, rotting, torn open as if by the gnawing of animals: human babies, and dlömic, and—

They were gone. A hideous lie, an illusion. He was bathed in sweat, and needed to scream. What had just happened to him? *Was* he mad? Or was something attacking his mind, some illness, some enchantment?

The spores?

Alyash and several others had been stung by the spores. But what if not all of them stung? What if some could not even be seen, or smelled or tasted, but were potent nonetheless? They had shoved and stumbled through *miles* of fungi. Of course, the spores were inside them. Could they brew visions in the mind? Neeps was hearing voices, and the Turach had seen that bladder-fungus move ...

'Now!' said Hercól, and flew forwards like the wind. The others bolted after him, weapons high, rushing heedless through the fungi, slashing through the dangling worms, moving like a scythe towards their goal. Pazel ran too, faster than he thought himself capable. He actually passed Ibjen and Neeps, and drew level with Bolutu. They jumped a stream, darted around several of the towering trees (how close together they were now!), slid down an eight-foot embankment of roots and globular fungi, leaped through a last tangle – and saw the whole party, standing still and aghast beside an orange pool.

It was not sunk into the ground but raised in fungal walls some five feet high, and in the centre lay Greysan Fulbreech. The rim of the pool was a mass of wiry tentacles that strained to reach the newcomers. Fulbreech was floating on his back. He was withered, and shirtless, and a rag that might have been part of his shirt was wadded and stuffed into his mouth. Bruises and burns marked his skin, along with cuts that looked raw and inflamed. His eyes were open but he barely moved. A weak groan escaped him. He did not even turn his head in their direction.

Lifting the torch, Neda raced around the pool, gazing beyond the towering trees. 'Arunis is not here!' she cried, desolate, enraged. 'The Nilstone is not here! *We have been following that bastard and no one else.*'

Even as she spoke the torch seemed to leap out of her hand. Neda whirled, lunged after it, and then the light was gone.

31

The Uses of Madness

Thasha knew they were under attack. Voices howled – more voices than there were people in the party – and hands were groping at her out of the darkness. A sword whistled, sickeningly close; blows were falling, bodies crashing to the ground. She tried to back away from the fighting, but someone collided with her, knocking her hard into the fern-fungi. Then all at once she was seeing again, but all she saw were shapes from a nightmare. Cats, hundreds and hundreds of them, famished, feral, converging on them from all sides. Thasha raised her arms before the onslaught; they were closing, leaping—

They vanished like soap bubbles as they struck.

A hand on her arm. She whirled. It was Pazel, embracing her, drawing her close. She leaned into him, whispered his name; he opened his mouth for a kiss.

And laughed. The flame-spittle of the trolls burst out of him, straight into her face. Thasha screamed and broke away.

She was not burned.

I'm dreaming. No – hallucinating. I'm mucking wide awake! With a tremendous effort she made herself stand still. Once again she was perfectly blind, but that was better than the alternative. Some of the others were still at it, shrieking in terror or in pain.

Thasha shouted at the top of her lungs: 'Stop fighting! It's in your head, your head! There's no one here but us and Fulbreech!'

Bolutu and Hercól were already shouting much the same thing.

'Stop fighting! Stop fighting! We're lighting another torch!' Then she heard Pazel say: 'Don't light it yet, Hercól! Look at the pool! Are you all seeing that, or is it just me?'

Thasha at least could see it: the pool where Fulbreech lay was starting to glow. The light came from the fungal walls, and rather than orange it was now an indistinct purple, a weird radiance that seemed only to strike the edges of things. Still it brightened, until they could see Fulbreech plainly, one another less so.

'Here is the torch – drenched,' said Myett, from the edge of the clearing.

'Something struck it from my hand,' said Neda. 'A globular thing. It flew out of the darkness as though someone had hurled it.'

'Hear me, people,' said Bolutu. 'We have been drugged. We are seeing and hearing what is not there. Do not trust your eyes. And for the love of Alifros, do not be guiled into attacking one another!'

'The trouble,' said Pazel, 'is that some of the dangers *are* real. Those white worms, for instance. And whatever struck the torch.'

'The fungus-trap holding the boy is real as well,' said Ensyl.

'And I know just the solution,' said Alyash. 'We'll find a long stick, see, and push his mucking head under the surface. Deceitful son of a whore! He's managed to betray us one last time. Arunis could be anywhere by now.'

'How do you propose to find out, if you kill the boy?' said Cayer Vispek.

But the bosun was suddenly distracted. 'Look up,' he murmured.

Whispered curses: dangling overhead was an enormous mass of criss-crossed vines, so laden with growths they looked almost like a second forest floor. And hanging on the underside of every surface were bats. They were tiny, no larger than hummingbirds, but their numbers were incalculable. Most dangled motionless, upside down, their wings enveloping their bodies like cabbage leaves. But a few strained their necks around to look at the travellers. Their eyes gleamed purple in the torchlight.

'Those!' said Neda suddenly. 'It was they who snuffed the torch!

Why would they burn themselves up, attacking a fire?'

'Light here seems to be the enemy,' said Bolutu. 'Or rather: our kind of light. If they live off the fungus, perhaps they do it a service, too. The pool's glow draws creatures near; the liquid catches them. And the bats – they eat something that thrives here, around this pool.'

'They're weighing down the vines,' said Alyash.

It was true that something was making the vines hang low and taut, as though under some heavy strain. 'It's not the bats,' said Pazel, 'they're too small, even if there are ten thousand up there. You could set a mansion on those blary vines, Mr Alyash.'

'There is something else,' said Ensyl, shielding her eyes. 'Something wide and smooth. I can't quite make it out, but it is enormous – far wider than this clearing.'

Hercól stepped away from the others. With a sidelong swipe of Ildraquin, he slashed away a yard or more of the wriggling tentacles. The other appendages writhed in distress, and the bats quivered and squeaked (more were waking; a few flitted about). Hercól raised the sword high. 'Watch your feet,' he told the others. Then he struck, lightning-fast, and a V-shaped chunk of the pool wall fell outwards. Hercól jumped back. The gelatinous substance began to ooze through the gap, and Fulbreech, floating like a raft, slid towards it as well.

They groped for sticks in the weird light and used them to drag the limp youth through the incision, and out of the worst of the spreading ooze. With the tip of Ildraquin, Hercól snagged a corner of the rag in Fulbreech's mouth and lifted. The rag came out; Fulbreech gagged and retched.

'Master Hercól,' he rasped, his voice a feeble mockery of the one that had, briefly, excited dreams in Thasha's heart. 'Master Alyash. It's really you, isn't it? By the Blessed Tree, you're not illusions, not ghosts.'

'Are you certain, Fulbreech?' said Alyash. 'I think we'd better prove it to you.'

The Simjan's face looked drowned: not in the substance of the pool, but in a boundless immensity of terror. 'I can't feel my limbs,' he said.

'That's all right, boy,' said Alyash. 'You won't be needing 'em.'

Fulbreech gazed helplessly at the bosun. 'He will not harm you without my consent,' said Hercól, 'and I will not give it, whether you help us or refuse. For I have done you a disservice, Fulbreech.'

Thasha, and most of the others, looked at him in shock. 'A grave disservice,' Hercól went on. 'I have had some opportunity to reflect on my mistake, these last days of travelling. How you came to be Arunis' creature I will never know. Were you madly ambitious as you seem? Or were you weak, like Mr Druffle, seduced into lowering your defences, until he made a puppet of you, colonised your mind? Do not speak yet! I will believe nothing you say. But the fact is that when I guessed whose work you did, I chose to leave you in his clutches, for weeks. It was the only way I could think of to locate Arunis' hiding place on the *Chathrand*. But in so doing I treated you as a pawn, just as Arunis did. I might have struck a deal with Ott, had you safely confined, asked Chadfallow and Lady Oggosk to attempt the rescue of your soul.'

'You don't know that he *needed* any rescuing,' said Thasha, her rage boiling over. 'You don't know that he *wanted* any.'

'And now I never shall,' said Hercól, 'unless we escape this place. Then, Fulbreech, I will seek help for you – again, whether you aid us now, or not.'

'Damn it, Hercól!' Pazel exploded. 'Why don't you make him your mucking heir and be done with it?'

'Pazel's right,' said Neeps. 'You're going too blary far.'

'Thashiziq!' said Ibjen suddenly. 'I hear voices. From the black water beneath the roots.'

Hercól waved imperiously for silence. 'What you must appreciate, Fulbreech,' he went on calmly, 'is that if you do not help us, we *cannot* prevail. And then you will be doomed. Your body will perish here, and your soul – what did he say would become of it, lad? He had a promise for you, didn't he?'

'They're calling me, calling me away,' whispered Ibjen.

Bolutu shot him a quick, distracted look. 'You're in *nuhzat*, lad. Be still and it will pass.'

Ibjen sank to the ground, hugging his knees. Thasha crouched down and held him, whispering, begging him to hush. Whatever Hercól was attempting she didn't dare interrupt.

Fulbreech's tongue slid over bloodless lips. 'I don't know what you want, Master Hercól,' he said.

'What I want is answers,' said Hercól, 'although I know you cannot give them if you still serve the mage. If that is the case we must fail, and perish here together. But even then I will help you.'

'How?'

'With a clean death,' said Hercól, 'and if I discover you in a lie I will do it instantly, for our time is very short.' Then, as if following a sudden impulse, he added, 'I will also do so at a word from Mr Undrabust. You may not be aware of it, Fulbreech, but he has a nose for lies. The best I have ever encountered.'

Neeps stared at him, shocked silent in his turn. Pazel reached out and squeezed his shoulder. *Courage, mate.* Hercól rested the tip of Ildraquin on Fulbreech's throat.

'Speak a little truth,' he said.

Fulbreech lay there, blinking and trembling. He licked his lips again. 'Arunis can use the Stone,' the youth whispered. 'He's already doing it. Through the *tol-chenni* we brought from Masalym. He has terrible powers now, worse than anything you've seen.'

'Then we're too Gods-damned late,' hissed Big Skip. But Ensyl, on his shoulder, hushed him quickly.

'He's keeping the forest dark,' said Fulbreech. 'He says it's always full of light – made by creatures, and plants, and mushrooms – just not the kind our eyes can see. Only the fireflies make our sort of light, and he's driven them into hiding. And he ... created this place around me. As a trap, in case you made it this far.'

'What is the danger here?' asked Hercól. 'The bats? The pool itself?'

Fulbreech shook his head slightly. 'He said that if I didn't know, I couldn't tell you. That's the truth, by all the Gods. But I know this: he has power from the Stone, but not control – not yet. The idiot really *is* mad – dangerously mad. And to use the Stone, Arunis has to reach into his mind and make him see what he wants.'

'How much does he know of us, boy?' said Lunja suddenly. 'Our numbers, our distance from him? Is he watching us even now?'

'No,' said Fulbreech. 'He has caught only glimpses of you, though they seemed to grow clearer with each day – as you grew closer, perhaps. When we stood on the shores of the glacier lake, he closed his eyes suddenly and cried, "Vadu! Vadu has drawn his knife, somewhere on the plain below! That buffoon is chasing us!" Then again, a day later, he stopped and pressed a hand to his forehead. He was furious, and I heard him growl: "So you are bringing *her*, are you, Counsellor?" I thought he meant Macadra, the sorceress from Bali Adro City: after all, we fled when he learned that she was coming for the Stone. But now I think he meant you, Thasha darling.'

'Enough of that talk,' snapped Hercól. 'Where is Arunis now?'

'Deeper inside the forest. Where the River of Shadows breaks through to the surface.'

'That is no help,' said Cayer Vispek. 'Which direction, and how far?'

Fulbreech shook his head again. 'I don't know. He would not tell me.'

Hercól and Neeps exchanged a glance. 'Continue,' said the swordsman.

Fulbreech coughed: it was like an old man's rattling wheeze. Then he lay still, gazing strangely at Hercól. 'Are you finished?' said the swordsman at last. 'Have you nothing more to tell?'

'You want to know how I came to be in his service?' said Fulbreech suddenly, and there was pride in his ruined voice. 'Perhaps you think he seized on some weakness. Oh no, Stanapeth, not at all. I went to *him*. In all that multitude at Thasha's wedding, I alone saw through his disguise, saw that he was the power behind the spectacle, the master of ceremonies, the one who would win.' He turned his head, gazing at them in defiance. 'And when you know that, do you linger on the losing side? Not if you've been poor. Not if you mean to go places in your life, to be something better than a clerk in a backwater kingdom on a humdrum isle.'

'You were *already* goin' places, you little bastard,' snarled Alyash. 'We'd seen to that.'

'The Secret Fist,' said Fulbreech. 'A priesthood of cut-throats, bowing to a crude stone idol named Sandor Ott. I would *never* have remained like you, Alyash, a cringing servant. When I guessed that Arunis was manipulating Ott's conspiracy, I walked right up to him, right there at the procession. I told him I was Ott's man, and would be his if the terms were better.'

'Were they?' asked Bolutu.

The Simjan's eyes widened, but he was no longer focusing on what was before them. 'Choosing sides,' he said. 'That was my talent; that was my only gift. I told you, Thasha: I placed all my trust in that gift, and I have never been wrong.'

'This time you were wrong, giant,' said Myett.

Fulbreech kept his gaze on Thasha. 'Cure me,' he said. 'I know you have the power. Cure me, heal my limbs, and I will tell you about the River of Shadows.'

'What about the River?' she asked.

'Don't listen to him, Thasha,' said Neeps. 'I doubt he knows any more than we do.'

'You know that it surfaces here, in this forest,' said Fulbreech, 'and you know that it touches many worlds, that if you fall into its depths you might wash up anywhere. But what good does that do you? I know something Arunis wishes no one to know. Something priceless to your quest. I know where the River touches the world of the dead.'

Bolutu turned him a sudden, piercing look. 'Yes,' said Fulbreech, 'I was there when Arunis discovered it; I saw his fury and disbelief. The world of the dead, Thasha. The one place that can save you. The place where the Nilstone belongs.'

'Where is this place?' demanded Hercól.

A vein pulsed on the youth's white forehead. 'Cure me,' he said to Thasha. 'It is a small deed for you.'

'Greysan,' she said, 'you're wrong about me. Everyone is, by the Pits.'

'Don't lie,' he said. 'Heal me, Thasha, let me walk. I can help you defeat him. With your power, and all I've learned—'

'I am not a mage,' she said.

There was steel in her voice. Fulbreech watched her a long time, and Pazel saw belief welling in his eyes, and then a new, colder look. 'None of you stand a chance, then,' he whispered. 'You're the walking dead. He's won.'

'Not while one of us draws breath,' said Hercól.

'You're dead,' said Fulbreech again. 'You've never known who you were fighting. You think he's just a beast, a monster, someone who hates for no reason. But he's not.'

'What in Pitfire is he, then?' said Pazel.

Fulbreech's eyes swivelled until they locked on Pazel. A ghastly smile appeared on his face. 'You should have guessed by now,' he said. 'Why, he's the same as you, Pathkendle. A natural scholar.'

Pazel looked as though he might get suddenly ill. Fulbreech's smile grew. 'Thasha talked a lot on that bed, when I let her. She told me what you loved as a child. Books, school, good marks. Treats for cleverness from your betters. And who were your betters? Old Chadfallow, of course, and all those captains who let a dirty Ormali set foot on their boats. And of course, Thasha herself. Tell me, Pazel, was it worth it? Did you ever earn your treat?'

Pazel leaped at him, quite out of his mind. It was all Neeps and Thasha could do to hold him back. Fulbreech watched them gleefully. 'Arunis is no different,' he said. 'He's been a student for three thousand years.'

'How many lies do you need, Hercól?' said Bolutu, furious. 'Arunis has been *torturing this world* for three thousand years. The North. The South. Kingdom after kingdom, war after war. Tell me he does not hate Alifros, Mr Fulbreech. Say that, if you dare.'

'He does not hate Alifros,' said the Simjan. 'He has no time for love or hate. He is a student, in the school where Gods are made. And those wars, those perished kingdoms, this last, total extermination—' Fulbreech's body shook with mirth. 'They're his exams.'

In the appalled silence that followed, Thasha knew suddenly that there were great regions within her where her mind dared not go. In one of them a woman was screaming. Thasha heard the scream like an echo from the depths of a cave.

'He promised to take me with him,' said Fulbreech. 'All the way out of Alifros, to the realm of the Gods. He lied, of course: that was the best way to ensure my services. There was never anything personal about it. How could a mind that old have feelings for the likes of us? A dead world. That's his project. Nothing else will suffice. He has to offer it up for inspection by his betters, you see. He called it a difficult school.'

Ildraquin slipped from Hercól's fingers. No one moved but Fulbreech, giggling in his madness. Then Ibjen crawled forwards on hands and knees, lifted the sword and stabbed down, through Fulbreech's stomach, into the earth.

Fulbreech gasped but did not scream. Thasha rushed forwards to pull the blade free, but Hercól stayed her with a hand. Too late. Removing the blade would only speed the Simjan's death.

Of course, the wound gushed all the same. Fulbreech tried and failed to lift his head. 'I can't feel a thing,' he croaked.

'But you are dying, all the same,' said Hercól.

'And your soul is damned,' said Jalantri.

'Who knows?' said Fulbreech, drooling blood now, and yet somehow still amused. Then his eyes found Thasha's once more. Through hideous expulsions of bile and blood, he said, 'You'll ... fight?'

'Fight Arunis?' said Thasha. 'Of course we will.'

Suddenly Fulbreech screamed. He convulsed, his paralysis ending with his life. But through the torment his eyes blazed with sudden defiance. With a terrible effort, choking on his own fluids, he spat out a last word.

'What was that?' said Bolutu, starting forwards. 'Did you say *Gurishal*?'

Fulbreech nodded. Then he raised a hand, shaking as with palsy, and Thasha took it, and held it as he died.

No one else made a sound. When Fulbreech was still at last, Thasha turned and looked blankly at Hercól.

'You asked for the truth,' she said.

All of this had happened by the light from the pool alone. But the strange ooze was draining away, and the purple light was dying. 'In a few minutes we'll be blind again,' said Alyash, his voice shaking. 'We need a plan, Stanapeth.'

'The plan has not changed,' said Hercól. 'Come, let us be off.'

'But friends!' cried Bolutu, 'didn't you hear his last word? Gurishal! The River of Shadows touches death's kingdom on Gurishal! Fulbreech has given us the key. Gurishal is where we can send the Nilstone out of Alifros for ever.'

'And before he came here, Arunis did not know,' said Dastu. Thasha and Pazel turned to face him, and for a moment there was no hatred between them, only wonder and amazement.

'Gods,' said Pazel, 'you must be right. He's been doing everything he can to get the Shaggat there, with the Nilstone in hand. And yet it's the one place in Alifros where *we* want the Stone to go.'

'He was being used,' said Dastu. 'Arunis the sorcerer was being used.'

'No wonder he was furious,' said Thasha.

Ibjen looked up at her, blinking back his tears. 'Fulbreech may have helped you in the end,' he said, 'but he betrayed you a moment before. He was calling out to Arunis, trying to get his attention, to tell him we stood by this pool. He started the moment you declared you could not heal him, Thashiziq. The voices told me: "Come away, come away, you're doomed, you're in the sorcerer's trap."'

'You did well to kill him,' said Neda. 'Don't weep; there is no shame in your act.'

Ibjen shook his head. 'It's not because of my oath,' he said. 'It's because I waited, hoping one of you would do it for me. That is worse. That is meaner.'

Hercól looked up: the darkness was descending like a black fog. 'No more delay,' he said. 'We must get away from here, away from those bats, before we try again with the torch.'

The elder Turach gazed at him heavily. 'And then?' he said.

'Then we backtrack to the trail we were marking,' said Hercól, 'and resume the search.'

'Resume!' laughed Alyash. 'Begin it, you mean! Only this time we've got piss-all to go by. Stanapeth, it's over. You can fool yourself that you might find a needle in a haystack – no, in a blary *barn* – if you've got a lodestone to drag around through the hay. But our lodestone was a cheat.'

'We must find the place where the River of Shadows breaks the surface,' said Hercól. 'What else would you counsel?'

'To follow our own trail back to the vine, that's what,' cried Alyash. 'And the vine to blessed daylight.'

Several of the soldiers, human and dlömic alike, nodded approvingly. Hercól looked at them in alarm. 'You know that to concede the Nilstone to Arunis means death to us all,' he said. 'Surely Fulbreech made that clear once again?'

'Let's just start walking,' pleaded Big Skip.

A furtive movement caught Thasha' eye: Jalantri was squeezing Neda's hand in his. She pulled away. Jalantri whispered something in Mzithrini that unsettled her even more. But before he finished there came a loud *pop*, like a child's toy cannon, and Jalantri howled in pain.

Something black and amorphous had struck the back of his head. He stumbled, groping at it. The thing slipped through his fingers again and again, and yet one end of it seemed embedded in his skin. At last he ripped it away, leaving a coin-sized wound.

Pop. Pop. Thasha felt a blow to her arm, and a sharp stab. An identical creature was there, wriggling, burrowing into her flesh. 'Leeches!' cried Dastu, as another struck his leg. 'But they're coming like cannon shot!'

Pop. Pop. Pop. 'The globe mushrooms!' said Ensyl, pointing. 'They're bursting out of them! Great Mother, there could be *thousands.*'

All at once the air was thick with the foul, biting creatures. Thasha felt them strike her again, in the shoulder, in the neck. 'Out of here!' bellowed Hercól. 'Get beyond the globes, beyond that ridge we descended! But then *stop and regroup*, for the love of Rin!'

Humans and dlömu were bolting in all directions. Neeps tripped over Fulbreech; Jalantri, his chest thick with leeches, shouted for Neda as he ran. Alyash was waving his pistol, of all things. Then Pazel slipped in the slime from the pool, and cried out as his wounded leg was wrenched. Thasha dived for him, grabbed his arm and dragged him, leeches and all, out through the fern-fungi, and under the fallen tree, and then—

'Cover your eyes!'

—right up the slope, the wall of exploding fungi, and on among the towering trees until she was sure nothing else was striking them.

Twenty feet from the pool, and it was nearly pitch black. 'Tear them off, Pazel!' she shouted.

'I am! I am!'

Gods, but they hurt. Eight, nine of them – and another in the small of her back. She was still trying to get a grip on it when she felt Pazel's fingers. He groped, squeezed, *ripped*: the leech was gone, along with a barbed mouthful of her skin. Then a match flared in the blackness, somewhere off to their left. It died, and Alyash bellowed in rage. Another match glowed, and this time Alyash managed to light the torch. 'Here, here, to me!' he bellowed. 'You heard Stanapeth! Regroup!'

Thasha and Pazel stumbled towards him. Others, by the sound of it, were doing the same. Then Alyash screamed as a flickering, flapping darkness took his arm. The torchlight disappeared. Thasha caught the stink of burning flesh.

'The bats!' cried Alyash. 'They attacked the torch! Devils in the flesh, they're suicidal!'

'Light it again! Light it again!'

'Ain't but half a dozen matches left—'

Another flared: Thasha saw Alyash's crazed eyes by its light – and then sudden motion, and darkness. 'Damn the mucking things!' cried the bosun. 'It's impossible! They *dive* on the flame!'

'Strike no more matches,' came Hercól's voice, suddenly. 'We must get further from their roosting place; there are simply too many here. Do not run, do not separate! But tell me you're here! Turachs! Where are you?'

'Here!' shouted the younger of the soldiers. 'Undrabust is with me. We're all right, we're just—'

'Vispek!' shouted Hercól. 'Jalantri! Neda Ygraël!'

Only Neda answered him – and from a surprising distance. Thasha heard Pazel's frightened gasp. 'Neda!' he shouted at the top of his lungs. 'Over here! Hurry, hurry!'

This time there was no answer at all. The bats flowed about them like water. Nothing was visible save the fading glow from the pool.

Footsteps crashed nearer, and then Neeps and the younger Turach found them, their blind hands groping. From farther off, the dlömic warriors shouted, drawing nearer.

'But the *sfvantskors*!' cried Pazel. 'I can't hear their voices any more!'

'Forget them,' said Alyash. 'They ran the wrong way.'

Furious, Pazel turned in the direction of Alyash's voice. 'She's my Gods-damned sister!' he shouted.

'She's a fanatic, a monster with a womb!'

A sword whined from its sheath. 'Pathkendle! No!' cried Hercól.

'You drawing a blade on me, *Muketch*?' snarled Alyash. 'Come on, then, I'll have your blary head!'

There was a horrible scream. But it came from neither Pazel nor Alyash. It was the Turach who was screaming, and his voice came from above them, rising by the second.

'It's the worms!' Pazel shouted. 'I'm fighting the mucking worms!'

Then there was no order of any kind. Every voice rose to howling; no one could see anyone; bodies smashed in all directions; Hercól's shouts for order fell on deaf ears. Thasha felt a tentacle graze her hand, then whip around her leg. She was rising; then her sword flashed and cut the tendril and she fell head first, and barely missed dying on her own sword. Up she leaped, stumbling, whirling, blind as death. The voices were already fewer, and all farther away. She cried out for Pazel, for Neeps and Hercól, but no one answered. From somewhere a fitful light appeared; she whirled towards it, a strange, pulsing, indistinct sort of light, but there were figures in it, struggling—

'Oh, Gods. Oh, sweet Rin.'

Not struggling. Making love. It was herself and Pazel she saw, naked under their cedar tree, her hands on the branch above them, her legs on either side of his thrusting hips.

It was Syrarys and Sandor Ott. The concubine looked at her suddenly, over the assassin's shoulder. 'Daughter,' she gasped.

Thasha fell to her knees. *Not real. Not true.* But she was weeping; it was a physical attack she was suffering, it was the spores, the darkness, the world that stabbed and stabbed again. She forced herself to her feet and pushed on, towards nothing, and then she heard Alyash and Hercól behind her, and they *were* fighting, and she turned and floundered towards them with the last of her strength.

'Idiot! Put it down, put it down!'

That was Hercól. Thasha tried to quicken her pace – and fell down the slope, back among the leeches, not stopping to fight them, not stopping for anything. There was the dying glow from the pool. And there was Hercól, collapsed against its rim, dragging himself after Alyash, who kept leaping out of his reach, and fumbling with matches, and something else—

'Fool! You can't shoot whatever's up there!'

'I can mucking well scare the bastards!'

'Don't do it, Alyash!'

A match flared. The bats descended on it immediately, but Alyash was quicker. He forced the tiny flame into the ignition chamber of his pistol, thrust it straight up through the mass of creatures and fired.

Bats erupted from the clearing in a boundless swarm. Alyash stood unharmed among them, laughing, triumphant – and then came a sound like a great sail ripped in two.

The flood lifted Thasha like a matchstick. The light was gone, the clearing gone; she flailed, helpless, borne away by the onslaught of water. Disarmed, nearly drowning, rolled head over heels through the fungi and leeches and drowning bats, grabbing at the larger growths only to find them ripped away, smashing through trees, tearing at roots with her fingernails. And still the water thundered down, as if a suspended lake were emptying into the forest.

A bladder-fungus, dangling over them, a monster of a growth. The trap had been sprung.

Her strong limbs were useless; her body struck tree after rock-hard tree. A part of her had always wondered what it could possibly feel like, to go down with a ship in a storm. This was the answer. Pain and blindness and sharp blows in the dark. She thought of Pazel and wished they'd made love long before.

Just let me see something (she was begging Rin like a schoolgirl). *I can die, we can fail, but let me see something, anything.* So many ways they might have died before, but not this way, in this pit of a forest, this unspeakable, dark hole—

A thought burst inside her. She stopped fighting, stilled by wonder. An insane, a delirious idea.

Look for me—

But hope was like that, wasn't it? A delirium that clouded your mind. A mist that protected you from the truth you couldn't bear to look at. Until something solid parted the mist: a cannonball, a reef, the words of a traitor with just minutes to live.

—*when a darkness comes beyond today's imagining.*

It was at that very moment that her hand caught something solid, and held. It was one of the worm-like tendrils, and though it strained terribly to pull free, to lift her up into the canopy and another sort of death, the rushing water was far stronger, and it became Thasha's lifeline, minute after blind, precious minute. And then her blindness came to an end.

Logic told her that she was hallucinating yet again, but her heart knew otherwise. At a great distance away through the flooded forest, a haze of light began to shine. It was wide and dispersed, like the stars on a cloudless night, except that these stars were blue, and moving, and as they neared her they lit up the forest as no starlight could. They were fireflies, and they broke over her in a blue wave, a second flood above the water, and before them flew a great dark owl. It circled Thasha once, then swept away into the darkness, and the storm of fireflies went with it. But some of the insects stayed, whirling above Thasha, showing her the great complexity of vines and upper branches of the trees, and the underside of the bottommost leaf layer, three hundred feet over her head.

When the water fell, it did so quickly, draining out through the root-mat beneath her feet. Fungi opened pores like puffy lips, spat out water and mud. When the water dropped below her waist Thasha released the tendril, watched it curl into a slender orifice high in the joint of an overhead branch. Trees with mouths. In some of those mouths were dlömic soldiers. In another, a young Turach marine, sent by his Emperor to the far side of the world on a secret mission, to fight (he was surely told) the enemies of the crown.

Dark or bright, I hate this place, she thought.

Then the fireflies drew closer together, and dropped nearer to the ground. As she watched, dumbfounded, they illuminated a path: one that began just over her head, and stretched away into the forest. Thasha couldn't help but smile. As in a dream, she set out walking, and the path vanished behind her as the little insects followed on her heels.

Some ten minutes had passed when she saw the owl again. It

was perched atop a high quartz rock that glittered in the light of the fireflies.

'You've lost your ship, I see,' said the owl. 'And it is yours, you know, regardless of the paperwork back in Etherhorde.'

Thasha stared at it a moment. 'I'm not imagining *you*,' she said, and raised her arms.

The owl dived straight at her, and Thasha did not flinch. Right before her face it suddenly fanned its wings dramatically, came to a near halt, and fell into her arms: a black mink.

A cry from deep in her chest escaped her, and she lifted the creature and hid her face in its fur. 'Ramachni. Ramachni. *Aya Rin*, it's been so long.'

'Oh dearest, that is such a charmingly human way to reckon time. I was just thinking that this has been the shortest night's sleep I could remember. But an eventful night, to be sure. Come, dry your eyes. There will be time for tears, and much else, when the fight is done.'

'Don't leave us again!'

The mage sat back in her hands. He fixed his immense black eyes on her, and there was a thousand times the depth and mystery in them as in the forest, and yet they were, as they ever had been, kind.

'You and I cannot be parted,' he said. 'Even if we leave the world of the living behind – minutes from now, or years – we shall do so together. Now walk, Thasha. Or better still, run, if your wounds will bear it. Many are suffering for your sake.'

His words were like a jolt out of a dream. She ran, with the mage in her arms, beneath the firefly-lit path, and in another five minutes she came to a small rise, above which the fireflies danced in a net of brilliance. Atop the rise, seated among seashell-like fungi, were some half a dozen of their party. She dashed among them, heart in her mouth. Ibjen. Neda. Bolutu. Big Skip. Lunja. And Neeps.

'Thasha!' he cried, jumping up to embrace her.

'But where – where are—'

Neeps pointed down the far side of the hill. There were two other firefly-paths snaking off into the forest. One of them was shrinking towards them, and upon it they could see the older Turach, Dastu and Cayer Vispek, running with one hand folded to his chest. When he saw Neda on the hillside, Vispek did something Thasha never would have believed of him: he sobbed. Hiding the reaction almost at once, he held out his arm, and Myett leaped to the ground. The humans and the ixchel gazed with wonder at Ramachni.

'The weasel-mage,' gasped the Turach. 'By the Blessed Tree, I thought Arunis had finished you off.'

'Not yet,' said Ramachni, baring his teeth.

'Hercól spoke of you,' said Cayer Vispek, 'a woken mink with the powers of a wizard. I did not believe him, but now—'

'I am a mink only in this world, Cayer,' said Ramachni, 'and even here I can take other forms, now and then. I know you believe that *that* can be done – you who crossed the Nelluroq as whales.'

'And died as humans, some of us,' said Vispek. 'Jalantri fell to the leeches, Neda Ygraël. He was gone before the water came.'

Now it was Neda's turn to fight back tears. Thasha reached to console her, but Neeps caught her arm, gently shaking his head. The two of them descended the hill, towards the last remaining path of fireflies. At first glance it appeared quite empty. Wordlessly, they started to run along its course, back into the forest. They could see where the light ended, just beyond that next tree, and then—

Hercól and Pazel, limping arm in arm, rounded the tree, and clinging to Hercól's shoulder was Ensyl. Seeing Neeps and Thasha, the ixchel woman pointed and cried out with joy. They rushed together, and Thasha for one made no attempt to hide her tears.

When she told them that Ramachni had come at last, Thasha thought her friends were close to tears themselves. 'He'll be stronger than ever,' said Pazel. 'He said he would be, when he came back.'

'The rest of us aren't so lucky, though,' said Neeps. 'Lunja is still alive, but the other dlömic soldiers are gone, and so's the younger Turach. And Alyash too, I suppose.'

'I'm not sorry for that,' said Pazel.

'Be sorry for the day he was truly lost,' said Hercól, 'though it was decades before your birth, and perhaps not so long after his own.'

'Lost to evil, you mean,' said Pazel. 'I understand. I saw into his master's mind, Ott's mind, you know.' He stopped a moment, his voice suddenly tight. 'I understand, but I can't forgive. Is that wrong of me, Hercól?'

'You are wrong only in being certain of what you can and cannot do,' said the swordsman. 'For now clear your minds, of rage and fear alike. Our work is not done. And here is one tool that remains to help us do it.' He touched the leather band across his shoulder. Ildraquin was still strapped to his back.

'Cayer Vispek kept his sword as well,' said Neeps, 'and Neda still has her dagger. That's all the weaponry left to us.'

'Then be glad I made you train with staves,' said Hercól, 'and find some, quickly. Put Big Skip on the task; he is a fine judge of anything resembling a club.'

It was then that they noticed the moaning sound overhead. It was the wind: something they had not heard once in the Infernal Forest.

'That change came quickly,' said Ensyl.

'Yes,' said Hercól, 'suspiciously so.'

The wind picked up speed. Leaning into it, they hurried back to the glowing hill. Even before they arrived Thasha could see what was happening: the fireflies were being carried off, dispersed, and the great darkness of the forest was returning.

But atop the hill Ramachni stood straight and calm, and the fireflies about him danced on unperturbed. As Thasha and the others drew near they stepped abruptly into quiet, windless air, as though they had passed through the wall of an inverted fishbowl, with Ramachni at the centre. But it was a tiny space in the darkness.

Once again Thasha felt as though she were standing on the floor of the sea.

Hercól knelt down before Ramachni. 'Beloved friend,' he said. 'Now I know that what I professed to others is the very truth: that despair alone brings ruin. Even with the Nilstone in hand, Arunis could not prevent your return.'

'On the contrary,' said Ramachni, 'I was able to return only *because* he had the Nilstone in hand – or rather because his idiot does. They are delving very deep into the River of Shadows, calling out to the Swarm, the force that would end all life on Alifros. But when you open a window you cannot always be sure who or what may blow through it. I was waiting outside that window. Arunis was not happy to see me.'

Big Skip, as it turned out, was already on the club-seeking task. He, Bolutu and Ibjen had scoured the area and managed to gather a number of heavy limbs. Soon everyone who lacked another weapon had a solid piece of wood in their hands.

'Arunis is experimenting now,' said Ramachni, 'but we are not too late. Remember that no matter what fell powers he has gained, his body is still that of a man. He will try to stop us from closing on him. But close we shall, and strike we shall, or die together in the attempt.'

Pazel walked to the edge of the sphere of becalmed air. He stretched out his hand until he felt the raging wind. 'It's still growing,' he called over his shoulder.

'My own strength has increased as well,' said Ramachni. 'There is nothing left but to test it. You have one march left ahead of you, travellers, but at least it will not be in the dark. Thasha, my champion, carry me; we must have words as we go.'

The survivors started down the hill, in the direction Ramachni indicated, and the globe of still air with its multitude of fireflies moved with it. Thasha walked in the lead, but off to one side, and the others kept their distance, knowing that *words* meant *words in private*. She tried to catch Pazel's eye, but only caught him wincing as he raised his wounded leg.

'Arunis knew just where to take the Stone,' said Ramachni. 'For many miles the River of Shadows flows under the skin of Alifros: first beneath the lake you crossed, then deep under the Ansyndra, one stream hidden by another. Only here in this forest does it churn to the surface. And it was at that very point that the Auru, the first fair tenders of life in this world, raised a watchtower after the Dawn War, lest evil things return to Alifros. It is only a ruin now, for evil did return, and triumphed for a time, and nearly all the great towers fell. But their ruins still mark the places where the River of Shadows touches Alifros. Much of the strangeness of this world has trickled in through such gaps. The spores that grew into the Infernal Forest are but one example.'

'And the Nilstone entered the same way, didn't it?'

'Yes, dearest,' said Ramachni.

Thasha smiled. 'I think you must be desperate,' she said. 'That was a straight answer, by Rin.'

'Wicked girl,' said Ramachni, pleased.

'Are you going to give me any more?' asked Thasha.

'It is not out of the question,' said the mage, 'but we are on the cusp of battle, and must speak of what may keep us alive. There is power in you, Thasha Isiq: we both know this. And Arunis knows it, too, and fears it.'

'But it isn't mine, is it?'

'Of course it is yours. Who else's?'

'Erithusmé's,' said Thasha. 'What are you pretending for, Ramachni? I don't know if she's my mother or something else to me entirely. But she's trying to use me, get into my head. Just like Arunis does to others, except that she would use me to do good. Although she's never managed to do much good in the past, as far as I can tell.'

Thasha knew how bitter she sounded. They marched on through the dripping forest, and for a time Ramachni made no answer. *Deny it, deny it!* Thasha wanted to scream.

But all Ramachni said was, 'It is you he fears most, ever since he first understood whom he faced, in that chamber on Dhola's Rib. Your power, your magic, far more than my own.'

'What are you talking about?' cried Thasha, no longer caring who heard them. 'I hardly know a thing about magic, and everything I do know I learned from you.'

'No, Thasha. Everything I know, I learned from you.'

She stared at him, appalled.

'Erithusmé is not your mother,' said Ramachni, 'and she is not trying to possess you, to force her way inside. For she has never been elsewhere, since your birth – since your conception. Thasha dearest, *you* are Erithusmé. I have no time to explain, but know this: you can draw on her power *if you want it*. Only if. No one can force you to do so, no one can demand it of you. Do you understand?'

'No I don't! What in the Nine Pits are you saying? I'm not Erithusmé, I'm Thasha Isiq!'

'Yes,' said Ramachni quietly, 'for as long as you wish to be.'

'What did he say to her?' whispered Neeps as he helped Pazel limp along. 'Look at her, she's crying.'

Pazel did not look; he was afraid his own face would be too revealing. What was wrong with Ramachni? Why would he shock her *now*? He felt furious at the mage, though a part of him knew there must be a reason. There were always mucking reasons. Vital, and cruel.

'Your leg's worse, eh?' said Neeps.

'Doesn't matter,' said Pazel. 'Don't say anything about it.'

Suddenly Lunja raised her hand. 'Listen!' she said.

A sound was reverberating through the forest: a huge, muffled *thump ... thump*. 'A heartbeat,' said Ibjen. The sound rose very quickly, until the giant trees themselves seemed to shake with it, and the more delicate mushrooms trembled with each *thump*.

'We are nearly there,' shouted Ramachni above the din. 'Fear nothing. You are stronger than you know, and Arunis has achieved too much by terror already.'

'That he has,' said Hercól. 'Lead on, Ramachni. We will give him no more easy victories.'

On they went, but not three minutes had passed when Pazel realised that Neeps had begun to sob.

'Mate? What's happened, what's wrong?'

'Bastard,' spat Neeps. 'He's doing this to me.'

'Doing what?'

Neeps drew a hand over his eyes. 'Showing me Marila,' he said. 'Captured, hurt . . . hurt by men.'

'It's a lie,' said Pazel, gripping him tightly by the arms. 'Keep your eyes open. Look at us, look at the trees, anything but what he shows you.'

'I'm trying, damn it!'

Pazel was about to say more, but then, without a moment's warning, he learned how hard it was to take his own advice. A picture sprang open in his mind, like a child's pop-up storybook, but utterly real. He saw Arunis cowering, and Thasha taking the Nilstone from his weakened hand – and death consuming her like some ghastly, wildfire mould . . .

Enraged, he looked at his companions. All save Ramachni were clearly suffering, their faces twisted with anguish and fear. Between the pulses of the unseen heart, Pazel heard Cayer Vispek and his sister, fighting in Mzithrini. Neda sounded almost out of her mind. 'She will use it to destroy us, destroy the Pentarchy, to finish her father's wars! I see Babqri burning, Cayer! I see our people thrown alive onto bonfires!'

'You see what he shows you, not what *is*. They are not our enemies, Neda Ygraël. We are none of us the people we were—'

'But the girl! She is not what she pretends to be! She has hidden her face from us all along! So many times we've been lied to, deceived—'

Letting go of Neeps, Pazel rushed forwards and grabbed Neda by the elbow. She whirled, raising her fist. Perhaps in that moment she would have struck at any face but his.

'Trust me,' he begged. 'Thasha won't do anything like that. I promise.'

Neda looked at him, torn by fury and pain. 'One Arquali defends the other,' she said.

Pazel was furious in turn. *Not that again*. He wanted to spit half a dozen retorts in her face, and was struggling against them all, when Bolutu cried, 'There, look there! Do you see it?'

Ahead of them, far above the fireflies, a light was shining down. It was the moon, the old yellow moon, and around it Pazel saw a few faint stars. 'A rip!' said Lunja. 'A hole in the tree cover!' And so it was: a jagged triangular gap, all the way to the open sky. As they stepped nearer, Pazel saw that something truly monstrous stood in that gap, pointing upwards like a great jagged stump.

The moonlight flooded the land below. After so much darkness it felt almost like emerging into sunshine. There was the river, the mighty Ansyndra, sweeping through a glittering curve. There were broad, grassy banks where no mushrooms grew. And on both sides of the river, and even within it, lay gargantuan carved stones. They were bricks, Pazel saw with astonishment: stone bricks the size of houses, grass and turf sprouting atop them, scattered like a child's building blocks across the land.

Now Pazel could see the thing piercing the tree cover. It was what they had taken for a hill, when they looked out across the forest from the crater's rim. But it was the remains of a circular tower, huge beyond reason, the curve so gradual that at first he took it for a flat wall. Almost nothing of it remained: just a shattered ring of cut stones that had formed its base. For most of the circumference the ring was but sixty or seventy feet tall. But on one side it still rose to dizzying heights, cutting through all four layers of the trees, and rising above the top-most by several hundred feet. The tower projected somewhat into the Ansyndra, so that the current broke and quickened around the wall. And there was, Pazel saw now, one more feature that had survived: a great stone staircase, dead ahead, leading up to a flat surface that must once have been a landing by the tower door.

At the top of those stairs stood Arunis and his madman.

Their backs were turned; they were facing the river. The idiot was hunched, knees slightly bent, arms crossed over his chest. Arunis stood with one hand clenched upon the idiot's scalp.

Ramachni glanced left and right at the fireflies. Silent as mist, they drifted away, and the wind wrapped around the party again: deliciously, then worryingly, cool.

Suddenly Arunis bellowed, shaking the idiot with great violence. 'It is *there*, animal! Call to it, call to it now!'

The heartbeat grew louder, faster. The idiot convulsed, like one in pain – and suddenly the river rose, churning, frothing around the base of the tower. Waves crashed against the ruin and the banks, and a dark hole opened in the river's surface. Then, just as suddenly, the water fell back into its normal course. Arunis struck the idiot on the head.

Ramachni's gaze was fixed on the sorcerer. His dark eyes gleamed in the moonlight, and his white fangs showed. 'Put me down, Thasha,' he said. She obeyed, and Pazel knew they could all feel it, the power compressed in that tiny form. Ramachni tossed his head about, slowly, like a much larger creature, and those nearest him stepped sideways, making room.

Pazel did not know what Ramachni was up to: something deadly, he hoped. He looked down at the branch Big Skip had provided: solid, but crooked and awkwardly long. *A stick*, he thought. *After all this, I'm going to rush Arunis with a stick.*

'Fight now, as never before!' cried Ramachni suddenly. Then he leaped into the air, and something about him changed, and he did not fall to earth again but ran above it, and about him Pazel saw a ghost-body forming. It was a monstrous bear, thundering through the grass and scattered trees, and before he knew it he and all the others were racing after him, their foes cornered at last.

The bear grew more solid and heavy as they ran, but Ramachni's tiny form was still visible within it, running and leaping with the same motions as the huge animal that surrounded him.

Pazel lost ground, as he knew he would. He could try to ignore the pain in his leg, but that did not make it work any better.

As soon as Ramachni bounded onto the stone staircase, Arunis whirled. He seized the idiot by the back of the neck. 'Slay them!' he howled. 'Kill them all!'

The idiot turned, looking at them blankly – and there it was, cradled against his chest: the black sphere of the Nilstone. All at once he screamed like a furious infant, and four tall, gaunt creatures rose out of the stone before him and flew down the stairs. They were vaguely human, with great mats of wiry hair and the fangs of jungle cats. But in a moment of sickening insight Pazel saw that their faces were identical: all four had the face of one the bird-watchers in the Conservatory, the one who had objected the loudest when Arunis claimed the idiot for his own.

Ramachni met the creatures on the stair. He cuffed the first off the side with one blow of his paw, and bore down on the second with his teeth, savaging it, and left its corpse where it fell. Hercól, Thasha and Cayer Vispek were on the stairs already, and leaped to attack the other creatures before they could spring. But above, Arunis was goading the idiot to renew the attack, beating him about the head and screaming, 'More, much more! Kill them instantly!'

The idiot bent nearly double, and his back heaved like a retching dog's. Once, twice – and then he vomited, and went on vomiting, an impossible flood of slick black oil. It raced down the staircase towards Ramachni, and just as it reached him, the whole sheet burst into flame.

Ramachni shouted a word of command. The flames died instantly, and the oil thinned to water and drained off the sides. Now the whole party was on the stairs. Hercól and Cayer Vispek had caught up with Ramachni, and the three of them were within twenty steps of the sorcerer and the fool. Then the idiot, his head cocked to one side, began waving his hand spasmodically before him.

This time three creatures appeared and flew to the attack. They were very different from the hags he had summoned before. These were creatures of mud and fire, but they were also mirror images of the attackers. There was a blazing bear for Ramachni, a mud-fire Hercól and a mud-fire Vispek. The clash was terrible. Pazel could not see clearly what happened to Hercól and Vispek, but Ramachni's huge foe caught him squarely, and the two bears rolled like a snarling, blazing boulder down the staircase, felling several of the party as they went. Pazel felt the rush of wind as they rolled past him. Lifting his head, he found the stair above him empty all the way to Arunis. With a feeling like he'd once had as a child, reaching for a pan on the stove that happened to be glowing an alluring red, he ran straight up the broken stones.

The idiot kept waving and moaning, and suddenly Pazel saw the creature's arm lengthen obscenely, and then the giant hairy hand with its scabs and black bitten thumbnail caught him cleanly, and more angry than frightened (of course this had happened, of course!) he was scooped from the staircase, hurled over the moonlit grass and stones – and plunged head first into the river.

Thasha had stopped to help Cayer Vispek fight his double. It grappled with him, strangling, howling in Vispek's own voice, and it barely seemed to feel her club. But when she landed a sound blow she felt its arm buckle slightly, and then Vispek, wriggling free, cried out in rage and slashed it to pieces with his sword. Thasha pulled him to his feet. Vispek, shocked, pointed past her. She whirled – and saw Pazel strike the river's surface, forty feet from shore.

Gods! Was he even conscious, after a fall like that? Thasha broke for the river. There was his hand, thank the Blessed Tree, but the river was violent, he was sucked under again, it would be the hardest swim of her life to reach him.

Then she saw that Ibjen was well ahead of her, boots off already, and like a diving cormorant he shot into the Ansyndra. Thasha's heart was torn. Pazel needed her, but the battle needed everyone. Still praying for her lover she charged back up the stairs.

The *tol-chenni*'s giant hand was still smashing and flailing, but now it was an armoured fist. Up it soared above her; down it came with a rending crash. She leaped; stone stairs were pulverised. Now she was falling, scrabbling to stop herself. She caught the black silhouette of the fist against the moon, it was plummeting again, she could not dodge it—

With a roar, Ramachni leaped above her, braced his bear's form against the blow. She raised her hands into his fur. *There*: oh Gods, the blow was crippling, lethal. The bear toppled onto its side, and with a shout of pain Ramachni abandoned it, leaped out as his old, mink self. The ghost-creature tumbled from the staircase, and vanished before it touched the ground.

Ramachni was dazed. Thasha grabbed him and leaped again, and the mailed fist struck where they had lain a moment before.

All of them had been driven to ground; the stones above them were now more rubble than staircase. With his left hand still on the idiot's neck, Arunis flexed the fingers of his right, and the mailed fist did the same. He was gaining control, and he leered, enjoying it. He spread his fingers wide; the idiot's ghastly hand did the same. Then the fingers started to grow, slithering down the ruined staircase, each one a serpent as thick as a man's body.

Hercól did not wait for them to close. He charged forwards with Ildraquin, right into their jaws, and Vispek was beside him, sword held high. The snakes proved clumsier than they looked: caught between serpent reflexes and Arunis' conscious control. Hercól danced between them; Ildraquin swept a figure eight, and two heads fell. Vispek's blade tore the throat of another. But the wound began to close almost before it could bleed, and already new heads were forming on the gushing necks.

Then Ramachni shook himself and sprang from Thasha's arms. A stinging, furious word left his mouth. The remaining snakes caught fire. The whole conjured arm jerked back and shrank away to nothing, and far above them Arunis cried in awful pain, cradling his own hand.

So there were costs for the power he'd seized.

Then Arunis stood again, and his gaunt face was mad with fury. He took hold of the idiot once more. This time nothing sudden happened; the sorcerer's face became quiet; the *tol-chenni* stopped his gestures and held still.

'On guard, on guard!' cried Ramachni suddenly. 'He is preparing something worse than all that has come before! I cannot tell what it will be, but— *Ah Mathrok!* Scatter, run!'

It was too late to run. Around them, a circular pit suddenly opened, deep and sheer. Bristling at the base of the pit were spikes – no, needles, needles of burnished steel, five or six feet long. The party huddled together; the space they occupied was barely large enough for them all. And then the rim of the pit – the inner rim, beside their feet – began to crumble.

Ramachni closed his eyes. At once the cracks in the earth stopped growing, and there were sighs of relief. But the mage remained very still and tense. Above them, Arunis and his slave tilted their heads together, in perfect synchrony, as if one brain were directing them both. Thasha saw Ramachni wince, and then the cracks once more began to spread.

The instant he struck the river Pazel knew that something was wrong. He kicked and flailed. He was a strong swimmer, but his wildest efforts barely lifted him to the surface; it was as if the water were partly air. There was a roaring below him, and a sense of infinite, rushing space.

He looked down into the Ansyndra, and thought the madness of the spores was infecting him anew: beneath his feet he saw a black tunnel, twisting down and away, a tunnel enclosing a cyclone. It was no illusion, he realised, horrified. He was seeing the River of Shadows, treading water above a hole in the world.

There was no escaping it. He had not yet begun to sink, but his terrified paddling had not moved him an inch towards shore – and suddenly there was no shore, for the Ansyndra had swept him downstream, to where the sheer stone wall jutted out into the river's path. Pazel threw out his hands as the current slapped him against the stone. For twenty feet he scraped along its slimy edge. Then, miraculously, his hands found something to grip.

It was only a thin vine, reaching down from a crack in the wall, and its tendrils began to break as soon as he seized it. But for a moment it stopped him. He gulped a breath, furious. A ridiculous death. Not even in the fight. And damn his stupidity, he was carrying *lead*! Mr Fiffengurt's blackjack was still there in his breeches, sewn into its special pocket. He couldn't spare either hand to cast it away.

Then he saw a dark streak below the surface. It was a dlömu, shooting towards him. A moment later Ibjen rose, treading water in a frenzy.

'This water's unnatural!' he cried. 'Even I can barely swim!'

'The vine's going to break,' Pazel shouted.

Ibjen turned in place, splashing desperately to hold still. 'We'll swim back together,' he said.

Pazel shook his head. 'I'm not strong enough. I'll have to go around the tower, downstream.'

But there was no more hope in that idea than in Ibjen's. Even if he managed to keep his head above water, the river would simply peel him away from the wall once he rounded the curve.

'*You* can still make it,' he shouted to Ibjen. 'Go on! Take care of Neeps and Thasha!'

Ibjen was staring at him strangely. 'I failed the prince,' he said, just audible over the water's roar.

'Ibjen, the vine—'

'I broke my oath to him. And to my mother. I'm paying now, like Vadu did.'

Ibjen's eyes, like those of the woman in Vasparhaven, were jet black. *In nuhzat again.* Was he aware of things around him, or in a different world altogether?

'Pazel,' he shouted suddenly, 'you're going to have to climb that wall.'

'Climb? You're mad! Sorry, I—'

The vine snapped like a shoelace. Pazel clawed at the stone, but already the current was whirling him on. He felt Ibjen seize him by the shoulders. 'Down, then,' gasped the boy. 'Hold your breath. Are you ready?'

Before Pazel could say *No!* the boy pushed him under. Kicking hard, he drove them both down the side of the wall. Descent was swift and easy; it was staying up that had been close to impossible. But with every inch they dropped there was less water, more black air, and now Pazel could feel the roaring cyclone, tearing along the side of the tower. It would lift them, bear them away like leaves. But Ibjen fought on, kicking with astonishing determination and strength, clawing at the water with his free arm, down and down.

And suddenly Pazel saw his goal. The river had undercut the tower's foundation; two or three of the mammoth stones had been torn completely away, and dim moonlight shone through the gap. It was a way through the wall, into the centre of the ruin.

But they would never make it. They were sliding past the gap already, and now the River of Shadows had replaced the Ansyndra almost entirely: the water felt as thin as spray. Beneath his feet, Pazel caught another glimpse of that vast windy cavern, winding away into eternity. There were walls, doors, windows. Lights in some of them. He saw a mountainscape at sunset; he saw two children with their noses pressed to glass, watching their struggle. He saw himself and Ibjen vanishing into that maelstrom, for ever.

Then, from somewhere, Ibjen found even greater strength. His limbs were a blur, his teeth were gritted, and with another blast of clarity Pazel found some last reserve of his own strength. For two or three yards, no more, they managed to move upstream. And just when Pazel knew that he could go no further, Ibjen shoved him bodily into the gap.

Pazel clung to the stone, found purchase, dragged himself forwards. The wind fought him terribly, wild surges of air tried to pull him back into the river. Howling inside, limbs straining beyond any effort in his life, he gained another inch, another foot, then turned and reached for Ibjen—

The dlömic boy was a speck, whirling away down the tunnel. A black leaf, a shade in a river of shades – dwindling, dissolving, gone.

'Hercól,' said Ramachni, 'can you leap over the pit?'

Thasha was aghast at the strain in his voice. The two mages were fighting to the death, and Arunis, it seemed, was the stronger. The edge of the pit was now just inches from their toes.

'Not that far, Master,' answered Hercól.

'Never mind, then, I will—'

Ramachni broke off, and his eyes opened. Then Thasha heard it: a whirling, whistling sound. Five feet above their heads, blades had appeared: long, heavy scimitar blades, parallel to the ground, spinning at unholy speed. Thasha could not count them: maybe a dozen, maybe more. Everyone crouched down, horrified. To reach for one of those blades would be to lose a hand. And now, as she had known that they would, the blades began to descend.

'Well,' said Ramachni, 'he has certainly mastered the Stone.'

His limbs were rigid, and his small body shook, and Thasha knew that he was trying to arrest both the blades and the advance of the pit. And yet the blades were still lowering, very gradually. 'You had best get to your knees,' said Ramachni.

They got to their knees, but the blades kept coming. They were almost invisible with speed, and through them Thasha saw Arunis gesturing at something beneath his feet, and then—

'Look out!'

Several large fragments of the staircase were moving towards them. Not quickly, not with aim or force; it was as if Arunis had reached the limits of the horrors he could control at once. The first stone dropped motionless before it had travelled halfway; two others fell and slid along the ground, toppling at last into the pit. Then a larger fragment rose, wobbling, teetering, like a stage magician's clumsy prop. Above, they heard Arunis groan with effort.

The stone flew at them – flew directly at *her*, Thasha realised. She raised her arms – but there was Hercól, pushing in front of her, absorbing the blow. The chunk of stone must have weighed more than he did, and it struck him dead-on. The top edged nicked one of the whirling blades; fragments of stone and steel flew among them; there were cries and sick sounds of impact. And before they knew what harm had come to whom, the blades dropped lower still.

Hercól was unconscious, the stone upon his arm, Ildraquin loose in his hand. Lunja was bleeding from her mouth. Earth crumbled into the pit, a little here, a little there. Among the crouched and bleeding bodies Thasha could no longer see Ramachni. But then she heard his voice in her mind.

I cannot stop him, Mistress. If you would help me, do it now.

Mistress? Help him? What could she do? He was mistaken; Arunis had fooled him like he had fooled everyone else at one point or another. She was not Erithusmé and never had been. She was a mortal girl in a trap. Weepy, weak, besotted with a boy who might already be dead, caught up in a fight that was never her own. Why had they lavished their love on her, their efforts, their belief? She heard the Mother Prohibitor's voice from her old, detested school, and knew that the ancient woman had, after all, known her better than she'd known herself. *Failure is not an accident. Not a thug who grabs you in an alley. It is an assignation in a darkened house. It is a choice.*

They were all pressed flat. Thasha suddenly found Neda gripping her hand, saw that she and Cayer Vispek had reached for others as well. They were praying, praying in Mzithrini. Why hadn't she studied the language harder? Pazel would laugh. It was a farewell, wasn't it? Something about knowledge in the last hour, peace when the fight was done.

Some of them had been cut; a mist of blood haloed the blades. Neda turned her head to Thasha. 'I am glad to die with you, warrior,' she said. 'I am glad you loved him, while you could.'

Something in Neda's voice changed Thasha for ever. There was no sign of daybreak, yet she was flooded with light, with certainty. She knew who she was, and who she had been; she knew that Arunis had been right to fear her. She could have swept him away like dust from her hands. She could have seized the Stone before he lifted a finger, pounded his body a mile into the earth, hurled him into the clouds and let him fall. She could feel the edges of that power, almost taste it on her tongue. It had slumbered inside her, untapped for years, laid away like firewood against the winter, this winter, this moment of need.

Thasha's eyes streamed with tears. All that power was waiting, but not for her. Yes, she had been Erithusmé. And Thasha Isiq – that girl had been an invention, a disguise, a hiding place when the sorceress stood cornered by her foes, expecting to be killed. Cornered (it must have been) very close to the big house on Maj Hill, in Etherhorde, where lived one admiral's wife, Clorisuela Isiq, longing for children she could never have. Thasha could picture the bargain: *a daughter born sound and healthy, in exchange for one chamber of her mind in which to hide my soul.* A pact between mage and mother, both desperate in their way. Had they known, even then, that they were creating a hollow shell, a child whom Erithusmé would slowly replace?

But like most desperate schemes, this one had failed. For the shell had *wanted* her life, wanted to breathe and dance and learn and love, and Erithusmé had been powerless to stop her. Year by year the mortal girl's mind had grown stronger, bolder, and the great mage had retreated. As with the Waking Spell, Erithusmé had misjudged the riotous strength of life, its habit of mutiny, its defiance. Thasha's mind called out to Ramachni, vicious with despair. *If only I had withered, died inside, the way you wanted. Then you'd have your champion, then you'd win.*

He answered fiercely: *No, Thasha! That was never the plan!*

But of course it was. Erithusmé would have had a new body, just as Arunis had once seized the body of a prison guard. And the whole, pointless shadow-play of Thasha's life, from her first breath in the midwife's hands to her shudder of joy in Pazel's arms – would have been expunged, spat out, blackened and unmade.

I'm so sorry, Ramachni. I can die for this fight. I can't go back and not have lived.

Thasha, you have felt her power; it is yours and yours alone, if only you—

No!

She blotted out his voice – and that other voice, that woman's. They were trying to take everything from her. Past, future, lovers, life. Worse, they were trying to make her renounce it. Maybe she could wish that her soul had died, leaving her body for Erithusmé. But she hadn't. She was here, a woken animal called *human*, and she would live until those blades struck her down.

'Hold fast!' cried Vispek suddenly. 'Neda and I are going to stand up. Our bodies may stop the blades, or deflect them—'

'No!' cried the others, trying to restrain them.

'Do not interfere! There is no other—'

'Wait, Cayer,' said Ramachni.

Atop the wall, behind Arunis and the idiot, a third figure appeared. It was Pazel, crawling up from the inside of the wall, rising unsteadily to his feet. Stealth in his movements, Fiffengurt's blackjack in his hand, and just as Thasha felt the first nick of the whirling blades he stepped forwards and struck the idiot a crushing blow to the head.

The blades were gone. The pit was gone. On the wall, the idiot crumpled, and the Nilstone slipped from his fingers. Arunis whirled and lunged at Pazel, lifted him by the neck – then tossed him down again as he saw his prize rolling slowly, inexorably, towards the edge of the wall.

Thasha gasped: her despair was gone as well. Everything had slowed except her mind, her hammering heart. She saw Arunis diving for the Nilstone; saw her hand groping along Hercól's twisted arm; saw the mage seize the Stone and topple with it over the wall; saw herself sprint forwards to meet him, weightless, almost laughing. She saw his lips move, his hands blackening where they gripped the Stone; saw a dark hole open in the river and something leap like a fish into the sky; saw the perfection in herself as she swung Ildraquin and severed Arunis' head from his body before he struck the ground.

32

A Fighting Chance

———

8 Modobrin 941

When they gathered around her she said nothing. Daybreak was nearing after all; the sky over the tower glowed, lamplight through musky wine. The corpse of the mage looked like any other. The Nilstone looked like a hole in the world, lying there on the grass between her knees. She could feel its draw, its invitation. Once before it had been her servant, and it would be so again. For a price.

Hercól was helped to her side; he bent down stiffly and kissed her on the brow. The others murmured, praised her deed. All save Pazel, who was still atop the wall, shooting glances at her, then looking quickly away.

Ramachni came next. His tongue flicked her arm like a tiny paintbrush. 'Dearest,' he said, 'can you have believed that I would join any scheme to make you wither and die?'

She gave him no answer, not even a glance.

'Mind you,' he said, 'what I *did* agree to gave me no joy. And the only person in all this world who could have persuaded me was you. I think you understand, now. We were minutes from death. Arunis had killed nearly everyone who opposed him, and wounded us terribly. His foul servants had chased us over land and sea, and cornered us at last in Etherhorde – on Maj Hill, to be exact. They were moving door to door, sniffing like bloodhounds, and he was there among them at the height of his powers. We had to think quickly, Mistress, and our options were few.'

Pazel touched his throat, wincing. He could still feel Arunis' fingers, dry and cruel as talons, and knew the mage had been on the point of snapping his neck. He sat down carefully atop the wall. They had done it, they had killed him. He had stopped believing the moment would come.

The first to reach him was Ensyl. She ran to his side, lifted his hand with effort, kissed his palm. He managed a brief, bone-weary smile. Ensyl ran across the wall and looked down.

'An inner staircase! So that's how you managed the climb. But Pazel, where is Ibjen? Did he drown?'

Pazel shook his head. 'The River took him. He could be anywhere, in any world. The same thing would have happened to me if he hadn't pushed me through that gap.'

Ensyl was silent a moment, then looked over her shoulder again. 'You have killed the idiot,' she said.

Pazel looked at the pale, twisted body. In death so very human. A prisoner, with a prisoner's filth and hair.

'Diadrelu said we'd all be killers before the end,' he said. 'I was always afraid she was right.'

'In a strange way, the idiot helped you do it, by knocking you into the river,' said Ensyl. 'I wonder if some part of him wanted it. To be a *tol-chenni* is surely a fate worse than death.'

Pazel shuddered. He looked down at Neeps, crouching at Thasha's side. They would cure him. They had to. It was impossible even to consider that they might fail.

'Admiral Isiq was away at sea,' said Ramachni, 'and the servants gone for the night. Clorisuela was alone. You bargained quickly, Mistress. You offered her a child: the one she could never have by natural means. But your power had limits. You could induce Clorisuela's body to form a new child in her womb, but you could not give that child a soul, as Nature does in her omnipotence. The only soul you had to offer was your own.

'But Clorisuela wanted nothing to do with creating such a creature – an infant with a mind twelve centuries old – and no entreaties on your part would move her. She said that it was perhaps time for your long life to end. "And if not," she said, "if you truly wish to hide within a daughter of mine, then you must *become* her. Change your own soul, and make it like that of a newborn. Hide your memories and your feelings and your magic away not just from others, *but from her as well, entirely*. Give her sixteen natural years – and one more after that to learn the truth. And finally, when those years have passed, let your memories and mind return to her only if she wants them – purely, and with no compulsion, and no regrets." Those were Clorisuela's terms. And you, Mistress, called them just, and agreed.'

Thasha stared into the blackness of the Stone. She was dimly aware that Neeps was beside her. His bruised hand on her shoulder, his lemon smell, his appalled face turned to Ramachni. She saw Neda come and bend down beside her and whisper a short prayer. She felt Pazel's eyes on her again.

'What was your part in this accord?' Hercól asked Ramachni.

'I pledged to watch over the girl as best I could,' said the mage, 'and to help when the time came for her to learn the truth. Yet even as I spoke my promise, Arunis attacked, and our spell of protection around the house buckled at his first assault. The timbers shook; the fire died in the hearth. We could wait no longer. Your eyes, Mistress, fell on Isiq's old mariner's clock, and in a matter of seconds you cast a flawless spell. When you opened the clock face, I saw my escape path: a tunnel back to the world I'd left so long ago, to become your student. That clock has ever since been my secret door into Alifros.

'The house shook again, and you turned to me for the last time. "Ramachni Fremken, the path to the future is dark, but I think I see you waiting for me upon it, far ahead through war and ruin, in a glade that is sunlit yet."

'Then you vanished, and Clorisuela gasped and placed a hand upon her stomach. "It is done," she said, "there is a child within me." Hearing that, I took my leave.'

'Then it's true,' said Neeps, putting his arms around her.

'Clorisuela *was* your mother. Do you hear me? Thasha?'

She leaned against him in silence. Her hand was still tight on Ildraquin. The sorcerer's blood was still drying on its blade.

'Why is the girl so solemn?' murmured Neda, staunching a wound on the Turach's arm. 'We have recovered the Nilstone, and killed the greatest enemy of North and South alike. This is victory, is it not?'

Lunja glanced at Thasha. One of her silver eyes was bruised and bloodshot. 'It is a victory,' she said, 'but not the last one, I think.'

'There ain't *never* a final victory,' said the old Turach with feeling. 'Not till you hang your sword over the mantle, anyway, and settle down to fat. And even then the fight can come looking for you. Remember the Great Peace, Miss Neda?'

The sworn enemies looked at each other. It seemed that either might have laughed, but neither did. 'Anyway,' said the Turach, 'don't mind the Isiq girl. She's just snipped a hairy daisy. The first one's always a shock.'

Cayer Vispek sat on the grass nearby, bare to the waist. Myett, behind him, was digging splinters from his wounded back. 'No,' she said, 'it is not yet time to celebrate. Arunis lies dead, but he has left us with the burden of the Stone. And from what I have seen, the wicked are drawn to it, like flies to a feast.'

'There is something else,' said Cayer Vispek. 'The dark thing that jumped from the river, and shot away into the sky. What was it? Arunis was looking that way even as he fell – even in the moment of his death. I have an idea that he was smiling.'

The old Turach bent over, spat blood into the grass. 'He ain't smiling now,' he said.

'I kept my promise,' said Ramachni. 'I guarded you in secret. But when Sandor Ott killed Clorisuela, I realised that the Isiqs were entangled far more deeply in the fate of Alifros than I had suspected. I was a fool not to have seen it: your choice of them, Mistress, had not been random at all. We knew Arunis wanted the

Nilstone, but you saw so much farther. How he was using the Shaggat, using Sandor Ott, using the very Empire of Arqual. And given such an enemy, you saw that no fortress in Alifros would ever be sufficient to guard the Nilstone. When you returned you would have to finish the great task of your life. You would have to take the Nilstone beyond this world.

'I did not know all that you intended, or how it was to be done. The *Chathrand* was a part of it: your old vessel, delivered with great reluctance into the hands of that Trading Family, so long ago. And of course this new being, this Thasha Isiq, would prove essential. So I sought help from the few I trusted: the Mother Prohibitor of the Lorg School, and the deposed Empress of Arqual, valiant Maisa, whose strength and goodness reminded me so much of your own.'

'And Maisa,' added Hercól, 'gave me into your service, Ramachni. At last! At last I know whom I have been guarding, teaching, scolding all these years.' He looked at Thasha, and though his voice held love and even humour, there was caution as well. 'I might have sparred with you more gently, mage, if I had known my peril.'

Ramachni sighed and bowed his head. '*That*, Mistress, is the story of your birth. By which I mean your rebirth, of course.' He looked up at her with his piercing eyes. 'But I think I am only confirming what you know. For surely you have called your memories back? Are you not yourself once more, Erithusmé?'

He did not see it; perhaps he did not dare. But Hercól should have understood, if he had seen her strike Arunis down. It was no magic, no wizard's spell. The calm, the focus, the timing of her sprint and swing. Not a step but as he'd taught her. No tools at her command but his own.

They were patient with her – she still had not moved or spoken – and she knew that for a time she must be patient with their unseeing. Cayer Vispek lugged the body of the sorcerer from her sight. Neda carried off the gory head. Hercól took Ildraquin from her hand and carefully rolled the Nilstone away. It left behind a trail of scalded grass.

Neeps scrambled up to the top of the wall. 'Come on, you,' he said. 'No more larking about up here.'

'I'm dizzy,' said Pazel.

'Then slide on your bum, one step at a time.' Neeps glanced down at Thasha and lowered his voice. 'You need to talk with her, mate. She's not doing well. In fact I'm not sure she's all there.'

Pazel looked at Thasha for a long time. 'I wonder,' he said at last.

Neeps extended a hand to help Pazel up. But just then Ramachni appeared, scurrying up the last steps, nimble again. He sat down on the stone before the tarboys and bared his teeth.

'A fine night's work,' he said. 'Thanks to you we are still on the path we chose together, so long ago. And it is clear to me now that you will let no fear or pain turn you from it. Hold your heads high, dearest friends.'

'Ramachni,' said Ensyl, 'what was the thing that leaped from the river? Was it what Arunis was seeking before we attacked?'

'Yes,' said Pazel, before Ramachni could answer. 'It was the Swarm. All along he's wanted to release it. And he managed to, with the help of the Nilstone, just before he died.'

Ramachni's black eyes closed a moment. 'I thought,' he said, 'to give you some time to savour this victory, to regain your feet, as it were. But I will not deceive you. Pazel is quite correct. The Swarm of Night has entered Alifros. Only a tiny piece of it, a little clot of darkness. But it does not belong in this world. It exists to guard the borders of the world of the dead, to stop the deceased from returning. Death makes it grow stronger, larger, and to death it will be drawn. But it was never meant to enter the living world, and I fear it will destroy any life it touches. Plants, or animals, or woken souls.'

'Like the Nilstone?' said Ensyl.

'More or less,' said Ramachni. 'But don't you see the danger? The Swarm both kills and feeds on death. The more it kills, the larger it will grow; the larger it grows, the more it will be able to kill, until at last it becomes a black wildfire no power can contain. Arunis may have perished, but his dream of a dead world is closer than ever to coming true.'

The others just looked at him, too exhausted to respond. Pazel was only dimly aware of his aching bruises, his trickling wounds. And the deeper aching of his mind: that he was numb to as well. Neeps sank to his knees with a deep sigh. Ensyl placed her palms on Pazel's leg and leaned into them, arms outstretched, like a runner propping herself up at the end of a race. But it wasn't the end, not yet.

Ramachni looked from one to another. 'Death has gained an advantage,' he said at last. 'But take heart, for we have gained two. Arunis is gone, and Erithusmé has returned. The one you called Thasha has made her choice, and opened herself to the mage's memories and powers.'

'She told you that?' asked Neeps.

'No, she has not spoken. I simply cannot account for our deliverance in any other way.' He looked down at the young woman slumped on the grass. 'In the days ahead she will show you the meaning of magic. And you who care for her must give as well. Give her your faith, and your aid. Without my mistress we cannot prevail – that is true beyond all doubt. But with her we stand a fighting chance.'

'I don't have any more fight in me, Ramachni,' said Neeps.

'Then sleep,' said Ramachni, 'and fear no evil tonight. Dream of your Marila, and the child you will one day hold.'

'Ramachni,' said Pazel, 'I saw the Swarm in the temple of Vasparhaven, in a *nuhzat* dream. It was huge, like a cyclone. How long do we have before it grows so large?'

'That will depend on how much death it finds to feed on.'

Ensyl looked down on the bloody earth. 'And that, perhaps, is why Arunis has laboured so long to plunge this world into war.'

A silence. Neeps and Pazel were struggling to do as Ramachni wanted, to hold up their chins, to have faith. Ramachni for his part was watching Thasha intently, as though waiting for a sign. 'Death will feed the Swarm, and war and hatred will feed Death,' he said at last. 'But there is another force in Alifros, a healing force, and it falls like rain upon the wildfire.' He turned and fixed his black eyes on Pazel. 'Get to your feet now, lad,' he said.

She sat in the grass and watched them descending. Ramachni scrambling ahead, then Neeps with Ensyl on his shoulder. Pazel took his time, but still she dropped her eyes after a moment, because the fool was seeking them, rather than a safe path down the broken stairs. That would be Pazel. He'd pass alive through the Nine Pits, and in the end still trip on his shoelaces. If he had any.

Cayer Vispek sang her a praise-song in Mzithrini, and Neda knelt and said that they were sisters, that their love for Pazel had made them so, that Thasha's children would have a godmother when they came. Thasha kept her eyes on the grass. There is hope downriver, Ramachni was saying; there is a place no evil has ever touched. Echoing words he hadn't read, giving her and the others a direction, a way out if they could find it. She felt the touch of his paw, the searing love he had for her, frozen in a being who could never love the way she thought of it, the senseless joys, the private laughter, the smell of sweat and cedarwood and the tree's rough bark against her back.

A firefly winked on like a lamp beside her foot. She reached out: the light was gone. She heard Ramachni telling the others that she just needed a little time, and that was true. She had not been around very long, after all. Not centuries, not millennia.

Birds were chattering, somewhere. Neeps came and went and smelled of lemons. Hercól was away at the edge of the forest, seeking something, seeking always and for ever. Big Skip began to talk of building a raft. And Pazel came eventually, nervous and awkward and afraid to sit down. He didn't speak, he was terrified, and she thought he understood more than any of them. But not the main thing, so when she was ready she touched his leg and looked up at him, and smiled. Hey, she said, it's just me.

Here ends

The River of Shadows

Book Three of *The Chathrand Voyage*.

The Story is concluded in

The Night of the Swarm

Book Four of *The Chathrand Voyage*.

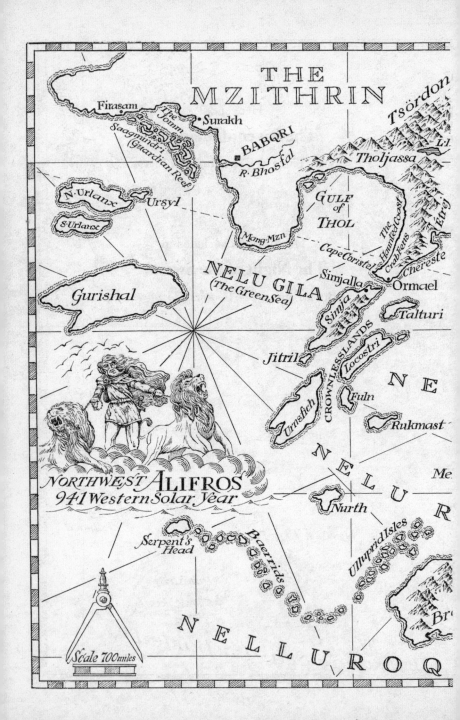

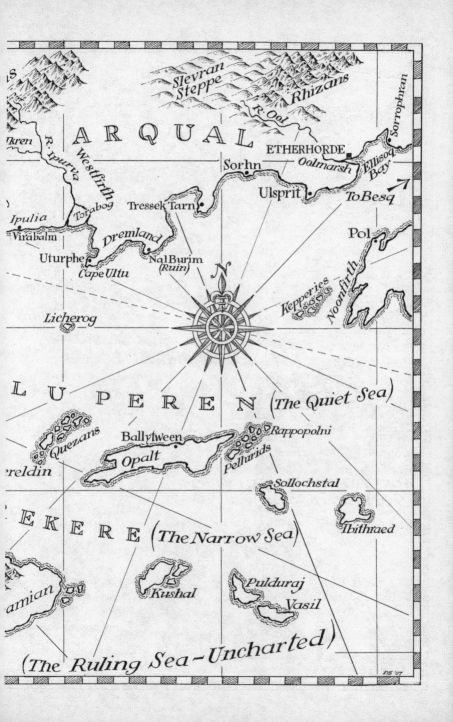

Acknowledgements

Each book is a wrestling match with human frailty, clocked by a merciless timekeeper, in a ring surrounded by an infinity of other rings, where different, often larger, struggles go on day and night. I'm keenly aware that those who helped with *The River of Shadows* had to slip out of their own rings, bruises and all, and step into my own.

My partner, Kiran Asher, read the novel before anyone, and kept me in food, health, good humour and at least minimal contact with the outside world: the latter was the hardest task, no doubt. Along with her insights, my mother Jan Redick, Stephen Klink, Holly Hanson and Edmund Zavada all read early drafts of this book, and provided marvellous feedback.

Sincere thanks also to my agent, John Jarrold, and editor, Simon Spanton, for their immense dedication, hard work and critical reflections at every stage. Likewise to Kaitlin Heller for her brilliant thoughts on the first draft.

I thank my father, John Redick, and sister, Katie Pugh, for their love and support. In addition, I would like to thank Betsy Mitchell and Tricia Pasternak of Del Rey, along with Veena Asher, Lisa Rogers, Bénédicte Lombardo, Bruce Hemmer, Brendan Plapp, Adam Shannon, Amy Heflin, Charlie Panayiotou, Paul Park, Tracy Winn, Michel Pagel and (last but never least) all my dear fellow writers at the Cushman club.